**It was all the youth could do
not to cry out in fright.
*What sort of magic is at work here?***

He waited by the window, ignoring his father's whispered commands to come away, and watched the guards work on the Bhrudwan, clearly convinced they were hurting him.

Eventually the two guards tired of their sport and disappeared into the darkness. A minute or so later they walked past the door of the cell, with a jangling of keys and whispered ribaldry. Up the stone stairs they clomped, then the trapdoor creaked open and closed.

As soon as the echoes died away the Bhrudwan let out a deep throaty rumble, then pulled savagely at his chains. Rather than jerking them, he maintained a constant pressure far longer than Leith would have believed possible. Mahnum joined his son at the window and watched in awe as, in a display of raw power, the warrior pulled himself free . . .

By *Russell Kirkpatrick*

The Fire of Heaven Trilogy

Across the Face of the World
In the Earth Abides the Flame
The Right Hand of God

RUSSELL KIRKPATRICK

IN *the* EARTH ABIDES *the* FLAME

www.orbitbooks.net

New York   London

Copyright © 2004 by Russell Kirkpatrick
Excerpt from *The Right Hand of God* copyright © 2005 by Russell Kirkpatrick. All rights reserved. Except as permitted under the U.S. Copyright Act of 1976, no part of this publication may be reproduced, distributed, or transmitted in any form or by any means, or stored in a data base or retrieval system, without the prior written permission of the publisher.

The moral right of the author has been asserted.

Orbit is an imprint of Hachette Book Group USA

The Orbit name and logo is a trademark of Little, Brown Book Group Ltd.

Orbit
Hachette Book Group USA
237 Park Avenue
New York, NY 10017
Visit our Web site at www.orbitbooks.net

Printed in the United States of America

Originally published by Voyager, Australia: 2004
First paperback edition published by Orbit, Great Britain: 2006
First Orbit edition in the USA: February 2008

10 9 8 7 6 5 4 3 2

*This volume is dedicated
to the other members of Aranui High School's
"cultural desert" (thanks Vince, 1978)*

CONTENTS

MAP 1: THE SIXTEEN KINGDOMS OF FALTHA

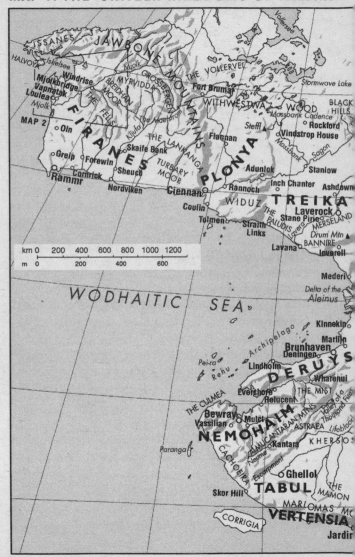

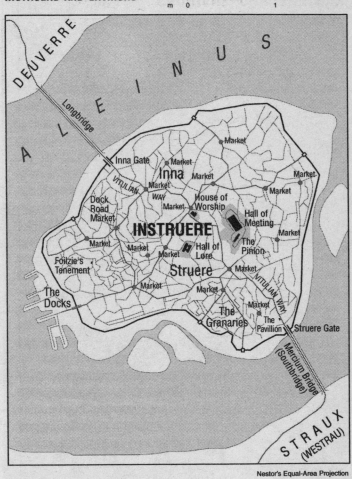

INSTRUERE AND ENVIRONS

Scale 1:50 000

km 0   1   2   3

m 0   1

DEUVERRE

A L E I N U S

Longbridge

Inna Gate   • Market

Inna   • Market

VITULIAN   Market

WAY

Market

• Market

• Market

Dock Road Market

House of Worship

Hall of Meeting

INSTRUERE

• Market

The Pinion

Market

• Market

• Market

Hall of Lore

Foïlzie's Tenement

Struere

• Market

• Market

VITULIAN WAY

• Market

The Docks

• Market

• Market

The Granaries

Market

The Pavilion

Struere Gate

Mercium Bridge (Southbridge)

S T R A U X

(WESTRAU)

Nestor's Equal-Area Projection

© University of Instruere

KANTARA AND ENVIRONS

km 0   1

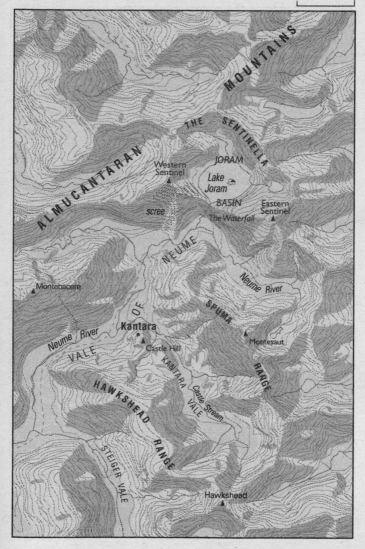

WODHAITIC SEA

Mederi
Rennet
Westhalba
Remeniet
DE
Instruere
Sivithar
Mercium
Oneiro
WESTRAU
Koamaru I.
Kinnekin
STRAUX
Motunui I.
Gatilion
Kanakananui I.
Albatross Point
Marlijn
Ranui I.
Nau I.
Schora Bay
VERIDIAN
BORDERS
Brunhaven
Deningen
Agrar
Archipelago
Lindholm
Thyborup
HAMADABAT
Rehu
DERUYS
THE
Qazez Maribat
NEXUS
FARRARIAN
Wainui
HEIGHTS
Whakatoke I.
EVERDALE
Waiotapu Wharenui
Astama I.
Cape Fairweather
KINEPUKOHURANGI
Tutua I.
(THE MIST)
Evershore
Mounga-atua
Bay of
Carabine
Bewray
Valley of a Thousand Fires
Sabkhat
Ocean Head
Fovea
Relucent
Bi'i Birkat
THE CULMEA
Murage
Ghadir Massab
Bewray
Rivals River
ASTRAEA
Fisherman's
Anthwitan
Akeldama
Lifeblood
Hook
NEMOHAIM
Mulct
(Hotel Dema)
KHERSOS
PLAINS OF
Vassilian
Iri
AMARE
The
Thousand
Arere
Neumlos
Sennrella
Springs
BADIYAT
Paranga I.
Kantara
Neume
Hawkshead
CACHOEIRA
Ni'itsa Top
Treachers Roads
ALMUCANTARAN MTS.
THE THWAITEBUL
Melon
Ghellol
Desolate Harbour
Skor Hill
TABUL
Sperare
THE
Volanosia Narrows
MAMON
The Dark Coast
MALOMAS
MOUNTAINS
JARDINES
CORRIGIA
VERTENSIA
Jardin
Sinnet
Potaccia
Fulmar Bright
Lone Tree Pt.
Stormsheltar
Feluccia
Haven

Scale 1:10 000 000
km 0   100   200   300   400   500   600

Nestor's Equal-Area Projection
© University of Instruere

Boundaries as at Treaty of Mercium
Governable Territory as at NA 1030
Movements into neighbouring territories
• Oasis

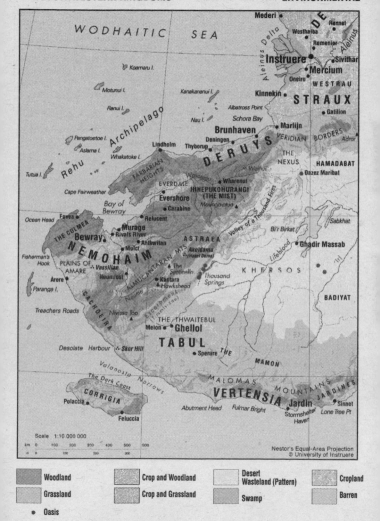

WODHAITIC SEA

DE
Mederi
Rennet
Westhalba
Aleines Delta
Remenier
Aleinus
Instruere
Sivithar
Mercium
Oneiro
WESTRAU
STRAUX
Kinnekin
Gatilion
Koamaru I.
Albatross Point
Motunui I.
Kanakananui I.
Schora Bay
Ranui I.
Nau I.
Brunhaven
Marlijn
Deningen
VERIDIAN
BORDERS
Pangatoetoe I.
Archipelago
Lindholm
Thyborup
DERUYS
Adror
Aslama I.
Whakatoke I.
HAMADABAT
Rehu
TAKBARIAN
Wanoit
THE
Oazez Maribat
Tutua I.
HEIGHTS
NEXUS
Cape Fairweather
EVERDALE
Wharenui
HINEPUKOHURANGI
Bay of
Evershore
(THE MIST)
Bewray
Carabine
Moumoohai
Ocean Head
Fovea
Relucent
ASTRAEA
Bi'r Birkat
Sabkhat
THE CULMEA
Murage
Bewray
Rivals River
Valley of a Thousand Fires
Mulct
Anthwitan
Akeldama
Ghadir Massab
NEMOHAIM
AJMILCANTAKAY MTS
(Hakel Dema)
Fisherman's
Lifeblood
Hook
PLAINS OF
Vassilian
The
KHERSOS
Ti'i
Arere
AMARE
Sentinelln
Neumost
Kantara
Thousand
Paranga I.
Hawkshead
Springs
BADIYAT
Treachers Roads
BACHOERA
Nivasa Top
THE THWAITEBUL
Melon
Ghellol
Desolate Harbour
Skar Hill
TABUL
THE
Valonoso Narrows
Sperare
MAMON
The Derk Coast
MALOMAS
MOUNTAINS
JARDINES
CORRIGIA
VERTENSIA
Jardin
Sinnet
Pelaccia
Abutment Head
Fulmar Bright
Stormshelter
Lone Tree Pt.
Haven
Feluccia

Scale 1:10 000 000
km 0   100   200   300   400   500   600
mi 0   100   200   300

Nestor's Equal-Area Projection
© University of Instruere

	Woodland		Crop and Woodland		Desert Wasteland (Pattern)		Cropland
	Grassland		Crop and Grassland		Swamp		Barren
•	Oasis						

PROLOGUE

USING THE BLUE FIRE LEFT DEORC panting, as always. These reports were not strictly necessary, but he could not avoid the contact if he wished to persuade the Undying Man of his continued fidelity, even though the fire took so much out of him. He sensed his master had become suspicious of him, but knew the Destroyer could not possibly know any details of his plans. Had those details been known, the fire would already have consumed him.

There was no way of telling how convincing his words had been. For a dreadful moment he had thought his master knew all about the four *Maghdi Dasht* and Deorc's reasons for sending them west in pursuit of the Falthan Trader. The Undying Man did not know about the Falthan, of course. Why should he? The Trader had been but one, and not the most important, of many people the Voice had interrogated in Andratan, and it was Deorc's task, not the Destroyer's, to keep track of those who had been questioned. So when Vaniyo the Bhrudwan Trader had reported the Falthan's escape, Deorc saw his chance. Indeed, he had no option but to have the man pursued, apart from telling the Destroyer that he had allowed someone to escape his impregnable castle. And that, quite simply, would have condemned him to death.

Sufficient reason for him to ensure the truth had to remain hidden.

Deorc of Jasweyah had taken a great risk in coming north to serve the Lord of Bhrudwo. Many years he had spent carving out a fiefdom in the Great Southern Mountains, a rugged country inland from the Fisher Coast, a country still beyond the Destroyer's long reach. But Deorc had seen the inevitable end of his success would be to attract the Undying Man's attention, and he knew the limits of his own strength. So, before Jasweyah could be invaded, he made a gift of his lands and people to Bhrudwo. His kinsmen called him a traitor, but he was soon safe in Andratan, soon being groomed to become the Destroyer's lieutenant, and he emerged from the dreadful castle to put down a rebellion led by his former countrymen. He'd surrendered his lands and suffered keenly the loss of his childhood friends: proving his loyalty to his new master necessitated his participation in their deaths. He had forsaken everything known to him in pursuit of the unknown.

It had been worth it. Oh, how his risk had been repaid! Absolute power within his own domain, a vast sphere of influence, the ability to command respect, his choice of women, licence to indulge his habits. Far more importantly, his new position gave him access to the deep secrets of the world, and with it membership of the most exclusive group of all, the magicians. Those who knew how the world really worked. Deorc of Jasweyah, son of a stablehand, had become Deorc, Keeper of Andratan, magician, a mere mortal no longer.

The crowning glory of it all was that now, of all times,

the Lord of Bhrudwo chose to reveal his intention to invade Faltha. The moment came within Deorc's lifetime and only a few years after he became the Keeper of Andratan. Deorc convinced himself he was part of the reason for this bold step, for finally, after a thousand years, his master had found someone he could trust. His great plan depended on the success of his faithful vassal. Deorc had a crucial part to play: he was to travel west to Instruere on a mission so secret the Destroyer would trust only a servant of the blue fire. What riches might fall into his hands! What new secrets might he uncover! And in the hidden depths of his mind he began to think about the ultimate betrayal.

But before he could leave, Vaniyo the Trader had come to him with news about the Falthan Trader's escape. What could be made of this? Vaniyo maintained that the Destroyer had shown great interest in something or someone called the "right hand." What might Deorc be able to do with such knowledge? He had no idea, as yet. But he had not risen to his exalted position by leaving important discoveries to others, so, after carefully concocting an ambiguous form of words, he approached Lord Vartal, his friend and trainer of disciples for the *Maghdi Dasht*.

Vartal shared Deorc's concern that a Falthan could contrive to escape from Andratan, and agreed the Undying Man need be alerted to the situation only if the man could not be captured. He spoke with Nimanek, his longtime lieutenant, and together they selected two of their most capable disciples. After ensuring that Vaniyo would not betray Deorc, the four *Maghdi* set off after the Trader on what promised to be a swift pursuit and an early recapture, followed by a lengthy interrogation conducted in the Keeper of Andratan's private quarters.

The pursuit had been swift, but there had been no re-capture. The four Lords of Fear traveled far beyond Deorc's reach, and what was supposedly a journey of mere weeks had taken over a year—so far. Many uncertainties centered around their disappearance. Had they been killed in some mishap? Had they betrayed him to the Undying Man? Were they playing some game of their own? These concerns now overshadowed in Deorc's mind the potential usefulness of any information the *Maghdi Dasht* might be able to win him.

He had found hints—tenuous threads, hard-won from detailed examination of the words of the Lord of Bhrudwo—that his master sought something in his invasion of Faltha. Something, or someone. Could it be the "right hand"? His master's motives for this risky and expensive invasion clearly went beyond the vast wealth he stood to control. The most obvious was revenge, never openly stated but underpinning every Bhrudwan attitude and action towards Faltha. Whatever small thrust Kannwar—yes, Deorc knew the name, even though his master believed it lost—whatever thrust he could make against the land of the First Men, favored of the Most High, he made with relish. The Undying Man prided himself on the rationality of his actions, but he seldom acted rationally in his dealings with Falthans. A blind spot, possibly his only one. Something to be exploited. And if his master sought something in Faltha other than the mere subjugation of his bitter enemies, then power would accrue to the man who found it first.

Perhaps this "right hand" was the key. Deorc, the Lord of Bhrudwo's right hand, could not miss the threat to his own position implicit in the name. So it was providential indeed—or a deliberate slight on his present right hand, an indication he was expendable—that the Undying Man should send Deorc to Faltha to act as the cornerstone of his great plan. Trust born of ignorance, and the position, the very life, of the Keeper of Andratan depended on keeping his master ignorant. And somewhere out there in the wilds of Faltha walked four men who carried knowledge that would give him the key, perhaps, to unimaginable power—or place him firmly in the pitiless hand of his master.

Deorc took a deep breath and extinguished the blue fire. These confrontations always left him weak and shaking. The Destroyer thought he alone knew the cost of magic, but Deorc had known it even before leaving Jasweyah. It was a mark of his strength that he chose, in his pride, to draw power from himself. Still, when he finally arrived in Instruere and began to order it to his satisfaction, he would have time to regain his strength and lay his traps.

Heaven defend anyone who found themselves in his way.

CHAPTER 1

THE GREAT CITY

LEITH STOOD SILENTLY on a narrow Instruian street, shaking with a deep, nameless emotion as the members of the Company finally reunited. First his father, then his distraught mother sought him out and they embraced, careless of anything but their grief, and bitter tears flowed.

They felt no joy at their narrow escape. The travelers had narrowly avoided the senseless violence that culminated in the death of the Fenni woman; and simply clung to each other, as much as anything reassuring themselves of the reality of their friends amidst the terror of the pursuit and the swiftness of Parlevaag's passing.

"It is over," Mahnum said quietly. "It is over." He repeated the words like an incantation designed to drive away despair.

"Yes, it is over; but I will not forget her sacrifice," said Kurr.

"Nor the hatred and evil that struck her down," Farr added bitterly.

Indrett lifted her tear-streaked face from her husband's breast, sobbing, her eyes filled with visions of her friend's horrific end. "She is dead!"

"Yet she died with honor, and in the eyes of the Fenni

has redeemed the death of her mate," Perdu said sternly, his voice gruff in the attempt to mask his own feelings. "Do not grieve! She wearied of life, and so gave it nobly so that we might live to continue our mission."

Indrett turned her eyes on him. "You mock her death!" she said, jaw clenched. "What meaning can it be given?"

"Perhaps no meaning for us, but who knows what meaning it had for her," said Hal. "At least she found rest."

"But it was senseless, senseless!" Still in shock, Indrett struggled to come to terms with what had just happened.

"Senseless according to you, maybe." Perdu turned to the coastlander woman. "Look past your First Men understandings. The Fenni would not regard Parlevaag's death as a tragedy. To them her sacrifice would be a thing of beauty, bringing final balance to her life. How do you know this was not the one thing to make sense to her, since her husband was taken in similar violence? Have you considered that maybe your friendship with her gave her the strength to do this thing? And now you want to make it a vile act?"

"I saw no beauty in it." The words were torn out of her. Leith could see the suffering in her eyes, as though she felt that harrowing sword piercing her own flesh, felt the life go out of herself, could still feel it, and could not stop her mind from recalling the savagery over and over again.

"But why didn't the soldiers on the wall come to our aid?" Stella asked, anger in her voice. "Why did they close the gates?"

"It was they as much as the Widuz who killed Parlevaag," Farr said. "Someone will answer for this cowardly act."

"What sort of place is this, where those sworn to protect instead shut the gates on us?"

"Perhaps they saw a threat approaching the city, and did not distinguish between us and the Widuz," Hal said quietly.

"Let us hope that the Iron Door will open for us more swiftly than did the gates of Instruere!" Kurr did not believe in omens, but even to his mind their time in the Great City had not begun well.

A few streets away a guard rose unsteadily to his feet amidst the shards of a broken jug, hand pressed against his badly bleeding head; all the while trying to explain with little coherence to his fellows the events that had led to this assault on his person.

Eventually he told his tale, and guards spread out to begin a search for anyone answering the sketchy description of his assailant. Assaults on the Instruian Guard were always taken seriously: this northern boy would likely face an unpleasant time in The Pinion when the guards found him.

Phemanderac found the travelers standing heedless on the Vitulian Way, the main road through the city from the Inna Gate. Leith introduced him to the Company, and his first counsel to them was to save their questions until after they found the relative safety of a narrow alley. There they hid, while all around them guards clamored in the open streets; but whether it was the general confusion or the Company's nondescript gray garb, they were not apprehended. Then, as the sun set, the guards were relieved and the search ceased.

In the mournful twilight the Company went out from

the Inna Gate to claim the body. Why no one had thought
to post a guard by the still form of Parlevaag, against the
chance the Company might reclaim her, none of them
could say. Perhaps the guardsmen had not yet connected
Leith with the disturbance at the Gate, though surely the
injured guard would have known. Whatever the reason,
the northerners were grateful.

Most travelers simply passed by Parlevaag, ignoring
the sight, though some gathered like carrion-beasts around
the still form, speculating on the explanation for such a re-
pugnant act within the shadow of their impregnable city.
"It's those uncivilized people from Deuverre," said one.
"Can't trust them as comes from the north," added another. "Animals they are, got no learnin' at all." The spectators scattered as the Company approached. No one
interfered when, after the fashion of the Fenni, they gathered sticks and dry grasses to make Parlevaag a pyre.
Perdu withdrew the Widuz sword from her body and cast
it into the river. Then tenderly, with reverence, they whispered their last goodbyes and set fire to the sacred mound.
Driven by the sea breeze, smoke from the pyre mingled
with that from the cook-fires of fishermen and itinerants,
casting a pall over Longbridge.

"The vultures gather on the city wall," Kurr muttered
to Farr as the flames reluctantly began their solemn task.

"Let them look," came his reply. "Their presence does
not dishonor her. She was worth more than any of them."

"I'll never understand why no one came to help."

"Such cowardice makes me ashamed to be Falthan,"
Farr said, bitterness in his voice.

Phemanderac grunted his agreement. "These 'people,'"—he made the word sound like an insult—"claim
to be direct descendants of the House of Landam. Furist,

the Arkhos of Landam, was as valiant a man as they are craven."

"Will we have any success in a city such as this has become?" the old farmer asked, doubt in his voice, as though in Parlevaag's death he read the death of their quest. "Where are the Watchers?"

Farr turned to Kurr. "My friend, you know more than I; but perhaps none of us knows very much. The fighting is over, and now the diplomacy begins. I must take a backseat and remain silent. If only Wira were still alive! His skill with words in tight places would serve the Company well."

The remaining Storrsen sighed. "If the diplomacy does not go well, all I can hope for is to die in battle against the Bhrudwans as honorably as did my brother."

Kurr did not reply. Instead he began to mutter to himself, loud enough for Leith at least to overhear him. "Why now? Why not when I was young and could wield a sword? Why now, when I am old and weak?" With a heavy sigh the old farmer turned and reentered the city upon which all their hopes rested, and the others followed behind him.

That evening the Company met Foilzie. After she heard their tale of the disaster outside the gate, she insisted the Company stay at her house, and offered them the refurbished rooms above the basement. "Don't pay me no money," she said, over their protestations. "Can't have you sleeping on the streets. The least I can do, since no one else in this city lifted a finger to help. Anyway, there's a curfew on, so you won't be allowed out after dark to look for somewhere else to stay."

"A curfew?" questioned the old farmer. "What is happening?"

"Escaigne is up to its old tricks," Foilzie said, as though that answered the question. She appeared not to notice, or to ignore, the quizzical looks her answer produced. If they had not been so exhausted the Company might have pursued the matter; but weeks afoot, days of flight and sudden sorrow proved too much for them, and they found their beds early.

The last of the northerners did not arise before noon the next day. After the midday meal they gathered in the basement to discuss their predicament. There Leith formally introduced Phemanderac to the group; and Leith explained in detail the tall man's role in their escape from Adunlok, a story which garnered the philosopher much praise from Mahnum and Indrett.

"I saw you!" the Trader said, face alight. "On the southern flank of Clovenchine you stood, and I thought you the enemy. I owe you thanks. Your playing of that instrument in the caverns below Adunlok saved my life." He pointed to the harp sitting across Phemanderac's shoulders, then explained how the unearthly sound distracted the champion of Widuz. "I would dearly love to hear you play it again."

Phemanderac smiled, and his absurdly long face lit up with a strange intensity. "Come with me this afternoon to the market," he said. "There I play the harp for the people; they gather to listen and I earn a little money."

"Enough to find better accommodation?" Stella asked. Her bed had been uncomfortable, lumpy and bug-ridden.

"We could certainly find more comfortable accommodation," Phemanderac acknowledged, "but we're unlikely to discover another landlady like Foilzie."

"Anyway," Perdu interrupted, "we may need the money for something more important than accommodation." He looked squarely at the tall philosopher. "Assuming, of course, that you're with us, and agree to use your wealth for the cause of the Company."

"Perhaps the Company, and its quest, are things we need to talk about." Phemanderac rose from a low couch and began to pace up and down the room. "I have many questions for you all."

Kurr stood up in his turn. "Can we trust you with the answers?"

"Trust me? What would I do with them that could damage you or your cause?"

"Sell them to the Instruians, for one thing." Kurr's voice took on an unexpectedly truculent note. "I'm sure the city guards would like to know a little more about us. I don't like traitors."

Phemanderac strode over to the old farmer, heat in his eyes. "This is advice only. That kind of talk will get you nowhere in this town. I spent three months here only last year, trying to get permission to view the archives in the Hall of Lore. The bureaucracy here is difficult to circumvent and impossible to hurry. You will have one chance only at the Iron Door. Talk like that will make enemies of your friends and render your task fruitless."

Leith tugged at a loose thread on his sleeve while he spoke. "I told Phemanderac everything. He is our friend! Kroptur said that we should discover friends in unlikely places. There aren't many more unlikely places than the Widuz fortress." His voice pleaded with them for understanding.

"And Kroptur also warned us we would meet people who seemed friendly but would hinder our cause," came the farmer's angry reply. "You were unwise to talk of our mission to anyone. There are few people we can trust!"

Leith's face reddened, and he sat down.

Phemanderac seemed untroubled by the harsh words. "In my opinion, a man who saves one of your Company from the pit of the Widuz, then delivers him safely to you and asks nothing in return, is a man worthy of trust. But no matter: the milk is out of the jug. What Leith says is true. I know about your quest. You seek to warn Faltha of the imminent Bhrudwan invasion, and have captured a Bhrudwan warrior to aid your cause. Where is he, by the way?"

Kurr said nothing, his lips a thin white line. The Acolyte was in fact held, trussed up, in one of the tenement's rooms, the door locked and barred, his bonds checked regularly. The old farmer most definitely did not feel safe around the Bhrudwan warrior, and the worry of keeping him safely restrained continued to eat away at him. They had concealed the nature of their captive from Foilzie, but it was undoubtedly only a matter of time before the Instruian woman discovered what manner of man was housed within her lodgings.

Phemanderac shrugged his shoulders. "I can help you," he said, "that is, if you want help. And, believe me, you'll need it. It takes a great deal of money—and persistence—to see the Council of Faltha. Once there, you will need someone to present your argument skilfully and concisely. Remember, you only get one chance."

"So what do you offer us?" Kurr said shortly. Leith could see and hear the old farmer's anger, but could think of no good reason for it. Perhaps something about Phemanderac's overweening self-confidence ruffled him.

The philosopher seemed unaware of the antagonism. "Money, lodgings, advice, a persuasive voice before the Council—and a number of other things of which I will not tell you yet, but are perhaps more valuable than anything else I have."

Hal stood, his movements jerky, and maneuvered himself to the center of the room. All eyes turned to him. "Do you see bribery as the best approach to the Council of Faltha?" he asked the philosopher.

Leith groaned, and buried his face in his hands.

"The best approach? It is the only approach. Without money they will not acknowledge your existence, let alone receive your suit. There are any number of minor officials who need to be paid off—in increasingly large amounts—before the Council will grant you an audience."

"Doesn't that bother you?" Hal stared up into Phemanderac's eyes well past the point of politeness. Leith could not help being reminded of his brother's confrontation with the Hermit. Back then, Hal had seemed so certain his way was the right way, and now appeared to be readying himself for another stubborn argument.

"Bother me? No. Should it?"

"I think it should. We are all forgetting the justice of our cause. We seek nothing for ourselves. Rather, we desire an audience with the Falthan Council because we have something to give them: time to prepare against the coming invasion. How could this threaten the Council? Why should they not see us? I think we should make it known we have information of great importance to them. Curiosity may do what money cannot."

Mahnum spoke, disapproval clear in his voice. "I counsel caution in approaching the Council of Faltha. Son, I told you the Voice on Andratan gloated over those Falthans he had suborned to his service. He gave me names, he showed me faces, faces I will never forget." He paused, taking a deep breath. "The Voice told me some of his agents have infiltrated even the Council of Faltha. He was quite explicit about it. Do you not think there is a risk that if we state our mission directly those corrupt members of the Council will hear of it, and simply advise the others not to see us?"

"Then they will reveal their true colors," Hal said. "Truth is more powerful than deception! Deceit wins many battles, but the fruits of its victories evaporate along with the lies it tells. Truth may suffer many defeats, but the victories it wins are permanent. We must tell the truth."

"The truth can be used against us," Mahnum countered. "Let me spell it out for you. The Council has sixteen members, one from each of the kingdoms of Faltha. Five countries—Sarista, Deuverre, Sna Vaztha, Haurn and Deruys—have loyal kings and their representatives on the Council follow that loyalty. We know that Haurn is a vassal state of Sna Vaztha, but the vote still counts separately on the Council. Another four of the kings have betrayed us to the Bhrudwans, but their ambassadors to the Council are still true. These are Plonya, Asgowan, Redana'a and Piskasia. The kings of Treika, Favony and Nemohaim are loyal to Faltha, or at least opposed to Bhrudwo, but their ambassadors are traitors. And four kingdoms—Vertensia, Straux, Tabul and our beloved Firanes—are betrayed by both king and councillor.

"This means there are eight of the Sixteen Kingdoms with traitors for monarchs. Faltha is in a perilous position.

"But the situation of the Council is not so desperate, though it might have become so by now, as it is over a year since I heard the Voice. Nine of the Councillors are loyal and seven are traitors. So, as long as things have remained the same, we should have the numbers to win the

Council. Hal, if we tell official after official that Faltha is in imminent danger of invasion, we will eventually encounter one who is in the pay of the enemy, or who is willing to sell the information to them. Then we will be barred from seeing the Council at all, or we will ourselves be betrayed when we get there. Let us be wise with the truth."

"Even if we are betrayed, we should tell the truth and not resort to bribery," Hal insisted. "Victory will come in the end."

"Refreshingly direct," Phemanderac commented, "but do you have the time to suffer the defeats until this supposed victory comes? I warn you, it may only take one defeat to render your task impossible." He continued pacing, as though possessed of vigor enough to fight the Bhrudwans right then. "Can we speak more frankly?" he said, "I too have a task, a mission I seek to complete, and to do so I need to open my heart to you. Shall we talk openly of our plans? Then, if you will not receive my help, I will walk away from you after promising never to tell anyone about your mission. I will swear an oath! But if I can convince you that I'm trustworthy, I would ask that you consider permitting me to join the Company."

Kurr looked around the room. He read tiredness in the faces of his charges, and he realized that this was not the best time to deal with important issues. What they all needed was rest or diversion, something to help them get over the weariness and shock they still felt. The tall stranger seemed to have more energy than the rest of them combined.

"We must talk about these things," the old farmer said, hoping his instinct was right, "but not now, not today. We're simply too exhausted to make good decisions.

Tomorrow morning we'll give Phemanderac the chance to explain himself, and he will hear all he wants to know. Until then, I would advise you all to seek sleep, or at least rest.

"We have much still to do," he continued. "I, for one, will begin searching for signs of my order. Somewhere in this forsaken city the Watchers must live, and unless they have completely abandoned their calling, they will be actively opposing any traitors against Faltha. Once I discover them, we may find that access to the Council of Faltha becomes much easier."

He sighed. "At least that's my hope. No other reason for a weary old man to have come this far."

"Get some rest, weary old man," Perdu said quietly, a hint of kindness in his words. "The Watchers will still be around tomorrow."

"Do you want to come to the market?" Phemanderac had spent the afternoon pacing the floor.

"Well, I don't need the rest," Leith said. *I can't sleep in this house, not now she's here. Perhaps if I go for a walk . . .*

"Come on, then." Before Leith could rise from his couch, the philosopher had slipped his harp over his shoulder and stood waiting by the door.

As they came out on to the landing at the top of the wooden stair, a voice rose from the floor below. "Where are you going?"

"Just to the market," Leith replied. "Phemanderac plays his harp for them most afternoons."

"Oh." The old farmer's voice sounded weary and strained. "Does he mind if I tag along?"

"Not at all," the philosopher said cheerfully.

"And us? Can we come?" Simultaneous inquiries emerged from other rooms.

"Of course!" Phemanderac told them, and laughed.

"So much for the Company's rest," said Kurr gruffly.

In the end only Perdu stayed in the tenement building, assigned to keep an eye on their prisoner. Everyone else took refuge in the multicolored gaiety of the market.

The site of the market, one of sixteen in the Great City—one for each kingdom, it was said, though undoubtedly the number was merely a coincidence—occupied the large open space at the intersection of three narrow lanes and a major thoroughfare. Stall owners set themselves up in a rough circle at the perimeter. There they peddled their produce and their wares, which ranged from necessities such as food and clothing through to the frivolous and even the downright dangerous. The central area showcased various entertainments. The more professional of these were funded by the stall owners—who paid the performers in the hope they would attract people away from the other markets—the others by coins collected from the spectators. The resulting cacophonous crush of both Instruians and visitors became a swirling sea of color and light best observed from one of the nearby rooftops, yet best experienced at ground level.

"Stay together," Phemanderac counseled them, "and keep your hands in your pockets. Don't buy anything, because I can get it cheaper for you."

"Why should we keep our hands in our pockets?" Indrett wanted to know. Wide-eyed, she gazed at delights unimagined, Rammr-born though she was. Few of them had imagined the Great City would be like this.

"Professional pickpockets. It's harder to pick a pocket if your hand is in it. If you relax your vigilance they'll take everything not actually tied to you. Stories are told about the best of them. Travelers have reported losing their undershirts without realizing 'til day's end."

Leith was beginning to recoganize the twinkle in Phemanderac's eye that accompanied these statements, but one or two of the others looked at the tall man doubtfully.

The Company spent an hour sampling the sights, sounds and smells of this, perhaps the brightest if not the largest market in Instruere. They saw fish taken from the river surrounding the city and fish from the sea two days' journey to the west. Larger and more varied than anything from the colder waters of the north were huge eels, strange fish with beards or wire-like protrusions from their heads, and crab-like fish with red bodies and huge claws. Food of every sort could be bought, cheaply if one was skilled at bargaining. Fruit of many shapes and colors, vegetables of all kinds, meats and livestock gathered from each of the Sixteen Kingdoms of Faltha. The Company watched hawkers trying to sell jewelry for the wrists, for the ankles, for the neck, the ears, the nose or virtually any protruding part of the body. They walked amongst crowds who applauded displays of juggling and acrobatics by a troupe of men from somewhere in the arid south; exotic dancing by young women—probably locals, Indrett decided—whose exuberance and lack of adequate clothing attracted quite a following; and listened to minstrels performing alone or in small groups on a variety of instruments, few of which were familiar to any of the Company. One of the more enthusiastic stall owners tried to sell them children's shoes, not desisting even when it was pointed out that they had no children with them. He stopped only when they agreed to buy four fretas' worth of sweetmeats and a decidedly amateurish painting of a mountainous landscape. The experience overwhelmed, exhilarated and unsettled the villagers from Loulea and their friends, leaving no time, it seemed, even to draw breath; and they soon lost themselves in the agreeably exciting chaos.

Phemanderac excused himself and made his way to the open space in the center of the market just vacated by the acrobats. Expectantly the crowd quieted down to what Leith would have described as a dull roar, and most turned to watch and listen. Of the Company, only Leith and his father knew what to expect.

The philosopher unlimbered his harp like a weapon, sat comfortably on the cobbles, then fitted one point of the triangle under his chin and placed another between his feet. He ran his fingers across the instrument, so lightly that at first it could not be heard over the noise of the crowd, and Mahnum felt a slight disappointment rise within him. He guessed much of the magic he had experienced came from the caverns of Adunlok, but anticipated more than this.

Phemanderac played a chord, the crowd hushed and the Trader discovered the magic was still there. Like liquid fire the notes dropped from the thin fingers, coalescing into a sound that set him trembling.

Leith, too, felt himself respond to the music, as he did every time he heard it, even though the sounds lacked the fullness lent them by the great caves under Adunlok. For a time the melody soared, then suddenly was reined in by a tight, syncopated rhythm unlike anything the Falthans had ever heard. All around the market people found themselves opened by the music, a sweet song that seemed to draw them into a more complete embrace than any of them had known. Even in a land where music was well recognized as able to affect the soul, Phemanderac's skill was deeply moving. Immersed in the sound, his listeners were granted the chance to forget their struggles for a time; some were presented with the opportunity to overcome them. His playing left no one untouched.

Other musicians began to join him, their sounds merging with those of the philosopher in harmony and counterpoint, until to Leith and Mahnum the music began at last to echo the solidity and complexity of the sound of Wambakalven. Some of the onlookers began to dance, seemingly unconscious to all but the rhythm. Indrett held her breath, absorbed by the beauty of what she heard; and at the back of her mind the Northern Lights danced. Stirred to the bone, Farr thought of the Vinkullen bards, cold and austere, and by how much this music surpassed them. Stella felt the notes from the harp flowing over and through her like some soothing autumn rain, granting relief from an oppressive summer. Kurr closed his eyes and stood quietly as he allowed himself to wish, honestly and openly for the first time, that Tinei was here to share the music with him. She would have loved music and market both.

Singing came after that, local musicians leading the crowd in old folk songs from the Golden Age, a gentler, richer time ended by the Bhrudwan invasion a thousand years ago. Phemanderac played with them for a while longer, then swung his harp over his shoulder and joined the Company. He fully understood the silence that greeted him. He remembered feeling the same way himself when he first heard the harp played by Pyrinius, his teacher, the day he determined he would master this difficult instrument. To speak after such playing would be to spoil the peace settling over them like a thick blanket.

Without a word they returned to their lodgings.

*   *   *

"All right, Phemanderac," Kurr said. Weariness bit deep into the old farmer's bones: he knew he ought to have spent the afternoon sleeping, but was honest enough to recoganize he would not have slept if he had stayed in their lodgings. "Forgive us for being perhaps a little over-protective of our mission, especially when it's obvious we need all the help we can get. You've earned the chance to speak, friend. Tell us about yourself. Where are you from, and what can you offer?"

The tall stranger settled back into his couch. The members of the Company spread themselves around the basement room, the fading natural light from the one small window already surpassed by two blazing tapers.

"I come from a place called Dhauria, a small country on the far side of Desicca, the *Khersos*, the Deep Desert of Faltha. I am the first—"

"Dhauria?" Mahnum interrupted, puzzled. "The Drowned Land? You come from the Drowned Land?"

Phemanderac was about to reply, but was beaten by Kurr. "You don't mean the Vale of Dona Mihst, surely?" His eyes sought an answer from either Mahnum or Phemanderac.

"How do you know of the Drowned Land?" the thin philosopher asked Mahnum.

"The Drowned Land is what remains of the Vale of the First Men, according to legend, with Dona Mihst as the capital," Mahnum replied to Kurr, who nodded. They both turned to Phemanderac.

"What do you know of Dhauria?" he asked them.

Kurr looked at Mahnum. "All the Watchers are taught the *Domaz Skreud*, which tells the tale of the Poisoning—*Dhaur Bitan*—in which Kannwar betrays the First Men and pulls the wrath of the Most High down on to the

Vale of Dona Mihst. It is the central history of the First Men, the ancestors of true Falthans. I related the story to the Company, though they may not remember it."

"Do all Firanese know this story?" Phemanderac asked. "Few I have met in Faltha admit to knowing it."

"I've not heard it in its fullness," Mahnum said. "I heard the name Dhauria from the Voice of Andratan."

"Leith told me of your adventure, and I can scarcely credit it. You were interrogated by the Voice, in that terrible castle, and yet you live? Surely in this, more than anything else, we can discern the hand of the Most High!"

"The hand of a greedy Trader, more like." The anger in Mahnum's voice was unmistakable. "Vaniyo may have saved me from the devices of the torturers, but he placed me in the merciless hands of the Bhrudwan warriors. At the very least, the deaths of innocents in a Favonian village can be laid at his feet."

"The shades of my father and my brother also have reason to be angry," Farr added, his tone bitter.

The old farmer appeared not to hear this last exchange. He took a step toward the couch upon which the lean, gaunt Dhaurian sat. "I thought, as do all the Watchers, that Dhauria was a myth, an imaginary place, and the story of its fall was allegorical of the corruption of man, serving to explain the hatred of the Destroyer and of Bhrudwo towards us." Kurr shook his head. "Yet you say this land of myth is your home?"

Phemanderac glanced at Kurr, then stared intently at Mahnum. "You have among you one who escaped the dread Keep of legend, yet you doubt the existence of my country?"

"Wait a moment!" Farr said. "Too many questions, and

not enough answers! There are others here who don't know what you're talking about. Let's sort this out."

Everyone sat down, leaving the Vinkullen man alone on his feet.

"Phemanderac: you come from this Dhauria country. Is Dhauria another name for one of the Sixteen?"

"No," the philosopher replied. "Dhauria is not one of the Sixteen Kingdoms, and has no seat on the Council. Yet according to the ancient writings every one of the Sixteen Kingdoms sprang from the inhabitants of Dhauria."

Farr persisted. "What do these other names mean?"

"The Drowned Land?" Mahnum said. "As far as I know, that is a literal interpretation of Dhauria."

"Not exactly," Phemanderac corrected, the scholar within getting the better of him. " 'Death Valley' is the exact translation, though I can see how the error occurred. 'Ria' is an old word meaning 'drowned valley.' "

"What about the other one?" Farr pressed. "The Vale of something or other?"

"The Vale of Dona Mihst," Phemanderac finished for him. "That was the name of my country before we were betrayed and the Most High sent a flood to drown us."

"Oh yes, I remember now. Kurr told us the story on Breidhan Moor." The lines cleared from Farr's brow.

"Well, now we've established where Phemanderac comes from—or, at least, where he claims to have come from," the old farmer said. "Even if we cannot yet credit it. Will it take the rest of the evening to hear why he wants to join the Company?"

"Not if I can help it," Phemanderac said, smiling widely. "But indulge me a moment first, if you will. This man, Leith's father, Mahnum: you've been on Andratan, you've heard the Voice. Can you be certain it was the Destroyer?"

Mahnum sighed. "I've been on Andratan, I've seen the fortress, I've visited the dungeons; I've heard the voice of one *claiming* to be the Destroyer. His voice was powerful. I've wondered ever since if it was indeed the ancient and Undying Man, or if in my weakened state I was merely more suggestible. I don't know."

"Yet here you are. People do not leave Andratan. We Dhaurians know this, for the Bhrudwans are our sworn enemies, and some of our number have been taken there. None have returned."

"It was a mistake," Mahnum said quietly. "They meant to make an end to me, and so the Voice told me everything about the coming Bhrudwan invasion, trying to ferret out information he hoped I had, secure in the knowledge his boastful words would die with me."

"My friend, they should build a statue to you." Phemanderac shook his head.

"After they listen to my story, it is my hope that they will be too busy building defenses to worry about statues."

The man from Dhauria told them about himself, continuing his interminable pacing as he did so. He was, he told them, the son of a blacksmith. His family lived in a small village a day's walk upvalley from the island of Dona Mihst, and as a youth he was apprenticed to his father. His mother, however, held higher hopes for her youngest son, and convinced her husband to send him to the School of the Prophets when he was sixteen years old. There he met Pyrinius, the most famous of all teachers, listened to the debates, heard the music, and lost his heart to learning. Twelve years he spent in the School, replacing his mentor when the old man died.

He paid special attention to one area of lore. Various old and long-neglected scrolls contained words from prophets generally regarded as mentally unbalanced by later generations and, in the opinion of most, not fit for serious study. Yet Pyrinius chose to question the general opinion, and began the exhaustive work of restoring the scrolls, convinced something of the utmost importance lay hidden in their obscure phrasings. Though he died before he discovered what it might be, he passed his passion and curiosity on to his disciple, and Phemanderac still vividly remembered the day when finally he realized what, or who, the common factor in all the writings actually was. More than anything he wished the old man had lived to share his triumph, for he, Phemanderac the blacksmith's son, had uncovered the secret of the Right Hand of the Most High.

Phemanderac continued his story, completely failing to notice Mahnum stiffen, then lean forward with mounting excitement. The Right Hand, explained the Dhaurian philosopher, is revealed in the scrolls to be a person, the representative of the Most High in the world—some prophets referred to the actual embodiment of the Most High, though the manuscripts were obscure on this point— who would appear at the moment of greatest danger to Faltha. His appearance would herald the thwarting of Bhrudwo's power, ushering in a new age of enlightenment when once again the Most High would concern Himself with the affairs of the First Men. Phemanderac called a meeting of the philosophers, the most senior of the prophets, to share his knowledge, but suffered a rude shock.

"We are not concerned with Falthan affairs," his sage elders told him. "These manuscripts are of dubious origin, are they not? It may be they were written by Falthans and brought here in the days when we of the Vale still had ill-advised contact with the north. So what if the Right

Hand appears? We need him not: we are of the Rehtal Clan, descendants of Sthane of the House of Saiwiz; we have access to the benefits of the Most High. Forget such studies, conceived as they were by an old man far advanced in his dotage, and return to the paths of wisdom."

The young philosopher argued against the judgment of his elders, but could not convince them of the validity of his growing interest in the Right Hand. They forbade him to pursue it, yet he continued reading the scrolls. They had the scrolls destroyed, a shocking act which pained him still, though he had memorized their contents. He expressed the desire to journey to Faltha in order to verify his theories, but this they would not allow, fearing contamination by the ideas and customs of lesser men. So, obeying his inner prompting, he departed from his family and the land of Dhauria without leave nearly three years ago, and crossed the Deep Desert alone. Aware of the parallel between his rebellion and that of Kannwar two thousand years earlier, he hoped his cause was more just than that of the black-hearted Destroyer.

About the same time I set out for Bhrudwo, Mahnum thought.

Phemanderac searched Faltha for knowledge of the Right Hand, but found none. "Only in the vaults of the Hall of Lore in Instruere might I have been able to find, perhaps, the evidence I sought, but the Council denied me access. I continued westwards, persuaded with ever-increasing urgency that time was short, pursuing the only clue as to the whereabouts of the Right Hand: a fragment of a riddle locating that which I seek '*in lowly vale on Cape of Fire.*'" This dragged another start from Mahnum, and one or two others of the Company, but he was too far gone in his story to notice.

He told them, "Unwittingly I strayed into the lands of the Widuz, who captured me there and took me to the fastness of Adunlok. Strangely, I was ignored in my cell while those around me were given to Helig Holth. Then Leith arrived in my cell, and when he told me his own strange story, everything fell into place. Firanes is the Cape of Fire, rendered in the old tongue; Loulea is the lowly vale . . ."

"And the Right Hand?" Mahnum asked, as breathless as though from a long run. He could not forget the terror which accompanied his inquisition on Andratan, nor could he erase from his mind the threats and the beatings by the Bhrudwans. Everything had been about the Right Hand. His breath came quickly, paused as he was on the brink of revelation. Maybe his two-year ordeal was about to make sense.

Phemanderac turned and faced him. "I was hoping you could tell me," he said.

Outside twilight gave way to darkness, and the Great City settled into another uneasy night. "I'm not sure what to make of all this," Kurr said. "If I understand you right, you say there exists right now in Faltha—from Loulea, no less—someone who presumably possesses magical powers, someone whom the Most High will use to subdue the Bhrudwans. I have to be honest with you; there was no such person there when I left, nor has there ever been. If such a one lived in Loulea, we would have brought him on our quest. Surely the Most High would have organized it so that he came with us?

"Or are you saying he *is* one of us? Take your pick: a Trader and his wife, by far the two most likely candidates, though by his own admission Mahnum does not know who this 'Right Hand' is. A young woman, a crippled youth and his younger brother, none of whom possess the qualities you imply. Our Haufuth—village headman—though a worthy man, is the least likely of all, and abandoned the quest on the borders of Firanes. Such we are. Not a hero amongst us." The old farmer leaned forward, his whole demeanor a challenge to the young Dhaurian.

Phemanderac held his ground. "Yet you defeated the Bhrudwan warriors and escaped from the Widuz, feats which the stoutest warrior might fail to accomplish." The philosopher raised his voice. "Ask yourselves: are those victories attributable to your own strength? Or is there another Hand positioning and protecting you? This Right Hand need not be strong in himself. A hand is, after all, merely the focus and outworking of the strength of the arm. It may be that the Right Hand is among us, and we—indeed, even he—do not recoganize it."

"It is far more likely our victories are due, at least in part, to the courage of our members, the sacrifices of Wira and Parlevaag, and a leadership determined to do what is right." Though Hal's voice remained soft, the words hung like a challenge in the room.

Phemanderac turned to him. "You do not believe my tale of the Right Hand?"

Hal smiled. "I believe that were all of us to simply do what we know to be right, there would be no need for the Right Hand. I listen to what I can hear of the Most High, and try to obey his words. If that is power, then so be it, but it is not a sword with which to strike at the Bhrudwan army. Rather, it is an ointment to apply to the wounds of life."

"Yet there is a power about you and your family. I can sense it."

"It is easy to mistake integrity for power," said Hal. "However, whatever you discern cannot run in our family, for I am adopted."

"Are you saying that the Right Hand is from Mahnum's family?" Kurr asked.

"I can do little more than guess at the moment," answered Phemanderac. "But I am certain he—or she—is one of the Company."

"A tale of coincidence misinterpreted by a hopeful scholar, if you ask me." Farr stood up, a mixture of puzzlement and disbelief on his face. "Like Hal says, we've come this far through hard work, courage and determination, not because of some hidden magician. We're here because of the sacrifices of good people, because Wira and Parlevaag gave their lives for us. The Council of Faltha will believe us because of the Bhrudwan captive and the testimony of this Trader. I say this man's words are irrelevant. He would do better to play his music in the marketplace, or go back to his homeland where they obviously appreciate this kind of talk."

"What's got under your skin?" Kurr turned to the Vinkullen man.

"Strong arms are always taken for granted, while the good talkers gather all the praise."

Kurr frowned. "Surely the time for strength is over? What we need now is someone with a clever turn of phrase."

"And what does the fighter do? Sit back while Mister Golden Tongue plays his harp for the Council?"

Kurr's frown deepened. This was like the bad old days before they met the Fodhram. He had neither realized just how much Withwestwa Wood had changed Farr, nor that the change might not be permanent.

Before he got another chance to speak, Phemanderac stood and walked over to the wooden stool upon which Farr sat. The Vinkullen man rose to meet him. There they stood, facing each other like jilted lovers or warriors about to duel, the willowy philosopher half a head taller even than his snowy-haired antagonist.

"Actually, I agree with you," Phemanderac said. The whole room let out a relieved breath. "No amount of talking could have brought the Company safely to Instruere. I just happen to believe that—well—you were guided by an unseen power. You were *meant* to join the Company; your part is not yet over. We may yet have to fight."

"Oh," Farr replied, a little too sweetly. "So the Most High is in charge, is he? And he planned it so I could join the Company?"

Phemanderac nodded enthusiastically, not seeing the trap.

"I joined the Company as a direct result of my father being murdered by the Bhrudwan bandits," the mountain man breathed, his voice dangerously quiet. Then his patience snapped. "Did the Most High plan that too? Did he watch as my father writhed on the ground, as he begged for mercy, while they cut him and cut him and cut him just for the fun of it? Was he shouting encouragement?" His river was in flood, and the despair in his voice struck at the souls of those in the basement. "Was my brother part of his special plan? When he died trying to save the Company, was this because he loved us, or was it because the Most High organized his death? I have no need for such a god! I will not worship Him! Give me a sharp enough sword and I will kill Him!"

Phemanderac lowered his eyes. "My friend, if you would only listen—"

"No, you listen! I've heard you mystics talk about the Most High as though he lived in the next house, but it's just talk! When something needs to be done you go quiet and leave it to someone like me, or Stella, or Mahnum, or Kurr. Ordinary people! Give me deeds, not words! Be quiet and get on with it—like Hal here. He doesn't blather on about the Right Hand, he just gets on and does it."

At the mention of his name, Hal dragged himself to his feet and shuffled over to the two men. "There is a time for talk, Farr," he said quietly, "but that talk will be before the Council, and it will be about our deeds: about Mahnum and Andratan, about the Company and the Bhrudwans, about Leith and the Widuz, about Phemanderac and his journey to Faltha. There is no need to rehearse it here."

He clucked about them like a hen fussing over frightened chicks. "Don't be in a hurry to blame the Most High for what happened. It is futile to debate what is in his mind. If he exists, and if he is interested, he will have something to say before this mission is completed."

"Are all our discussions going to end up like this?" Leith asked his brother late that night. For the first time in months he and Hal found themselves alone together, and while they shared sleeping quarters there were things he intended to ask, suspicions he needed to voice. "You know, as debates about faith?"

Hal shrugged. "In one sense, all the discussions we ever have are about our beliefs," he said. "We either carefully avoid it, thereby giving it shape by the space we leave; or we find that it creeps in whatever the subject."

"But no one really believes in the Most High, do they? That was for the old days, when people didn't know as much as we do now." This wasn't Leith's own argument:

he once heard someone say it, but couldn't remember who. There was something akin to hope in his question, and also a shade of regret.

"Have people really changed? I think we are the same as we ever were in every important respect. We still need friendship and wish to give it; we continue to search for answers but struggle to find them; we still settle for much less than we could achieve; we persist in allowing petty selfishness to dominate and crush our lives. Some people even in these days think the Most High helps them meet their needs."

Leith lifted his eyes to gaze into those of his brother. "I saw you that night at Bandits' Cave," he said, then held his breath.

"I know," said Hal, and waited.

"But what—what did you do to the Hermit? I saw the black wings, I heard you rebuke him; then the next thing he was ill and the Haufuth had to stay behind, just like you said." Leith looked his brother in the eye. "Who are you?"

"I am who I've always been: Hal, your brother. I don't possess any dark powers, if that's what concerns you. What happened to the Hermit was not evil, not really. He was wounded, yes, but the wounds allowed his inner pain to be operated upon. Remember that lamb we kept last year? His leg had been broken, but had not healed properly. If we had left him alone, he would not have lived another year. Instead I broke his leg again—remember? You became upset and called me all manner of hurtful names. But now he is alive and well, and no longer remembers his pain. Do you see? What the lamb considered cruel was simply kindness beyond his understanding. In the same way, the Hermit now has a chance to become healthier than he has ever been."

Something in the glibness of the explanation, something in the certainty of the answer, annoyed Leith, and the old resentment began to build within him. "I thought you were angry with the Hermit," he said. "None of us could understand you. He did nothing wrong."

"Not angry with him; afraid for him. I still am. He has not learned to harness his gifts. Like a wild horse he longs for the highest pastures, but does not have the discipline to get there. Not until he is broken to the bit and to the bridle will he ever make the journey."

Something began to form in Leith's mind. "Wait. If we are all lambs—including you—what gave you the right to break the Hermit's leg? How could you understand what none of the rest of us could? And when he is broken to the bit and bridle, who will ride him to the high pastures?"

Hal smiled. "Those are impressive questions. Like the Hermit, I hear things. But unlike him, I act only when I am given permission."

"From a cruel god? How can you stand it?"

Hal said nothing in the face of Leith's rising anger.

"I don't want to know a god who hurts people. I don't want anything to do with a god who breaks people's legs and calls it kindness. I don't want to know a god who abandons his people."

Hal turned to face his younger brother. "Like Mahnum our father abandoned us? Be patient, Leith. One day you will be able to forgive him."

"Only if I choose to," Leith shot back before he could stop himself. "Maybe he doesn't deserve to be forgiven. I hate all this talk of goodness and forgiveness and mercy. I'm sick of you and your ways, Hal. You always find a way to put yourself above me. You're *always* right, and I hate it. It's just an act, if you'd only admit it. Some big act to compensate for your crippled body. Well, nobody likes it. And you're not as innocent as you make out, brother. I've been watching you!"

Even as he spoke he knew that this wasn't the best way to do things, that Hal wasn't his main target, just one who wouldn't strike back. Nevertheless.

"Tell me, brother, how did we defeat three powerful Bhrudwan warrior-magicians? Phemanderac told me something of these Lords of Fear while we traveled through Treika and Deuverre. How could we possibly have beaten them? Where did their magic go? Kroptur warned us of the power of these Bhrudwans. I saw no power. What do you know about that, brother?"

Hal returned Leith's stare for a moment before answering. He still betrayed no loss of composure.

"They weren't exactly at the height of their powers, Leith. Weeks on Breidhan Moor without the provisions we had, without a guide, without an aurochs like Wisent. They had to abandon their horses. Perhaps their strength was weakened by all this."

Leith shook his head. "I know you, Hal. You are aware of more than you're telling me. What about the Bhrudwan we took captive? Mother tells me he escaped from his bonds, yet the Company recaptured him. And surely he wasn't so weak then! He was supposed to have struck you with a sword, yet there wasn't a cut on you when the others came to your rescue. Don't tell me any lies! You're doing something to him, aren't you; you're keeping him sedated, like you did to the village horse when she got sick last year. You're a magician, exactly like the Bhrudwans. You're not just some farmer's boy, not just some local village healer. You're not the Right Hand they're talking about, though, I know that: the Right Hand is supposed to be good. For all your talk of the Most High, you're not good. I've seen you, remember? I've seen the black wings, and no arrogant talk of kind cruelty makes a bad thing good. So if you're not the Right Hand, and if you're not a farmer's son, what are you, Hal? *What are you?*"

"You'll see," came the unconcerned reply. "One day you'll find out whether I really am good or evil. Until then, watch me if you must. Warn the others if you think I'm dangerous. But remember the words of Kroptur, the ones he spoke to you and me just before we left his house. Do you remember? *'Answer me this question,'* he said. *'Do ye two boys love each other?'* Do you have your answer yet, Leith? I have mine. Do you want to hear it?"

"No, I don't. Go away."

"I love you, Leith. I always will. Now, goodnight."

"You've done it again, you monster." Leith glared at his brother's turned back.

The Company spent the next day in further debate. The basement echoed to the sound of voices raised in frustration, entreaty and occasional anger as they discussed how to gain access to the Council of Faltha. Gradually it became clear Hal would lose the argument. Farr, Kurr and Phemanderac all agreed that bribery would achieve their aims, while the direct approach entailed a great deal of risk and would work only slowly, if at all. Hal countered by arguing that even if bribery helped them towards their goal, the methods used to achieve it might sour the result. The others tried to understand, paying Hal at least that much respect, but in the end his lone voice lost out to the wisdom of his elders. It was decided. The Company would bribe their way to the Council.

The members of the Company would seek employment in the Great City, in order to raise the amount required to buy off the vast number of officials between them and the Council of Faltha. Phemanderac declared himself optimistic he could find jobs in the market for a number of them, and that a few weeks of his playing would bring in a substantial sum. Mahnum trusted his Trader skills would enable him to buy and sell to his advantage. Indrett had observed few sellers of baked sweets at the market, so saw a potential opening for the sale of her baking. One by one, each member of the Company suggested ways of making money; each, if the truth be known, relieved to have something to do, something to distract their minds from the rigors and sadnesses of the journey that lay behind them.

True to his word, Phemanderac persuaded the stallholders to find jobs for a number of the Company. Leith and Hal were employed by the fishmonger; Hal as a general "fetch-and-carry-it" boy, Leith as a filleter. Across the open space Stella worked with the jeweler, a job seemingly tailor-made for her; within days she bargained with the customers like an old-timer. Indrett rented space at the end of the foodmarket, getting up early each day to bake honey cakes and other sweets, simple northern delicacies not before seen at a sophisticated Instruian market. When the others arose in the morning she was already gone, leaving behind a delicious aroma.

Each market day ended before sunset, when a nighttime curfew came into effect. This was unusual for Instruere, but the Great City was on an unofficial war footing with a rebel town or province—Leith was not clear which—called Escaigne. On each street corner stood a waist-high pole, like a broom handle planted in the earth; the signal pole for curfew. When the Council deemed the city unsafe, the City Guard placed red tags on every pole as a warning to citizens not to be seen on the streets after sunset, unless they had special dispensation. This custom had first been introduced during the time of the Bhrudwan occupation nearly a thousand years before, but was now used almost exclusively when the robbers and raiders of Escaigne infiltrated the city, making it unsafe—so the Council said—for the ordinary Instruian to be abroad.

Establishing exactly who these Escaignians threatening the mighty city actually were took the Company quite a deal of working out. According to some at the market who said they knew (rather than the many who ventured an opinion), Escaigne was a town somewhere in Straux which had been made poor under onerous taxes, and raided Instruere in order to survive. Others claimed it was a secret society philosophically opposed to the rule of the Council, with its headquarters out in the forests of southern Deuverre, or in the swamplands of the Maremma; while still others said a disaffected former member of the Council of Faltha had raised an army and sought to bring down the Council. Whichever was correct, all agreed that from time to time raiders stole from the city granaries, markets and coffers, and letters sent to the Council of Faltha from a place called Escaigne claimed responsibility. No matter how diligently the Instruian Guard searched the countryside no trace of this country, city or organization had been found, and no captive, however mercilessly tortured, ever divulged the location of this mysterious place. Escaigne was a thorn in the Council's ample flesh.

The curfew proved a major barrier to the Company in their pursuit of a hearing from the Council of Faltha. It was difficult to raise enough money during the day to survive and to put some aside into the "bribe fund" and, as well, find the time required between market's close and the beginning of curfew to actually pursue the officials who required bribing. Eventually Kurr decided that Mahnum, Farr, Perdu and he himself would spend their afternoons seeing officials in the Hall of Meeting, while the others continued to earn money at the market.

The Company had one difficult moment with Foilzie, who had initially not been told of their prisoner. She'd been angry, going so far as to threaten to tell the Instruian Guard, and was dissuaded only by promises that it was a temporary arrangement, until such time as the Council of Faltha could be persuaded to take charge of their captive. Hal told them Achtal would be no trouble, but the Company took no chances, keeping him locked in an annex to the basement used as a storeroom.

The old farmer took time aside from the others to search for the Watchers. But, as day followed day and he found no sign of them, he began to question Kroptur's sources of information. The Seer's words suggested nothing had been heard from the Watchers for some time, which now seemed something of an understatement. Kurr spoke with business leaders, prominent citizens and even members of the Instruian Guard, and learned only that few of them remembered the existence of such a group. Those who did laughed it off as little more than legend. The Watchers seemed to have vanished from Instruere.

At the end of the first week the Company decided to begin the long process of approaching officials to gain an audience with the Council of Faltha. They sought advice from others at the market. Though none of the stall-owners had themselves been before the Council they all knew someone who had, and were not reluctant to offer counsel.

"Spend as much as you can on the first official," some said. "That way, you'll pass over many in the line."

"Don't waste your money on anyone below the Assistant Secretary," others advised. "They'll bleed you dry, only to pass you on to one of their friends, getting you no closer to the Council."

They made the journey to the Hall of Meeting again and again, until Kurr knew every step of the way like he knew the road to his own farm back home. They tried first one strategy, then another, spending money as fast as they earned it. Petty official after petty official they saw, mindful always of the long line of people in the Appellants' Corridor waiting to see the Council . . . but after weary weeks of this it seemed the Company were little closer to finding the key to unlock the Iron Door of the Outer Chamber.

Hal kept his silence. The others avoided eye contact with him, especially Leith, who wanted to see as little of his insufferable face as possible.

And somewhere to the east the armies of Bhrudwo undoubtedly gathered.

CHAPTER 2

BEHIND THE IRON DOOR

"YOU'VE BEEN IN THE CITY over a month now, and you still don't know the rules?" the thin-faced man said in mock surprise. "How do you expect to gain an audience with the Council unless you demonstrate your earnestness with some form of monetary contribution? Look around you! Do you think we maintain such a large building and associated staff without some sort of assistance from appellants?"

The four men nodded mechanically; they had heard this line or variations on it from an uncountable number of officials during the previous weeks.

"No doubt you've seen the crowds of people waiting to be heard in the Appellants' Corridor. Some of them have paid large sums of money to put their cases to the Council. Do you ask me to prefer you over them? That wouldn't be right, would it?"

"But as we explained to your secretarial assistant, we're not just another group wanting some favor from the Council," Mahnum said patiently. "We have information of vital importance to all Falthans about a threat to the whole of Faltha."

"So he told me," came the smooth reply. "But you can't expect me to believe you if you won't tell me what this threat is, now can you? For all I know there may be no threat, and you may be a group of madmen come to destabilize the economy of this city. Or perhaps you invented the whole thing just to gain an audience with the Council! Be reasonable! You might be the threat yourselves!" He smirked at them, clearly pleased by his own cleverness.

"Listen, we'd pay you if we could, but our funds have dried up. Surely the occasional person gets to see the Council with a genuine need?" In spite of his vow to keep his temper tightly reined in, Kurr felt anger bubbling under the surface of his words.

"A genuine need? Many of those waiting in the corridor out there have genuine needs indeed. Why, there's a man out there whose father died without making a will, and whose brother has taken all his inheritance. If he doesn't get a judgment soon his whole family will be forced to beg for a living. Would you consider that a genuine need?"

"If we don't get a hearing, he may be forced to beg for his life," Farr muttered under his breath.

"Very well!" Kurr grated, realizing he was fast losing the battle for self-control. "Are you telling me we've got this far, but you're not willing to pass us on to the next official in the chain?"

"The next official?" The thin-faced man looked highly insulted, though the expression did not extend to mask the indifference in his eyes. "I'll remind you I am the personal secretary to the Appellant Division of the Council of Faltha. As such I can recommend directly to the Council anyone I so choose. And I do not choose to do so in your case. Good day."

A door opened in the small alcove in which they stood,

and a head poked around it. "Furoman! Can you not keep things quiet? I have a great deal of work to do!"

"I'm sorry, Arkhos, but these appellants are unusually persistent, and rude with it."

"Arkhos?" Mahnum whispered. "That title is reserved for Council Members alone!"

Instantly Kurr seized the opportunity. "Thank you, Furoman, for granting us an opportunity to see the great Arkhos. We'll take only a few moments." He led the other three men past the astounded personal secretary and through the door before Furoman could react. Bemused, the Arkhos closed the door behind them.

"Very clever," the middle-aged, dark-skinned, black-haired man acknowledged in a heavily accented voice. This man surely had to be a southerner, from one of the hot countries. "Unusually persistent appellants?" he said, a quizzical look on his face. "What do these unusually persistent appellants want with the Council of Faltha?"

Outside the door Furoman bellowed with rage at being tricked. "It seems our subterfuge hasn't done much for the noise level." Mahnum grinned.

Farr could not stop staring at the strange figure of the Arkhos. He had never seen anyone with such dark features, in total contrast to the blond-haired Firanese he had assumed ubiquitous. He had met *losian* who looked more like true Falthans than did this man.

Kurr stepped forward and stood before the Arkhos. "Who do we have the pleasure of meeting?"

"Of course; I must introduce myself. Saraskar, Arkhos of Sarista, the Saristrian representative on the Council of Faltha." He held out his hand.

"Kurr, farmer from Loulea, a town in the North March of Firanes," said the old farmer, his shoulders set proudly as he shook the proffered hand. "This is Mahnum, Trader from the same town; Farr of Mjolkbridge, a week's march from Loulea; and Perdu, originally also from Mjolkbridge but of late an adopted Fenni of Myrvidda. We're glad you could make the time to see us," he finished with gentle irony.

"Ordinarily I see no appellants until the Council itself sees them," came the reply, "but here you are. Sit down, all of you." The Company pulled couches away from the wall and sat gratefully on them. The last week had been full of waiting in corridors and standing outside doors.

"So, the famous Firanese have fallen into my lap!" Saraskar said, hands clasped under his chin, and the blood of four men went suddenly cold. "Let me see, how does the story go? These Firanese nearly provoked an international incident by crossing Longbridge without the necessary papers, pursued by barbarian warriors from the north who certainly didn't stop for documentation. These Firanese were admitted to the city by a fellow countryman who infiltrated Instruere without authorization, along with a companion whose status is as yet undetermined, but who plays a very skilful harp, as I myself can attest, having attended a number of his performances. Story accurate so far?"

"I'm astonished and flattered at the depth of your information," Kurr said, his face stiff with surprise. Their attempts at secrecy had all been for nothing!

"I merely repeat the story circulating through all the wormholes in this worm-ridden building." The dark-skinned representative from Sarista looked at them through shrewd and calculating eyes, as they tried to keep their apprehension from showing. "So, what is your suit?" the Arkhos asked, his tone giving nothing away.

The old farmer glanced across at Mahnum, who nodded.

"I'll explain what we want, then I'll outline our reasons," Kurr replied, then took a deep breath. *This could be our only chance*, he thought. *I must not get angry. If only Phemanderac and Hal were here.*

"We have come to Instruere to seek an audience with the Council because we believe Faltha is in immediate danger of being invaded by Bhrudwo."

Saraskar's eyes widened a little, but he showed no other reaction.

"We believe the Council of Faltha should immediately mobilize the armies of their member countries to face this threat, thereby defusing it or at least meeting it head-on. The depth of our belief in this situation is shown both from our long journey through the northern winter to Instruere, and from our continued struggle to be heard by the Council, even after our resources were exhausted."

"Forgive me for saying so," the Arkhos said in his deep, resonant voice, "but I find it unlikely that a group of farmers and artisans from the most westerly and—how shall I say it?—*undeveloped* of Falthan countries would know of a Bhrudwan threat when neither Sna Vaztha or Piskasia, who lie across the border from that land, have anything to say about it, at least to my knowledge. So I need to know what evidence you have. Should you convince me of the validity of your claims, I will ensure you gain an immediate audience with the Council, and I will support you openly. However, if your evidence is not substantial and incontrovertible, I will ensure that not only will you get no further hearing from any officials, but also that you are removed from Instruere itself to prevent the spread of any rumor and associated panic. Others might argue my responsibility would not end until your deaths. Do you understand?"

The four men nodded. Each of them knew the games were over, the tale they had borne for months now was about to be put to the test, and that lives were at stake. "That is fair," Kurr replied, "and prudent. Thank you for hearing us." He looked at Mahnum, who nodded, a barely perceptible movement of his head.

The old farmer took a deep breath, and wiped the palms of his hands on his cloak. "Two years ago now, Mahnum here was ordered by the then King of Firanes to travel to Bhrudwo disguised as a Trader, in order to investigate a report that a Bhrudwan army was being assembled. We are unsure from where this report came, though we suspect it originated from the royal household itself, who were, we believe, being infiltrated by Bhrudwan sympathizers. It may be that someone overheard a secret conversation, or a courtier resisted the bribery of a traitor. Whatever the reason, the king was disturbed, and so sent Mahnum, the son of Firanes' most famous Trader, to investigate." He glanced over at the Trader.

Mahnum took over the story. "I entered Bhrudwo easily enough, and it soon became obvious to me that there was a major upheaval in that vast land. I investigated further, and became convinced Bhrudwan men were being recruited for an army, but could not determine that army's identity or purpose. Then I was captured and taken to Andratan."

Saraskar's jaw tightened.

"On Andratan I was questioned, as they quaintly put it; then, marked for death, I was told the details of a vast and intricate plan for the conquest of Faltha. With unexpected assistance I managed to escape, bearing this knowledge with me back to Faltha. However, I was trailed home by four Bhrudwan warriors of the highest order, Lords of

Fear, whose task was to capture me and learn what I knew. They were most likely sent by some leader not associated with Andratan, because the Master of Andratan had already learned everything I knew.

"The warriors caught up with me just after I made it home to Loulea in Firanes, and took my wife and myself captive. However, I had told my sons what I had learned, and they organized a party of farmers and artisans, as you so rightly put it, to rescue us from the Bhrudwans if they could, and to warn Falthans about the coming invasion."

Kurr resumed the narrative. "A group of us pursued the Bhrudwans along the Westway, enlisting the help of Farr and Perdu here in the process. Just west of Vindstrop House, a town in the wild lands north of Treika, we ambushed the Bhrudwans and freed their captives. We also succeeded in capturing one of their number, and brought him to Instruere as a token that our story is true. We expect his interrogation will prove invaluable in confirming our story.

"Unfortunately, a marauding band of Widuz captured one of Mahnum's sons and took him south to a forest fortress. With assistance from the local forest-dwellers, Mahnum tracked them and helped set his son free. They were then pursued by the Widuz, who harried our Company until we reached the gates of Instruere, where the narrative joins with the story you know already."

The four men watched the Councillor closely, but the expression on the face of the Saristrian ambassador gave nothing away.

"We have two main pieces of evidence to substantiate our story," Mahnum said, filling the silence. "First, there is the Bhrudwan warrior currently held at a secret location in this city, whom we will produce for the Council's examination. His presence will surely serve to corroborate our tale, and warn the Council that something serious is about to happen. To my knowledge none of the Lords of Fear have been seen in Faltha since the end of the Bhrudwan occupation a thousand years ago.

"The second piece of evidence is the information I carry in my head. In his quest to learn what I knew, the inquisitor on Andratan gave me full details of the plans to infiltrate Falthan leadership at the highest levels. I can tell you which Falthan kings are corrupted, and even the names of Council members who are about to betray Faltha. I reveal this only because your name, Saraskar, is not among them." Mahnum smiled weakly. "It has been a long time to bear such terrible secrets, and I need to pass the information on to someone trustworthy who is in a position to act. So, you see, I know things that will destroy Falthan politics, and may mean the death of many people, if the information is misused. My life, and the lives of many others, are in your hands."

The Arkhos of Sarista tried to remain impassive, but his clasped hands shook and his knuckles were white. "The proper course is to report to the Firanese king, or to his Regent as I understand the present situation is. If they would not see you, you might try the Firanese ambassador. Were these roads tried?" His voice was unnaturally quiet.

"No, they were not." Mahnum spoke with care. "As I said, Arkhos, I know the names of all those who are traitors to Faltha. You may draw your own conclusions."

"And you would not have spoken to me if my name had been one of those mentioned on Andratan?"

"No."

"Are you sure the names are accurate?" Saraskar

asked. "In the time since you were on Andratan, could others not have been recruited to the Bhrudwan cause?"

"Perhaps," said Mahnum, doubt in his voice. "My inquisitor seemed certain of his information. Indeed, I gained the impression that he was the mastermind behind the whole thing."

"The Destroyer himself?" Saraskar looked skeptical.

The Trader shrugged his shoulders.

"Your life truly is in my hands," the ambassador agreed, standing suddenly and locking the door with a key attached to a chain about his waist. "You were foolish, perhaps, to reveal so much to me. Do you know what the Instruian method is for dealing with such situations?"

The four men shook their heads.

"They would take you to their deepest dungeon and there introduce you to a number of sophisticated instruments designed to assist you in telling them everything they wished to know about these names. Cruel but very effective, I am told. Then once your information was theirs, they would see no reason to keep you alive. In fact, they would see many reasons to make you dead. Do you understand me?"

Four heads nodded.

"Fortunately for you, I am not an Instruian, and I despise their methods, unworthy of the descendants of the First Men. Also to your good fortune, I am one of the few to whom this story could be told without guaranteeing your untimely deaths. But be assured: you are in greater danger in this city than you ever were on your undoubtedly hazardous journey here." He thought for a moment. "I am inclined to take your story seriously, if not yet wholly give credence to it, because it confirms a number of things I myself have suspected for some time, but have not been willing to believe.

"If you will give me the names of the traitors on the Council of Faltha, I will arrange a hearing for you, so you can accuse them to their face," the ambassador continued. "I am in no position to move against them, you understand. My powers here in Instruere are tightly prescribed, and I have only a few personal guards for my protection. I promise to reveal your secret to no one. But you must understand the danger to you is greater than any danger I face, for whether your story is true or not, those you accuse on the Council will seek your deaths in order to ensure that others do not hear your accusations. With this in mind, do you wish to continue? Or would you perhaps prefer to flee Instruere now, while you still can, and leave me to investigate the story?"

Mahnum turned to the others. "Can we risk it?" he breathed.

"We're committed now," Perdu answered. "If we refuse, he might betray us."

"And what better chance than this will we be able to manufacture?" Farr said. "We must risk everything or make a swift escape from Instruere."

"We'll probably have to do that anyway," said Kurr. "The Arkhos is right. If we accuse members of the Council, they will seek our deaths whether the Council believes us or not."

Mahnum stood. "I'll tell you the names," he said. "We'll see the Council."

The door closed on the four northerners, leaving Saraskar, Arkhos of Sarista, alone with his thoughts, and unrelievedly dark ones they were. The little things he had been trying to ignore—the knotted groups in the hallways, the reluctance of the Instruian Guard to take his orders, the rise and rise of the Arkhos of Nemohaim, the new-found wealth of some of his colleagues—now added up to betrayal. And within one day the traitors would be unmasked, for the Council would meet tomorrow and he would ensure the northerners gained a hearing for their tale.

But would that serve only to speed up the Bhrudwan plans? Surely deception on this scale must be well planned to remain so completely hidden. In that case, would the traitors not have plans to cope with an untimely exposure? And would they not deal harshly with the ones who accused them?

He was afraid; there was no doubting that. Perhaps if he had been in Instruere on his own . . . but Sarista was a thousand miles and more to the south, and his wife and his two dear girls would not remain separated from him, insisting that they accompany him to the famed city of Faltha. Now he was in danger, and therefore they were in danger also.

Would there be enough time to spirit them away? He sighed, knowing there would not. Permission had to be sought, papers signed, guards assigned to them; all this would take time. Could he delay the northerners until his family was safely out of Instruere?

Then he thought for a moment of the bravery these Firanese farmers had already shown, and he was ashamed. Ashamed, and angry; angry at his supposed friends and colleagues on the Council for betraying him, his countrymen, and all he stood for. He could not run. The Arkhos of Sarista needed to play his part in the defense of Faltha, and he needed to play it now.

That night the basement of Foilzie's tenement was the scene of much excited talk. After weeks of hard work and disappointment, the Council of Faltha would meet with them the next afternoon. Saraskar had specifically requested the attendance of all members of the Company, so each would have to ask for time away from their work. Saraskar of Sarista proved to be an important ally, promising to support their cause by sponsoring their appearance before the Council, though they could all see that this placed him in no small danger.

"We must face facts," Mahnum said soberly. "If things go ill, and we are not believed—or worse, we are believed but are judged against because of it—we run the risk of danger and even death. Saraskar explicitly warned us about that."

Farr leaned forward. "We must accept the risk. Wira and Parlevaag accepted it, and we should do no less."

"One way or another, tomorrow sees the end of our quest," Kurr stated. "So we should prepare for the long journey home. I think we have enough money for at least one horse, if not two. I saw some good specimens at the market, and I will make inquiries about them in the morning. Tonight I want you to pack up your belongings in preparation for a swift departure, if required."

"What will we do with the Bhrudwan once we've finished with the Council?" Perdu asked.

"Perhaps turn him over to the Council or to the Instruians to do with as they wish," Kurr answered. "I'm not sure. Let's deal with the first thing first, and concentrate on tomorrow. Winning the confidence of the Council is all-important."

Phemanderac chose that moment to come down the stairs to the basement, having just returned to the tenement. They immediately deluged him with the news, and he was eventually able to work out that the Company, through good fortune and Kurr's bold opportunism, had secured an appointment with the Council of Faltha. He rejoiced with them, then announced his own important news.

"You may have noticed this is my third consecutive late night out," the philosopher said. "I discovered a priceless treasure in the Hall of Lore: a vault in which are stored many early manuscripts regarding the activities and beliefs of the First Men. Unlike a year ago, when I was forbidden access, the Archivist has been of great help to me, allowing me freedom to study these valuable records, and even assisting me in transcribing and interpreting their obscure language. Apparently there is now no restriction on their use, though the Archivist tells me few people ever inquire of them."

"I wonder why," Farr said quietly.

"How did you avoid the curfew?" the old farmer asked him, the faintest hint of suspicion in his rough northern voice. The thin philosopher frowned, but chose not to take offense. *Be patient with Kurr*, Leith had advised him. *He is slow to trust, but is a good man.*

"Easily enough," he replied. "I don't know why this did not occur to me when last I sought permission to view the Archives. I simply struck up conversation with the Archivist who, as is the norm with these men, is ever eager to talk to another man of learning. He is very opinionated and a little conceited to go with it, but his friendship earned me one of these."

He held up a green tablet, about hand size, with the seal of the Council of Faltha set on it.

"A night pass!" Foilzie said, almost reverently. "I have friends who would pay you much money for that."

"I'm sorry, madam," Phemanderac replied, giving

Foilzie a slight bow. "This is the property of the Archivist—or, more correctly, his wife. Were it not returned, questions would be asked."

"Nevertheless, it will come in useful," Farr said.

"*Would* have come in useful," Kurr corrected. "You forget we no longer need to make the loathsome journey to the Hall of Meeting, save once more; so we do not need the pass. But it would have saved us much time."

"I am sorry," Phemanderac replied, his long face reddening slightly. He thought it best not to tell them he had come by the pass ten days earlier.

"Have you found anything important in the Archives?" Stella asked politely.

"I have found many things of wonder," Phemanderac replied with enthusiasm. "Books of poetry supposedly written by brothers of the House of Wenta, one of the original four houses; parchments upon which were written records of the dealings of Instruere, going back to within a hundred years of its foundation; an extensive treatise on good and evil which makes interesting reading: many such things lie unknown and unread within the vault. Apparently the House of Lore employed a team of scholars who transcribed and interpreted these works, but of late scholars are being replaced by guards, and the oldest manuscripts begin to decay."

Kurr said nothing. The scowl on his face, however, spoke volumes.

Phemanderac looked around at the Company. *They have lived for their quest for months now*, he thought; *lived and died for it. I cannot expect them to be interested in fragile old manuscripts that do not bear on their immediate predicament*. Nevertheless, he felt deep within there was something in that vault calling to him, something that wanted to be discovered and read. *How can I tell them that? How can I tell them that what I look for is more important even than the safety of this generation of Falthans?*

"No, I've found nothing you would consider important," he admitted. "Not yet. But I will."

Some time after breakfast the next morning strong hands knocked on the door of the tenement. The door went unanswered for a time, most of the Company being at the market. The remainder (Perdu, Stella, Mahnum and Kurr) expected Foilzie to answer it. The pounding grew louder and more persistent.

"I'll see who's there," Stella said eventually, hands pressed against her temples, and went to the door.

"Stella!" a great deep voice boomed. "It's good to find you safe and well! And the rest of the Company? How do they fare?"

"The Haufuth, it's the Haufuth!" Stella shouted excitedly back down the hall. "Haufuth, come in, come in!" She ran ahead of him, calling: "We have a guest!"

"Guests," the Haufuth corrected, striding in behind her. "My friend the Hermit is here also. Is there anything to eat?"

"We are all well," Stella said, answering his earlier question. "I'm home from the Market with a headache, but the others work there."

"It is good to see you fit and healthy again," Kurr said, shaking the Hermit's proffered hand, delight clear on his face. "Sit down, both of you, and break your fast. We have much to tell you."

"My friend," the Haufuth said as he smiled at Kurr, "you know I want to hear your story, though I fancy I know some of it already. But unless you have forgotten yourself completely, you will remember that the greater the tale, the more strength required to hear it, therefore the larger the breakfast to fuel the hearing. Will you at least let me sample the delights of Instruian fare before I collapse from starvation?"

Foilzie came to the table, and Kurr introduced her to the Loulean headman and the Hermit. "You will not be disappointed in this woman," the old farmer remarked as breakfast was served.

"Well, it seems like we've arrived just in time," the Haufuth commented between mouthfuls.

"Yes, the meeting is this very afternoon," said Mahnum. "How did you know about it? And how did you find us, friend?"

Kurr laughed. "Unless I am mistaken, our worthy headman refers to breakfast. Am I right?"

The Haufuth looked shamefaced.

"We spent three days wandering the city in search of you," he said, "and it was like looking for one patch of grass in an open field until we came across a certain market." The Haufuth grinned widely at them. "After that it was easy."

"It's good to see you again," Mahnum said to the big man. "But forgive me for asking, where is the rest of you?"

"Blame him," the Haufuth said, pointing at the Hermit. "He wouldn't let me sit down long enough to sustain my girth. Look at this!" He stood, placing a closed fist between his belt and his shirt, and the disappointment on his face was obvious. "Still," he continued, sitting down again with a thump, "if the fare in this city is the equal of what is set before me this morning, it won't take me long to recover."

*   *   *

The Hermit smiled. He had grown to appreciate the Haufuth in the time he had known him, and reflected that he had met the others only once, for a total of one day, and putting himself in their service was a somewhat risky thing to do after years of solitude. To counter that unease, however, he considered the excitement rising within him at the thought of taking such a risk. Here he sat, among people he hardly knew, with a door about to open to a new life. He determined he would meet it without flinching.

"What have you done with Wisent?" Perdu asked, worry edging his voice. "Did you find him lodgings?"

"We did indeed," replied the Haufuth, "but at a price! I hope the Company has money enough to pay for his keep: the stable-master was very specific in demanding that we pay him for the rental of two stalls and for the equivalent of two horses' upkeep. I had money enough only for three days."

"You gained a bargain," said Perdu, a smile on his face. "He eats at least as much as four. Now, if you will give me directions, I will go and visit him." In a moment the adopted Fenni left to reacquaint himself with his clan chief's generous gift.

The Haufuth and the Hermit listened while Kurr told them about the adventures of the Company—how they made the Southern Run, the ambush of the Bhrudwans and the loss of Wira, the long journey across Treika and Deuverre, the escape of Leith and Mahnum from Adunlok, and their race with the Widuz to the city walls, finishing with Parlevaag's death. Then they heard the trials endured by the Company in this city of cities, and were cheered to learn of the imminent appointment with the Council.

Kurr turned his attention to the blue-robed man from the edge of the wild. "And you? Have you recovered?"

"Recovered and more, thanks to your leader here," came the prompt answer, with genuine gratitude in the words. "And I am a hermit no longer—though I will continue to wear the name until I discover what I have become."

"You may not have long to wait," Mahnum said quietly. "Though if I were you I would give hasty thought to what name you would be known by, for after today . . ." He left the sentence unfinished, hanging there like a presage of the executioner's sword, as a reminder of what they were about to face.

The remainder of the Company worked only half a day at the market. As the reason for this became general knowledge a small crowd gathered around Indrett's stall.

"I told you they'd see you," one large woman held forth. "Just spend your money wisely, that's what I said. And see? A meeting with the Council, and inside a month. Unheard of!"

"Yes, but what will they say?" said another. "Who can know whether the Council will grant your boon? No amount of money buys the Council."

"Who can know?" echoed an elderly man. "But the Council is not what it was. If you would just tell us what your suit is, maybe we could give you advice . . ."

"Yes, tell us, tell us," the crowd demanded. But Indrett remained silent, as did all the Company, knowing just how quickly the news would spread if they were in any way indiscreet. As the crowd realized that no secrets were to be revealed, the merely curious drifted away. The friends Indrett had made remained, offering their silent support. And when she closed her stall and with the others made her way back to Foilzie's tenement, a few of them accompanied her.

The Company approached the Hall of Meeting in the early afternoon, accompanied by twenty or so of their acquaintances from the market. There were few words adequate to describe the Hall of Meeting, the crown jewel of Instruere, conceived and built at the zenith of her glory. Even now, with the golden age long past and the city of cities but a shadow of what she had been, when the skill and patience that constructed the great hall had long been forgotten, Instruians still took pride in this massive building. A detail of guards was permanently assigned to keeping the towering walls clean, risking life and limb on precarious scaffolding as they wiped (and in some cases chipped) the soil and soot of the city away from the elaborate sculptures that adorned them, or clung to the roof while scraping and scrubbing the slate.

The huge building was visible from practically every quarter of the city, intended by its architects to dominate Instruere, yet not in an aggressive fashion; instead it stood to remind the citizens of their commonality, of their part in the government of their new land. Indeed, in the golden age before the Bhrudwan invasion it was possible for the head of each family to meet in the vast Outer Chamber of the Hall of Meeting, which would seat five thousand in comfort. However, there had been no gatherings of the people for over a thousand years, and now it brooded over the city like the memory of a tyrant, its twin towers rising two hundred feet above them.

The Company was not summoned to the Council until late that afternoon. The appellants seen in the morning had taken an unusually long time to be dealt with. At least, this was the excuse offered by Furoman, the ostentatious personal secretary to the Appellant Division of the Council of Faltha. Privately Kurr wondered at this, especially since there was a two-hour gap between the exit of the last (and obviously disappointed) appellant and their call to pass through the Iron Door and approach the Council Chamber. At last, having been reduced to a state of extreme nervousness, they saw Furoman march importantly along the wide hallway, stop and motion for the Company to follow. They made their way past the line of appellants still waiting along the left side of the corridor, under the huge carvings and wide pillars Kurr had grown to hate. They could all feel the resentment in the eyes of the appellants: yet another group with money or influence bypassing the system. Around a sweeping bend the corridor went, then they were face to face with the Iron Door.

Tall as a ship, made from iron won from the Remparer Mountains hundreds of miles away, the Iron Door was of immense symbolic importance to the modern Instruians. It divided rulers from subjects, it enforced the hierarchies so important to a city of this magnitude, and in the process became a focus for the discontent and resentment that small people felt for the big people with the power to influence affairs. In the minds of the Instruian underclass the big people worked behind the Iron door; there the inscrutable decisions were made, and there the intolerable laws were passed. As Leith approached the width and height of the door, he felt its power as a strong repulsion, as though it did not want him to pass. He saw no discernible way through. But just as Furoman drew close enough to touch it, the mighty door rose slowly up into the ceiling amidst the shrieking of gears and clanking of chains. The Company walked under it. Leith glanced up: the door was at least ten feet thick.

Behind the Iron Door a great, high-ceilinged hall opened out before them, the famous Outer Chamber of the Hall of Meeting. The grandest and most expensive structure in Instruere, the intricately decorated walls of the Outer Chamber stretched away from the Company into the hazy distance, seeming to the apprehensive travelers like nothing so much as a huge ribbed gullet, swallowing them into the bloated stomach of the Council. Wide marble floors, inlaid with patterned tiles depicting scenes from the Vale of the First Men, led the eye to fluted columns and cream stone walls—the stone having been transported over five hundred miles from grim quarries at the northern extremity of the Remparer Mountains—and a high-vaulted roof. Up to this roof the eye was drawn, as indeed had been the plan of the great architects, a roof seemingly supported by two rows of statues depicting some great conflict.

Furoman followed their eyes, noted the expressions on their faces, and was satisfied: this place never failed to generate awe in those who first saw it, and proved an invaluable weapon in the hands of the Council, serving to cow appellants who might otherwise have given them trouble.

"The statues tell the story of the dealings of the Most High with the First Men," he said. "Not that provincials such as yourselves would be expected to know that venerable tale." The jibe was obviously designed to intimidate but, despite knowing this, the members of the Company found that in the presence of such magnificence they could not respond.

*   *   *

Leith found himself transfixed by the enormous wall-carvings stretching between floor and ceiling, and could make out elements of the story Kurr had told them on the road to Breidhan Moor. That dark shape must be gray-cloaked Kannwar, the Destroyer, kneeling with arms outstretched, about to take the Water of the Fountain in disobedience to the ban of the Most High. That faceless figure with the arrow nocked to the bow, marble feathers resting against cold cheek, was surely the Most High. The arrow was aimed at the outstretched arm of the Destroyer. The sculptor had managed to capture and communicate the sense of drama: the two figures on the brink of conflict, about to make eye contact; the water about to be drunk, the arrow about to be released, the doom about to be pronounced, the world about to be changed forever. Around them other carved figures watched the confrontation, the battle within their own hearts personified in this clash of good and evil, and they tried to choose which they preferred.

What do I choose? Leith asked himself. *The continued powerlessness of unquestioned obedience, or to take control by dipping my own hand into the fountain?*

"Come on, Leith," Hal whispered, tugging at Leith's sleeve. "The Council awaits us."

Through a wood-paneled door at the end of the hall they entered a deep but narrow room, the Inner Chamber of the Hall of Meeting, almost filled with a long table and chairs stretching from end to end. There were no other furnishings or adornments in the room, nothing but plain walls and a white ceiling. Near the center of the table sat the sixteen members of the Council of Faltha. While the Company was still some distance away their friend

Saraskar stood, then came over to them. He introduced himself to each member of the Company, repeating their names to himself as they spoke them; then led them to the others at the table.

The overwhelming tension in the room began to affect Leith even before he sat down, and he began to shake with fear. Not fear of the Councillors themselves, or not exactly; he was more afraid of the situation they found themselves in, of the uncertainty, afraid that he might do or say something to damn Faltha—or, more elementally, damn himself. The doom was about to be pronounced, the world was about to be changed forever. He sat on his hands, but his whole body shook so much he was sure the others would notice it. No one said anything: they were involved in their own struggles.

For it was not only a unique afternoon for the northerners. In calling the meeting Saraskar had been obliged to give an outline of the Company's request; and, though he had couched it in the vaguest terms possible, he knew that it had, as had been inevitable, warned the traitors that the game was up. He had seen the looks on their faces. In that sense the meeting itself was unnecessary, for Saraskar now had his confirmation. The words of the northerners were true—in essence, if not in detail. Faltha had been betrayed.

He had been granted so little time to prepare. One short night, a night on which even he could not break curfew without good reason, a night during which he was closely watched. No chance to meet with the loyalists—he already thought of them in those terms—who lived in various unattainable parts of the city. Time only to talk frankly with his frightened family and his servants; to solemnly tell them that they were in the gravest danger, from which there may be no escape. To flee the betrayed city would re-move the last defense Instruere had against the stratagems of Bhrudwo. His wife bit her lip, held him close and reas-sured him that she would do whatever was necessary. His girls cried. His servants made certain discreet preparations against his failure to persuade the Council, in the event the evil had gone further than the northern Trader asserted.

Saraskar used the time as well as he could, but not well enough. The Council had convened early that morning (just after sunrise, in fact), in order to make some impres-sion on the stream of appellants congesting the corridor of the Hall of Meeting. He had no opportunity to talk to the Arkhoi he knew to be loyal, other than the exchange of a few whispered comments; learning that they, like him, had no firm plan, and no chance to make one. On and on the day wore, the Council dealing swiftly with appellants under the firm hand of the Arkhos of Nemohaim, their leader. One of the traitors, Saraskar reminded himself. And the Arkhos of Nemohaim kept them busy as though to deny them any opportunity to discuss the coming meeting.

The northerners knew nothing of this. Some of the great men of the world were gathered in this room, about to judge their case. Leith flicked a glance in the direction of the Arkhos of Sarista, and in a moment of clarity read the fear on his face. His hopes sank. If this wise man feared the outcome, what hope did they have? What was likely to be their reward for accusing these powerful men of treachery? In a wild moment he hoped his father was wrong, had made it all up, that the benevolent caretakers of Faltha would forgive them their impudence and let them go.

To his left sat Hal. Behind him stood the Bhrudwan warrior, compelled to the Council under the close eye of

Farr and Perdu, his hands still bound. Hal had effected
some sort of change in the stern man, but the Company
was by no means ready to risk freeing him from his
bonds, so he stood there, a barely controlled explosion
just waiting for a spark. Surely here was evidence no
Council could ignore. Surely truth would win, just as Hal
argued it would. *Please, please, please*, Leith thought,
willing it to happen; *please, please, please* . . .

The meeting went wrong from the start. In spite of the importance of the moment—or perhaps because of it—the
hard faces staring at them from across the table daunted
most of the Company, who were reduced to staring at their
laps. The Haufuth found it particularly difficult, as he had
been in the city barely three days, and had not yet encountered the grimness characteristic of the Instruians.
Phemanderac found his scholarly arguments of no use, as
they were invariably interrupted long before the point he
so carefully tried to formulate emerged from its logical
construction. Farr and Perdu were content to leave the
talking to the others. Indrett and Stella, being women,
were tolerated in the Council only if they did not speak.
Thus within minutes Mahnum and Kurr became the effective spokesmen for the group, and found themselves
questioned sharply by several of the ambassadors. Then
Leith accidentally knocked over a carafe of water, and the
Arkhos of Tabul was forced to stop in the middle of an
elaborate dissertation on the ability to discern Bhrudwan
troop movements, having to mop up the spillage with his
own handkerchief.

   The Council Members insisted on questioning the
Bhrudwan themselves. One after another they fired questions at him, but the Acolyte simply refused to answer

them. *He doesn't understand the common tongue*, Leith shouted at them in his mind. *We told you that! Of course he can't answer!* When Hal attempted to answer for the Bhrudwan warrior, the questioner bade him keep silent. Hal tried to encourage them to approach him differently, without confronting him so blatantly. The Council would have none of it. Even Saraskar seemed to be losing patience.

A tremendously fat man, larger even than the Haufuth had been last winter, pulled himself to his feet by gripping the table, and began speaking with the Bhrudwan in another language. The warrior obviously understood, for he began to answer in the same tongue. The fat Councillor translated the questions and the answers: is an army planning to invade Faltha? No, Great Lord, there is no army. What are you doing in Faltha? I have traveled to this backward land to pursue a man who stole my master's fortune. Is that man in this room? Yes, Great Lord. He sits opposite you. To whom do you owe your allegiance? To Vartal, my Trader master. As one the members of the Company sprang to their feet to protest, but they were ordered to sit down. Leith felt as though he and his friends sat locked inside a cage.

"You are not telling us what the Bhrudwan is actually saying," Kurr complained to the fat Councillor once the charade finished.

"Are you questioning my honor?" came his sharp reply.

"Of course we are," the old farmer replied frankly. "We're questioning the honor of the Council of Faltha. That's why we're here."

"Do you believe his report?" Mahnum asked directly, addressing his question to the Council at large. "Surely even the appearance of a Bhrudwan warrior in Faltha speaks of danger?"

"I believe it," the fat Councillor said flatly. "For some reason of your own, perhaps to gain advantage in the exchange of goods, you bribed or coerced a Bhrudwan citizen to impugn the good name of the Council of Faltha. You are a Trader, are you not?"

"But his presence here?" Mahnum pressed.

"Is not unusual," the fat man insisted. "Many Bhrudwans travel through Faltha every year, on their way to the slave markets of Ghadir Massab."

"Traders, not warriors."

"Are you the expert on the affairs of southern Faltha, northerner? Perhaps you would care to explain to us how these Bhrudwan traders protect their cargo against desert thieves? Do they perhaps use warriors?" The fat Councillor's cruel voice cut at Mahnum, who had no reply.

"Where did you learn to speak Bhrudwan?" Saraskar asked the fat man.

"It was deemed necessary for someone on the Council to study the devices of the enemy," said the Arkhos.

"But if Bhrudwo is no threat, why study them?" Kurr shot out.

"Simple prudence," the fat man replied, but the answer was patently false.

This is not how it should be happening! thought Leith. *The Council should be listening sympathetically, and offering us aid—or taking this burden from us, and rushing out to organize their defenses against the invasion to come! What has gone wrong?*

Finally the Arkhos of Treika leaned forward and asked the question everybody was expecting. "Trader, you say you were given the names of various traitors within Faltha. Now, answer me carefully. Are there any such here in this room?"

Mahnum seemed undaunted by their treatment. "Yes, there are," he replied simply. Indrett's pride in her husband shone from her face.

"Then you have a responsibility to name them, so that we may judge the reliability—or otherwise—of your story."

So be it. They might as well be ordering our executions.

Gently he spoke. "There are seven traitors among the sixteen members of the Council of Faltha. They are the Arkhoi of Firanes, of Treika, of Favony, of Tabul, of Straux, of Nemohaim, and of Vertensia." He deliberately looked each man in the eye as he spoke their names. Two of their number would not respond to his gaze, while the others stared at him with a contempt bordering on hatred.

The room settled to complete stillness as all waited for the Trader to continue.

"I have told no one the details—how the treachery was committed, who was involved, how deep it all runs—not even my companions. I will now relate the acts of betrayal these men engaged in, as told to me on Andratan; acts that can be verified should anyone wish to do so." Mahnum spoke quickly, determined to say as much as possible before he was silenced. "The Arkhos of Firanes conspired with Wisula, now Regent, to murder the rightful king and usurp the succession. This was done on the suggestion of the Redana'an ambassador to the court at Rammr, a man who is in fact a Bhrudwan agent. That the Arkhos of Firanes and the Firanese Regent are both puppets of Bhrudwo can be confirmed by a number of the courtiers, who now live in fear." *How raw the words are*, Mahnum thought, *how roughly shaped; almost impossible to swallow, let alone digest.*

The Arkhos of Firanes, supposedly a servant of Loulea, and of all other Firanese villages, Mahnum reminded himself, openly sneered at his words. *This is wrong*, the Trader thought worriedly. *If only seven of the sixteen Councillors are traitors, why are they not fearful of their lives now their treachery is exposed?*

"The Arkhos of Treika authorized the shipment of Bhrudwan armaments to Instruere, to be used in an insurrection planned to coincide with the coming invasion." A hissing sound came from the aristocratic figure opposite Stella. "These weapons can be found in a private house he rents near Struere Gate."

"That's not true!" the Treikan ambassador cried. "He lies!"

"You told us those weapons were for the Instruian Guard, bought honestly in the markets of Tabul," Saraskar said quietly.

"They are, they are!" insisted the Arkhos of Treika.

"Then how did a man from Firanes learn of them?"

Mahnum continued relentlessly, as though reciting something burned into his mind. "The King of Tabul has placed an interdiction on the export of gold from the mines of Ghellol. This has angered the ruler of Vertensia, whose country depends on the revenue from gold exports through Jardin, the only deep-water port on the Southern Shores. The Arkhos of Tabul and the Arkhos of Vertensia have conspired together to circumvent that ban. When not in Instruere, they use Bhrudwan silver—which is not banned in Tabul, being as close to the markets of Ghadir Massab as it is—to bribe the Ghellol miners, and a steady supply of gold makes its way south across The Mamon to Vertensia.

The Vertensian king uses this gold to build an army, which he will use to annex Tabul. Apparently the Arkhos of Tabul does not know this part of the arrangement."

The two ambassadors turned to face each other, cheeks reddening, one man in embarrassment, the other in anger. Mahnum ignored them, and continued his implacable recitation.

"The Arkhos of Straux has been supplied with a number of willing bedfellows in exchange for information about the strength of the Westrau and Austrau divisions of the army, and the financial state of Straux. This he has done secretly, as the court of Straux is loyal to Faltha, though their king is a traitor and aids the Arkhos in his treachery."

The Arkhos of Straux stood to protest. "Wait until the man has finished," Saraskar snapped at him. "And when you do speak, perhaps you would care to explain your bawdy boasts the last time we met at this table." The Arkhos of Straux spluttered, but could clearly think of nothing to say.

Mahnum continued. "The Arkhos of Favony gained his appointment to the Council just over two years ago. He was a lowly official in one of the outlying villages in the foothills of Mount Porveiir until his elevation by the new ruler of that land. His father is a Bhrudwan spy, known to them as 'The Refiner' in honor of his ability, by spendthrift ways, to turn pure gold into dross. His son apparently has inherited that distinction, as well as the epithet, and has enormous gambling debts which Bhrudwo has offered to pay in return for his support.

"The Arkhos of Nemohaim is the leader of the rebellion. He was the first to betray his country, having traveled to Bhrudwo itself twice, the first time over four years ago. In fact, the Voice of Andratan told me that the Arkhos was a guest of the fortress even as we spoke. That would have been about eighteen months ago." Half a dozen heads turned to look at the man from Nemohaim. "This man recruited at least three of this Council to serve Bhrudwo."

Mahnum leaned on the table with his hands, as much to steady himself as to emphasize his words. Looking at the Company, he realized some of them would struggle to believe such a tale of corruption. What if Mahnum was wrong, they would think. They would not leave the room alive. Perhaps they were doomed even if he was right.

A thick silence hung over the table.

"Is he finished?" the Arkhos of Vertensia asked; then, without waiting for a reply, stood and spoke: "Why have we allowed such talk to spill across this hallowed table unchallenged? Not because of our fault, unless it be the fault of tolerance. Yet such pernicious rumors as these, each no doubt as easy to explain and as innocent of evil as that which concerns Vertensia, cannot be allowed to reach the general populace. I applaud the decision of the Arkhos of Sarista to sponsor these deluded outlanders in their bid to undermine sensible government; for if these rumors had first been spoken in the markets, many ill-bred people might even now be overcome by panic." He sat down, a confident look on his face.

Saraskar stood, and spoke in an imperious voice, a voice of command, a final gambit. "The allegations can be confirmed easily enough. There can be little doubt that seven of us here are traitors. I cannot believe we have been so blind as to allow this treachery to rise in our midst completely unchecked. Why have we closed our eyes to the actions of our fellows? I personally had many warnings, but chose to believe the lies I was told rather than the truth I could see. Well, now I can see the truth clearly in front of me. We have before us a Bhrudwan—admittedly a recalcitrant one, but a Bhrudwan nonetheless—clad in the garb of the *Magdhi Dasht*. What is he doing in Faltha? We have heard details all of us can confirm: for example, my colleague the Arkhos of Favony has always answered to the name 'Refiner,' for the reason given by this Firanese Trader who could not have possibly known it. So how does he know it?

"If this Trader is telling the truth, there are traitors among us. Why would such a group as this put their heads in the mouth of the lion if they were not convinced of the truth of their stories? For we all know they risk death by making such information public."

"This thing should not come to a vote," the Arkhos of Straux said, his voice a growl. His bald head spun round to face his accusers. "Who is to say that this is not an elaborate ploy on the part of an enemy—whether Bhrudwo or some Falthan country, it matters not—to distract us from their real plan? Though I would have thought they might have employed more convincing emissaries. Look at them. Women, old men and children!"

Farr shifted in his seat, clearly having difficulty restraining himself.

The fat Councillor placed a heavy hand on the shoulder of Saraskar, forcing him to his seat. "Sit down, my friend; you've had more time than enough to flesh out the lies of the enemies of this Council. I am the Arkhos of Nemohaim," he announced in a sneering, high-pitched wheeze. "Supposedly the chief conspirator in this band of evil traitors. The man who, according to our worthy friend here, traveled twice to Bhrudwo, though everyone knows I have trouble walking from one side of Instruere to the other. There are a number of facts I wish noted. First, this Mahnum is the son of a man executed by the Sna Vazthan king for interfering in the war between Haurn and Sna Vaztha. Our predecessors at this table spent much time discussing Modahl of Firanes; that is, before his untimely death." He sneered along the table at Mahnum.

"What is he talking about?" Leith asked his mother.

"A long story," she replied. "One of which even I don't know all the details."

"You see, this family has a history of interfering in Falthan politics, and suffering for it." His sickly-sweet voice menaced them all. "It is interesting to note that one Leith Mahnumsen is being sought by the Instruian Guard on a matter of common assault. I understand that this grandson of Modahl sits at this table as I speak."

With some shock Mahnum realized that this was a reference to his son's striking of the Instruian guard. *I hope he didn't die. But it was either that or forsaking his family and friends . . .* He took a deep breath and forced himself to look at the Arkhos of Nemohaim. *There is a distinct unsavoriness about this man's evil*, he thought as the little pig eyes bored into him. *The Bhrudwans seem to be evil but impersonal, as though it was their job; this man smells like a rotted carcass, a person going bad from the inside out. Can the other Council members not see it? Or are they cowed by it?*

How has he found this out? Mahnum asked himself. *And how does he make such noble and true deeds as those of my father and my son sound so insidious?* He could feel the will of the Council falling in behind the words of this foul creature. And now he, too, began to suspect there must

be some unknown fact bolstering this man's confidence
and that of his co-conspirators. Something that endangered
them all.

"I will not ask for all my rights as a member of this
Council, merely that the Firanese Trader and his son be
handed over to me for further questioning. As for the others, they can go free. For their safety, I will arrange an es-
cort which will conduct them to the borders of their own
land. Then, when I have finished questioning the son and
grandson of Modahl, perhaps they also might be released.
It is important that we discover and deal with the source of
these wild and dangerous accusations." The huge man sat
down with such violence that the table shook.

"My friend, you miss the point." Phemanderac was on
his feet, arms spread wide, palms on the table, his sharp
eyes level with those across from him. "The purpose of this
meeting is to discuss the Bhrudwan aggression threatening
Faltha. All your baseless posturing does is confirm that
threat. Here is the question: is Bhrudwo about to attack us?
If so, what should our response be? Anything else is irrelevant, though perhaps the Council might look to the loyalty of certain of its members.

"All that need be done is dispatch spies swiftly to verify the formation and location of the Bhrudwan army.
Mahnum here claims to know the timetable, and suggests
that these spies will not have to go far into enemy lands
to find this army. When word is received by the Council
that such an army indeed exists, all Faltha can be mobi-
lized. If not, you can have your discussion with Mahnum
about the source of the rumors.

"Or, as an alternative, you can hide irresponsibly behind indecision, or be bullied into compliance with the
wishes of this—this man of limited intellect. Then when

all comes crashing down around you, and your colleagues are revealed as murderous traitors, you can hope for a swift death. Though, in all likelihood, I suspect you will not be granted it. I would not care to be a member of the Council of Faltha on the day the Destroyer breaks down the Iron Door." The philosopher did not sit down immediately, remaining fixed in his pose, staring into the eyes of the Arkhos of Nemohaim.

The debate continued for an hour at least, but the further it went, the less confident Mahnum felt about the outcome. Several Council members not named as traitors sided with the Company, but urged caution in dealing with Bhrudwo for fear of provoking an attack. The revelations about their fellow Councillors appeared to have taken them by surprise, robbing them of conviction and coherence. However, the opponents of the Company knew no such confusion. They were aware that they fought for their very lives, which lent their speech an urgency and articulateness seldom seen in the Chamber of Debate. Phemanderac matched wits with them, Saraskar argued cogently but without much real force, and Mahnum reiterated what he had seen and heard, but to him they seemed unlikely to prevail. The threat was so numinous, so unlikely, few seemed prepared to risk their careers and the wrath of their peers by responding positively to it.

Eventually the talking stopped and the Company were ushered out into the hall beyond the Iron Door to await the verdict of the Council. It was over, and it had gone so badly.

"It is simply not possible they would ignore the evidence before their eyes!" Farr said angrily. "Was blindness a requirement for the position?"

"They would rather the evidence was not so," Hal said, speaking for the first time in at least an hour. "By doing nothing, they may hope things will correct themselves unaided. Such thinking is to be expected of those who never make important public decisions."

"So much for the Most High," Farr said. "We've done our part. Now the fools behind that door are about to undo it all, and the Most High is nowhere to be seen."

Hal turned to face the angry man. "Blindness is a disease not confined to members of the Council," he said mildly. "You do not see where you do not look."

"The Council has not decided yet," Stella said encouragingly. "They may decide in our favor after all."

The words were no sooner spoken than the Iron Door opened and they were summoned back into the Chamber. One look told them all they needed to know. Saraskar and six others sat to one side, crestfallen, surrounded by members of the Instruian Guard; while the remainder of the Council members formed a knot in the center of the room. As the Company approached, two of the Councillors assisted the Arkhos of Nemohaim to stand. He had been chosen to deliver the verdict. It was obviously one that pleased him.

"Worthy Firanese," he wheezed, the undercurrent of the words contradicting their literal meaning. "The Council of Faltha has come to a decision regarding the alleged invasion from Bhrudwo. We do not regard Bhrudwo as a threat, and can find no evidence to support the claims made by your Company."

The words hammered at the Company like blows from a huge fist.

"We have also made the decision to deal with the

rumors of traitors in high places. You have come to the appropriate place with your allegations, to your credit"— he seemed almost to choke on the words—"and so will not be punished for them. For now. However, if any member of your Company is proven to have spread any such rumor, he or she will be arrested immediately. You may now leave. You are not permitted to petition the Council again on this or any other matter."

"That's it?" Farr shouted. "We claw our way across the world only to be told by a slippery oaf that nothing will be done? Well, I can do something, at least!" and, in so saying, advanced on the huge man.

"Farr! Come back!" Kurr shouted, and grabbed for the mountain man's hand. "You'll only put yourself in prison. He is not worth the trouble!"

At the last moment Farr came to his senses. "So my father and my brother remain unavenged," he said in a hollow voice, "and within the year all this splendor will be in ruins. Well, at least that will afford me some satisfaction. I've never been in such a foul place." He allowed Kurr to guide him back to the others.

"My friends, I can say little to assist you at this time," Saraskar said quietly, his face a field of grief. "As you can see, someone has miscounted, and there are more than seven allied against us. This I promise you, all my personal resources will be invested in looking for further evidence of the threat you have revealed to us. Politics is an unreasonable business, and I am sorry you have been exposed to it. Do not blame yourself for your failure. It would take nothing less than the production of the Jugom Ark itself held in the hand of the Most High to convince the Council to act. Goodbye. And keep safe: the Arkhos of Nemohaim issues no idle threats."

"Goodbye," Kurr said slowly, glancing across the room at the obese man who had won the day. "We thank you for all your help."

The Company turned and left the room; behind them none of the Council save Saraskar and the Arkhos of Nemohaim watched them leave. Leith waited for the Council to shout, to lay hands on them, to imprison, question, torture them, but there was no shout. At the least he expected them to take Achtal the Bhrudwan from them; after all, they had declared him innocent. But nothing was said. With much creaking and clattering, and with a final hollow boom, the Iron Gate slammed down behind them.

CHAPTER 3

THE PINION

ALONG THE CORRIDOR WALKED the members of the Company, defeated, bereft of options, already turning their thoughts towards home. *Surely we have done all we can*, Perdu thought. *It is time I saw my family again, it is time I reported to my clan chief, it is time I told the Fenni of the bravery of Parlevaag's death.* The prospect of a Bhrudwan invasion seemed to be less believable in an ancient place like this Hall of Meeting. *And what if the invasion does come? The Fenni will survive.* And then the thought: *is Faltha really worth saving?*

Kurr knew the most sensible course of action would be to leave Instruere immediately and start the long journey home, yet his heart would not let him admit defeat. He began to review the conversation just concluded. Much of it had already evaporated from his mind, yet he sought some way he might better have presented their case. Rather than sealing the rightness of their cause, Mahnum's revelations about the duplicity within the Council seemed to weigh against the Company. Could it have been handled differently? Would it have been better to leave the traitors unnamed? Might they have fared better had they not brought the Bhrudwan with them? However he turned the options over in his mind, the questions remained unanswered.

The old farmer's sense of failure was replicated among the other northerners. From his vantage point at the rear of the Company Leith looked across at Stella. Her lustrous, shoulder-length hair hung over her face, hiding the eyes that just this morning had seemed to embrace the world with enthusiasm, but now were dark and quiet. Thinking about her, even after having shared this long journey with her, simply paralyzed him. He could not look openly at her, much less talk to her or offer her consolation.

His mother walked beside him, speaking only when spoken to, her thoughts obviously somewhere else. The sense of abandonment Leith had felt while his father was in Bhrudwo had been replaced by a dullness, a feeling of regret for what they had lost rather than a passion to revive it. During the last few days the family had said very little to each other, as though in mute acknowledgement of the change.

And Hal? Leith could not understand his brother. The decision of the Council should have dealt him and his precious faith in the Most High a severe blow. After all, he was the one who told the Company that the Most High would take care of it. Well, they had tried his way, telling the truth to the Council of Faltha, and had met with failure. But, far from being discouraged, Hal alone of the Company seemed unconcerned about the defeat. *Perhaps he has no other way of dealing with disappointment*, Leith thought in sudden comprehension. *Maybe he is less, not more, than the rest of us. Maybe he has no capacity to care*.

Perhaps he is right, Leith reflected further as they

walked out into the dusty streets of Instruere. *Here we are, a few moments after the Council decreed there is no Bhrudwan threat, and the markets are as full as ever.* On a sun-drenched afternoon like this, it was difficult to conceive of any threat to the small talk of the market-goers, the entertainments of the musicians and acrobats, the sights and smells of this city that seemed to grow from the very rock of the earth. These people, this city; they would go on forever.

The Company left the Hall of Meeting behind them and hurried down the Vitulian Way, past the thin spire of the House of Worship, towards home. Tall tenements on either side lost their color as the weary sun finally found the horizon, the last of her golden benediction lifting from the city, turning splendor to sullenness. Instruians melted from the streets, leaving them to the refuse and the dogs; the hour of curfew was nearly upon them.

Ahead and to their left a small group of men lounged against a low wall. As the Company approached, one man detached himself from the group and stepped into the center of the wide, deserted Way. "Halt!" he cried.

"Guards," Kurr muttered.

"No, not guards," Farr corrected him. "See, they do not wear the Instruian livery, but are dressed in the garb of the Straux." Most of southern Instruere was dominated by the drab but utilitarian brown of people from the most populous of the sixteen Falthan kingdoms, while northern Instruere was largely populated by those of Deuverre, who wore brighter colors. It was unusual to see people from Straux in northern Instruere, especially so near curfew when they could not possibly return home in time to avoid being picked up by the Instruian Guard.

"Well then, we shall see what they want," said Kurr.

"You should be in your houses," the man called to them. "Not walking the streets after curfew, an easy target for every band of ruffians!" He laughed, an unsettling sound. Kurr found himself wishing they had brought their swords.

"We return from an audience with the Council of Faltha, and as such have nothing to fear from the curfew," said Kurr boldly. "And as for ruffians, the Instruian Guard keep them off the streets."

This elicited another ugly laugh from the man barring their way, echoed by the others leaning against the wall. "Let us see if the Instruian Guard will protect them," one called.

The man in the street pulled his sword from its tattered scabbard. His fellows eased themselves away from the wall and on to the dusty road. Without a word they drew their swords, then spread out across the street. Helplessly the Company watched the leader signal to one of the others to step forward. "Show me which one."

This man had a bandage around his head, but Leith still recognized him as he walked towards the Company, sword held before him. With a sudden chill Leith knew the purpose of this confrontation.

"These *are* guards, only not in uniform!" Leith hissed in Kurr's ear. "He with the bandage is the one—" But it was too late. The man separated Leith from the others with the point of his sword. "This is the one we seek!" he cried in a harsh voice. "He is mine!"

"You have your orders," the leader said grimly. "Take him, his father—that one beside him—and the dark one there—yes, him. Leave the others for now. Obey orders or no bandage will be able to help you."

It was over in a moment. Before the Company could protest, Leith, Mahnum and the Bhrudwan warrior were taken from among them and marched into a side street at the point of a sword. While most of the ruffians melted into the shadows, four remained with the Company, ensuring there would be no pursuit.

After many long minutes one of the men barked: "On your way! Hurry home before the guards find you on the street!" To emphasize his words he cracked Farr a blow across the shoulders with the flat of his sword, then turned on his heel and ran with his fellows towards where the Hall of Meeting rose from the shadows.

Farr made to follow, but Kurr grasped him by the shoulder. "Think with your head, not your heart, my friend," he said quietly. "Those were guards, not brigands. They've taken our friends into custody. Remember what the Arkhos of Nemohaim said about Mahnum and his son?"

The Vinkullen man grunted, then spat on the ground in disgust. "What sort of place is this? The heart of fair Faltha is black. The sooner I'm home, the better I'll feel."

"But in the meantime we have companions who need help. Perdu," Kurr said, turning to the Fenni, "take the Company back to our lodgings. Farr and I will seek the aid of the Instruian Guard. There must be some who still resist corruption."

"I'm coming with you," Phemanderac said to Kurr, "at least as far as the House of Lore. The Archivist awaits me, and I would keep faith with him."

The other members of the Company cried out that they too wanted to seek the help of the guard, to do something to aid their friends.

"There is no use in your all coming," the old farmer

told them. "There's nothing you can do about this now. Go back and tell Foilzie what happened."

Kurr, Farr and Phemanderac started back up the Vitulian Way, leaving the others standing for a confused moment in the deserted street. Eventually, in a silence punctuated only by Indrett's sobs, the Company made the slow walk home to Foilzie's tenement.

Under a fiery sky, in the northern reaches of the vast steppes of Kanabar, brown-robed figures wielding cruelly barbed whips barked out orders, sending many thousands of warriors backwards and forward across the plain with mechanical precision. Andratan had decided this war would be the last ever fought, and was prepared to invest a little more time to ensure that both strategy and execution were perfect; thus the many weeks of maneuvers in the midst of this wasteland. The commanders were only too aware of the importance of perfection. He of Andratan was rumored to be coming personally to inspect his army, the first time he had left his fortress in living memory. Death would come to those who proved themselves inadequate. Whips cracked; ranks of soldiers wheeled left and right; swords were drawn, swords were sheathed. Incantations, shouted in strange tongues, reverberated across the dusty fields like curses leveled against life itself. They spared no effort. All were aware their biggest test would be the imminent visit of their Leader. Beside this, even the coming invasion itself held few fears.

"Just tell me what he's supposed to have done!" Kurr said, a little more loudly than he intended. To his mounting frustration, the guard continued to ignore him.

"We are Falthans! We come from Firanes! We are guaranteed our rights by the Treaty of Fealty!"

This last brought a response from the guard, a curling of his upper lip.

"I think we're forgetting an important fact about this city," Farr said to Kurr. With that, he turned to the guard seated behind his desk, pulled a number of coins from his purse and spread them on the table.

"Ah, the Firanese." The guard expertly scooped the money into a drawer as though it was second nature. "You're finally speaking valuably enough for me to hear."

"What happened to our companions? Why have they been arrested? With what have they been charged?" Kurr could feel himself reaching the end of his patience, never a very long road but particularly short late at night on the bleak day the Council rejected their petition, and their companions were snatched from the street.

"Three questions! I'm not sure I heard all three." The guard glanced pointedly towards Kurr's purse.

"Very well! I'll treat this as a donation to your wife and family."

"Think of it rather as a contribution to the coffers of the local innkeeper," the guard replied pleasantly. "You can see that I'm a busy man, so I'll be brief. Your friends have been arrested and imprisoned in a holding cell pending trial on charges of a most serious nature. According to a reliable witness one of the three assaulted an Instruian guard, rendering him incapable of executing his duty since. As you can no doubt appreciate, the government of this city views such actions with extreme seriousness."

"How badly is this guard hurt?" Kurr's already wrinkled forehead creased further.

"He sustained head injuries of a most—"

"Yes, I know; of a most serious nature. But tell me: how could a mere boy like Leith overcome a heavily armed guard? If this guard is anything like yourself, I cannot imagine anyone hurting him."

The flattery had no effect. "I merely pass on information."

Kurr sighed deeply, and pulled a small bag from his pocket. "How much to have him released?"

The guard looked shocked. "These charges are serious! You cannot hope to secure his release by bribing me."

"I'm sure the charges will be serious," Kurr said without a hint of irony in his voice. "Who then do I bribe?"

"My captain will know. Wait here a moment." The guard strode off down the corridor.

"So what now?" Farr asked. "What's to stop them bleeding us dry, then refusing to release Leith and his father anyway?"

"Nothing," the old farmer said, weariness blurring his voice. "If I had a suspicious mind, I'd be tempted to think that they sought to make it difficult for us to remain in Instruere. I have a feeling that if our secret is not known all over the city by now, it will be within the next few days."

Back down the corridor strode the guard, followed by his superior. Before he even reached Kurr and Farr he began lamenting the seriousness of the charges leveled against their friend, and how little he could do about it. Kurr shook his head. It looked like there would be many days like this ahead of them.

"This one is particularly dusty," Phemanderac said between sneezes. It took him only a few moments to remember what it was he disliked about searching through old manuscripts: his allergies had returned, as strong as ever.

"That is because it is from the storeroom next on the list for transcribing." The clipped voice of the Archivist came from behind a shelf of dilapidated parchments. "It is possibly two hundred years since anyone laid hands on the volumes in front of you."

Despite the dust, I was born for this, the philosopher affirmed as he leafed through the first of this latest stack of leather-bound books. *Forget the politics of nations: I am at home in storerooms deep under the ground. There is a music in these volumes, the music of the past; and I am one of the few who can hear it.* But as he read, his thoughts wandered back to the events of the day.

These thoughts were abruptly interrupted by the Archivist, who set an armful of books down on the chair beside the philosopher. "You missed these," the beak-nosed Instruian said politely. "They were at the back of the drawer. I myself have not seen them before. Perhaps they will be of some interest."

Phemanderac cast an eye across them; then suddenly slammed shut the volume he was perusing and pulled the chair with the pile of books over to where he sat. "Where did these come from?" he demanded.

The Archivist frowned. He appeared taken aback by the change in tone. "As I said, these lay at the back of the drawer from which you took the previous manuscripts."

"Yes, but where did they come from? How did they come to be in your archive?"

Gingerly the lean philosopher picked up the topmost book. A huge yellow sun setting behind a tall tower graced the aged leather cover.

"I do not know," said the Archivist. "The devices on the covers are unknown to me." He hefted the second book, a thick tome; on it the silhouette of some giant flying bird hung in front of a full-orbed moon.

"But not to me," Phemanderac murmured. "Oh, not to me. My friend, what you have here may be more valuable than all the gold and silver in this city."

"What are they?" the Archivist asked, his interest piqued.

"I have seen their like in the libraries of my home country; a set of ten volumes, of which five are missing," came his slow reply. "These, perhaps, are those five books."

"Are you certain?"

"If I am correct, we should find on the covers of the other three books a tall blue wave breaking over a slender spire, a golden arrow with long red feathers, and two hands clasped in friendship," Phemanderac recited.

As he spoke the Archivist spread the volumes out across the bench. Phemanderac drank in the books with hungry eyes.

"The five missing books," he announced quietly. "The Sun, the *Mariswan*, the Wave, the Arrow, and the Hands." He paused, and when he spoke again his voice was hoarse with emotion. "My life is complete."

"You have other books like these? What makes them so special?" The Archivist's voice trembled.

"I have never read the other books, though I have seen them," said the philosopher. "They are locked in a glass box, deep in the heart of the Hall of Lore in the land of my fathers, holy relics revered above all other treasures of our land. Each of them has a picture carved into the leather of its cover: the Fountain, the Vale, the Fire, the Cloud, and the Rock." As he recited their names he referred to a deeply ingrained visual memory, the covers spread in front of his eyes.

"Why are they valuable?"

"They are over two thousand years old," Phemanderac said. "What preserves them is beyond our power to discover; in all that time our scholars have not needed to transcribe them. They were authored in Dona Mihst, they are of the Vale of the First Men, and preserve the history and culture of our common ancestors. My country would be prepared to pay a fortune for them."

"And your country is—"

"Dhauria. What remains of the Vale of the First Men."

"But—that country is a country of myth!" The Archivist scratched his balding head. "I have been happy to entertain you in this library: goodness knows how few people care for the things of the past. But now you tell me you have walked out of myth and into my store of old books. How can I believe you?"

"It doesn't matter whether you do or you don't, for here I am. Dhauria I came from, a land beyond Desicca, the Deep Desert, and in that land the past is prized above the present, to our cost. In that land five books are our chief treasure. Now I discover that five more indeed exist, as Hauthius told us, and are within my grasp. Is this then a time for me to deceive you with needless falsehoods?"

"And these books reveal themselves at the exact time in which you come to Instruere? Is this not a coincidence too great for the imagination?"

"Of course not," said Phemanderac. "Far from being coincidental, it was inevitable. You said yourself this afternoon that I appeared determined to read everything in your archive. How could these books have remained hidden?"

The Archivist nodded, obviously recognizing the sense of the argument. "Let us for the moment assume you come from the Vale of the First Men. How were the books lost to your library?"

"We have always assumed they were destroyed by the great wave which drove the First Men from the Vale," Phemanderac said as he mused it over. "The other five, so the legend is told, were found floating on the waters by the few members of the Rehtal Clan who chose to remain in the Vale. But now I see that it was not so. Someone of those who remained in Dona Mihst must have removed them and brought them here, in violation of the command of the Most High. What harm has been done?"

"What is written in them?" The Archivist loved history, though even his passion met its match with this stranger, and he was eager to read the books. He reached out to take the Wave book.

"Wait a moment," Phemanderac commanded, and the Archivist withdrew his hand. "Books like these must be approached slowly, otherwise their contents will be taken too lightly. For two thousand years we have speculated as to the nature and subjects of the missing books. We knew their names, as they are referred to cryptically in the five works in our library, as Hauthius revealed to us, but he— and we—could guess at little of their contents. The *Book of the Sun* was believed to contain lists of those who passed into the presence of the Most High, translated after a life of devotion to Him. We knew the *Book of the Mariswan* by another name: the *Song of Losian*, the record of those who rejected the Fire of Life and left the Vale. We always supposed the *Book of the Clasped Hands* was a record of the *Domaz Skreud*, recording the disobedience of the First Men and the rise of the Destroyer, written by Weid of the House of Wenta. The *Book of the Golden Arrow* was the symbol of the righteous judgments of the Most High, and most scholars agreed it was a book of law. The *Book of the Wave*, it was thought, talked of the destruction of the Vale, or it might have been a symbol of the blessing of the Most High."

He drew a shallow breath through tension-whitened lips. "We are about to find out."

The Pinion was a long, low building near the center of the Great City, sited next to the much taller Hall of Meeting. Unlike the latter, it was plain and unadorned, with but one door at each end and few windows. The Instruian guards were housed within the one floor visible to the general population, and it was through this barracks Leith and Mahnum were taken. The boy cast a concerned eye over his father's limp form being dragged along in front of him. The Trader had tried the patience of the guards beyond what they had considered reasonable, which was not very far, and a blow to the head with the hilt of a sword had silenced him. Some way behind him the Bhrudwan came, silent and impassive. As Leith stumbled through the single room that seemed to stretch away forever, chafed and bruised from his bonds, heads glanced up to stare at his sandy hair, unusual in the city, and perhaps to wonder to themselves what part of Faltha this one came from. They would soon know. The Instruian guards were justifiably proud of their success in encouraging their guests to talk.

A spiral stone stair led down from the center of the long room to the lower levels of the building. While an official secret, the average Instruian knew enough about these lower levels to harbor a strong desire never to see them. Constructed by forced labor during the Bhrudwan occupation of Faltha a thousand years before, they were an exact copy of the lower levels of Andratan. Many terrible things had happened down the stair while the

Bhrudwans ruled Instruere. Instead of destroying it, as many survivors of that time urged them, the city rulers had made use of it; first for innocent purposes—storage of grain and the like—but lately it had begun to acquire a reputation equally as sinister as it had previously owned. Leith knew none of this as the guards propelled him down the torchlit stair, but the fear that had hovered around him since his arrest now settled on his shoulders like a black mantle.

At the bottom of the stair lay the lowest level of the building, and it was to this level they took Leith. *But I've recently escaped from this*, he thought as they thrust both him and the limp body of his father into a cell. *Instruere was supposed to be a refuge! We often talked of it as a place of hope, the end of our quest; and now I find myself in a dungeon fouler even than the one in Adunlok.* Like that fortress, each cell in The Pinion had a single window; but unlike Adunlok the window looked inward into darkness, not outward into light.

The door clanged shut. Leith nearly gagged as the stench from the cell overpowered him. When his eyes finally adjusted to the lack of light he noticed a communal toilet—little more than a bucket—in a corner near the door. It appeared not to have been emptied for some time. At the far end of the cell he could make out dim figures sitting, lying as if asleep or pacing up and down the inner wall.

"Welcome to the Pinion Inn," came a laconic voice from the far wall. "What law did you break to earn a holiday here?"

A thickset, middle-aged woman stepped forward, arm outstretched. "Name's Clothier. Yours?"

Leith shook her hand—or, more accurately, she shook his. Firmly. "I'm Leith, from the north," he squeaked.

Laughter came from nearby. "Don't mind Ma Clothier!" The speaker turned out to be an acne-scarred youth, hardly older than Leith. "Mine's Lennan. Come and meet the family."

Over the next few hours he got to know "the family" well as they traded stories. Fifteen people were crammed into an area slightly smaller than the Widuz cell Leith had shared with Phemanderac. Ma Clothier had been there the longest; at least six menses by her reckoning. "And it'll be a lot longer too," she growled. "None of my children care where I am. Even if they did, they couldn't afford to get me out."

"What are you here for?" Leith found himself warming to this woman and her "family."

"No idea." She shrugged. "They grabbed me on the street, then pow! Here I am."

"Stole her weight's worth of jewelry from Tower Market," Lennan whispered. "She's the scourge of the city." Respect for the broad-shouldered woman, tinged with something approaching love, filled his voice. Leith nodded.

"How about you?" Several curious faces turned his way.

The Archivist trimmed the candle as Phemanderac reached for the volume with the great blue wave on the cover. "Pyrinius was right, the old fool," he whispered. "He always said the Wave volume contained the *Domaz Skreud*. Here," he said, calling his companion over. "Listen to this," and he read:

Above those who fled the fire in the east
Stood a snowflecked fence; the skyline did it stain.
A fertile land and free lay sheltering beneath
White-walled rock flights floating o'er the plain.

The people of the Vale claim this verdant land
Where the history of hope may begin again.

The once proud upraised ramparts are no more.
The timeless towers tumbled to the ground.
Behind the fallen lichen-covered walls
No songs or careless laughter now abound.
Of the mountains and the sea and the strong-walled tower,
Of the pride-pillars three, only two can be found.

"It's a fragment of a lament, a song no doubt composed on the long march north and west to Faltha. These lines must have been added after the First Men left the Vale. They may even have been written here, in this very building. It destroys every theory held by scholars since the Five Books were first lost. It appears, rather than being complete before the destruction of the Vale, the Ten Books were still being written after Faltha was settled. But how could books still being written refer to the contents of other books authored, at least in part, thousands of miles away?" He looked up, puzzled. "Either the First Men who left the Vale and those of the House of Rehtal who remained behind had a much greater degree of contact than anyone imagined, or—or it would explain what Hauthius wrote about mind-sharing. Mind-sharing! Pyrinius always maintained Hauthius was far saner than most of the other scholars who sat in judgment on him." He laughed, oblivious of the fact that the Archivist could not possibly know to whom he referred. "They called Pyrinius the new Hauthius, and perhaps he was, perhaps he was.

"This is a book to be savored. It is too late in the evening to commence study on it now. Such treasures! It might be years before I leave this place." He closed the book almost reverently, then picked up the final volume, easing the dry pages apart with the caress of a lover.

As the minutes lengthened to hours and the hours stretched away into the night, Phemanderac pored over this last volume, the Book of the Golden Arrow, with the Archivist at his side. It was indeed a book of law, but a kind of law unguessed by the scholars and moralists of Dhauria. There were no legal requirements, no dates, times or amounts to be adhered to, no system of government based on the visible externalities of life such as existed in Faltha—and Dhauria—now. All discussion within the pages seemed based on the premise that the ultimate goal of humankind was to dwell together in unity, and every law was subservient to this goal. For Phemanderac, who specialized in the study of the evolution of moral codes, the book was a revelation, an explosion of light that left him breathless. *We were taught to set one day a month aside to honor the Most High, a day on which no work was to be done. But here it explains that the Workless Day is called Today; that we enter the Workless Day by resting from our own attempts to fulfill the moral code. So we fulfill the law every day, not once a month, by not trying to fulfill the law!*

He read on. Teachers in his own land regularly expounded the virtues of making offerings to the memory of the great Fountain. In fact, many insisted on a regular tithe, the *Teogothian* it was called, levied on the villagers and used to support the teachers and scholars themselves. *But here it says that the heart is bound by the tithe, but loosed by the gift freely given. Who could have guessed this? Have we completely misinterpreted the nature of the Most High? Are we worshipping some other god—or our own good deeds?*

His mind groped on the fringes of understanding. *The*

cold heart seeks to placate its gods with outward things, offering sacrifices, parading its goodness in public and then retreating to its private darkness. But here the fire-warmed heart rejects the bare bones of legislation in favor of attitudes inherited from the Most High, which then work their way out to the surface.

Dhauria was without doubt the most civilized place in the world, a fact confirmed by Phemanderac's travels. *What happens in this city would not be tolerated in my homeland. Yet according to this book we of Dhauria have been completely wrong! Our laws prohibit murder, yet do nothing about hate; punish adultery, yet condone betrayal; flay the skin, yet leave the heart untouched. We are no different to the Falthans or, indeed, the Bhrudwans, for that matter. Perhaps we're worse, living smug lives of dedication and service, our cold hearts undisturbed by the requirements of the law.*

He looked again at the cover of this book that left him stunned. *The Golden Arrow. The power of the Most High to be good; to be righteous, fired from his bow, piercing the skin of human endeavor, enflaming the human heart.* He lifted the precious book from the bench, his own heart beginning to burn. *I am tired of the laws that wrap themselves around my ankles like seaweed, drowning me with their lies, turning acts of love into mere acts of duty. What have we done to ourselves; oh, what have we done?*

A piece of parchment fell from the book and fluttered down on to the bench. On it was written, in a rough hand unlike the scholarly scribing of the book, the following doggerel:

> *Shaft of steel shot through with strength,*
> *Burning will of Mighty Name,*

Rod to rule o'er all rebellion,
Making nations whole again.

Hidden from rebellious hands,
Free from every fleshly claim,
Through the air, over water,
In the earth abides the flame.

Instantly Phemanderac laid aside the law of the Golden Arrow. He turned to the Archivist, who was reading from the *Book of the Sun*.

"What's this?"

The fleshy man studied the parchment and the verses on it, then looked at the thin stranger. "I don't know. I know nothing of these books."

"But it is clearly not part of the original book, so must have been added later. Think! Have you seen script from this hand before?"

"What is so important about a piece of parchment?" The Archivist seemed perplexed at the discoveries of treasure in his musty old rooms. Probably, if the truth were told, he found himself embarrassed to have some visiting scholar make these discoveries. Embarrassed, and perhaps a little resentful.

"What do you know about the Jugom Ark?"

"Pardon? The Jugom what? I know of no such thing."

"It was called the Arrow of Yoke."

"Oh, the Arrow!" The Archivist looked glad to be back on familiar ground. "Well, I know what everyone knows, of course, what they taught us at school; the Arrow was loosed in judgment by the Most High at the Destroyer, taking off his hand. It became a great heirloom of the First Men, and the guarantor of leadership to whomever possessed it. We were taught that Raupa and Furist, the two leaders of the First Men, fought over the Arrow, and this contention divided Faltha into northern and southern factions. Furist took the Arrow south out of knowledge, where it became lost." The Archivist scratched his head. "I was taught the Arrow was a symbol of the favor of the Most High, and in losing it Falthans lost contact with Him. Oh yes, and whoever wields the Arrow commands the unity of all Falthans. Whatever that means."

"Where could it be?" Phemanderac muttered. "Is that what all this is about? Unity?"

"Where could what be? The Arrow?"

"Have you seen other books containing the same handwriting? It really is most important."

The Archivist studied the lines for a long time, then stood slowly, walked over to a tall shelf and took a book down from it.

"What have you found?"

"Nothing really, just a suspicion. A far-fetched one at that. This book has within it a discussion of the evolution of script writing styles—look here," he said, directing Phemanderac to the page he had just found. "Here, at the top, is the commentary written in contemporary handwriting. This book was last copied . . ."—he referred to the cover—"about seventy years ago. See the straight lines and uprightness of the letters? If anything, the writing slopes a little to the left. Typical of the precision, the solemnity and conservatism that characterizes the typical Instruian script. And take a close look at the ligatures."

"Where?"

"That is my point: there are none. We did away with them centuries ago. Now, look at the parchment scrap. A cursive script with full, rounded letters, exhibiting a marked slope to the right. There is a definite musical lilt to the manuscript; the words flow together like a song. There are no books in this library written in such a script. It is too old. Remember, we re-copy each manuscript at least once every two hundred years.

"Now, follow this discussion. Here." A stubby finger pointed to the relevant passage. "'In the early years, learning was concentrated in the hands of the Scriveners, the most famous of whom was Dakru of the House of Wenta, the last to die of those who left the Vale.' It was he who composed the *Domaz Skreud*. What follows is a description of the style of script he used."

"Yes, we've heard of Dakru. No one in Dhauria has written a treatise on his writing style, however," Phemanderac acknowledged, impressed.

"I read this many years ago. Listen: 'Dakru had the endearing habit of adding little serifs to some of his capital letters, an elaborate idiosyncrasy often admired, but very difficult to copy.' Like this." He pointed to the scrap of parchment. "See the 'T' in 'Through'? This had to be written either by Dakru or by a skilled and meticulous copyist. And look at the ligatures! The 'fl' in 'fleshly' is almost a capital 'A.'"

He turned to the tall philosopher with puzzlement in his eyes. "There can be little doubt about it," he pronounced. "This piece of parchment is nearly two thousand years old."

Phemanderac nodded slowly. "I have never heard of even a fragment such as this lasting so long a time," he said almost to himself. "Except for the Five Books themselves. Perhaps it has been preserved by being held within the leaves of the Book of the Golden Arrow. Nevertheless, if you are right, it confirms my suspicions.

This is a riddle, written in the style of the fancies so popular in the Vale of the First Men. The only difference is this riddle is meant to be taken seriously."

"And the subject of the riddle?"

"The subject is without doubt the Jugom Ark, the Arrow of Yoke."

"I see no reference to the Arrow," the Archivist said.

"I would have thought the first two lines were quite sufficient: 'Shaft of steel shot through with strength/Burning will of Mighty Name.' To what else could they refer?"

The Archivist pursed his lips.

"Look at the cover of the book from which it fell," Phemanderac pressed on. "The Golden Arrow. Coincidence?

"And to what other meaning could the line 'Making peoples whole again' refer? The Unity of the Arrow, a common theme of the legend of the Jugom Ark. My friend, this follows the classic structure of the riddle: the first verse establishes the subject, while the second provides the information."

"Which is?" The Instruian scratched his forehead.

"The first couplet explains that the Arrow has been hidden, and hints at why," Phemanderac explained, trying not to sound condescending. "The second couplet is the riddle proper, telling us where to find it."

"Do you mean this riddle is like a map giving us the location of the great treasure?" Phemanderac noted the skepticism in the other's voice.

"That is exactly what it is."

The Archivist stood to his full height and folded his arms against his chest. "Then it is a flight of fancy, for in my mind there is no question the Arrow of Yoke never existed."

"Never existed? How can you say this of such an important part of our history? A little while ago you struggled to even remember what you knew about the Arrow. What makes you now say it is nothing but a myth?"

"Undoubtedly there was no such thing. We descendants of the First Men have always displayed the tendency to invest mere symbols with human faculties or even supernatural powers, as though trying to make up for that which we lost. Our legends are full of quests for this object or that place of fantasy: Kantara, the house of Everlasting Life; Bi'r Birkat, the liquid gold lake. Need I continue?"

"No. You've made your point. The scholars of Dhauria have made too many mistakes by interpreting obscure passages literally, and basing their doctrines and careers on them; perhaps I run the risk of compounding their mistakes."

Phemanderac's comments barely slowed the Archivist as he constructed his argument. "Even the *Fuirfad*, the indwelling of the Most High, may itself be only a symbol."

"The Firefall a symbol?" The philosopher tried to keep his indignation in check. "Even in Dhauria no one has dared to say such a thing. Some of us devote our lives to investigating the *Fuirfad*. Do you think we would do so if we saw it merely as a symbol?"

"There may have been lives of devotion to the *Fuirfad*, yet tonight you say you have discovered in my archives things that centuries of study have not revealed," the Archivist said, displaying his shrewdness. "Answer this. In all your years of study, have you ever experienced the Fire the way it is described in *Domaz Skreud*?"

The philosopher shook his head.

"In the two thousand years since the destruction of the Vale, has there even been one instance of anyone experiencing the Fire?"

"But that is consistent with what the Most High told us! Part of our punishment was to lose the Gift of Fire. Because we do not experience it now does not exclude the possibility of its existence then."

"No, but it does bring it into question. The writings are, in my view, entirely consistent with the human need to create mystery in order to justify morality—or lack of it."

"So you do not believe in the Most High?"

"I know of no one who does."

"Perhaps that accounts for the moral state of Instruere," came the caustic reply.

The Archivist raised his eyebrows. "A lack of belief in the Most High has in no way lessened my commitment to my own morals," he shot back. "The current moral state of this city is exactly what one would expect in a time of confusion when primitive beliefs are being exchanged for more human-honoring, life-affirming codes. Within a generation we will experience a golden age such as we have never before known."

"Sounds remarkably like Kantara or Bi'r Birkat to me," Phemanderac said, a little unkindly. "If you are so positive about the future, what are you doing studying the past?"

"My study of the past led me to these conclusions," the Archivist replied. "There was such cruelty and injustice among the sons of the First Men that I could only doubt the lofty claims they made for their ancestors. In my view the path to the future lies in rejecting the strictures of the past, and especially their religious dimension."

"Quite a view for an archivist to take!" Phemanderac chuckled. "But you have yet to persuade me of the inadequacy of the moral code, or the non-existence of the Jugom Ark. Failure to obey the code is the fault of the person, not the code. And as for the Arrow, and the possible existence of legendary things, you have yet to explore my assertion that I come from the remnants of the Vale of the First Men."

"That puzzles me," the Archivist admitted, "given that what you say is true, and not merely a misidentification based on generations of wishful thinking. I will have to take your word for it."

"Take my word? Surely oaths are part of the old moral code?"

"I never said the transition would be easy." The Archivist smiled as he issued his glib reply.

Phemanderac stood and stretched tired muscles. "Nevertheless, I value the discoveries we have made this night, the last perhaps more than all the others. Will you allow me to make a copy of the riddle?"

What passed for night settled on The Pinion, though the inquisitors in the central chamber seemed to need no sleep, and appeared to enjoy depriving their prisoners of it. Leith's cellmates eventually managed to drift into uneasy slumber, something that eluded him. Some time later Mahnum regained consciousness. The Bhrudwan had been taken from the cell perhaps an hour earlier. Leith caught a glimpse of him in the dim red glow of the central chamber, bent backwards over something in the shadows. *They are going to torture him.*

He related to his father the events that led to his striking the guard, and surmised it was for this crime he was imprisoned.

"No, that is but a pretext," Mahnum said. "You and I are here because of the reputation of your grandsire. The Bhrudwan is here because he may have knowledge the

Instruians can use. No doubt the Arkhos of Nemohaim ordered this."

"My grandsire?"

"Modahl. My father. A spy for the Firanese king, though not as secret a spy as I thought. So they talked about him behind the Iron Door! He must have been involved in more than he told us."

"My grandfather?"

"Leith, there is no mystery about this. My father was already a veteran when I was born, and was killed when I was young. I barely knew him. There's no more."

Leith detected something evasive in his father's voice. "Mother said there was a long story."

"She also said that much of it was not known," he replied shortly. "Now time presses us, my son, and we need to consider how we might escape this place. If only my head did not hurt so much!"

Leith waited patiently while his father sat on his haunches, deep in thought. He tried not to look at the cell door, through which the guards would come for him. But he could not help considering his fate. From somewhere in the darkness beyond the cell window the Bhrudwan warrior made small, agonized sounds. Leith found himself tensing at each indrawn breath. *If they cause a Lord of Fear so much pain, what will they do to me?*

Finally the sounds drew Leith to the far window. He stood and peered into the red-tinged darkness, where he could make out two shapes occupied in doing something dreadful to the Bhrudwan. What it was they did he could not tell, but they kept doing it for what seemed like hours.

So much for Hal's protection, Leith thought, and the beginnings of real fear began pulling at his bowels. *That will soon be me*. At that moment the Bhrudwan warrior lifted his head and, his face illuminated by a flickering torch, smiled at Leith in the midst of his torture.

It was all the youth could do not to cry out in fright. *What sort of magic is at work here?*

He waited by the window, ignoring his father's whispered commands to come away, and watched the guards work on the Bhrudwan, clearly convinced they were hurting him. The grunting and sighing continued, but now Leith knew it was pretense, he could hear the acting in the sounds.

Eventually the two guards tired of their sport and disappeared into the darkness. A minute or so later they walked past the door of the cell, with a jangling of keys and whispered ribaldry. Up the stone stairs they clomped, then the trapdoor creaked open and closed.

As soon as the echoes died away the Bhrudwan let out a deep throaty rumble, then pulled savagely at his chains. Rather than jerking them, he maintained a constant pressure far longer than Leith would have believed possible. Mahnum joined his son at the window and watched in awe as, in a display of raw power, the warrior pulled himself free of the machine that had held him fast.

"Perhaps you should go home," Phemanderac said after a long silence, noticing the sag in his companion's shoulders. "It must be well into the morning."

"I should," the Archivist replied. "But then you would have to leave also, for I have the keys. And before you say it, no, I do not trust you. I saw the covetous gleam in your eye when you discovered these books. If I left the keys with you, I am not sure you would be able to resist the temptation."

The philosopher laughed loudly. "I'm sure you're

right! Though truthfully I had not thought beyond remaining here as long as I could. I will not sleep even if I return home for the remaining few hours of darkness." He laughed again. "Given time," he said, clasping the Archivist's round shoulder with his large, bony hand, "I'm sure we could become friends."

"Then you agree to leave the books until tomorrow—or later today, I probably should say."

"Yes," Phemanderac said reluctantly. "I have no doubt they will be here when we return. They have hidden from us for two thousand years. A few more hours will not matter." Phemanderac took one last loving look at the pile of books; then, unable to resist, he spread them out across the bench so that all five covers were visible. Finally he turned and followed the Archivist through the many narrow twists and turns up and out of the old building.

Terrible noises abruptly recommenced from the central chamber of The Pinion. It seemed a third guard had gone to work somewhere in the chamber. Horrible as they were, Mahnum gave thanks, as the sounds served to mask the scraping of metal on metal as the Bhrudwan knotted his chains around the bars of the window.

"Will you be much longer?" Leith asked, unable to mask his anxiety. One or two of their fellow prisoners stirred as the agonized screams coming from the central chamber increased in volume: the torturer had apparently begun his work in earnest on the young woman who, Ma Clothier had told them, had been taken from the cell to make room for Mahnum and Leith.

The bars groaned in answer, frighteningly loud in a momentary silence. Under the relentless pressure exerted by the inhumanly strong warrior they bent inwards, further and further, until he had made just enough room for the two men to squeeze through. "Come on," Mahnum whispered. Unnecessarily, as Leith had already wriggled his way through the gap.

They emerged cautiously into the chamber itself, a cavernous room filled with a bewildering array of machines of various shapes and sizes, providing them with ample cover. The Bhrudwan was nowhere in sight. For a while the two northerners hid behind a large, barrel-shaped instrument, a machine with a purpose neither cared to guess at. They listened for any sound that might betray the presence of guards; but all they heard was soft whimpering from the far side of the chamber.

Suddenly there came the sound of boots on stone. Mahnum watched the purposeful stride of a guard from between the slats of the barrel. *Only one*, he thought. *Good*. Signaling for Leith to remain hidden, he flitted from hiding place to hiding place, following the guard; and as he did so he caught sight of the Bhrudwan, feigning unconsciousness, seemingly strapped to a wooden rack.

Ahead of him a chilling shriek rang out. As Mahnum emerged into the very center of the chamber, he saw the guard heft a red-hot branding iron above the shaking nakedness of a girl who could not possibly have been any older than Stella. Desperate, he spun around, and his eye fell on a foot-long metal spike on the flagstone floor. As he picked it up the girl cried out, an ear-splitting howl, and Mahnum cursed aloud. He raised the spike and, without a second thought, buried it deep between the guard's shoulders.

The guard grunted, then half turned, seemingly unaware that he had been dealt a mortal blow. He dropped to his knees, jerking the spike from Mahnum's hand, and tried to raise his head. His mouth dribbled blood. His unseeing eyes looked in Mahnum's direction. Then he expired with a gurgle and slumped to the floor.

Mahnum sighed with relief, thankful that little or no sound had been made. In a flash Leith rushed to his side, and stripped the guard of his short sword. With its tip forward he approached the girl, who stared at him with wide, terrified eyes. She screamed, a throat-wrenching sound, when Leith moved to cut through her bonds; and Mahnum winced, even though his mind told him the noise was exactly what any other guard would expect to hear.

The Loulean youth turned to walk towards the Bhrudwan, and found himself staring at the face of a prisoner watching from one of the cell windows. "Let us out," the man called. "Let us out!"

"Be quiet!" Leith signaled furiously to the man. "We don't want to be discovered!"

But the man would not be quiet. "Let me out!" he continued to cry, more and more loudly, and began rattling the bars of his cell.

Leith ran forward, waving the guard's sword threateningly. "Silence!" he shouted. The man withdrew somewhat from the window, but shouted all the more from the safety of his cell.

Now other prisoners awoke, and some joined in the shouting. A desperation haunted them, a bone-deep fear generated by the scenes constantly replayed before their eyes. There would be no keeping them silent.

"No," said Mahnum, exasperated. "No, no, no!" There was nothing else for it. He bent down and rifled through the pockets of the still-twitching guard, then found the keys he looked for on a belt clip. With a signal for Leith and the Bhrudwan to follow, he raced for the passage

leading back to the outer corridor. He would have to let
the prisoners out.

*If only they would keep quiet, perhaps we can still do
this*, Mahnum said to himself; but they would not be
quiet, each wanting release before the others. The first
door opened, and eight people bolted; but Mahnum noted
three or four more who cowered in the cell, obviously too
afraid of the guards to move.

*Perhaps the guards cannot hear the commotion, or
maybe they think it is the normal sound*, the Trader
thought, trying to reassure himself; but even as the
thought flicked through his mind, he heard the rough
sound of the trapdoor to the guardhouse opening. He hurried on, resisting the temptation to look behind him. The
second cell door would not open, so he abandoned it, ignoring the frightened wails of those inside, and went to
the third. Behind him came a cry: obviously a guard or
guards had discovered the freed prisoners. *This is all
going wrong*.

Now Leith emerged from the passage linking the central chamber and the outer corridor, sword raised. The
Bhrudwan followed him, naked, lacerated and bruised
about the face but otherwise not seriously injured. The
dark warrior brandished a steel bar found somewhere,
and looked grim and fierce, his purpling face a death
mask. Menace radiated from him like heat from a fire.
Mahnum reminded himself that this redoubtable killer
was but the least of the three Bhrudwans they had defeated on the slopes of Steffl.

The Pinion contained more cells than Mahnum could
possibly open in the time given to him. Having committed himself to this course, he threw open door after door,
but as he did so his doubts grew. How many deaths would

this cost? Prisoners poured out of the confined spaces, milling about in the corridor, but in each cell a few remained behind, simply too frightened to move.

A commotion echoed along the corridor to the right. Leith ran in that direction and, in a moment, was pitched headlong into a one-sided fight between two guards and a group of unarmed prisoners. Three lay sprawled on the floor, each injured in some way; though not fatally. The corridor was too narrow to deal strong blows. The others were being forced back to their cell, giving way before purposeful slashes and thrusts of the Instruian blades. With a strange shout on his lips Leith fell upon the guards.

Within moments the two guards lay on the floor, wounded by short, sharp strokes of Leith's sword. Leith stood panting and dizzy in the middle of the corridor. Smaller of frame, and with a shorter blade, the Loulean youth had enjoyed an insurmountable advantage in the confined corridor of The Pinion. He was allowed no time to enjoy it, however. The trapdoor opened and another guard came down the stair, took one look at the scene in the dungeons and ran swiftly back up to the guardhouse. Leith went in pursuit. As the trapdoor closed in front of him, he realized the hopelessness of their position.

He made his weary way back down to the corridor, and met the Bhrudwan there. The warrior, still naked but totally unconcerned, held the steel bar in his hand. Would he attack me? Leith wondered. Perhaps thinking of this killer as Hal's tame creature was a mistake. But then why would the Bhrudwan have saved him and his father both? There was so much fear in the air he could be sure of nothing.

Again the trapdoor scraped open, this time to admit a

horde of guards who poured quickly down the stair,
shouting as they came. He was trapped: the guards above,
the Bhrudwan below.

Leith made his choice and, with a shout, charged at the
Bhrudwan. To his relief the warrior drew aside and let him
pass, then followed as he ran a little way down the corridor.
Now they were pursued by the guards, each one armed with
a sharp, double-edged sword. Their enterprise was about to
founder.

In the middle of the night Indrett sat alone on her bed, unable to sleep, knowing beyond doubt that somewhere out
in the darkness the husband she loved and the son of their
flesh were in peril. The woman struggled with the weight
of her sorrows, made greater by love rediscovered on the
hard Western Road and the separation of both Widuz and
now Instruere.

A knock came at the door. It was Hal, who with great
effort had hauled himself up the stair from the basement.
"I know," he said, before Indrett could say anything.
"I've loosed Achtal's bonds. Achtal the Bhrudwan warrior," he explained in response to her quizzical look.
"Anything could be happening. Let's sit together. I'll
know if he dies."

The prisoners ransacked the central chamber, searching
for anything sharp or stout with which to defend themselves. Chains, branding irons, pieces of timber, anything
and everything that came to hand was claimed by the terrified captives. They were under no illusions as to what
the guards might do to them, and many of them began to
doubt the wisdom of having left their cells: not a few,

their courage failing them, took the opportunity to return to their prisons, to the jeers of their fellows.

Forced back by the guards, Leith and Mahnum found themselves first at the far end of the passage encircling the cells and then in the vestibule of the inner chamber. Behind them swarmed the freed prisoners. Wordlessly, the guards formed a wedge, drew their swords and marched inexorably down the passage and into the chamber as Mahnum and Leith moved aside. Before they could react, the guards found themselves in the center of the wrecked chamber, surrounded by angry prisoners.

For a moment all was silent. Then the leader barked a single word of command, and the guards laid about them. Though the prisoners fought with a will, they could not match the skill and weaponry of the fighters. One by one they fell, stunned, wounded and a few slain. Then guards began to fall among the bodies. Leith looked up to see the Bhrudwan warrior had entered the fray, wielding the steel bar to irresistible effect. The cries in that confined space grated horribly on Mahnum's ears, until he could stand it no longer.

"Follow me!" he called to the prisoners and, knocking a guard out of the way, made for the passage. It was time to attempt the longhouse, to make an end of this thing, one way or another.

Immediately Leith went to his father's side, glad to be out of the open space where he had been vulnerable to the superior swordsmanship of the enemy. The prisoners followed them as they ran from the central chamber, closely pursued by most of the guards. Two soldiers stood in the corridor, but they fell before the swords of Mahnum and Leith. At the rear of their ragged group the Bhrudwan held off the remaining guards single-handedly, felling many of them with vicious blows of his steel bar.

As if in a dream, Leith began to lose touch with the reality of their peril, and found himself thinking how impersonal all this fighting seemed. *These guards are nothing but faceless shapes falling before me. I have not looked into the eyes of anyone I've struck.* There was a darting move to his left. A slashing blow ripped his sleeve and nicked his arm, dragging him out of his hypnotic thoughts. Still more guards!

"Up and out!" Mahnum cried. "Follow me!" He made the stair, turned and saw, thankfully, that Leith was right behind him. The narrow corridor was crowded with people fighting at close quarters, where swords could not be swung. The shouts of pain, of fear and of exultation mingled into a harsh, ragged noise that drove him on up the stair.

In a moment he stood directly under the trapdoor, and looked down on the fighting below. The yellow regalia of the Instruian Guard, he saw, was seriously outnumbered, but the guards had an overwhelming superiority of weaponry. It was only a matter of time, Mahnum realized bitterly. Even the spinning steel bar of the Bhrudwan warrior would soon be buried under the disciplined blades of the Instruian Guard. Mahnum put his shoulder to the trapdoor, opened it and climbed the last few steps into the longhouse. To his astonishment it was empty.

The Arkhos of Nemohaim disliked being disturbed at night, especially when he had company. He was particularly unhappy to be interrupted when he had left explicit instructions with his servant to prevent any such disturbance.

"It is the Bhrudwan prisoner, my lord," his servant said respectfully, knowing that, depending on his master's mood, his life might be saved only by convincing the Arkhos of the gravity of the problem.

"What about him?" the Arkhos growled, out of breath and livid with rage. "He is not to be interfered with until the morning, when I will have sufficient time to attend to him!"

"Yes, my lord, but it appears some sort of rescue mission has been mounted to free him from The Pinion."

"Rescue mission? What is happening? Speak!"

Good: he now had his master's attention.

"It seems someone infiltrated The Pinion and freed the prisoners. At present the Instruian Guard is attempting to contain the riot. I thought you would want to be acquainted with the situation." The man held his breath and waited.

The Arkhos struggled with his nightgown as though it was his rage, and succeeded in buttoning it up. "You have done well," he said quietly, even pleasantly. "Send for my captain. I will dispatch my personal guard to deal with the situation. With good fortune we may capture further prizes to examine at our leisure." He licked his full lips. "Moreover, make it known that I will attend this disturbance personally and supervise the quelling of this riot."

"Yes, my lord." His servant nodded, then bowed and began to withdraw.

"And you, my little bird," the Arkhos said, turning to the pale, frightened figure cowering in the corner, "you will wait here until I return. Let that thought sharpen your desire." His red battle robe still fitted him—just—and, with it securely fastened, he left his room. His servant locked it behind him, then leaned on the door in relief as he watched the Arkhos stride purposefully down the corridor.

Is this some sort of trap?

Mahnum puzzled over the absence of guards in the longhouse. He had imagined there would be many more guards waiting for them here. However, it seemed most of the guards slept at their homes. Perhaps all the guards had gone below, or the others had gone to fetch their fellows from their beds. *Either way, we'll soon be out of this place and on our way home. The Instruians will not forget this night!* Thanking the luck that seemed still to be holding, he called Leith and the others forward.

Behind him the prisoners pushed, pressing together up the stair. An older man missed his footing and fell on to the well-worn stone steps. For a moment those below halted their frantic rush upward, but the carnage behind them grew louder, driving the terrified prisoners past the point of reason. Someone stepped on the old man's back, but his feeble shriek was drowned by the sound of fighting below.

The Trader scurried across the deserted guardroom to the door. Behind him Leith spoke tensely: "What about the Bhrudwan?"

"With the way things have turned out, we have a responsibility for many others now. The Bhrudwan can look after himself."

"That's not how I see it," Leith said. "You stay here with the others while I go back and search for him."

"You young fool! I only hope there is enough left after they've finished with you in order to hold a proper funeral."

"Yes, Father." Leith made a mock subservient gesture. "You're not the only one allowed to take risks."

People now poured out of the trapdoor. Leith saw that, in spite of his bravado, he had no hope of forcing his way down into The Pinion; so he waited anxiously as the flood of prisoners continued: the younger men first, then the older men and women, and finally a young mother and the remnants of her family. Many wore a strangely blank, frozen look on their faces, eyes glazed, shocked and un-comprehending, as a result of the violence below. Most simply milled about; a few comforted others, while one or two collapsed on to the wooden floor. A heavily built young man, carrying a bloody sword wrested from a guard, grabbed the trapdoor and slammed it down, then swiftly rammed the bolt home.

"What are you doing?" Leith cried.

"Stopping the guards coming up, that's what," the man replied gruffly.

"But—"

"There's no one left alive down there except the guards," growled the big man. "I saw them going from cell to cell, dragging out the prisoners and butchering them. They're all dead, poor sods."

There was a disbelieving, stunned silence. All dead? How could Instruians do this to their own?

"What about the man with the large steel bar?" After all this, with all the suffering and death, Leith couldn't believe that the Bhrudwan hadn't escaped.

The man shrugged his shoulders. "I didn't see him."

The Trader put his head in his hands. The Bhrudwan slain, and many more besides. Death seemed to be snapping at Mahnum's heels, following him across the world. A dreadful thought came to him: had the Destroyer delib-erately let him go as some sort of catalyst of destruction?

A lightning rod fashioned to attract the dark power of Bhrudwo?

Behind him came a sharp crack. Mahnum wheeled around: the sound came from the trapdoor.

"Quick! Everyone out of here!" he cried. Leith tried to herd the prisoners towards the door, but they moved slowly, far too slowly. Any moment now the guards would emerge from The Pinion.

With a splintering of wood and a loud roar a naked figure drove up through the trapdoor, bursting it open. In a smooth, swift movement he took his steel bar and wedged the broken doors shut, then turned his black, implacable eyes on the astonished Trader and his son. "Go now," he said.

They cajoled the prisoners—perhaps fifty at the most, Mahnum speculated, leaving at least the same number dead down in The Pinion—through the longhouse door and out into the clear, cool night. The Trader and his son took deep breaths of the sweet, sweet air, and wiped their swords clean on the hems of their tattered robes. Then they heard a faint clink, a tiny metallic sound. It came from the shadows on the far side of the open space between the longhouse and the Hall of Meeting. There was something in the shadows.

An unmistakable figure, large and menacing, strode out into the moonlight.

"So this is the brave rescue party," came the familiar, hateful, high-pitched wheeze. "Good. I shall enjoy discussing aspects of your attempted escape with you in a location of my choosing. Perhaps you will not find me so agreeable without the protection of the craven Arkhos of Sarista." He made no attempt to keep the note of gloating triumph out of his voice.

"Guards!" he cried.

Purple-cloaked, armored men stepped out from the shadows in perfect unison, long, curving scimitars at the ready. The laughter of the Arkhos of Nemohaim rolled softly across the compound.

CHAPTER 4

FIREFALL

TERRIFIED PRISONERS COWERED against the wall of the longhouse as the personal guard of the Arkhos of Nemohaim advanced menacingly across the dusty compound. Leith glanced desperately to the left and to the right, but there was no way of escape, the wooden wall stretching into the darkness on either side.

"Bhrudwans," said the naked warrior between Leith and his father. "*Bhrud achannin Aldh*. An order low." His lip curled in derision.

The guards stopped on a command, and parted to let the Arkhos through. The obese man stood about ten steps away, breathing heavily, surveying his prizes.

"Disarm them," he said. "Then slay all the prisoners but these three. And do not leave a mess: I don't want any questions." He withdrew through the line of guards, lifting his robes to avoid the dust. *This will be entertainment richer even than I had planned for this night*, he thought as a smile played on his full lips.

Instantly and with no visible effort three of the guards crossed the remaining space in obedience to their master's order. Leith's hand went to his sword. Without warning he was slammed up against the wall then slid to the ground with the wind knocked out of him. His weapon fell from his hand. For a few seconds he lay gasping. He forced himself to his feet, dizzy and nauseous, in time to witness Achtal the Bhrudwan, Leith's sword in his hand, face his three countrymen.

It had been Achtal who disarmed him, roughly but quickly, Leith realized. Still naked, yet clothed with a single-minded determination, the warrior marshaled his considerable strength and training. The first of his opponents lost his life by incautiously turning to his fellows for a fraction of a second. Perhaps he was surprised by the arrogance of the man's demeanor, or unsettled by his stance or some subtle hint of Bhrudwan training. Whatever the reason, his head fell to the earth before he could warn his comrades, leaving his body standing for a few unnatural moments. This distraction cost the two other Bhrudwans dearly. A moment's inattention; a sword-thrust; and their bodies slumped softly to the ground.

Turning to the prisoners, Achtal cried: "Run! Go!" Hesitant at first, but encouraged by what they had seen and aware of what would happen to them should they remain, the disheveled group edged away into the shadows.

"Guards!" the red-faced Arkhos shouted, then closed his mouth tight in frustration. "They're not important," he muttered.

Leith sucked air into his burning lungs, steadied his spinning head and glanced at Mahnum. "There's nothing we can do," the Trader said. "We're totally in his hands."

There was an inevitability about the way the remaining seven guards were dispatched. This is a combination of innate ability, strict training and pure aggression, Leith thought as he watched the Arkhos's personal guard fall before the Bhrudwan warrior. They were obviously reluctant to face him, knowing themselves in the presence of a warrior of the highest order, and therefore stood no chance. Although it was almost certainly his own life at stake should one of them defeat Achtal, Leith couldn't help feeling sorry for them, people like him, mere footsoldiers in a far larger game. They could not have suspected that they would face a Lord of Fear this night. Now if it had been the Arkhos at the sharp end of the sword, then he wouldn't have felt so sorry.

It was over very quickly. The Arkhos of Nemohaim became more and more incoherent as he screamed orders to his men. When the outcome became obvious he quickly backed away towards the Hall of Meeting and safety.

Not fast enough. The naked figure flashed across the compound, easily outdistancing the bulky man. Passing him, he turned and held his arms wide, with the blade extended even wider; as though shepherding a recalcitrant sheep back into the fold. Wild-eyed, the Arkhos looked right and left, searching in vain for a way of escape. Achtal advanced on him. The Arkhos backed away, straight into the grasp of Mahnum and Leith. Instantly a sword was at his throat. Terror paralyzed the Arkhos, turning his red face gray.

Achtal turned his head slightly and caught Mahnum's eye, then raised one eyebrow slightly. The question was obvious.

"No," said Leith, for some reason he couldn't understand. "No more killing."

"What?" Mahnum said, surprised. "You know what he was going to do to us!"

The Bhrudwan's eyebrows raised in puzzlement, his eyes edged with a dangerous anger.

The exercise of mercy strengthens the merciful, a re-membered voice echoed in Leith's mind.

"That doesn't mean we have to do it to him. This one can't do anything more to us. So, no." But even as he spoke, his mind cried out: *what are you trying to prove? That you are more moral than your brother?*

"Not now, perhaps, but—"

"I'm not killing a defenseless man!" Leith insisted. "Besides, if we kill the Arkhos of Nemohaim, we're likely to find ourselves back in The Pinion." He looked into the small, frightened eyes of their adversary. "Am I right?"

The Arkhos took a deep breath and swallowed twice, then nodded, clearly not able to trust his voice.

"How are you going to tell the Bhrudwan?" Mahnum asked. "He doesn't seem to be particularly merciful."

"If he wants to slay the Arkhos, I can't stop him," said Leith. "But I'll not agree to it."

He spun on his heel, very deliberately, and walked away. "Come on," he called over his shoulder. "We need to get back before dawn."

No one moved. Leith held his breath, but also held his course.

As he left the open space he heard movement behind him, but forced himself to continue without looking back. In a few moments he was joined by Achtal and his father. A red robe sat on the Bhrudwan's wide shoulders. Nothing was said on the long walk home.

The pale pre-dawn glow had begun its task of rolling away the heaviness of night when finally the three weary figures approached the tenement. For Leith the last hour had been the most trying of the night, more difficult than the night in The Pinion cell, far more difficult than the frantic battle under the longhouse, more difficult even than choosing life or death for the Arkhos of Nemohaim.

For in the hour it took them to walk from The Pinion to the tenement, Leith saw again the faces of those he had sent to their deaths. Up they rose, one after another, people with histories and friends, some dying at the end of his sword, some cut down before he could come to their aid. Faceless then but dead now, and now he could see their faces. The realization the world was unfriendly, he was not at the center of it, and that life was uncertain, death inevitable, with no guarantees of old age, settled on Leith like nightfall in a foreign land. He was going to die. Perhaps not like those just gone to their desperate, frightened deaths, but death would seek him out nonetheless. The faces of the dead had come to help him think about it.

In echo of his sorrow the clouds lowered over the grimy city and it began to rain.

Leith put his hand to the door, and let out a long sigh. Sanctuary in an oppressive world, for the moment at least.

"You've been released!" Kurr cried as they entered the tenement. "I would not have believed it!"

He must have been waiting here in the hall, unable to sleep, Leith realized. *Such is his care for us*. The discovery that the crusty old man would do such a thing was somehow humbling.

"Not released exactly," Mahnum said. "I doubt they had any intention of ever setting us free."

"So . . ." Kurr encouraged.

"So, wake everyone and assemble them here," Leith said in a voice that was his and yet not his. "We need to talk together."

The old farmer nodded slowly, as if his thoughts were elsewhere, then disappeared up the stair.

The story related by the Trader and his son amazed and encouraged the Company. There was sadness for the many lives lost, but great joy for the captives who escaped such a cruel place. "We fled The Pinion," Leith concluded, "only to walk into a trap laid by the Arkhos of Nemohaim."

At the mention of his name the Company leaned forward as one.

"He was waiting for us outside The Pinion, he and a contingent of guards wearing a livery I have not seen before in the city," Leith said.

"Bhrudwans," Mahnum spat out.

"Bhrudwans?" echoed Kurr. "What are Bhrudwans doing in Instruere?"

Hal spoke swiftly to Achtal in a rumbling language, and the Bhrudwan replied in kind. "*Bhrud achannin Aldh*," he said.

"Mercenaries," Hal interpreted. "Defectors from the Bhrudwan army, perhaps." Mahnum raised his eyebrows.

"Perhaps," Leith commented, "but they were under the command of the Arkhos of Nemohaim. Bhrudwans they might have been, but they were merely humans, and proved no match for the skills of Achtal. After he had dealt with them, he—" Leith hesitated.

"We let him go." Mahnum sighed. "Not my choice, I assure you; but Leith seemed to think we ought not slay someone without the means to defend himself." He fell silent, clearly troubled by some memory. Parlevaag's death, perhaps. Or maybe, considered Leith, her husband and the other Fenns cut down by the Bhrudwan raiders. Kroptur's messenger, tormented and dispatched by

Bhrudwan swords. A burning Favonian village. Screams. Shrieks. The smell of death.

His eyes cleared and looked into Leith's own. "Killing the defenseless is the territory of our enemies," he said.

"There's been more than enough of that," Hal said in agreement.

"But a habit seemingly adopted by many Falthans," the Haufuth observed in disgust. "Especially those living in Instruere."

"So the Arkhos was allowed to live," the Hermit said, a tinge of regret in his voice. "Our enemies will see such mercy as weakness to be exploited."

"Exercising such mercy strengthens the merciful," Hal interposed quickly.

Leith looked at him sharply. *I have the moral high ground, big brother, and you cannot reclaim it*. But he was disturbed by the similarity between his brother's words and those that had echoed through his mind when they had the Arkhos of Nemohaim at their mercy.

The Hermit shook his head at this apparent renewal of hostilities. "Irrespective of the morality involved, I would suggest we might expect a visit from the Arkhos in short order, accompanied by a full complement of the Instruian Guard."

This sobered the Company, who until then had not considered the consequences of the escape. "He won't be coming to thank us for sparing his life," Stella said.

"But we are not defenseless!" declared Farr, raising his sword. "Let them come! We will fight them!"

"We cannot," Kurr responded wearily. "Not unless we want to fight off the whole of Instruere, who will be told we threaten their city. We have to leave Instruere as soon as possible."

Perdu waited until the implications of this had settled on the Company, then observed: "They'll be watching the bridges. We'll not escape from Instruere either north or south. And they'll pass our descriptions around the city. We're trapped."

Two or three murmurs of assent came from around the room.

"Listen to you!" Foilzie said, hands on hips. "What's done is done, and plenty of time we'll have to discuss this when we're safe and sound. Until then, we'd best keep away from such arguments."

Stella was outraged. "You at least need not flee! Surely you have done no wrong in harboring us?"

"I'll not take the chance. Besides, you'll be needing a guide to escape this place."

"Escape? You have an idea?" Kurr rounded on her, hope in his eyes.

Doubt flickered across her well-worn face. "No. No, not really," she said, but it was plain she was thinking hard.

"Then we must pack and leave. We may not have much time." Kurr was clearly becoming agitated.

"Leave for where?" Mahnum asked. "It may be some time yet before the Arkhos finds out where we live. We will be better served by spending that time trying to come up with a plan."

"If we head out into the city streets we will be seen by the guards," said Perdu. "How big is this city? Are we sure the Arkhos and his guards do not know where we live? And if they don't, how long will it take for them to find us?"

Indrett grimaced. "No one at the market knows where we live, but you can be sure they'll be asked. Someone will let it slip they know us. The guards will concentrate their search in the tenements near the market. That should give us some time, surely. There are hundreds of tenements to search."

"It took three days for us to find you," the Haufuth added.

"At the least we must wait until Phemanderac returns," Stella said.

Kurr grunted. "Then let us put our heads together," he said.

Leith looked at his father, older and more haggard than the gentle, loving man he remembered. "We escaped The Pinion only to be trapped in another prison. How many people will die if we try to escape this time?"

His father gave him no answer.

With Foilzie keeping an intermittent lookout from high in the tenement, the Company remained in the basement all that day, trying out this idea or that suggestion, interrupted only by the return of Phemanderac; but by evening they had come to the end of their plans and admitted defeat. They were trapped. It didn't matter what they did, their great quest was in ashes. As the rain came down in torrents, beating at the shuttered tenement windows and hammering at the cobbles on the narrow lane outside, the Company sat in silence for the longest time, eyes open yet unseeing, the world of their own efforts and their hard work and all the discussions they had held coming to an end with no promise of anything but swift defeat. Many of them longed for home. Within Leith it was not just an ache for the northern air and a glimpse of a bush-clad hill, but also the haunting memory of a contented family, mother and father sitting quietly on the porch of their home while their boys wrestled together on the cool grass.

A large fire roared in the grate, around which the Company huddled against the unseasonably cold weather. Foilzie came down to join them when the gloom prevented her from keeping watch. The stone-walled basement was much warmer than the draughty upper floors of the old tenement. As evening wore on the air warmed in the room, becoming thick and close; heads began to nod, chins dropped forward on to chests. The Haufuth lay on a couch, soundly asleep, his breath whistling through his broad nose. Outside, the weather showed no sign of relenting.

What conversation remained centered on two groups. Kurr, Hal and Phemanderac talked through yet another fruitless rehash of the few options remaining, then in quiet tones spoke openly for the first time of the dissolution of the Company, hoping perhaps by ones and twos to escape the vigilance of the guards; while Indrett, Stella and Foilzie discussed life in hiding in Instruere. Indrett wondered aloud whether they would return to Loulea. She found the city quite to her taste, she told them. Perhaps they could blend in with the city-dwellers. She knew many of her friends at the market would be willing to help them. But hers was the only optimistic thought expressed amongst the Company, most of whom seemed no longer to care that the Arkhos of Nemohaim might come for them at any time. Perhaps some of them even welcomed it.

Eventually the debate died away, the Haufuth's snoring the only remaining sound competing with the crackle of the fire and patter of rain.

A log shifted in the grate; another, larger log resting on top of it came crashing down out of the hearth, coming to rest on the stone floor, flames playing along its length. No one stirred.

One moment the basement room was in flickering shadow, the only light coming from the dying fire; the next it was ablaze with a searing light that seemed to spring from the grate.

Leith awoke, startled. Through tightly shut eyes he saw a column of purest white light stab down into the room, and knew it was a dream. The column was yellow at the very edges, but whitely opaque in its thickness. A great weight seemed to force him downwards, crushing him against the cold stone floor. The youth tried to cry out, but his voice made no sound. A crackling and a roaring filled the air, so that even had he been able to cry out, his voice would have remained unheard.

Fiery yellow filaments sprang from the column of flame, flashing across the room. Leith saw the flash, but could not avoid the flame holding his death as it arced towards him, then slammed into him with the power of a waterfall, of a glacier, a falling mountain, pinning him to the floor like the flies Druin used to pin to the windowsill.

Now the roar grew so loud he thought his head would burst with the fullness of it. There was something in the sound, something human, something musical; Leith was reminded of the caverns under Adunlok and the sound of Phemanderac's harp, magnified beyond comprehension.

This is not real. This is a dream. I'll run with it and see where it takes me.

The flaming filament continued to pour into Leith, and now he realized his own body was glowing, burning yellow at the edges, shining white at the center. It was as though a fire had been set inside him and was burning its way out. The noise and the brightness increased well beyond what seemed possible, yet he did not burn, he was not consumed. For a moment he caught an impossible glimpse of the basement, with filaments of fire spreading out from the one central column, each filament burning a member of the Company.

"I have something to show you," a placid, rich voice spoke, quietly but seemingly loud enough to drown out the raging noise of the fire. "Do you wish to see it?"

Yes, Leith answered, the word coming out like fire.

Immediately a huge shape materialized in front of him, a massive cube. Leith lifted his head from his prone position and found he could see two facets stretching away into the infinite distance. He craned his neck further, but could not see the top of the cube, as the edge of the facets rose into the clouds. There was no way of telling what it was or what purpose it served. The cube was in the room, yet somehow Leith knew it was many times bigger than the tenement, or indeed the city.

This is a very vivid dream, he thought.

The voice spoke again, the richness of it thrilling through him like a draught of cool water on a hot summer night. "This is the love people bear for you," the voice said. "I want you to take a good look at it. See how wide, how high and how deep it is."

Love? For me? Who are you?

As he watched the block tilted downwards, or perhaps Leith rose above it in the manner of dreams. The wide flat top surface receded into the unguessable distance.

"Look more closely," the voice instructed him.

He looked closely, as he had been bidden, and saw a small scraping had been taken from the surface of the vast block.

"Do you see this?" said the voice. "This scraping

represents how much of this love you will use up in your lifetime. Now look at how much remains."

Leith looked, and the enormity of this love began to overwhelm him, forcing him under like a wave, driving him down to the bottom of the sea, drowning him.

"Nothing you do, no matter how foolish, how selfish, how evil, will exhaust the love your family and your friends have for you."

Why would I dream such a thing?

"Whenever you feel alone, unloved or forsaken, I will remind you of what you have seen."

The vision closed and the voice fell silent.

The little girl Indrett wept under the clear fire, her body shaking with the memory of what her father had done to her night after night all those years ago. Gradually, seeping into her dream-consciousness, came the remembrance of her friends the Northern Lights; and suddenly she could see them dancing in the fire above and around her, and could hear them singing:

> *The Northern Lights set to music*
> *brush soft across the stage;*
> *Behind the Lights a little girl*
> *flees her father's rage.*
> *Her pleas for help in nightly pain*
> *unnoticed by the sleeping,*
> *Are heard by one who hears such cries*
> *and sets his heart to weeping.*
>
> *He lays his scepter by his side*
> *and steps down from his throne;*
> *Ignoring every courtier*

he swiftly leaves his home.
Her name he calls as he approaches,
His presence as perfume;
The King of Kings, the Lord Most High,
a sentry in her room.

Outside the Lights dance slow and solemn,
the music whispers low;
The girl lies trembling in the dark,
afraid lest he should go.
His love he pours out selflessly,
to calm her heartfelt fears,
And every night he makes the journey
down throughout the years.

Within her heart there is a box,
The lid is shut down tight;
On suspicion that within
lie terrors of the night.
The time has come to take the key,
Against her fears to fight,
So good may grow from evil sown;
From the midst of darkness, Light.

So it was you all the time, she thought. *You are the Northern Lights. Why did I not recoganize you?*

"Because you were not ready for a father," came the reply. "I came to you in the only way you could bear."

Please don't leave, she begged the fire. By now she shook uncontrollably, as though the fire around her had turned to ice.

"I did not intend to," said the voice.

And you'll never leave me alone again?

"Never." The word resonated through the fullness of her mind, giving her the key with which to open the secret box she called her disgrace. *He said, never.* Her shaking stopped as she looked into the box, and saw no shame there. No shame at all.

Mahnum found himself flat on the floor, weaponless and assailed by an unseen foe. *They have brought some kind of flame with them,* the Trader thought. *Just like the Favonian village.* But the inimical sense of evil he had felt then was absent this time, and for some reason he felt no fear. This combination of factors told him he experienced a dream.

"Take off your shirt," a deep, resonant voice directed him. "I can't help you unless you do."

Help me with what? Who are you?

"You've always found it difficult to trust anyone, haven't you." It was not a question.

Only way to survive as a Trader, Mahnum replied abruptly.

"But that's all it is: survival. Take off your shirt."

But—

"While you're at it, take off your shoes as well. I'd like to do something about those feet."

Let me up, then.

"Can I trust you?" the voice said, rumbling with laughter. The fire lessened, and Mahnum found he was able to stagger up to his knees. With shaking fingers he stripped off his shirt.

"These scars have been giving you pain, haven't they," the voice commented.

Nothing to the pain within. You wouldn't believe the nightmares I have.

"I would. Andratan. Favony. Torrelstrommen. Breid-han Moor. Withwestwa Wood. I saw it all; it hurt me too. Now bend forward."

Mahnum laid his whip-scarred back open to whatever the voice chose to do. For a while nothing happened; then the Trader noted small lines of flame running across the floor. They traveled up his arms and legs, meeting on his back. The flames felt like the most soothing of ointments, the ministrations of countless supple fingers.

"Your feet."

Why are you doing this?

"A symbolic gesture. These are the outward scars. Will you let me?"

Yes, his heart shouted, before his mind could organize any defense.

"As I heal your feet, I heal your future. You shall be Faltha's servant. Your back shall bear her burdens. Your feet shall walk her paths. Will you give her your future?"

I will. Eagerly he slipped his shoes off, and held his feet to the flame.

The Hermit knelt before the flame, head bowed, hands outstretched. Dream or not, he was convinced of its reality. He knew such visions could be both dream and real.

"Oh my child, my child," the gentle, familiar voice lamented. "So long you've known me, yet you still don't know who I am."

Use me, use me, the man begged. *I want to be your servant.*

"And I had planned to use you," the voice responded, "yet you are not content with the role I have chosen for you. So be it. I will continue to call you; you will continue to hear my voice. One day, my child, you will discover that I am more than that which you have constructed."

Just let me be the least of all your servants, the Hermit petitioned.

"I hear your words," the voice said, not unkindly, "but I also see what is written on your heart. Even so, I embrace you. I will continue to fall on you with anointing, in the hope that one day I will be permitted to fill you."

I dedicate my life to you, the snowy-haired man vowed. *I will do whatever you ask.*

"So be it," came the response. "Let he who has no understanding be as one who is led by bit and bridle."

The Hermit did not understand the words of his master, but abased himself before him with a familiar, pleasant humility.

Bent over double by the force of the bright white fire, Stella found she could barely breathe. *What's happening?* she screamed. *Go away! Leave me alone!* This seemed different to her other nightmares, being pursued by shadowy strangers, grasped at by clumsy unseen hands, different and yet the same. Here her assailant was implied rather than visible, but an assailant nonetheless. She could not see him, but she knew he was there. *Go away!*

"But you've been calling me for years," a rich, sonorous voice spoke as though into the back of her mind. "Are you sure you want me to leave you?" An invisible hand took hold of her arm.

Wait a moment! Who are you? Let me go! Let me see you! Stella struggled against the overbearing weight of the light.

"It would be better if you saw yourself," the voice answered, and instantly the room disappeared.

She sat outside, a little way up a grassy hill, looking down on a scene she knew well. There in front of her lay the lake. Behind the small body of water stood the village of Loulea. As she sat there Stella began to cry, her heart aching at the sheer familiarity of it all, and the longing for home she had stifled within herself rose up and broke down her carefully constructed walls.

Through her tears she saw a group of children—no, not children, young men and women—swimming, socializing and relaxing at the shore of the lake. There stood sweet little Lonie, at least three inches taller than she remembered, her best friend Hermesa—with a new hairstyle—and Insusa, another girl from the village. With them were Hayne and Druin. She could never forget that face. They were talking: she listened closely.

"The water's still a little cold," Lonie said.

"Yaaah, you weakling," Druin teased her. "Go back and play with the babies. Us grown-ups can swim in the water."

"I've noticed you in the water much more recently," Hermesa said to Druin, tilting her head towards him as she spoke.

The broad-shouldered boy blushed slightly. "The lake's a good place in the summer."

"Or perhaps it is because now Stella has gone, no one can beat you across the lake?" Hermesa said sweetly.

Thank you, my friend! Stella wanted to shout.

"I miss her," Insusa said quietly. "And Leith. There's no one interesting around here now."

Druin will take that as a personal affront, Stella thought. Sure enough, he walked menacingly towards her.

"No one?" he said.

"Present company excepted," Insusa said politely. "We

all find you *very* interesting," she added, and the other girls laughed. The irony passed right over Druin, and he smiled at the unintended compliment.

"She used to sit on that rock," Hayne commented.

"And dive in," added Lonie. "With a big splash."

"Not as big as my splashes," Druin insisted, but no one was listening.

"I wonder what really happened to her," Hermesa said. "If she really wandered off and got lost in a blizzard, surely we would have found her body. And I don't remember a blizzard that night; do you?"

The others shook their heads.

"She could be a proper cow at times," Insusa added. "Acted as though she was the queen of Loulea, and we were all her servants." She turned to Druin. "I don't know how you put up with her for so long."

Stella wanted to rush down the hill and do something nasty to the girl, but found she could not move.

"Her mother was really broken-hearted about it. We hardly hear anything from her these days."

"Two birds with one stone!" Druin laughed.

"That's the problem if you're both clever and good-looking; you think you own the world. Too good for us, that's what she was." Insusa warmed to her subject. Stella waited for the others to contradict her, but they all nodded their heads in agreement. "Probably she ran away to find somewhere better, somewhere her talents would be appreciated."

That's not fair, Stella screamed inside. *Couldn't you see I was hurting?*

"The problem with Stella was that you couldn't tell what she was thinking," Hayne added. "I have trouble telling what any female is thinking—if they think at all."

Lonie cuffed him on the back of the head, and he rubbed it as though it had hurt. "Stella was totally closed. Is that what you thought?" He turned to Druin.

"I dunno," the big boy said. "Sometimes I thought she was scared of me. But she was so high and mighty, I don't think anyone could scare her."

I was scared of you, I was scared of you! Why couldn't you see you were tormenting me?

"I miss her too," Druin added. "But I don't miss her tongue."

Nor I your fists! Stella fumed.

"It was a good funeral," Hayne said. "Everybody cried."

"But she had no real friends," Hermesa commented.

What about you?

"I never knew what she really felt about things. She wouldn't let anyone get close to her. I'm glad I've got you now, Lonie," concluded Hermesa.

"Coming for a swim?" Hayne asked. He took off his shirt and stepped into the shallows. "Ooh, it's cold," he mocked Lonie. "I'm turning to ice." The others laughed.

Babies, all babies, Stella thought as she watched them frolic in the water; but her feet tingled at the thought of the cool water of the lake, and she longed to run down the hill and join them.

A cloud passed overhead, borne on a cool breeze. "Sometimes I think she's still here," Druin said, glancing around. "I feel like she's come back to haunt us." They all turned and looked up the hill, and for a moment Stella thought she would be discovered. But for some reason they appeared not to see her.

Was I really so selfish, so wrapped up in myself? she asked.

The voice did not reply.

But what about Druin? Stella pleaded. *He was mean to me; he never loved me.*

"You shut him out, so he reacted by being cruel. He thought that if he could hurt you, he could open you up. The more you closed up, the more he tried to hurt you. Of course he was to blame, but it is a hard truth to accept that the blame did not rest on him alone."

Who are you? How do you know these things?

The voice ignored the questions. "This is your home, and these are your people. Did you think that running away would change you, or change them? There is not a place far enough away that you can escape from yourself."

What is wrong with me?

"Nothing that a little fire won't fix. Will you open yourself to the Flame?"

Stella nodded her head miserably, and immediately found herself back on the floor of the basement, the fire pouring over her still, licking all around her as though seeking an entry point. She stretched out a hand and touched a yellow-orange flame; it detached from the filament of fire and burned painlessly on her hand. As she watched, blue-edged flames ran up her arms. Slowly, slowly.

While Perdu knew this was a dream, he valued it more for that; the Fenni taught that the dream world was in many ways more real than that experienced while awake.

I'm not interested in the god of the underworlders, he warned. *Not after all my time with the Fenni. Compared to them, your people are barely alive.*

"I'm not much interested in that god either," said the fire. "He seems petty and self-serving to me."

Small gods for small people. No offense, but I want my gods to be big, like the vast spaces of Myrvidda.

In answer the flames roared menacingly around the adopted Fenni, arching over him in a yellow-white sheet. Intimidated though he was, Perdu would see this through. *You're a far cry from the watered-down god we learned to reject in Mjolkbridge. You'd fit right in on the vidda, especially with all that fire. Why haven't I met you before?*

"Because one of us is too small," the flames roared.

Oh, really? I couldn't see you because you're too big?

The fire surrounding Perdu rose even higher, and the Fenni marveled that he was not consumed. "Ah, wisdom comes belatedly to the Fenni. Or is it the Falthan? When a man denies his heritage so vehemently, I begin to wonder from what he is trying to hide."

You're hardly likely to make a follower out of me by employing that sort of insult, Perdu snapped. *What a strange dream!*

"Not a follower?" the flames questioned, genuinely puzzled. "Yet here you are in Instruere."

Not by choice! Perdu commented wryly.

"They seemed like choices to me," the voice laughed in reply. "Keep making those choices, and we'll see where we end up."

The burning, the burning, the burning. Kurr took the dream-flames and wielded them like knives against his pain, hammering himself with the rightness of the fire, beating his weary, blackened heart. *Burn it all out, sear out the pain. I deserve to be punished.* Reality was much less painful than this searing dream, and therefore he mistrusted reality.

"You shouldn't be doing this," the voice said to him. "I didn't come to punish you. Don't use my flames to hurt yourself."

I want to be hurt. You know what I did to Tinei. You know I neglected her while I searched for answers. How can you say I don't need punishment? My soul will feel better when it bleeds.

"So you're the expert?" the voice said with the hint of a chuckle. "I've been looking for a few days off. Care to take over for a while?"

Don't taunt me. I've led these people into a trap: even now the Council may be planning our deaths. Deaths! For what purpose was Wira slain? Did Parlevaag die in vain? I have chosen wrong at every turn. Others suffer as a result of my failures.

"Get down off your throne!" the voice growled. "You are but a human leading humans. By what standards do you evaluate your efforts? Those of a god? Put down the fire and kneel. I have come to break you."

Break me? That I understand. Make it hurt.

"You do not understand. I brought with me a message for you."

Without warning another voice spoke; the gentle, lilting voice of the one he had loved all his adult life. "I forgive you," Tinei whispered. "I forgive you."

No, no, no! You can't forgive me! I've done wrong!

"I know, my love, my rock-man." She used her old name for him with all the tenderness he remembered. "That's why I'm forgiving you."

"There was absolutely no excuse for many of the things you did," the first voice insisted. As he spoke, images Kurr had thought were forgotten flashed through his mind, and his shame rose like a flash flood to drown him. "No excuse. So she forgives you. Put down your knife. If she chooses not to hurt you, why should you hurt yourself?"

Higher the wave of shame rose, then broke against him and receded, leaving him still standing. "You're tough, rock-man," her voice chuckled. "But not as tough as you fear."

The words were like battering rams, driving down on top of him, forcing him to his knees. The wave rose again, this time washing over him and knocking him to the floor. And all the time the flames beat at him.

An image rose in his mind; an image of Tinei coughing as she helped round up the sheep. Kurr realized that she should not be out there, but he had insisted on bringing sheep to the Midwinter feast . . .

She turned and looked towards him, compassion on her clear-eyed face. "I forgive you," she mouthed, her words whipped away by the cold wind. "I forgive you."

Suddenly, beyond a shadow of a doubt, Kurr knew that this was no fantasy. He saw what had actually happened. She had really said those words, out there that morning in the bitter cold; she had really meant them. He was undone.

As he lay there and wept out the pain and the long hard years of tight self-control, the flames flowed over him and through him, burning away the blackness, leavening the sorrow with sweetness.

You liar, the old farmer smiled through his tears. *You said you weren't going to hurt me.*

Fuir af Himinn! Phemanderac cried. Harp in hand, his music soared to the heavens, helping kindle the flames as they spread throughout the room. *Fire of Heaven!* He knew this was merely a dream; he even knew what had prompted it. Hadn't he and the Archivist recently argued about the truth of the Firefall? But oh, if only . . .

Pass me the salt, please, the Haufuth asked politely. He didn't understand where the table had come from, nor why fire spewed from the vases where flowers might have been expected to sit, but he was not going to object when the most perfect roast pig he had ever seen sat steaming on the table—so pure, so tender that it almost seemed to glow—and he occupied one of the two places set. This wasn't the first time he had dreamed about food, far from it; it was, however, by far the most vivid he had experienced recently.

"Certainly," replied the voice. Curiously, the Haufuth could not see his host, but the salt appeared before him nonetheless. He busied himself with the pig, and for a while his host remained politely quiet.

This is marvelous, the Haufuth commented eventually. *We do not get such good meat in Firanes*.

"No, you don't," the voice agreed with him. "I'm pleased to see that you are doing it justice."

The Haufuth nodded, wiping the juices from his chin.

"A word with you about the Company," the voice said. "You were the one I chose to lead it. Yet I've had to delay things here while I waited for you to arrive. What happened?"

What happened? I ran out of courage, that's what happened. I wasn't necessary, I was so tired, and I couldn't see why I should risk my life when I was practically irrelevant. He took another bite of pork.

"So you want courage? Why haven't you asked before?"

I didn't know I was allowed to. We were told you abandoned us after that fuss about the Vale.

"Yet here I am, abandoning you to this pig," retorted the voice. "Well, I'm here, and this pork is proof I can supply the desires of your heart."

What about the courage? I really could do with some of that.

"Look more closely at what you are eating," the voice said quietly.

Funny, the Haufuth thought, *I never noticed that before*. There was a flame set within the meat. *That's what is causing it to glow: I'm eating fire*. The dream-food stiffened his bones, as though a steel rod had been set in his backbone.

He laughed. *I hope I don't suffer indigestion.*

"Why are you so angry?" the voice asked. "What fills you with such rage?"

An exultation ran through Farr's veins. The basement, the whole tenement no doubt, had burned down, that much was clear. He had not had time to protect himself, let alone anyone else. So death was painless, after all. Soon he would be reunited with Wira, with his father and his mother. But in the meantime he had the chance to ask the questions that drove him.

You ask me why I am angry? You who watched Storr die? You who stood by while my mother wasted away in hopeless agony? You who sacrificed my brother for the good of the Company, then allowed our mission to fail? You ask me what fills me with rage? Come near and I will teach you justice!

Farr found his quarterstaff in his right hand. He hefted it, feeling its reassuring weight. The fire around him condensed into a human figure, which advanced slowly on him. *Yes!* Farr's heart sang. *This is my crown! Whether I win or lose, I will have fought the battle I have longed to fight!*

"Not so," said the figure of flame. "I am not the one you long to fight. Nevertheless, come and teach me justice."

Farr flipped his staff from hand to hand, as though it were a small twig. Never before had he felt such power as that which raced through his veins; never before had he been able to marshal all his powers of concentration to such a degree. He was ready.

With no warning he flicked the staff out at his opponent's head. The figure did not flinch. The quarterstaff met the fire with a loud report, then turned to ashes in his hand.

Oh, I forgot, Farr said mockingly. *You don't fight fair. Given the way you run things, I shouldn't have expected anything different.*

Weaponless, he sprang at the figure. Again the fiery shape did not flinch. Farr expected to be consumed like his staff as he grasped the white-hot arms; instead, he found them substantial, and he was able to hold them without pain.

So you're real after all, and not just a convenient fantasy of my imagination. Not that I could have imagined anything so evil, Farr taunted as he wrestled with the flame.

Crack! A hand seemingly came from nowhere and rattled against his head, leaving his ear stinging.

Not much of a reply, Farr crowed. *Now, give ear to my complaint.* He aimed a fist at the flickering yellow head, and the blow just missed its target. *You're supposed to be good; that's laughable. But I'll give you the benefit of the doubt for a moment. Wholly good, they say.* He ducked under a swinging arm. *Not only that, you are all-powerful.*

Then how do you explain the presence of evil in the world—other than my assertion that you cause it? He threw out a left which caught the figure in the midriff. *If you're good, why don't you stop it? Unless, of course, you can't.* Farr laughed as he landed another blow, sending the figure reeling.

"A well-aimed blow," the fiery figure replied, breathing heavily, "but not a fatal one." Farr followed up his strike, only to be met with a stiff forearm. "Let's assume that I am wholly good; let's also assume that such a concept might just be beyond your understanding, and that such goodness might appear cruel to one who is merely sentimental." Farr dived at the figure's legs, trying to catch it off guard; he came up with nothing but air. *Good is good*, he growled. *I know good when I see it.*

"Maybe so, maybe so. If I am good, evil must be something other than myself. Things other than myself exist: therefore it is at least possible that they are the source of the evil."

Farr glanced at the face of his adversary in surprise, a serious mistake. He never saw the blow that caught him under the chin, sending him spinning.

"I am the author of all life: but in order to have life, these things I have authored must have certain freedom in their choices, constrained only by circumstance. Evil is spawned in the matrix of choices made that I would not make."

What's this about freedom of choice? Did my mother have freedom to be well and healthy as she lay dying through the spring and summer? Why did creation not weep? Why did the clouds not fall down dead to the ground? He scrambled to his feet and grabbed the figure around the neck.

"The difference between you and a cloud is that you can choose not to be blown by my breeze. But your power is not infinite; you cannot create your own breeze." The flaming figure wriggled out of Farr's grip.

My mother did not choose death, yet it happened. If we are all destined to die, we have no real choices. Strike and counter-strike. Both men rested for a moment, blowing hard.

"Listen. By creating things other than myself, I have limited my power to that which will allow them freedom to choose. It's either that or become the thing you fear—a thing helpless before the wind. But what would you? I have chosen to give you the gift of death, and you have chosen not to understand it. Your mother understood it and welcomed it, even in the most desperate hours."

Welcomed it? Liar! She cried out for mercy and you did nothing! He caught his opponent a glancing blow on the shoulder.

"I did nothing but sit with her the whole time, sharing her pain. Do you think I abandoned you all, just because you chose to keep out of my breeze?" The figure drew its arm back, as though preparing to throw all its weight behind a punch. "Choose now to be honest with yourself. The reason the deaths of your parents and your brother have made you angry is because they have left you behind. You are angry at being abandoned. Well, I have not abandoned you. I will never leave your side, even if you ask me to. Does that make you angry?"

Farr saw the blow coming, but could do nothing to avoid it. At the very last moment he twisted his body enough that the force of it connected with his right elbow, and the joint dislocated with a sickening crunch. He fell to the floor, writhing with the pain.

"You are a mighty warrior," the voice said. "You have served me well, but as a leaf before the wind. Would you not rather be my servant by choice?"

What have you got in mind?

"Wait and see. But it is not all over yet, not by a long way."

Farr nodded, the nearest he could come to surrender.

"Good enough. Now, take your anger and place it in the fire."

Won't I be less of a warrior without it?

"Not at all. Anger will rob you of your greatest victories," the voice advised. "Into the fire with it." The flames drew close around the warrior.

Very well. He took his anger and threw it into the fire; then laughed great gouts of flame as he realized that he had thrown himself in bodily.

Leith's dream changed: for a few moments it was as though he hung suspended above the room, seeing somehow through the stone walls. The conflagration reached a tumultuous climax, interconnected columns of flame burning with a brightness beyond belief. Then, as abruptly as it had begun, the fire diminished, leaving for a moment one central column burning with an unmatched clarity, before winking out with a final pulsing crackle.

He awoke with a shudder. There, on the stone floor some distance from the hearth, lay the charred remains of a log that had fallen from the fire, a lone flame lingering upon it. As he watched, the little tongue of fire shrank; then, like the last breath of a dying man, it grew for a moment before disappearing, accompanied by a curling wisp of smoke.

CHAPTER 5

THE RIDDLE OF
THE ARROW

A SOLITARY TEAR OF REGRET slid from Foilzie's eye as she slipped the big, heavy key her husband had given her into the lock and turned it. *I never thought it would come to this*, she mused, running her hand across the splintered, heavy wooden door of the tenement. *Well, this house was a gift. It is time to let it go.*

She slipped the key into her pocket, then crossed the narrow street and joined the northerners waiting for her in the morning gloom. This might be the most dangerous part of this dangerous day: as the sun rose and people emerged from their houses, anyone seeking a desperate gang of murderers would find many willing helpers. A "desperate gang of murderers"! So had said the informant, an acquaintance of one of the Instruian Guard, that that was how the northerners were being described by the guards sent to apprehend them.

Well, they know where to find us, thanks to the fishmonger—or, leastwise, they did. Let's see them find us now.

She had prepared a bolthole for the northerners yesterday, but had been unsure whether they might use it. The

talk in the basement had been all discouragement and defeat, and Foilzie had been unable to make them appreciate the danger they were in. No, that was not right, they
did appreciate it; they just didn't seem to care. The decision of the Council and the scene of death at The Pinion
appeared to have emptied them of the strength to continue. *They have been at this for months*, she reminded
herself. *There's only so much a body can take without
refreshment.*

And then last night. Something had happened after
she'd left them in the basement, she was sure, having
shared breakfast with them this morning and listened to
their talk. The results were clear to see: listless and ap-
athetic yesterday, uncaring about their fate; energetic
and full of plans today, receptive to her offer of help.
Some decision, perhaps, or maybe one of them had offered some thought or speech of hope. *They'll need it
where I'm taking them*, she reflected. *Still, they—and
I—have no choice.*

Lennan shifted his weight carefully, perched uncomfortably on a pile of bricks. From his vantage point on a tenement roof he could see both sides of the street. He
watched Foilzie lock the door of her tenement, then
scurry across the morning-lit cobbles to the Company.

She's not like Ma Clothier, he thought bitterly. *Not
gentle like Ma. And this woman is still alive. I saw Ma
fall. I saw them hack at her while she begged them for
mercy. Those two didn't see it. They were too busy saving
themselves.* His thin lips set in a white line.

The news had flashed around Instruere the previous
day. Prisoners had risen up and taken The Pinion, slaying
many of the hated guards, initial rumors said, and many

citizens rejoiced to hear it. Later, more authoritative word spread, saying The Pinion had been stormed by enemies of the city, who killed both guard and prisoner mercilessly and without discrimination. Some said that this latter rumor had been spread by the city officials, but their voices were smothered by the insistence of others who claimed to have been there. Such a rumor, calculated to stir the patriotic passion of the city-dweller, took hold quickly among the dawn traders in the crowded tenements. Escaigne, they said. The rebels were making their final move.

Lennan heard both rumors. He knew the truth.

He eased himself forward a few more inches, as far as he dared. The bricks shifted underneath him. Away to his right, at the edge of sight, the northerners flitted down the narrowest of alleyways. A delicious thrill ran through his body as another, larger group came into view from the left, the direction of the Inna Gate, at least twenty of the Instruian Guard, fully armored, led by a vast figure in a flame-red robe. Then, marching along a shadowed street, came another division. To the right, a third. There, a fourth. At least eighty armed warriors arrayed to vanquish the Company, arriving a few minutes too late. Lennan eased himself away from the edge, went to the other side of the roof, and tracked the group's progress across the western quarter of the city. Whatever bolthole they found, Lennan would see it, and ensure it became their grave.

Hands signaling frantically in all directions, the long-suffering chief servant of the Arkhos of Nemohaim walked worriedly behind his master. He had never seen the man in so foul a temper. Nothing he said could ease his mood. He'd heard rumors, whispered silently among

the Arkhos's household, that the Arkhos had returned
robeless, his gross body shamefully exposed, humiliated beyond his ability to bear it. His precious personal
guard, gifted to him by his Bhrudwan allies, were gone;
the servant confirmed that report in the most unpleasant
of ways, having been part of the detail that had disposed
of the dog-harried corpses. He knew his master. The
Arkhos would not rest until he exacted extravagant revenge, abandoning all other responsibilities in the
process. Should anyone thwart him, they would die. If
any unfortunate got in his way, they would not have the
time to wish they had not. Any mistake, by friend or foe,
would be punished. His own life was in danger, dependent entirely on his performance, owing nothing to
sentiment.

He begged, implored, ordered and cajoled the Instruian Guard in order to gain support for his master. Initially
the guards were not keen for a further taste of battle, but
wheedling words in the right ears eventually secured
eighty soldiers for the task. They had spent the previous
day searching the city, and his worry had finally eased
when that stinking fish-seller gave him the information
he sought. Plans were laid, and the attack timed for dawn.
The Arkhos would have his revenge. Success was vital,
failure unconscionable.

His signals now brought the axemen to the front. An
imperious gesture from the Arkhos of Nemohaim sent
their axes ringing against the old oak door of the tenement. The sturdy wood withstood the four-axe onslaught
for a full minute before it splintered, then crashed inwards. In an instant two dozen soldiers poured through
the dark opening, trying to dismiss thoughts of steel bars
and double-handed swordsmen. They had heard the

rumors, embellished in the telling. But the huge red man was real, and had the power and will to order their deaths should they show the slightest sign of reluctance. It was folly to cross any member of the Council, death to cross this one.

It took less than a minute to secure the building, and within three minutes it was obvious the tenement was empty, not only of people, but of possessions.

"Burn it down," the Arkhos ordered in his wheezy hiss.

"But, my lord, the buildings on either side will also be consumed," his servant said before he could help himself. His moral inhibitions foolishly overrode his instinct for self-preservation. "Should we not at least warn the occupants?"

The Arkhos of Nemohaim was in no mood to brook any questioning of his will. He made no effort to control his black emotion. In the silence of the moment, as the chief servant realized that he was dead, he noticed a muscle twitching in his master's neck, as though something was alive under the skin.

"Burn it down," the Arkhos repeated, reaching out a meaty hand and grabbing his servant around the throat. He turned to one of the guards. "Start the fire with this."

As the fire roared from floor to floor and the piteous cries ceased, the Arkhos of Nemohaim surveyed his handiwork. The gnawing blackness inside him was in no way assuaged by the scene. *Let it all burn. It is their fault for living here, so close to them, and not reporting them to the guard. Let them die.*

"Block the entrances to the tenements on either side," he commanded. "They might be hiding in one of the buildings."

Distasteful as this was, no one dared disobey the monster in red. Sword-bearing guards beat back the desperate occupants as the fire took hold in the building to the right. To the left, the neighboring tenement stubbornly refused to burn. A man and a child emerged on the roof of the rightmost tenement: below them the building shifted, settling perceptibly lower. As the flames licked around the roof the man took his child and threw it bodily over fifteen feet of yawning space to the roof of the next building. The child cried out and lay still where it landed. The man set himself, then jumped. He fell at least three feet short, and plummeted to the ground with a shriek.

Not enough, the black madness cried. *Give me more.*

In the midst of all this came Lennan, who had watched the Company take refuge in a small outbuilding near the city wall. It had taken longer than anticipated to climb down from his vantage point. He was appalled at the sight of the burning buildings, and for a moment considered abandoning his revenge. *Coward*, the fire roared at him. *Take your destiny into your own hands.* His blood roaring in his throat, Lennan stepped out into the street.

Rough hands were laid on him the moment he ventured into the open, and one of the guards dragged him before the Arkhos.

"This is one who was in The Pinion," he said. "He is an associate of the ones you seek."

"I wasn't there!" Lennan cried. The guard cuffed him silent with a steel glove.

The Arkhos drew his sword. *Do it*, the blackness pleaded with him. *You know you want to.*

The guards drew back, leaving the wretched boy defenseless in the middle of the street. "I can tell you where they are!" he cried, trying to get this creature before him to hear reason. But it seemed the man was not listening.

The Arkhos advanced on the boy, who stumbled in his haste to escape. On came the Arkhos, slashing indiscriminately. Nemohaim had been a superb swordsman in his younger days, but displayed none of that talent today. The Captain of the Guard turned away, professional distaste mixed with horror at what was happening in plain view on the street. But he could not shut his ears to the grunts and screams, and the sound of steel on bone.

When he turned back, the Arkhos was fumbling with his sword, trying to slip it back into its scabbard, not having bothered to clean it first. The captain would assign to his junior the task of cleaning away the shapeless mess that besmirched the cobbles.

I feel better, the black madness whispered. "I feel better," the Arkhos of Nemohaim said. *For the moment.*

"Pheeeyeew," Stella remarked after careful consideration. "This place smells like a dead sheep."

Indrett smiled pleasantly at her. "That's because it is a dead sheep, dear," she said, pulling a greasy pelt, overlain with dust, out from under the young woman.

"Ugh," Stella added, after a little further consideration. "Where are we?"

"Looks like some sort of storage shed," Kurr said.

Foilzie nodded. "That it is. My Ferdie—may his soul be at peace—used this place to keep goods he bought until the price went up at market. Now sit tight, my loves, and don't you put so much as a toe into the open air until I return. Promise?"

The Company nodded as one. Anything, even the fetid

air in this cramped shed, was better than being on the streets today. Foilzie grunted and pulled the reluctant door shut behind her, leaving them alone.

Phemanderac waited for a full thirty seconds, then could contain himself no longer. "Is this a good time to discuss the future of Faltha and our role in it?"

"You have a fine sense of the dramatic," Kurr said. "I doubt you could have found anything that important in the records of a town such as this."

"But I have," the philosopher replied emphatically.

"Important to a scholar, perhaps."

"Why not judge the matter yourself? I want to present my findings to the Company. All of you should decide upon the merit or otherwise of what I have discovered. Understand, though, that however my words are received I shall assist you in your endeavors to escape this city; and if you see any hope in your quest, I will continue to give you whatever assistance I can. My pledge thus made, you can make a judgment without fear of my taking offense."

"Very well, then," Kurr said. "It appears we will be here for some time. Tell us what you have found out."

"First, let's summarize our knowledge," the philosopher suggested. "The Bhrudwans threaten to invade Faltha, and are conducting their preparations with the utmost secrecy. They have succeeded in infiltrating many of the Falthan kingdoms, and appear to have a majority of the Council of Faltha in their pay. The Arkhos of Nemohaim seems to be their leader.

"Mahnum the Trader was sent to Bhrudwo by the Firanese king to investigate a rumor of war heard at the court. Most likely this originated from Bhrudwan emissaries sent to enlist the king to their cause. In Bhrudwo

Mahnum was able to confirm the existence of a large army, and on Andratan learned the names of those who were set to betray Faltha, and something of the Bhrudwan timetable. He also learned the Voice of Andratan—who may be the Destroyer himself—is searching for information."

"He wanted to know all about the Right Hand," Mahnum confirmed. "I had no idea what he meant. I still don't.

"But while I think about it," he continued, "I have for some time intended to ask Achtal what the Bhrudwan warriors knew about the Right Hand. Their leader was relentless in his pursuit of knowledge about this Hand, and would not accept we knew nothing. I am convinced it was for this knowledge Indrett and I were taken captive and not merely disposed of."

All eyes turned to the Bhrudwan, who crouched unconcerned in a shadowy corner of the shed, still wearing the Arkhos of Nemohaim's red robe.

Hal spoke. "According to what Achtal has told me, his leader was playing a dangerous game. Their instructions came from Andratan, and referred merely to the elimination of the Trader and anyone else who might know of the Bhrudwan plans. However, there were those in Bhrudwo who might reward handsomely the one who brought them information about something Andratan itself had not discovered; that is, the Right Hand. So the leader of the raiding party kept the captives alive, hoping to gain that information or at least to hand the captives over to the highest bidder. There was one man, apparently, an ambitious and scheming individual, who was prepared to pay a great deal of money for such information."

"Why did Achtal not rebel at this, if his instructions from Andratan said otherwise?" Stella wanted to know.

"Bhrudwan warriors of this order are taught unquestioning obedience to their leader, so it never occurred to Achtal to disobey him. But during their travels he lost respect for his leader, and it is his opinion that this divided purpose robbed them of strength and led to their defeat."

"So what is this Right Hand, then?" Mahnum asked.

"Achtal knows no more than you do," Hal said. "He assumed it was some great weapon or fearsome warrior with the potential to deal the Bhrudwan cause a mighty blow. For a while he considered it might be you yourself," he said to his father.

Mahnum laughed. "If I am the Right Hand, and the Right Hand is a chief part of the Falthan defense, then Faltha is in serious danger."

Phemanderac resumed. "As I understand it there are others among us, such as the Hermit, who have become aware of the existence and significance, if not the identity, of the Right Hand."

"That is so," said the man in the pale blue robe, smiling widely. Instruere had been good to the Hermit, and he had taken the opportunity to mix with the countrymen of his birth, and relearn the social niceties he had forgotten in his years of self-imposed isolation. He had deliberately kept a low profile, spending much time away from the Company, observing them and allowing circumstances to take shape.

"In my solitude I heard the word of the Most High," he said positively. "Not in an audible voice, but fully formed as an impression in my mind, came the word that I should expect visitors. I was given two specific words for one of them, whom I should recognize when he came. I was also given a specific phrase, one which I had not heard before: 'the Right Hand of the Most High.'"

"Let's make this clear: no one had told you of this Right Hand?" Phemanderac wanted there to be no doubt as they tried to make sense of what was happening to them.

"I can verify that," the Haufuth interposed. "While he was convalescing the Hermit raised the subject with me a number of times—a large number of times. Actually," he added, "I think the Hermit believes he knows the identity of this Right Hand."

"I do," said the Hermit, "though this is through my own observation and suspicion, not through a direct word." He shot a glance at Hal, who said nothing. "And in my opinion the Right Hand is a member of your Company, the one to whom I delivered my words at Bandits' Cave."

Head down, apparently absorbed with something on the floor, Leith felt his face coloring at the attention of the Company. He remembered the words of the Hermit: "a high and lofty destiny . . . will rule over kingdoms . . . have come for such a time as this." He also remembered the unease the words caused him. They represented the kind of fantasy he entertained as a child, to dominate and rule over those whom he could not control, to be important, famous, loved by everyone . . . *This is not my destiny. I hope it is not my destiny. It would destroy me. Dreaming in the daylight.*

Leith raised his head, his chin forward, and faced his friends and family. "Those of you who know me know how unlikely it is I would turn out to be a great weapon or a mighty warrior. Let us all dismiss the notion, as I have already."

Unperturbed, the Hermit said: "Such an answer is precisely what I would expect from the Right Hand."

Phemanderac spoke. "When I first met Leith I told him

of the prophetic saying of Hauthius, a great sage and prophet of former times from my homeland, who many hundreds of years ago wrote the *Arminia Skreud*. It tells us a number of things: that the Bhrudwans will have dominion in Faltha; that they will be driven back by something called the Jugom Ark, which is an artefact wielded by the Hand of God, who is at present concealed, but is about to be revealed; and this Hand originates, the saying concludes, from Loulea Vale in Firanes."

"What it tells us depends on whether we believe in the accuracy of such prophecy." The Haufuth frowned as he spoke. "It tells me nothing at all. Moreover, it raises the possibility of making foolish decisions in trying to fulfill prophecy. We have come this far by honest endeavor and determination, not by giving way to ancient writings. I say this is not only a waste of time, it is potentially dangerous."

"Perhaps this is something we can debate once the information has been presented," Phemanderac said somewhat testily.

"If I read the riddle correctly," Mahnum said, "the Right Hand is the warrior, and the Jugom Ark is the weapon he uses."

Stella squirmed on her sheepskin seat. "I would like to hear more about this Jugom Ark. The name seems familiar. What is it?"

"The name should be familiar, if you remember anything from the history you were schooled in," Kurr growled. "So should the rest of the Company recognize it, unless they were asleep when I recited the *Domaz Skreud* to them. The Jugom Ark was the arrow with which the Most High vanquished the Destroyer, and was given to the First Men as a symbol of their unity."

"And, symbolically, was almost immediately lost—as

was the unity," commented the Haufuth wryly. "That's what we're fighting against. Rescuing Mahnum and Indrett from the Bhrudwans was nothing compared to the task of pulling the different Falthan factions together, complicated by the depredations of the traitors to Faltha. A unified Faltha would be able to drive back any Bhrudwan attack, in my opinion. But," the big man concluded, "it will never happen."

Phemanderac nodded enthusiastically. "Aside from your last point, I think you're exactly right. Unity is everything, unity is the key. How to achieve it in such a divided land as Faltha?" One look at the philosopher's face was enough to tell the question was rhetorical; the man from Dhauria thought he knew the answer and was working the Company into a position where they could see it also.

"Perhaps this saying of Phemanderac's is symbolic, and we are making the mistake of interpreting it literally." Leith leaned forward as he spoke. "The Jugom Ark is symbolic of the unity Faltha needs, which will come from the Hand of God, originating in Firanes. Well, we've already spoken of unity, and we came from Firanes. Maybe we've already done all that is required of us, and things are going wrong because we remain where we are no longer needed."

Leith could see the others considering this for a moment, then Phemanderac shook his head. "Plausible, but not in the nature of riddles. They are intended to be interpreted literally, if their code can be broken. The objects they mention are specific objects, their places are specific places, their people specific people, and so on.

"Let me add some more information. Buried in the Archives of Instruere are five ancient books, counterparts to five found in my homeland, and originating from there." He reached into a pocket, and pulled out a crumpled piece of paper. "In one of those books I found a further riddle, which I've copied:

> *Shaft of steel shot through with strength,*
> *Burning will of Mighty Name,*
> *Rod to rule o'er all rebellion,*
> *Making nations whole again.*
>
> *Hidden from rebellious hands,*
> *Free from every fleshly claim,*
> *Through the air, over water,*
> *In the earth abides the flame.*

"The riddle is about the Jugom Ark, the shaft of steel; its function is emphasized, that of bringing unity; and it is now hidden in a specific location, the clue to which suggests we need to go through air, over water and into the earth to find it. I am convinced of its existence. Though I suspect it has no magical powers of its own, it has that most elusive of powers—the ability to command unity, to bring enemies together as allies, to rally nations under its banner. If we could find this Arrow, we would be able to convince the Council, the kingdoms and the people to unite behind our cause."

Phemanderac spoke quietly, urgently, and the shed was silent save for his pressing words.

"I spent many hours reading obscure journals and writings in the Archives, and learned more than I cared to know about the government of Instruere, the entrapment of merchants who used false weights and measures, and the mediation of boundary disputes. In amongst all this, though, I found a journal written by Bewray of the House of Saiwiz, one of the First Men and the founder of Nemohaim, the most mysterious of the Sixteen Kingdoms of Faltha. According to the *Domaz Skreud* Bewray was given charge of the Jugom Ark when Furist and Raupa both coveted and fought over the precious thing, and took it away southwards with him when the First Men divided into northern and southern factions. But exactly where? Did he take it to Nemohaim?

"The answer was buried in the pages penned by Bewray. He founded the capital now named after him but, according to his account, he never lived there. Instead he went inland, accompanied only by his family and bearing the Jugom Ark, following the valley of the Neume, determined to travel to Mulct and make his home there. However, he was ambushed by bandits, and his children were slain. He kept the Arrow from his captives, but was forced to flee further inland, and decided that it had to be placed beyond the reach of friend or foe. Eventually, he made his way to the Almucantaran Mountains."

"Kantara," murmured the Haufuth. "It couldn't be."

"What?" Phemanderac spun around and grabbed the big man's arm. "Where did you hear that name?"

"Kantara is no secret!" the Haufuth said, surprised by the philosopher's vehemence. "Everyone knows about the legend of Kantara. It's a favorite tale of our children." The others nodded in confirmation.

"What is this legend?"

Stella spoke. "Kantara is a fantasy place, a place of peace, a castle surrounded by a quiet village and open fields, a place in heaven where good children go who die an untimely death. Once in a hundred years Kantara comes to earth, coming down from the clouds, and then mothers and fathers can visit their children again. No one ages in Kantara, no one dies; but no one can find it, no matter how hard they look, except for a day and a night once every hundred years." She sighed. "As children we used to paint pictures of the castle of Kantara, wreathed in mist, nestled on the clouds, with children looking longingly from the battlements, searching the horizon for their fathers and their mothers."

"So Kantara is no secret? The hiding place of the Jugom Ark a story for children?" Phemanderac scratched his head. "Perhaps that has proved the best disguise of all. Turned into a legend, people believe it doesn't exist."

"Kantara is the hiding place?" Kurr inquired. "Are you sure this again is not symbolic?"

"Having listened to this children's tale, I am sure that Bewray created this myth as a most effective hiding place. Your explanation of the Kantara story makes it even more likely that substance lies behind the myth."

"Let us understand this correctly," the blond-haired Hermit said. "The journal of Bewray names Kantara as the resting place of the Jugom Ark, is that so?"

"Indeed," Phemanderac replied.

"But does it tell us how to find this elusive place?"

"It does. Kantara lies at the head of the Vale of Neume, a great white castle on the slopes of Hawkshead, nestling between the Sentinella. According to his journal, Kantara is a real place."

"The Sentinella?"

"Two great peaks, said to guard the Arrow," said Phemanderac. "Though how two mountains might guard anything I was not able to ascertain."

The Hermit shrugged his shoulders. "And where specifically in Kantara is the Arrow to be found?"

"I have no idea; the journal does not say. For this we will have to rely on the riddle."

"So you suggest that the next stage of our mission is to find the Jugom Ark?" Indrett asked quietly.

Phemanderac nodded. "I don't think your endeavor is yet complete. You must find it, and with it unite all Faltha against the coming invasion. Why else was I brought across the deserts from Dhauria if not to aid you in this fashion? The kings, the Council, the people will listen when the Jugom Ark returns. They'll have to, the people will make them listen. At the very least, you must find it so that no others can make use of it for less lofty purposes."

Outside the wind picked up, bringing rain with it to buffet the little shed.

"Are there others searching for the Arrow?" Kurr asked.

"Not that I am aware of," the philosopher answered, "though I expect your movements will be monitored, and you may find that others guess your purpose unless you cloak it with deepest secrecy."

"There's an implication in your words I hope I do not misinterpret," said Perdu. "You encourage us to use the Jugom Ark to bring unity to Faltha. If I understood the conversation properly, you suggested the riddles say this task is reserved for the Right Hand. We've heard the Hermit speak of his inner voice, and he thinks one of us here in this room is the Right Hand. Are you really certain the Right Hand is to be found within the Company?"

Outside, the breeze had dropped; the morning was sultry, thick, heavy, building up perhaps to a storm in the afternoon. There was no noise apart from the patter of intermittent rain.

"I am," Phemanderac stated finally. "At least, I believe

the Right Hand lies within the Company, but it is not a specific person. Let me explain."

The previous evening, Phemanderac told them, he had fallen asleep by the fire in the basement, his veins pulsing with a thought sown into his mind earlier in the day. "It has possibly been there for weeks, perhaps as far back as Adunlok, when I first heard Leith's story and his answers to my questions about the Right Hand. And it has taken me all this time to realize what was right under my nose from the start. How foolish one can be! How blind!"

The thought that had come to his mind that afternoon, the one which had continued to preoccupy him, had been this: *a hand has five fingers*. That was all. A hand has five fingers. Then he thought about the Company, and those who originally set out from the Lowly Vale on the Cape of Fire: Leith, Hal, Stella, Kurr and the Haufuth . . . a hand has five fingers . . . and suddenly the Right Hand of the Most High was staring him in the face.

The Right Hand was not one person. It was this core group of the Company, a group whose destinies were intertwined in some special way. A Hand made up of five fingers, each weak on its own, but together able to take a powerful grip on Faltha and set her to rights.

He tried to dismiss the thought, challenging it in a hundred ways. *What about Mahnum and Indrett? They were also from Loulea.* They were but the foil that drew the Right Hand out of hiding, the prize that taught the Hand to cooperate, to close around its quarry. *What had the Company achieved?* Nothing except that which had been done through the Right Hand. Surviving the Roofed Road had been through Stella of the Hand. The healing of the Hermit: the Haufuth of the Hand. The defeat of the Bhrudwan warriors: Kurr's plan. Stella brought down a

Lord of Fear with a stone. Leith delivered the final blow. How many people could claim to have slain one of the Lords of Fear? Kurr and the Haufuth led the Company. Had he, Phemanderac, really rescued Leith from the Widuz fortress, or had it been the other way around? The philosopher was no longer sure. One thing was certain: their common adventures were forging the Loulean peasants into a formidable weapon. There could be little doubt. They were the Right Hand of the Most High.

For Leith the morning was taking on a dreamlike quality. He was tired, desperately tired, and weary of spirit. After the night in The Pinion, and the flight from the tenement, what he really wanted to do was sleep. The air was so close in the wooden shed, stifling the members of the Company, and Leith noticed others—Mahnum, Kurr, Perdu, the Haufuth—struggling to keep their heavy-lidded eyes open. Leith could not believe this "Right Hand," this supposedly mighty warrior, would be found in their ragged band of villagers. The Bhrudwan, perhaps; but he was not the greatest of warriors even in his own land. How could Achtal hope on his own to vanquish the brown horde to come? Stab them all to death with the Arrow?

Now Phemanderac moved on to tell them of the Five Books he had discovered in the Archives of Instruere. He explained his theory that each book contained a personality, an aspect of the Right Hand. The Sun book, full of fair songs of hope, he matched with Stella. The bittersweet nature of the *Mariswan* book, containing the "Song of Losian," gave him some pause; but eventually he read the personality of Leith in its pages. The *Book of the Clasped Hands*, with its blunt statements and sweeping summations, instantly reminded him of Kurr, without doubt. His personal favorite, the Golden Arrow book, carried within it many of the observations on life he had heard in the last few days from the lips of the Haufuth. Its laws were tempered with the kind of love Phemanderac had seen the big headman show. And the *Book of the Wave*, containing a treatise on appropriate government, exemplified by the righteous judgment executed on the Vale, was one he wished he could show to Hal. Five books, five fingers, one Hand.

Could it be? Was the world of ancient prophecies relevant to this small group of people hiding in a smelly storage shed? At what point had they walked out of their sensible, predictable world? If they could defeat Bhrudwo's elite and recapture Mahnum and Indrett, then perhaps . . . if only they weren't all so tired . . .

Foilzie returned just before noon to find the shed silent. For a brief moment she feared the worst. Tugging the door open in haste, she found the Company sprawled over the sheepskins, the soft-woven rugs and the sacks of cotton, all fast asleep. The old woman beckoned to the tall bald man beside her; they entered the shed, and closed the door behind them.

A lowering iron-gray sky hung threateningly behind the Bhrudwan army as it was put through its paces. The nervousness was palpable. From the most recent callow conscript to the general, a grizzled old man with blackened skin and steel for muscles, every member of the largest army ever assembled felt fear at the presence of their master. Like a living organism it moved back and forth across the sandblasted valley, not faltering for a moment when the flash of lightning and rumble of thunder gave way to a stinging, slashing rain; shedding a few soldiers here and there like flakes of dead skin, but completing drill after drill with a dreadful precision that struck awe into the small knot of observers on a rocky knoll. And in their midst a tall, black-draped figure exulted, raising first one arm, then both to the sky, as though drawing down elemental forces to his aid. Though the general knew it must be coincidence, he was almost ready to believe his master directed the storm, and he knew his army would so believe. Thus the legend would grow, giving courage to the fainthearted, inciting fearful respect in the ranks. Such fear, such courage would be needed to harness so vast, so diverse an army. The last drill concluded, the last shout echoed, the rain ceased as though shut off by a valve. The black figure stepped forward, held his sword high in his only hand, and a harsh cry of triumph swirled in the sultry sky. The trials were over. The invasion was about to begin.

CHAPTER 6

ESCAIGNE

"THESE ARE THE ONES," Foilzie said softly.

"These?" the man said, puzzled. "How could ones such as these . . ."

"What were you expecting? Unshaven, armor-girded warriors, swearing and cursing, fighting their enemies even as they sleep? These dear ones are doing things impossible for those of great strength. The stronger and more famous they become, the less suited they will be for their mission."

"So it is our job to . . ."

"To keep them hidden, to keep them unknown. That's why they need your help."

"Foilzie, my love," the man said tenderly, squeezing her arm, "both you and Ferdie, when he was alive, gave us so much. Without aid from you, and a few others like you, we could not have survived. How could we refuse you in your time of need?"

The old woman smiled widely. "I know you believe you owe Ferdie and I a debt," she said, "but don't do this because you want to pay me back, do it because you're convinced it's the right thing to do."

"I'm not so sure about that," he said, running his hand

over his shiny bald pate. "Foilzie, you are so trusting, it's easy for you to forget how important our secrecy is to us. Any betrayal will cost many lives."

"These ones have taken so many risks on your behalf, on everyone's behalf, even though they don't know you exist. It's time someone took a risk for them."

The man nodded. Foilzie was a simple, direct woman. One could always hear truth in her words, which was why she was beloved of Escaigne, of all the factions in that entangled place. Taking in the northerners was the right thing to do, even if ultimately they suffered for it. Still, he wasn't prepared to throw lives away carelessly. Someone would be assigned the task of watching these refugees.

The shed served as a safe hiding place for the Company that afternoon, where Leith was able to rest and recover fully from the trials of the previous forty-eight hours. According to Foilzie, the Instruian Guard still swarmed through the streets of the city, driving honest citizens into their homes with the fervor of their questioning. It remained unsafe to move until well after dark.

"But where are we to be taken?" Kurr's question was asked on behalf of them all.

"To Escaigne," said the bald man. "To safety."

"How far do we have to travel? How do we get past the guards on the streets and the watch they have placed on the bridges?" asked Indrett. Uncomfortable with the presence of the bald man, who kept his name to himself, the Company plied him with questions.

"We of Escaigne are skilled in avoiding the guards."

"Where is Escaigne? It is not one of the Sixteen Kingdoms of the Falthan Council." Phemanderac had studied the maps, traveling extensively through central Faltha in the previous year, encountering plenty of talk about this mysterious place, yet no one had been able to supply him with a satisfactory answer.

"No, it is not one of the Sixteen, yet it is Falthan territory; a sovereign state, yet without a king."

"We heard something of Escaigne in the market, yet everyone who told us of Escaigne had a different idea of what and where it was." Indrett shook her head.

"I can make nothing of this riddle," Kurr said.

"Good. There's a reason why we want the location of our state to remain a secret. Foilzie has kept you ignorant of Instruian history," said the bald man. "Nevertheless, I will seek to remedy this as we journey there. Shall we go?"

In answer the Company stood and made ready. The Haufuth was heard to mutter: "Whoever heard of a journey made on an empty stomach?"

Out into the deserted side streets they ventured. After a tense ten minutes or so they came to a part of the city Leith recognized: they were perhaps two hundred yards from the market when their guide stopped, produced a number of cloths and gave one to each of them. "Blindfolds," he said. "You must wear them on the journey. Escaigne is a secret."

Farr muttered darkly, but allowed himself to be blindfolded. Likely he realized that they had no choice; their lives depended on this man.

Leith tried to work out where they were being taken, but after a few turns he became thoroughly confused. For a time they walked on the cobbles of a road, then on the soft sand of an alleyway. At one point their guide whispered: "Down!" and they sank to their haunches, holding their breath, but Leith could neither see nor hear whatever it was they were hiding from. More sand followed, then they stopped while the man knocked, and listened in the silence for an answer which must have come because the man whispered something, then a door opened and the refugees were hurried inside a building.

"Your weapons may not be taken into Escaigne," said their guide.

"Then I will not be taken there," Farr responded harshly. "I go nowhere without my sword and my staff."

"So be it. Perhaps I could save time by summoning the Instruian Guard now? I don't think you grasp the situation you are in. You northerners either find sanctuary in Escaigne or face the wrath of Instruere. Rest assured you will go to your death in The Pinion with neither your sword nor your staff."

"Don't be a fool," Kurr said to the Vinkullen man. "Lay them down. We are not in a position of strength."

"I have never yet been disarmed by an enemy," Farr insisted stubbornly.

"Then it is fortunate that we are not your enemy," said their guide, "for you are about to be disarmed."

"Perhaps we could debate this further when we reach your land," said Farr.

"You may take your blindfolds off after your weapons are surrendered," their guide said in reply. "We are at the gates of Escaigne now."

"Already?" Kurr said, surprised. "But surely we have not yet left Instruere!"

"Lay down your arms, then take off your blindfolds," their guide repeated patiently. "Come and find rest in Escaigne."

Around Leith came the clatter of weapons falling to the floor. With little reluctance he shed the short, stubby blade he had acquired in The Pinion. His fingers loosened the knot holding the cloth across his eyes, and he blinked a few times. It was every bit as dark as when he had been blindfolded.

Along a pitch-black passage they went, following the echoing sound of their guide's footsteps.

"Who lives here?" said the old farmer suddenly. The words came as a shock, almost a violation of the close dark silence. Leith drew away from Kurr.

Unperturbed, their guide responded by throwing open a door at the end of the passage. Sudden light burst in upon the Company, and for a moment they could not make out details of the room they were in. Leith blinked, and blinked again. The windowless, dimly lit space was packed with people.

"Welcome to Escaigne!" cried their guide.

"But this is still Instruere!" said Kurr, clearly puzzled and a little angry. "How are we any better off here?"

One or two of the people in the room had risen to their feet. The bald man motioned for them to sit. "They do not know," he said. "Forgive them. They will speak better when they understand better."

He turned to Kurr. "This is *not* Instruere. Scattered throughout the city are small enclaves like this one, never more than two or three rooms, hidden from our enemies. This is Escaigne; they are all Escaigne, *we* are Escaigne. The Hidden Ones, entangled with the city, but separate from it."

"Come ye out from her, and be ye separate," said one of the people, a young man.

"Conform not to her ways, nor be tainted with her evil. In this way shall ye set her free," intoned the woman beside him.

"Ye are Escaigne, set apart for purity," said a third, an older voice from the far side of the room.

"Who lives here?" The bald man repeated Kurr's question. "Those persecuted and dispossessed by the rulers of the city. No one knows who the first one was, nor why he founded our place of refuge, yet here it is. For the best part of the last decade people have found their way to Escaigne. A man here, a woman there, a family. Gradually the numbers mounted. At first they saw their role as watchers, observing the increasing depravity of the city-dwellers, and they continued to risk visits to the city, but as the regime grew more vicious and the Council of Faltha seized control over Instruere, the people of Escaigne no longer took the risk. Many here have not slept a night in Instruere for a long time. One day soon there will be more of us who were born in Escaigne than those who have fled the city."

"Does the Council know of your existence?" Kurr asked.

"They know, indeed they know," said their guide. "We make sure they know. We want all Instruians to know there is a place of resistance, a place they can find sanctuary, a place from which we will emerge one day to take back what is rightfully ours. They know of Escaigne, and the Council fear us, but they do not know where we are. They do not suspect we are in their midst."

"How long will we be your guests?" Perdu asked.

"Those few of us who return to the city will keep our ears open. When your names are no longer mentioned, it will be safe for you to leave. Until then, your choice is darkness or death, I'm afraid."

"Don't you have sunlight in Escaigne? Don't you go out and watch the sunrise?" Perdu sounded nervous. This place must seem the complete negation of his beloved vidda.

"Very few of us come and go between Instruere and Escaigne. As for watching the sunrise, it can be arranged for you if you wish, but would be very risky. The Guard changes at sunrise."

Leith spoke up quickly, conscious of Perdu's discomfort. "Please arrange it," he said. "I find the dark quite unnerving."

Hearing these words, Phemanderac thought: *the boy matures, the finger grows longer.*

A wide, well-lit (though windowless, like all the rooms of Escaigne) antechamber was found for the Company, and once they were all seated, ordinary-looking people brought them food and drink. The tension that had gripped the northerners this long day oozed slowly away, and they began to relax. "Something puzzles me," the Haufuth said, in between his endeavors to stuff a haunch of roast lamb down his throat. "Where does such excellent food and drink come from? Surely you cannot grow food in the darkness?"

"Most unlike the Haufuth, to concern himself with such things," the Hermit said quietly.

"I'm surprised we haven't heard something before now," Kurr added. "Greatest risk he ever took, in my opinion, traveling from Bandits' Cave with an ascetic."

"I'm afraid I learned more from him than he from me," said the Hermit.

"Oh dear," Kurr said sadly. "Our village tailor is fully employed meeting the needs of our Haufuth. I'm afraid we can offer you no help."

"Ignore them," the Haufuth advised their host. "They

are merely jealous, not being as substantial personages as I. But I would like an answer to my question, if it please you. At least if you talk, they will be forced to remain silent."

"There is much about The Cache, as we call the food stores of Escaigne, that we keep secret," the bald man replied carefully. "Piece it together yourself. If, as you say, we cannot grow food here, we must get it from Instruere. We have access to the area called the Docks, where some of our sympathizers have their employment. We have an almost inexhaustible supply of wealth, as in Escaigne we hold all things in common. Have I supplied you with enough information?"

A number of further questions were asked, then their guide apologized and excused himself, leaving the Company alone in the room. The meal was finished in silence, each member occupied with his or her own thoughts . . .

Could it have been real? Had the dream beside the fire in Foilzie's tenement been real? Leith had been puzzling away at it all day. Such a vivid dream, he remembered every bit of it with a clarity he seldom experienced in waking life. The colors had been brighter than real life, the sounds rounder somehow, fuller, nothing like any other dream he had ever experienced. And that was the problem. The whole thing made him suspicious, made him feel he'd made it up. *What do I want most of all?* He could answer that honestly. To be appreciated, to be loved, without any threat that those who loved him would abandon him, however noble the cause, and spend two years chasing ghosts in the land of their enemies. Without the object of his love casting that love back in his face by telling all her friends and laughing at him. Without always being better than him, always being right, always having the last word, like a treatise on morality. The dream-fire had offered him the kind of love he wanted. It was too perfect. It had to be an invention of his own mind.

But oh, if only it was true . . .

The air in the chamber was perfectly still. Enraptured by the peace of the moment, Phemanderac untied his well-traveled harp from his knapsack and played a few liquid notes, soft to the edge of hearing. In the confined space the sound seemed to flavor the air, sweetening it with something akin to joy; they took in lungfuls of it.

No one moved, no one dared speak, as all sat spellbound under the glorious weight. Phemanderac's hand fell to his side. The silence, the absolute Escaignian silence, cocooned them. They were held in stasis.

"I had a dream last night," Stella said suddenly, and everybody's hearts skipped a beat. "Can anyone tell me . . ." Her voice tailed off as every face turned towards her, and embarrassment enflamed her neck and face.

"You had a dream?" Leith cried. "I also—"

"Hush!" Phemanderac said, steel in his voice. "If anyone has dreamed, let her keep it to herself." Leith pursed his lips. *Did others also hear the voice last night? Do they hear it tonight?* He did not ask the question: the moment was still too new, too precious to unwrap. *Perhaps, perhaps . . .*

For many long minutes nothing was said, but for Leith at least the moments were full of inexpressible longing.

"Perhaps we might debate the direction of our path from here," the Hermit said eventually. When no one responded, he continued: "No matter our opinion on the identity of the Right Hand, we must decide whether the Company has any further task to achieve. Do we seek out the Jugom Ark, like our friend Phemanderac suggests? Or do we consider we've done all we can? I must confess I'm sensing a calling to serve the people of Instruere, people like those forced to hide in places like this."

This stirred the old farmer Kurr into life. "Any further task to achieve? You may have some sense of success, my friend the Hermit, but I don't. Perhaps you could supply me with a list of the tasks we have successfully completed?"

"I note the presence of two former Bhrudwan captives amongst us," came the reply with just a touch of asperity.

"Granted," Kurr acknowledged. "But if that was all we had to do, I might already be home enjoying the delights of a Firanese spring."

The Haufuth joined the debate. "Let's be precise about this. Exactly what was the second of the two tasks the Company was given?"

"To save Faltha," came the blunt reply. "At the moment we can't even save ourselves."

"As I remember it, our task was a little less lofty. We set ourselves to present our knowledge to the Council of Faltha."

"Which has been done," the Hermit said quickly.

"This was to be linked to the presentation to the Council of a captured Bhrudwan, who would convince them of the Bhrudwan threat."

"Whose idea was that?" pressed the Hermit.

There was a pause as the Company thought about this. It had been such a long time ago. So much had happened since the night in the Haufuth's house when they had decided to leave . . .

"It was my idea," said Hal evenly.

Leith started; he thought his brother had been asleep.

He should be asleep, harboring his strength. Leith had seen how much their long journey had taken out of him.

"Your idea?" the Hermit said, the measured politeness in his voice belying his intent. "Why am I not surprised?"

Hal frowned, but said nothing. Indrett made to speak, but Mahnum put a hand on her shoulder and a finger to his lips.

"No matter the idea's origins, it was a good thought. But it failed because of Falthan politics and the treachery of ambassadors and kings." The Haufuth spoke with a heavy voice. "We never had a chance." He sighed.

"But does Faltha?" Mahnum inquired of them all. "Will Faltha be able to defend herself against the army that even now may stand on her borders? Because if not . . ."

"If the people had sufficient warning . . ." said Perdu.

"If the army could be readied in time . . ." added Farr.

"If they had any sort of leadership . . ." the Haufuth said.

"If, if, if!" Phemanderac lost patience. "Of course Faltha could match the Bhrudwans if they could raise an army now, and had the leaders to direct them. But the problem is that they do not! Faltha has Bhrudwans for leaders! They will ensure you are defenseless and un-aware, and will simply invite the Brown Army in to oc-cupy your cities! There will be no defense. There will be no battle. Instead there will be slaughter! If you imagine you have carried out your task to its completion, perhaps you will give me leave to return to my own country now, because I will not remain to watch Faltha's fair rivers run red with blood!"

"Please don't leave," said Leith, rising to his feet, not wanting his friend to be misunderstood. Phemanderac was, after a fashion, his responsibility. He had befriended the strange foreigner, and told him the Company's secrets. "We can't sit back now, thinking of our own safety, not when we know things vital to the survival of Faltha. Not when we've been given a path to tread which might lead us to our goal." *Sit down!* his timorous inner voice shrieked at him. *You're only a boy! Be quiet and learn from your betters!* Far from taking heed of the voice, Leith rejoiced to hear its desperation, and took heart. "Phemanderac says the Jugom Ark is a symbol of unity. Maybe he's right. Maybe the Jugom Ark will join Faltha under our leadership. I don't know. But we won't find out by remaining hidden until hauled out by cruel hands! I don't want to spend however much time we have left before the Bhrudwans come wondering whether I might have still been some use to Faltha, whether my friends and I might have saved her from destruction!" He clenched his fists, arms held rigid by his sides, and his voice filled the chamber, giving the others nowhere to hide from it. "I don't care about prophecies or swords. I don't care whether I'm young or old. I've been given the chance to do something good, and I want to do it. All my life I've wanted to do the right thing, and I've never quite managed to do it." His voice cracked, but he was heedless of it. "Something always gets me by the heel, and holds me back so I fall short, never quite measuring up. Well, I've had enough!" He took a deep breath. "I choose to do the right thing, just this once. Whether I succeed or fail, live or die, I will have chosen rightly! And if others choose as I do, maybe Faltha will not be totally lost, even if Bhrudwo should overrun her. Do you hear me? Are you listening? *Are you?*"

No one spoke.

Doubts echoed in his head as he spoke: *braggart* . . .

attention seeker . . . Hal might be able to get away with this sort of talk, he always had, but on Leith's tongue it sounded fatuous, almost offensive . . . *fool* . . .

"Phemanderac calls us the Right Hand. He says that a hand is made up of five fingers. I see more than five fingers here. Maybe we are two hands. I don't know. But I do know fingers are no use on their own. We will fail again without each other." He turned his gaze on them all in turn. His mother and father, faithful Perdu, the inscrutable face of the Hermit, the Haufuth and Kurr, Achtal the Bhrudwan Acolyte, Hal, whom nothing surprised, Phemanderac, with a wide smile and a wider love, Foilzie, who nodded her head to him; and Stella, oh Stella, who brought a catch to his throat, whose eyes shone so brightly they threatened to burn him away. "I love you," he said gently. "I love you. I love you all. I cannot tell you—I cannot . . ." he faltered, and sat down.

Someone pushed past him, knocking him to the floor. By the time he regained his place, the Hermit stood amongst them, eyes closed, face uplifted.

"Your journey is not yet finished!" he cried in a resonant tone. "You will travel through madness and mist, through the depths and to the heights, though a thousand fires assail you and the mountains shake under your feet. You shall pierce the veil of illusion and bend the root of magic to your will. Though scattered, you will gather; though divided, you will unite. And when the chance comes to take the fire into your hands, your grasp must be full of faith, unwavering and without doubt." The Hermit smiled then, and opened his eyes.

Though Leith expected something to follow such a speech, what happened next still shocked him. Eyebrows raised provocatively, the blue-robed man ran his eyes over the Company until they locked with Hal's. "Anything to say about that, cripple?"

Even Hal was surprised, Leith could tell, though he maintained a mild expression. Kurr leapt to his feet, followed by Farr and Perdu, all shouting at once. The Haufuth cried out for silence, but it was slow in coming.

"So discourtesy is repaid in kind." The village headman shook his head. "How can you expect us to take your words seriously when they are delivered in such a churlish manner?"

"You'll take them seriously when they start to come true. Don't expect me to apologize for the prophetic words I receive. I have reflected on events since first I met you northerners, and I realize I permitted myself to be influenced by your views. I must weigh my own humility against the incontrovertible words of the Most High. For the sake of Faltha, I shall speak out what I have been given."

"That's no excuse for rudeness," Stella snapped.

"Perhaps my comment was ill-advised," the Hermit allowed. "But I trust you find what I say more important than how I say it."

"That may be," said the Haufuth. "Tell me, Hermit; your prediction suggested we have more journeying to do. Fine, I can accept that. In his own way, Leith has already made a similar argument. But what was the rest of your prophecy about? If the Most High wishes to speak to us, why are his words not more helpful? Why not say: 'Travel east through Straux until you reach the Aleinus River, then turn north and walk for thirty days until you trip over a golden arrow,' or some such thing? Why wrap plain words so tightly in mystery that nothing can be unraveled from them?"

"Words, words. I say we ignore them," Farr said, with his characteristic bluntness. "Phemanderac offers us a path to travel. I say we travel it. I'll go to this country of Nemohaim, this place called Kantara, and try to find the Jugom Ark. It would be good to have some companions on the road. Anyone coming?"

"I'll come," a steady voice said. Stella, proud Stella, chin upraised, eyes wide and so alive. "Things can't have finished for us, just like that. We can't be going home yet."

"Oh my," said the Haufuth. "Herza would eat me alive if anything happened to her daughter. I'd better come with you."

"I'll come too," Leith added in haste, fearing he'd be left out.

"And I," came the gruff voice of the farmer. "No telling what mess you fools will get yourselves into without my help." He laughed, a clear, pure sound, with that hint of mischief Leith had mistaken for evil the day he'd been afraid of being locked in Kurr's barn.

"We will all be coming, I'm sure," Mahnum said. "There's no safety in this city for us now."

Leith glanced at his brother. There it was on his face, that superior look he always wore when he knew something no one else did.

"Hal? Will you come?" Asking Hal for a commitment was so unnerving it made Leith giddy. He remembered a similar conversation months ago in the house of the Haufuth, before they had even left Loulea, when it had been Hal confronting the adults afraid to make a decision, paralyzed as they were by the weight of responsibility. But it was typical of Hal that he was not discomfited in any way by the turn of events. *Look at the smile on his face!* It was as though he had been made *happy* by Leith assuming his role. *Curse him! Can he never show some humility?*

"If everyone's convinced by Phemanderac's theory of the Five of the Hand, then it seems I'm needed. Of course I'll come."

"Do you have doubts about Phemanderac's idea?" Leith bored in.

"No doubts at all," Hal replied sincerely, but Leith heard something evasive in his brother's answer.

Phemanderac stood, and the moment passed. "So all five of those who left Loulea together will continue to the end, along with the rest of the Company. It is fitting."

"I will not accompany you," the Hermit said. "The Most High has another mission for me. I am called to minister his word to the people of Instruere. Careless of the risks, heedless of the danger, I am to prepare the Great City for the coming of the Most High and his glorious Fire."

He seemed to be building to a declamation of some self-importance, and there had been enough wearying talk for one day. It was really a question of who would interrupt him first.

"We must leave with all speed," the Haufuth noted.

"We have a great number of things to prepare," added Kurr.

"And what about the Bhrudwan? What are we to do with him?" Leith was puzzled by the status of the warrior-wizard, who supposedly could kill them all. He was still bound, but since The Pinion it had been largely ceremonial. Given Hal was going to Nemohaim, wherever that was, would not Achtal want to accompany him? Could they stop him?

"Surely tomorrow morning will be early enough for

thinking about all these things," the Haufuth moaned. "I still have much work ahead in order to fix my tiredness and hunger."

"Tomorrow morning it is," Kurr said, laughing. "My, how we missed you these last few weeks. Without you, it's so hard to keep things in proper perspective!" He nodded to the big headman, then addressed them all. "We need to communicate our desire to our hosts, and ask for any assistance they can give us in escaping the Arkhos's net. Let us rest tonight, then be on our way tomorrow."

There was a tomorrow in Escaigne, but no sunrise. Perdu, the first of the Company to emerge from sleep, spent his waking moments, as he always did, thinking about his family—most likely camped somewhere in northern Myrvidda—then unwrapped the breakfast that had been left for them and roused the others.

"Rise and shine!" the adopted Fenni said. "Sorry I haven't opened any windows, but it's morning about a hundred yards from here, in another land. Come on, Haufuth. You're not really asleep: you snore a lot louder than that when you are." On he went, until a pillow to the back of the head shut him up.

Their host, the bald friend of Foilzie, returned as they finished breakfast. In answer to their inquiry, he told them the day was well under way, then casually informed his guests a gathering of Escaigne—a Collocation, he called it—had been called immediately in order to meet the Company. "It may be many days before you are able to return to Instruere," he said. "I thought, therefore, that you might like to be introduced to our people."

"I thought you said the people of Escaigne did not travel through Instruere," Kurr said, instantly suspicious.

"Indeed," came his reply. "So most will remain in Escaigne. But enough will come that we can have a Collocation."

"Why do we need this gathering?" Kurr pressed him. "We were anxious to try to sneak a small number of us past the guard on the Straux Bridge, the sooner the better. Why the delay?"

"There are some who would like to cast an eye over you," the bald man said. Leith detected a note of caution in his voice, something the others apparently missed, for no one offered any comment; so he stood, seeking to pursue it further.

"Are there leaders of Escaigne we have yet to meet?" Leith asked the bald man. "We would like the opportunity to reassure them of our trustworthiness and peaceful intent."

Their host pursed his lips. "I understand you were one of the warriors who raided The Pinion." Now everyone could hear the doubt in his voice. "A few of those who escaped made their way to Escaigne and told us of your endeavors. My leaders wish to be assured such bold warriors pose no threat to our security. As you can imagine, security is crucial underground. Seeing you, perhaps I could offer them the assurance they seek."

Leith laughed. "It would be well to remember that appearances are deceiving. Although, in my case at least, they are not. Where the skilful fail, the lucky may survive. I am no warrior."

"Yet the tales of your deeds, and those of your companions, have spread through Escaigne faster than fire. Whether they are exaggerated or not, I do not know, though I believe Foilzie; however, my leaders intend to find out the substance behind the rumor."

Now other members of the Company began to take an interest in the conversation, and both Kurr and the Haufuth stood. "There may be matters which it would not be wise to raise at a public meeting—or even in private," Leith said, as the two men came to stand beside him.

"Indeed," the bald man replied, and now his voice carried a hint of menace. "But if any information exists relevant to the survival of Escaigne, be assured we will obtain it."

"And if such information compromises us, we will hide it!" Farr boomed across the chamber.

"Peace, Farr," Kurr shot at him, but there was a gentleness in his voice designed to settle the mountain man while placating their host.

"There is something in what my comrade says," the Haufuth said. "We'll be careful in what we say. Remember, we are over a thousand miles from home, hidden in a hostile city, fugitives far from help. It's frustrating, I know, to have reached a decision and yet not be able to do anything about it. Let's set ourselves on being patient."

The Collocation was held later that morning in a large hall, formed with infinite skill and patience from the hollowed interiors of two adjacent tenements. When the Company arrived, having spent a harrowing hour dodging guards as they were escorted across the somber, shower-washed city, at least a hundred people stood against the unadorned walls of the hall. At least a hundred pairs of eyes appraised the northerners as they were led down the middle of the open space. There was something very strange, even unsettling, about this hall, as though everything within crowded close.

At the far end of the open space a group of perhaps a

dozen people sat on tall stools, all together on a low stage, and the Company was invited to join them.

"What is the purpose of this?" Farr whispered to Perdu. "The people gathered here will learn nothing from a meeting they cannot hear."

"Be assured our people will not miss a word," said a voice from the stage. "There is a reason we hold our meetings here."

"Perfect acoustics!" Phemanderac breathed. "All my life . . ." He turned as if to gaze behind him. "I wish I had brought my harp. I wish *someone* had not thought it might be a weapon and made me leave it at the door."

"Please, come up here and take a chair," said a voice from the stage. *Impossible!* Leith thought. *We are perhaps thirty paces from the speaker, yet we can hear his every word!*

But it was true. The walls of this carefully crafted space were peerless reflectors and amplifiers of sound; and every sound uttered, no matter how soft, was somehow enlarged, filled and focused so all might hear it. Every whisper, every cough, every shuffle of the feet. This, Leith realized, was the source of his discomfit, as the effect of the acoustics was to bring everything closer, as though a crowd of a hundred people leaned over his shoulder.

As soon as the members of the Company were seated on the stage, a tall, raven-haired man with sallow skin and pinched features stood and welcomed them. "I would remind everyone of the rules for the Collocation," he said solemnly. "There are to be no—"

"What's a collocation?" Stella whispered to Indrett.

"A Collocation is the formal gathering of Escaigne," was the abrupt answer. "We gather to decide matters judged too important for the Elders alone to decide."

"And these Elders are—"

"Those seated on the stage," the sallow man concluded for her. "Since you have finished speaking, I will proclaim the rules for the benefit of those unfamiliar with the Collocation. There are to be no Escaignian names mentioned. Only one voice is to be heard at a time, and other than this, there is to be no sound. No voice is to be raised in anger. Remember, if we are overheard, Escaigne is no more. The Presiding Elder is authorized to direct the Collocation. The gathering will be concluded by the taking of a vote. Are these rules acceptable?"

A woman stepped out from beside the wall.

"On behalf of the people, these rules are acceptable," she said formally, in a manner that told Leith he was witnessing a ritual.

"Very well. Let the Collocation begin."

Leith soon realized the meeting was being conducted to the advantage of the Escaignians—more specifically, the Elders—and against the Company. One after another people were called forward to ask questions. Polite questions they were, but carefully phrased, and delivered with a care that suggested others had taken a hand in their shaping. Answers were dissected by the Elders, mostly by the sallow man, obviously the Presiding Elder, and further questions then asked. It was outwardly amicable, with no direct malice that Leith could put his finger on; but something sinister lay behind this formal gathering, this slow questioning, something beyond the mere accumulation of information, Leith was sure of it.

"I was one of those freed when The Pinion was raided," said a young woman with long, lank hair and wide, almost bulbous eyes that at present were filled with a genuine thankfulness. "Would my rescuers identify themselves, so I might thank them?"

Feeling a little awkward, Leith stood; as did Mahnum and Achtal. Brief applause rippled through the hall, cut off by a gesture from the Presiding Elder. Obviously others who escaped the dungeons had also made their way to Escaigne. Leith sensed the attention of the Elders on him.

"Who devised the plan?" asked the sallow man.

"It wasn't a planned raid," Mahnum answered. "My son and I were prisoners of the Council, along with one of our comrades who was already undergoing questioning. If you know The Pinion, you know what that means. We were keen to avoid it ourselves, and the other prisoners seemed to be of like mind."

"And the warrior with the staff of steel? Which is he?"

"Need you ask?" Farr said, obviously tired of the Collocation.

The Presiding Elder turned to the woman with the wide eyes. "Which is he?"

She pointed to Achtal. "He is the one." There was something approaching awe in her childlike voice. "Thank you," she said. The Bhrudwan, understanding her intent if not her words, bowed stiffly.

"Is it true you are a Bhrudwan warrior, and you defected to Faltha?" a straw-haired man, little more than a youngster, wanted to know.

Achtal frowned, struggling with his reply. "Bhrudwan warrior, yes. Defect? I have no defect."

"Are you now a servant of Faltha?" Kurr paraphrased.

The Bhrudwan shook his head. "Servant of Hal, servant of Leith. None other."

Leith turned in surprise at this statement, and found the others had done the same. Hal was smiling broadly.

Servant of Leith? When had this happened? This was un-doubtedly more of Hal's doing. Not for the first time, Leith felt he had cause to doubt his crippled, seemingly innocent brother, who seemed to pull invisible strings attached to everything and everyone. Where had the Bhrudwan learned words of the common tongue? The questioning continued even as he considered this.

"Can you tell us how the Bhrudwan has become your servant?" the Presiding Elder asked, directing the question to Kurr.

"To do that would be to tell you what a group of Firanese are doing in Instruere," the farmer answered, choosing his words with care. He too was aware of some undercurrent, some danger. Something about this sallow-faced man bothered him . . .

"Then proceed," said the Elder, "and let us judge your case."

"Is there a case to be judged?" Leith responded sharply. Here was the nub of it. Were they on trial? Before anything else was said, they needed to discover why the Elders of the Escaigne desired a formal public meeting rather than a private discussion.

"You have been granted sanctuary in Escaigne, and a surety of safety. Without this you would certainly have perished in the city. By granting you sanctuary, knowing that the Arkhos of Nemohaim—the ruler of the city in all but name—is pursuing you, we have placed the security of our State in great danger. This meeting is called to judge whether you are worthy of such risk. I must warn you that if your Company is shown to be untrustworthy or any risk to us, we will have no hesitation in delivering you to the Arkhos, or putting you to death ourselves."

Leith nodded his head. *So that's what this is all about.*

"This is outrageous!" Kurr cried. "Had we known we were in such peril, we would have taken our chances with the Council!"

Leith moved in front of the old farmer, signaling his silence. Kurr sat down, nonplussed.

"Then we will satisfy your concerns, and ensure that your judgment is favorable," Leith said, trying to project solidity, sincerity, integrity. It was happening again; something boiled within him, seeking a way out. *This is a public show, with a public vote. If we rail against the morality of this trial, it will go badly for us.* He hoped the others would realize what he was doing.

"On Midwinter's Night last our village was raided by four Bhrudwan warriors, and Mahnum and Indrett, my parents, were taken captive." Leith was careful to let his emotions show, though in truth he couldn't have held them back. "Five of us set off in pursuit, and on the long and arduous path we were joined by others who had suffered at the hands of these raiders. We tackled and conquered the Westway in winter, a feat never attempted in living memory. We met and befriended the wild race of the Fenni, crossed the Jawbone Mountains, traversed the Southern Run, aided by the Fodhram, woodsmen of the north, and survived Mossbank Cadence, the first ever to do so. Then we ambushed the Bhrudwans at Mount Steffl, killing all but Achtal, whom we took captive, and rescued my father and mother. I was taken captive by the Widuz, a fierce warrior race, and while waiting in their dungeon for execution I met Phemanderac. Together we escaped. My father, who had pursued my captors, set the Widuz captives free. Eventually we all made our way to Instruere, chased by a Widuz war party."

As Leith recited their deeds, so briefly summarized, he

realized the list was bound to sound impressive. While his listeners might not know the people or places to which he referred, the sheer weight of achievements must be establishing their credibility. *Keep talking*, he encouraged himself. *They need to hear confidence in my voice.* He thought of Wira and how the young mountain man was able to defuse the tension at the Fenni campfire with bold but conciliatory talk. *Ah, Wira, we need you now!*

There followed numerous questions about their adventures upon the Westway, to which various members of the Company responded, and Leith could see a new regard settle on the faces of those in the hall. Eventually the sallow Presiding Elder cut short this questioning. Under his prompting the doings of the Company in Instruere became the focus of the meeting, and here Leith and the others were hard pressed to keep the keen minds of the Elders at bay.

"You say you rejoined your fellows within the walls of the city," said one of the Elders, a bushy-browed, black-bearded man, directing his gaze at Leith. "Yet you have not explained why you should have come here at all, nor why your Company did not simply return to Firanes when the Bhrudwans were defeated and your kinsmen were rescued." The man looked on Leith with an uncomfortably penetrating gaze.

Kurr shot Leith a warning glance, but he did not need the farmer to tell him of the danger masked by the polite questioning.

Ignoring the Elders, he rose from his chair, stepped forward and addressed the Collocation in clear tones.

"I will not hide from you the fact that we have a mission, and guard a great secret," he said, and the gathering leaned forward as one. "But on behalf of my companions

I plead with you to let our mission remain secret. We revealed it to the Council of Faltha, and were betrayed. We cannot take the risk of revealing it again, for even the Elders cannot be certain there is not a spy in your midst, one who might betray us to the Council."

Leith could feel the anger rise from the stage behind him.

"I am afraid of what might happen to my friends and to myself should this gathering find against us. But I am more afraid of what will happen to Escaigne, and to Instruere, and to all Faltha, should our mission be betrayed to the Council.

"This much I can reveal, for the Council already know it. My parents were not taken by the Bhrudwans by mere chance. Mahnum, my father, is a Trader, and was sent by the Firanese king to Bhrudwo to discover the truth about certain rumors. On the island of Andratan he learned that the armies of the Destroyer are being raised up once again, for a final deadly strike at Faltha, and at Instruere her heart; and that this heart is already blackened by treachery. He escaped to warn his king, but was recaptured before he could do so.

"After rescuing my parents, we continued to Instruere in the hope of warning the Council, and of persuading them of their peril. We believed the testimony of the Bhrudwan would sway the Council where our words perhaps would not. However, treachery was even more widespread than we knew, and the numbers were against us. There will be no defense of Faltha. Escaigne, Instruere, and all Faltha, lie open to be taken by the Destroyer whenever he wishes. Our chief opponent in the Council was the Arkhos of Nemohaim." A low murmur susurrated through the hall, silenced by a rap from the sallow man's staff.

"His men stopped us in the street and took three of us by force. No doubt the Arkhos wishes to learn why a Bhrudwan, trained for war and steeped in evil, would turn against his life-sworn master. My father and I attempted to secure his freedom; but as those who were there will doubtless recount, the Bhrudwan proved he could look after himself. Through his abilities we escaped The Pinion, but the Arkhos is all too aware of our actions and no doubt most keenly seeks an interview with us.

"We have not given up on alerting Falthans to their danger, and have formulated a plan which we believe may give us a chance of success. However, I must be honest with you. In order to execute this plan a number of us must leave as soon as we are able, yet we are not able even in the most general terms to tell you about our plan."

"Leave?" the Presiding Elder said. "Leave? You will be fortunate indeed if you are allowed to remain alive, here to dwell until your death, in order to preserve *our* secret, which is of much greater import than yours!"

"And take to our deaths the secret which might save all Faltha?" Leith responded. "You are not well enough hidden to escape the attention of the Bhrudwans. For when they have finished gnawing Instruian bones, they will come for you! I would not like to be an Elder charged with keeping the Bhrudwan warriors from crossing your threshold."

Without warning Leith leapt from the stage, ran lightly forward and took a young child into his arms. "This little one is safe here, but for how much longer? Perhaps the Arkhos might consider raising an army against Escaigne, if indeed he knows of its existence and our presence in your midst; perhaps, perhaps not. But the cruel death of this child is certain if the Destroyer wills it." Her wide-eyed mother put her hand to her mouth, imagining a heartless sword-thrust through the walls of a child's cot. "Those of you who witnessed the abilities of Achtal, do you doubt it? And I tell you earnestly that this Bhrudwan is a neophyte, and is overmatched by the greatest of Bhrudwan warriors. Who among you could stand against Achtal? Could your Elders defend this child when the Destroyer's death squads come for her?"

He placed the little girl back into the arms of her frightened mother.

Now the young Loulean walked among the Escaignians, pacing up and down the hall as he spoke, completely taken by the moment, dumbfounding the Company. "I said we have a chance, but every hour we tarry in debate, the armies of the Destroyer draw closer. Already we may be too late, and we may yet be unable to prevent the merciless hordes from overrunning your homes. I ask you to consider the innocents—the children of Faltha—whose right to a long and happy life will be taken from them should we remain as prisoners here."

Who is this speaking? Kurr asked himself, intrigued beyond reason even in the midst of their trial. *Not a year ago this lad was frightened of me and my barn, yet today he takes on powerful strangers armed with wit and courage.*

"Innocents?" cried a voice. "Who can be innocent in a land where people are forced to live in hiding, never to see the sun with the eyes of freedom? Why should we care for the fate of our jailers?" The venom from this voice from the shadows was felt throughout the hall, and again the Presiding Elder had to thump his staff on the floor of the stage.

"Indeed!" agreed the Elders, coming to their feet.

"The worries of Faltha do not concern us," one said. "They may die or they may live, and to some of us perhaps the former is their more preferable fate. Yet they may keep the brown army at bay, or even defeat them, irrespective of your warnings and plans. And should the city around us fall, we may still remain out of reach. Such a circumstance is eagerly desired by many in this hall, for we have lost friends and loved ones to the depredations of the lords of the city; and it is hard for us to imagine a regime more cruel than that which drove us to Escaigne."

Now Stella sprang up from her seat, and lifted her face to her adversaries, eyes aflame with passion. "The evil in Instruere has arisen as an outpost of the Great Evil to come. The Arkhos of Nemohaim, cruel as he is, is a puppet of the Destroyer who seeks to dwell in your nest and devour your offspring. Listen to me! If you want to strike at the Arkhos, the most powerful blow you can deliver is one aimed at his master. Let us go, aid us in escaping the grasp of the Arkhos of Nemohaim, and you will be delivering that blow!"

The Presiding Elder spoke. "We seek to deliver a more certain and a more immediate blow. For many years we have labored to prepare an army to reclaim our rightful place in the city, to take back our houses and our lands, to live again under the sun and the moon. And just when we are ready to release our army, by chance it seems, a group of people fall into our hands who possess knowledge and skills that would ensure our success. Come with us, aid us as we attack the city, help us rid the city of its evil once and for all, and you will have rewards and riches beyond measure. Then you would be free to pursue your mission, though I deem it would no longer be necessary, for the

Elders you see on this stage would be the Rulers of Instruere, and the Council of Faltha would be no more. We
would certainly prepare against the chance of a Bhrudwan invasion. Help us! History would remember you as
the brave liberators of the capital of the world!"

"Yet liberators may fall into evil, and Captains of
Freedom may impose harsh restraint on their subjects,"
Stella replied boldly, conciliation forgotten in pursuit of
truth. "Were we to sack the city in search of justice, our
noble aims would be undone by the suffering of innocents, and we would become like those we seek to replace. We are offered a choice between division and
unity, between your army which would undoubtedly lay
waste the city, and our quest which, if successful, will
unite all Faltha against our real enemy." She turned to the
gathered Escaignians, just as Leith had done, and held out
her arms. "A choice! Personal revenge or the wholeness
of Faltha. You choose!"

Snarling, the raven-haired Presiding Elder rapped his
staff three times on the stage. "An end to debate!" he
cried. "You have been presented with a choice! On this
choice we will vote, and on this vote the fate of these
strangers rests. Choose either to release them to pursue a
quest, the details of which they will not reveal, trusting
that they will not betray our existence and purpose to the
Council. Or choose to pursue our plan to attack the city
and revenge ourselves on our enemies, and leave our
guests either to fight with us or face death."

He strode down from the stage and laid his staff in the
middle of the wooden floor. "What say you? Those for
the strangers stand this side of the staff; those for the Elders stand on the other."

Stella sat down and watched as the Collocation slowly

sorted itself out into two camps. Those who had made up their minds moved to their preferred sides of the line, then stood there and stared at each other, some with undisguised animosity on their faces. Others, unsure of how they should vote, scanned the two groups for some clue; perhaps a friend whose opinion they trusted, or even an assessment of which group had the most support. After a minute or so only a few remained, vacillating between the two groups, but these few took an age to make their decision.

Frantically Stella tried to count the numbers in each group, but people were moving about, making the task difficult. The people favoring war seemed to outnumber the others, at least to Stella's worried gaze. The last of them finally made up her mind, and the crowd breathed a collective sigh.

"Tally the numbers," the sallow man boomed.

At this command the Escaignians paired off, one from the left side of the line linking with another to the right, and moved to the back of the hall. As the Company watched, both groups became smaller, until there were only a few in each, and still they paired off.

"It's a tie!" Farr whispered fiercely, forgetting that his words would carry to all in the hall. But even as he spoke, the last pair of Escaignians, one for the strangers, one for the Elders, walked swiftly away, leaving the center of the hall empty.

"Indeed," said the Presiding Elder, trying to remain calm in the face of this reversal. "It is a tie. Clarification!"

At his word one of the Elders stood and said: "In the case of a tie in a Collocation vote, the Elders shall decide the outcome."

The sallow man smiled.

"Clarification!" Leith barked, emboldened beyond reason. "Who makes up the Collocation?"

"All those called to the great hall," came the answer.

"Then we have yet to vote." He turned to the others. "Let's cast our votes!" He ran down from the stage and stood to the right of the line, and the Company followed him.

"There is no tie," Leith said. "The Collocation is therefore decided!"

"No!" screamed the sallow-faced man. He turned in desperation to his Eldership, then in anger strode into the center of the hall, standing opposite Leith on the other side of the line. One by one his Elders joined him, and the two groups faced each other across the floor.

Foilzie stepped forward, and held out her hand. At the same moment Leith recognized one of the Elders: the bald man who had been their guide into Escaigne. "Come," Foilzie said to him. "You know this is wrong."

He shook his head sorrowfully. "I can't show disloyalty. I have no choice."

"Yes you have. Just step over this line."

"I cannot," he said. He lowered his head to his breast, and stepped backwards into the shadows.

"Tally the numbers!" The cry was laced with triumph.

One by one they paired off, a member of the Company with one of the Elders. But long before the ritual reached its bitter end, the outcome was obvious. Leith and the Presiding Elder walked together to the far end of the hall, turned and looked back: the bald man stood alone.

"The Collocation is decided," said the Presiding Elder, then rapped his staff three times on the floor. "It is decided in favor of the Elders. The strangers shall serve in our army, or they shall not be allowed to live."

CHAPTER 7

MORALS AND MIRACLES

"CONDEMNED TO DIE?" LEITH cried bitterly. His shout rang like an accusation around the deserted room, heard only by the others of the Company and their newly assigned guards. His head swam with the effort expended during the Collocation, and he barely found the strength to follow the others as they were escorted from the great hall of Escaigne, taken through the city in the dead of night— no need to dodge guards at this hour—and deposited at their quarters, also Escaigne.

There they were placed under virtual arrest. Confined to one smallish room, they fretted and argued as they tried to come to terms with the events that had so swiftly overtaken them. Farr strode up and down. Kurr and Mahnum fired questions, comments and wild schemes across the room at each other. At odd times members of the Company would rail against the hasty words Leith and Stella had spoken, saying all the things Leith would expect them to say, would have said in their position: why had they not left it to their elders, how could they have presumed so much and so on. Leith listened dispassionately. He could do nothing else, they couldn't know what it was like trying to hold back the fountain of words.

Though his mind told him he should join the debate about their future, working out some way of avoiding the sentence passed on them, he could do nothing but lie on his cushion. He felt robbed of the will to act. *Since that stupid dream*, he thought, *I'm being used. I could stand it if someone would ask my permission!* He'd almost accepted that adulthood meant severe constraint of his actions, that he had to do many things he didn't want to do, but he'd never imagined he wouldn't be able to say his own words, think his own thoughts.

You did all you could, said his timid voice. *No one can blame you if the mission fails. Faltha just does not want to be saved.* Leith nodded his head. The Most High Himself could have expected no more from him. He'd done enough. Listening to the angry words Kurr was saying, perhaps he'd done far too much.

<Speak to the guards.>

It was such an ordinary voice, so like all the voices droning in the background, that Leith hardly noticed it. He raised his head, but none of the Company were looking in his direction, so he lowered it again.

<Speak to the guards.> The voice came more insistently this time. <Leith, talk to them.>

Leith stood. The others were involved in tight little conversations he was unlikely to have overheard. "Who said that?" he asked.

"Said what?" His father turned towards him.

"Nothing. I'm hearing things, voices, a voice."

"You're overwrought. Leith, no one could do more than you did. No one blames you for this. Rest now: perhaps later we can think about this, and talk it over. We'll think of something. The sentence will not be carried out for some time."

True, Leith thought: *the one concession the Presiding Elder made, on the insistence of his Eldership. No doubt he would have seen them executed there in the hall, if he'd had his way. What was it that made him our opponent?* There was something in this line of thinking, something that held a kernel of hope, but Leith was too exhausted to pursue it. He lay back on his cushion.

Face it, you're going to die. Leith sighed. *I wish I could at least look on the sun one last time.*

<You haven't much time. Just engage them in conversation!>

Leith shook his head. *Go away, leave me in peace.* He coughed, then cleared his throat. A sudden coughing fit bent him double. *Great: I'm going to choke to death while waiting to die.*

"Water?"

Leith turned over. One of the guards leaned over him, concern on his face, holding a ladle of water in his hand.

"Thank you," he said, and gulped greedily; which served only to worsen his cough. "I'll be right in a moment."

The water seemed to settle him down. Eventually he sat up. A few feet away the guard knelt, solicitous concern giving way to boredom.

What we need here is a miracle, Leith thought. *How about it? You're very good at giving dreams, and you said some clever words. How about getting us out of here?* He looked at the guard. *You could start with him.*

<No, *you* could start with him, like I suggested. One small step is all it needs. I know you're tired.>

You do it, thought Leith stubbornly. *This is bizarre.* And a dark, burning suspicion settled on him: *am I going mad? Will I end up like Stella's drunken brother, talking to myself all day?*

<Believe me, it'll be better than a miracle if you do it. It's you or no one. I have no other plans left.>

Leith shrugged his shoulders. *I'm not going to go to sleep now, anyway.* He opened his mouth to speak. *This is a foolish idea.*

<Tell me about it afterwards,> the voice said.

"How did you end up with this task?" Leith asked the guard, who started at the sound of his voice.

"Oh—I suppose they think it's good training for when we reclaim Instruere," he said after a moment's hesitation. "I'm going to be one of the important ones out there," he said with pride. "They might even put me in charge of the captives, once we've put the Great Harlot to the sword."

The guard was a mere boy, little older than Leith himself. Tall and thin, he had that look some boys get when they have grown too quickly; all stretched, a profusion of arms and legs, a giant Adam's apple, an unexpectedly deep voice. *Like Lanka from Brookside*, Leith reflected. *I dealt with him during the Midwinter Play.*

"When is the invasion scheduled?"

"I'm not allowed to say," the youth replied.

I bet he doesn't know, Leith thought.

"But it will be soon, and then we'll show them."

"Show them what?" He was talking for the sake of talking. *I've done what you wanted*, he said to the voice. *Enough?* No reply. There wouldn't be. It was all his imagination. He *was* going mad.

"Show them the Watchers should never have been driven down here, that's what." The youth thrust his pointed chin forward. "They need us. Only we can look after Faltha."

It actually took Leith a moment to realize what had been said. "The Watchers?" he said in a surprise-filled voice. "What do you know of the Watchers?"

"The Watchers are an ancient order, more important than kings, warriors or wise men," the boy said proudly. "Ever since the Bhrudwan invasion of Faltha over a thousand years ago, the Watchers have sought to warn people of decline and deca—dessa—I can never say that word," he said, flushed with embarrassment. "Anyway, we warn people when things get bad, and we watch for evil and corruption, and try to put it right. About ten years ago the Council of Faltha stole our houses and lands—well, my father's house and lands, actually; his and those of others like him. We escaped to Escaigne and ever since we've been planning how to get back again."

Out of the corner of his eye Leith saw Kurr sit up.

"I've heard of the Watchers," Leith said, trying to keep his voice level. "But I thought they were spread throughout Faltha."

"Yes, they are, but the others don't really count. Just old men playing games, my father says. We're the only ones who can bring the Council to justice."

The old farmer walked over casually, sat on his haunches and asked the youthful guard: "How many of the Escaignians belong to the Watchers?"

"Most of them," he responded. "My grandfather is one, of course, so is my father, and so are all the Elders."

"Your grandfather? Who is he?" Leith could tell that Kurr was angry, and thought he had just cause. The youth saw nothing untoward, and carried right on talking.

"My grandfather is the Presiding Elder," he said with satisfaction. "He rules Escaigne, and one day soon he will rule all of Instruere."

"You," Kurr pressed, "you call yourself a Watcher. Do you know why we are called Watchers?"

"Because we—"

"Because we watch and we don't talk!" The farmer shook his head in disgust. "The First Rule of the Watcher is that all names and identities remain secret, to be shared only with fellow Watchers, yet you have revealed your membership, and that of your father and your grandfather. How could you do such a thing?"

"But you are going to die soon! It can't do any harm! I—how do you know the First Rule?" Comprehension began to settle on the mind of the slow-witted youth.

"There is only one way I could possibly know the First Rule. Now, remind me: what is the Third Rule?"

"No Watcher—no Watcher may knowingly injure or prejudice the life of any fellow Watcher," the boy replied. "But—if you know the Rules, you must be Watchers. That means we cannot carry out the sentence." Leith imagined he heard regret in the words.

Still Kurr pressed the boy. "And the Second Rule?"

"All Watchers shall respond to the need of a fellow Watcher with whatever aid lies within their power."

"At least you learned your Rules," Kurr said. "A pity your teachers forgot to train you to listen and remain silent. Or perhaps they themselves have forgotten the skill? Certainly your grandfather showed little evidence of it.

"Now, boy, if you please, I'd like to speak to him, as one Watcher to another. Bring him to me! He cannot refuse: I am a Watcher of the Sixth Rank, and he must hear and honor my request with all diligence. And ask as many Elders as possible to attend. Be off with you now, boy!" His voice was as gruff as Leith had ever heard it, but that voice held few terrors for him now. The youth, however, was thoroughly cowed, and scurried away.

Kurr turned to Leith and slapped him on the leg. "I haven't enjoyed anything as much in a long time," he said. "Pompous fool! In a land of fools! I can understand ordinary folk finding their way here so as to avoid capture or death, but the Watchers made a covenant to resist evil, not to flee from it! No wonder I saw no sign of Watchers in Instruere. They were all hidden in Escaigne!"

Leith had just about caught up with events when the old farmer finished by clapping calloused hands on his young shoulders. "Well, my friend; we are back in business!"

"I have few alternatives, then, than to render you the aid you seek," the sallow-faced man said heavily, and the Elders lined up behind him frowned.

"You have none at all," Kurr corrected him.

"Sixth Rank! You have given me the secret words, so I am forced to believe you. How came you by six ranks in such a place as Firanes?"

Kurr shook his head. "Such arrogance! The world neither begins nor ends here, and many things of importance happen without Instruere being involved. Indeed, you are in danger of being passed by altogether. Nevertheless, I will tell you where I came by my rank. Three ranks I inherited from my father, Lornath of Sivithar; three I earned in forty years' service on the uncouth margins of the world, as you would have it. You yourself, the foremost Watcher in Instruere—sorry, in Escaigne—are only Sixth Rank. Know this: within a morning's ride of my home lives another Watcher, of the Seventh and highest Rank, my teacher; possibly the greatest of our order still alive in Faltha."

"Lornath of Sivithar? Your father?" The face of the Presiding Elder had turned a sickly yellow. "Sivithar on the banks of the Aleinus?"

"You know it? I am surprised! You appear to have spent your life hidden behind cowardly walls, not openly on the bank of the Great River. Sivithar is the place I was born. I am Straux by birth, and a southlander, yet have lived the greater part of my life in the north, and have not regretted it. Indeed, now that I look on the south, I see little to make me regret my father's choice."

Something was wrong with the Presiding Elder. "Lornath of Sivithar is my uncle," he muttered, choking on the words.

Now Kurr's face drained of color. "Your uncle?" The words were pulled with reluctance from his mouth. "Then you—it cannot be! Say it is not!"

"Your name was Kurnath in those days," the sallow-faced man said quietly, and with ill-disguised malice, and took a step back from the old farmer. "Cousin!" He spat the word out. "I never thought to see you again."

"Nor I you," Kurr responded hoarsely. "Your name I remember, but I will not sully my lips by repeating it. A final proof! Hold up your right hand!"

The hand was held up, and all could see the top joints of the third and fourth fingers were missing.

"You should have moved more quickly," was Kurr's only comment, but it was squeezed out from between compressed lips.

"And your aim should have been truer," came the bitter response.

"Had it been, you would not be here."

"Your manners have deteriorated with age," the sallow man said, his voice deep with anger.

"As has your wit."

The others, Company and Eldership alike, gaped in astonishment at this interchange. Clearly, these two knew each other, and neither enjoyed the knowing. What evil chance had thrown them together, and what hope of agreement did they have?

The Presiding Elder smiled then, a worse sight than his frown, as the obvious thought occurred to him. "I remind you of your position here. You are the prisoner, and I am your jailer. I have no doubt the Most High brought you here to provide me with entertainment in my final years, and entertainment I will extract from you."

"And I remind you of your duty as a Watcher, which must override all other claims, including those of revenge. There are witnesses here, Watchers themselves, who are duty-bound to hold you to your oath, should you feel inclined to break it. You may have me imprisoned in Escaigne, but I have you caged in something far stronger."

Mahnum stood. "Enough!" he cried. "This furthers nobody's agenda! Let us reduce this to the essentials. You, Kurr, have claimed assistance from the Watchers, a claim the Elders apparently cannot refuse; while you, the Presiding Elder, wish to refuse the claim. We have therefore reached an impasse. What does your Eldership say?"

"The laws of the Watchers were written for the Sunlands outside, and do not apply to the Escaignian darkness," said one.

"Yet if we abandon all law, what have we left to bring to Instruere save a regime more lawless than that which now holds sway?" another answered him.

"If we do not displace the Council of Faltha, we must resign ourselves to a dark doom!" the sallow-faced Presiding

Elder growled. "Years we have spent plotting our endeavor, and yet at the last you would abandon it all for the sake of a few words from unwelcome strangers!"

"Though not all are strangers to you, at least," said the bald man who had been the Company's original guide. "It is plain that you hold strong grievances against this man, and our rules say that such grievances should be aired and judged by the Eldership. In this fashion we may perhaps discover which of you is blameless in this matter, if either, and therefore which is to be trusted; and so we will decide our course. I would certainly vote as a Watcher myself, and a servant of Watchers, to support Kurnath in his request, even if it means disobedience to the Presiding Elder. But let us hear the stories behind this enmity, and so be guided in making our decision! What say the Eldership?"

The sallow-faced man turned on the bald man with a red gleam in his eye. "You were ever my opponent on the Eldership, and have never overcome the bitterness of my rulership over you. Why should we follow your advice?"

"Because it is good advice," Kurr said firmly. "I at least am prepared to have my case weighed, and I am confident that, even though I will make every effort to be fair, the Elders will decide right is on my side." He turned to his enemy and stared full into his face. "Do you have such confidence? Knowing what I do, you should not."

The Presiding Elder was backed into a corner, and he knew it. Desperately he looked from one face to another, and read that the Eldership had decided upon this course of action. Though he had been challenged, this was still his domain. The thought comforted him. It would simply be a matter of telling the story to his advantage.

*　　*　　*

The Elders met that night with the Company in a small brick-lined room, an annex to the great hall where the Collocation had been held, and there they listened, first to Kurr, then the sallow man.

The old farmer told them of life in Sivithar, of the many children who played by the south bank of the great River Aleinus, and of the hard times that befell them there. For a severe famine took hold in Straux; the crops failed, then failed again; the river shrank from its banks; and traders ceased bringing their goods to market. The people of Sivithar and the surrounding lands saw their prosperity and livelihoods evaporate. Gangs of hungry youths roamed the streets, menaced the already hard-pressed citizens, threatened property and took life. The leader of the foremost gang, Kurr told them, was none other than their Presiding Elder, his own cousin, the black sheep of the family.

Along with many others, Kurr joined one of the vigilante groups raised to counter the depredations of the gangs. Some of these groups, he admitted, were little better than those they opposed, but others maintained at least a semblance of integrity. As the drought and famine pinched in more tightly, the young Kurnath had been forced to learn swordplay, and on occasion defend his life. It had been on one such occasion that he faced the ruthless, unruly gang leader his cousin had become. He wounded him with a slashing blow of his sword as he drove him off.

"Some months after this the rains came," Kurr said, "and the famine ended in Sivithar. Then raiders from the west, out of Mercium and Instruere, came to steal our new-grown crops, for the drought still held in Westrau. Then all the gangs joined forces to repel these men, and for many days we were successful. Yet during the late-night watch they found a way through our defenses, killed many of us, and took the rest prisoner. Ever after it was believed we were betrayed. One of our number sold information to the raiders, enabling them to breach our defenses. This betrayer would have received neither imprisonment nor death as his reward, but riches and a new identity in another town—perhaps the one from where the raiders came. For a long time I believed my cousin perished in Sivithar, but now I learn that it is not so. Yet he was not among the prisoners. Not dead, nor a prisoner. The question I wish to ask him is this. How did he secure his escape?"

The sallow man rose slowly to his feet. Leith could see by the loose folds of skin round his throat that the Presiding Elder was old, at least as old as Kurr, and as the two men faced each other the family resemblance was obvious to all those in the room.

With gentle voice, and a subtlety of speech far beyond that which Kurr could manage, he outlined a story similar to that of the old farmer, but with a reversal of roles. It was Kurnath who headed a marauding band in the river city of Sivithar, and he who resisted him. As for the betrayal, he would not accuse the old farmer of it, but ever after, doubt had lingered in his mind. Why should Lornath have left Straux if not to protect his troublesome son? How could Lornath have afforded the journey north and west to Firanes? And now, beyond all belief Kurnath had returned, and his sins had caught up with him.

"The sentence of death on Kurnath and his gang will stand," said the Presiding Elder, "for it seems to me his new friends are like unto his old; violent and apt to evil. Why else would a Bhrudwan, a sworn enemy of all

Falthans, take up with them? Fellow Elders, it is my belief The Pinion breakout was merely a staged event in
order to allay our suspicions, and to provide an excuse to
have them brought to Escaigne. This man is ready now to
betray us to the Arkhos of Nemohaim and the Council of
Faltha, just as he betrayed Sivithar so many years ago."

He rounded on the bald man. "And you," he said, "you
were the one who brought them here, and for such com-
plicity I remove you from the Eldership." A gasp came
from the Company's guide. "You have barely escaped
sentence of death. Should I find you had knowledge of
their true character, I will extend their sentence to include
you and your family."

"A masterful performance!" Kurr cried bitterly, and
clapped mockingly. "One which does nothing to answer
the questions before us, but has served to rally your un-
derlings to your side." He turned to the knot of Elders.
"Can't you see what he has done? He has sung of his
power, and you skip to his tune without ever questioning
the lyric! Has he picked you for Eldership because of
your special abilities as chattels? For your inability to
construct and hold a single original thought? You are Elders under this man because you have no qualifications as
leaders! Because you are weak sheep who need a strong
shepherd, and the more he strikes you with his staff, the
better you like it! Fools! You have all the responsibility,
but none of the authority; all of the glory, but none of the
power. You are his stooges! Know this: in approving this
sentence of death, you doom Faltha to a slower and more
painful, but no less inevitable death. History will record
that a small group of spineless men were responsible for
the fall of Faltha!"

"Take him away," the sallow man said, and spat upon

the ground. "Take them all away. Let the sentence of death be carried out one day from hence in the Water Chamber. I have spoken."

Last time I follow your advice, Leith thought sourly.

"Well, at least I feel better for having said it," Kurr muttered quietly. It was some time later that day, though none of the Company could tell the exact hour, and the doorway to the small cell in which they sat shackled together was barred by the same two guards who had watched over their quarters. "But perhaps it was not the wisest conversation I have ever conducted."

Politely, no one said anything. They were still trying to come to terms with what they had heard.

"You never told us about any of this," the Haufuth said eventually. "Didn't you think it might have been relevant?"

"What little I remember of my years here and the long journey to Firanes is muddied and confused. Witness how long it took me to recognize Feerik—the Presiding Elder, my cousin—as he is named. Indeed, I'm sure I would be ignorant still had I not mentioned my father's name. Perhaps I should have remained ignorant. It was cruel chance that revealed my mortal enemy to me."

"Do you really hate him so much?" Stella asked.

"If you had seen the hungry faces, and how cynically he and his kind took from them . . . I tell you, I would have slain him cheerfully. Times were very hard. It was all so long ago, forty years and more, and I would gladly have remained unreminded of it. I never would have thought my actions then would cost my friends their lives."

"So now what?" Perdu asked. "We have decided on a course of action, but our way is blocked both by Instruere and by Escaigne."

"I do not have much respect for Escaigne," Farr said. "Their weapons are rudimentary and ill-kept, and their discipline is lax. We should be able to leave whenever we please."

"Success has made you overconfident," Kurr told him. "Where is your weapon? For all their failings, they succeeded in taking your sword from you."

"To my shame," Farr muttered. "The first enemy to do so. At least I surrendered it willingly."

"That won't make it any easier to reclaim," Mahnum commented. "And what chance do we have against Escaigne without our blades?"

"We cannot rely on force," said the Haufuth. "Any sort of conflict will result in the discovery of Escaigne."

"Good," growled Farr. "Let Instruere do our job for us."

"Get our enemies fighting against each other . . ." added Stella.

". . . then in the confusion we could make our escape from the city," the Hermit concluded.

"If only we could get out of these chains," Indrett reminded them.

"Then we can stand on the shores of the Aleinus and watch the whole place burn to the ground!" Perdu declared. The death of Parlevaag was still much on his mind.

"No, no!" cried Hal. "The only winners would be the Bhrudwans."

The Hermit groaned. "How could you possibly object to the destruction of our enemies?" He had tired of this sullen, self-righteous youth some time ago, and resented his role in the Company. One of the Arkhimm, the Five of the Hand! *Can they not see it? They give him a respect he does not deserve. Is it the pity he receives for his disabilities, or something more?* He had heard of such things: a person able to hold others in thrall, aided by divination or the casting of spells. "I do not wish to see anyone die, but we cannot protect everyone, not unless the Hand of God suddenly sprouts a thousand new fingers."

"There are hundreds of innocents in Escaigne. Do you not object to their destruction?"

The blue-robed Hermit shrugged his shoulders. "They will die anyway once the Bhrudwans take the city."

"If we could find a way out of Instruere without betraying Escaigne, would you take it?"

"Of course I would. If there was such a way. Do you know of one?"

Hal shook his head.

"Then I see no alternative."

After further debate the others agreed with the Hermit, with the exception of Hal and the Haufuth. "In a perfect world we would be able to save everyone," Kurr said. "But this world is not perfect, and people have died already on our quest. The Bhrudwans plan to kill far more, and enslave the rest. Even unarmed, we should be more than a match for our guards. Let us await our chance."

"So we escape Escaigne. Then what?" The Haufuth felt uneasy about this. They had a cell door to break through, and Escaignians to avoid, let alone the danger they would be in once they were loose in Instruere. Where was this illogical confidence coming from?

The farmer was firm. "Then we have another problem to solve. Until then, we can do nothing but wait."

Above Instruere twilight took hold, sending a sultry sun scurrying from a reddening sky. Curfew was about to be imposed on a reluctant, uneasy city for yet another night. The Arkhos of Nemohaim could barely control his agitation. An emissary of the Destroyer! Here in the city, flaunting his presence, as though Instruere was already his master's plaything. *Perhaps it is, perhaps it is*, the Arkhos thought as he hurried to the hastily-arranged meeting. Curse this weather! He had never known such a place as this for hot, humid days. He forced his sweaty bulk along the pillared corridor and waited impatiently while the Iron Door was raised. His teeth ground silently of their own accord as he saw the Council members waiting for him, immaculately dressed, and at the head of the table, his own accustomed place, sat the emissary he had only heard about this very afternoon. And here came the Arkhos's first shock.

Deorc!

Tall, raven-haired, square-jawed, fine-fingered, charismatic, with a golden tongue and power resting on his shoulders like a mantle. Deorc, Keeper of Andratan, one of the Destroyer's most trusted servants, recruited by the Bhrudwan high command ten years ago after ruthlessly putting down the bloody Jasweyah rebellion. A black reputation, well deserved. Acutely aware of his disadvantage, and that all eyes were on him, the Arkhos of Nemohaim found a seat between the Arkhoi of Straux and Treika. He longed to straighten out his red robe, or fiddle nervously with his tassels, or give his mind to the question of why his spies had not informed him as to the identity of the emissary. But, exercising the iron self-control that had given him his position, the self-control that seemed so often to have deserted him lately, he did none of these things. For Deorc had the sharpest mind he had ever encountered—save one, it hardly needed to be noted—perhaps overmatching his own. He must concentrate. *They have engineered this deliberately! Someone desires to replace me, and Deorc is in league with them, perhaps with the blessing of the master. I must work fast, find and trap the usurper, expose him to my benefit. Where intelligence fails, cunning and deceit will suffice.* His pigeyes closed to small slits, and rich excitement bubbled through his blood. *A game! A game to the death! A game I will win.*

He took a moment to look around the room at the faces he knew well, the traitors of Faltha, the group named so accurately by the Firanese Trader. Straux. Treika. Vertensia. Favony. Tabul. Firanes. Asgowan, his most loyal servant, whom even the Trader had not known about, the ally he kept secret even from the supposedly all-knowing Destroyer. And finally Haurn, his trump card, a timid, insignificant man bullied into betraying his Sna Vazthan masters the very day the puerile northerners came bearing their tales, and the one who swayed the vote against the loyalists. He looked them all in the eye. Here he received his second shock.

Asgowan!

With a supreme effort the Arkhos of Nemohaim forced himself to stand, and grate out the formal greeting to their guest. "An honor indeed to welcome our benefactor and our master's right hand." The words of the blessing came out like a death-curse. *Try harder! You must not get off-side with this man*, he told himself. *He holds your life in his hands!* Then, as he read the countenance of the Bhrudwan who rose to acknowledge his welcome, he received his third shock.

Without doubt, my death is in his eyes. They mean to replace me.

"Nemohaim," the emissary of the Destroyer said, nodding his head to indicate he should sit. "I regret that I have been kept waiting."

So blunt! So confident in his power! The plans are obviously well laid. Even with this revelation the excitement did not leave him; rather, it increased. He felt his whole body begin to shake with it. *Death is the ultimate experience*, he reminded himself. *It is the only thing that satisfies.*

He spread his hands wide in a gesture of resignation. "I too regret the situation," he said carefully, forcing himself to think only of the moment, to allow his cunning an opportunity to flourish. "Such a chance, that so highly esteemed a guest as yourself should arrive at the precise moment of my triumph. Nevertheless, I postponed the moment to be at your service. I would like to show you something at your earliest convenience, my lord, if you would." That had his interest. He had bought himself some time.

Deorc was displeased. "I come with important news, a message of such moment it could be entrusted to no messenger save me. I have endured months of hard riding and the foul climes of your uncouth land to deliver it to you, and am not pleased I have been accorded such dishonor as being made to wait for the likes of you." His brows closed together under a frowning forehead.

The Arkhos studied Deorc carefully. Outwardly he was just as he remembered from their one encounter on Andratan something over eighteen months ago, when the man from Nemohaim formally pledged his loyalty to the Dark Throne. The Keeper of Andratan had not been a man to trifle with then, and had clearly grown since in some intangible fashion. *I will have one chance only. Wait for the opening, then strike quickly.*

"Even so, you had to wait, and now I am here. If you would care to deliver your message, you can again be on your way, this time out of this hateful land." *There! He should not be the only one to show confidence.*

Deorc's eyes widened, but he said nothing to answer this impertinence. Instead, he spoke the message he had been sent to deliver, each word enunciated clearly, the meaning unmistakable.

"The date draws near when our master will embrace this land with his arms of blessing. The new High Command has proved efficient beyond hope. We are therefore ready sooner than we thought possible." *A clue! A new High Command, perhaps with Deorc at the head?* "I remind you of the position and power that will be yours should you remain faithful—and of the fate that awaits you should you be proved faithless." Did the Arkhos imagine the sidelong glance that Asgowan threw him? "We will march on Faltha within the month. By the turning of next spring our army will stand at your gates, and you will open them for us. The New Age will begin from that date." This was delivered with a brusqueness that told the Arkhos to expect something further.

"But surely you were not sent here to tell us this? Could it not have come through the usual channels?" the Arkhos of Asgowan asked ingenuously.

You've been put up to that speech, Nemohaim thought darkly. *Traitor! I've taught you too well! Yet the pupil is not yet greater than his master. I know you, and you will prove the weak link in this conspiracy.*

"Indeed!" Deorc went on. "I have been sent with a question, and it is for your leader." He turned squarely to the Arkhos of Nemohaim, and to his chagrin the Arkhos felt the sweat start out from his brow. *There is something in his eyes . . . Weakness, weakness! I must show no weakness!*

"Some months ago an expedition was sent to this land in pursuit of a Falthan Trader, one who carried secrets of the war effort and who sought to sell them to loyal Falthans, if he could find any." He sneered, leaving them all in no doubt about his view of traitors. "Four warriors of the Order of *Magdhi Dasht*, our most potent fighters, were sent, and should have recaptured their quarry without difficulty or delay. Yet we have heard no further report of them—save that one of them stood in this chamber only a few days ago." He gathered himself, then pounced. "Is this so?" he snapped.

Betrayed! Undoubtedly he should have passed on the information to Andratan, but he had hoped to capture and question this renegade himself, thereby gaining valuable information and increasing his prestige with the master. But his plan had failed. The accursed northerners had taken the Bhrudwan out from under his nose, and badly tweaked it in the process. Since then he had been consumed with revenge, a serious mistake, he could see that now. *Perhaps not fatal.* He looked at Asgowan, who could not keep the satisfied smirk from disfiguring his fetid face. *Now* that *is a fatal mistake.*

"It is indeed so, my lord," the Arkhos replied, seemingly unabashed. "And it would be interesting to be told how Andratan learned of something I withheld." He stared directly at Asgowan then, and was rewarded with a look of fear. *I will remember that look and savor it, should these be my last hours.* "It is in fact this matter that is the subject of my triumph. I merely wished to tie up all loose ends before I shared it with my lord. Your arrival in Instruere provides me with the opportunity to give you a priceless gift, one which I know will appeal to a man of your tastes."

Yes, you understand that. I know what you do in secret on your foul island; I made it my business to know. You won't be able to resist what I will offer you. The Arkhos allowed himself a single moment's relief. For the first time since the meeting started he saw a chance, and without further consideration he threw himself at that chance. In order to succeed, he had to make Deorc believe he had a plan, and was confident of success.

"Come with me now, my lord, if it is answers you seek; yes, and the rest of you can come also, though I know there are those among you who plot my downfall. Fools! Do you think I would not prepare against you? Come to The Pinion with me, all of you, and help me put the question to a special guest I have invited there."

"The Pinion, ah, The Pinion!" Deorc said, as though to himself, and he flexed his long-boned fingers. "Long have I desired to see it, even though rumors make it only a pale shadow of the dungeons on Andratan. I would have asked for a tour, even if you had not made this request. Why not, indeed? We will go there now."

You fool! Barely can you restrain your desire. So the Destroyer ensnared you, the whisper on Andratan said, and so I ensnare you. In the heat of your desire you will believe anything I tell you.

"Very well," the Arkhos said placidly. "I will lead the way. Follow us, fellow Councillors, I insist." With that he heaved himself to his feet and left the chamber, knowing he would be followed.

*   *   *

Time passed slowly as the Company waited for their chance. Phemanderac called successfully for his harp, having convinced the guards of its harmlessness, and now sat in one corner tuning it. One or two of the Company sat silent, engrossed in their own thoughts and reflections, but amongst the others a debate was in progress.

"Let's assume our mission was of at least some importance to the Most High," Perdu said. It was he who had begun this discussion.

"Let's first assume he exists!" the Haufuth countered. *A dream is only a dream.*

"That's what I'm talking about," Perdu persisted. "If he exists, you would think he would be interested in the welfare of his people, the descendants of the First Men. Therefore he would be concerned with our mission to warn Faltha. Right so far?"

The others nodded.

"Then why does he not lift us out of this prison? Why indeed allow us to fall into this trap? He is renowned in your legends as a performer of miracles, so where are they?"

"We could do with a miracle now," Indrett agreed.

"In my view, a god who does not demonstrate supernatural ability is no god at all, merely a human construction," the Haufuth said firmly. "We have seen no miracles thus far, just the result of honest endeavor coupled with a little luck; therefore, the Most High is merely wishful thinking."

Hal spoke up. "Have you considered the cost of miracles?" he asked.

"The cost of miracles? What cost?" they wanted to know.

"For every direct intervention in the world of humans, the Most High loses an opportunity to enrich our lives," he said. "The most important things that happen on this earth, the things that really count, are the choices we make. The simple, honest endeavors of ordinary people trying to cope with the bigness of life enables true beauty of character to form within them. No miracle can replicate that. If the Most High met every crisis with a miracle, our characters would remain stunted and childlike, and the world would be robbed of its chief beauty."

"Yet at least people would live," the Haufuth said, dismissing the lecture. "What good are people with true beauty of character if they are about to die?"

"In many cases that beauty is enhanced by death faced courageously, or embraced for the sake of a friend," Hal responded. "Yet death does not automatically follow when the Most High allows events to run their course."

"I don't want miracles," Leith said suddenly, taking them by surprise. They had thought him asleep. "I don't want magic. Or, at least, what I want is magic that doesn't really matter, that doesn't change things. I'm tired of being manipulated by things like prophecies."

"Why so afraid of the Realm of Fire?" the Hermit asked. "Does it interfere with your control over things? Too wild and unpredictable?"

"Look at prophecy. The day we came to Bandits' Cave you gave me two 'words,' as you called them. The first one came true. So did the two signs you gave me to confirm your words. It made me feel like someone else was in control of my life. It seemed like you were showing off your power."

"So they came true, did they? To be honest, I can't remember what they were."

Leith felt somewhat deflated. "The first was an important clue in our escape from Adunlok and the Widuz. Your two signs were just a dunking in a frozen pond and a secret never shared. The second prophecy hasn't yet come to pass."

"So you wouldn't listen to any more prophecies?"

"I didn't say that," Leith protested.

"You can't have it both ways," the Hermit said. "Any use of the Fire, either good or bad, comes with a claim on the life of those practicing it and those benefiting from it. The Fire gives you control over things, but the source of the Fire gains control over you. Miracles open you to the miraculous."

"So I feel controlled because I am being controlled?"

"Well . . . let us say you sense the existence of powers far greater than yours, and you feel crowded out."

"So do we follow the prophecy or not?" Farr asked. "I thought we decided all this. I don't care where our guidance comes from, what I want is to get on with it. Too much talk, not enough action!"

"We follow the prophecy," Kurr said. "And, if the Hermit is right, we fall under its spell."

"If falling under a non-existent spell is the worst of our fears, then perhaps things are looking up," said the Haufuth.

"Things will look up once we're out of this foul city," said Kurr.

"Very nice," said Deorc. His tongue clicked like a businessman ticking off an inventory. "A work of true beauty."

"Thank you," said the Arkhos of Nemohaim. He could sense the excitement of The Pinion's central chamber, but forced himself to keep his wits about him. As the Bhrud-wan became ever more engrossed in the undoubted attractions of this place, the Arkhos's mind raced constantly, in search of ways to press home his advantage.

"What's this one for?" the Keeper of Andratan asked his host. His hand rested on a small table with a vise-like apparatus attached to one end.

"That's one of mine," the Arkhos said proudly.

"How does it work?"

"The hands go here," said the Arkhos, indicating the metal apparatus. "The fingers are spread apart—like this. Would you put your hand here?"

Deorc keenly complied.

"Now, if I tighten these screws—not too tight? Good—the hand is held firmly. Each screw moves independently, so I can force the fingers apart—thus."

"Very nice." The Keeper winced as the screws were wound tighter.

"And if I pull this lever, the whole mechanism is released, and you can slide your fingers out. What do you think?"

"How far apart can the fingers be forced?" Deorc flexed his own fingers, and the Arkhos was surprised to see a dreamy look in his eyes.

"Four inches apart is standard, lord."

"Good. Order one of these made for me. I will collect it when I am here next, in the vanguard of the Bhrudwan army."

The Arkhos nodded.

"By the way, these instruments are far too clean."

"Yes, my lord."

"The most important weapon of torture is fear, not pain. Your goal is to make them think they are quite properly your plaything; forgotten, abandoned, beyond rescue, beyond help. The pain is only an added bonus." He licked his lips.

"We have many other instruments . . ."

"Yes, yes. I have seen them. No time for that now. Show me the prisoner."

Through the chamber they strode, followed by the other Arkhoi. In the far corner a young man, chained to the cold stone wall, cowered away from his captors. *Doesn't look like he'll give us much sport*, thought the Arkhos. *Pity: I need as large a distraction as possible*.

The Arkhos and the Bhrudwan went through with the game. "How long has he been down here?" asked Deorc.

"Not long, a day or so."

"Untouched?"

The Arkhos nodded. "He appears to be a simpleton. Someone from Escaigne has erred badly in sending this boy into Instruere. Finally we may learn the location of our encmy."

"What shall we start with?" With a wave of the hand Deorc indicated the chamber and the instruments contained therein.

"You choose, my lord."

"Good," the Bhrudwan said. "This is my favorite," he said after some consideration, indicating a plain, unadorned bench. "Do you have the gauze?"

"Of course, lord," the Arkhos replied. Personally, he thought the Water Funnel a little tame. As though his mind had been read, the Keeper of Andratan turned to the captive. "All I want to do is to give you a drink of water. A nice long drink of water." Somehow, in the saying of those few words, he communicated such menace that the prisoner's face drained of color.

"Watch what I do. Listen to what I say," he said to the

Arkhos. "I'll have him begging for mercy long before the first drink. Pass me the gauze. I want to explain how this works to our guest."

As the unfortunate young man was unchained, the Arkhos noticed the hands of the Bhrudwan. They were trembling.

Behind the two dark figures stood the rest of the Arkhoi, some bored, others horrified by what they were hearing and seeing in this cruel place. Rhynn, Arkhos of Asgowan, tried not to look. He hated this place and was only too aware of what they were about to see, having been down here once before at the invitation of the Arkhos of Nemohaim. But he had been given no choice. To have refused this trip, his instincts told him, would have put himself and his State at a great disadvantage with respect to the Council. Personally, he could see his influence with the Council of Faltha waning to the point of uselessness.

"Look carefully at the gauze. It's a fine metal mesh, with small hooks that slide easily down the throat, but catch against the skin, making it impossible to draw out without tearing tissue away with it. You can drink with the gauze in your throat, but you can't eat. Now, the longer you delay telling us what we want to know, the more we'll give you to drink, and the further the gauze will be forced down your throat. Nod if you understand what I mean."

The captive, paralyzed with fear, made no move. Deorc took the razor-sharp gauze and held it against the boy's thigh.

"Then let me assist your understanding."

With a flick of his wrist Deorc dragged the gauze across the pale, quivering skin. The boy shrieked. His torturer held a ragged, streaming strip of flesh close to the captive's face.

"Do you understand now?" he asked in a soft voice. This time the boy nodded vigorously.

As the Arkhos of Nemohaim had feared, the entertainment was all too brief—or, from Rhynn's perspective, mercifully short. The Bhrudwan's art, though appreciated by many in the chamber, was lost on him. The captive's mouth was forced open, and the gauze placed inside. Then water was poured down the throat, forcing the gauze down with it. The Bhrudwan was immensely skillful, keeping up an almost careless chatter while making sure the victim was able to answer questions. And beg for mercy, Rhynn noted. The Bhrudwan seemed to like that best.

This is what I risk if I betray the Council, Rhynn thought. *Yet how can I choose otherwise, now that the Council has accepted the authority of this monstrous man?*

"Escaigne. Where is Escaigne?" The questioning was relentless. "Pass me the funnel. If the gauze goes much further down we won't be able to retrieve it, and your life will be measured in days; long, messy, agonizing days you'll spend coughing up your own tissue . . . What did he say?"

"Entangled, my lord," said one of the guards.

"I wonder what that means?" The Bhrudwan scratched his head, puzzled.

The Arkhos of Nemohaim leaned across the convulsing form strapped to the table. "I think I know," he said, struggling to keep his voice level. "We are about to remove a major impediment to the plans of your master. Escaigne is entangled, as he says: entangled in Instruere. I have some more questions for our friend on the table, but he will tell us where in Instruere the Escaignians are hidden. A decade of deception is about to come to an end."

CHAPTER 8

THE WATER CHAMBER

"TIME PASSES SLOWLY," KURR OBSERVED. A sense of failure did battle in his heart with a growing fear, prompting his morose words.

Phemanderac laughed thinly. "Although if we are to die, it does not pass slowly enough."

"Whatever the outcome, I'll be glad to be rid of this loathsome city."

"It's not that bad! Where else can you find the excitement of the market?"

"The market was a surprise," Perdu admitted. "We don't have costermongers or fish-splitters on Myrvidda. We don't have The Pinion, either, and our people don't hide in fear from each other."

"We have long told stories of Fenni cruelty," Farr said pointedly. "This should not be strange to you."

"The Fenni deal harshly, but they deal swiftly and justly," he replied. "We hold no prisoners, we seldom engage in torture, and we defend our own with a passion."

"Do you miss them?"

"Of course I do," Perdu said softly. "Some of them especially. Don't you miss the Vinkullen?"

"I do," Farr replied, "but I miss the Great Wood more,

and the laughter of the Fodhram; and my brother most of all." He sighed. "I, too, want out of this repellent place."

"I like the city," Stella said. "There is nothing about our village that I miss, nothing at all."

"Not even your parents?" Hal wanted to know.

"Especially not them," the young woman said with distaste. "They were happy to sacrifice me to that brute Druin. I'm glad we left Loulea."

"Even if we die here?"

"Yes, Hal," she said emphatically. "Better quick death than slow death."

"You didn't know Druin as well as you thought," the cripple insisted.

"I knew him better than I wanted to," she replied acidly.

"It would be foolish to judge the city by the behavior of some of its leaders," said Indrett. "I lived in a city once, a fair city, the city of a king; corrupt at the core, but still a place of beauty. I loved Rammr. Instruere reminds me of it. Beautiful and deadly."

"Cities are peculiar places," Phemanderac offered. "Wherever people gather, great potential exists for good or for evil. Usually people just gravitate somewhere between those potentials, to mediocrity. Instruere was once a great city in the Golden Age of the First Men, with vision and high ideals; now, after centuries of mediocrity, it tends to evil. But do not judge her by today's face. If legend in any way reflects the truth, she was once the bastion of all that was worthy. She is worth saving."

"Perhaps any city should best be judged by people like Foilzie," the Haufuth said.

"What happened to her?" Leith asked. "One moment she was with us; the next she was taken away."

"I suspect the bald man had something to do with that.

They were friends, acquaintances from the past. He may have used his influence to save her from our fate."

"And us? Who will save us from our fate?"

"By attempting the quest, we have already avoided the worst fate," Hal said. "Anything more is a bonus."

"Well, I'm keen to earn as large a bonus as possible," Kurr said, inwardly shaking his head at the crippled boy's triteness. How could any of them have mistaken the lad's words for wisdom? "Perhaps our guards know something that could help us."

"Perhaps," Leith agreed, keeping his voice low. He hailed the guards, who sat at the entrance to their small room. The closer guard, an older man with a clump of gray hair, opened the door and came over to them.

"What can you tell us about the Water Chamber?" Kurr asked him.

"I am sorry, friend; I do not have the stomach for this business," he responded, shaking his head. "Better you remain ignorant of it. I voted for your freedom. I do not agree that men advocating freedom from evil should imprison others."

"Then set us free," Farr whispered, his voice intense. "It is within your power to do so."

"It is not," came his reply in guarded undertones. "My fellow guard is most keen to see your deaths, and keeps careful watch on me. And would you have me break my Watcher's Oath, and betray those who outrank me?"

"You break your oath by keeping us imprisoned," Kurr said, but he heard the truth in the guard's words. No Watcher would disobey the direct orders of a Watcher of the Sixth Rank who had been set over him.

"I can tell you about the Water Chamber." The younger guard sauntered over to them, a smirk on his wide face.

Another filled with a sense of his own importance, Kurr reflected. *How did the Watchers of Instruere stoop to such a state? And how did we in Firanes—including farsighted Kroptur—remain ignorant of it? Such information would have been of great benefit to us.*

"You don't realize the honor you are being given," the man said. "The Water Chamber has been used only three times since the foundation of Escaigne."

"Well, that makes me feel much better," Farr said quietly. The sense of menace coming from the mountain man caused the old farmer to catch his breath.

"I've been there," said the guard. "Out by the Docks. The Water Chamber is an old warehouse with a stone floor, long abandoned as the Great River silted and rose. Now the good citizens of Instruere flush their sewers into it. Oh, yes!" he crowed at their cries of dismay. "Because the Aleinus River is tidal at least a hundred miles above its mouth, the city can't just discharge its waste straight into it. Instead the effluent gathers in the Water Chamber, and is flushed out on the outgoing tide. Along with anyone placed there by Escaigne."

"Excellent!" Farr said. The guard nodded earnestly.

"So why do the Elders wait until tomorrow before showing us the Water Chamber?" Kurr asked.

"Isn't it obvious?" the guard said scornfully. "The sewers are fuller in the evenings. Not enough to drown you. Neap tide tonight. Stronger tide tomorrow. Better for flushing out the city's wastes. Well, perhaps 'better' isn't the word you people would use!" And he turned his back on the northerners, chuckling at his own joke.

"A most enjoyable evening," the Keeper of Andratan drawled. "I never thought to find such sophistication in the land of the First Men. You must come to Andratan some time—as my guest, of course."

"I am pleased our humble facilities were to your satisfaction, my lord," the Arkhos of Nemohaim replied. "We have much yet to learn from skilled and experienced operators such as yourself. I hope we can make time for this when Faltha becomes a Bhrudwan province." And he bade the unpleasant Bhrudwan a good night.

The sentiment was genuine. In spite of himself, he was impressed by Deorc's ability to extract information from the prisoner. The Bhrudwan seemed to know exactly how much terror to instill while not damaging him beyond his ability to be useful. By the end the prisoner had begged, and told them all they needed to know, including the exact location of every part of Escaigne he knew, and something even more valuable . . .

The decade-long mystery is solved, the Arkhos thought as he congratulated himself. For ten years the rulers of Instruere had tried to find this Escaigne, presuming it to be a rebel fortress somewhere in Straux or Deuverre. Time and again the treasures of Instruere had been raided, important people assassinated and plans sabotaged as though the perpetrators knew the city intimately. Few had been caught, and none had talked even under the most extreme form of questioning. Until now. The Arkhos of Nemohaim could hardly credit his good fortune.

The captive was apprehended by the guard in a granary, trying to steal grain. He claimed to be a petty thief, but none of the Arkhos's contacts knew of him. Moreover, the evidence suggested he was but one of a large, organized group, yet all the organized crime in Instruere paid a percentage of their profits to the Council. So to which group did this man belong? That had set the Arkhos thinking, and he had questioned the simpleton himself. He had trapped the captive into confessing he was from Escaigne. That was the breakthrough.

And now it all made sense. The lightning raids, the intimate knowledge, their ability to escape without being caught by the guards manning the bridges—all explained by the clue offered by the captive. Entangled. Simply the modern rendering of Escaigne. Escaigne was entangled with Instruere, hidden in pockets within the city, and Deorc had persuaded the prisoner to give them the location of the major enclaves. It would be a simple matter to place these locations under observation, the Escaignians unwittingly leading their enemies to those who remained undisclosed. And their prisoner had told them something else, the real point of the spear, a connection between a woman of Escaigne and a certain company of northerners, three of whom had been involved in the sack of The Pinion. A group that included the Bhrudwan warrior, who would become the Arkhos's gift to the Keeper of Andratan.

Deorc had enjoyed his entertainment immensely, that was clear, and had accepted the Arkhos's invitation to observe the conquest of Escaigne and the capture of the northerners. But there was a more pressing matter, and now, alone in the sumptuous surroundings of his private chambers, the Arkhos of Nemohaim recalled it with smug satisfaction. As the prisoner confessed, betraying Escaigne and the Company, the Arkhos of Asgowan tried to leave the chamber unnoticed. He didn't have the stomach for it, the weak fool. But the Arkhos of Nemohaim had been watching him, waiting for the moment of weakness, and in that moment he pounced.

"This is the man who informed on me!" he had cried, pointing to the thin, orange-robed figure as he sought to leave the chamber unobserved. "This is the one who accused me of betraying our masters! Bring him to me!"

He timed it perfectly. Rather than sating Deorc's appetite, the Escaignian prisoner had merely whetted it. It took only a suggestion on his part for the Keeper of Andratan to order the white-faced traitor from Asgowan to be bound and delivered up to him, for his pleasure. The other Arkhoi, too afraid to leave the chamber, watched as it was demonstrated to them where the real power in Faltha lay. The Arkhos of Nemohaim had not known where to look, it had all been so heady: at Asgowan as he screamed in tortured agony while being slowly torn apart; at his fellow collaborators as they watched with varying degrees of fear and horror; or at Deorc and the way in which his very soul fed on the suffering and torment. Such single-mindedness. Ah, Deorc and he could be a great force together, if things were different.

Afterwards he had ordered Saraskar imprisoned—a delicacy to be saved for a later date, or even to be presented to his master when he came to claim the city—and took a moment to gloat over the broken body of Asgowan, then left the chamber with Deorc. He summoned the Captain of the Guard, issued the surprised fellow some very detailed orders, then settled back to relax with the Keeper of Andratan before retiring. *A most satisfying evening*, he thought. *Triumph rises out of the ashes of disaster*.

"Something is amiss," Kurr announced as the Company gathered for their evening meal. That afternoon a discussion had taken place in the next room. According to the little Kurr could hear as he stood balanced on the shoulders of Farr and Achtal, attempting to get as close as possible to the small open space near the ceiling, there had been a meeting some time after the midday meal, held in the Collocation hall. Someone's nephew had apparently been taken prisoner, even though it was well known that sending him into the city at all was a grave risk. Well known to everybody, apparently, except the Elders, who had been so preoccupied with their prisoners they had not known about the boy's excursion to the granaries. He had been taken to The Pinion, and everyone knew what that meant.

Kurr had heard little of the remainder of the conversation, which came to an end when some sort of commander, perhaps one of the Elders, came into the room and barked orders. Most of this was unintelligible, except for the ending: "Prepare for Chance Three." Chance Three, the old farmer told them, was the traditional Watcher signal for flight.

"Flight? What is happening?" The Company gathered close around the old man, trying to understand this riddle.

"It seems obvious to me," the Hermit said. "They are afraid the captive will betray them."

"I think the Hermit has read the riddle correctly," said Mahnum. "Escaigne expects discovery, and is preparing to flee Instruere."

"Will they take us with them?" Stella asked.

"I doubt it," Indrett replied. "More likely, they will first dispose of us as they have planned."

"So we should be ready to act instantly."

"Yes," Kurr said gravely. "But our chances of success are diminished as the Escaignians become ever more vigilant."

"The chance was never very great," said the Haufuth.

"Escaigne has haunted us far too long," the Arkhos bayed at his troops. "Robbed your houses, stolen your treasures, bled this Great City dry. Escaigne is the reason our city is but a shadow of herself. Escaigne is the reason we have been weak. You have observed them moving among us, without knowing who they really are, and all their foul nests are now laid bare to your blades. They are defenseless before the power of your arm! Destroy them now, and you restore Instruere to her place as the mighty Power of Faltha. Root them out, ruthlessly and without mercy, and do not allow pity to weaken your hand. Men, women and children of this foul, treacherous society need to be cut out from among us. Raise your swords as a sign of your loyalty!"

With a great cry the massed Instruian guards drew their swords and thrust them skywards. *The loyalty of fools*, the Arkhos observed to himself. *They do the work of Bhrudwo, and will be rewarded by the curved blades of the Bhrudwans—after they have watched the sack of their beloved city and seen their loved ones enslaved.* His dark inner voice was content with this thought, and the expectation of finally dealing with Escaigne—and the Company from the north.

"I don't like the idea of killing fellow Instruians," said one guard at the back of the great throng as he held his sword aloft.

"Neither do I, my friend; and neither do most of the guard," said his companion. "But will you be the one to walk away and make yourself an example of disloyalty, or will I? You know this pig's reputation."

Both the guards shuddered, and shouted their support for the Arkhos of Nemohaim with renewed gusto.

The Company's last day in Escaigne was just like the first, beginning with a breakfast of bread and fruit. They were left to themselves: no one interfered with them, though the swords of the guards made it clear they were not free to leave their room, save for the necessary short trips to make their ablutions.

They had been patient, trusting that an opportunity would present itself; but the hours had passed one by one without a single chance.

What they had been waiting for, none of them was sure. Some chance—perhaps when both guards were in the room at once—to overwhelm them without giving a warning to Escaigne. Their guards, however, had been careful. Now there was no more time to be patient. Today was the day of their execution. Today was the day to take risks if they wanted to live.

"Wait just a little longer," Phemanderac argued. "It won't make any difference whether we try it now or later this afternoon. In the meantime anything could happen."

Farr could stand no more. "We have waited far too long already! At any time they could come for us. Then we will have more than two guards to contend with."

"But the guard said they have to wait until after high tide," the philosopher said. "According to my reckoning, that will be later tonight."

Leith sat in a corner of the room, toying with a piece of an orange. He had never seen an orange until he worked in the market. Less than six weeks ago. He shook his head: he was having trouble keeping his mind clear.

Unexpectedly, Stella came over and sat beside him. She had spoken little to him during their confinement; but he had seen, or imagined he had seen, her eyes on him from time to time and a strange expression on her face. He despaired of ever understanding girls, especially Stella, and had long given up wondering what he had done wrong. If this journey had taught him anything, it had taught him to hold his tongue when she was about. But today might be their last day, so what did it matter?

When Leith could endure the silence no longer, he asked: "Have you had breakfast?"

"No—well, yes," she said. "At least, I ate some bread. But not the fruit. I hate fruit."

"Do you?" he said. "I've eaten all mine. Do you want my bread? I haven't eaten any of my bread."

"Thank you," she said, and for a time there was silence again as Stella chewed on the crusty bread. *I can't believe this*, Leith thought. *Possibly the last morning of my life, and I'm consumed with anxiety about what I am going to say to Stella. Was there ever a bigger fool?*

"Do you think we will get out of this?" she asked him. "After everything we've been through together, this seems an awful way for things to finish."

"I hope they let us go," he said to her. "There are a few people back in Loulea I wish could hear our story."

"All the people that mean anything to me are here in this room," she said to him. Her face wore that strange expression again. She seemed to be wanting him to understand something.

Leith shrugged. "The Company has been through a great deal," he said. "I can't imagine it is all going to end here. There is still so much to do."

"That's what you said on the night of the Collocation," she said. "I've never heard you speak like that. Except perhaps that night we spent together on the ice. Remember that night?"

Leith grimaced and shook his head. "I don't know what came over me," he said.

Stella bit her lip. "Whatever it was, I liked it. So strong, so courageous."

Oh. Leith acted as though he hadn't heard. *No, that wasn't me, I'm hearing voices.* But he could not say the words, not to a girl whose drunken brother heard voices even while sober. He couldn't speak, and sat there dumbly as the moment passed. Her face closed up, a knife in his chest.

"Did you really have a dream that night in the basement?" he asked her suddenly.

"Yes," she whispered, and he could see in her eyes that she told the truth, and the truth meant a great deal to her. Whatever happened to her that night had affected her powerfully.

"Yes," she repeated. "It was more than a dream. I was really there, really hearing them. I know they said what I heard."

"Really where? What was said? Who said it?"

So, shyly at first, she told him about her vision. And as she spoke she clearly relived it, Leith could tell: every word, every nuance, as though the dream had taken up residence inside her head. Leith could feel the power of it, and could imagine how it must have worked on her. Tears formed in her eyes, and in his; and she saw them and knew he was not as hard, as closed as he seemed.

"I've not been honest with you," she said. "Deep down I do miss my home, and my parents, and everyone, even Druin. I don't want to miss them, but I do. Perhaps all the more since I learned how to love on our journey."

She means Wira, Leith thought, and his chest tightened. Her face seemed to be telling him something else, willing him to hear the words she could not say.

"I also had a dream," he said, pushing through his hurt. "Would it be all right—I mean, would you mind—if I told you about it?"

*   *   *

The Haufuth glanced over to where Leith and Stella sat, engaged in animated conversation. "Good to see them talking," he said.

"Mmmm," Kurr replied, swallowing the last of his bread. "About time. They've avoided each other ever since this started."

"You were young once. Don't you remember what it was like?"

"No," the old farmer said sadly. "I spent most of my youth trying to survive in Sivithar."

"They're sharing the secrets of their hearts," Phemanderac said. "There is danger in such talk. Sharing intimacy builds intimacy."

"They're young. What's wrong with that?" the Haufuth wanted to know.

"We need as few complications as possible on a journey like this one," came his reply.

"Then we certainly could have done without Escaigne," Kurr observed wryly.

Leith told Stella of his dream and what it meant to him, and did not attempt to keep the feeling out of his voice as he spoke. For a time he forgot about the girl at his side, as he saw again the solidity of the vision he had been given.

She heard the words and saw the dream with him, but most importantly felt the passion; and she knew beyond doubt he was capable of deep feelings, of giving and receiving love.

"Leith," she said, and her use of his name thrilled him to the bone. "I want to tell you something." She pushed her hair back from her temple in the way she always did, and to the boy from Loulea she appeared altogether lovely.

He looked into her eyes, her deep dark eyes. He knew what she was about to say.

He held his breath.

At that moment the door opened with a stunning crash, and people armed with swords burst into the room.

"So you believe you will be executed tonight?" cried the younger of their two guards. "I heard your talk, you know. Your reckoning is wrong. Did you idiots think you could outwit the Watchers? We heard what passes for your plans. They caused much mirth in Escaigne. We prepare to once again outwit the Instruian Guard. Did you think we would be distracted by a group of people such as you?"

The Company sat speechless.

"The tide comes in twice a day," the young man continued, no longer concealing the smile. "Did you forget that? It comes in this evening, yes, but it also comes in this morning. This evening would have been better, but this morning will do. Now stand and follow me. You have an appointment with the river."

Other men strode into the room, a dozen or more filling all the available space. Their faces swam in front of Leith's eyes. He seemed to have lost the strength in his legs. His eyes sought Stella's, desperate to explore the unspoken bond between them, but she had already been hauled to her feet and was being shepherded towards the door. Ashamed of his weakness, he allowed himself to be unfettered, then hauled himself up by sheer willpower and forced his overwhelmed and unwilling body to follow the others.

Out into the main room they went, where they were

divided into small groups by their captors. The Escaignians appeared agitated, anxious and in a hurry. Those at
the rear, including Leith, Kurr and the Haufuth, were
roughly handled as a consequence. Ahead, a frustrated
guard pushed Hal against a wall. As Leith watched, the
guard rammed a fist into his brother's stomach. Hal stifled a cry, but Leith did not. He tried to go to Hal's aid,
but was prevented by the guards keeping watch over him.
To his relief Stella threw herself at the bully, clutching at
his arm. Leith lost sight of her for a moment, then caught
a glimpse of her and Hal being taken through a door. He
saw nothing of the others.

"They've divided us up," Kurr growled. "I didn't expect that."

The Haufuth had the answer. "They need to get us
through Instruere undetected."

"There's more to it than that," argued the old farmer.
"Escaigne is under some sort of pressure. This is Chance
Three: they have been betrayed. Look! These people
carry their possessions with them. Over there, see that
family? And there!"

"Escaigne is being evacuated," the Haufuth agreed.

Through the door they were herded, and Escaigne closed
behind them. Ahead, the rest of the Company had already
disappeared out into the city, but the last three members of
the Company did not immediately follow them. The seconds lengthened into minutes, and still they waited. Finally
their guards were given the signal they sought, and Leith
and the others were taken out into the daylight.

The morning was heavily overcast with a strong sea
breeze driving in a thick drizzle, but the light was sufficient
to pain their eyes after the days in Escaigne. Heavy cloaks
would have afforded them more comfort, but since the

night of the Collocation the Company retained only the clothes they wore. Not only their weapons but their spare clothes, their money and all their other possessions were gone. Even Wisent the aurochs was beyond their reach.

The city seemed on edge this grim morning. A few people—far fewer than one would expect on any normal morning in the city—scurried this way and that, not risking prolonged exposure to the rain. Or maybe to the eyes that might be out on the street. There was no sign of the other members of the Company, and the old farmer began to suspect they were being taken to the Water Chamber by different routes in order to avoid detection. Neither could Kurr see any evidence of the Instruian Guard. Perhaps Escaigne had taken alarm unnecessarily, and there had been no betrayal after all.

The Arkhos of Nemohaim fumed with rage. Anyone with sense kept away from him. Servants with the misfortune to be summoned by the Arkhos performed their duties quickly and silently, each praying his or her performance would satisfy. Even Deorc, the Keeper of Andratan, was impressed by the sheer extravagance of the Falthan's towering anger. Fortunately for everyone concerned Deorc did not discern he was the subject of the Arkhos's rage. In this, the blackest of moods, when the dark voices took him and rationality faded into the background, the Arkhos was unable to muster up enough control to express his thoughts.

The overrated, meddling fool! The spies he set the previous evening told him Escaigne had been alerted, so he had prepared his plans, arranged his men and issued his orders, yet Deorc frustrated him at every turn, countermanded his orders, confused his men, tried his patience.

Then when reports flooded in, all with the same message—the Escaignians were coming out into the city—
the Arkhos sought to regain the upper hand in this
contest of wills by delaying his strike. He sent no signal
to his forces. No attempt was made to capture the Escaignians, to cut them off, or even to follow them. "Let
them go a while longer," he said, taking a gamble, a risk
calculated to impress upon the Bhrudwan his coolness
under pressure. "Let all the rats emerge from their holes
before we pounce. They will walk into our traps. Have
patience," he assured the impatient Deorc. But they had
not walked into the traps. With synchronized suddenness
the various groups of Escaignians around the city, all
under observation at a distance by the Instruian Guard,
simply disappeared.

"My master will hear about this," Deorc gloated. "If
you cannot redeem this situation quickly," the Keeper of
Andratan told him, "it may be me who replaces you. It
may be me who extinguishes you."

The Arkhos put a brave face on it, but he had been seriously compromised by the day's events. It galled him to
have been so publicly humiliated. He knew that unless
the situation was recovered quickly and spectacularly his
life would be miserable or short, or most likely both. But
what rankled most was he had been showing off in front
of this poseur, this dandy. Of course he should have ordered the attack earlier, but by delaying it as long as
possible he had hoped to dazzle the Bhrudwan. It was
Deorc's fault. He, not the Arkhos, should be made to pay
for this. And deep in the back of his mind the suspicion
began to form that the thin, foppish man had outwitted
him. After all, the Keeper of Andratan had made the long
journey from his castle in order to place his own man, As-

gowan, at the head of the Falthan Council. He had underestimated this man's capacity for politics.

As the two great men contended in thought, their captains willed them simply to make a decision. Every moment they delayed afforded the Escaignians longer to make good their escape, and the guard fretted with anxiety, failing to understand the circumstances that paralyzed them. In two instances local captains took matters into their own hands and captured a number of Escaignians, though the leaders eluded them. The other, more disciplined captains saw little or no action that morning.

The Escaignians had not been caught without a plan. It had been obvious to their leaders ever since the initial establishment of the rebel enclave that their existence depended entirely upon secrecy, and at some stage in their history they would be discovered or betrayed. So huge resources and effort were expended in preparing a parallel Escaigne, places of refuge in Instruere that not even the ordinary citizens of Escaigne knew about. Some were in the upper floors of tall tenement buildings, others in forgotten corners of warehouses, still others under the city in discarded sewers or old hiding places, legacies of the Bhrudwan occupation. As soon as news of their betrayal came to the Escaignian Eldership the long-laid plan was put into action. Provisions and possessions were transferred to the new hideaways, and gradually people were also moved. Though aware of the watch maintained by the Instruian Guard, they trusted their skills, long in the developing, in avoiding detection. Even with all of this, much work had still to be done when the guard moved in early on this bleak morning, catching Escaigne underprepared. For a time their situation was desperate, but for some unfathomable reason the guard did not press home their advantage and they were able to complete the move to the new Escaigne right under the noses of their enemies. For a while this would be seen as a triumph, but in reality their time was short. The days of Escaigne were numbered, as the Elders well understood. The most important secret, the concealment of Escaigne within Instruere, was now a known fact. Soon the guard would be assigned the task of searching every corner of every building in the vast city. It was time for Escaigne to take the offensive.

And that was according to plan.

Leith kept his mind from thinking very far ahead, concentrating instead on what happened around him. For a time he wondered how the Escaignians were going to get them through the walls of Instruere. After all, the sole gate to the Docks, where this Water Chamber waited for them, would undoubtedly be heavily guarded. Had he been feeling more himself he might have laughed at the coincidence which saw them use the same small gate he himself had used to get the Company into Instruere. If Kurr or the Haufuth remembered the gate they made no sign.

The guards led them around the wall for at least half an hour. Here, outside the city to the west, the air was markedly colder and the chilly gray rain pinned them to the dark wall. Eventually they came to a series of low buildings, where their Escaignian guards sought and found a small door in the side of an iron-clad shed. This in turn led to a narrow corridor between the buildings and the wall, barely wide enough for the Haufuth. It certainly would have been too narrow for the Loulean village headman as he had been before all this began.

The path led down into a depression, almost under the foundations of the wall, and Leith guessed they were close to the Water Chamber. His heart began to race as though something exciting rather than horrible was about to happen, and he turned his focus once again to his surroundings. A narrow, ill-formed path; walls of stone, brick, iron and thatch; the pungent smells of raw earth and waterlogged mud; the muffled sounds of the Docks at work, the more immediate sound of boots on stone, his reluctant feet drawing him ever forward.

Ahead and to their right rose a low thatch wall, the rear of someone's warehouse. Beyond, Leith could see the river. The journey was almost at an end. They passed the thatch wall.

With surprisingly little noise the narrow walled path filled with people. Suddenly everything was ruled by confusion. Figures shouted and pushed each other, and some exchanged blows. Leith found he was shouting too, trying to get somebody to explain to him what was happening. He took an elbow in the face from one of the Escaignian guards and fell stunned to the ground; above and around him the tussle continued. It took a moment for him to regain his senses. Behind him Kurr was dragged through the thatch wall, while to his right at least six figures bent over the Haufuth. Leith forced himself upright. He dived at the nearest figure and pulled him to the ground, then pummeled at the back of his bald head . . .

He sprang back and turned the man over, and found himself staring into the bruised face of their Escaignian guide. He groaned and put his hand to his head.

"I—I'm sorry," Leith stammered. "But what is happening?"

"Just follow me," the man said, picking himself up.

"Quickly." He parted the thatch, pulled himself through gingerly and beckoned for Leith to come with him.

The warehouse was nearly empty. Ahead of them Leith could see the Haufuth and the old farmer being escorted by a large group of people. He could not make out who they were. He could not think. It was as though his mind had slowed to a halt, overwhelmed by the combination of events around him. Faltha and Bhrudwo, Instruere and Escaigne, The Pinion and the dream of fire, Stella and the Water Chamber; the pressure had been relentless, and Leith simply wanted to lie down and close his eyes.

Through the warehouse they fled, out into the sheeting rain and along a wide muddy lane. A man with a wheelbarrow wandered along the other side of the road, seemingly ignorant of the weather around him and the small, lightly clad group scuttling past him. Somewhere off to the right people were buying and selling. The aroma of freshly caught fish came to them on the same salt-laden air that brought the urgent sound of the auctioneer and the murmur of bargain-hunters. Soon they passed out of hearing, taking a circuitous route through open spaces, narrow lanes and between large buildings.

At some stage during the journey Leith came back to himself. Again he asked the bald man what had happened, and this time he received an answer.

"The Elders made an unjust ruling, taking the easy way out instead of doing the right thing." He laughed shortly, and apologized to Leith. "I'm sorry if I sound like Foilzie; I've been listening to her since this time yesterday. She is certainly a forceful woman.

"You've seen how it is with Escaigne. We allowed our Presiding Elder too much power, and now Escaigne suffers the consequences. As an Elder I could do no more to stop his flight into folly, so I betrayed the Eldership and condemned myself by rescuing you. I am now an enemy of Escaigne."

"But where are the others?" Leith could see Kurr and the Haufuth, and caught a glimpse of others some distance ahead of them.

"I could save only three of you," said the bald man.

A feeling of doom settled on Leith's shoulders. "And the others?" His voice was harsher than he had intended.

The man shook his head in resignation. "Nothing I could do. The others have been taken to the Water Chamber. They are now beyond my help."

"Please," said an anguished Leith. "Please send someone back for them. Or let us go and find them."

"I cannot take the risk," said the bald man, his face drawn into a scowl. "You should be grateful for your own rescue."

"How can I be grateful when my parents are about to die?" *And not just my parents. There is another . . .*

The man grabbed Leith's arm and spun him around. The others gathered as Leith and the bald guide argued.

"Many families will suffer loss in the next few hours," the man said angrily. "I've paid the price for trying to help you. I have left my own sons in Escaigne. Do you think I will ever see them again?"

But Leith was beyond this kind of reasoning, and tried to pull away from his grip. "Let me go and find them!" he cried.

"We can't have this," said one of the renegade Escaignians sourly. "Fighting in the streets! As good a way of attracting attention as any I can think of." He looked with burning eyes into the face of his leader. "I know the place you intend to take these ones. If you will wait for us, I will take this one back to the Water Chamber with me."

The bald man considered for a moment. "Very well," he ground out. "But I will not wait long. Our unwillingness to kill their guards has made it dangerous for any of us to remain within reach of Escaigne. You have one hour."

The young man with fiery eyes took Leith by the hand. "Come quickly! It is at least twenty minutes back to the Water Chamber from here. We must hurry."

Alone in his quarters for the first time since returning from The Pinion, Saraskar, the Arkhos of Sarista, pursed his lips in thought. Whatever action he took had to be taken soon: he was already being guarded by one of Nemohaim's men, and by evening the streets would be filled with the city's guards and associates. Instruere was about to become a closed city. The reality? He was trapped, completely at the mercy of that fat animal. Nevertheless, his duty demanded he warn Sarista.

Saraskar grimaced with the difficulty of his decision. He would have to send one of his few trustworthy kinsmen, yet the likelihood of any messenger getting past the guards and across the bridge was slim indeed. And even if the miracle did happen and he managed to get a message through, he had been away from Sarista too long and could no longer vouch for the loyalty of his own king. If indeed his king still ruled. Perhaps this might all be for nothing.

There was no more time. He was delaying because the only decision he could make was distasteful, and would probably condemn the messenger he chose to torture and death in The Pinion. He took a piece of fine Vertensian paper from his drawer, dipped his quill in Favonian ink, wrote the message and sealed it with the Council seal. As he rose from his seat and called for his servant, Saraskar had no illusions about the level of protection this would afford his message.

Later that morning, after a short struggle, a dark-skinned foreigner claiming to carry a message sealed by the Council of Faltha was arrested as he tried to cross Southbridge. He was taken to The Pinion, where he refused under extreme provocation to further implicate his master. The message he carried, however, was more than enough to condemn the Arkhos of Sarista, already under observation for suspected treason against the Council of Faltha. Just after midday a detachment of the Instruian Guard marched quietly into the Saristrian quarters, and met no resistance as they rounded up the Arkhos, his family and his servants. Bitter tears were shed as his children were separated from their parents; but in truth their good-byes had already been said. The outcome, Saraskar and his advisers now knew, had been inevitable since the loyalists on the Council had decided to wait rather than act, thereby lending strength to their opponents. These good men underestimated the degree to which their colleagues on the Council had become corrupted. Now they would pay for that mistake with everything they had.

Indrett tried to sit up, but she was bound too tightly and could get no leverage. She did not have to sit up, however, in order to understand their position. As if preoccupied with more pressing things, their captors had hurriedly tied them hand and foot, and simply left them on the muddy floor of the chamber. A third of the way up the wall was a gray mark left by the previous night's effluent. In front of them the chamber opened out to the river, which lapped at the entrance. They could hear the chitinous clicking of river crabs in the distance. And, infusing everything like a foul poison, a dreadful charnel-smell reeking of the city. The few facts remaining in their lives were stark and inescapable.

"I need help over here," came Mahnum's voice from somewhere behind her. "My bonds are tight, but I may be able to slip them. Perhaps together we may be able to work them loose."

He hasn't given up! she thought. *He never has, and he never will.* He wasn't the cleverest man in Rammr, she reminded herself, he couldn't match wits with the court, but he was the bravest, the most passionate man she'd ever met. The realization that there were many things she needed to say to him flooded over her. *How much time do we have left?* She felt a wetness under her, the wetness of water spreading rapidly across the floor. Sobbing with the effort, Indrett tried to lever herself across the chamber towards the rich, deep voice she knew so well.

Ahead of her, on the edge of her vision, a bright light danced. Then another drifted on the margin of her focus. Forward she forced herself as the ropes cut into her wrists and calves. A cry of frustration escaped her lips as she realized she would not make it in time.

Around her the chamber was rimmed with white light, dappling on the water quickly filling the confined space. Into the light burst a tall silhouette, followed a moment later by another figure, the gods come to collect them, the Northern Lights come to sit with her one last time. Indrett turned and saw one of the figures draw a knife from his belt and raise it. Blinding light stabbed from the blade, forcing her eyes closed, but not before she heard a familiar voice call her name. Leith! Leith was here too. They would all go to meet the bright light together.

CHAPTER 9

SUNDERED

FAR TO THE EAST OF INSTRUERE, on the southern margins of Sna Vaztha and within a day's march of the Gap, the one pass from Faltha to Bhrudwo, a great waterfall hung suspended in midair. A bitter winter had rendered the Thunderfalls silent, had captured and squeezed the great water into submission by the cunning and patience of ice, humiliating the majestic waterfall as had not been done for a hundred years or more. There it hung at the eastern end of Sivera Alenskja, the hundred-league gorge of the Aleinus River, a towering sculpture in blue and white, mute testimony to Qali, the real ruler of the interior.

In the steep-sided gorge of Sivera Alenskja winter only now gave way to spring. The cruel cold heart of eastern Faltha froze the blood during the long slow winter, yet boiled it during the short hot summer. This year the winter was the deepest in memory, and the spring thaw that followed came on Sivera Alenskja with a pent-up violence unequaled in the Sixteen Kingdoms. Though little snow fell here, the ground froze and re-froze until the very stones heaved to the surface of the soil in crazy patterns, and subsurface water turned to vast ice lenses, expanding and forcing the ground itself

to bulge into the frigid air like the misshapen limbs of
the tortured. Sna Vazthans were trapped in their homes
by the brutal weather, and outside in the trackless frozen
wastes many wild animals perished miserably for lack
of food. Therefore no eyes, human or animal, beheld the
awesome spectacle to surpass all others, the day the
Thunderfalls loosed the bonds of winter.

A gentle breeze from the southeast, having traveled
across the comparatively warm region of Birinjh in western Bhrudwo, made its way over the Armatura, the lofty
mountain range dividing Faltha from her enemy. As it
funneled down the brown, treeless slopes it warmed still
further, then settled on the upper Aleinus valley and
brooded there a while. Under the influence of this breeze
the long ice-spikes started to drip, and the snow began to
aerate and melt. The Aleinus awoke from her slumber,
and applied enormous pressure to the ice at the head of
the Thunderfalls. After resisting for six days the ice gave
way. Abruptly the whole sculpture detached from the
rock and plummeted into the gorge. The resultant clamor
was possibly the loudest noise ever made in Faltha, but
no one heard it.

The vast lake that ponded in the upper Aleinus valley
was now released. An incalculable volume of water cascaded over the waterfall into the deep slot that was Sivera
Alenskja. Here ice and water combined to scrape the valley sides bare of the trees sheltering in her generous mi-
croclimate; topsoil was stripped away in many places,
and in a few instances the great deluge tore bedrock from
the sides of the canyon. The gorge reverberated with the
sound of water and ice, soil, rock and the trunks of once-
proud pines clashing, shredding and breaking apart.

Less than twelve hours after the fall of Thunderfalls,

Sivera Alenskja disgorged wave after wave of soil-rich, debris-laden, frothy brown water. Now humans and animals alike heard and soon saw this great natural event, and the sight and the sound struck fear into man and beast. The inhabitants of Adolina, a southern Sna Vazthan town at the entrance to the mighty gorge, built on two terraces, had little warning of the furious waters. What cryptic warning they did have came first from the dogs, all of whom bolted for the upper terrace. Many of the inhabitants of lower Adolina experienced an inexplicable unease, a deep, unsettling vibration that led them to abandon their homes for safety. Those who did not were caught in the swift brown flood.

On roared the river, cutting a swathe through the riverlands of Piskasia. Saumon and Tructa were devastated in their turn, but most people escaped unharmed. The flood bore on into Redana'a. Kaskyne, the capital, sited on a hill above the river valley, avoided the roiling calamity, but riverside hamlets were not so lucky. It was night now, and those asleep were taken by the river.

Through Vulture's Craw roared the mighty flood, its force redoubled, pinched between the Taproot Hills to the south and the taller Wodranian Mountains to the north. And early on the third morning after the melting of Thunderfalls a brown wall of water a hundred feet high surged irresistibly through the Gates of Aleinus and out into the everwide Central Plains, rich bottom lands divided between Favony, Asgowan, Deuverre and Straux. The Warden of the fortress on the northern flank of the Gates ordered the warning beacons to be lit, the first time in living memory; and from town to town, faster even than the flood, the dire message spread. Not a single life was lost west of the Gates.

Once out into the Central Plains, the Aleinus was ordinarily a wide, sluggish river, a tired, swollen thing resting from its labors among the mountains. The flood took some time to slow, but eventually did, becoming little more than a ripple followed by a color change and mile after mile of debris. However, the broad river could not contain the sheer volume of water. Over its banks the flood poured, depositing silt on fields far and wide.

The Great Plains were fashioned like an enormous shallow-sided bowl. In the center of the depression lay great marshes and huge lakes, and here the land was foul, allowing nothing to grow. This enormous bowl, named the Maremma, had a lip from which the water it contained would pour, and this lip was located near Plafond, the capital city of Deuverre. There was nothing on the ground to indicate why this should be so, as the gradient of the bowl was so slight as to be imperceptible. But if water was to escape the bowl, it had to do so at Plafond.

After many days of wandering through the Great Plains, the tame remnants of the once-mighty flood began to gather at Plafond, bringing much debris with them. Here, on the lip of the bowl, the bones of centuries-old trees from the steep slopes of Sivera Alenskja gathered, interlaced with smaller branches and driftwood accumulated on the long journey, and was cemented into place by the finest of the silt still not deposited by the river of rivers. A great wall was formed, only a few feet high but many miles wide; a dam that stretched right across the lip of the bowl, a barrier that held back both the waters of the flood and the not-inconsiderable late spring flow from the tributaries of the Aleinus. Included was the Branca, a mighty river in her own right that drained Asgowan, Haurn and the Borders to the far north. The water began to bank up behind the dam; slowly, insidiously, inexorably; and little or no water passed through.

A few days' journey downriver from Plafond was Instruere, the city of cities, lying in the arms of the river of rivers.

I have been bested, the Arkhos of Nemohaim admitted to himself. Bested from the moment the foul Bhrudwan Deorc came to Faltha with his plan to gain rulership of Instruere.

What galled the Arkhos the most was that he himself was to blame. He had handed Instruere to Deorc. The claw of the Destroyer was about to close over the city, and squeeze him out in the process. *But I can perhaps do a little squeezing of my own*, the fat man vowed. *Deorc will pay dearly for his presumption.*

He had played the game by Bhrudwan rules, shady though they were, and had lost. Escaigne had slipped through his fingers in the presence of the Keeper of Andratan. He had foolishly gambled all, and now the Council would install this *fool* as their leader. In one sense the Destroyer would have Faltha without fighting for it, though there would undoubtedly be resistance . . . too little, too late. The Arkhos gnashed his teeth in frustration as he replayed the fantasy in his mind, the scene in which he, as Faltha's most powerful man, opened the Iron Door to the Destroyer and handed him the scepter of the city. A few well-chosen words, filled with understatement, a dignified acknowledgement of the thanks due to him and an acceptance of the promised lieutenant's position. But that was all gone now. It was time to forget the rules, and fall back instead on the street-fighting skills he had learned in the slums of Bewray.

*   *   *

All that day and into the night the low dam held, and a small inland sea formed behind it. Plafond itself was unaffected, being on a low hill a mile or so to the west of the dam, but many river people, fishermen, farmers and their families, evacuated the lowlands. Local officials, their hands full with the emergency, did not think to warn those downriver—or, if they did, they assumed someone else had already taken care of it.

Downstream of the dam, of course, the river of rivers simply dried up.

It was a matter of time and the sheer weight of water. The natural dam would have given way eventually anyway, but its demise was hastened by the late arrival of the whole trunk of a forest giant, plucked from its proud position at the entrance to Vulture's Craw by the tail end of the flood. It clattered into the dam, splintering and dislodging timber in its path. With something akin to a sigh the dam was parted, and with an irresistible force the water ripped through it.

It took Leith a long time, far too long, to revive his mother. It had been the work of a moment to free the members of the Company trapped in the Water Chamber, but Indrett had taken in some foul water and for a few fraught moments she stopped breathing. The Escaignian who had come with Leith cleared her air passages and she breathed again almost immediately, but did not regain consciousness.

"How long did the bald man give us?" Leith asked.

"An hour," came the reply. "I don't know how much of that is left."

"Perhaps we can carry her," Perdu suggested, anxiety imprinted on his friendly face.

"Better than waiting here," Leith agreed. "The tide is still rising."

As they made to lift her she coughed, then opened her eyes to exclamations of relief from her companions. "Where is the light? Where is the light?" she asked, with something akin to regret, even desperation, in her voice.

"Just the sun coming through a hole in the roof," Leith said. "Can you walk? We have to leave here now."

Indrett needed assistance to stand, let alone walk, and in spite of her best efforts she held up the progress of the Company. "He said an hour," Leith chafed. "It must be all of that now since we left the others. Will he wait?"

The young Escaignian shrugged his shoulders. "Maybe he will, maybe he will not. Who can say how any of us will act? None of us have been in this situation before."

Phemandcrac came up behind them. "If we do not find a hiding place soon, we will be found by Escaigne or Instruere. I'm not sure which I'd rather have as a captor."

"If you had seen the inside of The Pinion, you would not be so unsure," Leith said grimly. "But I would prefer to remain free. We may yet find worse captors than either. Certainly we will if we cannot prevent the Bhrudwans from taking Faltha."

Leith had only a moment with Stella, but one glance was enough to know what had been kindled still burned. His heart leaped.

"Are you unharmed?" he asked her shyly.

"I'm all right," she said. "We haven't come this far together to fail now." She reached out her hand and took his.

Leith nodded, though he was finding it impossible to think as her fingers closed around his. "We must continue until we find the Jugom Ark at least."

"Oh, Leith, will you always misunderstand me?" Stella wondered aloud.

"We must leave," Mahnum said, bringing them back to the immediacy of their situation: they were still in danger.

"Then follow me!" the young Escaignian cried.

Out of the Water Chamber they ran, then ducked behind a row of buildings. To the left and to the right they went, time and again, trying to take the shortest route to the bald man and the rest of their companions without being seen, and with the added handicap of their Escaignian guide knowing the Docks little better than the Company. Down a narrow alleyway they went, only to freeze in their tracks when a brace of guards went running along the street at the far end. This held them up for precious moments, while Perdu, the quietest among them, ensured the way ahead was clear. They dashed across the open street, along and behind a row of low storage sheds similar to the one Foilzie owned in the city, and up another alleyway to emerge suddenly in the open space where they had left Kurr and the Haufuth in the care of the bald Escaignian. But their friends were no longer there.

"What now?" Leith asked the Escaignian.

"What now?" the other answered. His eyes flashed with casual mirth, a lightness incongruous with their desperate situation. "That depends on your goal, does it not?"

"Our first goal is to remain uncaught," said Farr tersely. Ever since they had left the Great Wood the old anxieties had come upon him again; by now he was stretched tight as a drumskin. "Then perhaps we will be afforded the leisure to consider our next move."

"No. Our first goal is to reunite with the others," Leith

stated firmly. "The worst thing that could happen now is for us to be divided."

"Then where have the others gone?" Perdu demanded. "Surely this man must know where his master intended to take us!"

"I don't think even he knew," the Escaignian admitted. "But he would not go back into Instruere, that is for certain. Death awaits him there. Perhaps he seeks transport to take you all across the river and into Straux or Deuverre."

"A boat! He must be looking for a boat! Or perhaps he found a hiding place here." Leith considered a moment, no longer so certain. *Or has he betrayed us?*

As if in confirmation of his fears, an armed man strode into the space between the sheds. To Leith's relief this man greeted the Escaignian as a friend, and for a moment the two talked together in their own language. Then the young man with the fiery eyes turned to the Company. "Follow me!" he said. "Or, more correctly, follow him. We have found a boat capable of taking you across the Aleinus."

With joy the Company was reunited. When it became apparent just how narrow the escape from the Water Chamber had been, everyone thanked the Escaignian for his help in rescuing them. "Does this mean you can no longer go back to Escaigne?" Stella asked.

The young man shrugged his shoulders, as he seemed wont to do. "I was getting sick of the darkness," he said, making ready to leave them.

"What is your name?" Indrett asked, now fully recovered. "Tell us, so we can thank you properly."

"You ought rather to thank this one," he said, indicating Leith. "But for his persistence, you would have been left to your fate. But my name? You must know that in Escaigne all names are kept secret."

"But this is not Escaigne!" cried Indrett.

"True, but it may be one day. Until that day, let it be enough that we are free." He waved to them, then went off up the rutted road, following the others.

Now only the bald man remained with the Company. "What of you?" Kurr asked him. "Will you not come with us? I know your Presiding Elder, and alone of those here can guess your fate should Escaigne find you."

The man shook his head sorrowfully, drips spraying from his hooked nose in the thick drizzle. "I cannot go with you. I have family in Escaigne, nieces and nephews and two sons. I will not leave while any chance remains of seeing them again."

"Then it remains only to thank you, bid you farewell and head for the south," Kurr responded. "Lead us to the boat."

The bald man smiled. "That I will do. We have been out in the open too long—"

A sound like someone striking a sack of corn, a wet *thwack*, pulled everyone's eyes towards the bald man, whose face registered surprise and shock. He took a step forward, then slumped to the ground, an arrow embedded deeply in his shoulderblade. As he fell, a second arrow flashed at chest height through the spot where he had been standing, grazing his head.

"Take cover!" Farr shouted, the first to come to his senses. "There is an archer over to our left, up on the wall!"

The Company dived for shelter. Farr and Mahnum dragged the wounded man away from danger. "The Guard!" Kurr hissed. "We are discovered! How badly is the man hurt?"

"Not that badly," the bald man himself answered,

though in a voice tight with pain. "I'll not die, though I'll not be going anywhere for a while either."

"He was shot from the wall? It must be at least a hundred yards away." Leith was puzzled.

"They don't wear their weapons as decoration, boy," Kurr said. "This is a dangerous place!"

Indrett went to inspect the arrow, but Farr said: "Don't touch it! Don't draw it out! Leave it there for a while. It will prevent him bleeding more seriously. Hal—do you have any experience with this sort of wound?"

Hal examined the wound, and nodded. "You have read it right," he said to Farr. "He should not be moved, but should be made comfortable until we can dig the arrow out."

"We have no time for that," Kurr told them urgently. "They know where we are, and no doubt have dispatched a regiment to deal with us. We cannot remain here."

"Then hide me in some dark corner and go to the boat," said the bald man. "They'll not do to me what they will do to you if you are found."

"Then let me take care of you," said a new voice. Leith and the others sprang up with surprise. It was Foilzie.

"I told you to wait by the boat," the bald Escaignian growled.

"My place is here, beside you," Foilzie answered simply. "A fat lot of good I'd do you down there."

"Then do something about this prickle in my shoulder, would you, and stop jawing me to death." His voice growled, but his face was bright.

Foilzie turned to the Company. "Go on, off with you, down the lane there to the boat. You can't stop here; you're getting in my way." And she turned her back on them and placed concerned hands on the bald man's shoulder.

"Oh, Rubin," she said quietly, as the others made a dash for the boat. "What have we gotten ourselves into?"

"Come this way," said Furoman, the personal secretary to the Appellant Division of the Council of Faltha, as he smiled his disconcerting smile. The Archivist shook his head slightly, wondering if he was doing the right thing, but followed anyway. Silently he rehearsed the speech he planned to make to Saraskar. *This man Phemanderac has made subversive inquiries about the government of Faltha, and I have heard he is linked to the northerners who are wanted for the debacle at The Pinion. I have information about this man that may be of assistance to you.* Yes, that sounded good. He had to admit it, he was nervous at the prospect of facing a member of the Council of Faltha. Stories abounded of people going missing after dealing with the Council. Everyone knew the Council were not what they had been in ages past. *Part of a necessary reorganization,* the Archivist told himself. *Getting rid of kingships and the old feudal system, and introducing a new democracy based on election to the Council of Faltha. Well past time. Still, I wouldn't be here in this cursed city if it wasn't for my family.* "There's a reward," his wife had said. "You'll be able to leave that dusty old library." What she really meant was they could leave that drafty old tenement. *Well, she is who she is. How can I refuse her?*

"This way," the secretary said, opening a door off the main corridor. "He'll see you now."

The Archivist took a deep breath. The moment was at hand. He walked through the door.

"Sit down," a high-pitched voice wheezed. "Sit down."

With those words the blood froze around the Archivist's heart. There at Saraskar's desk sat the Arkhos of Nemohaim, and he wore the widest smile.

The grassy bank, slippery with the morning rain, sloped steeply away towards the river. Perhaps this explained the slowness with which the Company made their way forward, though it may have been the delayed shock of the Water Chamber and the closeness with which death had brushed them; perhaps it was their reluctance to leave Foilzie and the bald man to the Instruian Guard, or even the fact of their undeniable tiredness. Whatever the reasons, they were far too slow.

There was the boat, a small dinghy down at the bottom of the slope, with Kurr, Hal and the Haufuth climbing in at the prow with a couple of Escaignians—Leith supposed they were Escaignians; yes, there was the bright-eyed young man who had led him to the Water Chamber—occupying the rest of the space. They would certainly never fit the whole Company in. In front of him the Hermit slipped on the muddy slope and fell to the ground, soiling his blue robe. Leith himself had to be careful of the treacherous ground as he lent the tall, aristocratic man his assistance. The Hermit regained his feet and brushed himself off. Leith turned to press on, his feet went completely from under him and he slid twenty feet down the slope, his fall arrested when his head slammed into the side of a small stone water trough.

Above him the short period of grace the Company had enjoyed ended with a suddenness that took their breath away. Into the grassy lane burst a contingent of the Instruian Guard, a few yards below the northerners. At the same moment those down in the boat yelled a warning, then hurriedly cast off from the shore as some of the guards scrambled down the slope. Seeing this, the guards turned and advanced up the slope towards the Company, who took to their heels in a desperate attempt to avoid capture. Only the Hermit had seen Leith fall. In the fear of the moment none of the others missed him from among them.

It seemed to take no time at all to flash past the place they had left Foilzie and the bald man, fear lending them a fleetness of foot they could have used earlier. They soon outdistanced their armor-encumbered pursuers. Phemanderac noted in passing that Foilzie must have found shelter.

"Where are we going?" Perdu gasped out from the front of the group. Behind him the Company stretched quite a way back down the wide muddy road, back to the Bhrudwan, who looked a little lost without Hal. "Where are we going?" he repeated. No one replied. Most were out of breath, spending all their energy on running. In truth no one could have provided an answer anyway.

Behind them the guards slowed to a walk, confident their prey would not escape. This was the Docks, to be sure, a veritable rabbit-warren of places to hide, but the ignorant northerners ran away from the walls of Instruere, towards the western end of the island where the arms of the Great River rejoined in their final reach to the sea. The captain smiled. He would enjoy this. And it would prove to be the perfect result to present to his new master, a final betrayal of the hated Arkhos of Nemohaim.

The sumptuous red leather chair seemed to wrap its arms around the Archivist as he waited for the Arkhos of Nemohaim to begin. He wanted to ask where Saraskar was, what was happening and why he was obviously not free to go, but could not loosen his tongue sufficiently to speak.

"You're probably wondering where the Arkhos of Sarista is, and why I have taken his place," the dreadful man wheezed from his black chair behind the desk. "Well, there's been a reorganization around here. I have been moved—shall we say, sideways—while the Arkhos has been relieved of his position. Very indiscreet, our friend has been." The Arkhos's jowls wobbled dangerously as he shook his head. "It is a foolish thing in this city to talk too freely to the wrong people." For a moment the wheezing stopped.

The fat man fiddled with a piece of paper on his desk. "Now, you were here to tell the Arkhos of Sarista about your encounter with one of the northerners, I believe. Specifically his discovery of information in the archives relevant to the Council of Faltha. I'm sorry he can't be here to hear your tale. I hope I will suffice in his stead. Be sure I will relay anything important to the Council. Speak to me and you speak to the Council."

His words were reassuring; the tone mild, conciliatory, designed to allay his fear of this legendary man, the fat Spider of Instruere; still, the Archivist was afraid.

"So the northerner discovered something important among that pile of rubbish? If there was something of such importance that Saraskar would grant you an audience, why was it not unearthed before now? Are you incompetent?"

"No, my lord," the Archivist stammered, his face flushing a bright red. "The visitor had knowledge I was not party to which enabled him to interpret some of our oldest and most obscure manuscripts."

"How could a provincial from Firanes know something the Archivist of Instruere does not?"

"Ah, but he does not come from Firanes, my lord," the Archivist said, stung by the insinuation. "He claimed not to have come from Faltha at all."

"From where, then? From Bhrudwo?"

This was better. He had information this slug wanted. "And my reward?"

"Your *reward*?" For a moment the Archivist feared the Arkhos would climb over the desk to get at him, but the man apparently thought better of it. "Your reward?" he repeated, thoughtfully this time. "Yes, I can suit a reward to the value of your information. Now, tell me where this man is from."

The Archivist wanted to pursue further the matter of the reward, but something in the face opposite his dissuaded him.

"He said he was from Dhauria, of the remnant of the Vale of the First Men." The words came out like a pearl from his lips, and the Archivist noted their effect on the pig-like eyes of the Arkhos of Nemohaim.

"Did he? Did he now? And what did you think of his claim, then?"

"Well, like you I don't believe a word of it," the Archivist replied carefully, "but he did have knowledge of the First Men that has died out in Faltha, knowledge no villager from the north could possibly know. He knows more than I do; more, if I might dare say it, than you yourself, my lord."

"So you don't believe him?" The Arkhos heaved himself to his feet, and came around from behind his desk until he stood directly in front of his visitor. "What if I were to tell you I myself have been to another place of legend, a place of equal renown, of even greater power? Would you disbelieve me as quickly as you disbelieved him?"

"What place is this, my lord?" The Archivist could barely speak in the face of the overpowering presence of the Arkhos, who appeared far more dangerous than any mere spider.

The huge man lifted his head proudly. "I have walked the blackest of all halls, plumbed the deepest of all pits, strode the highest of all walls. I have spoken with the Voice disembodied, and have eaten with he of the one hand. Do you know the answer to this riddle, man of learning?"

"Andratan," whispered the Archivist. "The Destroyer."

"Wonderful what a little learning can do for a man," said the Arkhos. "But learning can take you only so far. I offer you this reward. Pledge me your fealty, and you too can walk in the places of legend." *I need a new servant*, he thought. *This one will do nicely*.

"So if the man I met is indeed from the Vale, then he is your enemy."

"Not my enemy, but the enemy of the Destroyer. The enemy of Bhrudwo." *The truth as a lie—the best weapon of all. Tell this easily gulled mental weakling the truth and he will assume the man is our friend, because he will not believe I am a traitor.* "Our friend. I need to talk to him."

"That may take some doing, my lord. He intended to leave Instruere in order to follow up his discovery in the archives. He may have already done so."

"Indeed? What could be so important that he would want to leave so fair a city?" the Arkhos mused in a voice heavy with sarcasm.

"He is after an old relic. He believes, my lord, that he knows the location of the Jugom Ark, the Arrow of

Yoke." Another pearl cast in front of the Arkhos. *Perhaps this meeting will work out well after all*, he tried to tell himself, but he could not suppress the unease that rose up to fill his throat.

There was no mistaking the effect these words had on their hearer, nor the covetousness that sprang into the small round eyes as their import was absorbed. "The Arrow?" he breathed. For a few moments the huge Arkhos appeared quite unmanned.

The Archivist said nothing, but merely waited, trying to prevent his unease growing further.

"So that is their plan! With the Arrow, the weapon wielded by the Destroyer's deadly foe, I could . . ." He came to himself, and said no more of what was on his mind.

"So the legends multiply," he said eventually. "This must be disconcerting for a revisionist scholar such as yourself. Dhauria, Andratan, the Destroyer, the Jugom Ark. Next Kantara will come down from the clouds, or Bi'r Birkat will appear in front of our eyes. What say you? Do you still call these things legends?"

"Well, my lord," the Archivist said quietly, "you have yet to ask me the location of this Arrow."

"You *know*? He *told* you?"

"According to the words of Bewray of Nemohaim, the Guardian of the Arrow, words I saw with my own eyes, the Arrow rests in the Vale of Neume, between the two mountains known as the Sentinella, at a place named Kantara." The Archivist smiled. The third of his pearls. It was time he weighed in with a legend or two of his own.

If the fat man was surprised by this revelation he did not reveal it. "I am the Arkhos of Nemohaim," he said. "I represent Nemohaim to the Council of Faltha. I am a direct descendant of Bewray, the founder of Nemohaim. As such, I am a fit Guardian of the Arrow." He stood, as if announcing a decision to the Council. "I claim this heirloom as my own. No other man may lay hands on it, on pain of death. With it I will declare myself the enemy of Bhrudwo."

The Archivist sat stunned at this turn of events. *What does the fat man have planned?* he asked himself.

"I need a partner," the Arkhos said suddenly. "I need somebody like yourself, with the lore to guide us to the Arrow. I will pay you well. Will you come?"

History reached out an ancient hand and grabbed the Archivist, this doubter of myth, this rational man. The names of legend assaulted him like raiders of the heart. Dhauria, Andratan, Kantara. In the face of this overpowering desire he retained a small measure of equanimity.

"I want my family provided for," he said.

The Arkhos of Nemohaim reached into his robe and took out a small bag. He handed it to the Archivist. "Payment in advance," he said. "Open it."

With unsteady fingers he unpicked the knot in the drawstring to reveal one large nugget of solid gold. Pure Tabul gold, the like of which had not been seen in Instruere for a generation.

"Is that enough?" the fat man asked.

"I am your servant, my lord," said the Archivist.

Leith woke to find himself alone, totally alone. Wet and cold, he lay in the mud at the bottom of a grassy slope, unable for the moment to remember what he was doing there. His head hurt. He touched his temple and found blood on his fingers. The sight made him feel nauseous. Misty rain filtered down on him as the weather closed in, and he began to shiver where he lay. There was some reason why he should get to his feet, something urgent; but it eluded him. He worked away at it: Instruere . . . Escaigne . . . the Water Chamber . . .

He sat bolt upright. The motion made his stomach heave. How long had he been lying there? Where were the others? He crawled back out on to the grass and looked down at the river. The boat was gone. He turned away and began to climb the slope, slowly, gingerly; then stopped, disbelieving, and turned his aching head back to the river.

He rubbed his eyes, unable to comprehend what he was seeing.

"They're herding us," Perdu said bitterly. "Rounding us up like dumb animals, penning us up against the river. There's no escape."

"But at least there will be defense," Farr exclaimed. Each member of the Company wielded a stout length of timber, gleaned from a stack of building materials they passed some while ago.

"Can't we hide?" asked Indrett. "Sticks against swords doesn't sound like a winnable fight to me."

"Hide where? The guards are taking their time, exploring every house and every shed in their search for us. It's just a matter of time." The exhilaration of battle built within Farr, and all thought of flight or safety retreated from his mind.

"Then why not surrender to them? Perhaps they will deal with us leniently."

"Wishful thinking," Mahnum answered his wife. "They have not forgotten The Pinion. We wounded their pride. They will seek revenge, if only to prove to their citizens that they still retain control of the city."

"Has anyone seen Leith?" Stella asked quietly.

Heads turned this way and that, but it was obvious Leith was not amongst them. "Now where has that foolish boy got to?" Farr said.

"Who saw him last? Where was he when he was last seen?" Mahnum's voice was tight, urgent.

For a while no one answered as they thought, retracing their steps from the Water Chamber. One amongst the Company kept his thoughts to himself, thinking, *this is right. I will say nothing.*

"The last memory I have is of the Escaignian—not the bald one but the other one, the one who helped rescue us—thanking Leith as he left." Anxiety gripped Stella's heart.

"Was that before or after the bald one was shot?" Mahnum's voice betrayed his fear.

"Before, I'm sure. We must go back!" Stella cried. *He can't abandon me now!*

"Hold on!" Perdu shouted. "We can't all go rushing off. We need to stay together! Leith has thus far displayed enough sense not to have done anything foolish. Likely he is in a better position than us! Perhaps even now he is working on some plan to save us."

"Or perhaps he has tried to save himself," Farr said quietly. Stella rounded on him, eyes blazing.

"There is no time for this," Phemanderac said, and his voice carried authority. "Since I am not one of the Company, and therefore am dispensable, I will go and look for him. The rest of you stay together, as Perdu suggests. Keep out of sight of the guards. Hide if you can, fight if you must. Now is the time to trust what you have seen, to trust what you have felt. The Most High overshadows us, and for good or for ill he has a plan which involves you. He will provide a way of escape, but will not force you to take it. It simply depends on whether you are prepared to be patient and wait for his deliverance."

"I know what the Haufuth would say to that, were he here," commented Farr.

"Then it is just as well he is not here. I will be back with Leith as soon as I can," and saying this, he left them, darting down a side road.

"Shouldn't we follow him?" Indrett asked. "If he can find a way out of this maze, maybe we could all escape."

"He'll have a much greater chance on his own," her husband replied.

Leith found himself staring incredulously, unable to take his eyes from the scene.

The Aleinus River was completely dry.

It was not a trick of the light. It was not a fantasy of his mind. There in front of him, stretching out into the misty distance, lay the mighty Aleinus River, the Mother of Rivers; only there was no water flowing between her banks, just the odd pool in low-lying areas of light gray mud. Finally, released from his paralysis, Leith rushed down to the bank. Boats sat bottomed on the sand, fish flopped about on the mud, struggling for breath. The scene was eerie. *I thought it was mid-tide*, Leith thought. *But how long ago was that? How long have I been lying unconscious?* He was soaked through, but this rain could have achieved that in a matter of minutes. *Surely low tide did not empty the river? Water must continually come from upstream, that cannot be the answer.*

Whatever the explanation, he still needed to find the rest of the Company. Turning his back on the preposterous spectacle, he began to scramble up the bank.

Straight into a contingent of the Instruian Guard.

They were even more taken by surprise than he, and before their rough hands could close around him he had squirmed free and, half rolling, half falling, tumbled down the riverbank.

"Leith! This way, this way!" It was Phemanderac, also on the riverbank, about a hundred yards to his right.

The youth scrambled to his feet, the guards already halfway down the slope. Behind Phemanderac more guards came running.

"Look behind you!" Leith cried.

Now Phemanderac ran for his life, and in a moment they were together, surrounded by guards who were rapidly converging on them.

"The river!" Leith said. "We must go across the river!" He held out his arm, pointing over the bank. Phemanderac followed his arm, and his mouth opened wide. The guards looked up, then stopped in their tracks, stunned. For a moment no one moved, and in the silence Leith heard the cry of gulls as they came to take advantage of a most unexpected feast.

"Indeed, my friend; let us cross the river," Phemanderac said, and his voice rippled with laughter. The joy had come upon him, the first time since he had left the Vale, and he shook with the power of it. Leith made ready to jump down on to the sand, but the philosopher cried, "No! Don't jump. Trust me! Climb down the bank as best you can!"

So down the bank they clambered, fighting their way through the sedges and water plants, until their feet touched sand. Meanwhile the guards recovered their wits, having been awed for a moment at the sight of their river empty, seemingly at the command of the northerner; and were even now at the bank, perhaps ten feet above the pair below, making ready to follow them.

Leith and Phemanderac sprang away from the bank, the willowy philosopher leading the way, trying to avoid the treacherous mud. Behind them the first of the guards jumped from the bank and, to his chagrin, sank up to his knees in the soft sand.

"Fool!" his captain cried, but his words did not deter half a dozen others from jumping and suffering the same fate. "Pull them out!" he ordered the others, but the bank was too far above them. "Get down there and help them!" the exasperated captain said, then thought better of it as he saw his quarry making their escape. "Forget these fools. Chase those two northerners!"

They were by now a few hundred yards from the bank, and Leith was already exhausted. The ordeals of the last few days had stolen his reserves of strength, and the sucking sand and mud turned his legs rubbery. He lost one shoe, the result of a misplaced footstep, and as yet the far side of the river was not in view. Behind them the guards had made it to the riverbed, and were setting out on the chase.

"Keep going," Phemanderac panted beside him. "The run will tire them also."

Fear lent him further energy, but only for a time. Some distance and many minutes further on Leith came to a halt, hands on knees, gasping for air. They were near the center of the river now, and here the rising tide still filled a wide but shallow channel. The guards were three hundred yards or more behind, giving the fugitives a minute or so to rest.

"What happened to the river?" Leith asked between deep breaths.

"I thought you might be able to tell me!" Phemanderac replied. "You stuck out your arm, and there was no water!"

"I'm sure I didn't do it. What about the others?"

"Still trapped, I'm afraid."

Leith shook his head.

"Time to take to our feet again," the philosopher said, as the guards drew closer. "They're going slower now."

"So am I," Leith said.

The next hour was like a nightmare. While Phemanderac picked a way through the bog-like mud on all sides, Leith just plodded along behind him, concentrating simply on putting one foot in front of the other, his eyes on the philosopher's boots. He had no idea how far behind them the guards were.

Phemanderac had a better idea. The occasional glance behind told him the guards were faltering in their chase, but still close enough to prevent them stopping to rest. There was also the matter of keeping ahead of the guards once they made the shore.

Finally the line of the far bank came into view. Minutes later the two weary northerners climbed the steps to a small dock. As they made the safety of the wooden structure, figures came running out from the trees ahead.

"Leith! Phemanderac!" cried a familiar voice. "You're safe! But what of the others?" It was Kurr and the Haufuth, along with Hal and two of the Escaignians.

"The others are trapped back there," Leith replied in a drained monotone. "We barely made it here. There are guards close behind us."

They all cast their gaze over the waterless river, and at the edge of sight they could see the guards, fanned out into a long line, working their way towards them.

"No one here knows what has happened to the river," the Haufuth said. "We were about to launch the boat to come back and get the rest of you when the water simply drained away."

"We don't have time to wonder about it now," Kurr observed. "We need as much of a head start on those guards as we can get."

"But what about the others? Shouldn't we try to get back to Instruere and rescue them?" Phemanderac asked. He was preoccupied with the realization that the Five of the Hand was incomplete. The Book of the Golden Arrow talked constantly of the Five of the Hand, though there it was named the Arkhimm. What of Stella? Could the Arkhimm, the Five of the Hand, achieve anything at all when one of its components was missing? Would an expedition to recover the Jugom Ark be futile without her?

But Leith was not listening to the discussion, nor worrying about the Arrow. His eyes were fixed on an awesome sight upriver. One by one the others noticed his silence and turned to him, then followed his outstretched arm to see it too.

It was a brown smudge on the horizon, stretching from bank to bank and beyond; it was a roiling, frothing, debris-laden wall of water; it was the Aleinus returning to her bed.

"Run!" shouted one of the Escaignians. "Run for higher ground! The river returns!"

His voice broke the spell they were all under. As one they ran across the jetty and towards the trees planted on a low hill. Leith cast a glance over his shoulder. The wall of water had already drawn much closer, and ahead of it came a sound that would haunt him forever; a horrible grinding, gnashing noise that set his teeth on edge and drove him on between the trees and up to the crown of the low hill.

Down on the riverbed the Captain of the Guard had

watched the northerner stretch out his arm again. To his horror the wall of water responded to his gesture. He tried to block out the awful sound battering against his ears.

"The shore! The shore!" he shouted, but no one could hear him. He motioned for the others to follow, and ran hard for the Straux shoreline in the distance. To the left the wall of water approached at an incredible rate. His men would not make it to the safety of the far bank. Mercilessly he drove himself on, willing himself to safety. Behind him his men struggled forward, but in their panic one after another of them became mired in the thick mud and could do nothing but watch with terror-filled eyes the doom that rumbled towards them. Knowing there was little he could do for the men now, their captain redoubled his own efforts to survive. The dock was a hundred yards in front of him, then fifty, then twenty. On the crown of the hill Leith watched his race for life and, though the Instruian was an enemy bent on capturing or slaying him, he willed the man on.

The men trapped in the riverbed threw up their hands in a last futile defense as the water exploded over them. Most were killed instantly by the debris in the dark brown flood, while the others were drowned by the water that flowed many feet over their heads. The river stretched out a foamy arm towards the Captain of the Guard as he mounted the steps to the jetty, crooked a finger around his legs and dragged him cursing back into the swiftly flowing flood. As an afterthought the waters pulled the jetty itself away from the bank, sending it spiraling out into the center of the river.

The last few unsearched buildings were all that remained between the Company and the river. They would provide no refuge for the beleaguered northerners. The guards had continued their systematic search, and were undoubtedly closing in on them. So little time remained. No words were said now. They all knew each other too well to waste words.

From the direction of the river, behind them and somewhat to their left, came a shout. Some of the Instruian Guard had discovered them. Their slender hopes of avoiding capture were at an end. Only Achtal had not given up hope of escape, or perhaps his aggressive response came from instincts developed by his Bhrudwan training. He stepped forward from the group and hefted an improbably large log.

A sound intruded on their bleak thoughts. A murmur at first, it soon mounted to a roar. The guards down by the riverbank turned and looked upstream, then became extremely agitated, dropping their weapons or clasping them carelessly and running towards the Company. At the same moment the remainder of the guards emerged on to the street, drawn there by the fearsome noise, and there confronted the northerners. But for the moment no one struck a blow. Clearly, from the ever-increasing noise, some catastrophe was about to descend on them all.

The brown wall of water struck the island of Instruere with an earth-shaking blow, knocking many residents abroad that day to the ground. It surged around the low-lying land, ate at the very wall of Instruere at its eastern extremity, undermined and then overtopped the riverbank and surged through the Docks as the divided flood sought to reunite. Those unfortunate enough to be close to the shore were swept screaming to their deaths by the merciless, indiscriminate floodtide. Fishermen trying to earn an honest living, smugglers bringing gold and ivory traded with the savages from the unguessable south, members of the Instruian Guard trying to run to higher ground; all tried in vain to escape. The Company and the main body of the guard watched helplessly as the water took soldier after soldier down into its brown depths. Further and further up the surge came until the foam bubbled around the very feet of the Company, and then just as suddenly retreated as the main body of the flood passed them by, leaving a brownish residue on Farr's boots. The noise was indescribable. Though only a tithe of the stupendous sound of the Thunderfall, from which this calamity originated, all who heard the Aleinus return to its bed were rendered powerless, incapable of flight or even thought. The dreadful power clapped a vise-like grip on the mere humans who witnessed it, overtopping their senses by such a distance as to drown them in fear and wonder.

All except Achtal, the Bhrudwan warrior. He advanced on the guards, many of whom did not even see him, so powerfully engraved on their eyes and minds was the image of their fellows being pulled to their frightening fate.

Achtal swung the log in a wide arc, felling half a dozen of the guard. This served to waken the remainder, some thirty or more, who drew their swords. "Strike at the man, not at the weapon!" their leader cried, but in vain. So many of his men had ears full of that terrible sound that few took heed. Every blade that struck the swinging log bit deep into the wood, lodging there; Achtal jerked the log, plucking the swords from their owners' hands. Thus were a dozen or more rendered harmless.

The remainder struggled to empty their minds of the cataclysm that still echoed around them. As they came to themselves, they remembered the stories of this warrior's power and bloodthirstiness in the depths of The Pinion no more than a week earlier, and their courage flowed away from them like water. A number of them took a step or two backwards in the face of the Bhrudwan's onslaught. Seeing this, Farr gave a yell and sprang forward to join Achtal. Perdu, Mahnum and Stella followed a moment later.

This was more than enough for the shocked and disoriented Instruians. Their captain was gone with another contingent, perhaps claimed by the river; the rest stood here bereft of leadership, staring violent death in the face. To a man they turned and ran.

Farr let out a triumphant cry and made to pursue them, the lust for battle boiling in his blood. A shout from the Hermit stopped him. "Don't!" came the cry. "They are under some kind of spell, we all are. In a while they will come to their senses and pursue us again. We should make good our escape while we can!"

As one the Company recognized the wisdom in this advice. "Follow me!" the blue-robed man cried. "This road should lead away from the guards, at least." The Company followed the Hermit as they made their way away from that scene of fear and death, down a cobbled road which took them in a wide arc back towards the walled city in the distance.

CHAPTER 10

DERUYS

LATE SPRING WAS A WONDERFUL time to walk the narrow poplar-lined lanes and grassy meadows of Straux. However, Leith and the Arkhimm, the seekers of the Jugom Ark, did not have the leisure to appreciate them. The low country of Westrau stretched from the Aleinus, the Great River, more than seventy leagues south to the Veridian Borders, a mountain range which separated Straux from the arid interior of southern Faltha. Fertile and flat, Westrau province was comprised of cropland and woodland in equal measure. Many roads wound their way across these rich lands, shooting tendrils left and right to wooden farmhouses; houses that looked safe, homely and inviting to the little group making their careful way southwards.

A momentary spasm of homesickness seized Leith as they walked between two long rows of stately oaks. He thought of the Common oak, of all the long, lazy days he and his friends had played under its protective boughs. He remembered the late September storm that found him hiding under that great tree, sheltering from the rain and from the villagers who laughed at him. His longing weakened somewhat at the thought.

It was about noon on a cloudless day, the fifth following

their escape from Instruere. The tension and fear that had emanated from the city, enmeshing Leith, Hal, Kurr, the Haufuth and Phemanderac in its debilitating embrace, slowly faded away. Not that they were out of danger. Though the brooding evil of the city was now behind them, and the great flood had sundered them from both friend and foe, they were in no doubt they would be pursued. Nevertheless, all of them enjoyed the open lands they traveled through. Leith felt as though the air was lighter, or that lead weights had fallen from his limbs. *I ought to be leaping about and shouting*, he thought. *Or perhaps not*, he reflected, glancing at the sober faces of the two Escaignians who remained with them. They had lost much in the unmasking of their secret hideaway, and more in their rebellion against it. *There is too much uncertainty, too much loss to be truly happy.*

Yet he could not help himself. She had said—well, she hadn't actually said, but surely she *meant* she had feelings for him. His mind told him that Stella's regard ought to be a small thing when compared with the Bhrudwan threat, or the traitorous Council of Faltha, or even the Escaignian problem, but his heart said otherwise.

No matter what happened now, he was loved.

Leith stopped for a moment under one of the oaks. Sunshine, spring fragrance, a warm breeze, so different to the day he'd waited in vain for her under the Common oak. He ran his hand over the rough bark, remembering . . . but in his recollection Stella walked across the Common towards him, her face bright with love.

Three faces, the faces of his family, intruded on his vision. Did their love matter? His mother, Indrett, loved him, that he knew. But his father? Perhaps he did, but he had a peculiar way of showing it. Hal? Yes, Hal loved him, but it was a harsh love, too strong, a love that put him under too much pressure. Not that Hal demanded anything for himself; just the opposite. Instead, the realization hit Leith with some force: Hal's love demanded too much of him.

But in some way Stella's implied feelings for him meant something more. Well, his family *had* to love him. Stella, though, was the desire of his heart.

"Do you think they are all right?" Kurr asked the Haufuth for the fourth time that morning. And for the fourth time the big man answered, "I'm sure they are."

"One of us should have stayed with them," the old farmer said, also for the fourth time. Leith anticipated the answering grunt from his village headman.

"Still, what's done is done. We can't go back now."

Leith could not let this go on, the two older men were punishing themselves. "But where are we going?" he asked. The old farmer turned to him as they walked.

"We go to Kantara, like we discussed last night. We have no other choice. As the Haufuth said, it is the same choice we faced back in Loulea; to protect the ones we love, with no hope of final victory, or reach out and risk all. We must finish what we have been called to do."

"But where is Kantara? If it is anywhere?"

"We know that Kantara is in the mountains of Nemohaim, at the head of the Vale of Neume," Phemanderac said from directly behind them. Leith and the farmer both turned to regard the serious philosopher. "Bewray hid the Arrow there."

"Will it still be there for us to find?" the Haufuth said quizzically. "Surely it must have been found some time in the last two thousand years?"

"Finding it may be the least of our problems,"

Phemanderac admitted. "The sacred book spoke of some form of protection. Sentinels and guardians."

"Oh," said Leith. This was sounding worse every time they talked about it.

"It is my hope that the Arkhimm—the five fingers of the Right Hand—is constituted specially to spring the trap, or to find a way around the guardians," the philosopher continued. "Something about the combination of talents found amongst you, some blend of courage and cunning, of honesty and single-heartedness, of self-doubt and confidence . . ."

"You talk in riddles," Kurr said gruffly. "And anyway, if what you say is true, won't Stella's absence cause us a problem or two?"

"That's exactly what I'm afraid of," Phemanderac admitted. "Nevertheless, we cannot go back for her now. If the remainder of the Company contrive to escape the city and find us on the road to Kantara, well and good. Otherwise, we will face whatever we have to face, and overcome it, or not."

"First we have to find Nemohaim," Hal reminded them. "None of us have been southwest of Instruere. We have to pass through Straux and Deruys—two friendly countries, so the innkeeper told us—before we reach Nemohaim."

"Before that we have to find the main road," one of the Escaignians said gruffly. "We're not much help, we've not been out of Instruere in over a decade."

"Down this path until we come to a small village, then take the gravel road to the right until we come to a low hill; that's what the innkeeper said," recited the other Escaignian. "The Great South Road will be found on the far side of the hill."

"I thought he said the gravel road went off to the *left*," the Haufuth said.

"And how much further is this village?" the first, taller Escaignian inquired, the one with the bright eyes. "I think the innkeeper was too drunk to give us the correct directions."

"At breakfast time?" Leith looked doubtful.

"You were there last night," Kurr commented dryly. "You saw him. He drank more beer than the rest of the bar combined. I'm surprised he was able to get out of bed this morning."

The Haufuth shook his head and winced. It had been a lively evening. "He looked like a man who could hold his liquor."

"Still, I don't trust the directions he gave us," the shorter Escaignian insisted. "We should have found the village by now."

"You mean *this* village?" Kurr asked, pointing down the lane to where a few rude shelters were interspersed with the trees.

"Look for a gravel road," the taller Escaignian suggested.

"And then go right," said his companion.

"Left," corrected the Haufuth.

Kurr sighed.

"You will stand aside and let us pass," said the enormous man in his high-pitched, wheezy voice. "You have no authority to prevent our passage. Stand aside!" The Arkhos's temper skirled upwards towards breaking point. Beside him the Archivist stared nervously over the low sides of Southbridge into the lazy waters of the Aleinus River, trying not to pay too close attention to the conflict.

"It's for your own good, sir." Sweat poured off the forehead of the young guard, who knew this man by reputation. "Enemies of the State are abroad, and no one is to leave Instruere until they are located."

"Those are your orders?" The voice had a dangerous edge to it.

"Yes, my lord. I would not presume to stand in your way were I not obliged to do so." The guard's face paled visibly under the Arkhos's pig-eyed stare.

"So I am a prisoner in Instruere?"

The young guard did not speak, but the answer was obvious, visible on his face. Deorc had taken control, and meant to play with Nemohaim like a cat plays with a mouse. This youngster stood between the Arkhos and his freedom, between his life and death. *I'll have to be careful here*, the big man thought, but his thoughts were betrayed by the hot singing of his blood in his head.

"I am a prisoner and *you* are my jailer?" he asked quietly. He took a step closer to the young man, menacing, intimidating. Behind him his company shuffled their feet nervously.

"Don't draw your swords until I give the signal," the young guard said, motioning his men back.

The Arkhos of Nemohaim smiled, and laid his hand on the hilt of his sword. "That's right," he purred. "We don't need to involve anyone else in this. You see, I have to leave the city, and you have orders to prevent me. Let the matter be decided at the point of a sword."

The young guard had been badly outmaneuvered. He could command his troops to slay the Arkhos, but he would lose face before his company. Nemohaim once had a fearsome reputation as a swordsman, but had run to fat, and perhaps single combat would be the best way out of this. He had graduated third in the Academy, more than handy with the sword, and should be able to vanquish this cumbersome, slow man. Yet he had orders not to take this man's life if at all possible. There was no way out of his dilemma.

"So, lackbeard." The Arkhos spat the words out. "You will not fight me. Then take the coward's place and step aside!"

The calculated insult had its effect. Against his better judgment the young guard drew his weapon and adopted the half-crouch drilled into him at the Academy. At the sight of this the Arkhos of Nemohaim smiled. A neophyte. *I can predict every move, every response.*

The fight was short and bitter, the outcome never in doubt. Forward two steps came the youngster, leading with the left foot, and a feint to the right. A classic textbook opening. The Arkhos waited with his sharp blade. The sound of steel on bone made the Archivist turn away. For all practical purposes it was finished then, though the guard was valiant to the end. The Arkhos didn't have to kill him, but the blackness in the center of his being cried out for death, reminding him of Deorc's gloating smile and the death of all his hopes, and so he slashed the defenseless youth until he no longer moved, and then some more after that. The remainder of the Southbridge Guard melted away, and the Arkhos led the horrified Archivist, their five servants and their horses across the bridge into Straux.

"You have some skill with the blade, my lord," said one of the servants, bowing to the Arkhos before they mounted their horses. This servant pulled back the heavy cowling that had hidden his distinctive features, revealing the captain of the Instruian Guard. "You were right," he said. "It was important they did not recognize me."

"It is better the city thinks you lost in the flood," the Arkhos said, pausing to mop his brow.

"I almost was. I have never seen such power wielded by one man, my lord. He just raised his arm and the flood rose up. Fifteen of my best men were killed, cruelly drowned. We will have to be careful in the face of such miracles."

"I have met the boy you say caused the flood," the Arkhos of Nemohaim said in his chesty wheeze. "I saw him in the Inner Chamber of the Council of Faltha, and he performed no miracles then when a miracle would have served them well. But he comes from a powerful family, one we have had dealings with before. They must be destroyed before their interference can affect the plans I have laid. And when I have this Arrow I will destroy them all." His voice was implacable, but his gaze was on the city as he spoke.

The last flush of the setting sun found Leith and the others of the Arkhimm scrambling up a series of low hills topped by a single line of tall pine trees. This day had not worked out as they had hoped: misled by a hung-over innkeeper, they had expected to find the Great South Road by lunchtime and be safely in lodgings by now. Instead the seven of them spent an unpleasant afternoon lost, and Leith found the experience of being lost in a strange land extremely disconcerting. There had been arguments, and at one point the Haufuth and the old farmer came close to a serious falling-out. *Here we are on a quest to unify Faltha*, Leith thought wryly, *yet we can't agree amongst ourselves. Where are my fancy voices now?*

The day, which had started so promisingly, clouded over; the sky lowered as the cold west wind rose, until the dark green branches of the exposed pines still some distance above them swayed back and forth, groaning and creaking in the stiff breeze. Cold, tired, hungry and downhearted, Leith and the others finally crested the hill and gazed out over the twilight world of southern Westrau.

A hundred feet below them a silver ribbon of swiftly flowing water wound its way to the right, beside which Leith could make out a road—wider than any other they had seen in this country—surely the Great South Road. Far off to the right, in the hazy middle distance, twinkled the cozy new-lit lights of a large town, snugly nestled in the low arms of hilly outliers. The young Loulean's heart sank as he realized just how many hours it would take them to reach the safe haven of that town, and longer still until he was lying asleep in a bed.

A collective sigh came from the small group as they looked out from the hills towards their rest; then Kurr started down the steep slope to the road. Leith took a step forward to follow him. At that moment the sound of horses came from the left.

"Back to the trees," Kurr growled. "Better be careful. We don't know this country." Leith, who was by now some distance down the slope, made an undignified scramble back up to the trees as the riders came into view.

For a moment Leith did not believe what, or who, he was seeing. Surely there could be no other man of such size, or who wore red robes like those clearly visible in the fading light. Beside him he felt, rather than saw, Kurr stiffen in recognition, while just behind him Phemanderac gave a stifled cry, for down below on the Great South Road came the Arkhos of Nemohaim, accompanied by the Archivist (whom Phemanderac had recognized) and five well-armed attendants. They were riding their horses at a fast, mile-eating canter, and in a few moments they passed by and were hidden by the shadows off to the right.

Leith let out his breath in a slow, low whistle, and the tension that had gripped him since their arrival in Instruere clamped itself around his chest again.

Behind him Phemanderac shook his head. "Did you recognize the man immediately behind the Arkhos?" he asked Kurr.

The old farmer shrugged his shoulders.

"He's the man in charge of the Instruere Archive. He knows about the Jugom Ark," the philosopher said sadly.

Kurr took a moment to put it together. "So a man who knows the nature of our quest is in league with our chief foe, one who undoubtedly knows his way around the countryside of Nemohaim. This changes everything." The dour farmer's face wore a look of despondency. "Just when things were looking a little more straightforward."

"For all our problems, I'd rather be here than back in Instruere," said Leith quietly.

It was not until well after dark that the Arkhimm made it to the outskirts of the sprawling town, and immediately they settled into the familiar routine of seeking out the least-rowdy inn—with the extra proviso that tonight it should not have regally attired horses stabled nearby. After much cautious investigation they finally settled on The Reveler's Rest, a small inn set off the main road. In talking to the innkeeper they discovered the name of the town was Kinnekin, the largest town in southern Westrau, set roughly halfway between Instruere and the southern border of Straux. After arranging rooms for the night the hungry travelers sought meals, and in a little time (but still far too long for Leith) they were settled in a corner of the main bar-room, working their way through fare that was plain but had the special merit of being substantial. Leith eased off his boots and let the stiffness and strain drain from his tired feet. Beside him Phemanderac sat back in his chair and stretched aching limbs.

"Back in Dhauria we were taught walking is good for you," he said. "I can't imagine how they developed such a theory."

The Haufuth smiled. "I see the Arkhos of Nemohaim doesn't subscribe to the theory either."

"Perhaps the theory is intended only for large men," Kurr jibed.

The village headman turned to Leith, Hal and the two Escaignians. "I wonder whom he could possibly be referring to," he said, smiling ruefully.

"Not you, if that's your worry," the old farmer growled good-naturedly. "You've lost far too much weight to be named in the same breath as the Arkhos of Nemohaim."

"Well, I suggest if you don't want to lose any more, you consider finding horses," Leith said as tactfully as he could. Now the Haufuth had rejoined them the old farmer had given way to the headman's leadership, but he obviously did not find the transition easy.

"Horses would be an excellent idea," said the big headman. "If we only had enough money to purchase them! Most of our money is back in Instruere with the remainder of the Company."

The Company, thought Leith shamefacedly. He had spent very little time thinking about them—apart from Stella—and they were very probably having the worst time of it. Phemanderac had told him of the Company's precarious position, trapped between the river and the

Instruian Guard. Their only hope, expressed in hushed tones on their first night out from the Great City, was that the sudden flood afforded the Company an avenue of escape—or, failing that, if they had been captured they were still alive. *I'm so selfish*, he chastised himself. *I could have spared them* some *thought*. So he forced himself to give each one of them a moment, to capture an image of them in his mind. Indrett, his mother. Eyes bright with tears, waiting for her love to come home. Mahnum, his father, a figure carved from birch, now with a face. Farr, the Vinkullen man, strong eyes, a scowling brow, softening in the forest greenshade. And, beside him, his brother Wira, insubstantial now. Broad-shouldered and broad-hearted, with a hurt hidden deep inside. Perdu. Solid, forthright, eyes haunted by the separation from his family and his people. And behind him, the ghost of Parlevaag, frozen in the act of giving her life for them. The Hermit, cloaked with power, mysteries on his tongue. Curiously, the image of the Hermit was the least substantial of the Company. Achtal the Acolyte, flint-hard and ruthless, somehow inhuman but no longer an enemy. And Stella. His thoughts lingered on her image, and still lingered, until the food and the fire combined to send him to sleep.

An hour or two went by, as the four Louleans talked things over with Phemanderac and the Escaignians. Between them they had enough coinage for one fair pack-horse, so they decided that Kurr should seek one on the morrow. Conversation turned to Instruere, and the Escaignians talked about their lives, their families and their rebellion against the lords of the city. True to their custom, the two Escaignians would not reveal their names.

Names were powerful things, reflected Phemanderac. *Without them the two were merely representatives of their nation, unable to be approached too closely. Perhaps this was necessary in a place like Escaigne had been; a hidden society where trust was everything, betrayal spelled ruin and the corporate was more important than the individual, seeming to take on a life of its own. How unlike Dhauria*, he mused, *with its cult of the individual, the sophistry of its arguments, the rules still existing but unwritten, and maybe more powerful for all that. On second thought, perhaps Dhauria and Escaigne were not so dissimilar—hidden, self-absorbed, unaware of the wider world, and ultimately vulnerable. And Faltha? Faltha had enough good people to see the Sixteen Kingdoms through—if they could be raised up, if they could be organized to resist the darkness sweeping in from the east.* But underneath it all something nagged at him. Was the brown tide of Bhrudwo any darker than the blackness in Faltha's own heart? Which was the greater enemy? Who gathered around the great prize of Faltha, ready to pick the eyes from her corpse—the hawks from the east or the vultures of the west?

Outside the inn, in the darkness of a moonless night, shadowy figures flitted across the open spaces either side of the small building. Small movements served as signals as the black shadows surrounded the building, and seemingly random night-sounds guided them to predetermined positions.

The fire died down as the bar emptied, and the innkeeper, a jolly, round-faced fellow, set to washing the tankards. In the far corner the Arkhimm sat, on the edge of slumber, wearied by the miles and by the deeper sense of care. The door burst open with a crash. In rushed a large group of people led by a long-haired man wearing the livery of the Instruian Guard. Before the Arkhimm shook the sleep from their eyes they were surrounded by men with swords drawn menacingly, men who ignored the innkeeper's strident protests and leveled their steely eyes at the startled faces of their quarry.

"There'll be no trouble, barkeep," the long-haired man said evenly. "These men were just leaving."

"What do you want with us?" the Haufuth asked, trying unsuccessfully to keep the fear out of his voice.

"We're your friends," said the Instruian-robed man in a heavy colloquial accent, the sort Leith had heard in the markets of Instruere, and in tones that were anything but friendly. "We just want to make sure none of you northerners have any accidents on your way to your lodgings. Would be easy to stub a toe in the dark, see? Though not with us around." He smiled, and a few of his fellows laughed. "We'll look after you."

"We don't need looking after," said Kurr, his old belligerence evident in his posture, no doubt cursing his decision to leave his sword upstairs. It was a gift from the Escaignians, given on the south bank of the Aleinus, and now it would be gone. Along with what else? "We are lodging here tonight."

"Change of plans," the long-haired man said cheerfully. "Our master wants to meet you, and he's asked me to arrange it." He smiled wider, and Leith noticed an assortment of the man's teeth were missing. At that moment Leith hoped the losing of them had hurt him.

"And who is your master?"

Long-hair turned to his fellows. "This old'n's got a tongue in him! Talk us right through the night if we let him!" He turned back to Kurr with an air of mock civility. "However, sir, we don't 'ave the time to enjoy the beer, though they do say it's the best to be found in these parts," he said, nodding to the bemused publican. "Come on, then." He beckoned to the Arkhimm. "Let's go, and make it sharpish, or I'll make sharpish with you." He fingered his sword and laughed as though he had just made a great joke.

The Arkhimm had no choice. At swordpoint they filed past the bar and out into the still, cool night air, while two of the rogues went through their possessions. It was all too much for Leith, recaptured on the brink of escaping. The thought of returning to Instruere and The Pinion was unbearable. He began to cry softly.

Two or three miles out of Kinnekin, Long-hair and his men guided their prisoners away from the main road, through a high hedge behind which horses were tethered and into an open field. For an awful moment Leith thought the end had come.

"I am truly sorry for any inconvenience, but I had a fiction to propagate," said the long-haired man, all traces of a city accent gone. "I wanted the innkeeper to believe you had been reclaimed by the Instruians."

"Who are you?" Kurr asked in wonder. "What do you want with us?"

"Who I am is not important at this time," he replied. "What is important is the King of Deruys has sent for you, and you are to be taken to him. Do not despair! Your quest is known to us. We wish to aid rather than hinder you." He smiled at them, a rich, wide smile. "If we had not taken you when we did, you would have been recaptured by the Instruians. Now, if you will allow me, I will be rid of this foul raiment." He stepped into the shadows of the hedge and began to take off the livery of the Instruian Guard.

"The King of Deruys?" Kurr said.

"Our quest is known?" Shock registered on Phemanderac's face.

"You're not from Instruere?" the Escaignians asked with relief in their voices.

"You're still prisoners, you know," Long-hair said, wiping the blackener from his teeth. "My lord wishes to take counsel with you, and he is a most determined man."

"But why the disguise?" Leith asked.

"I'll answer your questions on the way to Deruys." He waved to his men, who handed their captives back their possessions. "Now mount up! We have still a long journey to make."

Stealthily the guardsmen surrounded the building, giving not a sign of their presence. They had done this sort of thing many times before: night raids on traitors, opponents of the Council, dragging them from their homes to the pitiless Pinion, there to be questioned and broken. Tonight was going to be a little more interesting, for the reputation of the northerners—they had bested a dozen Bhrudwans in hand-to-hand combat, according to reports—had only been enhanced by the hatred on the puffy face of the Arkhos of Nemohaim as he talked strategy with his guards. So they took extra care, ensuring the advantage of surprise was played to the fullest.

But it was they who were surprised when they broke down the door of The Reveler's Rest only to find an empty inn and an innkeeper who could only say: "But you already took them!"

They searched the inn, and found clothing that matched

that which the northerners had been wearing when they escaped Instruere. A few swords, a little money, nothing substantial. Fearing the wrath of the Arkhos, they took the unfortunate innkeeper aside and gave him their own special brand of assistance with his memory.

"So we have another enemy," the Arkhos ground out when he could trust himself to speak. "The northerners are in league with someone—someone powerful." It did not take the Arkhos long to arrive at the logical—the only—conclusion, fueled by hatred as he was.

"Deorc!" *The Destroyer, damn him to the pit of fire!*

"My lord?" The Captain of the Guard gave the Arkhos his full attention. It had been an exhausting night, ever since his men had seen the northerners coming into Kinnekin, and things had not gone well. For a few moments after delivering the bad news he had feared for his own life.

"My foe's hand is in this. It has his hallmarks. Treachery, cunning, stealth. We must be on our guard."

"Yes, my lord." Anything to placate the man.

"Send two of your men out on each road, north and south. I want to know exactly where they are. If we can keep up with them, they will lead us to the Arrow. My Arrow!"

"Now, my lord?" He should have known better, but it was late and he hadn't fully recovered from his narrow escape on the day of the flood.

Instead of exploding, the obese man simply turned his dead eyes on the Captain of the Guard. "Go now," he said in a voice devoid of inflection.

The Captain of the Guard went.

The journey to Brunhaven, capital of Deruys, took nine days. During that time Leith learned a great deal about the

Raving King of Deruys and, having heard the stories, was not at all sure he wanted to meet him. "Mad" was the most polite thing said about him. Apparently the monarch, on the throne nearly fifty years, had a habit of speaking obliquely. He had been wont to indulge in eccentric behavior until arthritis confined him to his castle, and even now his exploits, performed (often unwittingly) through his courtiers, the nobility, his guards or even his family, brought much mirth to the stolid kingdom. His madness, apparently, disguised a serious purpose.

None of this came direct from the long-haired Deruvian who, though sociable enough, kept his purpose to himself. Most of what the northerners gleaned about their intended host came from the idle talk around them, until their long-haired leader made them keep their peace. "It's enough that the king is what he is," he told them sternly. "Don't add to our embarrassment."

Late in the afternoon on the sixth day they crossed the border between Straux and Deruys, a footbridge over a small stream that came down from the purple highlands away to their left. The border guards made a half-hearted attempt to question them, until the long-haired man came forward. Leith distinctly saw their faces blanch, and noted the alacrity with which they waved the Deruvians through. The border guards had definitely heard of this cut-throat ruffian and his band, and were no doubt in his pay—or scared of what might be done to them.

"The Veridian Borders," Long-hair said as they rode across the bridge into Deruys, waving his arm airily at the purple smudge out to the east. "Beyond that lies the *Khersos*, the Deep Desert. Our way lies to the west, down to the coast."

"And between?" Leith looked out on the mountains

ahead of them, lower but more rumpled than the stern heights of the Veridian Borders.

"Between is the Mist," said Long-hair cryptically. Leith squinted at the lean young man in the service of the King of Deruys, but there was no guile in his face.

"Looks clear enough to me," the young northerner said pointedly.

"Their name for it. The land gets a lot of rain; most often it is shrouded in mist. It is not part of Deruys, not yet. Highlands, covered in bush, not good for farming. A few people live there."

"It's beautiful," said one of the Escaignians, watching the sun kiss the peaks in the distance. "I never imagined the outside world would be like this."

"I can't remember why we stayed in Escaigne," his partner remarked, turning in the saddle to face him. "Can you?"

"It escapes me."

Leith reflected a moment on the two Escaignians. So young they seemed, so vulnerable, removed as they were from their homeland. Last night they had sat apart, some distance away from the fire, talking quietly; trying to make some sense of the wide world. Of course they learned about it in Escaigne, but it was different—bigger, more complex—out here. They had not planned to go this far south, having decided on the dock just after the vast flood swept through that they would travel far enough to ensure that the northerners found the Road, then return to Escaigne; but they had been drawn into this journey, this quest, and as they continued it became clear to them that Escaigne itself was but one part of a much larger story.

The young man from Loulea wanted to reach out to these two people, to offer them some comfort or with wise words help explain their place in what was happening to their world; but he did not know their place, he did not have the words, and he knew of no way to reach them. He didn't even know their names. The taller man, probably aged in his early twenties, was the one who had led Leith to the Water Chamber, and the Loulean youth thought of him as "Bright-eyes": he seemed to wear a perpetual smile, and constantly had a cheerful comment ready to apply to any situation. The shorter of the two was not a man at all. It had been a shock to the Arkhimm to learn the second Escaignian was, in fact, a woman—though why it should have been surprising, Leith had been unsure on that first night south of Instruere when Bright-eyes had requested that his friend be given a separate room. After all, Stella and Indrett had traveled with the Company, hadn't they? Though neither traveled by choice, both became vital parts of their enterprise. Why should this woman be any different? Still, he had been so surprised he'd struggled to give the woman any mind-name, but finally settled on "Freckle," for self-evident reasons.

Kurr had tried to find out their real names, invoking his authority as a Watcher of the Sixth Rank; but apparently their training had been somewhat better than other Escaignians they had encountered, and they simply ignored him. They listened politely as Kurr and the Haufuth told them the story of their journey from Firanes and their trials in Instruere, and contributed what little they knew of Instruian and Escaignian history. Leith listened too, and wondered wryly whether this repetition of the story was the way legends were made. Already their deeds sounded heroic, completed by figures larger than life, when they had actually been unpleasant acts done out of necessity, costing lives—

and no doubt would cost more. Perhaps when the story had been told a thousand times he would be ten feet tall, the wielder of a mighty blade, before whom the doughtiest warriors of the world quailed in fear.

The sixth day ended in a blazing sunset and a warm bonfire under another black, moonless night. The next morning they came to a wide coastal plain and a main road with houses and small farms on either side, hiding behind well-manicured hedges and solid stone walls. Late the following day, after a hard ride, the travelers reined in at Brunhaven's North Gate.

Brunhaven was a glorious city, straight out of a child's painting of what a capital city should look like. The walls were low, and the city climbed upwards behind them; whether the buildings were taller the further back one went, or perhaps the city was built on a slope, the northerners could not tell. Whatever the reason, they could see spires with pennants fluttering, domes shining golden in the sun, crisp clean lines, order and tidiness everywhere. Leith looked in vain for a stray dog, a beggar or an open sewer as they rode quietly down the straight cobbled streets, the clatter of hooves on stone painfully loud in the still midday air. To the left and to the right small plots of flowers decorated the margins of the road, and beyond the splashes of green, red and yellow the squat whitewashed buildings sat in orderly rows. Looking down side streets one could catch glimpses of open grassy spaces. Leith took in a lungful of the air: no foulness, no reek. He could not help contrasting the white of Brunhaven with the brown and gray of Instruere, the quiet with the noise, the order with the chaos, the purposeful walk of the people with the aimlessness common in the Great City.

Above all, there was no sense of the malaise that Leith had learned to detect in Instruere.

Directly ahead of him Freckle turned to Bright-eyes. "What a dull place," she said, shaking her head.

The palace was situated on a piece of elevated ground near the center of the city, a high hill encircled by a white wall and a blue stream. Both the wall and the palace were constructed of white stone cunningly laid, producing a pattern pleasing to the eye, and from the wall a drawbridge was lowered so they could cross the stream.

"A real castle," Leith said. It was the first time Leith had considered a building beautiful.

"Just like the castles above Inverell," Kurr said to the Haufuth. "One day this too will lie in ruins."

A narrow cobbled path wound its way up the greensward to the palace proper, and up this path Longhair led his guests. The soldiers and courtiers all bowed formally to him, and he nodded his head to them. The great wooden palace doors were swung open by two tall guards in full regalia, trumpets were blown, formal words exchanged and the group ushered through a myriad of corridors to a large pillared and vaulted hall. The throne room.

Behind the throne a single arched stained-glass window cast multicolored light into the hall, illuminating the ranks of courtiers attending the king, the carved throne, the white-robed figure seated upon it and the golden crown set upon his head. The simplicity, the elegance, the beauty of it took Leith's breath away. Could this truly be happening to a village boy from the North March of Firanes? Now the King of Deruys stood and beckoned to the group, and Long-hair led them across the blood-red carpet to the dais upon which the throne stood.

Leith was uncomfortably conscious of their attire—their simple, travel-stained cloaks, their backpacks, their weary, grimy faces—in the midst of all this finery.

The Haufuth drew close to Kurr. "I wish Indrett were here," he whispered. "She spent most of her life in a palace. She'd know what to do."

"Say as little as possible, and speak truthfully when you do," the old farmer replied. "Deruys has no reputation for evildoing."

"Neither did Instruere," the village headman shot back.

The group mounted the steps to the throne, and Leith was able to get a good look at the Raving King of Deruys, as Long-hair's men had named him. He was an old man, Leith knew, at least seventy years old, but his fair face, framed by long white hair, was remarkably unlined. His face wore a slight smile, the eyes a rheumy vagueness. Leith had not known what to expect. The fashion with which their journey had been forcibly interrupted and the rumors of this man had not prepared him for the gentleness he read in the king.

"My son," the king said in a clear, pleasant voice; and, to the surprise of the Arkhimm, Long-hair stepped forward. "My lord," he said, and bowed.

"Gatherer of flowers and stones, be welcome in our halls. Have you planted them to see which will grow?" the king asked.

"No, my lord," said Long-hair. He appeared to expect this sort of question. "I left that task to those who have better skills at gardening."

The old man smiled. "And where is my queen?"

"Awaiting your command, my lord," came a low, rich voice from amongst the courtiers. "Just growing a few flowers of my own."

Leith looked at Phemanderac, who shrugged his shoulders in reply to the unspoken question.

The queen came forward and stood by her husband's throne. She was a much younger woman, short but slender, not much older than Leith's own mother, perhaps. But what took Leith's breath away was the look of keen intelligence on her face; the gaze of an eagle she had, and her formidable eyes gripped whomever they alighted on like the talons of a bird of prey.

She cast her gaze over the members of the Arkhimm, then turned to the king.

"Perhaps we should water them, my lord."

The king nodded sagely, then extended a hand to his guests. "Come and receive our blessing, travelers from afar," he said. "We extend the bounty of our kingdom to you."

"Does that extend as far as showing us the quickest way out?" Kurr inquired ironically.

The king was unperturbed. "Kurnath of Sivithar, late of Loulea in far Firanes, Watcher of the Sixth Rank; Warden Protector, sword-sharp and with a backbone of steel, be welcome. Seldom has one of your rank been seen in this court. You, however, are not the leader here."

"No, my lord," said the old farmer, bowing and stepping back, flushing red all the while.

"Haufuth of Loulea; Heart and Life, ox-couraged and deep as a wellspring, be welcome. You lead the hope of Faltha at the nexus of all times. This hall is not big enough for you."

The Haufuth's eyes narrowed, unsure whether he had

been praised or ridiculed, but he bowed in imitation of Kurr. The king smiled his pleasant smile.

"Phemanderac, Dominie of Dhauria, Water of Life, mist-cloaked and far-eyed, be welcome. You see too truly to be comfortable in our lands."

"True, my lord," said Phemanderac after he bowed. "But sight without understanding merely magnifies choice and increases confusion. I search for understanding to sharpen my sight."

The monarch of Deruys clapped his hands together and laughed aloud like a child. "See, my queen? Water them and watch them grow!"

"But don't pluck them untimely," she warned, her eyes on the gaunt philosopher, "or they will disease and die."

"My lady," the king said, "will you water these ones?" and he indicated the Escaignians.

"Assuredly, my lord. Ceau and Illyon, Watchers of the Second Rank, late of Escaigne; Rock and Pillar, dour bastions of the kind upon which Faltha will be rebuilt, be welcome. I grieve to have learned the fate of your nation."

Twin gasps came from the Escaignians at her words, as much for the speaking of their names as for the presaging of the fate of Escaigne.

"Do you have news for us, lady?" they asked her. "News of Escaigne?"

"I do," she said, "but it would be better received in private. The principle of rain in season is not mocked, though sometimes overmuch rain might fall. We would shelter you from the storm."

The king nodded again, and Leith began to suspect that the power in this kingdom did not wholly reside with him.

"Things are always as they seem," the king said, turning his old eyes on him, "if seeming is understood for what it is. Leith Mahnumsen, peasant of Loulea, the fire about to waken us all, be welcome. The match is ready to be set to the kindling."

"No, your majesty," Leith said, in a flash of insight, understanding that it would be acceptable to speak so, "the kindling is already alight." *I was wrong, after all. This man knows things like the Hermit knows them, but dresses them up so that others will not see the naked truth of his words.*

The king smiled shrewdly. "So you are a truth-speaker also? That is good news."

Leith took a moment to consider the naming of the Escaignians. Ceau and Illyon. *But which is which?*

The Deruvian king drew a deep breath. "Hal Mahnumsen, peasant of Loulea; Destroyer and Healer, be welcome. I assure you I know what can be spoken, and what must remain silent for fear of unmaking what it is."

Hal smiled at him and nodded.

Now the king addressed the Arkhimm as a group. "Warden Protector and your Heart and Life, the men who lead you, stand before me. I see the one who grasps the fire, and he who will water you all with knowledge. I acknowledge Rock and Pillar. I tremble before Destroyer and Healer. But where are the others? I desired so much to meet she of the Starlight, and also the Great Sufferer and her husband the Traveler, along with the Healer's Knight. Where is Faithful and True? What of He who Dares All? And the Soothsayer? Why do I not have the pleasure of their company?"

As the names were spoken Leith tried to use his insight to match them to the Company, but without much success.

"If you know the fate of Escaigne, you know where they are," said Kurr. "Which is perhaps a little more than we do."

"You might be well advised to look to your manners, old man," growled one of the king's guards. "The king will be given respect."

"When he earns it!" Kurr snapped. The courtesies had been nothing but an irritating distraction to him, exhausting his small store of patience. "We have a task to perform, and He Who Seems to Know Everything ought to know what will happen should we fail. He will earn our respect when he guides us to his borders and gives us aid in the completion of our mission!"

Instantly two guards of the king's house stepped forward and drew their swords, leveling their tips at the old farmer's throat. "He dies for those words, my king," said one of the guards.

"If you raise your hand against me, you raise your hand against Faltha!" Kurr was past reason. He had not spent weeks cooped up in Instruere, enduring the failure of their mission to the Council and the possible loss of the rest of the Company, just to listen to some clever wordsmith. "Then whose enemy have you become? Shall Deruys be aligned with Bhrudwo? Why has Deruys interfered with our mission?"

A low hiss echoed through the court.

"Forgive us, Haufuth," the king said, ignoring both Kurr and his guard. For a moment his eyes lost their rheumy film, and Leith read in them the same startling lucidity demonstrated by the queen. "I do indeed know the fate of your companions. They are locked in the gilded cage, but they sing still. A new man, a brown man, has the key, but does not yet know what he has captive. He has not discovered the entangled ones, but neither they nor the caged birds will be let out now.

"The man-mountain, the red man, has been displaced. He now hunts new quarry as a way of regaining favor with the keeper of the cage. Warden Protector, look to your laurels! The red man has a black heart."

"I know," Kurr said quietly. "We've seen him."

"So I sent my falcon out to gather up the stray birds, to protect them from the red man and to offer them whatever seed they require. As to flying south for the summer, members of a scattered flock far from their own land would do better to seek a guide who has flown those skies before."

"So we're supposed to be grateful?" Kurr's anger had not been assuaged. "Why capture us? Why not just offer us assistance?"

"Perhaps you haven't been listening," Long-hair said. "We know the importance of your mission . . ."

"Just how do you know?"

Long-hair took a sidelong glance at his father the king. "The Arkhos of Sarista managed to get a messenger out of Instruere two weeks ago, but another was intercepted and executed soon after. The story the successful messenger told alerted us, and we have been receiving reports from our own people in Instruere since then. The city is filled with rumor, but we think we can make out what has happened."

"Your people? Who are they?"

"Really, my friend, do you expect that to be answered in an open court? We gather news in order to be of use to passing strangers; that is all you need to know."

"So what happened?"

"Again, I must stress there is no guarantee that every-

one within earshot has the best interests of Deruys, Faltha
or your group at heart. It might be wiser to adjourn to private chambers if you mean to find out more."

"And tomorrow?" Kurr was determined not to let go.

"We will do what we can for you tomorrow. More than
that, we cannot promise."

The Arkhimm sat with the king's son in a small chamber.
They had taken a late lunch there, baked fish on a bed of
lettuce, and were now ready to listen to the king's pro-
posals. Except the king complained of a sudden headache
(though in describing his discommoded condition he was
by no means so direct), and left them with his son, Prince
Wiusago, Long-hair.

"He's not the only one with a headache," the Haufuth
complained when the king and his entourage left the
chamber. "How can you stand the constant brainwork?"

"Don't forget I was brought up with it," Wiusago said
defensively, brushing his long locks back out of his eyes.
"The Witenagemot dynasty prides itself on brainwork."
His voice took on a rueful note. "So what did they name
me? I have best friends named after wild animals, great
heroes of the past or particularly difficult feats of swordsmanship; but no, my parents decided 'wiseacre' would be
a good name for their eldest son." He laughed, and
looked at the door. "That's what my name means in Old
Deruvian. I thank you, Father."

With that the mood lightened somewhat, and the
Arkhimm learned a little of the ways and customs of the
Deruvians. Leith was puzzled by their habit of journeying to the coast to swim in the sea ("We consider it ther-
apeutic," Wiusago said in response to disbelieving stares
from Leith and the others: no one would ever consider

swimming in the wild, cold sea of Firanes). Phemanderac probed the prince about the uniformity of the architecture ("The Deruvians like order," was his short answer, "but you might like to ask my father about architecture, he's the authority. He built the palace wall himself when he was younger"). Eventually after a glass of wine and an easing of the tension that accompanied their capture, talk came back to the quest of the Arkhimm.

"We understand the seriousness of the situation," Longhair said. "Most of the kingdoms either dismiss the rumor of war as paranoia, or are themselves in league with Bhrudwo. We know of the betrayal of the Council of Faltha, though we have not heard from our ambassador—the Arkhos of Deruys, the king's own brother and my uncle—for nearly a fourweek. Let me assure you, by good fortune you have found the only court of any of the Sixteen Kingdoms which would both believe your story and be willing and able to lend you aid."

"What sort of aid might you lend, and how are we to pay it back?" the Haufuth wanted to know. "Most of all, how do you know of our quest when we ourselves are unsure of what it is we are trying to achieve?"

"You have not spoken openly of your quest, so we may not be able to suit aid to the specifics of your situation. However, we can guess the nature of your mission. You headed south when the danger comes from the east, so either you are running away—not a likely possibility, I might add," he said, looking sideways as Kurr bristled, "or you seek something or someone. Behind you comes the Arkhos of Nemohaim, until recently the man with the heart of Faltha in his hand. He is accompanied by the Captain of the Guard, said to have perished in the great flood, though obviously it is not so, and by a curious man whom we discover is the Archivist of Instruere. Now, the Captain of the Guard I can understand, if the Arkhos's purpose is to raise an army to retake Instruere for himself. But no, he travels south with all speed, making contact with none of his servants in Westrau, seeking someone if we read the signs right, and talking constantly to this Archivist. So we make inquiries about your party, and learn one among you spent much time with this Archivist, and is himself a Loremaster. In fact, some among us remember a man like him traveling north through Deruys two years ago, asking questions such as a master of lore might ask. So we reason that both your party and the Arkhos's band come south in search of some great heirloom."

Phemanderac pursed his lips and raised his eyebrows, tacit acknowledgement of the shrewdness of the prince's logic.

"Now I do not believe in heirlooms. Every kingdom has their legends of heirlooms lost, and from time to time various dreamers have made journeys in search of them, their adventures and their deaths adding to the legend. Legends are slippery things, difficult to grasp, always changing shape. I believe in solid things, the sky, the earth, man's evil and the necessity for bright steel, treaties, lies and international boundaries. However, my father sets little store by such things, and when presented with the evidence he suggested you might be pursuing a particular heirloom of legendary fame. Not in our kingdom, but in one further south. Do I aim my arrow accurately?"

"You have strung your bow with the correct heirloom," the Haufuth acknowledged. "Though, like you, I do not believe in such things. Yet there seems nothing else to be done. We are, after all, just a few northern peasants."

"Who, if the tales have not already assumed the status of legend, have defeated a band of Bhrudwan masters—I would give my inheritance to meet even one on the field of battle!—and liberated The Pinion of its prisoners. How wise that was I do not know, but it certainly was brave. Whatever you are, you cannot be simply a few northern peasants."

"Yet that is what we are," Kurr insisted. "Peasants with a past, perhaps, but peasants nonetheless. We tried to warn the Council of danger, only to find we were months too late. So now we seek the one thing that might convince the kingdoms of their danger. With it we could rid ourselves of this internal plague and then resist the Bhrudwan locusts."

"I still do not believe in the existence of this thing you seek," Long-hair said. "However, my father does. So will the Fathers of the Sixteen Kingdoms, even those who have asked the locusts to come and devour their lands. As far as I can see, it is the idea of this thing, the unity it embodies and its symbolism as the weapon of the Most High, used to defeat the Destroyer, that is the real power. It has no power inherent in itself. Is that true, Loremaster?"

Phemanderac nodded his head and smiled. "Writers of history make much of the unusual, and would undoubtedly have recorded—and embellished—any instances of miraculous or supernatural power resident in the thing itself. There are none."

"Then does the real heirloom have to be discovered? Would not some similar weapon serve the same purpose? After all, it is a common article. Why expose yourself to the risk, the delay and, in my view, the inevitable failure?

We have arrows aplenty in our armory, even gold-plated ones, should you desire. I'm sure we could spare you one."

The Haufuth's eyes widened, but Phemanderac shook his head. "A nice idea, but it wouldn't work, for two reasons. First, the Arrow was fletched with *mariswan* feathers. Unless you have seen one of those legendary beasts recently, we might be hard pressed to make our arrow look convincing."

"Would people have to get that close to it?" Prince Wiusago was reluctant to let go of his idea.

"Undoubtedly many, including our enemies, would seek to verify our claim, should we find it. But there is a second and more powerful reason. We ourselves would not believe in the authenticity of the arrow."

"Why should we? We would know it was a hoax." The prince looked a little puzzled.

"So much of this depends on faith," Phemanderac answered him. "If we ourselves were not convinced, how could we expect to convince others? And how could we lead an army of ordinary Falthans into battle against Bhrudwan soldiers while we knew we had deceived them? All the power of the Arrow lies in the fact of it being *the* Arrow."

"So are you saying your quest is more than a search for something to bring unity? Do you agree with my father that the Arrow is a symbol of the Most High returning to have dealings with the First Men?"

"We'll have to see what happens. But we can't wait for the miraculous Arrow to turn up in the Hall of Meeting in the fat hand of the Arkhos of Nemohaim. It sometimes falls to the hands of humans to fulfill the wishes of the Most High."

"Or to perpetuate the myth of his existence," Long-hair said, but he softened the words by smiling. "I remain unconvinced about the heirloom itself, but I understand the reasons for your rejection of my little scheme. I suspect my father would also have rejected it. Never mind, it kept the mind occupied for a space of time." The young man sighed.

Leith received a sudden insight into this man. Intelligent, skilful in battle, yet with no challenge against which to measure himself in a kingdom that prided itself on order and predictability. With a sense of awe he knew what the prince was about to say. Not magical foreknowledge, but foreknowledge nonetheless. Was all magic like this?

"Let me come with you," said Prince Wiusago. "I would like the chance to pursue a legend. That is, if unbelief does not disqualify one from the pursuit."

Kurr glanced at the Haufuth, his eyes narrowing. The village headman leaned forward.

"I suspect your father was going to compel you to come anyway, and that is why he feigned a headache— so his compulsion would not be necessary. I thank you for your offer of assistance, and I accept it. Would you convey that message to your father? Tell him also that in spite of his watering, we're still not that wet."

The Haufuth sat back in his couch, aware of the eyes on him. He smiled, and said: "Well, it's about time I earned my keep as leader of this noble quest."

Kurr laughed, and so did Leith, a shared sound that did much to ease their hearts.

Later Prince Wiusago returned to tell them the king had indeed offered his own son as guide for their journey, and recommended one other, whom they were to meet at the evening meal. They also learned the fate of the Company trapped in Instruere. "Apparently in the confusion caused by the flood they escaped the guard and made it back into the city, where they are hidden from both Escaigne and Instruere," Long-hair told them. "We know they are alive, but have no clue as to their whereabouts or purpose. The city is shut up tight now, and we will not be able to get information in or out. There is no way your friends will be able to follow you south."

"That's a pity," said Phemanderac. "One of them in particular ought to accompany us," and Leith knew he referred to Stella and the five-fingered Hand. Leith wished she was here, but for his own reasons.

"A pity, certainly," echoed the prince. "For I was given to understand there were swordsmen among you, and—forgive me—I do not see them."

"Forgive you?" the Haufuth stormed playfully. "Forgive you? I declare to you I wield a powerful knife and fork, and were you a lamb or a boar you would have been devoured long since!" He smiled, then sighed. "No swordsmen, I'm afraid. Perhaps Farr, but even he would be no match for your highness, if we are to believe the minstrels out in the hall. They've been singing your praises all afternoon. Quite tiresome, actually. Did you really do all those things?"

"Legends," the prince said amiably. "It's a tradition that the minstrels retell the old legends and weave the name of whatever modern warrior they fancy into the story. I've never actually killed anyone, though I've seen it done. We've had a few border skirmishes with the wild men who live in the Mist, the green mountains I pointed out to you yesterday. Still, I was hoping you had brought some skill with you. Surely you must have some ability. Or did the Bhrudwans fall at your feet?"

"Something like that, actually." Kurr chuckled. "Though really it was no laughing matter."

"What about Achtal? He can use a sword," said Leith.

"Even he would find it difficult to leave Instruere now," Phemanderac said. "Besides, I don't think his sword would be of much use in locating the Arrow."

"But he might have been of some use in keeping off the Arkhos of Nemohaim and his men," Kurr observed.

"So might we," the prince interjected. "With your leave—or without it, actually, for we have no love of this Arkhos—my father's best men will watch the roads for Nemohaim and his party, and ensure that he follows us no further."

"That would be excellent," said the Haufuth. "We thank you for all your help, and our anger at having our ease interrupted at The Reveler's Rest has been somewhat reduced. Now, if you would be so good as to leave us, we will make our preparations for the meal to come. One can't be underprepared for such an occasion," he said, licking his lips in an anticipatory fashion.

"Very well, my friend." The prince laughed. "Shall I leave you a knife with which to make another notch for your belt? We do provide something of a feast for visitors, unfortunately."

"Oh dear," said the Haufuth. "See what trials we endure on this journey? Lesser men would not survive."

"You will be more of a man after tonight's feast, I can promise you that."

"Then you had better leave me to prepare," the village headman said. "But don't forget to tell me when dinner is ready."

*   *   *

The feast was all that was promised and more. In all his wildest dreams Leith never imagined feasting at a king's table, an honored guest among nobility clothed in courtly finery, sitting in the Great Hall of a real castle while minstrels sang of his deeds and those of his friends. The songs were not entirely accurate, but Leith did not have the heart to correct the minstrels, who seemed to have made such an effort.

"Eat up, Leith," Phemanderac whispered in his ear. "The time may soon come when food itself is but a memory."

Leith heard the warning, but amidst the glamor and the revelry he could not take it seriously. On his right-hand side sat an older man, a senior courtier of some sort, who kept trying to draw out stories of their journey south and east from Firanes, but Leith resisted talking about the Company, unsure as to how much he was allowed to say. The courtier had a mop of wiry graying hair, a lopsided grin and penetrating brown eyes, and an uncanny skill in getting Leith to say more than he wanted to. He cast about him for a distraction, noticed several young women of the court eyeing him speculatively, and realized with a degree of discomfit there was to be dancing after the meal. Perhaps he could borrow the king's excuse and claim a headache: indeed, the small amount of wine he had drunk had made him a little light-headed.

His fears were groundless. To the chagrin of many of the daughters of the nobility the northerners were taken aside by the prince after the feasting had finished and introduced to a dark-skinned stranger with flashing eyes.

"This is Te Tuahangata," Prince Wiusago told them. "My father wants to know if you will accept him as a companion on your journey."

"Greetings," the dark-skinned man said, then leaned forward and touched noses with each of them in turn. Leith could sense his companions' unease with the custom, but did not refuse when his time came to greet the stranger.

"I don't want to give offense," the Haufuth said carefully, "but surely we will have to know much more about this man before we allow him to accompany us. He's obviously not from Deruys, so where is he from? And why should he wish to come on our journey?" The words were perhaps harsher than he intended, but it was late and he had consumed a glass too much wine.

The tall stranger frowned a little, but said nothing.

"Te Tuahangata is from the Mist. Believe me, the people of the Mist do not readily make contact with outsiders. You are being accorded an honor."

"If meeting outsiders is so distasteful to him, why does he want to come with us?" Kurr was too tired to be conciliatory.

"Perhaps you would care to ask him yourself," Te Tuahangata said with exaggerated politeness. "Over many years of concentrated effort he has been trained in the rudiments of your language. He speaks almost as well as a real person now."

"Oh," stuttered the Haufuth, embarrassed. "I'm sorry."

"Are all you civilized people the same?"

"Leave them alone, Tua. They don't know the history."

"They've undoubtedly made some history of their own, First Men cutting an arrogant swathe of well-intentioned ignorance across the supposedly wild and empty north. Still, they can't be held responsible, right?"

The prince's eyes edged with anger, but his voice carried something close to compassion. "We should keep these things private, my friend. They're at a disadvantage here."

"And it warms my heart. It's an uncomfortable feeling, isn't it, not knowing what's going on?"

Things were definitely not going well. "Perhaps we are ignorant, or arrogant," Leith said. "Most likely we are both. So if you choose to come with us, we would be happy to hear about it."

Te Tuahangata nodded curtly. "You need someone to get you through the Mist. I know all the hidden paths. My father says it would be good for my people to be involved in the affairs of this land. I will come with you." He turned on his heel and strode away.

Even Kurr was left a little breathless. "Does anyone remember accepting his offer?"

"Is he always so prickly?" The Haufuth had still not recovered from his embarrassment.

"He has good reason to be prickly, and a lot more besides," Prince Wiusago said solemnly. "You will hear it from him if you are patient, or probably even if you are not. All I will say is there has been war between his land and ours, and his father and mine are attempting to undo the many strands of the ancient enmity."

"Why do we need him as a guide?" Kurr wanted to know. "Nemohaim is directly south of Deruys, that much I remember. I thought you were going to lead us."

"I will, for some of the way. But if you want to avoid the main road and the chance of encountering the Arkhos of Nemohaim or his agents, then Tua knows another way to the Almucantaran Mountains."

"How much time will it add to our journey?" the Haufuth asked worriedly.

"It will save us at least a week, though it is a hard road.

The main road to Bewray, the capital of Nemohaim, goes south and west, while the mountains which are the subject of the Kantaran legends are east as well as south. Besides, the Mist is the most beautiful country in the world. It will do your heart good to travel through it."

"The Mist?" Leith said. "I've never thought mist was beautiful."

Long-hair smiled. "You'll see. I've been into the Mist many times, yet still I long to return."

Phemanderac looked intently at the prince, and smiled in turn. "My friend, I am almost certain that your judgment of the land's beauty is colored by the beauty of one of its inhabitants. Am I right?"

To Leith's surprise the prince blushed slightly and lowered his eyes. "She has my heart in her hand. I will see her again before the week is out, and I will take her to wife, no matter what the law says."

"The law?"

"It is getting late," Prince Wiusago said evasively, as if he had said too much. "We know that you are in haste, and will no doubt want to leave in the morning. I have much to do before I can go to bed: dances to dance, wine to drink, responsibilities to discharge. I will see you at sunrise."

After the door had closed, Kurr and the Haufuth exchanged looks. "This is all getting out of control," the old farmer said. "We seem to be deciding nothing. Increasingly our course appears set for us."

The huge headman grimaced sourly as he replied, "When were we ever in control?"

CHAPTER 11

CHILDREN OF THE MIST

THE ORDERLY ROWS OF WHITEWASHED houses looked a little gray under the leaden morning sky that greeted the travelers. Leith, Phemanderac, Hal, the Haufuth and Kurr were each provided with a horse. Leith thought for a moment of refusing, as his riding skills were rudimentary at best. He could envisage the discomfort that awaited him over the next few days; however, the others accepted quickly and he found himself mounting his steed, a small bay mare, before he could raise a coherent objection. The Escaignians could not ride, and shared the saddle with Te Tuahangata and Prince Wiusago. Gifts were given: food and drink, fresh raiment for their journey into the Mist and the Sun of the South, and weapons. Leith had been given a sword. He fiddled with his scabbard, and noticed with pleasure that the leather had been oiled and his sword was sharpened and polished. He hefted the blade, then laughed at himself: *quite the expert on weaponry!*

The Raving King of Deruys came with his wife to bid them farewell. "Walk when you cannot ride, and crawl when you cannot walk," he said in his inimitable style. "Ride through mist into legend; ride hard, and do not stop to sup at any fireside for the sake of your soul. The misty firesides shed too much light for people like us." His gaze, artfully unfocused, rested for a moment on his son.

"When you can be that directly indirect, why bother to speak plainly?" Long-hair muttered. "Yet I will stop by one fireside if I get the chance."

"Deruys will be by your side when the Arrow flies," said the queen in her rich voice. "We will not bow low to Bhrudwo."

The Arkhimm, now nine strong, rode down the cobbled path away from the tall white castle and the strangely enchanting King and Queen of Deruys. They were followed by half a dozen mounted servants, chattering excitedly amongst themselves. Guards saluted them with a great clash of swords on shields as they passed, for their beloved prince rode in their midst, and the northerners had been honored by the king.

Out in the streets the citizens of Brunhaven went about their business in their normal efficient manner, sparing not a second glance at the riders making their way out of the old city. The morning was a little cold for early summer this far south, but the wind was off the sea not many miles distant: an offshore cold current brought spring fogs and rains to the coastlands between here and the Culmea, a land to the southwest of Bewray in Nemohaim, still many hundreds of miles distant. Tall poplars and rowan trees bent away from the breeze as they passed through the city gates and found the southward road. An ominous sight they were to Leith, who thought them like bony fingers crooked to the east in some sort of beckoning call. A gray mood descended upon him, something akin to what assailed him on the forest paths of Adunlok. Now, as then, he was separated from his family, from those he loved and cared for, and was heading into an unknown land. When a mood like this found him, he would once have made his way to the lake near his village and skipped a few stones, alone with his brooding thoughts; but there was no such relief available on this road. He tried to isolate a part of his mind, keeping it for his reflections, while he answered the others with the rest. After a while it was obvious he had failed, and so he kept a sullen silence which seemed appropriate for such a sullen sky.

They rode all that day and on into the evening without incident, while Leith traveled the gray roads of the half-awake, and so missed some of the most beautiful sights of the whole journey. For here in southern Deruys cold and warm air mixed, causing mist and gentle rain, with soft light which subdued the landscape. Here they passed a still pool where tendrils of mist wound about sleeping willows; there they rode towards a golden patch where the sun broke through the clouds, her rays visible in the humid air. Animals and birds they heard and saw, and at the fresh smell of a green apple grove their heads jerked upwards as the scent surrounded them. All this passed before Leith's eyes, but failed to leave an impression on him.

Instead, through his mind passed the incidents since they had arrived at Instruere, the triumphs and the failures, and he found himself returning to one incident. As he thought more about it, he was left with an eerie feeling, a suspicion something had escaped his attention at the time, and answers were required. It was the same feeling he had experienced when Hal inflicted the Hermit with sickness.

What he remembered was Escaigne, and the Collocation; more specifically, his own words to the gathering. He did not remember exactly what he had said, but knew it had been impassioned and impressive, as though it was not he himself who said it. And this was the nub of what bothered him: perhaps truly he had not said it. Here he was, the sort of boy who could not ask Stella a simple question, and yet who dared to address a hall filled with strangers about life and death, purpose and loyalty. How likely was that? He thought of the night of Fire, and the few times since when he had experienced something similar: the voice that told him to speak to the Escaignian guard, for example. Had that voice spoken through him? Or had the experience itself lent him some sort of courage? Then he remembered the night he and Stella had spent on the ice, and how he had spoken to her, as if it had been Hal speaking through him. *Yes*, he thought. *The two are the same.*

This served to make him furious. *I will not be used by someone else!* he thought, not stopping for a moment to consider whether such a thing was likely, or indeed possible. *I will not be another's unwitting tool!* He could not put it into words, or even coherent thought, but he was tired of being seen through, of being totally predictable, of being thought shallow and being laughed at. A spoon for someone else's soup. He wanted some dignity, some mystery, some respect. *If I hear the voice again I will ignore it*, he decided.

He was pleased when the riding order continued to see him separated from his older brother.

Night came and eventually the party turned aside from the road. Wiusago led them to a small keep, occupied by a company of soldiers, and there they made their bed for the night. Leith thought he detected some animosity in the eyes of the soldiers, some hard looks directed at the strangers, particularly at Te Tuahangata, but eventually dismissed the thought from his mind. They were pleasant enough, the food was plain but wholesome, and the straw mattresses comfortable. Soon everything else was forgotten as sleep settled upon him.

The next day was a little brighter. The clouds lifted, though they had not disappeared, and on occasion they parted to let the warm sun shine down on them. The countryside was rolling now, the coastal plains having been left behind, and they drew near to green foothills that swept up to bush-clad mountains. Above and around the heights before them a deep mist hung like a hundred veils, shrouding their summits in mystery.

In the early afternoon Te Tuahangata reined in his horse and spoke to them. "Here we cross the border, leaving Deruys behind and entering the land of the Children. Anyone who harbors evil towards the Children will do well to leave it here, on this side of the border, for we are swift to reward faithfulness, swift to avenge treachery. I am your leader now; you will do as I say. This is a dangerous land."

Leith thought his speech abrupt and his tone peremptory, even arrogant, but Prince Wiusago merely nodded his head and reined in behind Te Tuahangata.

"There is something going on between those two," Kurr whispered to the Haufuth.

"Or something going on between Deruys and the misty place," the headman replied.

Now the road narrowed to a walking track, winding up through steep, rocky fields that supported few crops. No people were visible tilling the fields, and many had obviously been abandoned, as they had begun to revert to their natural state.

Te Tuahangata waved his arm to the left and to the

right. "See with what generosity Deruys grants us choice land in which to dwell!" he cried. Leith happened to be looking at Wiusago when this was said. The Deruvian prince winced, but made no reply.

"This is our land!" the dark-skinned Child of the Mist cried out in a loud voice, addressing someone or something other than the party with which he rode. "From the sea to the desert; from the plain to the mountain; from the soil to the sky. This is our land!" And with that uncontested assertion, he continued up the narrow track.

Perhaps half a mile below the forest Prince Wiusago pulled his horse to the left, and ascended a small green-turfed mound. The others did not follow, but waited as he dismounted, knelt for a moment on the crest of the mound, then, leading his horse, he rejoined them.

"What was that about?" Leith asked Phemanderac; but the philosopher did not know.

"We will leave our mounts here," Te Tuahangata announced. "They will be of no further use on our road." The Deruvian servants gathered the horses and, after a word of thanks from Wiusago, set out on the journey home to Brunhaven.

Now they drew close to the eaves of the forest, and Leith saw it was wholly different from the forests of Firanes. The trees here were not tall and slender, but shorter, squatter, older; gnarled, closely packed, a single, many-tendriled organism rather than a collection of stately individuals as one would find in the Great North Wood. Hanging from the branches were a profusion of sodden mosses and lichens, their somber shades like beards, adding to the feeling of great age. Above Leith the forest spread back up the slopes and into the mist, which inched long gray fingers down into the forested valleys. Here and there mist rose from folds in the hills, as though someone had set fire to the trees; and occasionally some great tree giant raised its head above the forest canopy, a silent sentinel standing starkly on guard, or an adult supervising a landscape of children. The forest floor was dark, much richer than the northern woods, and everywhere green ferns grew, many twice their height or more, raised on great stalks, while others spread wide and low across the ground. From everywhere came the sound of running water, and waterfalls could be glimpsed in the distance. Leith took a last look back out over the rolling hills and plains of Deruys, and in the distance the sea sparkled in the light of the sun. Then he turned to the forest.

In the Forest of the Mist Leith soon lost track of space and time. They could have been going north or south, east or west, and he would have been none the wiser. The narrow path went up and down, left and right, widened and narrowed, did everything in fact except go straight. It felt like late afternoon, but Leith could not be sure. He was not enjoying the forest. It seemed to him blacker even than his mood.

That night they made shelter in a grove of large, brown-trunked trees. In deference to the forest no fire was set: Te Tuahangata explained to them fire was only to be set in the hearth of their villages. "The nearest is still a day's ride away. Our people no longer dwell this close to the edge of the wood." Again the tension, again the pained look on the prince's face.

The land of Mist was almost wholly mountainous, though the peaks were not lofty enough to attract snow this far south except on the rarest occasions. The Children of the

Mist lived in long, narrow valleys between steep, high ridges, each valley connected to the next by a network of walking tracks so complex that any stranger to the land would become lost if not apprehended by the inhabitants. The forest was everywhere, even up to the shoulders of the highest peaks.

In from the *Khersos*, the Deep Desert, came the hot, dry wind. Above the mountains it met the cooler sea breezes which sprang from the cold offshore currents, and incessant mist and rain were the children of the union. The sun did shine on the land, but mainly in winter when the cold wind was in the ascendancy, and at the height of summer when the dry desert wind scorched the trees. In spring and autumn, when the balance was more equal, the sun might not be seen for weeks at a time.

This hardship had not bred a bitter people; far from it. The Children loved the blanket above them, as for centuries it had kept them hidden from those who would dispossess them. Even before other people came to Faltha, and the Children were alone with the land, they had seen the mist as the arbiter of their fate, their protection from the naked wrath and capriciousness of their gods. The Children were—or had been—a passionate people, given to fullness of love and of hate; and many of their people were yet of that disposition. Things changed, however, when the First Men came.

The First Men brought with them a desire for dominion, a mandate from their god some interpreted as justifying many things. And, what was perhaps even more dangerous, a number of good people who regarded it as their duty to incorporate the Children into the society of the First Men.

These good people taught the Children that land was a

commodity which could be carved up, then bought and sold, imparting the dubious gift of ownership to a people whose society was based on shared land use rights, not individual ownership. Then other people, not so good, came to buy the land, or take it if it was not for sale. Behind them came the army of Deruys, ever ready to protect its citizens. And with all these people, both good and bad, walked misunderstanding and sorrow.

Wars were fought in succeeding generations, and sorrow multiplied. Again and again the hot passion came down from the mountains, to be met by the coolly calculating armies of the coast. Where they met tears fell as young men died well or died badly, and nothing was resolved. The Children of the Mist and the First Men of Deruys became mortal enemies.

But now love offered them all a chance of reconciliation.

Not many years ago the elder prince of Deruys, leading a punitive expedition into the land of the Children, fought his way to the edge of the forest. Villages had been fired, and a number of his men, nursing their own hurts for family lost in the old conflicts, had done disgraceful things to the villagers who surrendered, shaming the prince. In order that some lives might be saved from the villages, he ordered the remaining captives be taken to Brunhaven, where they would be at least afforded some protection. This was done, though with great reluctance on the part of his soldiers, who sought the deaths of all their prisoners.

In Brunhaven it was discovered one of the young women taken captive was the daughter of the paramount chief of the Children. When the King of Deruys learned this he became greatly afraid, for he knew the paramount chief would come to rescue his daughter, and the bloodshed would be of a scale not seen even in this most bitter of conflicts. Well he knew the hidden forces in the land of Mist, for as a young man he had spied out the land and was aware the paramount chief held many forces in reserve. They were quite capable of laying siege to Brunhaven itself if they chose to put forth all their strength. For this reason he was greatly displeased with his elder son.

"It would have been better if the men had been allowed their way with these wretches," he told his son, "for now we are all in mortal danger." His elder son was then banished from the king's presence in disgrace, and the monarch retired to his rooms to think on his dilemma.

While the throne was so occupied, the younger prince of Deruys acted. He had seen the daughter of the paramount chief, and for the love of Brunhaven, weariness of the incessant warring and respect for her beauty and lineage, decided to take her back to her father. He could not, however, free her from the guard placed upon her without shedding blood, so decided upon a more risky plan. At night he departed from Brunhaven alone, and took the old paths to the Mist. There he was apprehended and at that moment nearly lost his life, for the Children were wrathful over the loss of their princess. Though he was not slain, he suffered many indignities, then was bound and taken to the dwelling of the paramount chief.

There the young prince explained what had happened—how the captives had been taken to Brunhaven to save their lives—and there repented of the dishonor done to the paramount chief and his daughter. The prince offered himself then as surety for the safety of the captives, and suggested the exchange of prisoners would solve the problem without any loss of honor or need for vengeance. The son of the paramount chief, however, sought his death, and all but persuaded his father. After much thought letters were sent, the exchange agreed to and the vehement objections of the paramount chief's son ignored if not silenced.

On a low knoll at the edge of the forest the exchange took place, all parties weaponless as an expression of good faith. The young prince and the daughter of the paramount chief looked upon each other that day and a bond formed between them, one which flourished in the months and years that followed as, alone of all the men of Deruys, the prince was given freedom to visit the land of the Mist. For a time, therefore, peace came to the lands between the desert and the sea, and the King of Deruys learned much from the wisdom and courage of his younger son.

But now pressure was being applied by settlers looking for land, and a number of border skirmishes blighted the fragile peace. Worse, the elder prince of Deruys had lost his life less than a year ago. Whether this had been by accident or by foul play could not be proved, the only sign of his passing being a riderless horse returned to Brunhaven.

And now the younger—the only—prince of Deruys rode again into the Mist, accompanied by the son of the paramount chief and a company of strangers from the north, on a journey so important it stood apart even from the old enmity.

It took the party a week to cross the deeply folded land. At night they stayed in the villages, and twice were welcomed with intricate ceremony on to sacred land where issues concerning the Children of the Mist were debated in and around houses adorned by intricate carvings. There their story was told, always to an attentive hearing. It appeared the Children reserved their mistrust, and in some cases hatred, for their neighbours the Deruvians, rather than for the First Men in general; also, they seemed to know something about the Bhrudwans. Wiusago explained to the northerners the mighty Bhrudwan army of a thousand years ago had penetrated this far south, and in these hills many atrocities occurred. "There is a sympathy here to our cause," he explained, "which is the main reason they tolerate our presence, I suppose."

On the sacred ground conversation was shared, feasts held (including an astonishing meal cooked by hot stones and no flame in earthen pits) and stories were told. Such stories! Stories of the younger days of the world, of the exploits of great heroes and of the travels of explorers; each one, it seemed to Leith, told with emphasis upon the extent and importance of their territory. It was as though the stories established some sort of right to the land. Songs were sung, strange songs which pulsed with a rhythm fiercer and hotter than the cool, lilting tunes of the north; and one memorable evening a contingent of warriors, clad only in flaxen skirts, performed a war dance. Spears flashed, thrusting high then dipping to bite imaginary enemies, choreographed perfectly with deep-throated shouts, foot-stamping and grotesque poking out of tongues. To the northerners these were the most frightening warriors they had seen on their journey: without the hidden menace of the Bhrudwan killing machines, perhaps, but much more physically imposing than the Instruian Guard. Leith wondered what manner of men the Deruvians were to have held out against them.

During the day Leith saw very few people, for the

paths took them along the ridges and quickly across the valleys. He was able in this shrouded land to forget for a while the threat to Faltha and what he might be expected to do in her defense. Silence by day, merriment and wonder by night. For the first time in months Leith found himself able to relax.

One morning the Arkhimm worked their way up a narrow, rock-strewn track beside a bright, youthful river. Ever afterwards Leith would associate his time in the land of Mist with an image of that swift-flowing stream. White-foaming shallows, placid blue-green depths, soft sandy beaches, rounded boulders larger than houses, water purer than light, colder than ice; all overhung by the dappled, fern-filled forest rearing up on both sides, framed by mist-cloaked hills.

In one place the stream squeezed between granite shoulders, and here a bridge of three ropes arched across the gap like fragile spidery filaments on a frosty morning.

"We cross here?" Leith asked, but even as he did a small, cheeky-faced boy ran past them, leapt on to the footrope and skipped lightly across with unconscious ease.

"It's a cold swim otherwise," Te Tuahangata told him wryly, laying a hand on the guide ropes.

Shame is an excellent motivator, Leith considered as he found himself perched on the swaying rope fifty feet above a jigsaw of swirling waters and outcrops of shining rock. A minute or so later he was able to complete the aphorism: *exhilaration is the reward*.

On the opposite bank of the stream the path wound more urgently upwards. Beside it, hidden by tree-high ferns and hill-high trees, the river rumbled down with an ever-increasing voice. The air grew cold. Ahead, bush, branch and fern shook with the force of a downvalley breeze. Leith drew his cloak tightly about himself as a protection against the obvious approach of inclement weather.

Around a sudden turn stood a waterfall. A great white pillar of foam it was, a plunge of vitality from the heart of the land. Here, near its mountain catchment, the river encountered a huge hundred-foot-high slab of granite, and dealt with it simply by leaping over it. Though neither the largest nor the highest fall Leith had seen, it was perhaps the most perfect. In a single great plunge the river fell from a narrow crack in the obdurate rock, tumbling, thundering, crashing down into a deep green pool. Delicate water-curtains like filigrees of lace draped themselves on either side of the main fall in contrast to the brutal roar of the river, beaded strings surrounding power with beauty. Moss-bearded rock walls rimmed the bowl of the fall, their sheerness failing to prevent ferns and even trees lodging in their cracks and crevices. The fierce downdraft created by the waterfall beat incessantly against the branches and fronds, sculpting them into strange shapes that flowed away from the booming water.

Leith noticed movements in the dark water of the pool, but for a moment could not identify them. With surprise, he realized children swam in the frigid waters around and even under the waterfall. Others scaled the prodigious cliff-heights to find narrow ledges, from which to launch spectacular dives into the pool, their splashes and their squeals of laughter barely heard against the thunder of the falls.

Here, amid this aching beauty, the Arkhimm sat and ate their midday meal.

"What is this place?" Phemanderac asked. Leith heard the awe in his voice, and was reminded for a moment of

the Wambakalven under Adunlok. But no harp-voice
would be heard here. Here a louder, more elemental
music prevailed.

"It is called Wainui," Te Tuahangata replied. "Bigwater, in your language."

"A prosaic name for such a place," the philosopher
said reverently. "So might the Fountain of Life have appeared in the youth of Dona Mihst."

The swimming children awoke in Leith a great homesickness. As he closed his eyes he saw the lake in the
warmth of summer, ringed by Loulea's children diving,
swimming, running, chasing, hiding, fighting, talking,
laughing; and with a gut-wrenching ache knew of a certainty such a scene was being played out far, far to the
north even now. No doubt some of the participants would
be his friends. And here he was, forced by circumstance
to be old before his time, sitting and watching others enjoying the fruits of what he sought to protect. An ineffa-
ble sense of loss filled his soul.

"Tomorrow we come to the end of our lands, and encounter the Valley of a Thousand Fires," Te Tuahangata
announced to them late that afternoon. "There I must
leave you, for it is forbidden for a Child of the Mist to set
foot in that valley, on pain of exile or death."

"Why should such a thing be?" Phemanderac asked
him. "How can a place be forbidden you?"

"I don't know," Tua replied, shrugging his shoulders. "It
is a foul place, beset by desert winds and in which great
fires burn, erupting from the ground or even from the tops
of mountains—but don't worry, you will not have to cross
it at its worst," he added, seeing the apprehension in their
faces. "I suppose we are kept out of there for our own good.

At any rate there is a boundary just beyond the edge of the forest beyond which no Child may walk."

"How much further to our goal?" Phemanderac wanted to know.

"I don't know the location of this Kantara, for I have not traveled in the mountains of Nemohaim," Te Tuahangata replied.

Wiusago spoke. "We have perhaps another two weeks at best, maybe more, before we climb down into the Vale of Neume. I have been there once, but only to the mouth of the valley and from the other direction; I am unfamiliar with what waits for us at its head.

"Now, my friend," he said, turning to Te Tuahangata, "I have seen nothing of your sister, though she must know I am here. Why has she not come to see me?"

Te Tuahangata frowned, and spread his palms wide. "Who knows women? Perhaps she has taken up with someone else."

"You and I both know how unlikely that is," the prince replied quietly, as the northerners struggled to apprehend the sense of the conversation. "You have not forgotten the words spoken over her and I on the green mound of Pohaturoa. There is no one else; there will never be anyone else for her or for me." A hard edge underlay his voice.

"I am a warrior, and give no credence to soothsayers." There was no mistaking the menace behind the words.

"I also am a warrior," Prince Wiusago asserted in his turn. "Yet I would rather fight an enemy than a friend."

"You lowlanders have little stomach for a fight. Not so we of the Mist." Fingers twitching, his hand hovered above the handle of his war club. "I will protect the honor of my sister."

From this Prince Wiusago knew that Te Tuahangata

alone stood between himself and his love. Her father would not have prevented that which his own soothsayer had predicted. He frowned; but the importance of their mission and the words of his father both forbade him challenging his fellow prince. "I question the wisdom of attempting to thwart your father's soothsayer," was all he allowed himself to say as he walked away. Behind him Te Tuahangata smiled.

Their last night in the land of the Mist was spent high on a steep ridge. The eastern margins of the land were sparsely inhabited, as they were more subject to the winds of the desert, though, paradoxically, they also suffered the severest rainfall. As a consequence of these winds the vegetation grew somewhat thinner, so their progress was a little quicker. Though at least two hours of sunlight (or what passed for sunlight in the late spring mist) remained, Te Tuahangata found a little clearing on the ridge and insisted they halt here, rather than continue over the divide and into the Valley of a Thousand Fires. "I will not spend a night in that valley," was all Te Tuahangata would say about his decision.

Leith awoke to deepest, darkest night, the moonlight unable to penetrate the blanket of mist wrapped about this ancient land. Something, some noise or other, had woken him. He struggled to his feet, vaguely uneasy. Beside him Phemanderac, Kurr and the Haufuth slept on. There was someone else awake, standing a little distance away. He could feel rather than see his presence.

"Who's there?" Leith whispered into the night.

In answer the sound of bare feet on soft earth drew closer. "It is I, Te Tuahangata," came the whispered reply. "Come with me. We have a meeting to attend."

Leith thought about refusing, but remembered how everyone acquiesced to this man's leadership. They were in his power, he could have them killed any time he wanted to. He had to trust him, to regard him as a friend. Just the same . . .

"You won't need your sword," said Te Tuahangata. "Come."

Leith followed as best he could, trying not to stumble on the treacherous ground. By his admittedly unreliable sense of distance they walked perhaps two hundred paces, then turned to the right and descended a slope. Ahead of them a hearth fire burned, beside which two figures warmed themselves. Something dreadful, a weight like fear but not quite, hovered over this place. Leith dragged his reluctant feet after Te Tuahangata.

"Step into the light," said a voice, "and let us see you."

Leith could do nothing but obey, and found himself standing in front of a man and a woman, the two oldest people he had ever seen. Te Tuahangata bowed low before them, and Leith did likewise. Then the man and the woman drew up to Te Tuahangata and touched noses with him in the same form of ritual greeting he himself had offered the Arkhimm in Brunhaven, and which had been repeated many times since on their journey through the Mist-lands. Leith found he was expected to do the same.

In the moment of touching the two old people many sensations settled on Leith. His breath mingled with theirs, and he smelled the richness of freshly turned earth, then the moist echo of a rain-laden morning breeze. Old eyes drew close to his, eyes yellow-rimmed and rheumy, but deep, steady and powerful. The touch of skin was soft, and somehow welcoming and comforting. Irrationally, he felt as though he had been embraced by the land and the sky themselves.

"Sit down, young one, and tell us why you journey through our lands." It was the woman who spoke, in a voice cracked with the passing of the years, but strong nonetheless. "We will hear of your travels."

As though spellbound, with neither the power nor the volition to resist, Leith found himself recounting their adventures one after another. No detail was spared, and it was many hours in the telling. Beside him Te Tuahangata listened with growing amazement. He had heard parts of this, but the telling in full of the exploits of the Company moved him powerfully. The two ancients listened with grave faces, saying nothing.

The man interrupted finally, just after Leith described the night of the Fire, when he had dreamed about the Most High and had received his promise of love.

"Ah, the Most High," sighed the old man. "Yes, this sounds outrageous enough to be one of his plans. Do you feel comfortable entrusting yourself to the will of this god?"

"Yes, of course," Leith answered defensively, then remembered the pact he had made the previous day when he decided to ignore the interfering voice should it speak to him again. "Well, perhaps not, but I can't see any other choices."

"Oh, there are other choices," said the old woman in a mysterious tone. "There are always choices."

"I don't see how," Leith replied, a touch of bitterness in his voice. "It seems I am easy to manipulate, and that whatever I do serves his purpose."

"Are you certain? Can you truthfully look back and say none of the choices were your own?" Her eyes looked into his, not allowing him to brush the question aside.

Leith took a long time to answer as he reviewed his adventures. "No, I cannot say that," he admitted finally.

"So what is this god like, the one you so unwillingly serve?" asked the man.

"What do you mean, what is he like? He is a god! How can I know what he is like?"

"Is he good or is he evil? Is he light and holiness, or is he dark and malevolent? Or is he neither good nor evil, but awesome, majestic beyond our comprehension? Some great dragon of the sea, ready to lash out at us with his poisonous tail the moment any of us break some unwritten, unguessable law simply by following the natural desires he gave us in the first place? Or is he simply a fool, too frightened to admit things are beyond his control and the notion of giving the gift of life to humans was a mistake?"

"None of those things," Leith said stubbornly.

"So what is he like, then?"

A number of glib answers came readily to Leith's tongue, but he tried and discarded each in turn as being dishonest. Dishonesty would not do in a place like this. In the end he shrugged his shoulders and said, "I don't know exactly."

"You don't know? You don't know? Do *any* of you know?" The old man's sudden incredulity stretched upwards towards rage. "It's the conceit of it all that makes us the angriest. For thousands of years we have lived here, grappling with the power in this place and in each other, and then you people come, asserting some sort of special relationship with the Most High. 'We are the First Men,' you claim. 'We are the chosen people.' As though we who lived before were something other than human!

"So what do the chosen people do? Not satisfied with

taking the choice lands by the Mother of Rivers for your own, you proceed to drive our kind out to the fringes of the world. You transform the land beyond recognition. Gone are the sweet-smelling lowlands in which the *mariswan* bred and blessed the land; in its place the slimy, silt-choked waters of the Maremma. You take our land still, smothering it with your parchments recording purchases and sales, using your pens to slice it up into parcels, red ink marking the places the land bleeds. Each parcel is so small it cannot contain within it all the seeds of survival, yet it is isolated from the parcels around it, and slowly it withers and dies."

A badly frightened Leith wondered what the passionate words meant. No reply came to his lips, but it seemed none was needed. There was anger here, but it was not directed at him; and he realized suddenly that they did not expect him to take the blame upon himself.

"There is a certain deer that lives in the high mountains south of the Valley of a Thousand Fires," the old man continued. "Even a hundred years ago it roamed freely over the foothills, through the misty valleys and down to the sea. But not now, not now." The speaker paused to wipe a tear from his eye. "Perhaps that is of no consequence to you. But the deer used to eat the seed of the mightiest trees, and in its belly the seed traveled hundreds of miles, so the trees could grow here, far away from the high mountains, in strange soil. And now, because of your inky knives, your fences and your hunting dogs, all brought to make real the blood-red lines on the parchments, the deer come no longer to the Children of the Mist. One by one the great trees die, as they will, and there is not enough seed to replace them. Our trees die. Our land is taken from us. Our people work harder and longer to coax any kind of life from the tired soil and yet are poorer than ever they were, and finally we are forced into small villages to live on charity and listen to the First Men tell us about the goodness of the Most High, while behind our backs they call us lazy and worse. We cannot walk on the cool grass of our home. We cannot shelter under the tall trees of our youth. We get no succor from the dried-up remnants of land we are so graciously given. But we are expected to be thankful. Would you be?"

"No," said Leith. "I would be angry."

The old man sighed. "To be angry takes great energy, and we who have lost our land have lost our energy. But we hurt, and we remember. We remember the treaties and wonder about a chosen people who seem so faithless, so selfish and so thoughtless. If your god is like you, I have no desire to make his acquaintance. But of course you don't know. You have no idea what this god of yours is like. All this has been done to us in the name of an unknown god."

The fire crackled and spat as it burned the green wood, and the flames it gave out were orange and yellow, lending an unnatural cast to the faces turned towards the old man.

"I have no answer to make to you," Leith said quietly, "so I will tell you how I feel. Is that all right?"

"That I cannot say until I hear your words and measure their truth."

Leith nodded his head, and a number of things hidden thus far came into focus. The Arkhimm had ahead of it an urgent task, an imperative mission, and any delay increased their peril. Yet there were things in Faltha deeper even than the Destroyer's lust for Instruere. He could not go on until he made a reply to this old man beside his fire.

If no reply came, the quest ended here. Something important was being shaped beside this fire.

Then, suddenly, Leith knew what to say. "Pass me that carving," he said, to the old man's surprise. "The one around your neck."

Reluctantly, the man drew it over his head and handed it to Leith.

It was of abstract design, a delicate swirl of waves and wind perhaps, or of a tree swaying in the morning breeze, carved in translucent stone of deepest green. It was altogether lovely, a treasure, and not lightly touched. As Leith drank in its beauty, the steely eyes of the old man softened measurably.

"Did you make this?"

"Yes," the old man said. "It took me six years."

"Do you have the tools?"

"I have had the tools since I was a youth," the man said proudly. "I carry them with me all the time."

"May I see them?"

Leith fingered the stone blades in his hand. Three roughly fashioned blades and the infinite skill and patience of this man had created a masterpiece out of a piece of rock. He shook his head in amazement.

"You made these tools." It was a statement, not a question, and the old man nodded his head.

"My rite of passage," he said simply.

"Tell me," said Leith. "Did you ever visit the markets of Instruere on your travels? Have you seen the fine implements on display there, tools made by master craftsmen the world over?"

A glance at the old man told him his guess had been right.

"Yet these are the tools you use? Why?"

The old man had the answer. "Because the old tools allow the skill of the master to be exposed. Only by harnessing the skill and patience needed to use such tools can the true beauty of the stone be revealed." The look of puzzlement on his face told Leith he was aware there was a trap in the words, but could not see what it was. Te Tuahangata, however, grinned and nodded his head.

"The First Men are a chosen people," Leith said in measured tones, "but not for the reason you might think. They are chosen not because of their strength, their toughness or their sharpness. They are chosen because their brittleness and bluntness allow the full glory of the Most High to shine forth. What is being made here is yet to be revealed, but when we all see it no one will think of praising the tools. All the First Men show is how weak we all are, how apt to crumble, how false when placed under pressure. We are your example, the tools who demonstrate the skill of the Most High.

"I am such a tool, it seems. In my village I am nothing, a boy not yet considered a man, a tongue-tied fool with a reputation for tears and fears. Yet it might be that I was plucked out of my village by the Most High, chosen above many far more qualified, far more deserving, and fashioned into a tool for his use. I have many rough edges, and splinter and chip when used, but the Most High is apparently doing something with me. To be chosen means to glorify Him, not to be glorified by Him. It is the carver, not the tools, who receives the praise. Please do not mistake the dullness of the tool for that of the carver."

After that the old man spent some time looking at his blades, saying nothing. Leith could not be certain, but he thought he could see a smile playing on the corners of the old man's mouth, and the suspicion began to grow within him that he had arrived at exactly the conclusion the old ones had wanted him to. Somehow the decision he had made in Deruys had been undone. The voice had spoken through him again. He was not entirely happy at the thought.

"What do you want with me?" Leith asked eventually. The question was addressed to the old man and the old woman, but not to them alone.

"That's what we wanted," said the old woman. "We wanted you to ask the question."

"And we wanted to ask you a boon," added the old man.

"What do I have that I can give you?" Leith said, puzzled.

"When you come into your own, remember the Children of the Mist," the old woman said. "Remember all those peoples who live in Faltha, yet are not of the First Men."

"What do you mean?" Leith wanted to know. He heard the words, but they made no sense.

"Just remember," said the man and the woman together. "Now we must go. Our children, our grandchildren, await us."

"Goodbye," said Leith, and embraced them in farewell.

"*He iti na Hinepukohurangi, e kata te po!*" cried the woman. "Although just a small offering from the Mist, the night laughs!"

Like shadows of the mist, the frail old couple seemed almost to dissolve where they stood, a trick of the flickering fire, no doubt. In the space of a heartbeat the glade was empty save Leith and Te Tuahangata. Leith took a deep breath and ran his fingers through his hair.

*   *   *

"Who were the man and the woman?" The sense of otherworldliness that had settled upon the two men was now slowly lifting from them.

"My ancestors."

"Your grandparents?" Leith hazarded a guess.

"No. Much older than that. My eldest ancestors."

"That's not possible. They would have to be hundreds—thousands—of years old."

"Who are you to come here and say what is possible?" Te Tuahangata was roused now, and his eyes flashed forth flame. "Do you see that tree over there? It was a sapling before you and your kind were expelled from the Vale. Up on that ridge—don't look, it's too dark to see—is a rock that has been there for all of living memory. They are my ancestors."

"Have I just been speaking with a tree and a rock?" Somehow, in this place, that did not seem entirely unlikely.

Te Tuahangata smiled. "Something like that. My ancestors do not walk the world as you and I do, but they have not yet left it. They guard the land for us, establishing our place, our right, our home. You've heard some of their stories as you've traveled through this land. But where the First Men have overrun us, the ancestors no longer walk. Understand that we, too, have our contact with the gods, but through the earth, not through the fire. Yet we are not loved the less because we were given earth, not fire; and now we sit and watch as fire scorches the earth. Do you wonder now why no fire may be set in this forest? Or why we are forbidden to descend to the Valley of a Thousand Fires?"

"But what of the fire the old ones set?"

"What fire?" Te Tuahangata asked. Leith spun round:

there was no fire, just darkness. No embers, no heat, no memory of a fire.

"So I've just been talking to ghosts?"

"No," said Te Tuahangata gently. "To them you are the ghost, not yet substantial enough to take your place in the land, scurrying across it and not a part of it. They are more real than you and I."

"But what was it all about?"

"You will know better than I," the Child of the Mist answered him. "And even if I knew, I would not tell you. Truth is most meaningful when discovered by the one seeking for it."

Together they made their way back to the silent camp, and Leith lay down again with his thoughts.

Te Tuahangata left the camp again and retraced his steps to the sacred grove. His eyes were hot and his face flushed.

"How could you?" he hissed into the darkness. "You have shamed the Children by appearing to a stranger! I was polite, as you asked, yet you betrayed our people. Never before have you spoken to the First Men. Why have you done so now?"

A voice, gentle as the night breeze, answered him from the darkness. "The season has changed, my little one."

"Are we undone?" Te Tuahangata thrust the question into the night.

"Everything is undone, and will be remade. See to it that your hands do not injure what is being done."

"But what about Deruys?" The question burst out of him. "When is the day of our revenge?"

There was no answer; the voice was gone, replaced by the gentle whisper of the wind in the trees.

*   *   *

Camp was struck just before dawn the next morning, but Te Tuahangata would not let them move on. He had already indicated to Leith he should remain silent about the events of last night, though Leith had already come to the same decision, and this latest move just added to his mystery and menace. "We will wait for the Song of Dawn," he said.

He led them up a nearby slope. After they had walked for about fifteen minutes he motioned for them to stop. The party found themselves in a somewhat open space: not open to the sun, but cleared of undergrowth. In the center of the clearing stood a huge tree. It was not tall, but it had the girth of many, many men, and put out roots and branches a prodigious distance on all sides.

"This is Eldest," said Te Tuahangata; and something in the phrase made Leith look closely at the tree. "He was here before the First Men came to Faltha. Here we will wait for the Song of Dawn."

As silence settled on the slowly lightening scene, Leith could make out sights and sounds he would otherwise have missed. On the branch of a tree to his right perched a small, perky bird, chattering quietly to itself; then, with a flick of a wonderful tail that spread wide like a queen's fan, it flitted past and found another branch a little closer to him. Other birds moved about invisibly in the forest canopy, and as the sun began to rise they started to sing. There was a rich, booming sound like the ringing of the bells of Brunhaven at sundown, but fuller, more liquid somehow. There were trilling songs, clicking sounds, piping tunes repeated, then echoed on the other side of the clearing in a different key. For a while Leith tried to isolate individual songs within the Song of Dawn, but could not. As the sun rose and played her beams upon the ancient forest the chorus rose to its height, and those listening in the clearing were moved to something approaching awe. And as the birds sang the mist drifted down from the heights to their left, flowing like smoke through the trees and rolling silently across the ground, so that Leith felt as though he beheld the dawning of the world's first day. An indefinable longing awoke within him, a longing for he knew not what; something about this country ate into his heart, called him into itself; but he was not at leisure to remain here and contemplate the calling. Another voice, purer and sharper to him than the thick green voice of the forest, called him forward to Kantara and beyond. He had heard this voice before, and it was edged with fire.

Reluctantly the Arkhimm left this place, this holy place, each consumed by his own thoughts, and climbed higher up the exposed ridge. The mist flicked insubstantial fingers at them, as though wanting to prevent the humans leaving its domain. Then the mist cleared away and they crested the ridge.

Ahead of them, at eye level and above, a bright sky stretched from left to right. Below them, far, far below, lay a landscape unlike any the northerners had ever seen. A wide valley of brown and gray earth, devoid of vegetation, pocked with craters, geysers and lakes, rimmed with lava flats, framed by huge volcanoes; a vast, ugly landscape which shimmered below them like a sweating, diseased animal. And the animal's breath came up the ridge to blast them with heat. A mere taste of what lay in store.

Gradually Leith became aware that a small knot of people awaited them some distance down the far side of the ridge. He noticed Prince Wiusago scramble frantically down through the stiff brown grass towards the group, calling out as he went. Te Tuahangata stiffened, and a scowl smeared his handsome features into a fearsome aspect. Leith gave thanks that it was not directed at him.

Waiting for the Arkhimm was the paramount chief of the Children, accompanied by two beweaponed attendants and a woman standing tall with an unconscious dignity. A great cloak of piebald feathers, intricately and skillfully woven, sat on the shoulders of the chief. On his weather-beaten face were the marks of a full tattoo. He rested an arm possessively on the woman's shoulder. It was she to whom Leith directed his gaze as they drew close. Thus he set eyes on Hinerangi, the most beloved of all the Children. Her hair was long, straight and dark, darker than anything he had seen, coal-black. Wide brown eyes were set either side of a small, upturned nose. But it was her mouth that glorified her face. As she smiled in recognition of the Prince of Deruys, her features assumed a beauty that Leith would have regarded as impossible in mortal woman. It was not beauty as those of Firanes would have regarded it. Instead, the woman appeared to have the ability to allow the joy in her spirit to shine on her face; and her smile was the means by which it gained access. The Arkhimm approached slowly, almost reverently, afraid, perhaps, to interrupt the tender meeting now taking place between Wiusago and the woman.

Te Tuahangata had no such qualms. "What do you mean by this, my father?" he stormed. Unmoved, the chief replied to his son's insolence with a steady stare of his own. Tua was not finished, however. He took the woman's hand from Wiusago's grasp and dragged her some distance apart from the others; intending, no doubt, to hold a private discussion with her.

"I would remind my son how much he detests humiliation," said the old man in a level voice, using the common speech to widen the audience to his son's discomfort. "I would ask him to consider how many generations it has been since the Children were led by a queen, and what implications his possible disinheritance might have. Has he considered, for example, whom the queen might choose for a consort?"

"You wouldn't," Te Tuahangata replied, injecting into his voice as much certainty as he could muster.

"Unquestionably I would," came the reply, and the certainty it contained was entirely natural. "My son, you have yet to demonstrate the self-control required to be paramount chief of the Children. Perhaps your sister might serve better in this role."

"But I—"

"Be silent and learn, my son. You are not yet ready for that which you desire. That is why I send you on a great mission to accompany the strangers from the north, and aid them in their quest."

"But we are not allowed into the valley—"

"It's true, Tua," said the woman, holding his right hand with both of hers. "I have spoken with the ancestors and they gave me a message to give to you."

"*You* spoke to them? They gave *you* a message?" Anger and bewilderment wrestled with each other on his face. "Why could they not speak to me? I have sought them long and fervently. Why do they not speak?"

"Because you have not yet learned to listen," came the ready answer from the lips of the chief.

"But a girl—"

"You have not yet learned to listen," the old man repeated. "And we have yet to greet our guests. Hold your tongue and shame us no more."

With a great effort Te Tuahangata restrained himself.

The woman spoke as she walked gracefully away from her brother, back towards Wiusago. "The ancestors said to me that nothing was forbidden us. Nothing is *tapu*. Our calling is more sacred than *tapu*. Do you understand? Nothing is *tapu*. The Children of the Mist are not to be bound."

Her father nodded and fixed his stern gaze on his son. "You will travel with the strangers, you will give them aid, and you will be my eyes and ears in the outer world. I wish to know what course of action to choose when the time comes to fight. I do not want the tide of war to sweep up and over our little land unchecked.

"Now, let us welcome our guests." The chief turned to the members of the Arkhimm with uncompromised dignity. "Please forgive our rudeness. We are not accustomed to making outsiders welcome in our land. Prince of Deruys, be twice welcome; and consider the words of the ancestors as you think on your heart's desire. Those from the north, recognize that we do you a great honor by allowing you to walk on our land. The number of strangers who have been embraced by the Mist in a thousand years can be summed by the number of trees in the grove under which we stand. Tua has explained something of your cause, but I would hear more. Spend an hour with me. Tell me of Faltha and Bhrudwo, and help me decide whether this is anything to concern the Children of the Mist."

He came forward then and greeted each of the Arkhimm in turn, lingering a little in his embrace of Wiusago. "You are our hope; you and my children," he said to the prince.

"I have given my life for such a hope," the prince said.

"And so have my children, one albeit reluctantly."

"Yet I have seen goodwill enough to hearten me," said the young man. "Pride and beauty have been given in great measure to you and your seed."

"Be patient yet a while longer, my child. You will not be cheated of your destiny."

Wiusago nodded solemnly. Then he and the Princess Hinerangi went aside some distance to spend the hour alone. Te Tuahangata glanced darkly in their direction once or twice, but said nothing.

The chief would not be gainsaid, even though Kurr, in particular, sounded anxious to get on with the journey. He was worried, he said, both by the immediate threat of the Arkhos of Nemohaim, whom he imagined would be even at this moment sweeping down the coast towards Bewray, and the (hopefully) less imminent but infinitely more dangerous threat of the Bhrudwan army. However, in the light of the honor done them, the Arkhimm stayed and shared a meal with the chief and his daughter.

Leith listened as Kurr, Phemanderac and the Haufuth attempted to convince him of the danger to his own people should Faltha fall. The noble old man was a little puzzled as to why the best course of action appeared to be flight to the south and, as his warriors did not use arrows, found it hard to give much credence to the Jugom Ark. What moved him when nothing else would, however, was his son's account of Leith's meeting with the ancestors.

This tale had not been told even to the Arkhimm, and caused much astonishment, and a little incredulity, when it was told to the chief. Phemanderac in particular clearly wanted to ask Leith many questions, but waited with increasing impatience as the chief sought to verify his vision.

Finally, at the end of the hour, the paramount chief stood and embraced Leith. "You have met he and she; Mother and Father, Earth and Sky, Eldest of us all. They have spoken to you and in so doing sanctified your quest. It is not insignificant that at the moment we consider involvement in the affairs of Faltha, our *tupuna* should speak to a Falthan, something they have never before done. I can do you no honor as great as that which they have done you; can offer you no blessing beyond that which you have received. But let it be known that this youth, the one on whom the favor of our Lord and Lady has been bestowed, I name land-friend; for he is truly one with this land. I have my sign. Commerce between my land and yours will increase, and one day soon this will be sealed by a marriage of prince and princess."

They bade the old man and his daughter goodbye, and the sadness in Wiusago's eyes was palpable. Nevertheless, he turned his feet with those of the Arkhimm towards the great valley which lay many thousands of feet below them, baking in the desert sun. A few minutes after they began their descent into the valley, Leith turned and looked back. The chief raised his arm in farewell. A moment later they crossed the boundary between the land of the Mist and the Valley of a Thousand Fires. There was no visible marker to indicate the border, yet Leith felt it keenly; as though he stepped from living soil on to mere dirt. He looked about him. No one else gave any sign that they had noticed the change. He could not read Te Tua-hangata's face.

CHAPTER 12

THE VALLEY OF A THOUSAND FIRES

THE VALLEY OF A THOUSAND FIRES lay long and narrow, northeast to southwest, three hundred miles in length and no more than fifty miles wide. The Arkhimm, the questers for the Jugom Ark, entered the valley from the west about halfway down its length. It lay along an ancient fissure in the surface of the earth, and here the deep fire that warmed the brittle skin upon which all humans lived burned close to the surface. Forces old and powerful beyond human comprehension pulled the land apart along this fissure, in places exposing the fire below. To the west of the valley the skin bunched up in folds, forming the land of the Mist, while to the north and south stark mountain ranges bounded the valley. Yet these mountains themselves were under long, slow and inexorable pressure. To the north the Veridian Borders, and to the south the Almucantaran Mountains, buckled upwards as the great rent in the earth sought passage. The land itself resisted the enormous pressure it was under, trying somehow to heal the wound, prevent the bleeding.

For here the earth bled. Deep fire welled up in scores,

perhaps hundreds of places. Along the eastern margin of the tear in the earth it erupted violently, forming volcanoes that filled the air with dust, ash and the reek of sulphur. Some were tall and proud, conical in shape, while from the flanks of others grew smaller parasitic cones. Still others looked like low-sided pits of ordure, violent blast furnaces that did not waste energy on the building of elegant peaks, but simply vomited their innards contemptuously into the sky. Where the fire rose through underground reservoirs the superheated water emerged from the earth's fragile crust as steamy geysers and fumaroles, or hot, sulphurous springs, or boiling mud pools, or fantastic combinations of them all. In other places the ground itself bubbled and heaved like skin stretched too tight over roiling corruption; bubbled and heaved, but held.

To the east of the valley lay *Khersos*, the Deep Desert, to which no country laid claim. In the center of this arid wasteland the sun held absolute sway, and no rain ever fell. Warm, dry air from the heart of the desert drifted slowly to the west, then grew even hotter as it descended the irregular edge of the Valley of a Thousand Fires and blanketed the valley floor in temperatures beyond belief. A number of streams found their way into the gaping wound from the north, south and west, forming a ribbon of lakes in the irregular floor of the valley. No water flowed into the ragged cut in the earth from the east, and no water flowed out from the Valley of a Thousand Fires; the greedy mouth swallowed all the moisture offered it.

This was the province the Arkhimm sought to penetrate, to survive in, to pass through.

Their descent into the Valley of a Thousand Fires rapidly became a nightmare, and soon everyone, even the guides, doubted the wisdom of choosing this path. Under a piercingly clear sky the nine-strong Arkhimm made their way down through waist-high clumps of sharp-edged brown grasses; *tussoci*, Prince Wiusago named them. For half an hour or so they encountered isolated clumps of straggly trees, outliers of the forest above, under which they received temporary shade; then these petered out altogether, leaving them at the mercy of the hot sun. She had not forgotten how powerless she had been to hinder them on the Westway in winter. Now these foolish creatures stumbled into territory not ruled by Qali—not ever touched by Qali—in the late summer at the height of her power, and she would make them pay for their folly.

Twin lakes sparkled invitingly immediately below them, and in the ever-increasing heat Leith found he had already pinned his hopes on them. He remembered the village smithy, how he lent his help there one afternoon, and had been scorched all down one side by the heat from the furnace. Appallingly hot, it became hotter as they descended; the heat coming not only from the sky but also from the earth.

The air grew fouler, more and more sulphurous, leaving a metallic taste in their mouths at each breath. *It would take more than a thousand fires to create this much heat*, thought Leith.

"This better be a good short cut," Kurr muttered.

Long before they reached the lakes, Leith's hopes faded. For rather than water, these lakes were filled with salt. All around them stood crazy pillars, arches and fantastic shapes, differentially eroded crags and pinnacles. The earth under their feet was painful to the touch, and crunched under their tread like broken glass. "Keep to the white rock," Wiusago advised. "No human can walk on the black rock."

In the heat of the day the Arkhimm were forced to take shelter, crouching between tall, asymmetrical shapes, their heads swathed in cloths dampened with small amounts of the precious water supply they carried on their backs. A gentle wind came up from the valley floor, many hundreds of feet below them. The breeze which would have been a blessing in any other land, here drove volcanic dust and noxious fumes before it, reducing them to a miserable state.

"It wasn't this bad last time I took this road," Prince Wiusago said.

"Last time? You say it's possible to survive?" The Haufuth was incredulous.

"Will we have enough water?" Kurr asked him.

"No," came the immediate and disconcerting reply. "But, believe it or not, there is water to be found in this valley a few days south of here. There we will have water enough for our comfort."

Late in the afternoon they set out again, though the air was still cruelly hot. "Stay close behind me," Wiusago warned. "Do not leave the trail. We are coming to treacherous parts."

"You mean it gets worse?" inquired the Haufuth. The heat affected him badly.

"Only if you stray from the path," reiterated the prince.

To the left and to the right Leith noticed small craters, some of which were filled with gray mud. As he watched, the mud popped and bubbled, as though it were merely porridge in his mother's pot.

"Careful," Wiusago called from the front. "If you step into one of the mud pools you'll lose your leg."

The surface of the rocky landscape surrounding them was an unfortunate collision of red, yellow, ocher-brown and green stains. Here and there steam arose from cracks in the ground; and once, to their right and some distance ahead, a great shot of steam roared up at least a hundred feet into the sky.

Thousands would flock to see a marvel such as that, thought Leith, *if only it were not here.*

Amid a landscape such as this it was difficult to think of anything else but survival. The Arkhimm had hoped to take time on their journey south to devise some plan, to discuss how they might decode the Riddle of the Arrow, which Phemanderac had repeated to them until it had become embedded in their minds; and how they might use the Arrow, once found, to unite the Falthans against their enemy. But the air was too hot to talk for long, the act of opening their mouths enough to scald their lungs. They had little to talk about in any case, the severity of the valley making it virtually impossible to concentrate for any length of time on a subject so esoteric as the future.

However, one substantial conversation took place on the afternoon of the second day, just after they resumed their march. Te Tuahangata had spent the morning walking silently, muttering to himself, drawing unpalatable conclusions if the look on his face was anything to go by. That afternoon he spoke to Wiusago.

"So you have traveled this road before." The tone was conversational, but Leith could sense the hidden menace. Wiusago was clearly aware of it.

"Only once, Tua," he said softly. "It's not a place we frequent."

"Now why would anyone come here even once?"

"Reconnaissance, Tua. Some years ago, when things were much worse, my father thought we might attack you from this direction."

"But your sense of honor held you back." Te Tuahangata's words hung heavy in the air with sarcasm.

"Something like that."

"Nothing to do with the fact that no army could survive a retreat."

"Retreat?" Wiusago bristled.

"Just think of it," Te Tuahangata continued. "Dragging your wounded and defeated warriors back through this valley. No opportunity to bury your dead. A task to match your undoubted talents."

"We wouldn't have attacked you without the proper declarations."

"Then, fool, you would not have had to worry about a retreat, for none of you would have survived the battle."

Wiusago bit his lip and said nothing.

"And as for declarations, what about Otane-atua?" Tuahangata halted, turned and stood quietly in front of Wiusago, legs apart, hands on hips.

"Where?" the prince said, momentarily puzzled.

"The place you call Giantwood. Remember? Or are such acts of treachery against defenseless villages so numerous that you forget their names? Because we do not!"

"My brother was severely punished for what he did."

"So was the Otane village. But at least your brother deserved what he received."

"My friend, we have rehearsed these grievances many times. It is my fear that one day we will again cross swords rather than words. I do not understand your world, I freely admit that, but I do not wish to destroy it."

"That is not enough!" Te Tuahangata snapped. "It is our land! From the sea to the desert; from the plain to the mountain; from the soil to the sky. It is our land! Yet you have destroyed our spirit by making us live in a fenced forest. You want us where you can control us, so we can do nothing unpredictable. You have our land, our riches, in the palm of your hand." He spat on the ground. "And still you are unsatisfied. You hunger after our women! Is there nothing you will not take?"

This was too much for Prince Wiusago. His hand flashed to his sword-hilt and, before any of the Arkhimm could interfere, he lunged forward. But this was what Te Tuahangata waited for, had planned for. He sought and found the handle of his warclub, dived to the left and in the one motion sent it whistling towards Wiusago's unprotected head.

Or to where his head had been an instant earlier. Now Wiusago held his sword point mere inches away from Te Tuahangata's chest, while Tua's club hovered just behind Wiusago's ear.

For a long moment all was in stasis, while the Arkhimm gathered its collective wits.

Still neither combatant moved, and it was clear that either man could kill the other with instant swiftness.

The Haufuth moved with exaggerated slowness, stepping up to the two foes.

"You are both men of honor," he said quietly. "Put your weapons away."

Neither man responded.

"It takes greater courage to follow your reason than your passion," the Haufuth pressed. "I tell you, for the good of all people everywhere, put your weapons away!"

Prince Wiusago resheathed his gleaming blade. Te Tuahangata made no move.

"Does the son of the paramount chief have no more wisdom than a child?" the Haufuth inquired gently.

"Craven!" Te Tuahangata ground out.

"I will not expend the future of our lands on the passion of the moment," Wiusago stated flatly. His eyes were dark with suppressed anger. "I would not have my affianced brotherless."

"Coward!" spat Te Tuahangata. "You are not worthy of Hinerangi. I will oppose this marriage with my life! I swear by the—"

"Do not make any oaths," said the Haufuth urgently. "I've heard about the results of oathtaking. In a generation both your countries would be laid waste. Hear me! Your kings sent you on this mission, so you are both under my authority. Listen to my judgment! I am within my rights to have you both slain for your shameful behavior. Don't try my patience!"

Leith held his breath. *Slay them? The Haufuth was bluffing. Would the two men guess?*

Te Tuahangata would not be deterred. "What makes you think you could match weapons with me, fat man?"

"Review the evidence!" the Haufuth snapped impatiently, as though this were nothing more than a spat between children. "How else do you explain the deaths of four Bhrudwan warriors, the like of whom you have not seen, nor could you hope to match. Surely this should give even a foolhardy youth such as you some small cause for doubt?"

The dark-skinned warrior was about to reply, when Kurr added: "Disobey the Haufuth and you disobey your father. Do you think this is wise? With you disgraced, who remains to oppose the marriage of Wiusago and Hinerangi?"

"It is so, old man," acknowledged Te Tuahangata. He looked on his opponent with narrowed eyes for a moment longer—to Leith a moment too long, suggesting a hatred that was partly habit, partly theatrical—then lowered his warclub. "This *mere* calls out for his blood. I will have to give it more powerful reasons than I have yet heard to prevent it satisfying its hunger." He stepped away from the prince. A moment later the journey resumed, Wiusago in the lead, Te Tuahangata at the rear, nursing a face like the fall of a great tree.

On the evening of their second day the travelers finally reached the valley bottom, the area where water would flow. Amazingly, even here in the zenith of the valley's heat, vegetation raised tentative fronds, leaves and branches into the shriveling air. Though virtually rainless for most of the year, it was no true desert. Were it not for the heat borrowed from the east and the uniformly arid, friable volcanic soil, this part of Faltha would have been relatively fertile. As well as the *dissotis* flourishing happily under scattered steam spouts, small clumps of all-but-dead *tussoci* hid from the scorching sun behind the larger rocks, and the occasional thorn bush asserted itself defiantly. Leith once thought he saw a butterfly, a small, yellow-winged thing, but on further thought it was probably a trick of the light, which here reflected from mica and obsidian as though the rocks were too hot for the light itself to come to rest.

Life perseveres even in the valley of death, Leith thought morosely. *It doesn't have the sense to let go even when it is obviously going to lose. Sustained by the force of habit alone . . . Just like me, here, one foot placed in front of the other, walking mindlessly to who knows where when all I really want is to be back in Loulea, playing by the Common oak with Hayne and Hermesa and Lonie and Druin and Stella . . .*

In his mind, as clearly as if he was there, Leith imagined himself sheltering from the wind and rain under the spreading branches of the Common oak. Around him the North March landscape, the very opposite of the Valley of a Thousand Fires: the greensward of the Common, the great Tree, the bustling sounds of the village—*his* village—preparing for a long autumn night; and the rain, blessed rain, filtering down from the gentle soft-lit sky, soaking, drenching, preserving . . . His heart ached with longing.

Then a changing wind blew through his daydream, sending his peaceful thoughts scurrying for shelter. The rain hardened and began to lean in from the north. The ache in his heart focused, became clearer, attached itself to a name, a face. Stella. She was to meet him here. And he *waited* and *waited* and *waited* and *waited* and *waited*—the words kept time with the regular tread of his boots on the merciless rock—and *waited* and *waited* and she did not come. They were laughing at him; everyone laughed at him . . .

He sat in front of the fire in their small house, waiting, whittling away at a slender piece of birch, hardly able to control the shaking in his hands; for the *one* he *loved* the *most* was *gone*, and the face he tried to carve stayed blank . . . His father was never coming back; he was abandoned . . .

Now he and Hal and Stella walked in the silence of a Mjolkbridge night, past *house* after *house* after *house*: Hal stopped and sent them on; but fear and frustration constricted his chest—he couldn't breathe, let alone speak . . . Everything remained unsaid . . . Worse, his silences were used against him . . .

Stella and he sat down on the ice, and after a while she began to shiver . . . without thinking, he put his arm around her and drew her close, then opened his mouth.

The words of eloquence issuing forth were not his. His spirit cried out abjectly while his mouth moved without his volition . . . The *inner whim*per re*mained* un*heard* . . . Meanwhile the ice creaked and groaned as it drifted further away from the Company . . .

Was everything that happened to him a metaphor?

She smiled at him in the House of Escaigne, and he knew he would give his whole world for that smile. *You are accepted,* it said; *no longer on the outside, no longer the secret subject of the world's mocking laughter, no longer the one ignored by everyone.* His heart was ready to break with happiness—as long as he kept the little voice of protest lodged in the core of his being under control; *it's not you she loves, it's the other voice, the other voice, Hal's voice, the voice of the Most High, cruel god, puppeteer* . . .

Then unseen hands jerk the strings and Escaignians come, separate the Company, take Stella one way and he another, his father one way and he another, Hal one way and he another . . . The ice creaks and groans . . . Swords flash in the sun as his father mutters: "They send me to my death . . ." Rough hands grab him, pull him away from the slopes of Steffl . . . The room reverberates with the crash of unseen figures, and as he struggles he watches them drag his mother out through the door . . .

And—oh, cruel god—he follows good, sensible, decent Hal through the cavernous darkness until he stands by the Hermit's crib; watches, uncomprehending, as his brother stretches out an arm . . . Blue fire flashes . . . The Hermit collapses in the grip of his sickness . . . And in such fashion does the Most High treat *he* who *speaks* with a *voice* of his *own* . . .

<Aren't you being a little ridiculous?> the hated voice inquired of him.

Shut up, Leith snapped, masking his surprise with anger.

The voice obeyed him, as though it was a product of his own tortured mind.

The trail followed by the Arkhimm was not made by humans. Instead, Wiusago explained on the following day, the valley was crisscrossed by a network of game trails made by mostly small—but a few extremely large—animals in search of water. For, here and there in this wasteland, water could be found. In most cases it was foul, brackish stuff oozing up from under the ground, but occasionally, wonderfully pure water bubbled from the dead earth; and here nature congregated: wide-spreading acacia trees, verdant carpets of green, flocks of enthusiastic bird life, swarms of insects feeding feverishly on the flesh of animal herds. The dramas of life played themselves out on small bright patches amidst the valley of death.

But the travelers saw no animals and scant evidence of their existence, other than a little spoor, and the ubiquitous, helpful trails. Having listened to Wiusago's descriptions of them, even allowing a little for the exaggeration of stories retold, Leith found himself pleased about this. Two-headed, fire-breathing lizards; snakes that launched themselves at their prey from trees, stiff like spears; huge cats armed with teeth and claws to tear and to rend; and even the small animals threatened, with bite and sting and itch, to undo the unwary traveler.

As the cruel desert sun set in a rack of fire on the third night out from the Mist, the Arkhimm descended by a narrow path into the head of a deep sandstone gully. Prince Wiusago's face lit up with a smile, and even Te Tuahangata gave him grudging acknowledgement. About what, Leith was unsure. He appeared to have missed a conversation about their route. Whatever, Wiusago was now receiving congratulations. "The *wadi* proved to be real," he said. "I trust the *gueltas* will so prove." The happiness in his face was undeniable.

The sandstone gully, Wiusago's *wadi*, made almost a straight path southeast. In the few remaining minutes of light—the violent twilight here was so much shorter than the languid evenings the northerners were accustomed to—Leith examined their strange surroundings. Smooth pale granite-like rock lined the floor of the *wadi*, and though there were small, regular cracks in the rock, they were filled with sand. The ever-deepening gully floor was perhaps twenty yards wide, framed by somber cliffs fitted out in subtle shades of tan and ocher, stretching already a hundred feet or more into the swiftly darkening sky. The effect was ominous, forbidding, as though the existence of such a chasm was evidence that this country was home to creatures more powerful than they. In a matter of minutes darkness flowed like a river down the *wadi* towards them, and the only light came from the narrow star-studded sky far above. A few minutes more and they could go no further.

Later that night a half-moon peeped over the edge of the cliffs and shed pale light down into the *wadi*; by its light they made good time for perhaps an hour. As the moon dropped behind the other cliff Te Tuahangata said: "No evidence of this *gueltas*. Without it we will not survive."

"At least the cliffs will keep the sun off our backs tomorrow," Wiusago said, unwilling to concede.

Just before dawn the Arkhimm commenced their weary journey once more, putting on their packs like unshoulderable burdens. Very little was said, as though energy wasted on words could prove to be the difference between death and survival; but weariness rather than prudence dictated the lack of conversation.

Dimly the Haufuth realized that he should make some attempt at promoting friendliness amongst his diverse charges, particularly between the Deruvian and the man from the Mist, but somehow he could not muster the energy. The Escaignians talked seldom, and then almost exclusively between themselves; and the Haufuth wondered on the twist of fate which had sent them on a journey that must be bringing inconceivable experiences for the city man and woman at every turn. Kurr, as ever, was a great comfort. For a moment he had a mental picture of himself and the old farmer sitting together in the corner of a graveyard, and his first reaction to this picture was a wistful longing for the verdancy, the richness, the regularity of his home. But then the vision sharpened; he could see the old man's face, and the grief it held was so great and so transparent he caught his breath. How much had the dear old man given up for him, for them all? The question gave him a moment's pause. Phemanderac, the tall stranger upon whom their quest seemed so much to depend, had withdrawn into himself; his lips moving from time to time as though reciting the riddles and mysteries gleaned from the Instruian Archives. The Haufuth laughed at the incongruity of his own position. A solid, dour man of the land, a conservative without doubt; here trusting a mystic from one fairytale land, chasing this mystic's personal vision into a second land of fireside stories. The big headman could no longer recall the force of the arguments which persuaded him on this course of action. Only one thing reassured him. In all his adventures he had encountered human beings who did familiar things—good, wicked or indifferent—but recognizable at least, even if on a larger scale than he saw in his own village. Apparently the fairy stories were truth intertwined with lies. What made people seek to explain things with reference to the supernatural? He laughed again to himself. All this thinking made him feel very hungry . . .

After the desolation of the valley floor, the day's journey along the steadily deepening *wadi* was almost enjoyable. While not recovered enough to talk yet, the members of the Arkhimm at least took notice of their surroundings. Early in the morning they saw a small group of what at first looked like rabbits sheltering in the shade directly under the left and steeper cliff. As they drew nearer, however, Leith could see that, while they were the color of rabbits, they looked more like short-cared, squatnosed moles, a family of timid animals avoiding the sun. Father and mother were there, along with three—no, four—children, chattering nervously at the approach of strangers. Once they decided these humans were no threat, the mole-like animals resumed nibbling on the sparse grasses that grew at the base of the cliff, glancing querulously upwards between bites.

"Dassies," Wiusago said, almost fondly. "Rock hyrax is their proper name, but that sounds too grand for such foolish animals as they."

Now the *wadi* began to swing left, then right, so that the rising sun made highlights of rocky outcrops on the cliff faces, and in that light Leith could see trailing shrubbery of some sort growing from crags and crevices high above. The almost regular brickwork of the *wadi* walls, overlaid with the unexpected greenery, made the passage they now threaded seem like a secret lane between castle walls, or a dusty Instruian street meandering between faceless tenements.

From the left and from the right other *wadi* joined the main channel, as evidently all drainage in this area tended southeast. To the eyes of the northerners, in whose own lands the evidence of water abounded, it was almost incomprehensible that such great chasms as these *wadi* could be the work of water. The steady rains and brimming rivers of Firanes had created no works like these, yet here they were in this arid, seemingly waterless landscape. Could these chasms be a relic of a wetter time? Perhaps. But, more likely, the absence of ground cover made the rock, for all its apparent hardness, vulnerable to the cut and thrust of whatever water made its way here. Added to this was the infrequency, but great magnitude, of rainfall here on the desert margin. Wiusago had heard stories told of sudden thunderstorms in which the continuous roaring left its hearers deaf for days afterwards, of *wadi* full to overflowing with raging floods, of whole mountainsides eroded away in an afternoon. Wiusago did not believe them, he said, but Leith had his doubts about this.

Finally, in the middle of the day, the Crown Prince found what he was looking for. Here the sheer-walled *wadi* was perhaps three hundred feet deep, or more; and, high above the travelers, it admitted only a narrow sliver of light. Yet there was ample light to discover the little pool of water set deep in the *wadi* sandstone floor. Perhaps thirty feet by twenty, it cooled the very air around it. At its edge six tall cypress trees grew, gnarled with age, last remnants of a once-forested landscape, of a milder climate. It sat directly across their path. With shouts of delight the travelers threw off their burdens, ran forward and plunged down the steepish slope into the pool. Even Te Tuahangata smiled as he emerged, his face cleaned of travel grime. "You found your *gueltas*," he said to Prince Wiusago, with thankfulness in his voice.

While the others enjoyed the discovery, drinking their fill, refilling their water-skins, shouting and laughing as though the mechanism of their tongues had simply required lubrication, Leith wandered away in search of solitude. For him there was little to celebrate in the finding of a scum-encrusted pond, when the bigger mysteries remained hidden. If the voice in his fire-dream came only to enslave him, where could he find release? Was there a voice that would declare him free? Or was his life one long abandonment to the whims of others?

Around a turn in the *wadi* he found two smaller pools, set perhaps ten feet down in the sandstone. Above him the sun was almost directly overhead, yet in a few places shone directly on the *wadi* floor. One of those places was the closer of the two pools, which sparkled prettily at the bottom of the light shaft. Two silent cypresses stood guard over this precious jewel.

Something scrabbled around at the very edge of the pool, at the bottom of a smooth, steep slope. Leith squinted against the light, and eventually made out that it was a dassie, a rock hyrax. Little more than a baby. He watched. It tried frantically to climb out from the *gueltas*, but could get only a little way up the slope before it tumbled back down to the water's edge. All the while it made high-pitched, mewing noises of distress.

The scene grabbed at Leith's throat like an ambush. The pitiful dassie was trapped, unable to get away. *It could be part of the family we saw earlier this morning,* he thought. Even though he knew the thought was unreasonable, he hung on to it as though immersed in some kind of madness. It had been abandoned, left here to die in the hot sun by those who loved it but could not help it. And all that remained for the poor dassie to do was to struggle in vain against its fate.

Something snapped in Leith.

"No! No!" he cried, scrambling down the slope. He must save it, return it to its family. Something had to be done about this, some attempt made to change a world where such things could be allowed to happen by powerful forces who spoke in reasonable voices about hurting things for their own good. He worked his way towards the terrified animal, which backed away from him in fear. The sun reflected fiercely in the water-lens of the pool, and in a moment Leith was drenched with sweat.

"Come here," he said encouragingly, and held out his hand. The tiny creature cowered away from him, consumed by terror. "Come on," Leith said, in as gentle a voice as he could muster, "don't you know what's good for you?"

Then everything happened at once. A shadow crossed between Leith and the dassie. He looked up to see a huge winged shape wheeling above him. The dassie let out a terrified scream, suddenly cut off. Leith whirled around, expecting to see the animal in the clutches of a predatory bird; instead all he could see was the dassie itself, rigid in the throes of death.

"What? What?" Leith cried in agony of spirit, as though he witnessed his own death.

The tiny animal did not move.

"Wake up; please wake up," he whispered pleadingly with it. Still it did not move.

"I've killed it," Leith said quietly; then he cried out: "I've killed it!"

The cry contained all his soul.

When the others, startled by the cry echoing around the canyon walls, came across the scene, it took them some time to work out what had happened. Distraught, in some inner torment, Leith could tell them nothing. The dassie they took and laid to rest under a rocky shelf.

"What's up with him?" Kurr asked gruffly, obviously concealing concern.

"We all need a rest," the Haufuth said gently.

The old farmer grunted. "We haven't got time for rest."

"But we may not be able to go on at this pace. I'm still somewhere in the mountains of Firanes, my old friend. I haven't caught up with Instruere yet. I can hardly believe that Mahnum and Indrett were rescued, and I just want to sit down and have a good long talk with everyone, and something to eat."

"But you persevere. You don't end up making strange noises at dead animals. The boy's too weak."

"Kurr, you've been toughened by life. We've learned things about your youth you perhaps would not have shared with us. Would you have Leith go through such things as you have? Isn't the point of all this we're doing so people like him won't have to go through those things?"

Kurr pursed his lips, but said nothing.

"In fact, he is going through a greater hardship than you ever did. He is a different person than the one who left Loulea months ago. He will be a man before this is over. Perhaps he grapples with issues you have not had to face." He paused, then looked shrewdly at the hollowed face of his friend. "Perhaps with issues you refuse to face."

Kurr opened his mouth to reply, but the Haufuth stopped him. "If we haven't got time for rest, we haven't got time for discussions like this. This valley is a hard place, my friend. Speak harshly of another only if you will allow others to speak harshly of you. Now, come!" And with that the village headman took up his pack and made to continue on their journey.

This man is changing, Kurr reflected, his anger tempered by the truth he had heard. *Leith is changing. One of us needs to remain the same!*

Later that afternoon the *wadi* emptied out into a large, shallow depression, the cliffs on either side vanishing to become part of an escarpment running away east and west. Ahead of them lay a shimmering emptiness, which through the early afternoon resolved itself into the last thing any of them expected in this place, the bone-dry pit of torment.

A lake.

The lake—if in truth it was a lake—stretched fully fifty miles from north to south, though it varied with the seasons: in what passed for winter it expanded to cover immense salt flats that lay to the east, quadrupling its size. It occupied a large depression, in shape more like a horse's trough than anything else. This trough contained a unique substance not quite liquid, not quite solid, a combination of alkaline water and extremely caustic soda. The mixture was obviously deadly, as the shore was littered with the corpses of small birds which had, for the most part accidentally, alighted upon it.

Irregular dull-pink blotches dappled the gray lake surface like ghastly exhumations of blood, now sun-dried. These blotches were colonies of some hardy plant growth which, unbelievably, could survive the life-choking soda. Interrupting the pink blotches, large soda-rimmed craters testified to the violent escape of foul vapors from deep beneath the surface. The fiercest of winds could raise only small ripples in the glutinous waters. Above the lake surface superheated air shimmered, through which could be made out steaming volcanoes lined along the far side of the lake. As the air spread away from the lake center it carried the awful, acrid stench of soda to the desperate travelers hurrying past her lethal shores.

This was perhaps the foulest of all the places Leith had seen on his adventures, more ominous than the forests of Widuz, more forbidding by far than the gloomy heights of Rhinn na Torridon, home of decaying castles, more inimical even than the depths of The Pinion, for all its cruelty and despair. There was something dispassionately efficient about the violence permeating this valley, something opposed to life itself brooding over—or in—these fetid waters.

It was late in the day when disaster struck. Perhaps they would have been wiser to have rested during the heat of the day, though the *wadi* had provided such effective shelter the travelers decided to press onwards. It had seemed a sensible decision at the time.

Whoever placed himself at the head of the group found it difficult to determine where land ended and lake began, so gray and solid-looking was its surface; but the crust of soda was treacherously thin in places. The Escaignians, who were taking their turn leading, stayed well away, so they thought, from the water: but not far enough. From near the rear of the Arkhimm, dust-choked, dehydrated and weary beyond the power to express it, Leith heard a cry of fear, then a soft splash. One of the Escaignians broke through the gray soda crust of the lake and fell, hands, knees and face, into the sulphurous ooze beneath.

Gentle hands pulled him free of the clinging ooze and carried him to the relative safety and shelter of an overhanging wind-carved rock. But it was already too late for Bright-eyes, and everyone knew it.

On his horribly burned face, arms and legs rose angry red blisters, which coalesced and turned black while they watched helplessly. The Haufuth tried pouring a flask of their precious water on the dreadful burns, but this only brought forth terrible screams from the doomed man. The flesh on his extremities seemed literally to melt away before their horrified eyes. Leith turned to his brother, a question forming on his lips. In the face of such suffering, Leith forgot his suspicions of his brother, and was prepared to ask his help but, as if Hal read his mind, he shook his head to answer the unspoken question. There was a tightness to his brother's face and neck, as though he was fighting against something—and losing. His face seemed carved from stone, a featureless copy of the volcanic rock to the right of the cursed path through this cursed land. Leith even tried the voice of fire, calling out for help in his head, a form of prayer, he supposed; but no answer came to him, no vision came to their rescue.

No hope of a miracle, then.

Leith had never watched a man die in such terrible agony, and with the foreknowledge that he was dying. It was a dreadful thing. "He has been boiled alive," said

Phemanderac sadly. "It would have been better if we had not pulled him out."

Though he had known the bright-eyed man less than three weeks, the Loulean youth felt responsible for the man's suffering as if it was a personal failure on his part, as though there was something he ought to be doing, but was not doing it. He remembered the swift moments he and Bright-eyes shared on the way to the Water Chamber, as the man who now writhed on the path before them led him to rescue the Company from the rising waters. He recalled the Escaignian telling them how he tired of the darkness of his hidden home. He remembered his last words had been about freedom.

As the evening set in he wished it would end quickly, but it did not. Worst of all, worse than the screams, the ragged breathing of burned lungs, worse than the horrific wounds, was the knowledge there was nothing they could do.

Bright-eyes did not talk; indeed, near the end he could not. *If it had been me*, Leith admitted to himself, *I would be begging everyone to do something*. But in spite of the man's brave silence, his suffering was obvious. Long before they finally closed the eyes of the corpse and began to look for a safe burial site, Leith had begun to ask why. *Why? The two other deaths—Wira and Parlevaag—I can understand. The nobility of their sacrifices were precious gifts to us. But this? A life taken by the whim of the Most High. The Escaignian died without ever revealing his name. Did he matter that little?* Leith could not believe in divine love here in this godforsaken place. There was no sense of purpose here, no plan, only wildness, danger and fear.

Just like the dassie. Killed by an uncaring hand. And though Leith's mind tried to tell him it was just a coincidence, that this was a harsh land and death a constant threat, something deeper within him than mere reason laid the blame squarely on the voice in his head. But there was something else, something that worried at Leith until it crystallized just as the sun went down. Did Hal's shake of his head signify an inability to do anything, an impotence to heal, or did the struggle etched on his brother's face represent a refusal to intervene, tested by the man's screams? Was this another of those moments where Hal's "kindness" wore the clothes of cruelty?

They laid the unfortunate Escaignian to rest on a slab of hard volcanic rock and covered him with stones. The Arkhimm did not take the risk of wandering around this dangerous place in order to find soft ground for a proper burial. One deadly encounter with this valley was more than enough.

"Oh, Ceau!" cried the remaining Escaignian. "You should have stayed in Escaigne. You should have stayed where you were safe!"

"Escaigne is no longer a safe place," Phemanderac observed quietly. "Faltha is no longer a safe place."

Fine words were said over the body and tears were shed, but afterwards Leith could recall neither the words themselves nor who spoke them. They had given his gray-bleak heart no cheer in this desolation of spirit.

Not until many days later was Leith coherent enough to realize that by naming Ceau her companion, Illyon the Escaignian had given them her name.

The next day witnessed a discovery that under different circumstances could have brought great joy to the hearts of the Arkhimm. In the middle of the morning, an hour before they needed to seek shelter from the hottest part of the day, they rounded a bend in the game trail and came across a small arm of the lake, perhaps a mile across. At first this served only to dismay them further, for now they would be forced to find a way around it amongst broken rock and boiling springs. *Is there nothing in this valley that is not dangerous?* thought Leith bitterly. Then one of them—Kurr, Leith later recalled—noticed movement on a tiny island, perhaps a hundred yards across, on the near side of the inlet.

On the island were many thousands of birds. They were the largest winged animals they had seen in the valley. At first all Leith could see was a riotous confusion of pink, but gradually he began to pick out individuals. These birds were quite unlike anything he had ever seen, or heard of. Six feet from the tip of their long, bulbous bills to the three toes on their webbed feet, gawkily thin, with ridiculous long necks and legs so narrow they seemed in perilous danger of snapping in two. Their soft pink bodies, set midway between the extremities, were enfolded by cerise, almost vermilion wings, tipped in black. In happier times Leith would have laughed at these awkward, almost preposterous birds.

But then he saw one of the birds in flight, and in an instant laughter was replaced by awe. For in the air this ridiculous fowl became an elegant avian, more graceful than a swan, flying straight as an arrow. And it was of an arrow that these birds reminded him, somehow.

In spite of their need to hurry, the Arkhimm slowed, and on occasion stopped completely, to observe these fantastic birds in action. Leith noticed a group acting strangely, launching themselves into the air with a series of ungainly steps, then flying close to the far cliffs and swooping to the left and to the right, as though trapped between invisible walls. Suddenly one of the great birds soared up above the others without any apparent effort; and as the Arkhimm gazed on in wonderment it rose higher and higher without even moving its wings. One by one the other birds found this hidden current of air, and each ascended the cliff face as though drawn up by a piece of string. Now the first disappeared over the top of the cliff, followed by the others.

By now the trail drew closer to the island, and they were no more than a hundred yards from the bird colony, close enough to see that the birds were nesting. Underneath the seething pink mass, small, gray-feathered chicks sought food and shelter, receiving both from their huge parents. Then something gave the sentry-birds fright, and panic flashed through the colony. Within a moment ten thousand birds erupted into the air like a river of flame shooting into the deep blue sky; the deepest fire of all in the Valley of a Thousand Fires.

Of them all, Phemanderac was the most affected. As the birds wheeled overhead, satisfying themselves there was no danger, he sank to his knees, heedless of the dangerous path, and in a whisper said "*Mariswan*," as though the word had a deep inner meaning for him.

It had been a majestic sight, no doubting that. But Leith would have exchanged it for another day of Brighteyes' company, for the erasure of the man's screams, for the easing of the creeping guilt that threatened to inure him to whatever beauty and joy the stone-faced Most High decided to taunt them with.

Two interminable days later the Valley of a Thousand Fires came to an abrupt end. Ahead rose slope after slope, up to great clouded tops, from which small streams trickled tentatively into the merciless depression. Leith let out a vast sigh, relieved to be setting his foot to the upward path, away from the valley. The last few days had drained him of whatever self-belief he had picked up in Instruere, leaving him feeling small, young and vulnerable. Head down, he had eyes only for the trail ahead, and the Arkhimm's booted feet. As the group began to climb out of the valley of their torment, Leith dropped a little way behind the others.

In response to an uncomfortable feeling between his shoulderblades—the kind one gets when one is being watched by an enemy—he turned to look one last time down into the troubled cauldron below. At that moment a gust of wind parted the steam around them and Leith found himself face to face with a fearsome stranger.

His features were that of a vulture. Deep-set eyes, a hooked nose and a long, straggling gray beard framed by a cowled white robe that covered him from head to foot. On his crimson belt were strange designs, unpleasant to the eye; two curved swords hung from it. In his gnarled hand he held a staff.

Such details were gained in but a moment. There was no time to alert the remainder of the Arkhimm, who no doubt continued their progress up the path. No words were exchanged between Leith and the apparition, yet he knew this was a warrior of the *Khersos*, the Deep Desert, that Prince Wiusago had told them about the previous evening around a cold campsite. The old stories were apparently true, as all the old stories seemed to be turning out to be. The man raised his face to Leith's, complete rejection engraved upon it; then extended the staff towards him and began to scream harsh, high-pitched words in his own tongue. The Arkhimm, who had drifted back down the path to check on Leith, stopped in their tracks at the sound. They were all aware this was a curse from the heart of the desert, laid on strangers fortunate enough to survive its perils. With this came the realization that undoubtedly they had been shadowed since their descent from the land of the Mist by a figure (or figures, more likely) wishing their departure from the valley and waiting to observe them die or leave. Such malice worked in the voice and fumed across the face that Leith could not endure it, having instead to turn his head. Phemanderac alone remained impassive, observing the display of unprovoked aggression until, with a contempt borne of a fundamental belief in his superiority, the white-robed man spat on the ground at their feet and turned away.

On reflection Leith realized there was a great evil in what the man had done. Yes, they were interlopers, trespassers on his land; and by the very nature of the environment, the desert dwellers would be unused to such transgression. The white-robed warrior was cursing difference, was railing against the very existence of people other than his kind, of places other than his own. Leith's last thought before he dismissed the incident from his mind (only one and not the most serious of those they encountered in the valley) was to reassure himself of the rightness of their cause against the Bhrudwans.

CHAPTER 13

ECCLESIA

TURMOIL AND CONFUSION GRIPPED the Great City as the remnants of the Company drew near the walls. Floodwaters swept through Instruere in a few chaotic minutes and, while the battlements kept out the vast wall of water, confining it to the river channels north and south of the city, inevitably some of the muddy, froth-capped sludge surged through the sewers and drains of the town, filling basements and overflowing on to streets. The water sent housewives scurrying for buckets and mops, the menfolk for sandbags, the unoccupied for the battlements. The Guard were called away to deal with the flooding of the longhouse. The rumor flashing around the city suggested water had gotten into The Pinion ("and a good thing too," went the gossip. "Needs a good cleaning out"). There appeared to have been some disturbance over in the Docks, occupying the remaining guards, so those Instruians milling about on the walls and congregating by the gates were left largely unsupervised.

It was as though the guard just melted away. At first Indrett thought the byways of the Docks cleared of guardsmen because the Bhrudwan had put them to flight. However, as they came closer to the walls and the Dock

Gate, she could see a general calamity. Individuals and families ran in either direction through the gate, and many of them were wet to the skin. *The river*, she thought; *the river flooded. That was the water down by the docks*. She imagined what would have happened if they had not escaped the Water Chamber, and swallowed convulsively, managing to keep down the bile that had risen to choke her.

"Now's our chance," cried Farr. "Let's go, before the guards come back!" He seemed about to break into a run.

Mahnum pulled him by the arm. "Not so hasty! It would be better if we simply walked in, slow but purposeful. Let's not attract attention to ourselves."

Farr scowled, but accepted the advice.

"Once we're in, where do we hide?" Perdu asked.

"Let's get in first," Stella said, somewhat nervously. There were still one or two guards about, though their attention seemed drawn elsewhere. "We might find somewhere to hide in the confusion."

"But what about Leith?" Indrett asked, anxiety lacing her voice. "What about the others?"

"You want to go back?" Farr pointed behind them, back to the Docks, where the guards still swarmed. "He's probably safer than we are. I don't think they're going to like what the Bhrudwan did to them, when they get time enough to think about it."

The Company walked under the arched gateway, taking care to mingle with the steady stream of people making their way from the Docks to the city. Involuntarily, Stella held her breath as she passed though the gate. After the series of reversals the Company had suffered since they entered this place, it was easy to imagine recapture. Yet, for all that, the young Loulean woman rejoiced as they found familiar streets. The newness, the noise and clutter, the grandeur, the excitement, all contributed to her feeling of freedom. She thought of Leith and the way he had changed since they came to Instruere: *who would have thought that such a quiet boy had so much depth! And his deeds in The Pinion. He's already a hero. Loulea really was a bad place. He's more mature now. He probably loves the city as much as I do.* For the first time she regretted the things she had heard, and said, about Leith. *They don't know him like I do. I didn't know him like I do now. I hope he's all right.*

Walking about in the city, the Company observed how little real damage had been done by the flood. Here and there pools of water lay, but in general a few people did the work, while the majority stood in groups talking about it. The sudden flood was but the latest, and by no means the most momentous, of a series of strange happenings over which the populace chewed. The raid on The Pinion and the tweaking of the guards' collective nose by the impudent northerners, the unmasking and subsequent escape of Escaigne, and the sudden disappearance of the city's real power, the Arkhos of Nemohaim; all signaled their city was undergoing some momentous change. As for the disappearance of the hated Arkhos, it was more than a rumor according to the most reliable sources, and the city was apparently in new hands. Whose, no one could be sure. Perhaps the Council had not yet appointed a new head. Perhaps the Council itself had been replaced! Just by lingering near knots of people talking intently the Company learned many things of importance to them.

It took them about half an hour to get to the market. There stood the usual stands, refreshing in their familiarity, although as yet most were closed, stallholders and customers no doubt off dealing with the aftermath of the flood. And there stood something else, someone else who brought cheer and gladness to the hearts of the Company.

"Foilzie!"

Oblivious of the single guard in the open square, who seemed more concerned with a fight between a couple of ruffians than checking the faces that drifted past, the Company ran over to the old woman standing in the shadows. Stella and Indrett found her glad embrace, and men and women alike shared a few tears.

"How is your Escaignian friend? Is he all right?" Perdu asked.

"You'll see him in a bit," Foilzie replied. "It'd be best if we took ourselves away from here, my dears. Soldiers asked questions earlier this morning, and we've had our fill of them. This way!"

They ducked down a narrow alley between tall tenements, heading in the general direction of Foilzie's house. There a grim surprise awaited the Company, who had not witnessed the burning. The old woman relayed to them the shocking story, as told to her by others in her street who had seen something of the Arkhos's rage.

"Who did this?" In spite of the story he had just heard, Farr could not believe it. The ruins smoldered still; the three-floored building now half its former height, blackened posts draped with burned boards, surrounded by charred rubble. This is where they had slept, eaten and shared their hopes for the last two months.

"The Instruian Guard burned it down. The Arkhos of Nemohaim ordered it. They were looking for you."

"What a foul city," he ground out. "They should have burned the whole town to the ground."

"It's only a house," Foilzie said, as the Company made to console her. "It was a gift. It has served its purpose. A small loss compared to what my neighbors suffered."

But even as she told them of her misfortune, a strangely joyful light played in her eyes. The Company followed her gaze. There, walking through the wreck of the tenement, arm in a sling, the bald Escaignian came towards them. His eyes, however, were only for Foilzie.

He had recovered enough food from the basement, which remained relatively undamaged, to make a rudimentary meal of cold meats, salad and fruit. The meat tasted a little of smoke, but nobody minded. There they sat, surrounded by rubble, eating together, laughing together. It seemed so strange, yet so familiar. *These two are our kind of people*, Stella thought. Yet, as she watched Farr eat, she had to acknowledge the Company was not a "kind of people." A more unlikely group could not be imagined: Perdu, the Hermit, Mahnum and Indrett, Farr the fighter, Foilzie and the Escaignian, and the rock-silent Bhrudwan warrior. For a moment she allowed herself the luxury of thinking about the others: Kurr, Hal, the Haufuth, the strange Phemanderac, Leith . . .

"Where to now?" Farr asked. "The fuss about this flooding will be over soon. They'll be out looking for us again presently. Can we get out of this place?"

"You mean Instruere? I don't think we should," Mahnum told him. "The others will go south, seeking the Jugom Ark. If they have any sense, they won't try to come back for us until their quest has succeeded, or . . . I think we should wait for them."

"Why wait? Why not try to join them? What chance have they of success without us?"

Perdu laughed bitterly. "Farr Storrsen, you will never

change, for which I give thanks. We can neither help them nor hinder them. They have no chance of success at all, unless they are favored by the gods. From what I can see, they retain the gods' favor." He talked as if instructing a child. "Has Farr Storrsen lost faith?"

"Mjolkbridge has lost things more important than faith," the Vinkullen man replied bitterly. "Evil men came riding through and slashed our innocence to death on the street."

Stella looked more closely at the young mountain man. Something obviously bothered him—well, there was a great deal which bothered them all, she acknowledged, as her mind dwelt for a moment on those not amongst them—but he had lost the composure she had seen in the days and weeks after he suffered the loss of his brother.

Farr stood, setting aside his bowl, his food unfinished and unregarded. "Ever since we arrived in this dreadful city we have done nothing but run and hide, or beg for an audience with people who ought to have been begging us for our help. I've run out of patience with people who do nothing but obstruct us, pursue us and imprison us in an attempt to stop us helping them! Listen, I know you people regard me as a hothead. Maybe there is a reason! I've seen my father cut down and butchered. I've seen my brother sacrifice himself for the good of our cause. I am not willing to see their deaths lose meaning by our running away and hiding again. Either we take the southern road in search of the crazy philosopher's Arrow, or we stay put right here." He waved his hand around, indicating the basement.

"But the guard will know where—"

The Vinkullen man did not give Mahnum a chance to

continue. "So we are to be on the run from now on, then? Do we run back to Firanes, to our villages and our families? Or do we find somewhere to make a stand, to put down roots, to be Falthans again, even if it is only until the Brown Army comes to the gate?"

"I am of a mind with you," said the bald Escaignian. "I have thought long about this. The whole history of Escaigne is one of running, of hiding. These last ten years I have lived in fear, using the cover of darkness to creep from one part of Escaigne to another. I will run no more. I will hide no more! Here I will live. Here in the heart of Faltha I assert my Falthan-ness. I will rise from the ashes of fear and here make my stand."

"Do you mean here in Instruere, or—" Again Mahnum was interrupted.

"No, I mean here. Right here in the ashes of this house." He looked to Foilzie.

"I am too old to run and too large to hide." The Instruian woman smiled as she spoke. "If the guards feel threatened by an old woman, then let them come and deal with that threat in public. It is time Instruere realized what she has become. Old man, I will stand with you."

As Stella listened to the words of the tough old woman, she realized that Foilzie herself was a symbol of the great old city. Too old to run and too large to hide, she sat at the heart of things like the world's mother, gathering Faltha to her. And beneath her harsh voice and her wrinkled skin she had a decent heart, and something more. As long as Instruere was made up of people like Foilzie, Faltha still had hope.

"So what is the feeling amongst us?" Mahnum asked the Company.

"I'll stay," Stella said flatly. "I've done nothing wrong."

"I will wait here for my boys," said Indrett wearily. "Let's see what happens when the others come back."

The Hermit pulled his blue robe close about him. "This is where I am called to be," he said with certainty. "I have been led from my cave to this city for some great purpose. I shall not leave until it is accomplished."

"Some great purpose?" Mahnum echoed quietly.

"I have seen it," the blue-robed man continued, either missing or ignoring the nuance in the Trader's voice. "The Most High is doing a new thing in these days. Behold, he is about to dwell with men, and once again call them his children. I am his herald. He has spoken. I have heard it! 'Tear down the walls, mend the ancient bridges, open the doors of the houses and get ready to welcome your king!' He has whispered to me in the silence of my cave. I will shout it from the rooftops of this city!"

Mahnum pursed his lips but said nothing.

"The closer I am to Myrvidda, the better I will feel," Perdu said. "I am mindful of my clan chief's instructions to me, for I have not yet reported to him of the Bhrudwans' deaths. But until the Company is dissolved, I believe it would be his wish that I remain here." There was a heaviness in his voice that Stella identified with; perhaps her own losses enabled her to hear it.

"I think we should stay here in Instruere," said Mahnum. "Our mission was to warn Faltha, and we still might achieve it while we remain. If we go into hiding, our message unrecognized, many may pay for it with their lives."

To their surprise the Bhrudwan acolyte, Achtal, sprang to his feet. "I serve Hal," he announced. "I serve the Company!" He looked around the group, his expression unreadable. "We drive the Bhrudwo from Instruere." His mouth snapped shut and he sat down with an easy grace, evident now he was finally allowed to have his hands free.

The members of the Company looked at each other, conscious for the first time that they had no leaders. Kurr and the Haufuth were gone. They waited for a decision to come.

"There is another reason we should stay here," Perdu said, thinking as he spoke. "I heard people at the gate talking about the demise of the Arkhos of Nemohaim. If he's really fallen from power, then we have little to fear, surely?"

Is this bravado? Stella wondered. *Is it some crazy reaction to days of being cooped up in Escaigne? To a series of unlikely escapes from imprisonment and death? Or have we simply had enough?*

Eventually, Mahnum said, "Well, since no one wants to leave, we stay here. But where, exactly . . ."

"No better place than right here, at least for the next little while," said Foilzie. "The basement's fine—smells of smoke, but it's fine—and maybe the guard won't think to look here."

The others agreed with her. Perhaps it was weariness, or the onset of shock, or the influence of this foreign place, that led the members of the Company to disregard their peril for the moment. In their hearts, however, they knew that discovery, arrest, even possible death, might be only a matter of time.

Red-faced, out of breath and more than a little nervous, the guard opened the door to the Inner Chamber. There, seated alone, was a man few in the city had seen, but who already controlled their destinies. The guard wiped his sweaty palms on the front of his uniform, waiting for the dread moment when the man would look up and acknowledge him, but the man did not look up. The man in the Inner Chamber was tall, angular and dark-skinned, perhaps thirty years of age. His features were simplicity itself. Large brown eyes, small, slightly upturned nose, a wide, full mouth, high cheekbones and unblemished skin; no extraneous feature to draw the eye away from his gaze. It was a face of command, a face of authority. There would be no mistaking the intent of one who owned such a face. The face of a man capable of great good, or great evil. A face to inspire awe—or fear.

As the guard watched, the man stretched out his arms over a bowl filled with a black liquid, and began chanting something in a low undertone. Clearly some sort of ritual was being enacted. *I should not be here*, his mind screamed. *I should not be seeing this!* But he had been ordered to the Inner Chamber, shown in by the man's own personal secretary. He could not leave now.

Something strange began to happen to the bowl. As if in answer to the rhythm of the chant, a blue flame rose from the surface of the liquid, flickered, steadied and began to pulse brighter. The chanting continued, swelling slightly; then, when it held the flame at about a foot in height, abruptly it ceased. The flame did not waver.

Now quickly, urgently, the man spoke to the flame; or, at least, that is what he appeared to be doing. The speech was high-pitched and sibilant, and in no tongue the guard could recognize, though he was, like many in cosmopolitan Instruere, something of a polyglot. In fact, his ability with languages had seen his swift rise through the ranks of the Instruian Guard, until he had attained his present rank; but he had never heard a language like the one he was hearing now. The man paused; then, incredibly, the flame answered him. Drawing his breath in sharply, the guard looked with stunned amazement at the scene. The noise invoked a tiny flicker in the flame, but immediately it steadied itself.

The voice from the flame spoke in the same language as used by the man in the Inner Chamber. It repeated the same phrase three times, as if issuing important instructions it wanted followed. The man spoke again, with more confidence now, as though offering assurances the instructions were understood and would be enacted. Then, without warning, the flame flared brightly; the guard could feel the heat of it. For a moment he gained the distinct impression the flame was searching the room, aware of his presence and trying to locate him. The sensation almost unmanned him. He could have sworn the flame leaned towards him and extended a small probing tongue of blue fire; or perhaps it was the result of some unfelt draft in this ancient building. Whatever the reason, the man spoke to the flame once again, waited a moment, then drew his hands slowly together over the bowl. The flame disappeared the instant they touched.

The man pushed the bowl away from him, then leaned back in his chair and closed his eyes. *Now what? Do I wait here until I am acknowledged? Does he even know I am here?*

The guard waited until he could stand it no longer. "My lord," he said, more than a little frightened at how querulous his voice sounded. "We have found no trace of the Arkhos of Nemohaim."

The man at his desk continued in his trancelike state, giving no indication he heard the guard, or was even aware of his presence.

"We looked everywhere," said the guard, sweat breaking out on his brow.

This statement was greeted with the tiniest tightening around the eyes.

They say this man is far more cruel than the Arkhos of Nemohaim, said a fearful voice in the guard's mind. *What do I do now?*

"We have received a report from the Southbridge Guard," he said, in a vain attempt to fill the gaping silence. "Does my lord wish to hear it?"

In response the man opened his eyes, turned his head slowly and fixed his single-minded stare on the unfortunate guard. "Did you knock before entering?" he said mildly, in a rich, fatherly voice.

"No, my lord. The urgency—"

"You make a mistake if you presume to judge what is urgent," the man said, his voice showing a little anger. "That is not for you to decide."

"Yes, my lord." *This is not going well.*

"Your report is known to me. The captain of the Southbridge Guard reported the death of one of his officers, and the probable escape of the Arkhos of Nemohaim. You will recall your detachment was charged with his capture. He also claimed the Arkhos was aided by a number of accomplices. You no doubt have their names."

Fear gripped him around the temples and tightened. "No, my lord." The admission came out as a whisper.

The face did not change, but this gave the guard no reason to hope.

"Is your report—such as it is—ready to present?" The man's voice was now tight, controlled, clipped, dangerous.

"Yes, my lord, I can tell you what we have learned—"

"Are you telling me it has not been written?"

The guard found it difficult to speak.

"Do you have a family?" the man asked.

"Yes, my lord. Two girls and a boy."

"What are they going to do now that their father has no employment?"

"My lord?" His temples throbbed with fear.

"Such frightful lack of competence is, no doubt, a legacy of my predecessor. I will not permit it to continue. Let us hope you discover some hitherto hidden skill in order to provide for your dependents. No, do not presume to speak. I will not always be so forgiving. You are dismissed from the service of Instruere. Now, go."

After the miserable guard had left, Deorc called his servant to his side. "Furoman, gather the Council together. We will meet at sunset tonight. Have the arrangements we discussed been made?"

"Yes, my lord," said Saraskar's former secretary. He wore a particularly evil smile.

"Good. I have spoken with our master. We have no time to waste."

The first few people who came to the basement were not too much of a surprise, just two or three friends accompanying Indrett as she returned from the market later that morning, keen to hear her story and share some of the local gossip. Others, seeing the burned tenement reoccupied and knowing the story of its burning, came to look at those who had invaded The Pinion and invoked the ire of the Arkhos of Nemohaim. The visitors brought food with them, good plain food, drink and good cheer; and the blackened walls echoed with laughter, little people rejoicing that the big people were not having things all their own way.

The surprise came when, rather than dropping, the

number of visitors to the basement increased throughout the day. Something of a carnival atmosphere settled over them, enhanced when a number of Phemanderac's musical acquaintances arrived and began to play; and by the evening it seemed to Indrett that the whole of the market had taken up residence in the room. And not just the market-goers: Mahnum recognized amongst the crowd some of those who had been rescued from The Pinion. It was clear the people of Instruere had taken the northerners into their hearts.

That first unforgettable night was spent talking, laughing and singing. Unobserved perhaps by the majority of those present, something unusual began to happen. The crowd divided into smaller and smaller groups, most comprising no more than two or three people sitting or standing close together, discussing the events in the city, what might happen in the future; talking, hesitantly at first, about their own hopes and dreams, and of the warnings brought to Instruere by the northerners. They quite forgot about their houses and their daily tasks. The unexpected boldness of the normally self-interested Instruians in associating with the northern "criminals," their expression of defiance in the face of the guard and the Council, were deliciously intoxicating.

Though most of the visitors left before midnight, they all returned to the basement at daybreak, bringing more food with them. There would be no market today—or, more accurately, the market was set up in Foilzie's blackened basement. Breakfast and lunch were shared, those with plenty giving of their bounty to those who had little or none. Carpenters, seemingly appearing from nowhere, began repairing the fire-damage, while others produced carpets, chairs, couches, curtains and drapes. The musicians began anew, and the crowd swelled until it could no longer be contained in the tenement basement, spilling out on to the narrow street.

At first the members of the Company were too tired to do anything except attend to the needs of their visitors. Then, when the realization that something was happening settled on them, they began to speculate about it. Farr was strongly of the opinion the crowd should be dispersed, fearing at any moment the attention of the Instruian Guard would be attracted to them. While agreeing with him, most of the others were too fascinated to be really frightened, and took comfort from the sheer number of people gathered in and around the basement. Surely there was not enough room in The Pinion, indeed, in the Hall of Lore, to contain the crowd! But Farr's warning at least elicited volunteers from those gathered who kept watch for any sign of the guard. None were seen that day.

Mahnum wandered around the basement, unsure of what was going on, and what, if anything, should be done about it. "My grandfather told us of the old days, before the Council ran everything," one old man was saying. "Back then a Warden had command of the guard, and there weren't so many of them either. A Warden, just like Furist and Raupa decided. If it was good enough for the First Men, it should be good enough now."

Not three feet away a young woman spoke with vehemence. "The Most High is real," she said, the intensity on her face daring any of her listeners to disagree. "I've *felt* Him. You just close your eyes and reach out with your soul."

"But what does that have to do with the Bhrudwan armies?" asked a thin young man. "You can stand on the battlements and reach out with your soul as much as you like, but the arrows'll make a pincushion of you just the same. We need weapons, not feelings."

In one corner of the room Stella described the journey of the Company to an interested group of listeners, a fair proportion of them young men not insensitive to the unusual northern beauty of the speaker. "We cut the ropes of the bridge," she was saying, "and two of the Bhrudwans fell. So we really only had one to fight. Even so, he would have killed us all but for the bravery of Wira. He's the one I told you about, hair as white as—well, as white. Tall and strong. Anyway, we captured the Bhrudwan. There he is, over there." She pointed to where Achtal stood impassively beside Indrett. Her listeners were impressed, and a number of them imagined an army of powerfully built warriors like the Bhrudwan just a few yards away. They had all heard of his exploits in The Pinion. "He was the least of the warriors we fought," Stella told them.

"Something has to be done," said one of the men with bravado. "If the Council won't do something, we will. Perhaps the Bhrudwan could give lessons or something, and we could learn to fight like him." A chorus of agreement rose from the others, not wishing to be outdone. "After all, we're all—well, most of us, anyway—just as strong as him. We've got the potential. We just need the chance." His speech was rewarded with a smile. The talk continued through the evening, and the second night repeated the pattern of the first. As the evening wore on, the overt market noise subsided into earnest discussion. The talk could perhaps be classified as political and religious; but that is only to say that people talked about what was most important to them.

Late that night the Hermit, clad as ever in his blue robe, stood in front of the assembled people and spoke.

"Good people of Instruere," he said, his incisive tone quieting the crowd, "this gathering is taking place in fulfillment of something spoken to me many nights ago. In a vision I heard a voice crying out: 'The people will join together in their search for me.' This is the voice of the Most High, who in these days is doing a new thing. He is about to return to his people, and has appointed us to tear down the walls, mend the ancient bridges, throw wide the doors of the houses and get ready to welcome our king. Can you not sense it? Does your spirit not feel restless even as I speak? Does not your heart beat faster? It was for this purpose that we of the north were called to you. It is here that the Most High will return. We are to be the spearhead of the new move of God. Let these thoughts lead you as you talk together."

As abruptly as he had begun, the Hermit finished his short speech, smiled briefly and moved back into the crowd.

"Who was 'e?" one man said to another, to be answered with a shrug.

"He said he heard the voice of the Most High!" a woman said to her neighbor, excitement in her voice. "He can tell the future!"

"Nonsense!" said an old man. "What has the Most High got to do with us? We'll put this town to rights without his help. And if he tries to interfere, he'll find things not to his liking." Reaction to the Hermit's speech buzzed around the room.

"What was that about?" Perdu whispered to Mahnum, not a little unsettled. "What does he mean by this talk of the Most High?"

"I don't know," the Trader replied. "If the Haufuth

were here, I would ask him. He has spent most time with the man."

"I see our friend has suddenly become a northerner."

"But what he said does help explain what is happening here," Indrett added. "What if Hal was right? What if the Most High simply requires our presence here, and it is not necessary to persuade the Council of our cause? What if the people themselves are going to prepare for his coming?"

"But *whose* coming, I wonder?" said Farr, intruding on their conversation. "The Right Hand, or the Most High Himself? Or, as is most likely, the Destroyer and the armies of Bhrudwo? And how should we prepare? Do we decorate the city walls, or build our defenses?" He paused, weighing the effect of his words on their hearers. "Make no mistake," he said. "Everything depends on our choice."

Deorc strode into the Inner Chamber, having been satisfied by Furoman that everything was ready. For what he had planned it would not do to be unprepared, as chance was the enemy of success. As he sat, he cast an assessing eye over the gathering of the Council. The division between Falthan loyalists and Bhrudwan sympathizers was clear, and fear had done its work: the size of the latter was far larger than the former. The elegant Bhrudwan wondered how any Councillor could remain a loyalist. *Surely they must know what is in store for them?* He could not conceive that any man, knowing he was betrayed and a trap lay unsprung in front of him—indeed, that he himself had unwittingly helped set it—would nevertheless walk open-eyed into it. *They are fools. They do not deserve their seats. I do Faltha a favor this day.*

"Welcome to the first session of the new Council of Faltha," he began. He pitched his voice carefully, in the way the Bhrudwan Voicemasters had taught him. As he spoke, his voice shaped the thought: *you are privileged to be here. It is an honor that at any moment could be taken from you. Do not forget it*. And, by his art, he wove the thought into his voice. "We have much work to do, and must first face a most unpleasant task—"

"Who are you, and what gives you the right to command this Council?" It was a direct challenge, and it came from the group of four loyalists seated at the far side of the table.

The Voiceskill is a two-edged gift, his masters had taught him. *When the spell is strong, you have the power of command. But when the spell is broken, deception fails and your intentions become clear. Above all else*, they emphasized, *do not allow stray thoughts to pollute the purity of your voice*.

It had been a shocking interruption, ripping across the table and momentarily unnerving him. The loyalists might be fools, but they were strong—or perhaps they lacked the imagination to be controlled. He tightened his grip.

"Until I am elected to headship of the Council, I am nothing," he admitted. *But let there be no doubt as to my right to be here*. "However, I was asked to chair the Council in the absence of the Arkhos of Nemohaim by a quorum of Councillors at an emergency meeting. The paperwork is all here. Examine it: you'll find it is all in order." *You are trapped. You are excluded. You are humiliated. You do not have the strength to oppose me*.

He turned to the majority of the Councillors, and prepared to resume his carefully planned speech.

With an agony of effort, resisting the compulsion laid so

heavily upon him, one of the loyalists spoke. "But you—
you are a Bhrudwan. How can you command the Council?"

And you are a fool who commands nothing! his
thought snapped before he could stop it. The unsettling effect of his angry thought would be diminished if he did not
speak for a moment; but then the compulsion of his voice
would be lessened. He decided to take the risk. In this situation he could not afford to lose control for a second.

"Where I have come from is of no moment. It is where
I am going, and Instruere with me, that is important." His
words were for his own party. *I am Progress. I am Power.
You who are little will do well to align yourself with me.*
Now he addressed the enemy. "It is not *my* loyalty that is
in question today. *I* submit to the will of the Council.
There are, however, some among us who do not." *The
loyalists are on trial today. You will decide their fate. Already you taste the fruits of power.*

He paused. His authority here was not being seriously
questioned. If it came to a vote, there would be no doubt
about the outcome. However, he had something much
less passive in mind. The northerners had stood in this
room and accused the Council of treachery, and because
of that fool Nemohaim the slur uttered here remained
unanswered. Until now.

"We have a responsibility to our people. You have
sought the friendship of Bhrudwo, and my presence here
is a confirmation that you have found it. You can regard
us as perhaps a seventeenth kingdom. And all of us
here—well, all except our unwise colleagues—realize
the supposed enmity between Faltha and Bhrudwo was a
fallacy invented to serve the conservative interests in
Faltha. It never represented anything real." All the time
he wound soothing, encouraging thoughts into his words.

You are doing the right thing. We must have unity; we must rid ourselves of division. You are the courageous ones, forging a new path for all Falthans to tread. It was hard for him not to laugh inwardly at the absurdity of it all, but he maintained his concentration so the Word-weave would not fail.

"However, we cannot be seen to tolerate division within our ranks. If we are to go forward, we are to go forward together. Therefore, I now call for a statement of unity." *Choose wisely, for this is life and death. Life, with prestige, power, rewards beyond your ability to imagine, access to the dark secrets . . . or death, slow and dark with pain, a fear-filled fall into futility, your name a byword to the peoples, your family . . .* "Those among you who choose, on behalf of your kingdoms, to press forward into the new Faltha, do so by standing to acknowledge me as the Head of the Council, in replacement of the traitorous Nemohaim. Those who choose the old Faltha, remain seated."

Immediately the Bhrudwan-bought Councillors stood, playing their part well. Along with the remaining six of the original seven traitors named by Mahnum—the Arkhoi of Firanes, Treika, Favony, Tabul, Straux and Vertensia—stood Haurn the Craven, along with new replacements for Nemohaim and Asgowan. Two other Arkhoi, Plonya and Deuverre, cast their lot with the traitors when it became apparent who held the power in the Council. The knot of four loyalists—the Arkhoi of Deruys, Redana'a, Sna Vaztha and Piskasia, sadly missing Sarista—remained seated, staring at their colleagues whom they had recently discovered they did not know at all, tensely awaiting the outcome. They knew this man meant them ill.

"The choice is made. An example will be made of those who have betrayed the will of the Council, so the people of

Instruere clearly understand the penalty of resistance. Furo-man!" he called out.

In an instant his new servant stood at his side. The loyalists recognized the man as the Arkhos of Sarista's secretary, and his presence here confirmed the news of Saraskar's death. As if Furoman read their minds, he favored them with a smirk both irritating and insulting. *Our executioner*, the loyalists realized.

"Bind these men," Deorc instructed. With the Word-weave, the loyalists heard their deaths pronounced.

The Arkhos of Piskasia could stand it no longer. "Please," he said, stifling a whimper, "could you tell me some more about the new Faltha you have planned? There might be something I can do to help." Fear-forced tears coursed down his cheeks, but he was past caring about humiliation. A life of plenty on the wide, fertile Piskasian plains had not prepared him for this extremity.

Perfect, Deorc gloated. *This will bind the Council to me more effectively even than fear.*

"You wish to recant?" he asked the miserable Piskasian, who could only nod with relief.

"You will serve a probationary period undergoing correction. If you prove yourself apt to teaching, you may be reinstated to the Council. However, if you betray us, we will deal swiftly with you." *I hold absolute sway here. Perfect obedience to my every word may see mercy extended to you. But, if mercy is denied, you will die like a rat in a sewer, without ceremony or lament.* He paused, gauging the effect of his Wordweave. The three remaining loyalists looked on their fellow with a mixture of pity and scorn, while Deorc's allies, though trying to remain impassive, could not hide their respect from the Word-master. He had them in the palm of his hand.

*   *   *

The daily assembly at Foilzie's basement did not remain unobserved by the authorities. The Hermit realized early on the third day that the gatherings were being watched. Members of the Instruian Guard had been posted at either end of the narrow lane, and would stop and question people at random. *Fools*, the Hermit thought. *If you were to come down hard on us now, you might prevent what is to come. But caution and ignorance have bound you, and despite yourselves you too serve the will of the Most High.*

Vigilant as the Instruian Guard were, they missed the escape of Achtal, the Bhrudwan warrior. Some time on that third morning he slipped away. With all that was going on, the Company did not see the need to search for him, nor could they have compelled him to return with them had he chosen not to. *He's served his purpose, and that not very well*, Perdu reflected. *He can't do us any harm now*. Vaguely he wondered how Hal might feel about the Bhrudwan's desertion, but thought about it no further than that.

To Stella, these days were better than holidays or Midsummer, more exciting even than the seven-year gathering when the whole of the North March would meet in the old walled town of Vapnatak. At last, she considered, everything was beginning to turn out all right. Leith and the others were gone, and the hurt of their desertion clawed at her deeply; but every day she met new and exciting people from all over the Great City, and with a pride she could not conceal she found herself at the center of it all. The story of the Roofed Road was told again and again, and Stella delighted in the fact that many people found comfort and strength in the tale. It didn't seem to matter to them whether it was true or false—occasionally she overheard the story being told with gross exaggeration—because the value of it seemed to lie in its ability to inspire faith in its hearers. "Imagine!" they would say. "Just a wisp of a girl, and she knocked a great warrior into the river!"

The Hermit began to speak to the crowd on a nightly basis, and his messages were mystical but direct. "The days when you conceived of the Most High as an invisible god are over," he would announce, and the people would quiet down to listen. "This is a new season, the dawn of a whole new day. For two thousand years the descendants of the First Men have labored under a deception, having been taught the Most High had abandoned them. This served them well, for they did not have to consider his claims on them; they could continue satisfying their own desires without interference. This I considered during the many years I have spent alone in contemplation, learning to hear his voice. And this is what he says: 'Soon, very soon, you shall meet me face to face. Only do not close your heart to me, do not whisper words of unbelief, as those who remain unconvinced will be left behind. They will be swept aside as I, the Most High, come to establish my kingdom. But those who remain faithful will find themselves administering that kingdom. Instruere will once again be my city, and I will dwell here, just as I dwelled in Dona Mihst of old. Only open your gates to me! Prepare me room!'"

Gradually the people were coming to accept this teaching. The signs appeared to bear witness to the Hermit's message. The city was certainly in a time of ferment, and the guard was everywhere, but a number of the old Arkhoi were no longer seen in the city. "We've got a new man," some said; and it was true, confirmed by the most reliable of sources, though no one had yet seen him.

"The fat man has been put to death in his own dungeon," some commentators asserted, while this was contradicted by those who claimed he had fled the city ignominiously. Everyone was agreed the truth of either rumor would be a blessing. Nobody could be worse than the Arkhos of Nemohaim. Undoubtedly Instruere was in a state of flux; everything seemed to be up for renegotiation. Perhaps, the gossip ran, it was as the man in the blue robes said: all this was necessary to make way for the Most High!

"What?" the informant would say. "You haven't heard the blue-robed man speak? You must come down to the basement. The basement, dear. Down a way from the Dock Road Market. Come with me tomorrow morning!"

As the days went on, the Hermit began to interweave prophecy with his teaching. He would pause, then point a finger into the crowd. "You there! Yes, you in the brown cloak! The Most High would say this to you: 'I see your pain, my son, and I offer you my comfort.' You are about to move into a season of great blessing, when everything you have lost will be returned to you tenfold. Do you believe?"

And the brown-cloaked one would inevitably reply: "Yes, I believe!" The effect was startling, and people began to come from every part of the city to hear the man in the blue robe speak.

The debate within the Company was fierce. "His words are accurate," Perdu argued, "and they bring comfort and encouragement to their hearers. How could they be wrong?"

"That's fine, as far as it goes," Farr answered him. "I've got no complaint with people feeling better. But what he says is so general, so cloaked in vague language, that he could say it to anyone and it would be true. I see no evidence that the Hermit is the mouthpiece of the Most High."

"Yet he was accurate with his words to Leith," Indrett said, and told them Leith's story. "I think he hears the truth and speaks it out. Just look at the people coming to the basement! Surely the hand of the Most High is upon us!"

"Of course he hears the truth," Mahnum said. His opposition to the Hermit's speeches had become consistent and vehement. "But that does not give him the right to use it like a conjurer. And when did we make the decision to trust this man to be our spokesman?"

"I am in no doubt," the bald Escaignian declared. "This man expresses the wishes and hopes of my people. Open the doors wide! Prepare for his coming!"

Foilzie was not so sure. "It don't feel right to me," she said, but could not explain what she meant.

"You're just afraid of change," the Escaignian said to her. "So you have chosen to stick to what you know."

"You might be right," the old woman agreed reluctantly. "But surely we should set store by tradition?"

"No!" The man from Escaigne was adamant. "Tradition is the sterile grave of good ideas. Escaigne started out as a good idea but became a tradition, ineffective and evil in the end. Traditions need uprooting. Escaigne needed uprooting. We need uprooting!"

Even as the debate continued, things began happening that put the validity of the Hermit's speaking beyond doubt. He was amazingly effective at picking out the members of the guard infiltrating the crowd and exposing them. His words of prophecy continued to be regarded as accurate. And then, a fortnight or so after the gatherings started, the shaking began.

It started in the front row, where the people were packed in most closely. As the Hermit spoke, people began to shake. It happened simultaneously in two places. Then to the left and to the right others began to quiver, some with their hands and arms, others with their whole bodies. "Look!" the Hermit cried, his eyes bright with promise. "Look! It is the fire of the Most High! He comes! He comes!" Some of the women began to laugh, and Mahnum cringed inwardly, for now the Hermit went too far. What had he done? But then he realized that the women were not laughing at the shaking people. Indeed, they shook themselves. The laughter seemed to be part of the whole happening.

"Catch the fire! Catch the fire!" the Hermit cried. "Open wide the door of your heart!"

"I thought the Most High was coming in the flesh," said one man. "What's all this about my heart?"

The Hermit turned on him. "You are the flesh. If you let the fire of the Most High fall on you, consume you, he will have indeed come in the flesh. He comes to dwell in Instruere, and you yourselves are his houses!"

The bald Escaignian stood in front of the crowd, and he shook from head to toe. "My friend . . . is right," he said, forcing the words to come. "The fire . . . has . . . fallen! The Most High . . . is in me. Don't . . . resist him. Open wide . . . your heart!"

Foilzie looked on in dismay.

The phenomenon spread until perhaps a quarter of the gathering, maybe up to a hundred people, were taken to varying degrees by the shaking and the laughter. The Hermit said nothing, merely standing in front of them with outstretched arms as though he was the conduit through which the power proceeded.

* * *

Late that night a few of the Company sat around the fire. The meeting had finished, the assembly had gone home, and the Hermit rested at the far end of the basement.

"What has happened?" Mahnum asked. "Far from readying us to defend against Bhrudwo, this . . . I don't know what to call it . . . has made us more vulnerable."

"The Most High has come," Indrett said. "What else could it be? He has brought us from the north for this very purpose, and now he returns to his faithful people."

"But this wasn't part of the quest!" Mahnum argued. "We have laid aside what we were supposed to do, and have been carried away into selfish indulgence!"

"I would not have believed you, of all people, would have argued against a visitation of the Most High," said his wife in a voice not without irony. "All your life you have talked of him as though he was your ally."

A voice drifted over from the other end of the room. "This is what the Most High says to you, son of Modahl: 'Curb your jealousy. Allow others to experience what you yourself have experienced. Do not keep me to yourself.'"

Mahnum bit his lip and said nothing.

Stella spoke diffidently. "Remember the night of fire?" she asked. "Remember the dreams? Leith and I dreamed about the Most High that night. You dreamed too, I am certain of it. I feel I ought not to speak of it—I am not sure I would have told you what happened even if I was allowed. Is it the same with the rest of you? Did you dream too?"

Her words were answered by the nodding of heads. No one had forgotten that night. The fact that it had been a shared experience seemed to make it so much more real to them.

She continued, pressing home her point. "If we were granted the fire, how can we refuse others the experience?"

"That has about it the ring of truth," Perdu said quietly. "I suggest we operate on the belief that the Hermit speaks truly, and see where our faith takes us. After all, it is what we have been doing since the quest began, is it not?"

The issue was debated further, but the crucial moment passed. The Company, with one or two exceptions, put their trust in the words of the Hermit.

"The Keeper of Andratan has achieved your first purpose, O my lord," the small, brown-robed man reported. "He has the Council of Faltha in his hands, and Instruere with it. The Instruian Guard treat his word—your word through him—as law."

The hot south wind of Birinjh flicked a lock of jet-black hair into the hearer's eye, and unconsciously he pushed it away from his plucked eyebrow with his one hand.

"We need not worry the Council with this," Deorc said softly as the Councillors filed out of the Inner Chamber. "Anything that came before the old Council is now my responsibility, so I will deal with it."

The relief on the face of the Arkhos of Straux was palpable. A very capable man, he and the Arkhos of Sarista had been overloaded with much of the trivial work of the Council. Now that Saraskar had gone—a source of sadness to the Arkhos of Straux, though he understood the necessity—there was simply too much to do. With the recent campaign to expose and destroy Escaigne ending in disaster, followed immediately by the damage caused by the flood and the disorder that accompanied it, his few resources were fully committed. And now an increasing number of guards were being drawn off to observe—not to intervene, much less terminate—a gathering of disaffected citizens that might—might!—turn into some kind of rabble rebellion. The loss of these guards simply taxed him beyond his limits, and he had seriously considered protesting.

But now he did not have to. Deorc said he would take care of it, and this meant he would have his guards again. There was much cleaning to be done, for example. The longhouse in particular was in a terrible state. As yet no one had been able to get down into The Pinion. It would take weeks for the water to clear from the dungeons, and heaven knew how much longer after that before it would again be usable.

He heaved a sigh as he made his way to his private quarters. The reality of political office was much different to the substance of the dreams of a youth from Straux. The dead weight of tradition and precedent, the seemingly incontrovertible need to continue doing things the way they had always been done, simply swamped the young man he had been. His associates were often unsavory, people without scruples and with strange personal appetites to support, and everyone had vested interests in virtually everything. His own scruples had suffered, he knew that, and they had been abandoned with a tinge of regret; but his idealism had been subsumed by the pragmatism of the needs of the Sixteen Kingdoms, and by and large he approved of the change. Sixteen Councillors, each one selected by the king of the country they represented, supplied with a small staff and an annual income, which could be altered or withdrawn at the king's pleasure. Because of his king's proximity to Instruere (Mercium was two days' journey southwest of the Great City) the Arkhos of Straux was particularly vulnerable to this, and more than once he had been threatened with replacement.

It had been about two years previously that the King of Straux had traveled to Instruere, bringing with him the notion of enlisting Bhrudwan help with the governance of the Sixteen Kingdoms. After overcoming his initial resistance to the idea—what child from Straux had not been taught to abhor the hated occupiers of long ago?—his administrator's soul saw the advantages of the arrangement. The imposition of unity where none existed, and would never exist if the kingdoms were left alone; the offer of financial assistance and the promise of legalized trade; and the infusion of new and vigorous ideas into what was undoubtedly a dying Falthan culture. The extra inducements offered him were hardly necessary, indeed somewhat insulting; but he took them anyway so his king and country would not lose face. Or so he told himself.

The Arkhos of Nemohaim, a repulsive man whom he had never liked, took him aside at the end of the next Council and welcomed him into the group he named the Falthan Patriots. He was surprised and a little chagrined to learn he was not the first Councillor so approached. "Of course, we of necessity required such a one as you," the fat man said, his breath wheezing. "I'm so glad you chose the path of progress." Perhaps he had imagined the subtle threat fringing his words: *we can replace you at any time if your performance leaves anything to be desired.*

From that time the Patriots met secretly, for fear of alerting the traditional element of the Council; and by the time those foolish northerners presented their distorted information to them all, the Patriots were well prepared. The removal and elimination of the old loyalists was necessary, and he thoroughly approved. Those were the ones who asked the awkward questions, insisting that the chain of command be followed, that every Councillor be accountable to the Council, and other such tiresome and time-wasting restrictions. Hadn't they realized their job was to get things done? Some of the others might not care, but he was determined to make his mark on Falthan affairs, and already he sensed time was running out.

So now the Arkhos of Nemohaim was gone (for that, if nothing else, he owed a debt to the Bhrudwan), leaving the city in chaos. Curse the misfortune that allowed crises to coincide with a change of leadership! However, if Deorc took care of the petty disturbances, he could get on with the more pressing tasks. It was with relief and not a little satisfaction that the Arkhos of Straux reached his private quarters, summoned his secretary and began work on a revised guard roster.

It was at the beginning of the third week that the basement gathering began to be known as the Ecclesia. The identity of the one who bestowed the name was never recorded, but within two or three days of the name being given it was the shorthand used in conversations all around the city. The Ecclesia became the dominant subject of discussion not just with the general populace, but also with a range of special-interest groups from the Council of Faltha through to underground political groups, including the remnants of Escaigne. Many such groups sent unannounced representatives to Foilzie's basement to look for ways to control the Ecclesia, to bend it to their own ends. People from all sectors of society converged on this new movement: the rich and cynical, to acquaint themselves with the source of the gossip or simply to mock the spectacle; the depressed and destitute, seeking against hope and reason for the one thing that would make all the difference; the Instruian middle class, frightened by the turmoil and the rumors in their city, frustrated by their inability to achieve their goals. And amidst them all, people looking for the Most High.

Stella watched them all come to the basement. She listened to them talk, listened to their ideas and dreams, their hopes and fears; and, where she could, tried to explain what the Ecclesia was about. At first this was difficult, for no one was really sure what was happening. Later, however, she and the other members of the Company became proficient in introducing people to the Ecclesia.

"For two thousand years the Most High has remained remote from human affairs," she said to a group of first-time visitors. "But not any more. He wants to reveal himself to the sons and daughters of the First Men, and he has begun right here, in this basement. From here it will spread throughout Instruere, throughout Faltha."

"How does he reveal himself?" an older lady wanted to know.

"Come back tonight; you'll see people shaking and laughing as they are touched by his fire."

"What's all that got to do with religion?" asked another. "That sort of stuff's just a put-on."

"The Hermit says that whenever the Most High comes to dwell in a person, our weak, mortal flesh cannot bear it. We can't hold it in. He says it's no surprise such things manifest, with the power contained within us."

In the few days the Company had been involved in giving this explanation, they had come to expect most people would leave at this point. After two thousand years of religious indifference, some just couldn't conceive of a hands-on religion like this. "The doubters will mock, and many will leave," the Hermit warned them. "But we are better off without them. Their presence in the basement offends the spirit of the Most High, and dampens the fire. Let them go! We have our hands full with believers." And that certainly was true.

Near the back of the group stood a tall, dark-skinned man with fine, even delicate features. "What do you plan to do with this 'fire' you have placed among the people? How will you shape it?" His plucked eyebrows arched together as he pitched his question.

"Ah—we have no plans for anything," Stella replied, momentarily disconcerted. "There's been talk about the Council of Faltha, but the Hermit says our mission is spiritual, not physical. I guess everyone knows we came here from Firanes to warn the Council about the coming Bhrudwan invasion, but were ignored. It looks to us like the Most High has a different plan for our defense than we imagined."

"You going to laugh them to death?" suggested one bored youth at the fringe of the crowd, but no one joined with his mirth.

"Tell me," said the dark-skinned man. "Is the fire for Bhrudwans too?" He directed his eyes at Stella, and for a moment it seemed to her his real intent had been masked by the words: *tell me: could you fall in love with a Bhrudwan?* She shook off her momentary foolishness. "I don't see why not," she answered, smiling. "Perhaps that is his plan. Perhaps if they find the fire, they will not want to attack."

"Perhaps you're right," he said; and as he spoke she could tell from his eyes that he would be one to receive the fire.

CHAPTER 14

CASTLE IN THE CLOUDS

LEITH THOUGHT THEY WOULD never make the brow of the hill, the long, slow hill they had been climbing all that afternoon, but finally, as the sky began to purple, the slope gave way to the hill's crown. He and the Arkhimm were rewarded with a distant view of the Almucantaran Mountains. Three days they had messed about in the broken maze of foothills that led southwards from the Valley of a Thousand Fires, climbing steadily all the while. The path was in serious disrepair and they lost it at least half a dozen times. Heavy rain during the winter was no doubt responsible for the state of the path, seldom used at the best of times. Years could pass without the tread of human feet, according to Prince Wiusago, and consequently the Arkhimm fought their way through thistle and briar. The third time they lost the track almost proved disastrous. They found themselves above a sheer bluff overlooking a steep-sided gorge, and spent an afternoon working back up a cruelly steep ridge. But now the Almucantaran Mountains, closer on their right, stretched away to the left, impossibly sheer snow-tipped peaks fading into the hazy distance. There, on the edge of sight, towering storm clouds straddled the mountains like dark riders astride their pale mounts. And between them and their goal lay ridge after wooded ridge, green into blue into purple like waves of the sea fading into the misty distance, a sight disturbingly similar to the wild North March surf during a spring westerly. An inhuman place, a place in which a man might drown.

Prince Wiusago frowned as he looked out over the sea of ridges and valleys ahead of them. He had been here once before, perhaps seven years ago, when he had been learning the warrior's craft, and others had been responsible for the route they took.

"I thought I would be able to find a way through for us," he admitted to the others. "But I remember virtually nothing. I'm afraid I might not be of much use to you."

"Great," said Te Tuahangata. Kurr groaned, Phemanderac frowned. The others said nothing, but the prince's bleak words served to increase their already overwhelming sense of insignificance in this vast, pathless land. The full history of this mountainous region was not known to any of them. Wiusago, as prince of Deruys, knew some of it, and Te Tuahangata was aware perhaps of even more, and so both kept silent. The land ahead was a place of dread, a place of death, a place of destruction beyond the knowledge of the Arkhimm. They would not win its crossing easily.

The Arkhimm rested that night on the high ridge bordering the land of Astraea. In the morning they started down the ridge in the general direction of the highest of the Almucantaran Mountains, in the absence of any better plan.

The Arkhos of Nemohaim had been having a rough time. After he and his band had lost contact with the northerners in Straux, having failed to resolve the strange affair of

The Reveler's Rest in Kinnekin, they took time to search thoroughly through southern Straux and into the broken country of coastal Deruys. He was tempted to stop at Brunhaven and inquire of the Deruvian king whether any northern travelers had been seen within his borders; but he abandoned the thought, realizing the foolishly Falthan-loyal King of Deruys would be unlikely to supply him with any information; and even if he did, it was likely to be so cryptic as to be unusable. So in great frustration he and his entourage thundered through Brunhaven just after dawn on a gray morning, looking to the inhabitants like a group of maniacal avengers.

It was after Brunhaven the troubles began. No peasant, no farmer, no one on the road, claimed to have seen his quarry, however roughly questioned. Undoubtedly the northerners had obtained horses by now, and were probably making better time than he. Of necessity, he traveled somewhat slower than others might. The Arkhos of Nemohaim was a frustrated man.

His temper did not improve when, a week south of Brunhaven and in the Southern Marches of Deruys, within sight of the mountains of his home, they were held up and robbed by a surprisingly large and well-armed band of highwaymen. Their food, money and weaponry were taken; yet, incredibly, they were left unharmed and with their horses even though they were defenseless. It was not until he reflected on this in a calmer mood that he realized these were soldiers, not highwaymen. But if the raid was inspired by Deorc, why did he not take the opportunity to have him finished off? And if it was not Deorc seeking to harry him, who was it?

The reason they were left with their horses became perfectly obvious later on that miserable day. Up in the mountains to the east dark storm clouds brooded, drenching the western margins of the ill-reputed land of Mist with late spring rains. Swift streams brought that water rushing down to the sea in foaming brown torrents: one such river appeared to have destroyed the bridge crossing it, leaving a few boards tenuously attached to each other.

"It will take our weight, my lord, and perhaps yours; but it will not support the horses'." The Captain of the Guard still smarted from the indignity of the morning's ambush. He spoke diffidently, fearing to raise the Arkhos's ire.

"How far to the next bridge over this stream?" The Arkhos of Nemohaim chose not to indulge in the luxury of anger.

"My lord, there is no other bridge."

The Arkhos scowled, but inside he knew fear. Not because of the delay this would cause, but because he knew this was the only bridge—this was, after all, his own country—and had forgotten. He did not forget things like this. The fear came because this was not the first time he had read in himself signs his supreme efficiency was disintegrating, falling apart from the inside out; the ultimate disaster for such a man as he.

"Yes, yes," he said brusquely. "Then we must abandon the horses and walk."

"My lord?"

"This will add a week to our journey." The Arkhos recovered himself by being brutally honest. "Unless we can procure horses on the other side of this stream."

"You are the Arkhos of Nemohaim," said the Archivist. "Surely horses will be made available for you? Every peasant in the land would regard it as an honor."

"Not here, and not in Nemohaim," said the Captain of

the Guard. "Here the people are fiercely independent. They pride themselves on it. We will get nothing without paying for it. The king himself would not be able to command a horse."

"So how—"

"Did I say anything about paying for them?" said the Arkhos. Really, this scholar was astonishingly naive. He looked forward to the day when the Archivist became unnecessary.

For two days the Arkhimm maintained their direction by the simple expedient of sighting the mountains from the ridgetops. It became obvious that this continual traipsing up and down ridges, rather than being able to follow the valleys, would cost them both time and strength; but there seemed no alternative. What disconcerted Leith most was that after two days' walking the mountains remained exactly the same distance away.

Then the weather closed in. Pale clouds came towards them from all sides, forming an unbroken roof over their heads. They opened to pour water in the sort of torrential deluge that at home would have sent Leith, who loved the rain, scurrying outside in wonder and delight. But not here. Here the rain beat at the ground like hammers on an anvil, as though the heavens sought to cleanse the land, or strip it bare, or drive the interlopers into the ground.

The Arkhimm could no longer sight the Almucantaran Mountains from the ridgetops. Indeed, such was the force of the rain, and such was its duration, they could not contemplate ascending the ridges. They kept to the valleys, seeking shelter and some semblance of dryness, while avoiding the streams that boiled into torrents even as they watched. Their progress was slow. Worse, they had no means to ascertain whether their exertions were for good or ill, whether they drew closer to or further from their goal, which discouraged them deeply.

The rain kept up for two days and a night. By the morning of the second day no article of clothing, whether worn or carried, remained dry. It proved impossible to sustain a fire in such weather. In spite of the increased pressure to make progress, with Kantara and the Jugom Ark ahead of them and the Bhrudwan threat behind, the Arkhimm elected to stay where they were that long day.

They found shelter of sorts in a hollow at the side of a rocky outcrop, though it was more of a concavity than a cave. What wind there was bent the gray rain-curtain somewhat to the west, away from where they sheltered, but the rock itself was wet and cold, and the travelers were altogether lost and miserable. Within their limited field of vision were a few moss-bearded mountain birch trees, some kind of flaxen bush, much larger than those which grew in the North March, and a rocky descent, down which milky water tracked to the valley bottom streambed, which rumbled with water-power. Of the ridge behind and the heights in front of them the travelers could see nothing.

"If I'd wanted weather like this I would have gone north, not south," Kurr grumbled, flicking water-drops from his nose.

"This lot could push off a hundred miles north, where it's needed," said the Haufuth. "What manner of country is this, where mist, drought and flood are close neighbors?"

"This is indeed an unexpected and unfortunate storm," Prince Wiusago agreed. "I am afraid I have led you astray."

Leith asked the question that bothered him. "If the

Most High has appointed this task for us, and has foreseen our journey, why has he not provided good weather for it? Why doesn't he do something about this storm? Why doesn't he supply a path to guide us?"

"Come to that, why allow the Jugom Ark to be hidden here?" Phemanderac commented. "It would have been far easier for it to have been rediscovered in Instruere."

"Exactly," said Leith.

The philosopher took his harp from across his shoulders, unwrapped it and played a few chords. "I wonder whether it has anything to do with us," he said thoughtfully. "Perhaps something needs to be formed within us, something which is brought forth only by hardship. Maybe the Right Hand is knit together by the sinews of struggle."

"So we're here for the Most High to remake us," said Leith quietly.

"All of life is a making," Phemanderac responded as he rewrapped his harp against the foul weather. "In this case, however, we may be partly aware of the purpose."

"What if we don't want to be remade? What if we don't like being someone else's plaything?"

"Then I doubt the Most High can achieve his purpose. You can't prevent yourself from being changed. After all, everything changes you to some degree. But you can thwart Him."

"Good," said Leith quietly. *If you leave me alone, I'll leave you alone.*

After a while the discussion extended into an examination of their quest. The Haufuth, as was his wont, argued against the influence of the Most High, supported at times by Te Tuahangata. After his initial outburst Leith remained quiet, and Hal, who had suffered more than the others during the trek of the last month, slept quietly at the foot of the outcrop. The Escaignian woman had said nothing for days, and remained silent now, staring into the grayness within and without: the reality of the world outside Instruere, bright with life and dark with death, had unnerved her. Phemanderac led a spirited defense of the Most High, while Kurr revealed that he had thought carefully about these matters by admitting he now felt a sense of destiny. The Jugom Ark *had* to be found, he argued; it *would* be found; it was their *destiny* to find it. Hardships were irrelevant. The only way they would fail to meet with their destiny was to stop moving, to give up.

"We have stopped moving," commented Wiusago.

"Have you given up?" Kurr asked him, eyebrows arched.

"I would like to. Though we have water aplenty, the answer to our prayers of only a few days ago, we are about to run out of food. We are going to have to live off the land. I see no problem when the weather is dry. Tua and I can hunt, and perhaps you northerners have skill in this area, as you have in so many others; but while it rains the animals remain in their dens, their lodges and their burrows, and even the birds do not venture abroad. Our path is unclear, and the rain will without doubt have brought down slips and raised rivers until the valleys are impassable. We are lost. We are wet. Soon we will be hungry. How can we go on?"

"Yet we are alive!" declared Te Tuahangata. "We cannot give up now!"

"I agree with you, my friend," said the Prince of Deruys. "I see no reason to go on except that we cannot contemplate failure. I said I would *like* to give up; I did not say I *would* give up. If this rain would but relent for a moment, we would be on our way once again."

As though to mock his words a huge clap of thunder reverberated around the valley, and the rain redoubled in intensity. In what seemed only a few minutes water began to cascade from the rock behind them. The air around them boomed with the fall of rocks and water, and from the flood that had once been a stream came the appalling sound of rocks grinding together, tearing at and seemingly shattering the valley into pieces. The small gray world about them appeared to be tearing itself apart. Then, just as it appeared as though everything was about to explode, the rain stopped.

As though a veil parted, the clouds lifted, the grayness lightened, the far slopes of the valley came into view. The travelers lost the sense that they were drowning in the very air. However, the water poured from every ledge, down every slope and showed no sign of abating: a thousand waterfalls coruscated from misty heights, seeking out the valley floor.

Prince Wiusago smiled at Te Tuahangata, his antagonist. "I have gained heart from you, my friend," he said. "Shall we go?"

Early the next morning they came to the confluence of two rivers. The stream they followed ran into a larger, broad-bottomed river with narrow flats on either side, flanked by steep-sloped mountains. It reminded Leith of the Mjolk River up near Windrise, except where the Mjolk was a collection of narrow, braided streams interwoven with broad shingle bars, these rivers were tumultuous floods, stretching from bank to bank. The clouds remained, but withheld their rain, and the Arkhimm could continue their journey.

"It's just as well we're on the correct side of this

stream," Kurr observed as they struck across the river flats. "We'd never cross it in its present state."

"But the same will apply to the next stream that bisects our path," the Haufuth responded. "We will be delayed eventually."

Prince Wiusago, who was perhaps fifty yards ahead of them, stopped and bent over, examining something on the ground. "Come!" he called to them. "Look what I've found!"

The prince held up what he had found in the half-light. He stood to one side of a symmetrical cone perhaps fifty feet high. Leith and the others made towards him.

"It's a shield," he told them, rather unnecessarily, as they came up to him. "Look at the device!" On the shield, which was mostly red in color, was a cross of white, over-laid by a jagged yellow line like a lightning-stroke. "This is an ancient shield of Tabul."

In a moment they all made discoveries of their own. Strewn about them lay the remnants of a great battle: swords, shields, helms; boots, mail-shirts and sundry clothes; staves, arrows and other weapons of war. The cone to their left was a huge cairn, placed above a mass grave containing many warriors, valiant and forgotten. Wherever the Arkhimm wandered on the river flat they found articles of war, bearing the lightning devices of Nemohaim, the yellow sun of Tabul, or, more seldom, the sable simplicity of the Pei-ra. As they moved about, Prince Wiusago and Te Tuahangata put aside their re-luctance and told them what they knew of the ancient wars.

In a number of places throughout Faltha, they said, during the formative years after their expulsion from the Vale, the various houses of the First Men contended with each other for land and resources. The bitterest and most protracted battles took place here, in the land formerly known as The Peira, a triangle of land wedged between the Valley of a Thousand Fires to the north, Nemohaim to the west and Tabul, the arid kingdom south of the Deep Desert, to the east. There had been people here before the First Men came, an industrious but not a numerous race called the Pei-ra, naming themselves after the land they loved. Their land was claimed by Nemohaim and Tabul both and, to establish their claims, both kingdoms sent settlers to this land to take possession of it. The Pei-ra quickly became skilled in the art of war, particularly those aspects involving stealth, ambush and betrayal, and they fought for their lives, harried like some small animal wedged between two rocks. It took hundreds of years and many bitter battles for Nemohaim to wrest control of The Peira from Tabul—and from the people called Pei-ra, though nobody thought to write them into the records of war—and it would have taken much longer but for the chance discovery of gold far to the east in southern Tabul, a chance which robbed the Tabuls of many of their fighting men.

The final battle fought in this land, at this very spot barely a generation ago, was perhaps the bloodiest ever fought in Faltha. Each side had at least two thousand casualties on each day of the fighting, which lasted six frightful days before Tabul abandoned the field. The dead had not been buried, for the forgotten Pei-ra came upon the victorious Nemohaimians with bitter fury in a final assault, allowing their own blood to be shed in what seemed careless abandonment, until the very ground turned red beneath them. The Pei-ra fought long and valiantly, but incrementally they were forced southwards until they faced the might of Nemohaim with their backs to the south coast. Then, with great anguish of spirit, the survivors abandoned the land they loved and found habitation on a large island a hundred miles or more out to sea; and the once-proud people became pirates, highwaymen of the seas, scavengers picking over the leavings of the First Men. So Nemohaim took possession of the land, naming it Astraea in recognition of the justice of their cause.

But the Nemohaimians never settled in their hard-won land. Their young king had taken a chance wound in the war and, though only minor, this wound became infected and he died before they could take him back to Bewray. A curse, it was said. A bitter wrangle developed over the succession, for his oldest sons were twins, the younger being much the more fit to rule than the older, but denied the throne because of the laws of succession, even though his twin would willingly have ceded the kingdom to him. The prospect of being a prince to his minutes-older brother's king did not suit this proud youth, and he plunged Nemohaim into a costly civil war. At the height of this war the Pei-ra swarmed ashore to give them battle, and a great engagement took place at Vassilian, in the north of the Plains of Amare, nigh to Bewray itself. There the army of Pei-ra was finally broken, but at great cost to the Nemohaimians; and after this they no longer had the reach to grasp the land of Astraea. Neither did the Pei-ra, of whose army only a handful returned to their island fortress. And the men of Tabul had found something else to fight about.

From that time the land of Astraea had a name of evil portent; and even when Nemohaim regained its former strength it did not put forth to settle the lands to its north-

east. The earth still ran with the blood of soldiers, the sayings went; the ground was cursed, and those who ventured by chance or design into that land seldom returned.

None of the Arkhimm had heard the sayings, though
Wiusago knew something of this history, and counseled
his fellow travelers to be careful. This, he reasoned, was
because of the physical dangers: the chance of becoming
lost, or falling from the steep-sided hills, or twisting an
ankle on the stony ground. He did not suspect himself of
fearing the land for other reasons.

As the two fighting men spoke Leith fancied he could
see the wraiths of warriors trading blows amid the thorny
trees and wide, well-grassed flats.

"This is an eerie place," Kurr said.

"The sheer numbers involved here frightens me," Phemanderac said quietly. "But even more concerning is the
image of such a conflict about the walls of Instruere."

As if to echo the somber mood, the clouds lowered a
little, and a light drizzle filtered down.

The Arkhimm took their leave of this grim scene, but
not before arming themselves with the best of the equip-
ment. Armor and helmets they found, barely heavier than
their normal clothes, fitting easily into their packs. More
importantly, many of the blades were of the highest quality, and Leith chose a short sword that had survived the
passage of years with no blemish.

"That blade was made for a noble or even a king,"
Prince Wiusago said. "We have no craft in Faltha today to
match it. Look at the black hilt: it was owned by a Peiran.
This is a weapon to grace the best swordsman."

"Then you'd better have it," said Leith quickly, smiling. "I have just enough skill to draw it from its scabbard
without cutting myself."

"I've found one more to my liking," came his answer. "You keep it. Perhaps one day I might have the leisure to teach you how to use it. In the meantime, that blade will intimidate any swordsman with sufficient knowledge to recognize it. That may keep you safer than any skill I could impart."

"What would Bhrudwan rule be like?" Leith asked Phemanderac later that day. The sky was still low, but the light rain had stopped, and conditions for travel were pleasant. They were working their way upriver, using the narrowing river flats to strike southwards towards the mountains.

"Bhrudwan rule?" The philosopher looked at Leith blankly for a moment, as though waking from a reverie. "Bhrudwan rule? The thought cannot be contemplated."

"We have to think about it," Leith insisted, "if only to help us resist it."

"You have seen the Council of Faltha, and in particular the Arkhos of Nemohaim. Their actions give you some idea, for they learned the art of government from their Bhrudwan masters. Yet they are pale imitations of the Destroyer and his lieutenants, who would rather annihilate Falthans than subjugate them. They would begin by pressing the able-bodied of Faltha into service as slaves to exploit the resources of the land. That is, if any remained after a conflict with Bhrudwo. The best and fairest of Falthan children would be taken from their parents and transported to Bhrudwo, to be remade into something horrible. A thousand years ago they made the mistake of trying to govern Faltha as a nation: this time they would more likely treat it merely as a source of raw materials for Bhrudwo. There would be no hope for the remainder, who might be allowed to live if killing them proved too much trouble. And whoever lived would be traumatized beyond measure by what they would see in the war. Villages, castles, cities and provinces razed. People killed, and worse, by an army intent on spreading word of their ruthlessness, their efficiency, their skill and their rapacious hunger. The Destroyer would come to Faltha to gloat over our destruction, as if the death of the First Men could somehow spite the face of the Most High. But he would not remain here. Instead, he would bequeath Faltha to the most faithful of his henchmen, with instructions to make our suffering a lingering one, but to destroy us all in the end.

"Then he would gather his forces and assault Dhauria. In his fear he imagines the place of his humiliation, the country within which the Most High once dwelt, to be much stronger than it is; therefore he will not make war with us until he has subdued all other enemies. But we are weak, having rationalized the Destroyer out of existence, and wholly unprepared for the force of hatred he would unleash upon us. We would fall before him, and the Destroyer would kill us all, before coming to make his home in Dona Mihst. There he would gnaw the bones of history, tormenting himself with the judgment of the Most High until his life became an unending weariness. His fate would indeed be just, but of no comfort to the thousands who would die, or to the few who remain alive.

"Even then, if we fail in our quest, the Most High would not completely abandon Faltha and Dhauria to their long fate. A remnant would be raised up to oppose the Destroyer; if not in this age, then in the next. He will not see darkness wholly conquer. But in the meantime much that is beautiful, praiseworthy, or loved even if it is plain, will be lost. Loulea will be no more. Disaster will descend on the innocent without explanation. Unlike you, the villagers will have no one to ask 'why' before they die."

"I don't want that to happen," said Leith. "But I cannot believe the Most High's chief weapon against the Destroyer is a group of villagers from Firanes. How heartless to take such a risk with all of Faltha! I would feel much better if the best of Falthans were part of his plan."

"We do not know all of the thoughts of the Most High. It may be he has other plans being enacted at this moment—or perhaps we are indeed the only hope. Who knows? But the best of Faltha have already deferred to you villagers, and so I tend to think if we fail, Faltha will be irrevocably lost. Whatever is raised up in the ages to come will not have the benefit of what we are now. They will look back on our simple pleasures with envy, regarding us as a legendary, classical age of truth and beauty."

"Then I will resist the Bhrudwans with everything I have," Leith declared, moved by Phemanderac's words. "But I feel as though the Most High is claiming me, whether I want him to or not, and I am losing myself in the process. Why does it have to be that way?"

Phemanderac walked for a time, deep in thought, trying to shape a reply to Leith's question. He was aware the young man was deeply troubled, and the fears he had discerned in the youth from the moment he met him in a Widuz dungeon were coming to the surface.

The travelers made their way through a narrow belt of broad-crowned trees, closer now to the mountain flanks than the foam-flecked river. Deciding on a response to Leith, the philosopher turned to him. As he opened his mouth to speak a heavy black shape dropped from the branches above them, landing between Leith and Phemanderac.

"Beware! Look out!" came cries from all around them, as the Arkhimm became aware of the danger in their midst. The warnings came far too late. Leith swept out his new-found sword, but even as he did so he knew he was far too slow, and wondered why he was not already dead.

"Hold!" cried Hal.

Leith looked on the black-robed form beside him. Recognition came slowly, mainly because he was simply not expecting to see this particular person in the mournful wasteland of Astraea. It was Achtal, the Bhrudwan.

Hal hobbled to his side as the others stepped away, unsure of him. Leith watched Hal and the Bhrudwan embrace, then exchange words, and with surprise noticed Achtal's poor condition. His black robe was worn, travel-stained with mud and worse, torn to tatters around his feet. There were fresh scars on his exposed forearms, neck and cheeks; and he looked thinner around the throat, as though he had been starved.

"Achtal tells me he left the Company three days after we did," Hal reported to them after some minutes' conversation with the Bhrudwan. "He says his place is by my side, and so he had to find us. When he left them the Company were well, had eluded pursuit, and were together in Instruere trying to decide what to do next. They had agreed not to hazard an escape from the city, because they believed they still had a role to play there. Achtal took his leave from them, and forced his way across Southbridge. It was difficult to achieve, the more

so because he tried not to take any lives. In this he succeeded, but at some cost to himself. Outdistancing the
pursuit on foot, he took a horse some distance south of
the city and set out after us. He would have overtaken
us quickly—in fact, he believes he may have seen us in
the distance—but the horse he stole pulled up lame, and
he fell into the hands of his pursuers.

"They treated him roughly, but he bided his time, and
made an escape when his captors relaxed their vigilance.
This time he could not avoid spilling blood, slaying two
of the guard. He took one of their horses, and applied his
tracking skills to find and follow our trail, but the day he
lost meant he arrived in Kinnekin too late. We had already left in Prince Wiusago's company. He continued
southwards towards Brunhaven, and there he lost the
trail.

"He spent three days searching for news of our passing, though he describes it as 'sensing the trail of his master.' To his surprise he eventually discovered we had gone
inland, and recovered our trail on the borders of the Mist.
Anxious to avoid drawing pursuit after us, he first made
sure the Instruians went south before he ventured too far
inland."

"The Instruian Guard would not have gotten very
far if they tried to enter the Mist," Te Tuahangata said
confidently.

"It is so," Hal agreed. "Though Achtal did not know
that being unaware of the reputation of the people of the
Mist. It appears the Children remembered the tales we
told them of our companions remaining in Instruere, or
perhaps gained insight from some other source, for they
did not hinder him in his journey through the Mist. From
there he followed our path through the Valley of a Thou-

sand Fires and on into Astraea. He thinks he must have passed us in the night. He saw us from afar across the river flats, but at that distance could not be sure we were not of the guard. So he waited in the trees until he could be certain."

"Be welcome, Achtal," the Haufuth said formally, acknowledging the Bhrudwan. "You have endured hard trials in the service of your new master, and have proved yourself faithful. I name you now as a companion of the Arkhimm, and bind you to the purpose of our quest."

As Hal translated, the imposing warrior nodded gravely. Then he spoke.

"Achtal will serve," he said. "Achtal will repay trust, make right his wrongs. But Achtal serve his master Hal, not Arkhimm. If Hal serve Arkhimm, Achtal serve Arkhimm."

"Fair enough," the bulky headman replied. "Hal is one of the Arkhimm. I see no problem with the arrangement. As a token his service is accepted, he may eat his fill from what remains of our stores."

"Good," said Kurr, sloughing off his pack. "It's about time we stopped anyway. My knee is giving me fits."

That evening, while the travelers built a fire and prepared their meal, Hal tended Kurr's knee and Achtal's various wounds. They slept beside a small lake that in the still hour of dawn became a perfect mirror, reflecting the lower slopes and thick cloud cover. The following morning saw them working their way through a patch of bush barring their way. The valley ahead began to rise more sharply, and on both sides the mountains hemmed them in closely. The clouds remained low, preventing any sighting of their objective, but even if the

skies had been clear they could not have climbed the
ridge to their left, such was its steepness. To their right,
the river was still full, surging brownly from bank to
bank, in places the color of tea. "Leaf-stain," Hal speculated. From folds and gullies in the mountains poured
waterfalls, sluicing the rain from the shoulders and tops
of the steep-sided peaks hidden far above them. Mist
rose like smoke from the bases of these falls, swirling
along the mountainsides, entwining itself among the
deep beech rainforests.

Some time before lunch they broke through the bush
and scrub, and found themselves beside the river. It narrowed here, to perhaps only a hundred yards across, and
the level had subsided somewhat: looking back downriver, Leith noticed that the river had forked. They had
taken the left-hand fork without knowing it, and were
now following the smaller of the two streams.

"If we knew where we were, it might matter which
fork we took," Prince Wiusago said when Leith drew it to
his attention. "But since we don't, we might as well
continue on up this valley." There was a trace of self-
deprecation, even of bitterness, in his normally light-
hearted voice, and his long hair hung lankly over his
shoulders in the misty morning.

They took lunch there on the banks of the stream, listening to hidden birds exchange liquid notes in the bush
behind them. The song hung long in the still, humid air,
and peace settled on them all like spring snow. *We might
be in the wrong place, but it feels right*, Leith thought.

With a wrench they moved off again, and for the rest
of the afternoon and all the next day made good time, following a narrow strip of land between the river and the
bush. Late that day, however, they came to their first

check, a fast-flowing stream lying directly across their path. It took them an hour to find a crossing, well upstream, where the water flowed noisily through a gorge so narrow they could leap across it. The return downstream was fraught with difficulty, as in places the water flowed hard against a cliff: at one point Leith found himself up to his chest in water so cold it seemed to burn him, clinging to a rocky outcrop as he edged his way around a bluff.

"Chin up, Leith!" Phemanderac called to him from the safety of a pebbly beach a few yards downstream. "Lucky the rain stopped, or the water would be over your head!"

"And if the rains hadn't come at all, we could have paddled through the stream two hours ago."

"If this is the hardest obstacle we have to overcome, then—Leith!"

The youth lost his grip, and suddenly he disappeared from Phemanderac's view. "Leith!"

A moment later he reappeared, held above the water by a Bhrudwan hand. The philosopher drew a deep breath, and in that moment the man from Dona Mihst, the scholar who loved only his books, realized the depth of the regard he had for the Loulean youth. *Strange*, he considered. *He's no student. We have nothing in common. Why the friendship?* In a moment he had the answer: *Perhaps our shared danger, our shared destiny, has forged bonds between us.* He chose not to examine his answer further.

Late the next morning the Arkhimm came to the headwaters of the river. The land about them had the appearance of having been blasted by some giant engine of war. Impossibly steep great gray walls, roughly chiseled by wind, rain, frost and ice, overhung them like the walls of an impregnable fortress. Thin water-curtains were the walls' only adornment. The cloud-shrouded heights above might hold snow—it certainly felt cold enough down in the bowl at the valley's head—but there was no way of telling.

"Where to now?" Kurr asked Wiusago. His question hung like an accusation in the misty air.

"Up," came the terse reply.

"The hills are less steep off to the right," Te Tua-hangata said. "We could hazard a climb there."

"Come, then," said the Haufuth. "I'm getting sick of these hills. It's time we found the Almucantaran Mountains. I don't imagine the Bhrudwan army will wait forever."

That afternoon their luck seemed to turn: a little way up the broken slope of the ridge before them, they came across the vestiges of a path. Without doubt it was man-made. It took a winding route across the face of the slope and back, in places carved with great labor into the exposed bedrock bones of this hard-edged land. Up and up they climbed, until the sound of rushing water in the valley below receded beyond hearing. When Leith next looked up, they were almost into the clouds. A minute later the wet, cold fog slipped around their shoulders like a shawl. "Keep close," the prince called from somewhere ahead. Leith hardly heard him.

It wasn't Prince Wiusago's fault they missed the path. Nobody, no matter how experienced a guide, could have held them to the narrow path, gray on gray, in such a fog. It was so thick Leith's legs seemed to disappear into it, and he could not see Phemanderac in front of him or the Bhrudwan behind. In fact, not until some time after they veered left when the path went sharply right did they realize their mistake.

"I should have been leading," Te Tuahangata said sullenly, as they perched precariously on the mountainside, trying to decide their next move. "I've spent half my life in the mist."

"But have even you seen fog as thick as this? We have nothing like it in Loulea." The Haufuth gave Te Tuahangata an opportunity to agree with him, in order to redeem the Deruvian prince.

To his relief the Child of the Mist shrugged his shoulders. "We stay home in mist like this."

"But we don't have that luxury," Kurr reminded them. "At the very least we must find shelter. A night on this ridge could kill us."

Even as he spoke the light dimmed noticeably. High above them the sun dipped behind the mountain peaks. A cold wind like the breath of ice stirred Leith's mist-moistened hair.

"Can we go back down?" he asked.

"You saw the path we took," Kurr answered grimly. "Hard enough to hold to in the middle of the day. It would be madness to attempt it at night. Better we should chance it up here."

"Then let's take advantage of the light that remains," encouraged the Haufuth. "Wiusago, find us a path!"

There was no path to be found, but they discovered the next best thing. Up ahead the slope flattened out, as though they had reached the ridgetop. Here a few hardy plants braved the wind and the fog, bordering numerous sad tarns. It was a gloomy place, but at least there was no danger of them falling to their deaths. Along the ridgetop they searched, looking for any kind of shelter. Eventually, on the edge of night, they came across a rocky outcrop that offered some shelter from the wind. There, in the lee of the rock, they made a cold, cheerless and uncomfortable camp.

Leith awoke from the briefest of sleeps with a crick in his neck, the legacy of ill-placed rocks. Unable to light a fire, the travelers had huddled close together for warmth, but Leith's back was as cold as if Druin had shoved snow down his cloak. They had a miserable breakfast together in the misty morning, then made ready to travel.

"Doesn't the sun ever shine here?" the Haufuth complained.

"Seems like we've wandered back into the land of Mist by mistake," Kurr said.

"Have we?" Alarm registered in Leith's voice.

"No." Tua laughed. "We don't have mountains like this at home. And there the mist is warmer, friendlier somehow. I don't know how to read these clouds at all."

"Nevertheless, we must find a way forward—or back," Wiusago said, wandering over with his pack on his shoulders. "Another night of this will do us serious harm."

"Last night did me serious harm," said Leith, half-jokingly. "My back aches with the cold."

Kurr looked at him with concern in his eyes. "Then let's get moving. A brisk walk will do you the world of good."

"We'll go back to the right and find the path," said Prince Wiusago confidently. "We'll be off this mountain in no time. Beyond that—well, we'll see."

They started back in the direction from which they'd come, or as near to it as they could judge. Within a few minutes, however, they realized their error, coming out above a sheer drop into the swirling mist. Whichever right-handed way they took led them nowhere but to bluffs, ravines or cliffs. In this fashion most of the morning passed by, and it approached the middle of the day when they stood once more by the rocky outcrop.

"I can't understand it," Leith heard Wiusago mutter. "I would have staked my life on us having come up the ridge from the left. But where is the path? How did we get up here?"

Te Tuahangata scratched his head, then nodded in agreement. "It is a puzzle beyond my wits to solve. I was born to the Mist, and I too cannot see how we turned completely around last evening; yet turn around we must have, for all the ways to our right are wrong."

"Then we must go left," Kurr said. "We were lost before; I can't see how even finding the path will make us found."

In an unspoken agreement, the travelers refused to eat lunch by the outcrop. They took a quick bite to eat as they struck out to their left. In a moment they were ascending the ridge: higher and higher it took them, deep into the heart of the cloud. Like drunken sots they staggered through the mist, each one clinging to the next, making little headway but at least keeping safe. Finally, Wiusago turned to the others and called a halt.

"We can climb no further," he said, his boots scrunching through a late-lying snow patch as he walked back to where the group had gathered. "We are at a mountain top. Every direction is down."

"A mountain top? It didn't seem that steep!" Leith was puzzled.

"We have wound our way up. But now I am not at all

sure how to get us down." Wiusago motioned them to follow him to a pile of fractured rock, where he bade them look around. To their left a knife-edged ridge sloped sharply downwards into the mist: it would take the skill of a mountain goat to avoid falling if they took that path. Ahead the way was not quite so steep, but the rock was broken into a scree slope, rocky rubble falling away into unguessable depths. Back the way they had come, off to their right, the rock seemed more solid. However, none of them would submit to returning to that cruel outcrop. Behind them lay a shelf a few yards wide, beyond which the ground dropped away in the sheerest cliff.

Hal made his way to the front of the group. For the first time in weeks Leith took a really good look at his older brother, and was shocked at what he saw. The effort of keeping up with these fit, experienced mountain men of the south had drained him more than Leith could have imagined. His cheeks were dreadfully hollow, his eyes were set back in his head, and he rubbed the back of one knee as he spoke.

How much more of this can he take? Why have none of the others commented on his state?

"Achtal wants us to try the scree slope," the cripple told them. He breathed with some difficulty. "He says in his experience such slopes do not usually lead to cliffs or dead ends. They need a flat base to sustain the weight of the rock above."

"But how do we get down?" Kurr asked. The others could read the statement in his eyes: it would be foolish to try to climb down a slope at once so steep and so unstable.

Hal had the answer ready. "Achtal will show us. He says that with care we should all be able to descend in safety." The Bhrudwan interrupted, speaking in his own tongue. Hal spoke for him: "He adds that running a scree slope is one of the most exciting challenges a man can face. We should count it a privilege to be measured against something like this." Beside Hal, the Bhrudwan smiled. He had never been seen to smile: it certainly improved the look of him.

"He can show us," the Haufuth said doubtfully. "I hope he remembers that not all of us are the physical specimen he is."

"He remembers," Hal replied, with just a hint of hardness in his voice. "He says he would not suggest anything that involved serious risk to his master."

The Haufuth gave way. Venturing a few yards on to the slope, Achtal demonstrated the scree-running technique, while Hal interpreted. "'Don't run straight down, or you will build up too much speed and fall. Zig-zag across the slope and back, like this. Stay in areas of rocks of similar size: larger rocks are slower to move, and will trip you if you strike a field of them suddenly. Keep your eyes open and look ahead. Don't worry about dislodging small stones. The slope will slide down with you a little way, that is normal. But if you set a large rock rolling, call out a warning to those below you. That is the greatest danger. Keep your speed down; walk if you must. But once you are used to it you can run fast, like this.'" And with that Achtal was off into the mist in a few huge bounds.

A moment later he reappeared, battling hard to ascend the unstable slope. His expression was a question: will you try it?

"I see no other alternative," Prince Wiusago advised them.

*   *   *

It was without doubt the most frightening, the most ex-
hilarating thing Leith had ever done. To make himself
take the first step down that exceedingly steep slope took
everything he had; and still that would not have been
enough, if it had not been for the sight of Hal struggling
down the slope, gracelessly but successfully. The first
minute or so was very bad: it felt like he was continually
losing his balance, falling forward. Suddenly, however,
he mastered it and was away. The slope roared past him
as he took larger and larger strides, cutting down at an increasingly steep angle. Small stones lodged in his boots,
but he gave them no heed. Flashing past Hal and Achtal,
he let go a cry of sheerest joy and gave himself completely to the slope.

The mist thinned as he sprinted across and down the
scree, well ahead of the others. To his left, still a way
down, surrounded by mist but temporarily open to his
view, he could make out a basin, with a small blue lake
set like a diamond in a ring. A breeze ruffled the water.
He caught a glimpse of a wooded island in the center of
the lake, then he turned away to the right, into another
patch of fog. Down and down he went, leaving the others
far behind, unable to think of anything but the freedom,
the pleasure, the passion of his feet on the slope, the cold
wind in his hair. His pack felt weightless on his back. Another glimpse to the left. Already he was level with the
lake. If he had wanted he could have made his way to it,
but he did not want. The lake drained into a small stream,
which flowed through a spout to the top of a cliff, then
dropped down out of sight, no doubt as a waterfall, into a
further patch of mist. Out of his eye's corner he caught a
glint of light, as though the sun reflected from a rope or
filament stretched across the spout. The moment's inat-

tention cost him a stumble. He had blundered into a patch of large rocks, but nothing was going to interfere with his run down the mountain, and he regained his balance without effort. Now the lake was gone, well behind him, up and to the left, and he plunged into heavy mist once more. But only for a minute or so. Then, without warning or transition, he came out into blue sky, and came to a stop in wonder.

The view spread before him hammered at his senses. He had imagined he might be nearly at the bottom of the slope, but he was wrong. It stretched down below him for at least another thousand feet—and at the bottom was not the valley floor, but further mist. How high was he? How high had they been on the mountain top? He cast his gaze further, and saw a tangled knot of mountain ranges snaking away in confusion to all points of the compass. Wooded on their lower slopes, they stretched upwards to snow-tipped peaks that flamed in the midday sun. Cloud-carpets flowed down the valleys like wide, slow rivers. In the few gaps afforded by the mist, Leith could make out silver streams and deep green forests. It was an altogether wild land, a land to assault the mind with its size, steepness and majesty.

Then Leith saw the castle.

In the valley opposite, surrounded by sheer mountains, a hillock raised itself just above the clouds that matted the forest floor. On the hillock stood a white-walled castle. Though it was two, perhaps three miles away, Leith could see every detail. Bright flags snapped in the breeze, flying above many slender turreted towers; themselves raised upon inner and outer walls, in which were set great gates; window after window, wall after wall, bastion upon rampart, battlement surmounting bulwark. It spoke of power, of grandeur, of stateliness. It was altogether lovely, the most beautiful thing shaped by human hands Leith had ever seen. *If* it had been shaped by human hands. Leith quite forgot the scree slope.

He still stood there when the others came upon him. Wordlessly, he indicated the object of his gaze. One by one the Arkhimm were transfixed by the sight below them.

For a long time no one dared name what they saw. They had searched for it in increasing desperation, and had found it at the moment when they were completely lost. It was the castle of legend, the place to where young children who died were taken, the place that appeared to mortal eyes only once in a hundred years.

Finally, Phemanderac spoke for them all.

"Kantara," he breathed, in a voice choked with awe.

CHAPTER 15

THE GUARDIANS

KANTARA STOOD BEFORE THEM, a newly revealed pearl sparkling in the summer sun; then, from behind them, a cold wind brought with it swirling mist, hiding the castle from their sight like a conjuring trick. At once the spell holding the Arkhimm broke and they began to descend the scree slope once more. But they were not free of Kantara's allure.

Leith pelted down the slope for all he was worth. But no matter how fast he ran, the descending mist stayed just ahead. Once or twice he thought he caught a glimpse of the castle, but whenever he steadied to make sure, the mist drew across him as though mocking his desire. The slope lessened, and he came down into forested areas; in another moment he was in the valley mist, where the scree came to an end in a boulder field above a lively stream. There he waited for the others, breathing hard. The descent, including the pause to gaze at the white castle, had taken less than fifteen minutes.

Picking their way down the little stream took about half an hour. "What a fine place this would be if the sun shone on it," Prince Wiusago said as he clambered over impossibly large rocks.

"Not as fine a place as the one we go to," responded Phemanderac.

"I suppose there is no doubt?" Kurr put in. "About the castle, I mean. It is Kantara, isn't it?"

"If it is not, then we can ask them for directions," Wiusago said. "But from what little I have heard about Nemohaim, the upper Neume valley is virtually uninhabited. It must be Kantara."

"Where is the upper Neume valley?" asked Leith, momentarily confused. "I thought we were looking for the Almucantaran Mountains."

"We were, but we appear to have stumbled upon them rather by accident," said Prince Wiusago. "Although I daresay most rivers in Astraea come from the mountains, so by simply traveling upriver we were bound to find them. The River Neume springs from the same source, but flows southeast, away from us, before turning north to find the sea near Bewray. The legend says that Kantara can be found in the Vale of Neume."

They came to a flat, open place on the valley floor. Here they rested for a while amidst signs of a recent forest fire; though, with the amount of rain this valley obviously received, it was hard to imagine fire taking hold. But scarred trees and blackened, stubby grass told their own testimony.

"Do we try to reach the castle today?" Wiusago asked Te Tuahangata as they lay back on the damp grass. "We have about three hours of daylight remaining, and perhaps two miles to go."

"The people in the castle must have some access to the valley," Tua replied carefully, "which means there will more than likely be a path. If we give ourselves an hour or so to find it, we could be at the gates before dark. If we

don't find it, we should make camp somewhere sheltered
and hidden."

"I don't know, though," the Haufuth said, yawning. "It
may not have been much for you, but coming down that
shingle slide has worn me out."

"Six months ago you wouldn't have been able to do it
at all," remarked Kurr. "Be thankful you made it, at
least."

"I'm merely saying we should make camp here and
get a good sleep. Then tomorrow we can search for this
castle with enthusiasm."

As they spoke thin sunlight shone about them as a
small draft of air momentarily parted the mist-veil. The
air was thicker down in the valley, Leith noticed; and
much hotter than the biting cold of the mountain top. Or
perhaps the run down the slide had tired him more than
he credited.

"It would be best if we carried on," Phemanderac argued, but his voice carried little conviction. "Think of
good food and a nice warm, soft bed. A real night's
sleep."

"I'm thinking, I'm thinking," said the big man. "I'm
thinking maybe we won't receive a welcome from these
people, coming as we are to claim their treasure. Maybe
we'll get bread and water, and the chill of a cold dungeon
wall on our backs. I'd rather take sleep now, when I need
it, than run the risk of another night like last night. Don't
you others feel the need for rest?" His voice had a
strangely soporific quality. Beside him the Escaignian
closed her eyes, and her chest moved up and down in a
regular rhythm.

Some distance away, near the edge of the glade, Achtal
and Hal were arguing; or, at least, the Bhrudwan was

talking and gesticulating wildly at the cripple. Leith tried to follow the course of the discussion, but found it slipping away into sleep . . .

"Listen, everyone! Listen carefully!" Hal stood among them, talking loudly and clearly. "Achtal says there is some kind of enchantment in the valley, a sleeping enchantment laid to trap unwary travelers. He says he has come across them before, in Bhrudwo. We must not go to sleep. We must not! Can you hear me?"

One or two of the Arkhimm stirred, raising tired faces and weary, sleep-laden eyes in the direction of the voice. "Enchantment?" Phemanderac said. "I've been trained. I'd recognize any enchantment—"

Suddenly he jerked himself to his feet. "You're right!" he cried. "How could I have missed it!" He turned to Hal and the Bhrudwan. "Shake them awake! They must not remain asleep!"

"It's in the valley mist," Hal said. "Achtal says that it has no effect while we are moving; but when we stop the spell begins to work."

"Magic in Faltha!" Phemanderac said, shaking his head. "It's the first time I've come across it."

The philosopher shook his head again, trying to clear the weariness from his mind. The call to sleep was elusive, seductive, just on the edge of consciousness but once the choice was made to fight it, once he was upright and moving again, his head cleared. Within moments the others had been raised, with the exception of one. A minute later eight alert and somewhat frightened men stood around the prone body of the Escaignian woman.

"How could that happen?" whispered the Haufuth. "It can't have; I won't believe it. We're just overtired."

"Then how do you explain her?" Kurr wanted to know,

pointing at the Escaignian. Hal and Phemanderac were
bent over her, and the philosopher whispered words in
her ear. She stirred slightly, but did not wake.

"I—I . . ." The big man stopped. Already, in spite of
his awareness, he could feel waves of lassitude washing
over him again, as though the air itself wanted to enfold
him. "We can't stay here," he got out through thick lips.

"That's right," Hal said tightly. "If we remain much
longer in this place, we'll never leave it. We must move on!"

"And leave our friend?" Leith asked. "We can't! She's
been faithful! We've already left her companion."

"It may be that the Kantarans can help us," Phemanderac said. "It is my guess the inhabitants of that castle
laid this enchantment on the valley. It is a simple matter
if one knows how. Rudimentary magic was taught in
Dona Mihst, and though I was not much interested in it—
Pyrinius tried to dissuade me from ever using it—I found
magic an easy skill to learn. I do know that only the ones
who made the spell can break it. Almost certainly the
only hope for this woman is for us to find the mistweaver
and persuade him—or her—to free her."

"Tall man is right," boomed Achtal, his loud voice like
a desecration smeared across the seductive silence of the
forest floor. "Leave fallen one, seek spell-maker and
break spell. Killing spell-maker will break spell." Leith
had always been nervous of the casual indifference with
which the Bhrudwan referred to life and death, and had
listened in fear to his father relate the tale of his capture
and journey. But perhaps killing would be the only way.

"I won't believe it," said the Haufuth stubbornly, as they
made their way from the glade. "It's not right. It doesn't
feel right. If things like that can happen, who's to say

what is possible? How can one believe anything? It's like the world has turned inside out."

"Proper magic feels a little like that," Phemanderac agreed, "but it is not as bad as ill-magic, so Pyrinius taught me. Proper magic merely uses the earth's natural processes and enhances them, or makes us more susceptible to them. What more natural thing than for travelers to feel tired and sleepy in a warm valley floor sheltered from the wind? Ill-magic, though, cuts across nature, making things that are not into things that are."

"I thought you didn't go to the classes," Kurr teased him. "How do you know so much?"

"I didn't say I avoided the classes, just that my *idominic* tried to keep my attention on other things. Everyone in Dhauria knows as much," the philosopher said. "And the First Men brought the knowledge with them to Faltha. But at some time in the distant past it was abandoned, along with their belief in the Most High. The two go together, you see. Believe in the existence of a power outside nature, and you must allow the possibility that nature itself can be changed by that power—or by other powers with insight." Phemanderac spoke to Kurr, but his words were directed at the burly headman.

"I've seen magic already on our journeys," Leith said, keeping the edge of his eye on Hal. "Of the ill kind. It was monstrous, and I have never had it satisfactorily explained to me." The image of a pair of wings—black against the blue fire—was firmly fixed in Leith's mind.

"When was this?" the Haufuth asked him. "Tell me about it."

"It is not mine to tell," Leith said, reluctant to name Hal directly. "One among us knows much more about it, since it was of his working."

Hal did not take the opportunity thus presented. Leith did not expect him to. *They probably think I mean Phemanderac*, Leith realized. *But I can't take the words back now.*

A few minutes later they came upon the path. A narrow, graveled walkway, not wide enough for wagon or cart, but unmistakable nonetheless. After half an hour on this path, working their way steeply upvalley beside a small stream casting itself down a staircase of rapids, Hal touched Leith lightly on the shoulder, drawing him slowly back through the travelers until they walked alone at the rear of the group.

"It is time we cleared this up," he said, looking with dark eyes on his younger brother. "There is much between us."

"The little matter of magic in the Hermit's cave, for one," Leith replied, as though the incident had been a personal affront. "It must have been ill-magic you used on him. You made him sick."

"We've talked about this, remember? I was given permission to do what I did, and it worked for the Hermit's good, and for the Haufuth. Do you think that otherwise we would have this man with us now?"

"That's not the point, and you know it. When we were trying to see the Council of Faltha you yourself argued against using immoral means to achieve our goal. 'No bribery,' you said. But at Bandits' Cave you used ill-magic to achieve your ends. How can a moral perfectionist like you live with such a contradiction?" Leith thrust the words at his brother like knife-blades. *Bleed! Show some vulnerability! Admit you are wrong! How can I love you if you're not fallible?*

"But, Leith, I did not use ill-magic on the Hermit. Listen

as I tell you the truth. The Hermit had been bitten by a black fly a day or so previously. All I did was speed the natural workings of the poison so his illness might be recognized and healed while help was at hand. It was proper magic, for want of a better description. Would you rather I had ignored his plight and left him to die in agony a day or so after we'd left?"

"No!" cried Leith, and one or two of the others turned to see what troubled him. "You can't get out of this so easily!"

"Is something the matter, Leith?" Kurr called back.

"Of course there is," came his reply. "But I'll work through it myself." Clearly stung by the unearned rebuke, the old farmer turned back to the path.

"Of course you shouldn't have left him," Leith whispered fiercely to his brother. "But you are a healer. Why did you not stop the natural workings of the poison so that he got better?"

"That would have been ill-magic, Leith," said Hal, not unkindly. "Did you not hear Phemanderac? Ill-magic works against nature. I could not have sped his healing until the Fodhram man returned with a natural agent I could work with—unless you believe I should have used ill-magic. Did I do right?" There was a slightly aggrieved note in his voice.

"After the bark arrived, why didn't you heal him completely then?"

"You know the answer to that. His natural recovery aided the Haufuth. Please, Leith, I did not harm him. I sped up the passage of the poison, sparing him many hours of convulsions. I aided his initial recovery, stopping only when he was out of danger, and I brought two men back from the brink of self-despair. Why do you accuse me?"

Leith would not give up. "What about the black wings?"

"I took on the form of the poison while I worked with it," replied Hal. "Black fly, black wings. It is not really very deep magic. I am no beast. I am as I have always been. Since I was very young I have been able to do such things. What is my fault?"

"That you have no fault! How can you expect me to have regard for one who remains so totally unapproachable? You're like the Most High, lofty and aloof, only interfering in our affairs when it suits you; fiddling with us to achieve your own inscrutable purposes. I find myself speaking with your voice! I hear your thoughts in my head! Or not you—the Most High—what does it matter? I want to be left alone! I'd rather be caught in my own follies than be used like some poison, used unwittingly to scourge someone else! What are your—his—plans to enhance me? How much will it hurt?" He looked his brother in the eye, half-blinded by the tears in his own. "Not as much as *you* hurt me!"

Hal waited a moment, dignifying Leith's feelings with silence. Then he replied: "Has it ever occurred to you that what you mistake for evil might actually be good? That your fear of losing yourself blinds you to what might benefit you?"

"Oh, so I'm not good enough at the moment, is that it?" Leith felt a desperate need to be angry at something.

Hal smiled in reply. "Simply being alive changes you, for good or ill. You can't avoid it. Even our friend the Hermit couldn't avoid it."

"But I had a dream," said Leith. "People love me—I saw how much. Nothing I could do would separate me from it."

"A vision of truth, indeed. But to love someone is a

different thing to having his trust," said Hal quietly, and Leith noted a peculiar twist to his brother's smile. However, the moment passed Leith by. He was where he had always been: on the losing end of an exchange with his brother.

The mist thickened about them as they climbed, but they met no one on the path, and the enchantment did not assail them while they walked. "It is growing darker," Wiusago commented. "Dusk draws near."

A moment later he gave a shout: he had come out above the mist, or it had drawn back, and in a moment the Arkhimm stood below the walls of the castle.

Tall beyond reason, the white walls stretched up to ramparts so far above them that the soldiers with crossbows trained on them could hardly be discerned. At their highest the walls supported massive turrets that sprouted from the very rock, leaning far out over the northerners as though shadowing them in fear. It was a majestic place, a terrible place; a place like the Outer Chamber of the Hall of Meeting, only far larger; designed to quail the spirit, to be bigger than the hearts of men.

"It's only a wall," Kurr said to nobody in particular.

The wall had in it a great opening, an arched entrance way barred by a portcullis more indomitable than the Iron Door of the Outer Chamber. Faces appeared through the interwoven bars.

"Strangers!" cried a strongly accented voice. "What is your business here?"

Wiusago looked to the others for advice as to how to answer; the others returned his stare blankly. Should they state their quest openly, or dissemble by spinning some other story?

"Are we safe from enchantment here?" Kurr whispered.

"No," Phemanderac replied, "but now I'm prepared for them."

While they debated the portcullis drew up soundlessly, and three heralds rode out on pure white horses. Their gear shone in the late afternoon sunlight, their silken clothes were of red and green, their spears long and held at the ready, the proud, high-stepping horses made no noise on the lush grass. The foremost herald dismounted and stood before them.

"Welcome, strangers," the herald said courteously. "You have journeyed through the mist, and must be very tired. Can we assist you in any way?" His voice was soft, gentle, polite, almost womanly.

A broad grin spread across the Haufuth's face. The offer of help was much more than he had hoped for. It looked like their fears had been unfounded.

But Phemanderac laughed. "Come now!" he said, mirth lacing his words. "Have you no more skill than that? Or is it because you are so far away from your master?"

The Haufuth stared at the philosopher, open-mouthed. "Have you gone out of your mind?"

But his laughter had broken the spell. The three heralds and their horses vanished.

"Illusion," said Phemanderac in the deep silence that followed, as though he instructed a class. "A pretty trick. Suggestion operating directly on our minds. We are susceptible because we expect the miraculous in a place such as this. I wonder what else around here is illusion?" As the others gaped in wonder he walked up to the castle wall. "Only the best illusionists can make a shape solid," he said thoughtfully. "I'm willing to bet you can't make an illusion this size solid. Am I right?" He made to strike the wall with his hand.

The castle disappeared before their eyes.

Leith cried out in fear and astonishment.

Phemanderac shrugged his shoulders apologetically. "I had to give him a chance to retain his dignity."

In place of the castle lay a grassy slope, leading up to a rude hut. At its door stood a young woman with a wide smile.

"You would not have discovered us had my father been here," she said. "Come on in. Welcome, travelers, to Kantara castle. Unless you'd like the other one back?"

Phemanderac strode up the hill: the others remained rooted to the spot. He turned back to them. "I think we'd better go inside. The quest, remember?"

Inside the hut two slatted beds occupied the near wall. The one window looked out over the hillslope and down on to the mist rising from the hollows. A large fireplace was set in the opposite wall, with the only two chairs in the small room positioned either side of it. The woman herself was probably about twenty years old: her blonde hair, ivory skin and teeth were perfect.

"Have a seat," she said, smiling still. As she motioned with her hands, six more chairs appeared.

"Solid?" Phemanderac asked, eyebrows raised.

"Not till my father gets home." She laughed, a golden sound.

"Cut that out," said Phemanderac. "Just be yourself."

Leith held his breath, expecting the woman to dissolve into an old crone, or a dragon. But she did not. Phemanderac looked hard at her, and his eyes widened.

"All right," he said. "But put on some proper clothes. You never know what might cause you to lose your grip on the illusion. We'll turn around, if you like."

Looking somewhat discomfited, the woman turned away and started rummaging in a large chest beside her bed.

*   *   *

By the time the Arkhimm turned back, the woman was bustling about the cabin, lighting lamps and tidying away various articles. She smiled at them again, her composure in place.

"I'd better have your names, then," she said equably. "Then, when my father returns, we can talk."

"There is the small matter of our companion," Phemanderac said quietly. "I'm sure you know about her; spiders always know when their prey falls into the web."

"Where else do you think my father has gone?" the woman responded, surprised. "We would not have left your friend out there, not in the rainy season."

"But he would expect to find nine bodies," said Phemanderac patiently. "How did he plan to bring them all back here?"

"That is something you should ask him," said the woman, standing. As she stood the door of the hut opened, admitting a small, misshapen figure. "Father!" she cried, clapping her hands. "We have guests."

The figure came into the lamplight and stood before the Arkhimm. Not much more than four feet tall, back bent, face gnarled and worn, a long white beard, hair like straw; he wore ill-fitting clothes of green, with a floppy hat of the palest blue. The effect was comical rather than alarming.

First he looked at his daughter, then gestured with his left hand. "Put the castle back," he snarled. "Never know who's wandering about. If fools like these can find our house, then who can tell what might come knocking at our door?" He stamped his foot in apparent anger. "I must attend to your training, my girl. What would your mother have said?"

Fixing his beady eyes on the company, he asked them: "How did you get past my fences?"

"Be careful," whispered Phemanderac. "This man is not what he seems. His appearance is designed to throw us off guard. He is dangerous."

"Aye, I am dangerous!" the dwarf-man said swiftly. "Particularly to those who do not answer my questions! You!" he cried, pointing to Phemanderac. "Are you the leader? Answer my questions!"

"No, my lord; I am not the leader. But it is agreed I should speak for our group, it having been decided that others of our number might daunt you with their words."

"What? Daunt me?" The little face turned purple with apoplexy. "Do not bluff me! There is not one among you with wit enough to understand, let alone match my skill. How dare you challenge me!"

The tall philosopher shrugged his shoulders. Leith watched him, nervous and a little disoriented by events, fervently hoping his friend was as much in charge of the situation as he seemed.

"Then you might care to consider how we evaded your nets," he answered calmly.

"Not all of you!" the old man crowed. "I entrapped one of you. What thaumaturge would leave a companion snared without freeing her? Unless he had not the power!"

"Or unless he wished first to deal with the daughter before he took the measure of her father," replied Phemanderac casually. "Thank you for bringing our servant back. She was warned, but chose to ignore us. Her embarrassment at being snared by one as feeble as you will be a just and sufficient punishment."

"How did you get past my fences?" the dwarf-man almost screamed.

"Another thing," Phemanderac continued, ignoring the question, "you can stop all this posturing. It does you no credit. I know you are no more a wizened old man than your daughter has a perfect female form. I know your names: I read them in a book two thousand years old. You are Maendraga and Belladonna."

"Who are you?" shrieked the old gnome. "How came you by such knowledge?"

"Not until you resume your natural forms," Phemanderac demanded. "Then we will see if something can't be salvaged from our relationship."

The old man nodded to his daughter. As Leith watched, their forms began to shimmer and flicker, flowing into new shapes. The man grew, his back unhunched and his paunch shrank, until he appeared to them as a lean, balding man in his middle forties. The transformation in the woman was more subtle. Her edges hardened a little, a few blemishes became visible, her trunk thickened slightly and a small gap appeared between her front teeth. Leith could see no other changes.

"Satisfied?" said the man in a mellifluous tone. *Do not question me too closely*, his voice seemed to say.

"The voice as well," said Phemanderac wearily. "Your Wordweave will not work on us. Our quest is urgent. We have no time for games."

"And I am hungry," added the Haufuth.

"Very well, then," said the magician, in a voice tight with tension. "By some art beyond my telling, you know our names. Would you do us the courtesy of telling us yours, and enlighten us about the nature of your business here? It must be something important, to bring to Kantara the only Falthan magicians I have ever seen. I suppose you're not going to tell me how you eluded all the traps I

set downvalley. I could detect no sense of their having
been disturbed."

Phemanderac smiled. "We must have our secrets," he
said blandly. "But our names are no secret—and, unlike
yours, not the subject of legend. I am Phemanderac. My
companions are my master the Haufuth of Loulea, his adviser Kurr, and the brothers Leith and Hal, all from Firanes. Their knight Achtal, as you have no doubt
discerned, is a Bhrudwan. Take a moment to assess his
power, and ask yourself how a Lord of Fear serves us.
Prince Wiusago of Deruys stands here for the southern
kingdoms, while Te Tuahangata is of the Mist. Our sleeping servant is of Instruere, and so you can understand her
ignorance of your arts."

"And you? You have given me your name, but not
your country. I know Falthans, and I know Bhrudwans.
You do not remind me of either."

"That is because I am neither. I am Phemanderac the
Traveler, the first man to leave Dona Mihst and journey
in Faltha for nearly two thousand years."

"Dona Mihst? The Vale?"

"Of course." Phemanderac sighed, as though despair-
ing of his charge's instruction. "Of the House of Sthane.
Drawn here on a matter that concerns you greatly,
Guardians of the Arrow." *Now we hit the mark*, he
thought. *This is the most risky moment.*

"Arrow?" the man named Maendraga said quietly, his
face revealing nothing. "I have no bow in the house. We do
not hunt. Our food is gathered in other ways. But you have
a purpose here. What is the name of your company?"

"You will have guessed it already; but you might as
well hear it from our lips. Ware yourselves, for we are the
Arkhimm. Our quest is none other than the Jugom Ark."

Despite his control, Maendraga took a step backwards and cast a warning glance at his daughter.

"There is no use denying it," Phemanderac insisted. "Or would you prefer my master attended to your interrogation?"

"No, that won't be required," the woman, Belladonna, said hastily. Her father glowered at her, but said nothing. "From parent to child the teaching has passed from the time Bewray appointed the first guardians. We know who you are. I knew who you were even before you reached our walls. It could be said we have been waiting for you. But you will need to supply proof before you are given the secret of our knowledge. And do not think to force it from us: no power can make us reveal the reason for our existence in such a place as this."

"So the story that Bewray's children were killed by bandits is false?"

"Of course," the woman said.

"And you are Bewray's descendants." *The puzzle comes together*, Phemanderac thought.

"From time to time we have taken husbands or wives from the few who have stumbled on this place, or have sought them among the shepherds of the Vale of Neume further to the south. But, yes, we are Bewray's children."

So that's how the Kantaran legend was shaped. "And he left you here as guardians of his—the First Men's—most sacred possession."

"Yes."

"Then you will know that in a time of great need the Arrow will again be revealed." The philosopher's voice rose, and took on a commanding tone. "That time is upon us. Here are the tokens. A Bhrudwan warrior of the highest order stands among us, now our servant, but once sent to Loulea to find the Right Hand of the Most High."

Maendraga and Belladonna reacted to the name: he drew in his breath, her eyes widened.

"The Right Hand will be revealed when Bhrudwo threatens Faltha. Achtal is the token that Bhrudwo indeed threatens us. As we speak, the Brown Army may be pouring through the Gap. If they are not resisted with the combined might of the Sixteen Kingdoms, they will surge across Faltha like a brown flood and lay this land waste.

"But the Sixteen Kingdoms will not resist. Already their leaders are in the pay of the Destroyer. Many Instruians have hidden from their treacherous leaders: the woman asleep outside your door is one such. She is our second token.

"At this time the Right Hand will be revealed. Two years ago I left my home in Dona Mihst to search for the Right Hand of the Most High. I, Phemanderac of Dhauria, am the third token.

"I have this lore to offer you, in confirmation of my knowledge:

> *Through the air, over water,*
> *In the earth abides the flame.*

"You recognize the couplet, part of the Riddle of the Arrow. It is known to us and no others apart from yourselves, who learned it on your mother's knee. To solve the riddle and recover the Arrow, then to use it to unite Faltha against Bhrudwo, is our quest. What say you to that, guardians?"

"Just this," said Maendraga, and Leith was surprised to see real fear in his face. "Where is the girl? I see four of the Arkhimm. Where is the fifth? You cannot hazard the Jugom Ark unless all Five of the Hand are present. I cannot allow it."

"She is detained in Instruere by powerful enemies. We cannot wait for her release. Things have fallen out as they have, and we cannot retrace our steps. We will hazard the Arrow with just four of the Arkhimm, and whatever assistance the others of our number can offer them."

"You will not," Maendraga said sadly. "Your tokens suffice to prove your worthiness to be on this quest. Be aware that were the five of you here, nothing would gladden my heart and that of my daughter more than giving you the secret of the Jugom Ark. But you must have the girl. Will you not go and get the girl? Get the girl, please."

"Have you not listened? We cannot spare the time. In the months it would take to return here our cause would be lost. We might have the Arrow, but no one would remain to be commanded. Give us the secret, and we will be on our way. Then you can lay down your guardianship and rejoin the world of men, as has been your long desire."

"We will do nothing without the girl. You know we will not. What kind of guardian are you, that you would lose the girl, then attempt to browbeat me into discharging my responsibility as badly as you have?"

Phemanderac smiled. "You are too close to the mark for comfort," he said. "I have done well, but not well enough, it seems. Nevertheless, we must press on."

"It seems, then, your command of enchantment will be measured against mine," said Maendraga grimly. "Shall we begin?"

"Please, not until after dinner," pleaded the Haufuth. "Can't this wait just a little while?"

To his surprise Leith heard other words behind those the Haufuth spoke. *Sit down! Discharge your duty with honor! Pay your guests some respect!* Had the words been directed at him, he would have had no choice but to obey them. The compulsion was strong. A suspicion grew in Leith: he remembered the timbre of the voice.

"What are you doing?" Leith whispered to his brother.

"Enhancing," came the reply.

"I can see why they acknowledge you as master," Maendraga replied to the headman, deep respect in his voice. "I obey not through compulsion, but because you are correct, which of course lends power to your words. I have been an ungracious host to such diverse representatives of the First Men—and others." He bowed to them. "Daughter, prepare these travelers a worthy supper, while I go and tend their companion." Stiffly, with a great weight of care on his shoulders, he strode from the room.

"Here, let me help you," Hal offered to Belladonna. "I know how to prepare food to my master's liking. It doesn't pay to get him angry."

Phemanderac had no opportunity to discuss his strategy with the others while the meal was prepared and eaten. He relied on their good sense, and the silence of Illyon the Escaignian, who would undoubtedly remember nothing of her enchantment. Maendraga and Belladonna never left them alone, as though it was part of their purpose to prevent the Arkhimm conferring together.

Maendraga and Phemanderac fenced with each other all through the meal, as though weighing each other up: it was clear they would do battle after dinner was over. What form the battle would take was a mystery to Leith. However, now his brother had revealed himself as a magician, he had fewer concerns as to the outcome. In fact, he wondered if it mattered at all. Was the Jugom Ark somewhere in this house? He doubted it. Why the necessity for the riddle if the Arrow could be found so simply? Leith was attentive to the conversation for any clue as to how the riddle might be solved. As he listened, it became clear to him that Phemanderac saw their only chance was to persuade the guardians to part with their secret.

"The Arrow is not here, that is plain," said Phemanderac. "But you know where it is."

"Of course," Belladonna acknowledged. "It would be a poor guardian that knew not the location of that which she guarded."

"It cannot be far from here," he pressed.

"I see no logic or reason that requires it to be close."

"Well, you have to guard it. How can you guard the Arrow if it is far away?"

"Is magic limited by distance?" Maendraga answered.

"It is limited by the power and imagination of the magician," replied Phemanderac, "and distance is a limitation of power not easily overcome. Is the Arrow subject to illusion? Can you make it seem to be what it is not?"

Maendraga pursed his lips. "I've never tried," he said frankly. "I doubt it very much."

"Pass the pork," interrupted the Haufuth, playing his role of disinterested but powerful leader to the hilt.

"The riddle is geographical, is it not? The answer is in the form of a location?"

"Perhaps," replied the wily guardian. "Or perhaps it is metaphorical: air, water, earth and fire, the four elements. By what route did you come to Kantara?"

"Through Deruys and the Mist, then down the Valley of a Thousand Fires and past Astraea. Ah. I see what you mean. Are you telling us that the solution depends on the way in which Kantara is approached?"

"So you came to Kantara from the north," Maendraga said, smiling. "That explains how you avoided my snares, except one. The north-way is little used."

As the conversation progressed a seed of suspicion, of insight, began to take root in Leith's mind. He could not name it, not yet; but it was there. He deliberately ignored it, leaving it to grow at its own pace.

"A mere technicality," Phemanderac said. "But obviously you expect any seekers of the Arrow to approach from the south, from Nemohaim, traveling up the Vale of Neume. You did not expect us."

"I did not. But I expected someone. Here is some news that might be of interest to you. My nets across the Neume have been sprung by someone competent in mastering illusion. Another party approaches Kantara."

He paused and gauged the effect of this announcement on the Arkhimm, and was not displeased with the result. *Nemohaim*, Kurr mouthed to Phemanderac, who nodded a reply.

"These are ones who would thwart our quest. They are sponsored by Bhrudwo. We must find the Jugom Ark ahead of them!"

"They will have as little success as you will, I assure you. It still comes back to this. Bring the girl to me! I must see the fulfillment of the Arkhimm before I can guide you to the Arrow."

"Tell me," said Leith, his face carefully expressionless, his voice devoid of inflection. "Are there any waterfalls around here?"

Phemanderac turned to him, a puzzled expression on his face.

"Countless thousands, my friend," Maendraga replied. And Leith caught what he was looking for: the slightest hint of Wordweave. *Don't ask about waterfalls.* No one who was not looking for those words would have heard them. The magician had been unable to keep his thoughts out of his voice. Indeed, he was probably unaware he had betrayed the location of the Jugom Ark; but, if Leith was right in his suspicion, that was exactly what Maendraga had done.

"Of course there are," Leith said. "I didn't expect you to cave in and tell me." He chose the words with care, and watched his man closely. Again he saw what he hoped to see; the slightest narrowing of the eyes, the merest whitening of the knuckles. He kept any expression of satisfaction or joy from his face, trying to appear young and naive. It was very easy to do so.

Everyone helped clear the dishes away, then the travelers found seats on chairs provided by Maendraga (they didn't ask where they came from, but they appeared solid enough). The guardian and the philosopher faced each other, eyes locked. Hal sat beside Leith, an indecipherable look on his face.

"We're a long way from home," the cripple said to his brother. "Don't be too surprised that there should exist things we don't know about."

I don't know about, you mean, Leith thought, but he held his tongue.

"Now then," Phemanderac said quietly. "Explain to me how you will prevent us discovering the Arrow of Yoke."

"Immediately after you've explained to me how you plan to gain the information necessary," said Maendraga pleasantly. "Be warned: I will kill anyone who gains this information in the absence of the full complement of the Right Hand."

Leith, who was about to speak, held his tongue.

"I can do it," said the guardian. "Not all my arts concern illusion. Being slain by magic is not pleasant." The Wordweave came through strongly: *give up this quest. I do not want to slay you, but I will.*

"No doubt you can," said Phemanderac, carelessly replying to the Wordweave. "No doubt you can."

"Can he do it?" Leith asked his brother.

"It is possible. If he can see the seeds of disease or ill-health in us, he could simply enhance them until they became the dominant force in our bodies. Similar, in fact, to what happened to the Hermit."

Something was wrong with Phemanderac: his eyes had glazed over and his jaw drooped slackly. "No doubt you can," he repeated.

"Fool!" crowed Maendraga. "He replied to my thought, and so became ensnared by it. What will you do now, Haufuth?" He turned to face the village headman.

Hal narrowed his eyes in concentration: the Haufuth shrugged his shoulders, apparently unconcerned, and Phemanderac's eyes cleared in an instant. "Not much of a Wordweave, really," he said. *I overmatch you: speak the truth!* Maendraga spun round, shocked.

"You overmatch me," he said incautiously, then realizing his error, gave such a shriek the cabin shook.

"You have spoken the truth," Phemanderac said, "and have fallen into my trap. Really, Maendraga, we used to play this game as children. Is your art grown so feeble?" But Maendraga could not move or speak. The weaving had rendered him incapable of volition.

Belladonna rose wearily. "I suppose now he is held in

thrall of the truth, you will ask him to reveal the location of the Arrow; and no doubt he will. But it is a mistake, I warn you; and I will oppose you with my life, small though my own powers be."

Phemanderac readied himself to put the question. The solution to the riddle! His scholar's mind ached to have that answer in its compass.

Unregarded in the drama of the moment, Hal turned to Leith. "Does he have to reveal the secret?" he whispered.

"I don't think so," Leith replied carefully, his hand in front of his face.

"Good," Hal whispered. "Revealing it this way would break him." He leaned forward as though keen to know the outcome of the moment.

"Maendraga!" Phemanderac commanded. "Tell me the location of the Jugom Ark!"

The question hung in the thick air of the cabin. Behind them, Belladonna busied herself setting the fire, obviously unwilling to watch the humiliation of her father.

"The location!" the philosopher pressed. "Where is the Arrow?"

Words came from the guardian's mouth. "I . . . will not . . . tell you," he whispered.

"What?" Phemanderac roared. Belladonna gasped, and clapped her hand over her mouth. "Impossible! You must tell the truth! You cannot resist!" Leith's friend was beside himself.

"Nevertheless . . . I will not . . . tell you," came the reply.

The man from Dona Mihst tried rephrasing the question, but could not break the resistance of the guardian. With a curse he sat down heavily on his chair, which promptly disappeared.

"That'll be sore in the morning," Belladonna said

tartly, as the philosopher tried to recover his dignity. "Now release my father, then do what he asks and bring back the girl."

"You are released," Phemanderac said, defeat in his voice. "I did not think resistance to a Truthweave was possible."

"Neither did I," said Maendraga, his face pale. "But I give thanks that it proved to be so. I felt such a power— I felt as though I might have done anything. I do not know where it came from."

"Stalemate then," the Haufuth said. "Maybe we will continue this game in the morning; but for now I am going to rest. Do you think you could shape an illusion solid enough to support me as I sleep?"

Maendraga laughed, having recovered in an instant. "It will be the sorest test yet of my powers, but I will try."

"Good," said the big man. "Just warn me if you're about to lose the illusion."

Leith waited until all slept, then crawled quietly over to where Phemanderac lay. A shake of the shoulder sufficed to wake him. Leith put his finger to his lips, then spoke quietly.

"I have it," he said.

The philosopher's eyes widened, asking the question: *are you sure?* Leith shrugged his shoulders: *I think so.*

Phemanderac nodded, then turned over. But he did not sleep.

The Arkhimm slept long into the morning, except Phemanderac who took an early walk. He was beside himself with impatience, waiting to meet with the young

Loulean; but took time to check for enchantments, and found none. Leith woke to a dull and wet morning. Mist enveloped the hut in gloom. *If one can believe one's eyes*, he thought. There was no sign of the two guardians.

They took a light breakfast from their own̄ meager supplies. Phemanderac returned as they were leaving the table (except the Haufuth, who was busy inspecting their supplies in search of a second helping). Immediately he took Leith aside.

"What have you learned?" he asked eagerly. "Do you have the secret? Have you solved the riddle?"

"I think so," said Leith. "You see, it has to do with—"

At that moment the door opened, and Maendraga and Belladonna came in. Both wore robes: the pale blue robe lent Maendraga a regal dignity, while the simple gray shift complemented Belladonna's beauty. Phemanderac ground his teeth in frustration.

"We didn't interrupt anything important, did we?" Maendraga asked with glee. "You want to be careful. I know a spell that can make words hang in the air long after they are spoken."

Phemanderac grimaced. "That, among other reasons, is why we are about to take our leave. We are the Arkhimm, the questers for the Jugom Ark. We have endured trials and deprivation to get this far, and will tolerate your obstinacy no longer. If the Most High wants us to find the Arrow, he will guide us himself."

Maendraga raised an eyebrow. Clearly, the game was not over. "We will come with you." Belladonna smiled. *Beautiful and deadly*, Leith realized.

"I don't think so," Phemanderac answered. "We've had enough of your help."

"I gather, then, you think you have some idea as to where the Arrow might be."

"Not really. But your news about others in the valley means we cannot wait. We must seek the Arrow."

"Have you told them we are leaving?" the Haufuth said to Phemanderac, still playing his part well. "We were to have been on our way by now."

Within the hour the Arkhimm took their leave of the guardians' cabin, but not of the guardians themselves. They needed food, and gained supplies in exchange for allowing Maendraga and Belladonna to accompany them. The young woman closed the door of the hut, and with a gesture her father restored the illusion of the great castle: they spent the next few minutes walking down a hallway and through a courtyard to the arched gate, and out into the sunshine.

Phemanderac walked just behind Leith, who of necessity led the group. "I hope you're right," he muttered under his breath. "We're relying on you."

CHAPTER 16

IN THE EARTH ABIDES THE FLAME

"CAN YOU RETRACE OUR STEPS?" Leith whispered to Wiusago as the travelers wound their way down the path from Kantara. Away to their left, down in a little ravine, the silver stream bubbled and fussed.

"Retrace them? Certainly. Anything to be gone from this witchy place." The practical Deruvian had been profoundly disturbed by the encounter with the guardians.

"Then do so. Take us to the foot of the scree slide."

In silence they came to the mouth of the glorious valley. At any other time Leith would have enjoyed the sight of the little stream leaping down a set of stair-like rapids, the bright water glinting in the sudden sunlight. Instead, surreptitiously he moved from one member of the Arkhimm to another, making eye contact and trying to reassure them without words, for fear of the guardians. It was a difficult task, made all the more difficult by the fact he himself was in need of reassurance. If he was honest, he had little more than intuition to go on, that and something he had seen without really looking at it. He had racked his memory, trying to force it to show him what he wanted it to reveal, but he couldn't be sure. The guardian seemed to have confirmed what he thought, but who was to say that was not part of Maendraga's plan? Phemanderac and Hal also communicated confidence to their companions: it made Leith feel sick to his stomach. *Please, I don't want to let them down.* Funny, he could raise no enthusiasm now about the plight of Faltha. All that mattered was that he keep faith with his friends, that his risk pay off. He couldn't stand it if—

<It's a matter of trust,> a voice exploded into his mind.

He looked around, but no one had their eye on him. With all that had happened in this valley, he suspected for a moment the guardian, or Phemanderac, or Hal, had spoken directly into his mind. But no; he could remember the sound of that voice.

After all I've said to you, why are you speaking to me?

<I have had to put up with a lot worse than you.>

But I said I didn't want to hear your voice.

<True. But have you considered that I might be able to see your motives? That while a part of your mind wants to shut me out, you really want to hear from me?>

Can we talk about this later? Right now I have to think about—in fact, you could probably tell me if I'm right or not.

<I could, but I won't.>

Right. You're going to better me while playing with thousands of lives.

<Leith, most people need to become more dependent on others. You, however, need to find some independence. You hover on the edge of adulthood; and you will all of your life, unless you take responsibility yourself. That is why you are involved in this.>

So it's up to me? You're not going to intervene?

<It all stands or falls right here.>

The Jugom Ark, the Bhrudwan invasion, the whole lot?

<It's a matter of trust. Trust me, trust your friends, trust yourself. You may yet prove sufficient.>

They stopped for a few moments' rest in the burned-out glade. Leith dearly wanted to talk to someone, but the presence of Maendraga and Belladonna among them prevented him.

The magician turned to Leith and looked him in the eyes, appraising him. It seemed to Leith he had little regard for what he saw. "Where to now, young master?" he asked abruptly. "You haven't been fooling anyone."

"That depends," Leith retorted, angry and more than a little rattled, "on what you plan to do if I'm right."

"Nothing. If the Arkhimm find the Arrow without my help, I will not interfere."

"In that case we go to the right, upvalley. I'm looking for something." He looked squarely at the guardian, then decided to hazard another guess. "You've never been there, have you? None of you have."

"No."

"That's why you're coming. Because if we find it, you want to see it."

"If you had lived all your life in the service of an object, wouldn't you want to see it?"

Leith smiled and tried another hunch. "Many times you've doubted its existence, haven't you?"

Maendraga smiled wanly. "Since my wife died, I've hardly believed in it at all. I must see it! I must learn whether my life and the many lives before me were wasted."

"So you think I know where it is?" By now all the travelers attended the conversation.

"I'm not sure. I feel unmade. Part of me wants you to find it, hope against hope, for it is hidden so cleverly even knowledge of the Arrow's whereabouts does not guarantee its possession. But another part of me wants it to remain undiscovered until the Arkhimm is complete. Why, oh why did you not bring the girl?"

"It must be strange," Leith reflected, "being a Guardian of the Arrow. To never see it. Or to see it and find out you had a purpose only when that purpose ended. I don't understand why the Arrow needed a guardian."

"Bewray did not want it found until the time was right. He was a Seer, of course, or he would never have hidden it. It should have been found, you know, at the time of the first Bhrudwan invasion a thousand years ago. An expedition came, just like yours, only the Five of the Hand was complete. They discovered from one of my ancestors the location of the Arrow, but could not recover it. The way is very difficult. So the Bhrudwans triumphed, and now you come again, just like Bewray foretold. And if you do not succeed—"

"Another group will come in a thousand years' time," Leith finished for him. "And in the meantime countless lives will be lost, and everyone will suffer, because of the failings of a few, or even one. Why does the Most High not pick his representatives more carefully?"

"Perhaps the task is beyond any of them," Belladonna offered dolefully.

"We will never find out whether it is beyond us if we remain here," said the Haufuth. "It is time we got moving again."

The valley mist rolled back, then dissolved in the morning sun, clearing away as though the guardians had no more use for it. Steam rose like smoke from folds and gullies in the valley walls; whether from evaporation or from the deep pools under the numerous waterfalls, Leith could not tell. He imagined little cottages set in hidden valleys, smoke spiraling from chimneys, laughter and play inside, and he found himself longing for rest from his labors, some peace and solitude, relief from the expectations of others. Not for the first time he returned in his mind to the days before his father was sent to Bhrudwo, to the time before the shining knights took his father away.

This brooding is doing me no good.

In the clear morning air the true grandeur of the upper Neume valley stood revealed. The mountains were impossibly high, impossibly steep. Not as tall, perhaps, as the heights of Grossbergen far to the north, but their bulk was more immediate, more oppressively daunting, because of the precipitousness of the lower slopes. The sheerest faces wore no cover, bare gray giant-hewn stone vaulting skyward; while slightly gentler angles managed to hold soil, bushes and trees. At about three thousand feet above the valley floor the forest ended: above the treeline brown grasses grew up to the shoulders of the mountains on either side. Higher than this Leith could not see. From every mountainside waterfalls sprang, and though they were not overfull as on the previous two days, their fragile beauty was enhanced for it. Ahead of them, at the head of the Vale, two great snow-tipped peaks towered above them, rising almost as high again as at their shoulders, the lower slopes of the rightmost peak hidden by a bluff jutting out from the rock wall. On the leftmost massif he could make out a huge scar slicing down from just under the peak to near the valley floor. *Be patient, be patient*, he told himself, as he waited for the bulk of the other peak to come into view.

Nearly six months' walking in the wilds of the world should have conditioned Leith to be patient; however, he could not help but continue to glance ahead, craning his neck as if it would make the difference.

"What are you looking for?" Belladonna asked him. Leith listened carefully, but could detect no suggestion or coercion in her voice.

"I think you know. I'm looking for water falling from a high place."

"So serious, yet so young," and she laughed. This time Leith heard something beside the bare words, and he did not dare examine it, except to realize a woman with such control over her voice must have meant to say what she said. He tried not to blush, though he knew she said what she said in order to distract him.

Suddenly, above the ridge in front of them, it sprang into view, the topmost stair of a waterfall that fell ribbon-like from a hidden basin set between the two great peaks, still a league away. Leith let out a relieved sigh. "That's it, isn't it," he asked Belladonna, but it was more of a statement than a question.

Maendraga answered for her. "So it seems you've discerned something from what I said, or from some knowledge of your own. What else do you know?"

"Let's walk on until the whole thing is visible," the youth replied boldly. "I want to see it."

This landscape affected the senses cumulatively. In the clear mountain air the slopes appeared to steepen, the peaks grew in size and the waterfalls crashed and foamed until their ears were full of the sound. Yet the forest did not alleviate their sense of smallness. The huge, spreading pines, firs and beeches towered over them, enfolding them in leaf-rustle and birdsong, one vast entity on a scale even the mountains could not match. The Vale of Neume, surrounded by the Almucantaran Mountains, was not a place mortals could suffer easily.

"How do you live with all this?" Leith asked Maendraga, waving an arm around him.

"You learn to break it down into manageable segments," the magician replied, intuitively understanding Leith's question. "It helps that my magic allows me to control parts of it, such as the mist, otherwise I think the land would be too burdensome. I must admit I have wondered what the rest of the world is like."

"Insipid," relied Phemanderac instantly. "Compared to this, anyway."

"Compared to that waterfall, anything else is bound to be insipid," added Prince Wiusago. As they talked, they rounded the spur, and the head of the Neume valley came into view. The two peaks were revealed as enormous sentinels, standing guard over some secret set between them. Where their spreading ridges met a waterfall issued, seemingly spouting forth from the rock itself, a thrilling cascade plunging to the valley floor two thousand feet below in three great leaps, each larger than the one above.

"It is beautiful," Te Tuahangata murmured. "Beside this, all other cataracts are mere driblets of water."

"Yes, it is beautiful," said Leith, and he did not keep the grimness from his voice. "It is beautiful, and we've got to climb it."

The Arkhimm and their companions ate lunch as near to the base of the great fall as they could get without being drenched by the spray. Away to their left a stream gurgled out from a narrow valley, while above it the scree slope they had used to enter the valley stretched upwards until blocked from their sight by a ridge. However, the place was dominated by the waterfall. It leapt down at them from unguessable heights, and the roar it made as it plunged into its pool belied the fact it carried relatively little water. By craning their necks they could make out the highest of the three steps almost directly above them. Leith focused on one splash of water and tried to follow its progress down the cliff face. It slammed into a stone step, was thrust away from the slope, sparkling as it dropped, diamond-like, through space, then again bounced from the wall and took the long, slow plunge down into the black pool at the foot of the cliff.

"Climb that?" said the Haufuth. "It's hard enough even to look at it."

"Does it have a name?" Te Tuahangata asked Maendraga.

"No. All the other falls have names. I don't know who named them. One of my forefathers, most likely. But this, the Father of all, has no name. It is the Waterfall."

"But the basin above has a name," said his daughter slowly, carefully, as if afraid to give away the secret. "It is called Joram."

"Perhaps someone might like to explain what this has to do with our quest?" Kurr asked plaintively. "It's all very nice—though I prefer something a little quieter and more restrained, myself—but I see no Arrow."

"All right," said Leith. Now the time had come to explain himself, he became self-conscious, keenly feeling the risk of ridicule he ran. He cleared his throat, then began.

"Walk this through with me. The only way to approach Kantara from the north is through the Mist, the desert or the Valley of a Thousand Fires. We all know how difficult that was. My guess is that Bewray and the guardians he appointed discounted the possibility of people approaching the Arrow from that direction, and so their defenses were slight, as we found out. Instead, they expect the few travelers who come to the Vale of Neume to approach it from the south, from Nemohaim, and their webs would deal with them. After all, there is supposedly no knowledge of magic in Faltha." Here Leith could not help but cast a sidelong glance in the direction of his brother. "At least, the guardians would be alerted that someone approached them. That's the way we would have gone if Prince Wiusago hadn't diverted us in Kinnekin. We might not have gotten this far.

"So if the defenses are concentrated in the south to prevent access to this valley, I guessed the Arrow might be located in the north, at the head of the Vale.

"Now the riddle becomes important:

> *Through the air, over water,*
> *In the earth abides the flame.*

"It is a map of words, telling us more specifically the location of the Arrow. My guess is, had the Arkhimm been complete, the guardians would have led us here, told us to climb the falls and left us to figure the rest out for ourselves. We have to go through air, over water, and find the flame in the ground. That could be anywhere. But what the guardians were not expecting was that we would come down that scree slide. But come down it we did, and because I was well ahead of the rest of you I saw the resting place of the Jugom Ark, without realizing it at the time."

Maendraga pursed his lips. "It seems a lucky chance,

if indeed chance it was. I wonder if the Most High has not compensated the quest for the missing girl."

Leith continued. "Did anyone else see the lake on our way down? I thought not. I only saw it for a few moments. Away to my left it was, lying in a basin between two ridges, with a small island at its center. The water drained out in a deep gut between the ridges, and disappeared over a cliff. I could not see where it went." He turned and looked up at the waterfall. "I can now. This waterfall drains the lake far above us. To get to the island in the middle of the lake, where I expect we will find a cave, we must climb the cliff beside this fall and find a way across the water to the island. I guess we must choose carefully which side of the waterfall to ascend, as one side will be unclimbable. That's why the first quest for the Arrow a thousand years ago failed, wasn't it?" He turned to the magician and his daughter.

"Yes, it was," Maendraga confirmed.

"They chose the wrong cliff, and either gave up or fell to their deaths. But the other cliff, the one they did not choose, is the correct way."

"But how do you know all this?" Phemanderac asked him, bewildered by the breaks in his logic.

"On my way down the scree slide I saw something else. Stretched above the gap where the water drains the lake was a thin, gleaming wire. I wondered about it at the time. But I think now that it provides access from the correct side of the cliff to the location of a hidden boat."

"A rope?" Wiusago repeated. "But what prevents an adventurer from simply circumnavigating the lake and coming on the boat that way?"

"I don't know," Leith said. "I hadn't thought of that."

"There is an impassable bluff on the lake's shore,"

Maendraga said. "Or so we've been taught. Bewray judged it easier for questers to hazard the rope than try to surmount the bluff."

"So *now* you're talking," Phemanderac said with some bitterness. "You might then want to explain why the illusions of the guardians were not defense enough. Why did he not simply leave the Arrow with you?"

Maendraga spoke with sudden solemnity. "The guardians are not enough for the Arrow. You see, Bewray wanted the Arrow defended with physical as well as magical snares. He reasoned that most of those who master the magic arts are likely to be too old to surmount the natural obstacles he placed in their path. This was done to prevent the servants of the Destroyer seeking to discover the Arrow and availing themselves of its power. So he placed it in a virtually inaccessible location, as the young man has guessed. In a cave on an island, in the middle of an ice-cold lake, locked between high mountains accessible only by scaling a waterfall and navigating a rope stretched across a deadly drop. That is the task before you."

"And how do we choose the correct side of the cliff to climb?" Prince Wiusago asked.

Maendraga stared at him with a most penetrating gaze. "It is the Random. Even the guardians do not know."

"What?" nine voices asked him in unison.

"Random. The most powerful defense of all. The snare that caught the questers a thousand years ago."

"I understand," said Leith slowly. "We are supposed to guess which cliff to climb. If we get it right, we are obviously the Chosen of the Most High."

"Yes," said Maendraga, smiling and turning to the Haufuth, the one he thought of as master. "You have been well served by bringing one with such intelligence.

He is right. Bewray judged chance might achieve what snares might not. He told no one the correct route up the cliff, but provided a choice, so giving the Most High an effective way to prevent unworthy claimants to the Arrow from reaching their goal."

"The guardians believe the Most High will speak to the Arkhimm, telling them which of the routes to take," added Belladonna.

"So, what it comes down to is this," Phemanderac summarized: "choose the correct path up the cliff, thereby solving the Random. Then cross the rope—*through the air*—take a boat over the lake—*over water*—to an island, enter a cave—*in the earth*—where we shall find the Arrow—*abides the flame*."

"I don't want to bring up the obvious," said the Haufuth sadly, "but there may be one or two of us who might have some trouble with the task."

"Yes," Kurr agreed. "I should have done this many years ago, and you should have done it many meals ago."

"Very funny."

"But deadly accurate," said Te Tuahangata. "Frankly, neither of you would make it up the cliff."

"Then what do we do?" asked Leith.

Everyone turned to him.

"That's what we were going to ask *you*," the Haufuth said.

I don't want to ask you, you know that. I'm only asking because I have no choice. I can't give them what they want.

<It's nice to be wanted,> said the voice dryly.

I'm sorry. But will you tell me which of the cliff faces we should climb?

<Neither.>

Neither? Then what?

<You have the answer. Just think carefully. You have to get up to the lake you saw yesterday. It was beautiful, was it not?>

An image of the rippling waters flashed across Leith's mind, just as he had seen it from the scree slope . . .

Oh. But isn't that cheating?

<There are no laws to break. If you can find the Jugom Ark, you have fulfilled the quest.>

Leith looked up into the inscrutable face of Maendraga. "Tell me," he said. "The scree slide wasn't there in Bewray's time, or even a thousand years ago, was it?"

"No. It appeared in my grandfather's time, after a month of torrential rain. The land was scarred in many places, but none worse than the one above us . . ." His words faltered as comprehension dawned on him.

"We came down the slide, and it appeared to me the lake was easily reachable from it, if from nowhere else," said Leith. "But can we climb back up the scree?"

"Are you saying we should avoid the cliff altogether?" Kurr exclaimed. "Is that allowed?"

"Random exists to ensure the rightful claimants find the Jugom Ark, nothing more. It is a matter of chance." Leith spoke earnestly to Kurr, and as he did so, suddenly, incongruously, an image of himself as a boy working in Kurr's barn flitted across his mind. As a boy? It was less than a year ago. He shut the image away and continued. "If we have been granted the good fortune to avoid making that choice, has not Random fulfilled its function? Is it not clear that we are led by the Most High?"

"We certainly cannot attempt the cliff," said Prince

Wiusago. "Had I known we would face such a test, I could have brought ten or a dozen of my best soldiers, skilled in mountain-work and rope-craft. With their help we might have made the crest of the cliff. But I am uncertain myself of making the climb, raised though I was in the hills of northern Deruys where scaling hills was the play of boys. I fail to see how the northerners could scale more than fifty feet. It would be an unnecessary casting away of life. And if I was to gain the cliff top, what then? Would I gain access to this relic, in the absence of the Five of the Hand? I think not. No; we must take the proffered scree slope or turn around and make our way back north towards home."

"Then let us make our decision," said Te Tuahangata. "For myself, I do not fear this little mountain wall. But I think the prince is right regarding the northerners. I suggest we try the scree slope."

"And I," agreed Wiusago. "What say the Arkhimm?"

"I want to know what Achtal thinks," said Phemanderac. "Can we climb the slope? It seemed insubstantial and treacherous to me. What does the Bhrudwan say?"

Hal turned to his companion. "Can we scale the stony slope?"

The fierce Bhrudwan looked with a practiced eye at the visible section of the scree slope, then turned to Hal. "Difficult. Two steps up, one step down. Take rest of the day."

"There is another reason to avoid the cliff face," Belladonna said unexpectedly. "Look! See the mare's-tails high in the southern sky? They foretell the weather. Rain from the south, they say, within the next twelve hours. It might burst upon you before you attained the top of the cliff; and it would pluck you from the face and dash you to the ground."

Maendraga turned on his daughter. "You depart from

the ways of wisdom! What, or who, has turned your head? How shall they be affirmed as the Chosen unless they choose correctly at the Random? They must take the test."

"Must we?" countered Phemanderac, and his suspicion of the magician returned. "You strengthen our resolve to avoid this test. What does it matter to us if you do not believe? Yet my heart tells me you shall not see the relic you have guarded most zealously, unless you accompany us on our climb. And logic defies you! By random chance we came from the north and, unlooked for, we found the location of our quarry. Is this not the randomness your test was designed to determine?"

"We have debated long enough," said the Haufuth. "We will re-climb the scree, whether the guardians will it or not. And we will begin now." With that, he repacked the remainder of his lunch, and slung his pack on his back.

"He must be serious about this," said Kurr quietly, "to have sacrificed his meal."

"I'm glad we do not risk the cliff," said Phemanderac. "I would have been compelled to leave my harp behind."

Te Tuahangata frowned, the nearest he could come to a smile. "Light-heartedness masks true feelings. You are a strange people, you northerners! Yet I have enjoyed my journey with you, and will follow you until the end."

"Then let us leave," Maendraga growled. "I have no wish to be in the open when the weather arrives."

The task began easily enough, though tramping up the stream-bed took longer than Leith remembered. An hour passed before they reached the base of the shingle slope, and there his heart almost failed him. How could it have been so impossibly steep? Up and up it stretched, and as they contemplated it, gathering whatever inner strength they had, a small stone slithered down the incline and clattered past them into the stream.

With increasing weariness the travelers forged their way up the initial slope. They began by tackling it head-on, striking straight up the slope; but a few minutes left many of them gasping for breath. Leith's legs shook uncontrollably, and his ankles ached with the pressure of anchoring him to the scree. After this they zig-zagged across the incline, each sweep taking many minutes and gaining them but little ground. After an impossibly long time of this labor, Leith looked down, to find they had risen only a few hundred feet above the valley floor. Already the sun began to quarter towards the horizon.

"I don't like this," Kurr said worriedly during one of their frequent halts. "The Haufuth is about done in, and even I, an outdoorsman, am finding the will to go on more and more elusive."

"I would find it harder to go back," retorted Te Tuahangata.

"Tua has his fear of being shamed to impel him forward," commented Prince Wiusago. "I have my love for my father. I suggest each of us explore deep within ourselves now and find something to keep us going. Whatever it is, we will meet it again only by conquering this slope."

Across and back, across and back. Sun behind, harsh heat rising from the gray stone slope. Legs screaming their ache. Achtal stopping to help the Haufuth. Hal ahead, legs crabbing efficiently up the slide. Rocks dislodged, sliding into ankles, calves, knees; rattling their way down the slope behind them, crashing into trees hundreds of feet below. Packs threatening to tip them backwards, send them falling, falling. No talk, just the ragged sound of labored breathing ahead and behind. Across and back, across and back. Kurr staggers and falls; the Escaignian thrusts out an arm and grabs him. No breath even to express thanks. Only the Bhrudwan and, surprisingly, Belladonna seem relatively untroubled. Payback time for months of borrowing on reserves now depleted. Unable to think with any coherence. Across and back. Maendraga turns and points: with care they pivot and look to the southern horizon, where a dark smudge spreads wide across the sky, reaching out to swallow the sun. Deep, deep breath, then back to the slope, the random rock-patterns flowing slowly under their boots. Across and back. Down behind them mist gathers in the shadowed valleys, puffs from deep stream-scoured folds, curls up the valley walls. Sun dives towards the mountains. Shadows lengthen, stretch out towards the ant-like figures on the rock-face, hesitate, then leap at them like hungry predators. Sun touches a mountain peak. Across and back, across—

"Nearly there!" someone ahead has the energy to cry.

Sobbing with the effort, Leith forces his legs on by pushing his hands down on his unwilling knees. The Haufuth is all in: Achtal helps him up the slope. Then they stop.

"Leith!" Prince Wiusago calls. "Is this what you saw?"

There, to their right and perhaps fifty feet below them, lay the basin Leith had seen the day before. It was dark and colorless now, as the sun slipped behind the ridge opposite the travelers. They could make out the island, vague in the gathering dusk.

"Yes, this is it," he said wearily.

"We can't go any further," Wiusago stated firmly. "It would take some time to find the rope, and none of us are in any condition to attempt it. We are going to have to spend a night up here."

"A cold and wet night, I fear," said Maendraga. "An ominous night to wait in Joram's arms. The storm is upon us."

As if his words called it down, drizzle began to fall from a leaden sky. Far to the west the sun sank below the horizon, and deep gloom rushed up the Vale of Neume towards them.

"Can't you fashion an illusion solid enough to shelter us?" Leith asked him.

"And who will sustain it when I am asleep?" Maendraga asked him a little shortly. "Or are you suggesting I remain awake all night?"

"Father," said Belladonna quietly. "There's nothing you can do about it now. Here we are, the first guardians to look upon the sacred lake. Let that satisfy you."

"I've heard too many disquieting things about this basin and the mountains that support her to be satisfied," Maendraga grunted in reply.

The Arkhimm and their companions worked their way down to the lakeshore, and began a search for shelter. To their left the bluff rose into the gathering darkness, sloping steeply away from the lake, the naked rock metallic in the fading light. No shelter there. A miserable gray rain-curtain slanted in from the south.

"Over here!" Hal called.

The cripple had discovered a ledge near the lake shore, over to the right. It was part of a ridge which swept down from the mountainside they had climbed, vanishing in the murk ahead of them. It promised little shelter, but perhaps it would keep out the worst of the rain.

During the long night the wind rose and howled all about them in a demented rage. Whenever the wind died, the rain soaked the company, few of whom could find more than a few moments' sleep. In his uneasy dreams Leith found himself caught under the great waterfall, or rolling, tumbling down the scree, falling with no hope of stopping. Whenever he awoke it was to the roar of the wind and the slash of rain.

"Can't you conjure something to keep this rain and wind off our backs?" he heard Maendraga say at some point in the darkness.

"Hardly. I can barely tie my own shoelaces," came the Haufuth's weary reply.

"Are you not the leader? Did you not do the magic in my house?" The voice carried a note of surprise.

"I am the leader, but I know no magic. I'm sorry for the deception, but it seemed necessary at the time."

A woman's laugh came from the darkness. "I wondered how a northern peasant had become an adept at the magic arts," she said. "It seemed so unlikely. So who is the magician?"

"No one," replied the headman. "But Phemanderac can recognize it, seemingly."

"Then how—how did I become caught in the Truthspell? A spell of that power takes years of training." Genuine puzzlement lined Maendraga's voice. Leith was learning to recoganize magic in speech—the Wordweave, Kroptur had called it—and through it discern between truth and falsehood.

"He says he didn't study magic. I suppose he was lucky."

"Luck?" the magician growled. "Luck does not exist."

"Neither does sleep, apparently," growled Phemanderac from further away. "Can you people quiet down a little? You're interrupting the noise of the rain."

Eventually the night petered out into a drab, wet morning. The storm blew itself out some time in the night, but the cloud lowered about them. Conditions were similar to when the Arkhimm had passed the lake two days earlier. A misty drizzle filtered straight down from a gray ceiling, beading clothes, hair and skin with water.

"It doesn't look quite so beautiful in the fog," Tua remarked.

A few yards away the lake lapped gently, quietly, at a stony shore. Despite what Tua said, Leith could see beauty in the way the perfectly clear water played with the gray, brown and white stones. The surface of the lake shimmered slightly, stirred by the faintest of breezes; further away it reflected the diffused gray above, until perhaps a hundred yards from shore it merged seamlessly with the fog. By the shore to their left the ghostly outline of a stunted tree counterpointed the gentle linelessness of lake and sky.

Breakfast was eaten, then the remnants packed away, in silence. No one had remained dry through the night, and the persistent moisture managed to penetrate their packs and dampen their clothes. Leith stretched uncomfortably, his body having not yet forgotten the exertions of the previous afternoon.

"We'd better go and look at this rope, then," said the Haufuth casually. "Leith?"

"To our right," said the young man. Instinctively he knew the village headman was attempting to lighten the mood, and tried himself to match his leader's tone, but they had the elements themselves to overcome. The day of their testing had arrived, and Leith knew in spite of his thorough preparation on the fields and hills and in the cities and dungeons of Faltha, he was not ready for the examination. The tone of the day was somber, and their mood echoed it.

They followed the lake shore about a hundred yards to their right until it came hard up against a spur of rock. A little way ahead a small stream found its way out of the lake and ran gurgling towards the spur, which allowed the stream through a deep, narrow slot. It looked to the company as though a giant axe had cleaved the ridge in two. Again a sense of smallness assailed them, encouraging them to regard themselves as misfits in a landscape writ too large. *Interlopers, intruders*, the land seemed to whisper. *Trespassers! You do not belong here.*

"Who said that?" Phemanderac cried out. Behind him Maendraga blanched and stood still.

"Someone is projecting a voice-thought. Who is it?" the disconcerted philosopher said.

"It is no man," Maendraga said, genuine fear thinning his normally inscrutable voice. "It is the land itself. My grandfather warned me of this. He said if the sacred lake felt the tread of the unworthy, it would cry out against the intruders until the very rock itself rose up to destroy them. I did not believe him, of course—I know the limits of magic as well as anyone—but the voice we hear does not come from human lips or mind."

"But we are not trespassing! We have been called here!" Leith said desperately.

"It seems that you are wrong," Maendraga pronounced. "There are unworthy feet in this holy place. I should have known. My heart misgave me from the start. It was folly to come here. We will not escape." He sat down on a wet rock outcrop.

"Nothing has changed," declared the Haufuth. "If that voice was anything at all, it was a phantom, a shadow, another illusion set here to discourage seekers of the Arrow. It will take more than whispers to deter me! I will not leave here until we have the Jugom Ark."

Yet the whispering continued: *Trespassers! Intruders! Begone from this place!* It was all Leith could do to ignore it. His sense of foreboding, of imminent disaster, grew stronger.

As they drew close to the slot through which the lake drained, Leith caught sight of their first objective. A rope of sorts had been strung over the chasm—through what endeavor, he could not guess—and anchored in the mountain bedrock at each end. The others made way for him. He stepped on to the top of the spur, then quickly sank to his knees: to his right the ground dropped away vertically into the mist, and the gray emptiness sucked at him the same way as had Helig Holth, the great sinkhole of Adunlok. He gritted his teeth and decided not to look in that direction again.

"Bit of a drop to the right, the top of the waterfall cliff, I expect," he said as casually as he could. "I'm going to have a look at the rope."

But it was not rope. Or, at least, it was a cord; but a cord made from three steel strands, somehow woven together. He shook it, and raindrops scattered as the cord rippled into the distance. In a moment the ripple returned, reduced but still noticeable. "About a hundred feet across," he announced.

Leith had always been fascinated with ropes, but this

one did not fascinate him. Slick with moisture, it offered
a tenuous handhold at best. He took a deep breath, slid his
hands along the wire, then pushed out with his legs.

Nausea instantly gripped him as his body swung back
and forth. His hands closed tightly on the cord. He looked
steadfastly up at them, refusing to look down. There was
rock a yard or so under his feet, he knew, but he also
knew that if he fell nothing would prevent him tumbling
into the chasm below. He would then be dragged by the
stream out over the lip of the cliff and pitched into white-
gray space . . . he would be dead as soon as he hit the first
step.

"Leith! Get back!" Kurr cried. "There must be an easier way!"

"We're all going to have to do it some time," came another voice: Tua's, probably. "Loosen your grip a little!
Slide your hands along the rope!"

How could he dare to loosen his grip even the tiniest
amount? He hung two thousand feet above the Vale of
Neume. His mind shrieked at him to hold on tighter,
tighter, tighter!

"Leith! Listen! I don't know what possessed you to go
first, but Tua is right!" It was Prince Wiusago. He could
not turn to look. "If you keep gripping the wire tightly,
your hands will lose their strength! Slide along the rope!"

I shall die, he thought, but he loosened his grip a little.
The cable was not taut, and the weight of his body, combined with the slickness of the moisture on it, caused him
to slide forward. It was a sickening feeling.

He stopped above the middle of the chasm. He took a
look down below his feet. He shouldn't have, of course,
but he did. For a second all was giddiness and vertigo,
then the view resolved itself into a foaming white stream,

shining black rocks, curling mist and the top of the waterfall. At that moment he nearly let go.

"Hand over hand, Leith. Hand over hand!" someone shouted to him. "You can't come back now! You must go on! Hurry!"

This must be a dream!

He tried to assemble his shattered mind into some sort of working order. *Hand over hand*, he told himself. *Take your left hand from the cable and place it in front of the right.* He could feel the muscles in his hand tensing up; his shoulders ached agonizingly, his legs dangled uselessly below him. He had been on the rope perhaps a minute. His hands refused to obey his mind.

"Leith! Hand over hand!" Cries, sharp and urgent; but whether they came from behind him or from within his mind, he could not tell.

Suddenly his left hand slipped from the cable. He clung on with his right, groping with his left hand for the rope. For an endless moment he hung: then his hand found the cable.

"That's right! And again!"

This time his muscles obeyed his mind, or the voices behind him, or both. Hand over hand he struggled towards the far spur. There it was, looming blackly through the mist. Twenty feet. Fifteen feet. His grip slipped a little, and he began sliding back down the cable. With an immense effort, he arrested his movement, then hung swaying while he recovered. Forward again, hand over hand, eyes closed now, concentrating fiercely, trying to feel rock under his feet. Release grip, swing forward, grab the cable, rest; release grip, swing forward, grab the cable, rest . . . then his right hand met the rock ahead, and his feet kicked against rock below at the same instant.

There he faced his most perilous moment. He opened his eyes. Somehow he had to swing himself up on to the spur, and there was no one to help him. He was all done in, he knew he hadn't the energy to lift himself up. There was no foothold on the rock from which to gain purchase. The knowledge dawned on him that he had come to the end of his strength. Then, on top of all this, the rope began to sway and jerk in his hands.

Now his life was measured in moments. He could taste death. A yawning blackness, a palpable thing, hovered just below him, reaching up with a black grasp. He could feel nothing but his hands. *So close!* his mind said, and the thought seemed far away. *So close! You were almost worthy. Almost.* It was over. He lost the feeling in his fingers, and they began to slip from the jerking cable. He let go.

He fell.

He fell back into the strong one-armed embrace of the Bhrudwan Achtal, who had swung across the cable behind him the moment it became clear he would not make it. That strong arm propelled him up on to the spur. A moment later, the Bhrudwan was up there with him, laying the frightened youth on the cold wet rock.

"Is he all right?" Hal called across the chasm. His voice barely carried. The Bhrudwan signaled his answer by an upraised arm.

"He's all right," Hal told the others, his relief obvious.

"A little courage is a dangerous thing," Te Tuahangata said quietly, but his voice carried respect rather than rebuke.

Prince Wiusago nodded. "Foolish or not, he has shown us the way with a brave deed. Let us prove ourselves worthy to follow him."

*   *   *

One at a time the questers measured their courage against the steel cable. Te Tuahangata went first, followed by strong-shouldered Kurr, who proved surprisingly adept at the crossing. Hal went next. His crossing took the longest, because he found it difficult to grip the cable with his crippled hand, and the Bhrudwan was forced to come out on the rope a little way to bring him safely in. Then came the Escaignian, who spluttered and cursed her way over the chasm. Willing hands hauled her to safety, where she lay beside Leith's twitching form. Phemanderac took his time before beginning, withdrawing to the still place within to insulate himself from his fear. "Leave your harp behind!" Wiusago told him; but the philosopher could not part with it, even though he knew it would unbalance him. Finally he struck out across the gulf and, in what seemed a moment later, found himself on the far side. He could never remember how he got there.

Now came the moment they all secretly feared: it was the Haufuth's turn to attempt the crossing. Wiusago steadied the big man, but it was obvious he did not have the strength in his arms and hands to support his considerable bulk.

"Wait!" came a cry from the far side. It was Hal. "Achtal says he has the strength for one further crossing. Let him help you!" Without waiting for any acknowledgement the Bhrudwan swung out over the chasm, slid gracefully to the lowest point of the cable, then swung powerfully, hand over fist, to the frightened headman's side.

"On my shoulders," the warrior said; and the Haufuth had no choice but to obey. The Bhrudwan lifted him with apparent ease, but how could he return over the rope with the huge form clinging to his back? Wiusago shook his head: when he next looked, the Bhrudwan was halfway across.

Achtal brought his incredible strength and powers of concentration into focus. The stress on his shoulders was intolerable. It would pull him from the rope if he allowed its force to concentrate. So he dissipated it by continuing forward at a fast rate, swinging hand over hand, throwing his legs back and forth, making the dead weight on his back work in his favor. With a last great effort he swung upwards into the arms of his astonished comrades.

Wiusago motioned to Maendraga, offering him the next passage. The magician shook his head. "I have done wrong to come this far," he said. "I am the only guardian to set foot here in two thousand years, and I have done so unworthily. I will be a part of this cursed quest no longer."

At that his daughter drew in her breath sharply. "My father, I cannot agree with you. These folk have demonstrated nothing but courage, imagination and faith. They seek nothing for themselves, and risk all for Faltha. If the Most High will not honor deeds such as theirs, then he does not deserve such servants. I will cross the rope."

"No! You will not! I forbid it!" cried the magician, his voice edged with panic. "Remain here with me!"

"You may have given in to despair, but I have not," Belladonna said quietly. "Remain here and wait for us. We will bring the Jugom Ark back with us." With that, she put her hand to the cable.

"No!" cried Maendraga. "No!" He made to drag her from the rope. Swiftly Prince Wiusago pinioned his arms behind his back.

"Let her go. There is nothing you can do save send her to her death. Wait here for us."

When at last the magician's daughter reached the far

side, Wiusago left Maendraga and made his way to the
others. The cable taxed him sorely and, trained from
childhood as he was, he marveled at the northerners' ac-
complishment. However, sooner than he had feared, it was
over. Ten questers stood together on the far side of the
cable; only one remained behind.

"I thought I was dead," said Leith, thanking the Bhrudwan. He had taken some little time to awaken from his
swoon, and felt a mixture of relief and humiliation. Apart
from the Haufuth, who was too humble to feel ashamed,
he had been the only one to require the Bhrudwan's assistance. Even Hal had done better than he.

"You are alive," Achtal stated. "You will continue."

The travelers rested for many minutes, then their
thoughts turned away from the cable and on to the next
step of their quest.

"Over water," Phemanderac reminded them. "There
should be a boat somewhere about."

The ten adventurers cast about for the boat. "There is
a boat, I presume?" Kurr asked. "The magician was
telling the truth?"

"I don't know," said Phemanderac, turning to Belladonna. He opened his mouth to ask her, but saw the
young woman stood facing the way they had come—the
way her father had refused to go—and noticed she was
quietly weeping. His heart softened. "Come," he said tenderly. "We need your help."

"I have never before willingly disobeyed him," she
said sadly. "Yet he is wrong, the stubborn old fool knows
he is wrong. If my mother had been here, she would have
told him so. He would have listened. She was the real
guardian."

A shout came from further along the lake shore. "Over here! Over here!"

"Perhaps we will talk more later," Phemanderac said gently, respectfully. Belladonna nodded, then followed the gaunt philosopher in the direction of the others.

The Escaignian stood proudly beside the boat she had discovered in a stand of dwarf-bush. "There is some enchantment about it," said Phemanderac in wonder, as they examined the strange craft. "How else could it have been preserved here for two thousand years?"

Kurr nodded in amazement. "Looks like the yawls used by the fishermen of Varec Beach. Not the same though—this has neither mast nor overlapping timbers. Is it safe?"

"Touch the wood!" The magician's daughter followed her own suggestion. "There is a power of preservation in the wood. It is a very strong magic! It is a difficult enough matter to speed a natural process such as decay, but to inhibit it! Such power is required! I would not have dreamed it could be done."

"Yet here is our transport," declared the Haufuth, fingering one of the two small paddles lying in the boat. "Or, at least, here is transport for some of us. How many will that boat carry?"

The water-wise Prince of Deruys looked carefully at the yawl. "It was designed to bear five people; one in the bow, two in the center and two in the stern. Consequent on the number of the Arkhimm, I suppose. Unless it has magic to keep it afloat, I would not exceed that number."

"Two trips, then!" the Haufuth said. "We'd better get on with it. My stomach tells me we have passed lunchtime already. I want to be off this mountain before nightfall."

Hesitantly Belladonna pushed her way to the front of the assembled group. "I doubt the wisdom of any other than the Arkhimm taking ship," she said quietly but firmly. "The island is a most holy place. Who knows what might happen if one who is not appointed steps ashore? A powerful magic has been set in this place. I can feel it; my father was certain of it. I for one will wait here. It will be enough to greet the Arrow when it returns. And why should extra people be needed? If the Five of the Hand do not suffice, I do not know who else might claim the Jugom Ark."

"Yet we are four only, not five," said the Haufuth. "Who shall stand for Stella? Or is it unnecessary?"

"The boat takes five, not four. Do not risk the island's wrath!" Belladonna said anxiously. "Five should go!"

"Then Phemanderac shall accompany us, since this is more his quest than anyone's," the Haufuth decided. "And we had better be quick about it! I don't like all this talk about wrath. Listen now! Do you hear it?" The Haufuth was right: *Go no further!* came the whisper. *Trespassers! Intruders! Curse the ground no more!*

"Illusion," said Phemanderac sternly. "Ignore it." But that was easier said than done. The insubstantial words ground on Leith's nerves until they shrieked in agreement: *I'm leaving! Just let me go peacefully!*

They cast off in the yawl. Leith and Phemanderac took up the paddles, and for a while splashed about dangerously until they synchronized their efforts. After that the paddles made little enough noise, dampened by the fine drizzle falling like quiet tears. The mist parted ahead of them, closed in behind, and within minutes they had lost sight of the shore. Then the thought struck them all at once. How in this sightless fog would they find the island?

No words were said. The Five of the Hand beheld the fear in each other's eyes.

Phemanderac and Leith kept paddling, but they could not be sure they rowed a straight course. And would even a straight course find the island? In this place of magic they could imagine all their courses being thwarted, the mist taking them around and around the lake without ever sighting land, or holding them prisoners in the same spot, ensnared between the island and the shore, suspended evermore as punishment for daring this place . . .

Now Leith would have been glad to hear the voice of fire; even a rebuke from that voice would have been better than the heavy silence enfolding them. Doubt encircled the Arkhimm like a tangible thing. "It's a matter of trust," the voice had said; but now that voice echoed only faintly, enfeebled by the damp gray mist. Trust alone would not suffice against such an unearthly place as this was.

"It was clear here two days ago," he said quietly. "The mist does not hang here forever."

"Let us pass, will you!" Kurr cried aloud. "We have the right! We have come to reclaim for Faltha what is hers!" His voice was swallowed echoless in the mist, and a moment after it was as if he had never spoken.

"Better not to speak," said the Haufuth. The mist seemed to draw in closer than ever.

"Illusion," Phemanderac reminded them. Of the five, only he and Hal seemed relatively unaffected by the haunting fog. "Don't give in to it. It is a spell laid here two thousand years ago, and it is indiscriminate as to whom it affects. Its only power is to force us to turn back."

While Leith's mind acknowledged the good sense of the philosopher's argument, his emotions quivered as they continued into the mist.

Now the way seemed dark and uncertain ahead, as though they paddled into an inimical force. Behind them the mist lightened, offering them a sure escape back to the shore. The only thing that kept Leith paddling in the face of this fear was the shame of being the first to give way, but while Phemanderac paddled steadily beside him, he would do the same. In the end the voice had been right. It all came down to trust. These men would not have led him here if his death was the inevitable outcome. The Most High would not set a puzzle that could not be solved. So many people had expressed their faith in him: the Hermit, the Fodhram (dear Axehaft!), Foilzie and the Escaignian, and his own parents. And others had opposed them: the Widuz, the Arkhos of Nemohaim, the Council of Faltha. Such wrongness surely emphasized the rightness of their cause. They would get through the mist, they would find the island, because they must.

Out of the cheerless slate-gray curtain loomed a black shape, and another. Leith cried aloud: what new shades had been sent to oppose them? Phemanderac also cried, but not with fear.

"Land! It is the island!"

"Thank goodness," breathed the Haufuth. "A journey like that makes it hard to disbelieve in the supernatural."

"It's a matter of trust, really," Kurr said quietly. Leith looked sharply in his direction, but the old farmer gave no indication he had meant anything by it.

The dark looming shapes resolved into ghostly trees, the island shore appeared ahead of them and the keel of their small boat grounded itself on stones. The island was little more than a mound jutting out from the lake, a pile of rock upon which a thin veneer of soil had found fragile anchorage, providing a foothold to ferns, grasses and a few larger trees. They walked all around it, taking about five minutes. Perhaps a hundred yards across, surely no larger, the island seemed to hold no special terror. Half an hour later the small island still held no terror, but apparently it also held no cave.

With mounting apprehension the Five of the Hand scurried about the island, searching for anything resembling the opening of a cave. "Through air, over water, in the earth!" Phemanderac repeated again and again, as though he expected the repetition to conjure the cave into existence. "It has to be here!"

"Does it?" Kurr countered. "None of the guardians have been up here since Bewray placed the Arrow here. What do they know?"

"They know the Jugom Ark is on this island," said Leith boldly. "It's part of what Bewray told them. The Arrow is here, in the earth."

"Could it be *buried*?" the Haufuth asked, horrified. "It would take days to dig up the island."

"More likely it is that the land itself has changed." Kurr's face was set like stone. "Two thousand years is a long time, far too long to entrust something as precious as the Jugom Ark to mere stone. Think of the scree slope. It wasn't part of the Riddle of the Arrow, yet we used it. What if the island has been worn down?"

"Possibly—but far more likely still is the possibility that the lake level has been raised. The entrance to the cave might now be offshore, under the water. What would we do then?" Phemanderac was given serious pause by his own question.

The five figures searched the island in increasing despair. An indeterminate time passed, and as they searched the gloom deepened around them. They hadn't eaten,

though in the tension of the moment even the Haufuth had
forgotten that; but they also forgot the progress of the hours.
Leith had seen the same three trees, the same half-dozen
bushes, the same bleak black rocks and the same pebbly
shore for far too long. It wasn't working out. All their
dreams were dissolving at the last possible moment. He remembered how he had been gripped by depression after
they were rejected by the Council of Faltha. He felt like that
now. Yet they had gone on then, another alternative had presented itself. Maybe it would again.

By unspoken mutual consent they sat themselves down
just under the rocky peak. The Haufuth brought out from
his jacket a small green apple for each of them, and they
munched quietly as the light slowly faded.

The village headman finished his apple, and cast the
remains down the slope towards the water. He spoke reluctantly. "We'd best be getting back." He received four
morose grunts in reply.

Kurr threw his apple core down at his feet, into a little
scrubby thicket they had checked a dozen times. Leith
had scratches on his arms from the thorny bush-lawyer.
The core clattered through the thicket and a second later
plunked on rock.

"I'm not staying here tonight," continued the Haufuth.
"We'll camp back on the shore and decide what we'll do
then." He turned towards the boat; Leith, Hal and Phemanderac followed him.

But Kurr scrabbled about in the thicket for a minute,
then called out to the others, who were making their way
towards the shore. Already the Haufuth had disappeared
into the mist.

"There might be another reason why we can't see the
cave," he called. Something in his tone caused Leith to

jerk around. "It might be that vegetation—say, a thicket of thorn bushes—grew up around the entrance, masking it from sight."

"We've looked in all the thickets—" the Haufuth began. There was a pause, then four gray figures scrambled back up the rock to where Kurr held aside a long, thorny branch, revealing a round, dark hole.

"In the earth," he said triumphantly.

The hole turned out to be a vertical drop of six feet to a smooth rock floor, on which rested a fresh apple core. The Haufuth went first, followed by Kurr, Leith, Hal and Phemanderac. The five men felt rather than saw their way down a narrow cavity descending into the gut-rock of the island. "This is not natural," the old farmer said unnecessarily: the smooth-sided walls and floor testified to the truth of his words.

Fifty yards or so on the cavity widened; ahead a soft glow illuminated a spherical chamber. "We're probably under the lake," Leith said, but nobody heard him. Their quest was on the brink of success.

Without words the Five of the Hand filed into the chamber. It was just large enough to accommodate them. In the center of the chamber a small rock sat on the floor; or, more correctly, the floor rose into a small rock table. The glow came from the stone table. No, from the arrow on the stone table. A small arrow, about two feet long, fletched with feathers. Glowing dull red, as though it was hot. The Arrow. The Jugom Ark.

"Look at it! It is beautiful," Phemanderac breathed. Slender, perfectly proportioned, feathered with the rare plumage of the *mariswan*, a metal shaft which gave off a rosy light: altogether lovely, beauty disguising a severe justice.

"Why does it glow?" asked the Haufuth. "Is it hot?"

"Illusion," answered the thin philosopher. "The final protection. But we need not worry. We are the Arkhimm. It will not burn us."

Kurr was decidedly uncomfortable with the glibness of this explanation. After all, Phemanderac was not the one who would be picking it up. The old farmer could feel the heat from his position a few feet away.

"Don't touch it!" The Haufuth extended a hand towards the Arrow, and Kurr's urgent warning came a moment too late. The big man didn't touch it, but his hand strayed too close for a moment too long, and he jerked it back with a howl.

"Let me look at it," said Hal tightly. "Let me see your hand."

"I didn't touch it!" But he held out his hand for Hal to see, and already it blistered, one large, watery blister to each finger. "My hand hurts! Why is it so hot?"

"I don't know, I don't know," said Hal. "But we must get you out of here, out to the lake, and put it in cold water." He led the headman to the exit. As they reached the hole the Arrow flared up, bursting into flame, flooding the tiny chamber with unbearable light and heat. "Don't leave the chamber!" Phemanderac shouted. "It'll kill us if we're less than five!"

"But my hand—all right, I'll stay." The big man was almost sobbing with the pain. "Let's find a way to fetch this Arrow and get out of here."

One after another the Five of the Hand stretched out their hands, but none could get near the Arrow of Yoke.

Phemanderac cried out in frustration. "In the earth lies

the flame! But who can carry a fire in his hands? What is making it so hot anyway? What are we to do?" Even retreating into his still small place, supposedly making him impervious to such pain, made no difference.

"Perhaps this is why we needed all five of us from Loulea!" exclaimed the Haufuth, shaking his hand back and forth to ward off the pain. "Had Stella come with us, we might already have claimed the Arrow. Now we may never—" here he grimaced with the pain, "we may never complete our quest."

"So near!" Phemanderac wailed. "How can this be happening?"

<Now, about this matter of trust,> said the voice of fire without warning. <It's time we took it a little further.>

Leith shuddered where he stood: he still had not become conditioned to someone else's voice in his mind. *You're about to ask me to do something extremely foolish, aren't you?*

<Pick up the Arrow. Pick it up! It's what you're here for.>

But I'll burn!

<Only if you don't grasp it firmly. It was not made for a hesitant touch. Some things burn you unless you take a firm grip of them.>

Leith recognized that the words were intended to carry something profound, but it was lost on him at this fraught moment. *It was made for your hand, wasn't it?*

<Mine, and Kannwar's. The Destroyer's. Are you going to pick it up, or do I have to wait another thousand years? And while you delay, the Haufuth suffers. His hand needs treating, you know.>

You never give me any choice; that's why I hate all

this. I'd rather do this because I want to, not because you make me.

<Of course you have a choice. Just leave with the others, telling them nothing. Get your leader's hand seen to. Make your way back to Instruere and fight against the Brown men, or go back to Firanes. I will tell no one about you. I am patient; I can wait for the next appointment.>

I can't do that. I can't leave when doing so would cost lives.

<You could. People do it more often than you might think.>

But I couldn't.

<Then pick up the Arrow. I'll bear the consequences.>

Just bear the pain.

<Do it before you have time to think about it.>

The voice closed off in his mind, leaving him alone to think through his dilemma. The voice had spoken of choices, but there was no real choice. His hand would burn, of that he was certain; but it seemed he would have to pay the price in order to avoid having countless deaths on his conscience. Then maybe they could be rid of this whole business.

Now for it! he thought glumly.

Leith put out his hand—

—and closed it tightly about the Arrow, clenching his teeth as he did so; but he felt no pain. The Jugom Ark flared, then died back. Beside him the others gasped. He lifted the Arrow and held it out, barely believing that it lay clasped in his hand, fire guttering along its length.

"We must leave this place," he said calmly, keeping the joy from his voice for fear it might be interpreted as pride. "The Haufuth's hand must be attended to." Nodding in wonder, the five moved carefully, respectfully, away from the holy place, the empty stone table, bearing with them the talisman of their time, the Arrow. The glow accompanied them.

The answer was obvious, but just as obvious was that the question needed to be asked. Kurr asked it. "Did it—does it hurt?"

Leith shook his head.

"How can that be?" said the Haufuth. "Look at my hand!"

"I see it clearly now," Phemanderac interrupted excitedly, his mind racing as they came to the cave entrance. "Leith, you were the Appointed One. Only one hand can hold the Arrow at a time: that's why Furist and Raupa, the leaders of the First Men who escaped the wrath of the Most High and led them into Faltha, came to blows over it. That hand is yours. More so because of your relationship with Stella."

Leith's head spun round, but he could see little of the philosopher's expression in the dark. "What relationship?"

"You've shared intimacy."

Leith reddened, and at the same moment the Arrow burst into renewed flame. "That's not true. We haven't—"

"I don't mean that! But you told her your dream on the night of fire, didn't you? And she told you hers?"

Leith nodded his head, still red in the face.

"Sharing intimate knowledge binds you together. It did, did it not? In some intangible way you may have brought enough of her essence with you to allow you to pick up the Arrow without hurt."

The Loulean youth shrugged his shoulders: he doubted

the argument, but had nothing to counter it with. *Let it rest: get the Haufuth to safety first. Time enough for talk later.*

One by one the five exhausted and emotion-racked men struggled up and out of the cave, and found themselves standing in the day's gloaming. It was nearly dark and raining steadily. Out in the cold air, free of its cave for the first time in two thousand years, the Jugom Ark flickered and flamed, shedding enough light for them to find their way down to the boat. At the stern Hal ministered to the Haufuth's burned hand. He encouraged the big man to hang his arm over the side, his hand in the icy, numbing water. After a few minutes he drew it out, and Hal applied an ointment from the pouch he had left in the boat. Leith had been holding the Arrow tightly for half an hour or more, but ignored the ache in his own hand and, settling himself in the yawl's prow, lifted the Arrow high to light their way through the fog. Thus those on the shore beheld the return of the Arkhimm, bearing aloft their treasure and the consummation of their quest.

But no cheer came across the waters, a fact that puzzled Leith. Surely the others watched for them? In silence they beached the boat, but there was no sign of their friends. Then, to their relief, black shapes materialized from the cloak of the mist.

"There you are at last!" the Haufuth called to the closest of them. "We have it! We have the Arrow!"

The shape resolved itself into that of a truly obese man, flanked by sword-wielding guards. A smile played on his cruel face.

"And you will deliver it to its rightful owner," said the Arkhos of Nemohaim. "And then you will die."

CHAPTER 17

THE SENTINELS' REVENGE

LEITH COULD DO NOTHING BUT WEEP with frustration as the soldiers of the Instruian Guard strode forward through the mist, bearing bright torches. Before them they shepherded the members of the Quest of the Arrow with their swords, having no more regard for them than if they were Kurr's stupid sheep, not some of the great heroes and nobles of their time. The Captain of the Guard, the man whom Leith had willed towards safety on the day of the big flood, stood before them with Belladonna as his prisoner, his arm wrapped about her shoulders, his knife-wielding hand at her throat. Beside him a younger guard held Phemanderac from behind.

To Leith the story of events seemed clear. The Instruians obviously captured Belladonna first, then used threats on her life to keep the others in line. Leith could think of no other reason sufficient to prevent the Bhrudwan, and no doubt Prince Wiusago or Te Tuahangata, from engaging in a death-fight with the guards. Absently he recognized the change in the Bhrudwan. Before becoming the servant of Hal he would have fought still, sacrificing the magician's daughter in the process.

The Arkhos of Nemohaim resembled a bloated spider settled smugly in the center of his web as he surveyed the fruit of his plans. He had correctly identified the northerners' weakness—an unreasoning belief in the rightness of their cause, and an associated trust in the guiding hand of myth and legend. Destiny. *Fools!* They assumed they were invulnerable, and so gave no thought to the powers arrayed against them. Such a small matter to capture horses and ride into Bewray, there to gather resources from his king—new, swifter horses, many provisions, and permission to ride to the Vale of Neume. Initially it surprised him to encounter spells set to trap the unwary; but his time in the castle of Andratan had served him well. No enchantment on earth could undo him, of that he was certain. True, he lost a couple of men. Seeing one of his soldiers burst into flame was a frightening moment, and the counter-spell he delivered was a moment too late to save the man (he wondered whether the momentary pleasure he experienced at the sight might have delayed his reaction), but he himself came through untouched. The Archivist's unbelief had been sorely tested, however, and during the scholar's whining moments of self-doubt the Arkhos found himself wishing the flames had consumed the Archivist instead.

Nevertheless, they won through to the Vale of Neume, there discovering that the northerners, accompanied by the guardians, were but a few hours ahead of them, having found a way into the Vale from the north. He laughed aloud then, for this made his task so much easier: all he needed to do was to follow the northerners to the Jugom

Ark, thank them politely, and take the Arrow from them. Then home to Instruere, where the Council and the entire city would rally behind him as he deposed the insolent Deorc. By this action, brave and brazen, his place at the right hand of the Destroyer would be assured.

"You no doubt wonder how I managed to ascend the mountain," he said. His breath, never very full, rattled in his throat at this altitude while he taunted his captives. "You wonder also at my presence on this side of the steel rope. How did I dare it?" He laughed, and the cruel sound cut the Arkhimm like knives.

"Arrogant fools! Did you think only yourselves capable of effort in pursuit of a goal? Is it not conceivable that if a rabble of northerners can climb a hill, their pursuers, trained warriors in the main, could follow them? By watching your feeble efforts with the rope, we might be able to emulate or surpass them? Such foolishness will reap its reward, as you will soon discover."

"What business do you have with this Arrow?" Kurr demanded. He was not daunted by this blusterer.

"What business? What business?" the huge man screamed, his face reddened, the blackness within him howled. "The Arrow is mine by right! I am the Arkhos of Nemohaim, descended from the stock of Bewray. This is my land! You are the trespassers!" He advanced on his captives, stabbing a fat finger in the direction of the old farmer. "I was—I *am* the ruler of the Council of Faltha: who else has a better claim on this heirloom than I? Certainly not a bunch of ragged peasants with delusions of grandeur!

"You thought you would be the saviors of Faltha. You will not. You thought you would deliver us from the clutches of evil Bhrudwo. Simpletons! Faltha needs

deliverance from arrogance like yours. Your simplistic view
of things is not wanted here—as if Faltha is wholly good,
or Bhrudwo wholly evil! Yes, I have been to Bhrudwo. Yes,
I count Kannwar, he who is erroneously named the Destroyer, among my allies. Who would not become friends
with such strength and purpose, given the chance? Who
would not accept assistance from such power, if assistance
is offered? Not fools like you! You would have us locked in
the past, secure in self-righteousness, rejecting a future
filled with possibilities for those with vision to grasp them.
You would make us all peasants. Well, I am no peasant! I
will not tolerate interference from such as you!"

Leith held the Jugom Ark tightly, breathing deeply to
calm his emotions. Already he noticed the Arrow was in
tune with his feelings, enflaming when his passions were
aroused, sinking into quiescence otherwise. He gave the
Arkhos only half an ear, for there was another voice im-
pinging on his consciousness. Not the voice of fire, the
voice which had impelled him to pick up the Arrow, but
the sound of the land itself, the expression of the potent
spell Bewray had placed here. *Unclean!* it screamed
silently. *Unworthy!* it cried. *Cleanse the land of this de-
filement! Destroy the intruders!* He listened to the words
for a while with mounting fear. Though in his heart Leith
knew the land's wrath was not directed at him or any of
his party—that from the beginning the whispering in
Joram basin had been directed at the Arkhos and his companions—he feared the land would not, could not discriminate between the trespassers and the rightful
claimants to the Arrow. He wondered that the magic-
trained Arkhos of Nemohaim could not hear the silent
voice. Perhaps his own hold on the Jugom Ark sensitized
him to the enchantment, and he heard clearly what others

could not. Behind him, above him in the fog-bound darkness, power built. Of what kind, or for what purpose, he could not guess. But something was going to happen.

"Don't surrender the Arrow to him," said Belladonna, struggling to speak against the knife-edge at her throat. "Hands like his should not sully the Jugom Ark."

"Then you will die," the Arkhos said, turning to her with a sneer.

"We're dead anyway, according to you. Why then should we obey you out of fear?"

The fat man's face leered at the young woman. "Perhaps, my dainty, your imagination might suggest a number of reasons. Or, if it does not, let me help you. I could have you wishing for death, in such pain you could not speak to beg for your release. Or maybe I could find some other use for you, perhaps as a reward to my men for a job well done, or even keep you for myself for a time, while you continued to please me. A woman like you would soon wish for death, any sort of death, rather than that kind of life. Do you see any reason to obey me now?"

Belladonna blanched, but returned his stare with a brave face.

"Is this the speech of one who would take Faltha into the future?" the Haufuth asked incredulously. "Does the new Faltha have no further need of morality?"

"Morality is but another vain attempt to control the lives of others," said the Archivist wearily. "It is a chain holding back the progress of all free people. Your goodness is just a cloak for fear and self-interest."

"Look, I don't have the patience to bandy words with you," said Phemanderac in steely tones, straining against his captor. "Good is still good, and wickedness is still wickedness, no matter what you call it. You have in your vaults a treatise on good and evil that would turn your heart, if only you would open yourself to it, but you favor your own wisdom over the combined wisdom of the ancients. Don't accuse *us* of arrogance! But enough! I will talk to the huntsman, not one of his dogs." He turned in his captor's grasp to look at the Arkhos of Nemohaim.

"You call the Arrow yours, and claim it by right of descent from those that bore it to this place. But that is not what the books and scrolls say. They tell us the Most High himself gave the Jugom Ark to the First Men as a symbol of unity, and it will be used to call all Faltha together in times of war. Two thousand years after it was hidden, the Arrow has now been found. And, at the moment of its finding, Faltha is threatened by the twin forces of evil: an invasion from without, and treachery from within. Yet you would use it to further your own selfish ends, making it a symbol of division, setting true Falthans against their traitorous masters. You have no right to touch the weapon of your master's punishment. Begone, before calamity befalls you!"

The Arkhos laughed then, a deep laugh that threatened to send him into a coughing fit. "Dear me," he chuckled, turning to his servants. "Such entertainment, and as yet no steel has been set to their flesh!" Within, his black voice cried out for their blood. *Give them to me!* "No right? No right? I have the right conferred by might, if no other. And it is a right I am ready to exercise!"

His face changed then, and he opened his arms wide in a gesture of conciliation. Behind him his shadow widened, appearing like a monstrous embrace in the torchlight. "Yet I can be merciful as well as just! Though your lives are forfeit for touching the Heirloom of Nemohaim, I might grant you pardon, if only you surrender the treasure freely to me. Just give me the Arrow, and you may all go your way."

He speaks in lies, Leith realized. *But why? Why beg for what he can take by force? Unless . . . maybe he fears the Arrow itself, wrested from us rather than given to him.* A glance at Phemanderac told Leith that he, too, struggled to comprehend the Arkhos's motive. He looked down at his hand: the Jugom Ark glimmered faintly in the dark.

Far above and behind him the power built towards a climax. *Hold him just a moment longer!*

Following his hunch, Leith took a step forward in the direction of the Arkhos, and held the Jugom Ark aloft, allowing it to glow a little brighter. "Why weary yourself with words?" he said pointedly. "Just come and get it! I am only a boy, and you have many guards at your command. What holds you back?"

For an instant the Arkhos's mask slipped, and the look he shot at Leith was a look of pure hatred. "You vermin! How could you have been allowed to live? Why were you not drowned at birth?" he said vehemently. Then, though his inner voice cried out for more, the Arkhos wrestled back control of his mind. "But here you are now," he said quietly, "and as my vision for a new Faltha is being questioned here, I will prove it is based on fairness beyond your wit to encompass. You may all go free, all of you, even those who have dared to raise their voice against the Arkhos of Nemohaim, if you but give me the Arrow. Give it to me!"

Leith nodded and walked forward. Belladonna let out a cry of anguish, clearly perceiving the youth was about to relinquish the Jugom Ark. For the same reason the philosopher struggled with his captor. But they could do nothing. Leith knelt before a rock, placed the Arrow there and withdrew.

"My hand is sore," he said conversationally. "I do not relinquish my claim to the Jugom Ark."

He stepped away. Behind him the mountains yammered.

"Mine!" the Arkhos cried; and, rushing forward, he picked up the Arrow.

And held it aloft.

And screamed and screamed and screamed as the Jugom Ark roared out in flame, engulfed his hand and arm, and seared his skin to the bone. The horrible sound reverberated around the Joram, shaking it like an earthquake. And indeed the earth shook. As the Captain of the Guard rushed to his maimed master's side, a boulder came leaping, crashing down from the heights far above, hurtling past them and diving into the lake with a great splash.

The Arrow fell to the ground with a clatter.

The earth rocked again. Leith was thrown down, then clambered to his feet, searching for the Arrow in the dark. If only it still glowed, he might be able to find it! All around them smaller stones rained down. Splashes extended far out into the lake, the water made choppy by the shaking earth.

Still the Arkhos screamed, an unearthly sound coming from somewhere in the darkness, a cry most like the howling of a wounded animal; the very sound of tortured agony. The noise increased rather than diminished in intensity, amplified and reflected by the amphitheatre-like basin around them. Rubble continued to slide into the lake.

"What's happening?" cried the Haufuth. A guard motioned for him to remain silent, but the Instruians were also in confusion. Their master gave them no thought, and their captain was occupied tending him, leaving them alone and leaderless. They did not know what to do, stand fast or flee.

"The Sentinels have awakened," said Belladonna.

"Sentinels?" Kurr inquired urgently amidst the confusion.

"Yes. For the two guardians there are two Sentinels. The two great mountains themselves, between whose arms Joram basin is set. The power is concentrated in them—"

"Be quiet!" yelled a guard, and cuffed her across the forehead. At that moment something dark and feral exploded at him. Achtal, the Bhrudwan, had made his way stealthily through the darkness and now drove his shoulder into the guard's midriff. Down the man went. His head smacked on the rough stony ground, and moved no more.

"Don't kill anyone! Don't shed blood here!" Belladonna warned them all, but her words were swallowed up in the rage of the land and the shrieking of the Arkhos of Nemohaim. Guard and Arkhimm moved through the night, trying to find and slay, or hide and escape. Torches bobbed here and there. Gravel crunched under feet. Dark figures—Leith one of them—tried to keep still as men (friend or foe, who could tell?) ran past in the fog.

Of them all Phemanderac was in the most perilous position. The Captain of the Guard had released Belladonna to aid his master, and she made good her escape, aided by Achtal. But the philosopher was held still by a guard, who now debated with himself whether to strike his captive down. There was none to guide him in the confusion: if only his captain was near! Nevertheless he made his decision, drew out a long knife and made ready to thrust it into the breast of the man he held.

"Release the prisoner!" came his captain's voice from behind. "He is of no importance. I need you to help me with the Arkhos."

Grateful for the guidance, the guard let go his grip, thrust Phemanderac away and turned to his captain. But it was too dark to see clearly, and the voice came again: "Come this way! Quickly!" He stumbled forward in his haste to obey; then he stumbled again, for his haste led him to the very edge of the great precipice. With no hope of arresting his momentum the guard pitched forward into nothingness. For a moment his wail of terror mixed with the cries of his Arkhos, then the fog claimed him and he was heard from no more.

Belladonna came out of the darkness and pulled Phemanderac to his feet.

"Your voice?" he said admiringly.

She nodded. "His blood was not spilled in the holy place," she said.

"Quite."

"It's all right, you don't have to thank me," she said somewhat testily. "If he'd seen through my ruse he would have chopped me to pieces, but I suppose it was worth the risk." She turned and stalked away into the riotous night, her shoulders hunched together angrily.

"But—but I am thankful," the philosopher stammered into the blackness, knowing she wouldn't hear him. *She's as prickly as her father.*

With a thunderous crash the basin shook again, writhing under his feet as though it was about to split asunder. Far above him Phemanderac could see a faint red glow. Perhaps the mountains themselves were on fire, responding to the peril of the Jugom Ark and the violence being done in the Joram below them. Where were the

others? In a panic now, he flung himself forward; then remembered the precipice just in time. He struck out off to
the right, seeking the others. In a moment he crashed into
a dark figure, winding himself. A guard, who now lay unconscious beneath him. *Where were the others?* Down
crashed a rock, shattering at his feet, showering him with
splinters and shards. *The mountain is coming apart: it is
perilous to remain here. Where is Leith? Where is the
Arrow?*

By chance, or by nothing at all, would Leith be able to
find the Jugom Ark now. Heedless of the commotion
around him, of the fighting and struggling, of the sobbing
and whimpering of the Arkhos, of the cataclysmic rage of
the Sentinels, he scrabbled about in the blackness trying
to find the Arrow by feel. It was slipping away. Moment
by moment the feel of it in his hand slid away from his
memory. Would he ever again be able to pick it up,
should he find it? Maybe he had done wrong by laying it
down, and now it hid from him, and would not have him
back, and all was lost. An idea came to him, from the land
itself perhaps, or from some other presence in this place.
*Fix your mind on it! Think of final victory, and the cast-
ing down of your foes!* He did so, and in that moment a
light flared a few yards away. There it was, down near the
stream that drained the lake. He scrambled down towards
it; then the earth heaved again, more violently this time,
and he was pitched upon his face. In a moment his head
cleared, and he raised it. The Arrow instantly flared in answer to his thought. But to his surprise it was further
away, and he realized it was sliding down into the stream.
In seconds it would be swallowed up, lost. Another explosion, a massive cracking sound like the ice on the

Southern Run and, to his horror, the earth parted. A deeper blackness amid the pitch of night. The stream was snared; the crack snaked back to the lake itself and began to empty Joram basin of water.

"No!" Leith cried, and hurtled down the slope. Another quake threw the Arrow into the air. Surely this time it would fall into the raging torrent and the black crack, but no! It hung on the very edge. A sour-sweet smell came up from the riven rock. Praying the earth would be still for just a moment longer, Leith reached the little shelf on which the Arrow perched. Without hesitation, disregarding the fate of the Arkhos, he took the Jugom Ark up in his hand; and again it did not burn him.

Now he turned up the slope, but the indiscriminate earth was not about to part with any of its prey so easily. The ground shook, and shook again. Leith fought to keep his balance, to keep from pitching backwards into the roaring abyss. Down on hands and knees, now down on his belly, he clung to the rock, trying to crawl forward, upwards. The earth shook again, this time jerking him sideways, rattling his jaw. *Up, up to safety*. Something pitched past him, crashing into the rocks below at the edge of the widening crack, emitting a groan as it landed, not resisting the slow pull of the blackness, slipping helplessly into the chasm while Leith watched, unable to lend any aid. *Who was that? Enemy or friend?*

The rumblings and shakings continued throughout the long night. As far as he could judge, Leith found himself on the eastern shore of the lake. Or, what had once been the lake, since now it had been drained away into the earth. For a time he wandered here and there, searching for his friends, but always walking with care lest he fall down some new-made chasm or stumble over the precipice that he knew was somewhere to his right. From time to time he called out, though he knew the risk he took. Should any of the Instruians remain alive in the basin and on his side of the earth-crack, he would be betraying his presence to them. For that reason he kept tight rein on his emotions, even though he felt close to panic; and the Arrow, comfortably warm in his hand, gave off nothing more than a faint red glow. But in that long, cold night filled with earth-anger and loneliness, Leith found none of his companions, and eventually, some time before dawn, he found a sheltered cavity near the chasm and, casting himself down carelessly, sought sleep.

Though the Captain of the Guard had some skill at setting bones and salving wounds, the horrific burns suffered by his master, the Arkhos of Nemohaim, were beyond him. They had some medical supplies, but these were down in the Vale of Neume with their horses, out of their reach until the morning. The Arkhos's arm had been severely scalded by the flame, and blisters overlaid melted skin up to the elbow. Those would heal in time, and gave the captain no great concern. Far more serious was the right hand, in which he had vainly clutched the Arrow for a brief moment. The golden shaft had burned through the flesh like a hot knife through lard, and the hand-bones were exposed in a line across what remained of his palm. There was surprisingly little blood, the heat of the arrow-shaft having effectively cauterized the wound, but for a while it appeared the Arkhos might die of shock. The Captain of the Guard had seen it happen. A sword wound, the loss of a limb, not life-threatening in itself, yet killing the victim because his body reacted too violently. Once the screaming and bellowing had died away, the

Arkhos had sat down and studied his hurt; and then shock set in. So the captain forced the Arkhos to his feet, making him walk about, keeping him awake, conscious, moving, until one of his men could tear up a shirt to form a makeshift bandage.

It was a fearsome struggle, but the Arkhos emerged from the far side of his pain with icy-calm emotions and a clear head. Clearer, indeed, than at any time since Deorc had come to Instruere. The deadly touch of the Arrow had brought him to his senses. He was not the kind of man who needed to rely on magic or devices of any kind. If he was to reclaim power he would do it on the strength of his personality, his ruthlessness and cunning. The Jugom Ark would have helped—still would help, if he could find some way to grasp it, or to control the one who was able to grasp it. But, he asked himself, had he really been so unsure of himself that he had been unwilling to match wits with Deorc unless he had the Arrow in his hand?

Give me Deorc. Give me them all! cried the black void within him. Surprisingly, even horribly, the Arkhos realized this inner part of him had enjoyed the pain, had wanted more, had sucked and sucked at him, as though trying to draw life from him. *Death is the ultimate experience*, he reminded himself. *It is the only thing that satisfies*. His own death, when it finally came, would be the most pleasurable experience of his life.

As the darkness gave way to the gray light of dawn, the Arkhos of Nemohaim felt strong enough to stand and look about him. Of the dozen Instruian guards and soldiers of Nemohaim that had made up his party, only four were left: himself, the Captain of the Guard, and two foot soldiers, one from Instruere and one from Bewray. The Archivist was lost to the great chasm that had opened up in their midst. Had he not fallen, the Arkhos would have ordered him thrown in, gold nugget and all.

And of the enemy there was no sign. The mist had thinned a little, so he could see maybe two hundred yards: none but the four of his party could be seen on this, the west side of the chasm; and on the far side, in a little hollow open in their direction, one body lay crumpled and still, hazy in the mist but obviously dead. Whether one of the northerners or one of his own men, he could not determine at this distance.

It was time to lay plans, and as his remaining Instruian foot soldier changed the bandage, the Arkhos of Nemo-haim called his faithful captain to his side. "We will have to assume at least one, and probably most, of the north-erners are alive," he said quietly. "Have you determined whether we can pass this chasm and pursue them?"

"The crack has riven the basin in two, my lord. It con-tinues from here right up to the cliffs behind the lake. There is no way to pass."

"Yet pass we must," said the Arkhos. "There is no going back down to the Vale, at least not for me. How could I pass the steel cable with a hand like this?" He held it up, a pink, oozing mass of flesh and bone.

"My lord, the cable is no more. Both it and the deep cut it spanned were swallowed up in the chasm that lies be-fore us. As we are on this side of it, nothing but a section of broken ground prevents us returning to our horses." From the tone of his voice it was obvious what counsel he would offer. "Horsed, we might be able to offer some sort of pursuit. However, you will not be able to sustain a long journey on foot in your weakened condition."

The Arkhos nodded quietly. "Perhaps the enemy might yet come to us. If they have lost any of their number, surely they will search the basin for them. All we have to do is to hide ourselves, then take one of the searchers captive. With one in our power, all will be in our power."

"If we cannot pass the chasm, neither can they, my lord," the captain reminded his master. "Though we might perhaps shoot anyone who ventures too close to the chasm. Dunay here is handy with a bow."

"What good would that do us?" growled the Arkhos, though the thought of such an act, even if only for revenge, caused his blood to sing in his ears. *Give them to me! Give them all to me!* "Could your man do it?"

"I have seen him do much better than hit a man-size target at a hundred paces," came the ready reply.

"Might we be able to wound him only, thereby attracting the others? It is the Arrow-holding boy I want. If I can get him to surrender to me, or if we could shoot him, our trip will not have been in vain."

"My lord, I readily admit my fear of this boy. I saw him on the day of the flood. The water of the Aleinus dried up at his outstretched arm, and returned to drown my men in response to the same command. He is a magician of some sort, a worker of miracles. Great power is in his arm. You saw how he held the Arrow, my lord, hot though it was, to no hurt."

"I saw."

"Then perhaps we would be better to attempt one of the others . . ."

"We will attempt whoever comes within range of our arrows," said the Arkhos. "We will hold them within range by the threat of death. Then we will force this boy-magician to give us the Arrow."

"We still have the problem of the chasm," pointed out the Captain of the Guard.

"If we provide him with enough incentive, perhaps the young miracle-worker will deal with that problem himself," said the Arkhos flatly.

As the darkness paled towards dawn, suffusing the mist with the gentlest of light, the Haufuth began to look about him and take stock of the calamity that had unfolded. He stood on a low shoulder of the eastern Sentinel, on the far side of the chasm from the scree slide. The mountain above him was quieter now, but still shook occasionally. The mist had thinned somewhat. Not enough to see the whole of Joram basin, but enough for him to see his friends.

Directly below him sat Kurr, Te Tuahangata, Prince Wiusago and the Escaignian in a little four-cornered arrangement, talking quietly together as they had been doing for hours now, ever since they returned from their last futile search for Leith. Some distance away, near the edge of sight and as near to the newly opened chasm as she dared, Belladonna stood, a forlorn figure; no doubt trying to discover what might have become of her father. Of Hal and the Bhrudwan he could see nothing: undoubtedly they continued the search long past hope or reason. There was no hope. The Haufuth himself had seen the figure of Leith tumble down the rocky slope into the widening ravine.

"The Sentinels have taken revenge on us," Phemanderac had said sadly when the worst of the confusion was over and they gathered at the edge of the basin in comparative safety. "The sacred site of the Arrow was violated, and the wildfire magic hidden in the hills burst forth to protect the Jugom Ark against an unholy touch.

The great crack in the earth swallowed the Arrow, taking it back underground."

"And it has taken Leith too," the Haufuth said. His heart mourned. "I saw him fall."

"I saw *someone* fall," ventured the Escaignian. "But was it Leith?"

"The glow of the Arrow fell with him," the big man confirmed. "He is lost."

"But why? Why?" Phemanderac fretted. "We did nothing wrong; I'm convinced of it. We *were* the chosen ones. Why did the Sentinels destroy our quest?"

"Perhaps they could not discriminate between friend and foe," Kurr suggested. His voice was grief-lined, as though the boy meant more to him than he had realized. "We all heard their whispered threats."

"I wonder if my father was right," Belladonna said quietly.

So much sadness here, the Haufuth thought.

"He said the girl was needed. He said the Arkhimm was incomplete. Maybe the mountains might not have rejected us if we had been up here alone, but when the others came, we were all deemed unholy."

"Whatever the explanation, we have lost Leith; and with him the hope of saving Faltha." A deep depression had settled then on the Haufuth, as the burden of failed leadership began to weigh on him.

"Nevertheless, we will go and look for him," Hal had said firmly. "If my brother is to be found, we will find him. Who will come with me?"

So they had searched and searched, stumbling in their weariness and sorrow, wandering back and forth between the chasm and the eastern edge of the basin until it seemed the night could not possibly last any longer. In his despair the Haufuth was reminded of the times during his childhood when he had mislaid something precious, usually something of his father's, and of the sick feeling nestled in the pit of his stomach as he searched in increasing futility for the object in question. He remembered the bargains he made with the Most High, what he promised to do for him if the object was found. Then, just as it did now, his anxiety had evolved into frustration and finally despair when he realized the god was against him. Then, as now, he had not found what he looked for. But now at least he made no bargains.

Sighing at his foolish recollections, the big headman made his way down to the others.

The Captain of the Guard barely had time to hunker down on his haunches and Dunay to fit an arrow to his bow, when the figure in the little alcove across the chasm began to move. At first he thought it was wounded, but after a few moments he realized the figure stretched as though it had endured an uncomfortable night.

"My lord!" he called urgently.

Instantly the Arkhos woke, and maneuvered himself to his captain's side. If he was in pain from the dreadful wound to his hand, he did not show it. *A truly remarkable man*, thought the Captain of the Guard, admiration momentarily overcoming his distaste for the man.

"He is alive," he whispered, pointing across the ravine. A moment later he added: "It is one of the northerners."

"It is the boy himself," said the Arkhos, wonderment in his voice. *So close! Delivered into my hands. The fates honor the rightness of my cause*. Deep within him his black voice cried out for blood. *Kill him! He's the one who humiliated you!*

. "I will not," he said clearly in answer, unaware that he had spoken aloud. "I will have him alive."

Leith stretched again, trying unsuccessfully to remove the knotted pain in his muscles. Beside him the Arrow lay quietly. He grasped it without fear, and the Jugom Ark flickered redly in his hand. *Live magic*, he thought. *Or not magic, but something more holy. The touch of the Most High remains in the Arrow. With such a touch, what is it capable of?* Slowly he unwound himself, rising to his feet.

"I have him at the tip of my arrow," Dunay reported flatly. "Shall I shoot?"

"Await the order of your captain," the Arkhos of Nemohaim replied.

His first task would be to find the others, Leith knew. If any of the others had survived the night. *I would exchange the Arrow and all the power it holds for their lives*, he thought, directing it almost as a plea to the Owner of the Arrow. As if in answer, he realized such an exchange was exactly the sort of thing the Most High might require of him, at the right time, when the exchange would ransom Faltha, not his friends. *I've seen Faltha*, Leith thought morosely. *I'd rather have my friends.*

<And your brother? What of him?>

Need you ask?

<No. But you need answer.>

Yes, then. Yes. I would surrender the Arrow and the power it promises in order to see my brother alive.

<Good. I will remind you of this.>

The voice left him then, as though satisfied that something significant had taken place. Leith yawned, reached inward for courage to face what he must face—even if it included discovering he alone survived the night—and made to begin his search.

"Captain!" Dunay whispered urgently. "I can shoot to wound."

"Hold your arrow," the Arkhos said tightly. Then, immersed in the deliberate irony of his words, he stood, making himself visible to the figure on the opposite side of the chasm. *I couldn't hold it. Let's see if you can.*

"Don't move!" a voice cried across the ravine. Leith stiffened at the sound of the Arkhos's hated voice. "We have arrows trained on you," it continued, "and we will not hesitate to use them if you do not do exactly as I say. Nod if you understand."

Without turning to face his tormentor, Leith could see the triumphant face in his mind, its pig-eyes glistening with evil delight. *Even yesterday I would have been vulnerable to this*, he thought. But not today. Not after he had picked up the Jugom Ark. After that risk, that terror, and with the awe in which he held the Arrow of Yoke, the threat of an ordinary arrow did not seem to touch him the way he would have expected. All this flickered past his mind in a moment, leaving him free to nod deliberately. He still had a task to complete, after all.

The Arkhos stepped forward eagerly, his arm outstretched. "Come," he called to Leith. "Come, grandson of Modahl. Come across the gulf to us. Join us! Or, if you cannot, throw the Arrow over to us."

Leith sensed an offer in those words, an invitation to betrayal. He turned around and faced the huge, obese man.

"The gulf between us is too wide. I could never join

you." His voice was sharp and clear, his words carried the recognition of their double meaning.

"My lord," whispered the Captain of the Guard, "someone comes." He pointed across the chasm where, in the mist above and behind the Firanese boy, shadowy figures moved.

"Lie flat on the ground," the Arkhos ordered Leith. "Any movement will attract the attention of my archers. Do it!" The Arkhos waited just long enough to see Leith obey his word, then he, too, took shelter. Underneath him the ground rumbled, moving slightly.

Down to where they could see the edge of the chasm came Kurr and Phemanderac, looking for any sign of their friend and companion and the Arrow he bore, determined to search even the depths of the ravine if they could. The old farmer held on to the unraveling threads of his emotions, his whole life, as he looked down into the black wound below them. Tears blurred his vision throughout the morning's search, tears Kurr thought he would never shed again after the death of Tinei his wife and heart's-love, but Leith's loss brought his own sorrow to the surface, and with it a burgeoning despair. It had seemed so much a part of his destiny, his traveling to Firanes so many years ago, meeting and being trained by Kroptur, the only Watcher of the Seventh Rank alive in Faltha. Then being on hand when the events leading to the revelation of the Right Hand of the Most High began, having a part in those events, then discovering he himself was a finger of God, one of the Five of the Hand. One of the Arkhimm. It was the culmination of his life's work. Even Tinei's death, which freed him to accompany the others west and south to Instruere and beyond, was necessary, sorrowful though it had been. Everything had been given meaning by the Jugom Ark. And now that it was lost, along with the only one who could hold it, the fragile structures of his recent beliefs had come tumbling down. He was on his own again in a raw and unreasoning world, where destinies evaporated and life had no meaning, and nothing and no one heard their prayers, and Tinei had died in vain.

The rock under his feet shook as the mountains above them stirred, as though offering their own answer to his mood. The faintest of whispers rippled across the Joram. A threat, a warning, the words indistinct. Kurr felt weak at the knees, as he had done every time since the Sentinels began to shake, taking revenge for the desecration of their sacred valley. In a moment the ground stopped moving. He went to take another step, then a great roaring rose from the depths of the earth. For a moment everything was held in some sort of stasis, while the world about them consisted only of the rock-wrenching sound. Kurr and Phemanderac clung to each other without realizing it. Then the earth heaved and buckled, throwing them both to the ground.

And it heaved again, and again, and the rocks crumbled under their prone bodies. All thought of searching for anyone left them. Terror-filled, they sought only to escape the quaking earth all around them, as it became clear the Sentinels had not finished with them yet. They had to flee, yet they could not even rise. The roaring and the shaking merged until sound and movement became as one, battering them as they lay.

As the basin pitched and spun around him, Leith could do nothing but grab hold of the sharp rock edges of the shallow depression he had slept in. He flattened himself against the rock, holding on for his life, buffeted and bruised, sobbing with fright, unable to take the chance to escape amidst the confusion of his enemies. Even in this extremity he refused to let go of the Arrow, though it meant he risked being pitched into the chasm.

Again and again the Arkhos picked himself up from the ground, only to be thrown down again by the agonized earth. The wound on his hand reopened and began to bleed, but he hardly noticed it. A great rage at being thwarted allowed no space for any fear he might have felt. "Shoot! Shoot!" he cried to his archer, but his voice was swallowed by the ear-numbing noise. Dunay could not have shot in any case, as he lay flat on his back, the wind knocked out of him by a hard fall. The Captain of the Guard was nowhere to be seen.

"Get out of here!" Phemanderac cried in Kurr's ear. "Now!" At any moment the mountains themselves and the basin between them might go sliding down into the Vale of Neume. A few stumbles at a time, made in between the worst of the shocks, were all the pair could manage.

Leith buried his head close to the rock, so did not see the chasm close up, a great wound healed in a powerful, astonishing instant. The solid rock rolled like waves of the sea, flowing from left and right as each Sentinel sent power down into the earth's very roots. The ravine filled with rock, leaving no trace of the fissure that a moment before had divided the Arkhos and his men from the questers for the Arrow.

Leith lost his grip on the Jugom Ark. It went bouncing away out of sight, soundless amidst the surrounding din. He turned his head to follow its path and cracked his temple on a temporary swelling of rock. The darkness roared, and his mind went out like a doused candle.

Some time later he awoke, and the world about him had changed. The mist dissolved under the gaze of the morning sun, which squatted low over him like an angry father. The ground still shook, but not as vigorously as before, and the tremors were intermittent now. His first coherent thought was about the Arrow. *Where is it?* He tried to stand, fell on to all fours and was noisily sick on the bare rocks. A little while later he raised himself to his feet, gingerly and with care so as not to send his head spinning again. There was a strong metallic taste in his mouth.

A bizarre landscape unfolded before him. What had once been—what had only yesterday been—a place of sacred beauty was now a chaotic wreck, testimony to the wrath of the magic Bewray had woven into the fabric of the rock. The island in which the Arrow had been hidden was gone, along with the lake that had surrounded it. The basin of the Joram was now a rock-pit, like the quarry at the head of White Forks valley a few miles to the west and north of Vapnatak; all cliffs and angularity, with newly faceted black boulders lying where they had fallen. Rock-slides continued to tumble boulders and stones down into the crumpled hollow.

Leith craned his aching head skywards, and there stood the Sentinels revealed. Stern heights towered above him, to the left and to the right, but both peaks were hidden in wispy cloud, as though reluctant to give up all vestiges of secrecy. "What have you done to my friends!" he shouted at them. They did not reply, and the effort nearly made him black out again.

A few yards behind him the basin ended abruptly, and the land fell two thousand feet to the Vale of Neume, smoking hazily in the morning sun. Leith swallowed. He had not realized how close to the edge he had been.

A noise like the rattle of a rock just behind him made him jerk his head around. It was for that reason as much as the sight of a large robed figure not five yards away that he fainted.

In this fashion did Maendraga, Guardian of the Jugom Ark, come upon Leith of Loulea, the sole remaining member of the Arkhimm.

CHAPTER 18

STELLA'S CHOICE

THE SMILING, DARK-HAIRED MAN had indeed received the fire, the first to do so under Stella's tutelage. She merely asked the Most High to meet his needs, and as she extended her hand towards him he fell to the ground, seemingly unconscious. Concerned, Stella moved to help him rise, but the Hermit himself stepped in. "Let him lie there and soak for a while," advised the blue-robed man. "He'll laugh later."

"What's happening to him?" Stella asked, uneasy at the increasingly strange sights she was seeing in the Ecclesia. "Is he one of the Blessed?"

"Yes, he is one of the Blessed," confirmed the Hermit. "The anointing of power is strong on him. He is marked out for a high destiny, and his deeds will be heard the world over. But leave him for now. He communes with the Most High in his own way."

Half an hour later the dark-haired man, having recovered, sought Stella out. "Thank you for what you have given me," he said politely. *I am innocent, I am obvious; don't think too hard about who I am or what I'm doing.* The Wordweave was subtly applied, and Stella was unaware of it.

"That's all right," she replied, smiling herself. "Though it was the Most High, not me. The Hermit says you are one of the Blessed."

"Oh?" His fine features registered surprise. "What are the Blessed?"

"They are the ones who will play leading roles in the re-birth of this city," Stella said earnestly. "He said there is an anointing of power on you."

"Did he? I should very much like to meet this man. Would you be able to arrange it for me?" *There is some-one else I would like to meet even more.*

"I can ask him," she said sweetly. "Would you like me to be there too?" Now why had she said that?

"I haven't asked you your name," the handsome man said. "Do you have one? And where are you from? You are no Instruian, that is for certain." He smiled as he asked the questions, but the Wordweave probed deeper: *you will have no secrets from me.*

Stella found herself talking with this fascinating man, and with little prompting telling him about their adventures, sharing with him her part in their endeavor. She took him to her primitive home in the cold north, sparing him none of her scorn for the place of her birth, then on along the Westway through Mjolkbridge and Windrise, past the Fenni and into the danger of the Roofed Road. She dwelt for a while on events in Bandits' Cave, surprising herself with her recollections; for some reason her companion listened to the tale of Hal and the Hermit with particular interest. Then she described their adventures on the Southern Run, and the battle with the Bhrudwans; again the man listened carefully, asking seemingly artless questions designed to reveal the strength of the northerners. Then, skilfully interrupting her as she moved on to matters known to him, he told her of himself. His name was Tanghin, he said; he was from Bhrudwo, a land far to the east, a nephew of the King of Jasweyah and a man of great wealth. "I am here on my master's business, to deal with the Council of Faltha," he said, the greater deceit being in the perfect truth of the words. "I will be here for some months. I hope I have the chance to get to know you better."

"I hope so too," said Stella, a little breathlessly.

"Do you really think the Ecclesia can bring about the changes you say?" Tanghin shaped his voice to sound naively skeptical.

"All change starts at the personal level," replied the Hermit earnestly. "Once you have changed from the inside, once you have caught the fire, then you can do anything. And a city of people like that, united in purpose and vision behind the man of God—what could they not accomplish?"

"Ah yes, the man of God. You are that man?" *What do you really think?*

"I am merely he who prepares the way," answered the Hermit humbly. "I am the fire-starter. But the fire is the important thing, not the man."

"So what happens next?"

"I have no idea," came the candid reply. "But I do know the Most High has a part for you to play. Will you play that part?"

"And what part is that?" Tanghin leaned forward in his chair, projecting passionate interest.

"You are a leader of men; it is written all over you. You are a man of many gifts. But you stand on the knife-edge of decision. To follow the Way of Fire will cost you everything. Your allegiance to your country, your position, and much of your wealth. But what you gain will be far greater: a chance to serve the Most High, and to see the presence of the Most High established once again amongst the First Men of Faltha." Now the Hermit leaned forward, and spread his arms wide. "I see you in a vision. You have your arm outstretched, and fire falls on Falthans—yes, even the Council of Faltha burns at your command. The true power of life or death is in your hands."

You speak truly. Aloud, he said: "I want to see all Faltha burn," and as he spoke his smile spread wider.

Stella watched and listened as the two men talked. Undoubtedly this man Tanghin was destined for greatness in the Ecclesia. Indeed, he could even be the man of god the Hermit talked about. And she had given him the fire! Surely now they would begin to take her seriously, and treat her as something more than a child.

As they talked, her thoughts drifted away. She was so thankful now that Wira and she had not married. She was sorry for his fate, but she was free to serve the Ecclesia, and Tanghin was a handsome man of substance . . .

As late summer matured into autumn, the Ecclesia grew beyond Foilzie's basement, forcing the Company to take lodgings across the street. The Hermit was in complete control now, taking counsel only seldom, and that with a group of "elders," as he called them—they were all men, and some were barely out of their teens—most of whom Stella barely knew. Meetings started in other parts of the city, each placed under the care of an elder. When asked why he neglected the northerners in choosing his leadership, the Hermit would reply, in a kindly tone: "The fire has started here in this city. Why should not the Instruians set the torch to Instruere?" And to his closest advisers he would add, more sharply: "Though my companions have a great anointing, they are proud and unwilling to let go of their understanding of the cause. The Most High can do nothing with them until they come to repentance. They must submit to the leadership." And his elders would nod wisely, pleased with the notion of the northerners under their authority.

In those days the man called Tanghin rose high in the regard of the Hermit, showing himself to be wise and a leader of men, not allowing sentiment to cloud his judgment. Thus he was appointed an elder, to the delight of Stella, though she could not help but wonder at the speed of his elevation; and he was given charge of the meeting at the Talman market, in the north of the old city of Inna, near the northern gate. Long hours he and the Hermit spent in conversation, and the blue-robed visionary learned much from his trusted adviser. "You have great experience in the governance of men," said the Hermit, "and I am grateful the Most High has married you to our cause."

Tanghin smiled, and replied: "I have written to my king, telling him I resign from his service. From now on I will work here in Instruere to see that the fire spreads. And, indeed I seek to be married to your cause in a way your prophetic tongue no doubt anticipated. I will seek the hand of the northern girl Stella. Would you grant me leave to do so?"

Then the Hermit smiled also, and gave his blessing to the match. For Stella was in the palm of his hand, and by this marriage he would bind Tanghin to him.

It was a night typical of all nights at the Ecclesia. Hundreds packed in and around the basement to hear the

Hermit speak, and to receive the fire for themselves. On this night a man Stella had never seen before stepped on to the stage. He was dressed in the garb of a peasant.

"Now they are coming even from outside the city!" she whispered in wonder to Tanghin, who nodded in agreement.

The peasant brought forth a shallow bowl filled with water, and set it on the platform beside him. "There will be a great shaking," he cried, "a great shaking; and the basin will be shaken, and water will be spilled." Grasping the bowl with both hands, he shook it to emphasize his words, spilling its contents on to the platform. "The Arrow will be found, and it will be protected by the two Great Ones. Many will try to lay their hands upon it, but only one will carry it." He turned to the Hermit. "That's all I received," he said.

Now the Hermit rose to his feet. "This is what the Most High says," he intoned, interpreting the vision. "A great shaking is coming, in which he will shake the hearts of men everywhere, but beginning here in the basin of Faltha. It has already begun! Behold the beginning of the shaking!" He spread his arms wide, indicating the people standing before him. "From here it will overflow into all Faltha, an outpouring of the presence of the Most High, shaking men out of their lethargy. The Arrow mentioned by our friend is the will of the Most High, the direction he wants us to go, which will soon be revealed by two among us who will be called great. Seek that revelation, brethren, for it will bring you honor. Yet in the end only *one* man will be shown worthy, and to him the direction of the Ecclesia will be entrusted." This last he said in such a way that there could be no doubt as to who he believed that one to be.

Another prophecy went like this. "One is soon to be

revealed, in whose hand the Arrow will flame," cried a woman in the throes of ecstasy. "He will lead us into battle with our enemies, and we will conquer them. Many will fall in that day; only remain true to the end, and you will see the victory."

"This is what the Most High says," said the blue-robed Hermit. "Only one man will carry the true direction for the Ecclesia, and thus for all of Faltha. He will burn with the fire of the Most High, and his fire will sweep through Faltha, setting alight many hearts. With the fire in their hearts, the people of Faltha will have the courage to face their inner enemy—whether it is a spirit of doubt, or of fear, or of rebellion. If they persevere, never giving up, they will defeat these enemies, and drive them out."

Later that night the Trader sat down with his beautiful wife. Tonight they talked of serious things: the fate of their sons, the uncertainty of their quest, and the meaning of the unlooked-for Ecclesia. Mahnum shook his head. "It's not right. It just doesn't feel right. I wasn't dragged halfway across Faltha in order to listen to the ravings of a mystic."

"You're wrong," said his wife. "The Most High used the only method that would have brought you here. If someone had come to Loulea and told you to travel here to receive the fire of the Most High, would you have made the journey?"

Mahnum shook his head. "But why me? Why us? Surely there were people in Instruere who could have kindled the fire?"

"Perhaps not," said Indrett. "Perhaps our hearts were the most open. Perhaps we were the best the Most High could find. And look! Our Company was gathered from many places, not just Loulea. Why do you think that is?

Could it not be that the Most High wants them to take the fire back to their own lands?"

"But what of Hal and Leith and the others? What about the quest for the Jugom Ark?"

"That's just the symbol. You've heard the prophecies about the Arrow; it signifies the direction that the man of god will take us in. We have the reality here. And I wouldn't be surprised if the Arkhimm return to Instruere with representatives of the southern kingdoms. It would fit the pattern. Then, after they catch the fire, the Most High can send them back to their own lands."

"Do you prophesy?" asked Mahnum, intrigued. He had never seen her like this before.

"Call it a prophecy if you like," she said.

"You've changed. I'm not sure I like it."

"You need to change," she retorted, "and you're rejecting the one thing that can help you do it."

"I'm not so sure. I think maybe our one hope has gone south with our sons. I wish my father were alive, he always saw true. He would know what to do."

"Sit down, Stella," said Indrett kindly. "Tell me what troubles you."

"Indrett, I don't know what to do," the young woman gushed. "My friend Tanghin has come to me with a proposal of marriage."

"Marriage?" Indrett exclaimed, bewildered. She knew Tanghin, of course. Everyone in the Ecclesia had seen this well-spoken, forceful stranger. But he and Stella? How had this happened? *She is not ready for life yet!*

"I'm so excited I can hardly keep still," Stella was saying. "Yet something worries me. Something burns in the pit of my stomach, a feeling of unease. It's there all the time, whenever I'm with him. Oh, Indrett! I'm afraid the feeling will never go away, and I will never be happy with him. What should I do?"

Stella raised her eyes to those of the older woman, and noticed the paleness of her face. Belatedly she considered the older woman might be tired—too tired, probably, to talk about Tanghin this late at night. "I'm sorry, Indrett," she murmured. "I can see by your face you are weary. Perhaps we can talk another time."

"I am weary." Indrett sighed. "You may think that is why I am drawn of face, if you wish; but there is another reason. Stella, would you hear the truth?"

"I would," came the reply. "But aren't you going to congratulate me about my news?"

"No, I won't," said the older woman, and Stella gasped with surprise.

"But he's so handsome! Well favored in mind and body, with power and possessions to offer security to any woman he chooses. He could choose any, and yet he has chosen me! And," she added, as though an afterthought, "he is one of the Blessed now. I could not imagine a more different man to Druin back home. If I had to pick between them, I know who I'd choose!"

"But you do not have to choose," said Indrett urgently. "Listen, now. I have a story you need to hear. Will you listen? Will you hear the truth?"

"I have already said I will," she said, snapping the words a little. *How can she not wish me well? I have made a match far above my station. Could it be she is jealous?*

"I was young once, and I can still remember what it is like, though you might not think so. My father was one of the many servants who lived and worked at the court of the Firanese king at Rammr. All his life he never became more than a footman to the Duke of Nordviken. He was fortunate compared with his relations and school fellows, some of whom were reduced to begging on the streets for a living, but in his ambition he did not see it so. We were not rich, but we always had food on the table. After my mother died my father went to pieces, and would have lost his place at court altogether if my older brothers had not already begun work there for the duke. He made life very hard for all of us, and when I reached an age where I might have expected to attract promises of marriage, my father drove them away.

"His frustrated ambition was more than he could bear. By day he had to serve at the court among those he sought to emulate, and when he came home at night he— he . . . did things to his children. Wrong things." Indrett faltered. "He sought to exercise a different kind of power over us. We became part of his fantasy world, his unwilling subjects. We were the only ones he could bend to his will. It drove my oldest brother mad."

Indrett's beautiful face stared straight ahead, and her features were drawn and gaunt. It was the one thing she did not want to talk about, but knew she must, and compelled herself to continue.

"By that time I had become a lady-in-waiting to the queen herself, and they all said I was a beauty; yet the years slipped by and still I had no lover but my father. There were those who sought to take my love without first taking my hand in marriage, but in horror I refused them all. I continued to rise in the favor of the queen, surpassing all the other ladies, even the duchesses themselves, and those who visited the court often mistook me for one of the princesses. Yet my father was never satisfied. We were servants still, with no titles or lands, and no honor, or so he thought; yet we had less honor because of his grumbling, and eventually he was forced out of his job.

"At that time the eldest son of King Clymanaea came of age, and with the consent of his father he began courting me. Such a thing was unheard of, that a prince might marry a commoner, but the king and queen ignored the gossip. I was flattered. Who would not be? So I welcomed the prince's interest. My father was beside himself with excitement, seeing in this his chance to gain in a single stroke what he had missed out on all his life.

"Oh, Stella! For a while I seriously contemplated marrying the prince. Had I done so, there is every chance I would be the ruler of Firanes at this moment; for the prince became King Prosala I, and died young. But down through the dark years of my childhood I had grown to know myself, my likes and dislikes, my strengths and weaknesses; and I knew that I could not live in a palace forever. I did not want my every move subject to public scrutiny. I did not want to be known as the 'commoner princess.' Oh, the prince was nice enough. Handsome, cunning, if a little slow. At times I even enjoyed his company. But because I knew myself, in the end I came to realize I did not want to marry him.

"My father was furious, and beat me until my brothers had to haul him off me. See here?" She indicated a small white scar under her chin. "A legacy of his wrath. There are others. I suppose that decided me in the end. I did not want to be defined by him or anyone else. The footman's biddable daughter. The prince's wife. I needed no husband to give me worth! I would not be forced into marriage by a father who saw me as a means to an end! Who used me as a means of self-gratification!"

The young woman watched uncomfortably as the older woman sobbed quietly.

"Stella, I know you understand me. You are part of a family that doesn't work properly. You had to put up with your brother and his drinking, your parents and the slow death of their relationship. Like me, your deepest desires spring from this. You want to be as far away from your family as possible. So did I! But to give in to this desire, this fear, is only another kind of victory for them. I was determined my father would not shape my life in that fashion. I would not marry, I decided, but neither would I run.

"Then one day a man from the north—a great Trader, the most famous of his day—came to court with his son to celebrate midwinter. Modahl the Trader! Everyone had heard his fame, everyone knew the stories told of his exploits. Yet I had eyes only for his son, Mahnum. Stella, he was everything I wanted. Not security: I already had that. But he was excitement, and comfort, and a sharp mind, and courtesy, and honesty, and companionship; and he returned my love. He had nothing to offer me but a woodsman's hut in the cold and primitive north, but I wanted him, not some position or fulfillment. So we married, and went to live in Loulea."

Stella drew a deep breath. "Have you been happy?" she asked.

"Yes—and no," came the slow answer. "He is all I could ever have wanted in a friend and a lover, but there have been many times, especially lately when he has traveled far away, when I have felt a certain lack. I wonder now whether any one person can be everything to you. I don't know; I think perhaps all this commotion about the Most High is part of the answer. To be pleasing to the Most High—now that would be something to satisfy the heart."

"So you found the right man for you. What if Tanghin is the right man for me?"

"Stella, something about that man troubles me. He is well mannered and intelligent, and there is no denying that he is rich and powerful. But he is a manipulator. He says exactly the right things. He is too calculating, as though he knows exactly how to get what he wants. In fact, he is a lot like you, only much more cunning."

"Like me? I thought we were completely different." Stella did not enjoy the turn of the conversation.

"You show all the signs of a trapped woman, one without power. I saw them at the Firanese court. Having no position of their own, and being controlled by men of power, they learned how to demand things by not asking. The suggestion that something was amiss, the merest hint as to what it was, the sulking and tears if it was not granted. I have seen powerful men completely tamed by such measures."

"You have just described my mother," said Stella sadly.

"And I have just described you."

"But I don't want to be like my mother!" she said vehemently.

"See? Again you define yourself by a negative, by comparison with someone else. Who do you want to be like? Who amongst your friends and acquaintances is most like who you want to be in the future?"

Stella flushed a little. "You," she said finally. "Well, you did ask."

It was Indrett's turn to be nonplussed. "Then listen to me," she said eventually.

"I'm listening," said Stella, "though I'm not enjoying what I'm hearing."

"Oh, Stella; you can't marry Tanghin. Not now, not when you still have so much growing up to do. It would be a constant battle between the two of you, each trying to get the other to do what he or she wanted. Eventually one of you would win—probably him, because you have been used to a life of submission, and he a life of power. Then you would be lost forever."

"Then who? Who do I marry?"

"No one. Don't marry anyone. Don't marry Tanghin, don't marry a Vinkullen woodsman, don't marry a Loulean peasant. Love someone first, then if you want to love him for the rest of your life, marry him. But don't get married for the sake of marriage, for the fear of being alone."

"But I want to *do* something! I want to *be* someone!" Stella cried. "At least Tanghin *is* someone!"

"And we are not? You silly little girl," Indrett replied, and again Stella sensed that Indrett spoke more to herself. "Don't you realize those things don't matter? At the end of your life the measure of success is whether or not you've done well in the little things, the mundane things. Things like these: did you obey those who needed obeying? Were you merciful and just with those under your care? Was your conduct honorable? Did you truly love— not the feeling, but the act? Did you give yourself to things like passion, ambition and success, or did you give your life to people? Stella, whoever is cherished by another, that person *is* someone."

The young woman nodded.

"I watched my father die. After the life I endured because of that dreadful man, after all he put me through, I still cried that night. Mostly because of the terrible waste.

He spent his whole life trying to be someone, and failed at the more important things. I saw him die in the knowledge that he was alone, he had won no earthly friends; and when his eyes closed that last time he knew they would not open on the other side to look on the Most High. He had lost his last chance at loving, and being loved, and only darkness awaited him. He had lost everything, Stella; everything worth keeping. Do you understand? It doesn't matter whether the people you are supposed to love live in a village or a palace, the job of loving them is just the same. It is not *where* you are, but *who* you are that counts."

Slow tears rolled down Stella's cheeks. "Is there no easy way to live?" she said, half-pleadingly.

"Not if you really want to live," Indrett replied hesitantly, as if she herself unwrapped this truth for the first time. "We who have endured capture and pursuit, hunger and thirst, and have watched companions die, should not deny the truth of this. Here we are, in Instruere. Would you rather all this had not happened, and that we remained in Loulea?"

"No!" said Stella passionately. "I've been waiting for this all my life."

Indrett nodded. "In a strange way, so have I," she said quietly.

Then talk ceased, as they sat together, holding hands, thinking about what had passed and what might still be to come.

The two men walked quietly, even furtively, down one of the many corridors associated with the Hall of Lore. They were Council members, the Arkhoi of Vertensia and Piskasia; and they walked quietly because of the propensity of their new master, Deorc, the Keeper of Andratan, to appear anywhere without warning.

"I hear he's found a girl amongst them," said Vertensia. "That's what is keeping him away."

"Whatever the cause, I can't thank it enough," Piskasia replied fervently. "The man is an abomination."

"Keep your treason to yourself," came the half-hearted rebuke. "You know what he does to those who stand in his way. You mustn't do anything to prejudice your recent conversion from the loyalists."

The Arkhos of Piskasia shuddered. Along with the other Council members he had been forced to watch the execution of the remaining loyalists, and found it extremely distasteful, even though his chest burned with relief that he escaped the flames that had licked the limbs of his former friends. Deruys, Redana'a and Sna Vaztha died nobly, and Redana'a had fixed Favony, a distant kinsman, with a gaze at once pitying and convicting. He had turned guiltily from that stare.

The Council sent immediately for replacements. While the kings of Deruys, Redana'a and Sna Vaztha might be suspicious, there was little they could do about it; and none of them would wish to be without a representative on the Council of Faltha. The replacement from Deruys would arrive within two or three weeks— Deorc had said he had a strategy to deal with him— while the other two would take months. By then, if what Deorc said about the Bhrudwan schedule was correct, they would be too late.

"She's a looker, that's for certain," Vertensia said quietly, even wistfully. Piskasia, remembering his companion's unsavory reputation, shuddered. "I can understand why Deorc wants her."

"Why, have you seen her?" Piskasia asked, curious despite himself.

"I have, and so have you. She's one of the northerners who came to accuse us. Remember her? Raven-black hair, flames for eyes. A bit young, but the fresher for it. If I was to meet her alone in one of these corridors, I wouldn't be answerable for my actions."

Around a corner they swung, and there, standing in the center of the corridor, was Deorc, his expression unreadable. The Arkhos of Vertensia turned white with fear.

"You would answer for any rash action, my colleague," said the Keeper of Andratan levelly. "Therefore you will control yourself, for you know the penalty for foolishness, especially with what is mine."

Vertensia had reason enough to fear. He had just made an enemy of the one man he needed to befriend. But his fear went beyond reason. There was a hidden power in the words this man spoke which turned his courage to water, leaving him vulnerable to every command or suggestion the man made.

"You will take no action against the northern girl, or against any one of the Ecclesia, or against any of their meetings. Let it be known they have the favor of the Council, and in them we see the hope of restoring Instruere to her former glory and pre-eminence amongst the cities of the world." His voice was firm, steel-sharp, slicing neatly through any objections the two Councillors might raise. "Then, my friend Vertensia, you will report to my office. I have thought of something to occupy those hands that otherwise might get you into serious trouble."

Not even waiting for a reply, the handsome man strode off, leaving the Arkhoi alone to contemplate his will.

* * *

Mahnum and Indrett had agreed to face Stella with their concerns about her relationship with Tanghin. They had met with the girl in their room late at night. In the Ecclesia, late at night was the only time available for talking. However, the conversation was not going well.

"Will you take me back to Loulea?" Stella asked pointedly.

"Once Leith and Hal return, we will all go back to our homes," Mahnum replied. "You are our responsibility. Therefore you will come back with us."

"Surely the Haufuth took me on this adventure?" said Stella. "Is it not for him to say what should happen to me?"

"You are right," Indrett replied. "But it would be remiss of him to do anything other than take you home to your parents."

"Unless I was married, of course," she said.

"He would not give his consent."

"Perhaps not, but the Hermit would." Stella was angry now, and she used her answers as weapons to wound her friends.

"The Hermit is not your guardian. You are the responsibility of the Haufuth."

"Not so! I have pledged allegiance to the fire and the Hermit, and I am one of the Blessed. Neither the Haufuth nor my parents have dominion over me any longer."

"So you would get married without your parents' blessing, and against the will of your village headman, simply to avoid returning to Loulea?" Indrett tried to control her fury.

"Do you doubt it? Instruere is the center of the world, and right now is the center of time. Here and now the fire is falling, and you want me to crawl back to the woods and become a simple village girl again? I was fashioned for more than that! I will not pass up the chance to change the world!"

"So you would disobey us all to follow your god?" Mahnum asked quietly, and everyone knew so much hinged on the answer.

"I would," said Stella, "and such is the Hermit's counsel. He says that of all our Company only I have shown the commitment necessary to carry the fire."

"Then by your words is the movement itself condemned," said Mahnum. "The Most High would not require you to commit evil in order to achieve good. My mind is at rest. I have long felt uneasy about the strange tree the Hermit is growing, and now I can see some of its fruit, I will not partake of it."

"It is evil only according to your outdated traditions!" Stella spat. "I would give up my parents, my friends, even life itself, for a touch of the fire!"

"As long as it suited your purposes," said Indrett angrily. "You know nothing of true sacrifice. I have heard enough. From now on, I forbid you to see Tanghin without one of us present. I only hope you do not represent the best of the movement, or I will have to agree with my husband. Now, go to your room and think a while on what we have said."

After she stormed from the room, the husband and wife stared at each other for a time. The meeting had not gone well, they knew it; and her decision hung in the balance.

Stella returned to her room in a dreadful state. How could following the Most High be so difficult? She had loved and respected Mahnum and Indrett, even before this quest began; but no more. She could see it now. They were tools of the enemy, the dark forces the Hermit always talked about, the spiritual Bhrudwo that had dominated Instruere for a thousand years. Stuck in their traditions, their old ways of thinking, how could they be expected to see the new thing the Most High was doing? Of course they would counsel her to take the safe course, and to run no risks, because that is how they themselves had chosen to live. She should have seen it before! They had passed up life in the court of Firanes for the safety and tedium of the North March. *Well, that was their choice, but they are not going to force it on me! I will take the risk! I will do something with my life! I will not return like a scolded puppy to Loulea, there to become the property of the village brute!*

As the tears streamed from her eyes, Stella found herself pulling her pack out from under her bed. Hardly thinking about what she was daring to do, she packed a change of clothes and a few small personal items, then drew the ropes tight. She put on her dark travel cloak, then shouldered her pack. As it settled on her back she thought clearly for a moment, reminded of the quest and the danger they had all thought hung over Faltha; she laughed it off, reassuring herself about just how wrong they had all been. The future was one of peace, not war. And across the city Tanghin waited.

Her room was on the second floor of the tenement, and one or two of the others had not yet gone to bed. Intuitively Stella knew what she had decided to do ought to be done quickly, before she had the chance to reflect on it, but she was forced to wait the best part of an hour before all the doors below were closed. That time was torture for her, as she tried to resist her childish fears. *What will my mother say? She thinks I'm dead anyway. What if*

Tanghin doesn't want me? Of course he wants me, none of the others do! And so on until she gathered the shredded rags of her fears, knitted them into something approaching courage, and quietly left the tenement.

The sun set in red flame, spreading an unearthly orange cast over the Brownlands. A black army, vast as thought, poured like ants on the march over the hills and hollows. In the van strode the Honor Guard of Andratan, thirteen thirteens, each robed in the garb of a *Maghdi Dasht*, the most fearsome of all Bhrudwan warriors. And at their head marched the Ancient One, the Undying Man, Blackheart, Kannwar One-Hand the Destroyer, the foe of the Most High.

As night fell the army halted, and the Destroyer went aside with his Honor Guard. There, on a bleak rock that served as an altar, they prepared the blue flame; blood and oil intermingling in a sacred bowl to allow the wielder of magic to stretch out his senses over thousands of miles. Tonight the Destroyer responded to the summons of his lieutenant Deorc.

The unwavering blue flame spoke in Deorc's measured tones. "I have done as you commanded," said the disembodied voice. "I have divided the city against itself, and have set enmity in the hearts of the northerners. While some of them are temporarily out of my grasp, I wait with the trap baited, my finger on the spring. It only requires their return for the trap to be sprung. Then, my lord, the city will destroy itself just as Dona Mihst destroyed itself so long ago."

"Will they return?" asked the Destroyer.

"They must. I have not been able to discover their purpose, but I suspect they are in league with the Arkhos of Nemohaim. They will return with strength to join their companions, but that strength will spring the trap and unleash Falthan against Falthan. I will save the Arkhos for you."

"Good," said the Undying Man. "You have pleased me."

"My lord, you have taught me all I know," purred Deorc.

First Stella checked the basement, but Tanghin was not there; only a few groups of people remained, engaged in conversation. According to a man she knew only vaguely he had left some time ago.

She knew where his lodgings were, but they were a long way away and it was the middle of the night, in a city that nominally at least still observed a curfew, and in which murder was almost a nightly occurrence. Nearly then did she abandon her wild plan and return home; but she could not bear the imagined sight of those self-satisfied, superior faces issuing further instructions designed to hem her life in. So onward she went, down roads and through alleys that looked menacingly unfamiliar in the darkness.

Perhaps an hour later a sobbing and badly frightened Stella reached Tanghin's lodgings. In truth she had encountered nothing other than a scavenging dog, but it had unnerved her, and the girl who had defied the Bhrudwan warriors on the Roofed Road could find no trace of that courage now. To her surprise and fear two members of the Instruian Guard stepped out of the deeper shadows as she approached the tenement.

"What are you doing here?" they asked roughly. This was a wealthy area of town, they knew all the residents, and this girl was not one of them. Then, as she moved into the half-light, they both knew who she was.

"I'm here to see Tanghin," she said, more timidly than she would have liked.

"Tanghin?" One guard looked at the other, and Stella thought she read surprise on his face; but it was gone in a moment, if it had ever been there. "Tanghin's not here."

"Where is he, then?"

"He's gone to speak with the Council," was his unexpected reply.

"The Council?" Stella echoed feebly.

The guards had their instructions: "If the northern girl comes looking for Tanghin, then bring her to me," their master had said. "That's right," one said. "Would you like to see him?"

"I'm going to find him," said Stella determinedly.

"We're coming with you."

"Why? I'll be all right." But in truth she was glad they insisted. The company of the guards was better than facing the dark city night alone.

It took half an hour to make their way to the Hall of Lore. Patrols stopped them at regular intervals, and Stella was astonished at the extent to which the Instruian Guard controlled the sleeping city. She had assumed the fall of the Arkhos of Nemohaim, and the growth of the Ecclesia, had robbed the guard of its potency. At least that's what the Hermit had said, and Stella had seen few of them about for ages; but here they were, numbers undiminished. Why had the Ecclesia been allowed to grow unmolested if the guard still controlled the city? A strange sense of foreboding closed around her as they approached the squat black outline of the Hall of Lore.

Down cold, unlighted corridors they tramped, until they came to a half-open door. The guards stepped back, knowing something of their master's business and so uncertain as to whether to knock; but Stella rushed forward and stepped through the door.

There, in a small room, sat Tanghin, hunched over a burning bowl. From somewhere in the room came the sound of someone talking, the sound of stone on stone. Then, as she closed the door, the talking stopped abruptly and the blue flame flickered wildly. Tanghin turned and faced her.

It was Tanghin, but it did not look like him. It was as though a mask had slipped off his normally gentle face, revealing some hideous entity underneath, a dead man's face; or, Stella thought with shock, just like the Snaer mask in the Midwinter Play, implacably black, the caricature of evil.

The face spoke, as the features reassembled themselves into some semblance of the man she thought she knew. "Stella," it said, mouthing the word like a profanity. "So you have come to me. I knew you would."

She put her hands to her mouth and shrieked once.

"You fool," he gloated at her as her world fell apart. "You weak-minded fool. Your degradation is complete. Far from being one of the Blessed, you are cursed! Didn't you know I command people with my words? Haven't you heard of the Wordweave? You have done my bidding ever since I set eyes on you, and you will do so from now until the day you die. Come then! Scream if you must! My master and I will enjoy your terror!"

But she could not scream. Anger, not fear, had risen to choke her; and in an instant of insight she realized that she had been a fool, but no worse. She had been tricked by an evil man, and her weaknesses had made her vulnerable to him, but she was not evil, she would resist this foul man with everything she had.

"Come nearer!" the man she had known as Tanghin commanded, and she was powerless to resist his hold over her. "Look into the flame! My master would know you."

As she stared, the blue flame reached out a tendril. Its touch was shockingly cold, unlike the warmth of the flame on the Night of Fire. *Hold on to that thought!* she told herself as the blue flame probed everywhere, everywhere, inside and out, unlocking her secrets, laying her bare. Her nerves shrieked in agony at the touch, and she held on to her sanity only by centering herself on the yellow-orange flames of her dream.

In the dusk of the Brownlands, the *Maghdi Dasht* watched in wonderment as their leader stiffened, then let out a great cry. "My enemy! My enemy!" he cried in the ancient tongue. Recovering himself, he spoke into the flame: "Keep her for me. The enemy has set something within her, and I must find out what it is. She is keeping secrets from me, and no one can keep secrets from the sacred flame."

"Secrets, my lord?" Deorc replied bemusedly. "She has no secrets from me. The Wordweave makes that impossible."

"Nevertheless!" The fearsome voice boomed out of the blue flame, the tendril broke contact with Stella, and she withdrew. Tanghin drew his hands slowly together over the bowl, and the flame disappeared.

"Well, Stella," he said. "It appears that you are claimed by one even greater than I. Great is the honor you are done!" There was malice in that voice, and something else: the merest edge of bitterness.

All she could say was: "Wh–who?"

"You naive fool. Don't you yet realize who you have become involved with? I am Deorc, Keeper of Andratan, head of the Council of Faltha and new Lord of Instruere. Tanghin was simply a figment of my imagination. And yours, girl; and yours. You wanted him to be real. Do you like this reality?"

Dumbly, Stella shook her head.

"And my master?" Deorc continued mercilessly. "My master is the Destroyer himself. It is he who wants you for his own. Think on that as you wait in chains for his arrival!"

CHAPTER 19

THE LAKE OF GOLD

LATE ON THE THIRD DAY north of Kantara and the Joram, Kurr saw the pursuit. They had taken it easy thus far, their progress along the maze of steep-sided valleys, across cold mountain streams and through deep forests more like a wake than a journey. Nothing much was said. The Arkhimm had failed. They had lost one of their members, found but lost forever the Jugom Ark, and with it perhaps their last chance to influence the outcome of the great war that must soon explode across Faltha, if it had not already begun. Disconsolate, distressed and drained of all purpose, their thoughts dwelt on grief, failure and humiliation. As they withdrew into themselves like a pack of hibernating animals, their pace slackened, their wills faltered.

The Arkhimm felt lost from the outset of their journey home. Fear and futility forced them from the basin, scene of their failure, and took them many leagues before they stopped to take counsel among themselves and taste together the bitterness of their defeat. As far as anyone could tell they took a generally eastward path, steering away from the setting sun. But they were not certain. Even Te Tuahangata and Prince Wiusago could not be precise in such an immense landscape. None of them knew what lay to the east of the Almucantaran Mountains. The desert, perhaps, or Tabul. Should they get through the mountains.

Two days' forced marching brought them to the end of the mountains and of their strength. Bella wept openly and often at the loss of her father, and did little more than totter along at the tail of the group. In particular, the members of the original Company that had left Loulea so long ago—Kurr, the Haufuth, Hal—had, with no purpose to drive them on, reached their extremity. When his mind cleared enough to think, Kurr wondered at the crippled Hal's taciturn visage, his silence where once he would have asserted continued faith in the Most High and their mission. From this, above even the evidence of his own senses, the old farmer judged their mission finally over. The Arrow was lost. Instruere, then all of Faltha, would fall to the brown hordes. They would sooner or later all face a bleak and hopeless death. They did not even have their instinct for self-preservation to keep them alive.

The third day came as an extension of the first two. The morning sun saw the Arkhimm straggling across a plateau between the mountains and the bright blue distance. They were much lower now than when in the Almucantaran Mountains, and the temperature grew warmer with every eastward step. By noon it had become uncomfortably hot; by late afternoon the temperature still rose, reminding Kurr of the Valley of a Thousand Fires. He turned and gazed back at the mountains, now receding as though Kantara, the Joram and the wrath of the Sentinels were only a bad memory, his mind reverberating with longing for the coolness and the rain.

So it was that he saw four figures outlined against the

setting sun. The second figure was unmistakably obese, and walked with that particular shuffling gait . . .

"We're being followed!" he cried. "The Arkhos of Nemohaim pursues us!"

At the same moment Prince Wiusago, leading the Company, uttered a cry of his own. "Beware! Step back!"

They had come to the edge of a cliff, a great escarpment stretching left and right further than the eye could see. Below them two thousand feet of warm, hazy air obscured the semi-arid lands rolling away into the gathering eastern gloom. One more step and Wiusago would have fallen.

"Did you hear me?" Kurr insisted from the rear of the group. "The Arkhos is behind us!"

The great gulf in front of them held the Arkhimm for a few moments longer, then the warning the old farmer had spoken registered in their weary minds.

"Behind us!" Kurr repeated, pointing.

Phemanderac groaned. "We need rest. Won't he ever give up?"

"He probably thinks we have the Jugom Ark."

"Perhaps he has it?" Belladonna suggested.

"I've seen enough of this man not to want to wait around and ask him," the philosopher said grimly. "We must keep moving."

"With this cliff beside us? With a new moon above? It doesn't bear thinking about," moaned the Haufuth.

"We have no choice," Phemanderac said. "The quest may be over, but that is no reason to sit here and await death."

For one or two of the Arkhimm death seemed almost preferable to the pointless future, but they said nothing. With the little energy left to them they stumbled across the plateau, always taking care to keep some distance between themselves and the edge of the escarpment to their right.

In the cool dark of night Kurr called a halt. "Phemanderac, we cannot continue," he said emphatically. "We're asleep on our feet. We must rest."

The philosopher grunted a reluctant agreement.

"We should move away from the cliff," offered Wiusago. "That way, if the Arkhos and his men still continue their pursuit, they may pass by without discovering us."

"It's a faint hope," Kurr said, "but we can go no further."

The first brush of dawn woke them from fretful slumber, from dreams of falling, dreams of loss. Kurr cast a nervous eye over the plateau to the north and to the south, but could see no sign of their pursuers. After sharing a cold breakfast from their negligible remnant of supplies, the Arkhimm shuffled northwards along the escarpment ridge like the condemned making their last walk to the place of execution. Throughout that day and the next they saw no sign of the Arkhos and his men, but suffered terribly from the heat and lack of water: few streams and no shelter interrupted the unrelieved flatness of the tableland. At times they barely moved forward.

Of all the Arkhimm, Te Tuahangata seemed the most troubled. While physically he, Belladonna and Prince Wiusago were the least affected of the group—excepting Achtal, of course—the warrior of the Mist struggled within himself. "This reminds me . . . there's something I should remember."

"What is it?" Wiusago asked him.

Te Tuahangata turned on his old adversary and frowned, his hollow eyes shadowed from the afternoon sun.

"I can't remember," he said.

Wiusago looked beyond him, to the south, straining his vision to penetrate the heathaze. "Perhaps we could ask the Arkhos of Nemohaim," he said quietly.

Eight heads jerked southwards, eight pairs of eyes searched and saw. Perhaps half a mile behind them lay their pursuit.

"Why do we run?" Achtal asked. Phemanderac started. These were the first words heard from the Bhrudwan since they had left the desecrated basin. "There are only four."

"I don't know," said Hal slowly. "Why do we flee this man?"

"They have weapons," said the Haufuth.

"But so do we," Te Tuahangata reminded them. "I have my *mere*, Wiusago here has his sword, and the Bhrudwan is a warrior with or without steel."

"So why are we running?" Belladonna asked.

"I—I can't say," said Phemanderac in wonder, as though he was awakening from a dream. "We have nothing to fear from them."

"What spell have we been under?" Kurr asked.

"Look!" Hal cried. "Here, to the right!" He pointed to a deep notch in the plateau, snaking down towards the cliff. "A path. Perhaps it will take us to the bottom of the escarpment."

"Why don't we stand and fight?" Te Tuahangata insisted. "I've never run from an enemy before." The others heard the shame in his voice; the question continued to echo in their minds.

Why did we run? Undoubtedly the shock of the witchery of Joram basin, Phemanderac reasoned. The dreadful loss of Leith—a grief he had not yet examined—losing the Jugom Ark, failing in their purpose . . . everything contributed to their flight like heralds of defeat. Yet hadn't the Arkhos been defeated also? Was he pursuing them, or was he running too?

"No!" Hal cried, his dark eyes pleading with them. "There has been enough death! On our quest we have defended ourselves, killing others only when necessary. Never have we struck the first blow. If we attack now, we make ourselves over in the image of our enemies. If they catch us, then we fight. Until then, let us continue to flee them. Please! No more killing."

"I've lost my father," Belladonna said simply. "You people are all I have left. I don't want to lose you."

Te Tuahangata sighed. "Then let's get on. Every moment we stand here brings this Arkhos closer. If you don't want to fight him, then we'd better keep ahead of him."

The cleft in the plateau did indeed lead to the escarpment. By some artifice of nature the smooth-sided gut sliced down the cliff at an angle, providing a steep but navigable path for their aching feet. After a moment's hesitation, Kurr led them down into the gully, half walking, half sliding towards the setting sun.

"This would be no place to be caught in a storm," said the long-haired Prince Wiusago grimly. "I imagine water pours off the plateau down this canyon."

"But where does the rest of the water go?" Kurr asked. "We're still not far from the Almucantaran Mountains. Their eastern slopes must drain down into this plateau, and we've all seen how much water those mountains soak from the sky. But we saw nothing more than the occasional brook. Where are the mighty rivers?"

"This whole land unnerves me," said Illyon the Escaignian. The others turned in surprise: like Hal, she had said little on this journey, as though she mistrusted her voice out here beyond the safe walls of her former home. As if to confirm this, she added: "I could not have imagined the violence in the outside world."

Phemanderac thought about the Escaignian for a moment. *What was her purpose here? Why had she been called?* For it was becoming clearer to him that, just as he himself had been lured across the world by an ancient rhyme, behind which he clearly saw the hand of the Most High, so others had been summoned. The Five of the Hand called from Loulea. Then the Storrsen brothers, Perdu of Myrvidda, and the Hermit of Bandits' Cave had joined the Company. Mahnum and Indrett had been reunited with their family. And others joined the quest for the Jugom Ark: Wiusago, Te Tuahangata, Illyon the Escaignian, and Belladonna.

Bella.

Bella, with her truthsense, her magic, her eyes . . . She reminded him of the women of Dona Mihst. But she was not as mean-spirited, as ingrown as they. Though born and raised in an isolated valley, far from civilization, she had a heart that encompassed the world. Compassion enough for every need. Love enough . . .

How do I know that?

Something more, some important truth lurked just below the surface of his imagination. It had to do with being called, with their quest, with a continuing purpose. *The quest for the Jugom Ark is dead. There is no purpose.* But even as he said it in his mind, he realized the untruth of it. Something remained. It nagged him, taunted him, but he couldn't fish it out. *Be patient,* he told himself. *It'll come to you if you wait.*

Before they were halfway down the fissure, a shout

from above told them they had been seen. At the very top of the cleft stood the Arkhos of Nemohaim and the remnants of his soldiers, murky in the gloaming. Behind them the sun set in red flame, bringing down darkness like a curtain.

"They won't risk such a descent in darkness," said Prince Wiusago confidently. "We can make camp at the base of the cliff." Relieved sighs came from among the travelers.

"That's if we ourselves can make it down before full-night," Bella said urgently.

With an assortment of bruises the Arkhimm arrived at the bottom of the cleft and found level ground. Caution drove them a little further, until the last light of the sun was erased by black night and their weariness could no longer be denied. There, on a piece of exposed rock a few hundred yards from the cliff, they ate the last of their provisions and took a swallow each of water from the last stream they had crossed, small and brackish, a day before.

That night they dreamed of water. It trickled, spumed and gushed through their dreams.

They were up before dawn. Nothing to eat and nothing to drink made for a quick start. But as the light grew, they discovered the reason for their dreams.

To their left, the great cliff spouted water.

In places it leached from the sheer wall, dribbling down the sandstone, drying up before it reached the bottom. Elsewhere it emerged with greater force, spurting from the cliff like it was poured from some great bucket. In a couple of places it cascaded down with the full force of a river, giant waterfalls pouring the blood of the mountains down into the arid plains ahead.

"Thousand Springs," muttered Prince Wiusago. "Now I understand."

"Understand what?" inquired Te Tuahangata.

"The old stories. Do you tell it in the Mist? The one about the Water-carrier?"

In answer Tua's eyes widened. "One of our Land-stories," he said. "I've been trying to remember something for the last two days. I wondered what it was. I didn't know you had stolen it."

"Borrowed, my friend. Borrowed. We don't steal everything."

Te Tuahangata grunted in reply.

Their path northwards kept them close to the escarpment, and crossed many streams. At each one they paused to drink, as though it were the last, and marveled at the sight of the water pouring from the cliff.

"So? Are you going to keep us in suspense?" the Haufuth asked the two southerners. "What is this story of the Water-carrier?"

"You'd better tell it, Tua," said Wiusago graciously.

Te Tuahangata nodded, then began.

"It is told in *Hinepukohurangi*, the Mist, that once all land was as ours: a place where humans lived in the embrace of earth and sky, where rain falls as a communion between Mother and Father, Earth and Sky themselves. But then one day the greatest of our warriors, Haputa by name, tired of this embrace, and called his family to him. 'Brothers and sisters,' he said, 'You know my prowess. I am always in the forefront of battle. Never have I suffered defeat.

" 'Yet now I have run out of foes, and the land has grown small,' Haputa said, and his family acknowledged the fairness of his boast. 'This is what I have purposed in

my heart to do. I will find another land, and there I will
breathe easier. Perhaps there I will find foes worthy of
my battle-skill.'

"His family were greatly saddened, and tried to dissuade him from his purpose, but he would not be swayed.
At the next turning of the moon he said farewell to his
family and journeyed alone to the east, far from the lands
he had called home. And not once during that journey did
he meet another person.

"Finally he found a fair land, a great valley scooped
from the earth by the digging-stick of the gods. Vast
mountains ringed the land, which was latticed by fair
rivers and gem-like lakes. It was more beautiful than
story can tell. Here indeed was room for a warrior like
Haputa to breathe, to rejoice, to find ease for his heart.

"And for a season his heart did find rest: as he walked
among the giant whitewood trees and listened to their
slow speech; as he watched the white heron fish for her
supper; as he lay on the grass and let the mist wash over
him. But in the winter his sorrow returned, and his pride
grew, and he purposed a dark deed in his heart. He took
his warclub, with which he had taken the heads of many
famous warriors, and raised it above his head.

" 'Hear me!' he cried, and the gods bent their ears to listen to their favorite son. 'There is no one to challenge me
amongst those who live on the earth! I have been succored
by Earth-Mother and Sky-Father, but I need them no
longer! I declare battle against them, for I desire the place
amongst the stars their embrace hides from me!'

"The gods then ran in fear, for there was none among
them who could face the battle-skill of Haputa in his
pride and wrath. But Sky-Father and Earth-Mother continued in their embrace, and for the sake of the land they

did not move. In anger, without thought, he swung his warclub and with one blow drove Earth-Mother and Sky-Father apart.

"At that moment the mist rose and vanished, and behold! Haputa stood on a mountain top, arms outstretched in triumph over a sunlit and beautiful land. And the stars circled around his head. He shouted a great boast: '*Te tama whakaete turanga rau, i titi te upoko ki te kura a rangi!* The young man who forces his way on to a hundred standing places, whose head is emblazoned with the glow of heaven!'

"And the land, bereaved of the embrace of Earth and Sky, became angry at his boast. Without the mist to dampen down its anger, the land erupted in flame. Many great mountains burst asunder, and the lifeblood of the land flowed across the valley like rivers. Here was a violence Haputa could not fight, and though he ran through the land like a fiery spirit, he could not salve the wounds he had caused. He then called on Earth-Mother and Sky-Father, inviting them to resume their embrace, but they would not. Though he repented of his folly, Haputa could not repair his ill-work.

"The gods took conference together, and decided to allow Haputa to make restitution. Pooling their power they drew a line across the land with their digging-stick, and where the line was drawn the land rose up in one piece, making a high cliff. This the gods struck with their stick, and where the rock was struck water sprang forth. They took their stick and reshaped it, making a large basin. Then they turned to the remorseful warrior, and spoke.

"'Hear us, Haputa, O greatest of warriors,' said the gods. 'In your pride you have driven apart our Mother and

Father, and now they will never again have children. As a result the land suffers. Without the mist the land bleeds, and will die unless the wounds are salved.

" 'Therefore, this is your task. You will take this basin and gather water from the Thousand Springs, then take it to the valley and put out the Thousand Fires. As long as you continue, the land will heal. But if you should tire, the land will die.'

"Haputa thanked the gods, for here at last was a task he could measure himself against. He took the basin on his shoulders, gathered water from the Thousand Springs and poured it over the red wounds of the once-beautiful valley. In this fashion was the land-violence ameliorated, and the valley regained some of its beauty.

"But in the long advance of years the Water-carrier Haputa learned that his flesh, though mighty, was mortal. He labored without rest, but he could never carry enough water to bring complete healing to the land. And as he grew old, his shoulders would not bear what they could when he was young. Thus it was that Haputa put aside his eternal task, and returned to the Mist, where his *whanau* greeted him with joy.

"But though Haputa the warrior lived, the Valley of a Thousand Fires died. The unassuaged flames of land's-blood and the heat of the desert sun boiled the waters, desiccated the trees, burned the animals until no life remained. The valley became a place of death, a memorial to the boastfulness of youth, the frailty of old age and the futility of strength. Thus the valley is held sacred to the people of the Mist, and none may enter it save in the greatest of need."

Te Tuahangata finished his recital, smiled and wiped his sweaty hands on his bare chest. "The tale never fails to move me," he said self-consciously. "I descend in direct line from Haputa the Water-carrier."

And forever strive to match his deeds, Phemanderac thought. The words were as plain as if Te Tuahangata spoke them aloud.

"The tale I heard names Thousand Springs as a sacred place," said Prince Wiusago as they walked on. "The ambassador from Tabul told us his people never approach it, though it lies on the borders of his country." He waved his arm vaguely to the southeast, where the semi-arid land rolled into the heat haze.

"Then does no one dwell near enough to appreciate its beauty?" Belladonna asked.

Wiusago glanced over his shoulder, measuring the distance they had come from the base of the cleft that gave them egress from the escarpment. The Arkhos and his men were yet to appear. "None," he answered. "Though it is said the wild men of *Khersos*, the Deep Desert, revere Thousand Springs as the source of the Lifeblood, a river that flows without failing through their forsaken lands. They live to the east," he added, answering Kurr's look of concern, "and have nothing to do with the descendants of the First Men, pursuing their own strange purposes out of our knowledge."

"We saw one," said Phemanderac. His statement incited general amazement. "In the Valley of a Thousand Fires, do you remember? He wore a white robe, and his face was as a bird of prey. He carried two swords and a staff. I think he shadowed us all the time we were in the valley, and he was glad to see us leave."

Phemanderac also looked over his shoulder as he talked, wondering what had become of the Arkhos. *He should have completed the descent by now!* So he did not see those in front of him suddenly halt. He walked blindly into the back of Belladonna, who stood rigid.

There, in front of the Arkhimm, was a wild, white-robed figure. As if raised from the dust by Phemanderac's words.

The figure gave a harsh cry, and in answer a hundred more like him sprang from within shadows, behind rocks, out from cracks in the earth. All sword-armed, poised for slaughter.

No one of the Arkhimm had to give the order to flee. They could not possibly stand against the violence written across a hundred implacable faces. None of them, not Wiusago, not Te Tuahangata, not even Achtal, considered opposing the grouped force of the wild men. As one they turned and ran.

"The Sanusi, the wild ones . . ." Wiusago gasped out as they ran. "They are angry that . . . we desecrate Thousand Springs. Ruthless . . . will kill their enemies." His words, and even more the look of fear on his proud face, spurred them on.

Achtal paused a moment, gathered Hal in the crook of his arm, then slung him over his muscular back. Of them all, only the Bhrudwan retained a measure of self-possession.

After a few moments of wildest panic, Phemanderac remembered Belladonna and her magic, her powers of illusion. Frantically he sought her. There she was, just ahead of him. What happened next brought horror to his heart. He cried out her name and she turned to him, responding to the urgency in his voice; but in the act of turning she stumbled and pitched forward, cracking her head on a rock. Without even a cry she collapsed, and blood began to seep from her temple.

The philosopher cried out in despair. Without pausing in his flight, Prince Wiusago bent down, gathered the still form in his arms and ran on.

Up ahead the Arkhos of Nemohaim and his soldiers had made the bottom of the escarpment, but he and his men were gathered up by the frantic Arkhimm as they sprinted past. In a moment of unlikeliest farce Phemanderac found himself running beside the outsized frame of the Arkhos himself, as the obese man clawed at the air in front of him as though trying to part it with his arms. He too had seen the danger. He too knew something of the reputation of these desert marauders.

Behind them the Sanusi came, stepping quickly, lightly, reverently over the sandy earth. Their gait unhurried, their mien untroubled, their purpose clear. As they came they wound their killing veils about their heads.

"I can run no further," rasped the Arkhos of Nemohaim, his face purple. "Let us put aside enmity—for now—and do something about these wild men. Perhaps they want nothing more than our food."

Phemanderac cast a glance over the Arkhimm: they had come to the end of their endurance. Nothing drove them on but fear, and it was not enough. Whatever this enemy wanted, it must be faced.

A few yards ahead lay a stone-field, large rocks strewn about randomly. The gaunt, exhausted philosopher signaled to the others, motioning them to take cover. He had scant moments left before the tribesmen came to exact revenge. Taking stock of the situation, he added up their fighting potential: Te Tuahangata and Prince Wiusago, the three Instruian soldiers remaining to the Arkhos, Achtal the Bhrudwan . . . He realized the Bhrudwan warrior was gone, was nowhere to be seen, had deserted them.

Phemanderac the philosopher had always believed his life was special, charmed somehow; that he was being prepared by the Most High for some great service to the world. He maintained complete faith in a manifest destiny even when rejected by the learned men of Dona Mihst, choosing to leave Dhauria and begin scouring Faltha for signs of the Right Hand of the Most High. And he had found him—them. For a few glorious, heady weeks, he had believed with all his heart that the consummation of his life was imminent, he was to be an important part of the salvation of Faltha, the remaking of the world, and perhaps the redemption of his own morally stagnant people. Then Leith had been lost in the Joram, the Arrow, the Arrow . . . oh, what hope had risen within him when he beheld the Jugom Ark! But the Arrow had fallen into ruin, and for the first time in his life the cold wind of doubt blew across the landscape of his mind, threatening his carefully constructed mental dwelling places. And now . . . he could barely believe what was happening. They were trapped— no, they had been *herded*—and were ready for slaughter. Belladonna lay lifeless in Wiusago's arms. The remainder of the Arkhimm would die violently, cruelly, and the promise of redemption would die with them. Achtal, their only hope of resistance, had left them to their fate.

He could not believe that it was about to end this way.

"Where's Achtal?" Kurr cried. The veiled tribesmen were only a few yards away.

"Gone!" came Phemanderac's lorn cry. Cheated hope stole his courage, and the hero of Helig Holth had nothing left to give.

"How are we to make a defense?" Hal asked quietly. He had not given up.

"Draw your weapons," said Te Tuahangata. "Stand back

to back. Make them come to you. Pick one man and look him in the eye. The real battleground is in the mind. Intimidate him with your confidence. Banish fear from your thoughts." He sounded like he was reciting an old battle creed—one even he had little confidence in.

"We've just finished running away from them," observed Illyon bitterly in the silence before battle. "How do we convince them we're not frightened?"

"Like this!" cried Te Tuahangata. He leapt forward on to a rock in full view of the white-robed tribesmen. Brandishing his great warclub in one hand, he shouted in a tone of utmost belligerence: *"Kaore e pau, he ika unahi nui!"* Even as his challenge hung in the air, he unwound a string from around his waist and began to whirl it above his head. Immediately a ghastly ululation rang out as a small shell on the end of the string whipped around and around. The tribesmen took an involuntary step backwards, then determinedly strode forward and gathered just beyond sword-reach.

For a moment everyone stood still. Then the line of veiled tribesmen parted and their leader stepped forward. He unwound his veil and sheathed his curved scimitar as he did so.

He means to parley, Kurr realized.

One of the Arkhos of Nemohaim's men leapt forward with a snarl, and aimed a vicious sword-blow at the defenseless tribesman. Kurr's cry of dismay had hardly been issued when a knife cut through the air and buried itself in the Instruian's face, stopping the blow short and sending the Arkhos's man tumbling to the ground, where he twitched for a second or two.

The leader of the tribesmen had not moved to defend himself.

Kurr spun around on the Arkhos of Nemohaim. "I hope that wasn't your idea!" he shouted, but he read deception and murder in the pig-eyes and thus received his answer.

The white-robed leader faced Te Tuahangata, who remained poised on the rock. "I would release you all," he said in a heavily accented version of the common tongue, "but because of this man's cowardice I will not." He kicked the corpse lying at his feet.

The desert warrior turned to the rest of his captives. "We watched you drink from the sacred springs. For that crime your lives are forfeit. How dare you take water from the source of our Lifeblood? We heard your telling of the legend of Haputa, him whom we name a-Hamiagsheikh, Desert-maker and Water-bearer, Father of Life. In reverence to the legend, we will allow the tale-teller to go free." He turned and raised his palms to his forehead, then spread them wide in a gesture of respect. "We would have released you all, after telling you never to drink from these springs again, but our anger is rekindled by the craven blow struck by your companion. Apart from the tale-teller, you will be bound and taken to Ghadir Massab, where you will be sold as slaves."

"While my friends are bound, I will not remain free," Te Tuahangata declared hotly. "And what right do you have to command us? We are free men in the service of our own chiefs. Who are you that you should hinder us?"

Behind the tribal leader his men grumbled angrily. "Silence!" the man commanded as he wound his veil about his head. "This is our land, and you may not desecrate the source of Lifeblood. Ever since the days the fools from Tabul polluted the river in their search for gold, we have claimed sovereignty over this river, from Thousand

Springs in the west to Namakhzar in the east, nigh the borders of Sarista. This is our land, Hamadabat and Badiyat, and we say what happens here! Once you descended the Timmis-zao, you came into our land and will be judged by our laws. You should be put to death. Remember our mercy."

But Tua would not be silenced. "Then put us to death!" he challenged. "You've decided to make money from selling us. I would rather die than be a slave!"

The tribesman nodded to one of his fellows, who pulled from his back a long whip. Quicker than any of the Arkhimm could credit, he flicked it at Te Tuahangata, who collapsed with a yell of pain and an open wound across his back.

"All right," Kurr conceded. "No more. We'll come quietly."

The tribesmen produced ropes and trussed the captives tightly. From a dry watercourse a number of tribesmen led tall, load-bearing animals similar to horses but with much longer necks and a large bulge in the center of their backs. Each captive was placed on an animal, just in front of the bulge. They slung Belladonna across the back of another, her head bleeding heavily. Then they led the beasts forward, and made their way into the desert with their booty.

By the end of the second day they had left all recognizable features behind them. The escarpment was gone, having sunk beyond the horizon some time ago. Foothills radiating from the escarpment had given way to scattered mounds, then disappeared altogether. Behind, below and ahead the captives could see nothing but black gravel. No vegetation, no sign of life. No rock, nothing at all to raise itself more than a few inches above the uniform surface. Nothing except themselves. Even the horizons had vanished in the heat, obscured by a shimmering whiteness so much like water more than one of the captives leaned longingly towards it. A hot wind blew intermittently from the north, and the tribesmen aimed themselves into it as though they had no other means of navigation. When the wind faded there was absolutely no sound apart from the soft padding of the beasts. It was a land to daunt the stoutest heart.

Motion lost its meaning. There was no *fast*, no *slow*, just the desert drifting slowly past them. The heat ceased to be hot, so dry was it, a desiccating wind that bit grimly at any exposed flesh. The captives were covered with veils, but still their skin began to blacken. They knew no time apart from night and day. At irregular intervals an acacia tree might hover above the hidden horizon, or perhaps it was just a vain imagination. Above them the only feature in the blueness was the angry white sun, which sank far too slowly to the western horizon. As it finally set it swelled in size, turning yellow then a brilliant red, pulled into an egg-shape by the ground below it, then disappeared, swallowed by the hungry earth. With surprising speed darkness spread over the plains, and finally the immensity of the *reg* desert was reduced to human proportions. Kurr sagged from sudden relief.

That night Belladonna stirred, and the captives knew for certain she was not dead. The tribesmen offered her what healing they possessed, but it was obvious her head wound was serious. She breathed, she took in food and water, but that was all. The light in her eyes had gone out.

The second day out from the escarpment seemed worse than the first. Heat, thirst, fear, heat. The captives began to hallucinate. Here, in the depths of *Khersos*, the Deep Desert, even the tribesmen did not easily travel. However, they seemed pressed by some need. Kurr could not understand their language, but he could sense their urgency. They traveled in a straight line, as if to have taken a longer route—perhaps following the Lifeblood, for example—would defeat their purpose.

None of the captives remembered anything beyond the third day.

When Kurr came to himself again the tribesmen were feeding their captives. It was near sunset, and the featureless *reg* had given way to scrub and sand. Ahead and to the left of them lay a vaster mirage than any seen in his hallucinations, a great golden lake. Its pure, stern beauty made his heart ache.

"Behold Bi'r Birkat, the Lake of Gold!" cried the leader of the tribesmen. "Here lies the wealth of nations, and none may gather it. Below us is Ghadir Massab, the city of the Sanusi. We have arrived in time for Haj Kahal, the summer gathering of the Sanusi. You will fetch good prices at the slave market."

Kurr rubbed his aching eyes to clear them. The lake lay there still, stubborn in its refusal to shift like the other mirages. Of all his dreams this was the most strange— except perhaps the hallucination that a rock followed them. Even now he could see it in his mind's eye . . .

The captives were taken down to the city. Nestled against the southern shore of the golden lake, Ghadir Massab was at first impression little more than a collection of tents and other temporary structures. The traffic of beasts such as those that had borne the captives, along with mules, horses and people, raised a choking dust into the air. And here noise spoke of humans about their everyday business, deafening after the hallowed silence of the desert.

Phemanderac tried to talk to Kurr through cracked lips, but was nudged into silence with the butt end of a whip. They had all tasted the edge of the whip, around their legs, on their backs, but none suffered like Te Tuahangata, whose wound obviously pained him still. Kurr wanted to ask him how he fared, but the watchfulness of the guards defeated him.

Just after sunrise the next morning the captives were led from their tents on the fringes of Ghadir Massab and into the city. Even at this early hour there was much activity. People bought and sold their wares in animated, often argumentative voices; they sang and danced to the music of the *imzad*, a single-stringed violin according to Phemanderac; others prepared food or fed animals—cattle and sheep, as well as the pack-animals. And there were many dogs, which scavenged for food on the impromptu streets between the tents.

But in the center of the city there were no tents. Ghadir Massab was more than a temporary village. Circling its heart was a stone wall twice the height of a man, and within it were many buildings. However, what made this city different to all others was the material used in the construction of these buildings. They were all made of pure gold.

Two children and a man with a many-tailed whip stood on a golden platform. A large crowd of men gathered in front of the platform. After watching for a moment, Phemanderac realized that this was the slave market.

Without provocation, the whip came down on the back

of one of the small figures. She cried out, then collapsed on to the stage. In disgust the man with the whip kicked at the squirming form, sending it falling from the stage. Ahead Hal gasped and began to struggle, obviously wanting to get to the prostrate figure. A blow with the butt of a whip stopped him.

With this much wealth, why do they need to sell slaves? the philosopher wondered. *And what makes them so cruel?*

From behind their veils men bid for the flesh of their less fortunate fellows, and when they bought what they needed they departed without a backward glance. As the morning wore on the crowd thinned, raising a vain hope in Phemanderac's breast that none would remain to bid for them, but such hope proved groundless. More than a hundred men remained when the strangers from beyond Timmis-zao were hauled up on to the platform, the men stripped to the waist and paraded to meet the judgment of potential buyers.

The response to these strangers was perhaps predictable: much laughter, but few bids. Even when Belladonna's still form was laid out at the front of the platform, interest was difficult to generate. The leader of the tribesmen, who acted as auctioneer, tried his best, but the buyers were obviously suspicious of the work capacity and hardiness of his goods. Belladonna's stillness seemed to confirm their suspicions. Phemanderac ached to go to her side, to salve her wound which would undoubtedly be infected, but ropes held him fast.

From the back of the assembled crowd came a bid which got the tribesman's attention. The bidder was a big man in a dark blue robe; his black veil obscured his desert features. Phemanderac had seen a few men with such raiment. From what little he could gather, they came from somewhere a long way away.

His suspicion was confirmed when bargaining began. The two men had to use the common tongue, so the captives could follow most of the negotiations.

"Six *nentachki?*" the man in the blue robe said incredulously. "I want twelve slaves, not fifty. One *nentachki* and two bars of salt."

The tribesman spat extravagantly on the ground in front of the golden platform. "One?" he said, his voice rising. "One? Do you think we want for wealth? Look around you! Do you see any lack?"

"You cannot deceive me," came the patient reply. "I know you are allowed to take from Bi'r Birkat only as much gold as your *marabout* allows. And I have heard your holy man is frugal. One *nentachki* and four bars of salt."

"I have eleven workers here, not twelve, and I would not part with them for less than four *nentachki*. Eight days we have borne them across the desert. Would you have us make no profit at all?"

"They do not look like Sanusi," said the man in the blue robe warily. "You Falthans all look the same. How do I know they can work? Two *nentachki*."

"Just look at them!" pleaded the tribesman. "Look at this one!" He pointed to Prince Wiusago. "If you know about such flesh, you will know an unmarked one is rare. It shows an obedient and hard-working slave. We have had much profit from this one. Three *nentachki* and six bars of salt."

From somewhere behind them music swirled on the gathering desert wind. New arrivals swelled the Hamadabat carnival, which by evening would be a riot of color and sound.

"If they are so good, why do you sell them? I am not sure I believe you, but my master wishes me to conclude business quickly. Give me those eleven and one other—that girl will do—and I will be on my way. Three *nentachki*."

"We sell them because we must," said the tribesman, shrugging his shoulders in a worldly gesture of hopelessness. "When the *dessica* wind comes, bringing drought with it, what can a man do except draw the strings of his tent closer? Three *nentachki* it is. But why do you want the girl?" He pointed to the child who had fallen from the stage some time earlier, now sitting alone and crying nearby.

"My master said twelve, including three women who could bear children. She will do as well as any other." The voice was flat, hard, callous. Phemanderac quailed inwardly at the sound. How long would he last as a slave? A week? A day?

Business was concluded with a touching of fingers to palms, then to the chest. Then the captives, numbering eight Arkhimm, the Arkos of Nemohaim and his two remaining soldiers, and the crying child, were roped together and led away to meet their new owner. Behind them another Sanusi climbed on to the platform and offered his chattel for sale. None of the captives looked back on that fearful place.

The blue-robed man dragged them at a cruel speed out through the walls of the City of Gold, through the dusty streets of Ghadir Massab, passing through markets where water-sellers and salt merchants plied their wares, then out into the desert and the midday sun, taking them to the place by three large rocks where his master waited with a train of the hump-backed beasts. The new slaves were forced to mount them, and preparations were made for their departure. Servants watered the beasts first, then themselves. The slaves got a sip of what was left.

The master, also wearing a blue robe, congratulated his servant on his purchase in a voice that to Phemanderac sounded strange, yet not so strange. Then he came over and looked up at the philosopher, and for a moment Phemanderac's heart stopped.

It was Achtal the Bhrudwan, and he had a twinkle in his eye.

CHAPTER 20

HEALING HAND

DARKNESS SWIRLED INTO LIGHT. Dull red light, brutal white light. Leith screwed his eyes tightly shut. But the red light did not go away, so he opened them again, and found himself staring into the concerned face of Maendraga.

"Have you seen her?" he said in a hoarse voice. "Have you seen my daughter?"

It was all the youth could do to raise himself to a sitting position. "The last I saw Belladonna, she had escaped the guard who had captured her," he said carefully. "She was helping to rescue my companions."

"Who were the ones who desecrated Joram basin?"

"You mean those who attacked us? The ones who have chased us since we left Instruere. The Arkhos of Nemohaim."

"The ones who broke through my snares in the Vale of Neume?"

Leith nodded.

"What happened here? Where are the others? I have searched Joram basin. Friend and foe alike seem to have vanished. Where are they?" His voice had none of its customary control.

"I don't know," Leith said despairingly, fighting back

the bile that threatened to rise into his throat. "The whole mountain just dissolved. Belladonna said it was the Sentinels. People fell off the cliff, or into the great chasm. I don't know if anyone escaped. I don't know why I'm still alive."

"Bella was right," said Maendraga. "The Sentinels were set in place to destroy the unworthy. But were the unworthy ones your party or those who followed you here? Perhaps both." Reproach shone from his eyes. "You should not have come here. I warned you."

"Yet we found the Jugom Ark," said Leith quietly.

"You found it?" His eyes widened.

"We found it in a cave on the island, and I bore it back to the shore. There we were waylaid by the Arkhos and his men."

"You bore it?"

"I did."

"The first since Bewray," Maendraga said. He took a deep breath, then wiped his hands on his cloak.

"Where is it now?"

Leith shrugged his weary shoulders. "I don't know. Lost down the chasm, under a rock somewhere. It could be anywhere. I lost hold of it when the earth shook. It's gone now."

Yet even as he said the words, he knew it was not lost, that all he had to do was think about the Arrow, attune his mind to it, and it would be found. He was linked to it now; he would never lose it again.

But did he want it found? Did it matter, now that his brother and his companions were lost? Did anything matter? *Of course it does*, he told himself. *This is more important than any of us*. But the thought made him feel worse, not better. Duty over love once again.

"Lost?" Maendraga cried in anguish. "Swallowed by the earth? It cannot be!"

The youth could not tell whether the magician referred to the Arrow or to his daughter. Perhaps he meant both. Leith held out his hand and thought on the Arrow. The familiar tingling rippled across the palm of his right hand. Some distance ahead, slightly to the right and amongst a pile of detritus, the Arrow flared in answer.

In a moment they stood beside it, the Jugom Ark flaming quietly as though waiting confidently for the hand it knew to pick it up. Maendraga bent down to touch it, but drew his hand away even as Leith barked a warning.

"It burns," he said. "It burns anyone but me. I don't know why."

"Here lies my life," said the magician. "At least I thought so, before—yet I am not stirred. I don't know what I expected. The Arrow is filled with magic, a great sustaining power, as would be expected of an object that had rested in the hand of the Most High. But it is not alive. Any one person is worth more than this relic." As he spoke he closed his eyes, and Leith could tell the one person he thought of was Bella.

"Little value, yet great value," said Leith. "If it proves able to deliver Faltha from the Bhrudwans."

"It will do no such thing," the magician said absently, his mind still elsewhere. "People under the guidance of the Most High will do that. The Arrow is a tool, a symbol, nothing more."

Leith bent over and grasped the Arrow firmly and without hesitation, not allowing any doubts to cloud his mind. The shaft was cool to the touch.

"How did you escape the Arkhos and his men?" Leith asked. "We thought you had been captured, or worse."

"I created an illusion just before they came upon me. I suggested that I looked like a large rock, so they just ignored me. They must have taken Belladonna by surprise."

"They must have," Leith echoed hollowly, his grief reserved for a less pressing time. "But we can't remain here, not with the Arkhos somewhere about."

"I will remain here long enough to find my Bella. I do not believe they would have been able to kill her. Perhaps she left the basin. I will find evidence—" A thought struck him, and he turned to the young man.

"You found the Jugom Ark just by sensing it. Can you do the same for your companions?"

Leith shook his head automatically. "No, I—"

"You must try!" The force of the words shook Leith like the rumbling of mountains.

He tried. For hours the man and the boy wandered the chaotic wreckage of Joram basin, searching for their loved ones, calling their names. They both watched the Jugom Ark for any indication it could help them in their search, but it did nothing other than give off a small, constant flame, reflecting Leith's bitterness of spirit. He tried to summon the voice in his head, but all he received in answer was a headache. They found no sign of those they searched for, though in truth Leith wondered how anyone might leave a sign of their passage on such a landscape as this.

"She is not dead," Maendraga asserted time and again. "She knows how to protect herself. She is alive. No Falthan could kill her."

But what about the Sentinels' magic? Who could stand against that? Leith wanted to ask, but he dared not. There was precious little room in his heart for hope.

Noon passed and the bitter afternoon hung about them,

gray and cold. "We should leave the mountain soon," Leith said gently. "We do not know what happened to the Arkhos and his men. It would not be safe to remain here another night."

"Yes, we must move on," Maendraga concurred reluctantly. "We must take the Arrow back to the Great City, so at least her loss will not have been for nothing." The former guardian of the Arrow choked back a sob.

He doesn't know what to believe, Leith realized.

The two men looked at each other then, and there, on the shattered remains of the sacred mountain, they shared their sorrow silently, and without words forged the bonds of a partnership that might sustain them until the end.

Their fledgling partnership was sorely tested even before they left the basin. Leith and Maendraga could not agree on which way to go. Leith favored the direct route northwards, retracing the steps of the Arkhimm through The Peira, the Valley of a Thousand Fires, the land of the Mist and Deruys. When Leith recounted the perils of the route, Maendraga flatly refused to accompany him. "It is my clear duty to go where the Jugom Ark goes," he said, "but I will not be party to foolishness. We would be better served to journey down the Vale of Neume to Bewray, and there take ship for Instruere. Besides, if any of the Arkhos's men remain, they must have gone the way you have suggested. At least, none came past me, nor did anyone use the scree slide. We must return to my house and gather provisions for our journey."

Leith argued hard and long, but at last saw the sense in the older man's arguments and acquiesced. *Carrying this thing has not made me any cleverer*, he thought.

They spent a few minutes building a rock cairn in

memorial to their lost companions. "Not that anyone will ever come up here to see it," Maendraga said in a voice of stone. They left Joram basin and made the long descent down the scree slope. Numbed by sorrow, Leith found it held none of the excitement of his previous descent. As they made their way down the weather cleared, but the castle was not visible.

Maendraga shrugged. "Nothing to protect now."

At the bottom of the scree slope they made a fortunate discovery, for here was where the Arkhos had left his horses. Prime steeds they were, all in superb condition, though clearly spooked by the earthquakes and rockfalls high above them. They appeared to have taken no other harm from their night in the open with nothing but grass to eat. Encouraged by their good luck, Maendraga and Leith chose the two best horses, and let the others go free.

The Jugom Ark proved itself a difficult companion. Leith found he had to hold the steel shaft tightly; any easing of his grip and the heat of the Arrow bit into his skin. After a few hours his hand and wrist ached beyond belief, and neither frequent changes of hand nor setting it down on stone (it set fire to grass) alleviated his pain much. As they neared Maendraga's cabin his arm resembled Hal's, all twisted and useless-looking. The memory sent emotions cascading through his body, and he twisted himself tighter to hold them out.

The next few days were for Leith a numbed succession of mounts and dismounts, of riding, eating and sleeping, of hours alone with his thoughts, his weariness and his grief. *I would surrender the Arrow and the power it promises in order to see my brother again*, he thought bitterly. *Faltha is nothing. Just a collection of self-interested kings ruling over ignorant people, all manipulated by a traitorous council that might as well be Bhrudwan. What remained to be saved? The only worthwhile products of Faltha died trying to save it. Did it always have to be this way? Did the best have to be sacrificed to save the worthless?* In a flash of intuition Leith saw the truth of it. Only the best could die for the others because only the best saw anything good in them, anything worth dying for. All other martyrs died for *their* cause, *their* struggle, *their* beliefs. Selfish deaths. Like his own quest. Here he was, not because he really wanted to save Faltha, but because he wanted to appear courageous and virtuous in front of his friends. He wanted to prove to others—no, ultimately to himself—that he was important. But now he could see he was completely unimportant, totally unnecessary. Yes, there had to be someone to carry the Arrow north. But the only talent required for that task was the ability to keep going, and he doubted his ability to do even this.

How many others did you ask to do this? he asked the voice within. *How many others do you have lined up in case I fail?*

<You already know of the Arkhimm a thousand years ago. There have been others.>

And in a thousand years' time will there be another Arkhimm to complete the task? To succeed where we fail?

The voice did not answer him.

The Vale of Neume took them initially away from their goal. Bewray, the capital city of Nemohaim, was many days' ride to the northwest, but the steep-sided valley cut a determined path to the southwest through the grandest scenery he'd yet encountered. Everything here was on the largest scale, inhuman in scope. Towering above him were steep, vertiginous slopes, too steep for his eye in his present mood; mountains that seemed improbably tall, made yet more intimidating by the knowledge further bulk towered behind the shoulders blocking his view. Vistas perhaps more suited to a giant than to a person like him. He could imagine the vast figure of the Most High striding down the valley, looking like the carving in the Hall of Lore in Instruere, mountain shoulders coming no higher than his waist, able to see beyond them to distant lands. In any other mood, at any other time Leith would have allowed such primal beauty to affect him. Now it barely registered on his troubled mind. Afterwards he could not recall clearly a single scene from the Vale of Neume, perhaps the most searingly beautiful place in Faltha.

Perhaps he had become accustomed to the Arrow—or it to him—for he found, as they traveled, it became easier to hold, demanding less effort, less apt to burn him if he relaxed his grip forgetfully. Leith had not the energy to examine why this should be so, and perhaps he would not have cared had he known.

Four days into their journey he had exchanged few words with Maendraga beyond the necessary communications required by politeness. *I loved him, I loved him*, he repeated in his mind and muttered under his breath, grinding it into the fabric of his consciousness: "I loved him, I loved him." Which soon became *I left him, I left him*; and finally *I killed him, I killed him, I killed him*. All the time he knew he had not killed his brother, that Hal had chosen this road himself, as clearly, if not more so, than Leith himself had; but he felt guilty, and could not stand the inner tension of this nameless guilt, so gave it a name. Indifference. Jealousy. Neglect.

Murder.

That evening they camped in a boxwood thicket. The weather had turned, becoming perceptibly warmer as they rode down the valley, away from the knot of high mountains surrounding Kantara. At this end of the Vale of Neume it was still summer. The air was warm and thick, the rain that fell in the afternoons caressed them rather than assaulting them like all the northern rains Leith had ever known. Wildflowers dotted the landscape: daisies and buttercups interspersed with tall flowers that looked like red-hot pokers, others richly scented with delicate trumpets, still others clumped in bushes, the flowers hanging down like dancers with wide, frilly dresses. Above them birds roosted, arguing noisily over the prime perches. But while Leith saw these things, he did not smell the flowers, did not feel the summer, did not hear the songs in the birds' calls.

"Want to talk about it?"

Leith spun around, heart in his mouth. It was Maendraga, back from gathering wood for the fire. Leith grimaced: he had been staring at nothing for ten minutes, and had not even taken their food out from his pack.

"Talk about what?" he said quickly. But he knew, and knew Maendraga knew.

"We need to talk."

"No," said Leith firmly. "You'll only say it wasn't my fault. You'll use reason and logic to make me feel better. You'll remind me you lost your only daughter, but she chose her own destiny and it would be foolish to blame yourself. You'll expect me to adopt the same attitude towards losing my only brother. But while he was with me I treated him badly. You don't know what he had to put up with. Jealousy, hatred, fear. I couldn't see it then, but I can see it now. So I don't want to hear your arguments. I need to feel the way I feel. I feel like I killed him. Leave me alone." The Jugom Ark flamed angrily in his hand.

Maendraga opened his mouth and shut it again.

Clearly that was, in fact, precisely what he was going to say. He turned away and busied himself with preparing the fire.

As the mountains shrank to hills and the landscape took on dimensions less disturbing to the human eye, Maendraga the magician began to consider a problem that obviously had not occurred to the boy. How, here in the land of Nemohaim, where the Jugom Ark was central to folklore, were they to prevent people taking a dangerous interest in it—and them?

Initially he considered illusion, and even fashioned a tentative invisibility with which to cloak the Arrow. Long before it was substantial enough to apply he abandoned it, knowing his thaumaturgy was no match for the power that made the Ark. Something touched by that Hand would always be visible. And, he reasoned further, it was the Arrow's time. Hidden for two thousand years, it was about to be revealed. He could do nothing to prevent that.

The solution, therefore, appeared to lie in avoiding people. But this was no solution. Neither he nor Leith had been this way, and therefore knew of no unpopulated paths. Worse, they had to go to Bewray, the capital city of Nemohaim situated at the mouth of the river they followed seawards, in order to take ship for Instruere. Maendraga shuddered: he had never been among more than a few people at a time.

Could the Arrow be covered or otherwise disguised? He thought not. The heat coming from the flames was real heat, and he had no doubt any covering would burn. Finally he shared his concerns with Leith, who shrugged his shoulders and mumbled: "I don't care. We have to go north. It doesn't matter."

They were noticed, of course, long before they came to the first of many villages, but were left alone by fearful, superstitious locals. Maendraga noticed this, and also noticed the messengers sent northwards ahead of them. Perhaps the youngster had been right, he considered. Perhaps they should have gone back the way he had come, but if he admitted the truth to himself he had not wanted to spend a moment longer in that malevolent place. Instead he had chosen the sanctuary of his cabin so as not to face the accusing shade of his dead wife, her voice filled with reproach, demanding to know what he had done with their daughter. But she had been there, too, in the cabin they had shared, so he left with the bearer of the Arrow. And his wife's voice came with them. During the warm days of late summer he spoke to her, becoming careless of his privacy.

Ah, Nena. Ah, my love. I told her, but she wouldn't listen to me. Just like you. You never really listened to me. You know, she looks just like you, my beautiful girl does, your eyes, your hair, your lips . . . and now I've lost you both. Please forgive me! I'll put it right, I'll find you rest! We never should have married, knowing what we knew. But I will yet find your name a home, yours and Bella's . . .

Maendraga had reasons for going to Bewray he had not told his young companion.

The arrest came in a small town a day's ride south of Bewray. Leith saw the soldiers approach on horseback, but neither he nor Maendraga made any effort to turn aside or seek a hiding place. Instead emotionlessly, fatalistically, they watched the approach of the armed men.

"Excuse me, sir," said a polite yet firm voice from

behind them. It continued as they whirled around, as they stared at the speaker, a tall, fair-headed man with his sword drawn, point leveled at them, an apologetic look on his face. "Persons answering your description are wanted at the White Palace to answer questions about criminal activity," he said, clearly enunciating each word as though afraid of misunderstanding. Unexpectedly, he broke into a smile and relaxed. "It would be safer for you if you came with me now, than if we had to send the soldiery down here to fetch you. They don't have the same regard for life as I."

"But—but we have to find the Aslaman . . ." Maendraga stuttered.

"It's all right, we'll come with you," said Leith quickly, overriding the magician's protests. "I was expecting this, or something like it." His companion returned him a puzzled glance, but Leith put his hand to his lips. The soldiers had drawn up, ready to enforce the commands of their leader.

"I agree with your young friend," said the fair-headed man amiably. "It is better to keep silence in a strange country."

"Criminal activity?" Maendraga said, still flustered. "We've done nothing wrong!"

"I have," said Leith. He'd never felt like this before: he could sense the danger all around him, but at the same time could tell it did not touch him. He felt safer facing the point of a sword in a foreign place than he ever had in his home village. Or perhaps now he had lost his friends, he didn't care. "I've done many things wrong," he said reflectively, "things that hurt my closest friends, even my family." As he spoke, it seemed as though clouds of grief and self-pity rolled away from him. "But I'm sure the King of Nemohaim doesn't want to talk to us about those. He wants us because I look like someone you've been told to keep a watch out for, and I carry something he wants to see. A few weeks ago the Arkhos of Nemohaim passed through Bewray, and left descriptions of a number of people he wanted arrested on sight. No, don't answer me; I know I'm right."

Maendraga stared at him, astonished. A small crowd of villagers gathered around them, attracted by the sight of bright steel and in the anticipation of spilled blood.

"Perhaps you are, sir," said their captor, a hint of puzzlement in his voice. "But why would you admit guilt here in public?"

"I'm guilty of being one of those the Arkhos wanted detained," corrected Leith. "Nothing more. So let's get on with the detaining. I've lots of things to do yet, and I can't stay here long. And don't bother asking me to give you my treasure. It would only destroy you."

"Of course not; it is for the hand of my lord." Their fair-headed captor looked at them a little sheepishly. "Can I—can we—perhaps you would . . . ?"

Leith smiled, and as he thrust the Arrow aloft it burst into bright flame, its crackling the only sound in a hallowed silence.

"Thank you, sir," said the fair-haired man.

It had been a long time, more than a month in fact, since Leith had been in a city, but it took him little time to adjust to the noise and bustle of Bewray. Less of a city and more a collection of towns, it sprawled in an undisciplined, disheveled fashion over three low hills squatting shamefacedly between land and sea. An ancient place, as ancient as Instruere, yet Bewray had no architecture, no beauty to boast about apart from the palace which sat atop the central hill. Surrounded by stately firs, it overlooked the town like a bloated insect resting from feeding on the remnants of its prey. The town was a trading center, a thoroughfare, a place to which everyone went to make money, a filthy, shabby place few lived in by choice. Leith, who had grown used to the streets, markets and intrigue of Instruere, found the place a little drab, a little pedestrian. For Maendraga, however, just being in close proximity to thousands of people was overwhelming. In the weeks it took them to ride down from the Vale of Neume to the northern coast, Maendraga had asked Leith repeatedly what Bewray would be like, but none of his taciturn answers prepared him for this. There was nothing but humanity and its detritus. Tall tenements, narrow streets, heat and dust, fumes from the open sewers, noise and movement; no peace, no solitude, no breathing space. The magician constantly felt his clothes fitted him too tightly, as though his surroundings were about to strangle him.

"Well, here we are in Bewray, walking to our deaths most probably," Maendraga mumbled as they rode quietly up the road to the White Palace. "I could have used the Wordweave to get us out of this."

"I know that," Leith said, almost laughing. His manner caused the older man to turn and face him.

"Where's the sullen boy of the last week? Why couldn't you have been a little brighter when we needed it?" he asked, a little aggrieved.

Leith laughed again. "I've just realized something I should have seen months ago, much earlier on in our journeying," he said. "You see, each country we travel through has someone important waiting, someone we need to make contact with."

"Someone? What do you mean?"

"I'm not exactly sure why yet, but all lands and peoples are being drawn into this quest. It's as though we've gone around Faltha gathering people."

"You make it sound mystical. You're just a northern peasant, not god's chosen instrument."

"Just like you're a shepherd from Nemohaim. Remember this?" He held out the Jugom Ark.

"Perhaps the Arrow gathers people to itself." Having lived his life under the shadow of Bewray's legacy, and the training he instituted, Maendraga was prepared to believe anything about the Arrow.

"So it stands to reason that someone awaits us here," Leith continued. "Let's go and meet him—or her."

Yes, thought Leith excitedly. *Why did I not see this earlier?* He ticked them off in his mind. As he named each name, it clicked into place in his mind. *Farr of Mjolkbridge, Perdu of the Fenni, the Hermit, Axehaft of the Fodhram, Achtal the Bhrudwan, Phemanderac of Dhauria, Jethart from Inch Chanter, even the Widuz leader who pursued us to Instruere. Then Foilzie of Instruere, the bald man of Escaigne, Prince Wiusago of Deruys, Te Tuahangata from the Mist, Maendraga and Belladonna of Kantara.* He breathed out. A great pressure had been released. Quite a collection, he reflected. Not all of them gathered yet, not all even allied to the cause, but all necessary. *Someone awaits us here, I know it.*

And then, as realization opened before him like a dormant flower reawakened by spring, Leith saw his place in the great deeds that had been, and were about to be performed. He was a flashpoint, a spark, a gatherer. *For what?* But even as he formed the question, he knew it didn't matter. He had found his place. He could wait and see what happened.

I remember the Hermit promising me a great destiny, he thought. *Nothing could be greater than being a part of this*. Then his head snapped up as another thought hit him. So preoccupied was he that he hardly noticed as they dismounted, and were led through the great portals of the White Palace, along a magnificent gallery to the throne room. Why would he still be gathering people if those he'd already gathered were dead? *They can't be dead! Phemanderac, Achtal, Wiusago, Te Tuahangata, Belladonna and the others—Kurr, the Haufuth and Hal. Surely they are still alive!*

I am not a murderer. I hated him, but no more.

As they walked down the mosaic-tiled floor of the vaulted throne room, as they passed assembled courtiers, soldiers and advisers dressed in stately robes, and as the soldiers forced them to their knees in front of the King of Nemohaim, Leith could hardly keep from shouting with joy. *I know, I finally know what this is all about!* He knew who he was, and what he was supposed to do. Even failure in this task would be better than not knowing what this was all about.

He was returned to the doings of the moment by a barked warning from one of the soldiers. The king spoke. Leith looked around him, but the fair-haired man was nowhere to be seen.

"You *will* answer our question!" shouted the king. "Why did you pursue our servant the Arkhos of Nemohaim?"

Leith wanted to answer immediately, not least because he saw there might be serious consequences if he did not, but too many things were happening inside his head. Chambers and compartments opened in his mind as he watched. The Jugom Ark was involved in some way, as were the words of the Hermit, the wisdom of

Phemanderac, the magic and Wordweave of Belladonna and Maendraga, the compassion and kindness of his brother, and behind all the voice. The Voice of the Most High, he admitted to himself for the first time. He was—they all were—stones suddenly magnetized, lodestones others would follow. And with the certainty came other things, thoughts he wanted to explore . . .

But there was no time. A soldier, dressed in ceremonial battle armor smelling of alcohol and cleaning fluid, forced him to his feet. "We can loosen his tongue for you, my lord," he declared.

Leith forced his mind back to the present. He had no miraculous powers, no mechanism for invulnerability, no means of protection from the King of Nemohaim and the power-lust evident in his eyes; none except knowledge. But it would be enough.

"There's no need," he said quietly, with absolute conviction. "We face here an impasse. You, the King of Nemohaim, want the Jugom Ark for some purpose of your own. Something to do with conquest and domination, no doubt. You guessed the nature of your Arkhos's quest, and would have taken it from him if he had returned with it."

The king said nothing, but his eyes were edged with anger.

"However, I have returned with it. Your problem is that you cannot take this thing from me, for I am its rightful bearer. You could try. Perhaps you could kill me and my friend. Did you recognize the last of the guardians of Kantara, by the way? But you could not stand the fire of life contained within the Arrow. Or could you? You are, after all, the king. But what do you know of the Most High? Would you care to try?"

Leith watched the royal face carefully. He saw the

eyes widen a little, as greed replaced anger, only to narrow with doubt and fear.

"Why don't you ask one of your loyal soldiers to try?" Leith baited. "Perhaps the one who sought to loosen my tongue? If he can handle this thing, perhaps you can too."

The king had to try, Leith knew. He held out the Jugom Ark. Flames flickered along its steel shaft, bringing no pain even as it rested lightly in his palm. *It's a matter of trust.*

"Take the Arrow," the monarch ordered.

The soldier did not move.

"Take it!" the king snapped, furious at the disobedience.

One of his advisers summoned up the courage to approach the throne. "My lord . . ." he began tremulously.

"What is it, Geinor?" The king's voice wavered dangerously. He was clearly in a black mood.

"M— my lord, there are stories, legends, tales about this Arrow . . . it may be dangerous, as he says . . ." The old man lapsed into a frightened silence.

The King of Nemohaim leaned forward, his thin, acne-scarred face flushed.

"Are you saying that either we or our subjects would be afraid of our greatest national treasure, unearthed after all these years and brought to our hand?"

"No, my lord," said the adviser, falling into the trap.

"Then as one of my loyal subjects, bring me the Arrow."

The face of the elderly counselor whitened, while the alcohol-soaked soldier mopped his brow. Leith had hoped the king would choose the younger man over the older.

The king's adviser, clearly terrified of the Jugom Ark, nonetheless was even more afraid of the wrath of his master. He reached out a shaking hand, forced it against the heat from the Arrow, and touched it. Instantly the whole throne room was lit up by flame, and a shriek of agony echoed through the White Palace. There, writhing on the floor, lay the counselor, clutching at his maimed hand.

Leith turned to the shaken king.

"You are a coward," he pronounced, in a voice laced with sorrow, anger and judgment. "You would order another to bear the pain of your own misdeeds. I have nothing to say to you, except that you have this day lost the respect of your people."

He turned to the badly burned man, and as he did so, he heard Hal's voice in his mind. *Enhancement*. Enhancement? What was that about? Then he remembered: black wings, the Hermit dying and being healed, the Haufuth unexpectedly dominating Maendraga the magician. In a flash he knew.

"Bring me ointment!" he cried.

"Ointment is no use here," someone said. "He'll die of that wound." Nevertheless, ointment was fetched and given to Leith. No one else moved.

Here we go, he thought, and spread ointment on to the burnt remains of the old man's hand. The man himself had passed out, and his body was clammy. He took the Arrow and laid it on the man's hand. *I'm looking for some enhancement here*, he said. The Jugom Ark flared briefly in response, and Leith stepped back.

The man's hand was whole, as though the burn had never been.

Absolute silence enveloped the throne room.

Leith wondered if, just for that moment, he had sprouted wings.

"The touch of the Arrow can either burn or heal," he spoke into the silence. "Which of these happens to you depends on what you are made of."

He took a deep breath, then sighed. *Well, Hal, I always wondered what it would be like to be like you. I guess I'm about to find out, and I'm not sure I'm going to enjoy it.*

It seemed almost possible that no one in the throne room would ever move, ever speak again, that they would all stand here in stunned stasis until the end of the world.

But there was no time. "Bring me the fair-haired man who brought us to the palace," Leith barked.

"Yes, my lord," said the drunken soldier, correctly assessing the shift in power that had just taken place. Without turning to acknowledge his king, he left the room. Meanwhile Geinor, the king's adviser, stirred into consciousness and stared dumbly at his hand. The King of Nemohaim, his authority usurped by the demonstration of power witnessed by his whole court, slumped back on his splendid throne and said nothing.

Maendraga knelt beside the old man, running his fingers across the now-whole hand. "It's not an illusion," he said quietly. He turned his head to look at Leith, who shrugged his shoulders, unsure as to how to deal with the magician's obvious regard.

The soldier returned with the fair-headed man, whose eyes widened as he took in the scene in the throne room. He had obviously been told of events, for he went straight to the old counselor.

"Are you all right?" he asked the old man.

"Graig," said the counselor, taking the other's hand and rising to his feet. "My son. I am all right."

"This is your father?" asked Leith.

"It is, and I thank you for what has happened here."

"Then I have found here what I sought," Leith said. "Come!" He indicated the son and his father, and the magician. "We need to talk, and I won't abide this place a moment longer."

It proved easy enough for the four of them to leave the White Palace. The story, or at least a garbled version of it, ran before them, and they simply walked out, unchallenged by soldier or courtier. Reluctant to attract further attention, Leith found and paid for lodgings at a dosshouse near the docks. He would have preferred somewhere more pleasant, a little less rundown, but he had almost no money. Little remained of the store the Arkhimm had brought south with them—he had almost forgotten to pick it up when they stopped off at the magician's cottage. The landlord, sensing the man with the money was a stranger, sought to charge them an outrageous amount for one night's stay.

"It's for the best," said Maendraga. "Tomorrow we need to find an Aslaman pilot who will take us north, and the wharves are just outside our window." After a sleepless night spent first telling Geinor the counselor and his son Graig of their quest, then having to listen to raucous singing from the tavern below and brawling out on the streets, the magician was less sure it had been a good idea. "Still, at least we have enough money to hire an outrigger," he said.

"How do you know all this?" Leith asked, curious and half annoyed that again someone else seemed to be making the decisions. "I thought you'd never been beyond the Vale of Neume. Where did you learn about pilots and ships? And who are the Aslamen?"

"The guardians come from mixed stock," said the magician quietly. "My wife was an Aslaman, a disgraced outcast. She came to the Vale of Neume in search of food, and found me."

"Oh." Leith heard the pain, and his own hurt made him reluctant to probe. "An outcast."

"Yes. Her father was—" He stopped, then turned to the youth, a frown on his face. "You've kept your pain private. I think I'll do the same."

"Fair enough." Leith shrugged his shoulders, apparently unconcerned.

"Leith, don't forget I have a truthsense. You really want to talk about it . . ."

"Is that so?" Leith retorted, bristling. "Where I come from such an intrusion into people's privacy would be called impolite at the least."

Maendraga turned away, visibly hurt.

<The boy who grew up in Loulea would not have done that to a friend,> said the voice.

Then the boy has grown up, Leith thought flatly. But the shadow on his heart did not lift.

"I'm sorry," he said to the magician. "I'm having difficulty dealing with this Arrow business and what it's doing to me, but that's no excuse."

"All that, and the loss of your brother," said Maendraga in an understanding tone.

Leith closed his eyes in exasperation at his own thoughtlessness. He explained to Maendraga his idea that his brother, the magician's daughter, and the rest of the Arkhimm were not dead. Too hurt yet to hope, Maendraga merely grunted a curt "We'll see," and began preparing to leave.

"What I said last night still stands," Leith said to Geinor and Graig. "We need to take the Arrow back to Instruere, where people from every part of Faltha are being assembled. Something is going to happen that neither the Council of

Faltha nor the Bhrudwans themselves anticipate. Whatever happens at Instruere will draw in every other country. All of the Sixteen Kingdoms will follow, as will the *losian* such as the people of the Mist, the Pei-ra, the Fodhram and the Fenni. If the peoples refuse the summons, and the Bhrudwans overcome us, no one in Faltha will escape the dark tide. You are not far enough away here in Nemohaim."

"We were far enough away last time," said Geinor. He had made up his mind: he would follow the bearer of the Arrow, but his fine, analytical mind sought to understand the situation. Things were clearly far worse than their own intelligence had led them to believe. Or lied to them about. His own king was many things but not a traitor, not yet anyway, of that he was certain, but the true situation had nonetheless not been known.

"Do you think it is by accident that the Arkhimm came from the furthest reaches of Faltha? If the Bhrudwans overrun us, my own country of Firanes will not be safe, and we are further from Instruere than you." Leith frowned, then sighed. "Sometimes, when I listen to my own rhetoric, I fear I am exaggerating. I've never seen a war."

The old counselor shook his head. "Pray fervently you never see one," he said. "It is impossible to tell you how cruel men can be; and it does not matter which side is right, both sides will be cruel. It is the nature of the aggressor to want to destroy their enemy, and of the invaded nation to exact terrible revenge. I have seen it, in my own lifetime, at Vassilian on the Plains of Amare. I was there when we routed the Pei-ra, and taught them a lesson. The only problem with the lesson was that none of the Pei-ra lived to take news home to their king."

"So you'll come?" Maendraga asked impatiently.

"Of course I'll come. Do you think I could again serve

my king after what happened? Do you think my son could remain a soldier and forever bear the shame of how his liege-lord betrayed his father?"

"But you come because of the Arrow," Leith said flatly.

"Because of the Arrow," Geinor agreed.

The wharves—a name dignifying a confused array of rotting timbers and broken piles—jutted out into the Bay of Bewray like a row of broken teeth. Tied to them floated a collection of decrepit fishing boats, a few of which were being caulked by old salts and their apprentices. Maendraga, Leith, Geinor and Graig wandered along the largest of the wharves, and at intervals the magician asked the fishermen, "Pilots from Aslama?" only to receive in response a shake of the head.

"Where's Aslama?" Leith asked him.

Maendraga pointed uncertainly out into the bay.

"That's the Wodhaitic Sea," said Leith patiently, reminding himself that the older man knew nothing of Faltha's geography.

"And out there is Aslama, or so my wife told me," said the magician stubbornly. "The islands of Aslama, off the coast of Nemohaim, where no one works more than an hour a day and it is never cold. Or so she said."

"Sounds like paradise," said Leith sullenly, a suspicion growing in his mind. "Tell me—and this is just an idle thought—your obvious desire to see these islands had nothing to do with suggesting this route north to Instruere, did it?"

Maendraga grinned at him. "Of course it did." Then his face sobered, and he added: "Aslaman custom requires that the dead be honored on their home island. I would like to see that custom honored."

"But you said she was an outcast."

"Yes, she was. We'll see what happens. But it's a moot point, since it seems there is no Aslaman ship in the harbor."

"What about one of those?" Leith asked, pointing to the dilapidated boats moored all around them.

"From what Nena told me, the Aslamen are not particularly keen to meet strangers. She told me dark tales of how they treat uninvited visitors to their lands. Now that I have seen the fear in the faces of the seamen I have asked about Aslama, I believe her. We'd never get a boat to take us out there."

"Then how were you expecting to get them to agree to take us north to Instruere?"

"They will want to honor my wife's and my daughter's death," he said simply.

"Excuse me," said a voice from beside them. "I hear you're lookin' for an Aslaman pilot."

There had been some strife between the Aslamen and the White Palace, the old salt told them, which explained why no outriggers tied up at the wharves. "Them as run the palace had their reasons, but they don't bother tellin' us," he said in his strong local accent.

"They don't tell me either," muttered Geinor. "I wonder how much else they haven't told us."

"Anywise," continued the fisherman, "the canoes don't come here now. Anchor round the coast a ways, do their tradin' in secret and get on their way unmarked by th' officials. Like it better that way, I reckon."

"So how do we find one?" Maendraga asked.

"I'd take y' meself, if I weren't goin' out on the boats

today," he said, a look of cunning on his craggy face. "A man's got t' feed his family."

Geinor took over. "Of course he does," he said. "And we'd want you to be rewarded for taking us to the Aslamen pilots, and missing out on all that good fishing." He took a purse from the folds of his robe and made to open it.

"Then you've got yerselfs a guide," said the old salt happily. "Fish ain't bitin', anyhow."

They left immediately, taking the northeast road out of the city, over a range of low, grassy hills. Within four hours of leaving the wharves, they were descending towards a small village which boasted a single wharf.

"Rivals River," announced the old salt. "Or, to name it proper, Afon-yr-Eifl. Not that many remember real names nowtimes."

"I've never heard it called anything but Rivals," said Graig.

"Everyone disremembers the past," said the fisherman sullenly. "We forget who we are, an' we become nobody, ruled by fools who send boys to war when there's nothin' left worth fightin' for."

"Did you lose your son at Vassilian?" asked Geinor gently.

"Just two girls left now, married off they are to worthless bide-a-beds. Lost three of 'em, my three boys," said the fisherman matter-of-factly. "And for what? No one tells us why, no one says sorry, they just wait 'til the next crop is grown and harvest them too. I say forget war! Remember the old ways. Remember the old names, the old language. Be true to what we know."

Leith looked at the old man sideways. *Not as old as all that*, he considered. *And not half as provincial as he affects. This man knows something about life.*

"Well, here we are," he said. "You're in luck. There's a boat at the wharf now—look, the pilot's castin' off. If you hurry, you might catch him."

The four travelers began to run.

"Goodbye now!" the old salt cried after them, laughter in his voice. "Goodbye! *Fuir af Himmin!*"

Leith spun around to gaze at the small, retreating figure. Who else had farewelled them with that cry? *Kroptur*. The hair on the back of his head rose as he realized the old fisherman was one of the Watchers, that he had *known*, he had been waiting for them. He had not asked about the blazing Arrow so conspicuous in Leith's hand. He had not needed to.

I wish I had asked his name.

The four men made it to the wharf, breathless and anxious, just as the canoe began to pull out. After shouting and gesticulating for a few frantic moments, they were able to get the pilot to bring the canoe around. It was more than a simple canoe. Hollowed from a huge hardwood forest giant, the canoe was at least fifty feet long and six feet wide. Attached to each side were smaller trunks, held out at some distance from the main hull. The cargo was stacked in the back, some way ahead of which four brown-skinned, bare-chested, bemuscled men rowed with wide paddles. At the bow stood the pilot, also bare-chested but wearing an elaborate, feathered headdress. A single sail was fixed to the main hull.

Now this is what I thought I would see on my travels, thought Leith, as he stared at the strange figures in the canoe.

The canoe hove to beside them, and the pilot stepped forward, one foot in the canoe and the other on the wharf.

He said nothing, but stared at them belligerently, as though daring them to speak.

"We want passage to Straux," Maendraga said, a little Wordweave in his voice. "Will you take us?" *We have power and money. You would do well not to refuse us.*

The brown-skinned pilot turned to his men and spoke in an incomprehensible tongue. *Though I suppose Phemanderac would understand it,* Leith thought, then with a pang realized just how much he missed the gaunt philosopher.

The pilot turned to face them, folded his arms proudly across his chest and shook his head vehemently.

Maendraga grunted in exasperation. "We must go north. It is very important! We need your help. We will pay well. Will you not take us?" *Do as I ask. I am being reasonable at present; don't make me angry.*

This time the pilot laughed, and again shook his head.

The magician turned to Leith. "Am I losing my touch?" he asked plaintively.

"No, I felt the Wordweave. But perhaps they are impervious to it," Leith replied. The pilot signaled to his crew, and they began stroking with their paddles, maneuvering the canoe away from the wharf.

"Wait!" Maendraga cried. "I have a name to bury. Aid her in finding rest!"

The pilot barked an order. The canoe spun around in its own length and again drew close to the wharf. This time the pilot regarded Maendraga with a wary eye.

"A name?" he said. "What name?"

"Nena," said the magician.

At the sound of that name, one of the oarsmen cried out. The eyes of the pilot narrowed.

"Outcast," he said.

"But Aslaman," replied Maendraga.

The pilot reluctantly nodded his head in acknowledgement. "Come and bury her name on the sacred shore, where she may find rest," he said by way of invitation.

As they got awkwardly into the boat, Leith noticed that the oarsman who cried out had tears in his eyes.

GLOSSARY

AS = Ancient Straux
CT = Common Tongue
FA = Favonian
FI = Firanese
FM = First Men
FN = Fenni
JS = Jasweyan
M = Mist
MB = Middle Bhrudwan
NM = Nemohaimian
OB = Old Bhrudwan
OD = Old Deruvian
OF = Old Falthan
OSV = Old Sna Vazthan
OT = Old Treikan
P = Pei-ran
S = Sanusi
ST = Straux
WZ = Widuz

Academy, the: Instruian institution to train guardsmen in the arts of swordfighting and self-defense.

Achtal (**Arck**-tahl) aka the Acolyte: Personal name of the young Bhrudwan acolyte, a Lord of Fear. [OB *death dealer*]

Adolina (A-doh-**lee**-nuh): A small town at the western end of Sivera Alenskja, the great gorge of the Aleinus River; first dwelling place in Faltha of the First Men. [FM *idyll*]

Adunlok (Ah-**doon**-lock): Fortress of the Widuz, built around a deep sinkhole just south of Cloventop. [WZ *down look*]

a-Hami-ag-sheikh (ah-**har**-mee-agg-**shake**): Sanusi name for Haputa the water-carrier. [S *desert king*]

Aleinus (Ar-lay-**ee**-niss): Great River of Faltha with headwaters in the Aldhras Mountains, then flows through central Faltha. [FM *barrier*]

Aleinus Gates (Ar-lay-**ee**-niss): Place where Aleinus River emerges from Vulture's Craw, surrounded by high cliffs. [FM *barrier*]

Almucantaran Mountains (Ell-moo-kan-**tah**-ran): A dense knot of high mountains in eastern and southern Nemohaim. [FM *mountains of the dream*]

Amare, Plains of (Ah-**mar**-ay): Densely populated lowland to the west of Bewray in Nemohaim, site of many battles. [NM *wind*]

Andratan Island, keep (**Ann**-druh-tan): Island off the coast of Bhrudwo, home of the Destroyer. [OB *dread*]

Appellant Division: Sub-committee of the Council of Faltha charged with managing appeals to the Council.

Appellants' Corridor: Corridor in the Hall of Meeting where those seeking a ruling from the Council of Faltha gather to wait their turn.

Archives, the: Collection of historical material housed in the Hall of Lore.

Archivist, the: Person in charge of the Instruian Archives.

Arkhimm, the (Ar-kim): The five members of the Company who set out to retrieve the Jugom Ark. [FM *five of the arrow*]

Arkhos (Ar-coss): Leader of a clan in the Vale of Youth; later coming to mean an ambassador to the Council of Faltha. [FM *arrow-bearer*]

Armatura, the (**Ar**-muh-**too**-ruh): Lofty and impenetrable mountain range separating Faltha from Bhrudwo, runs between The Gap and Dhauria along an ancient fault. [FM *armored hills*]

Arminia Skreud (Ar-**min**-ee-uh **Skroyd**): Scroll of prophecies by Arminius of Dhauria. [FM *Arminius' scroll*]

Arrow of Yoke: Alternative name and literal translation of the Jugom Ark.

Asgowan (Az-**gouw**-in): One of the Sixteen Kingdoms of Faltha, located north of Deuverre. [FM *horse country*]

Aslama (**Az**-la-muh): Nemohaimian name for Rehu Archipelago, an extensive island chain to the north of Nemohaim and Deruys. [NM *spoiled islands*]

Aslaman (**Ass**-la-muhn): Nemohaimian name for the inhabitants of Aslama. [NM *spoiled men*]

Astraea (Az-**tray**-uh): Nemohaimian name for an old *losian* kingdom, home of the Pei-ra until they were driven out by Nemohaim. [NM *spoils of war*]

Aurochs (**Or**-rocks): Legendary wild ox, found only on the inland moors of Firanes. [FN *urus*]

Austrau (**Orst**-rouw): Eastern and less populous of the two provinces of Straux. [FM *east wheat field*]

Axehaft aka Leader: The Warden of the Fodhram, from Fernthicket.

Badiyat (**Bard**-i-**yat**): Eastern province of the Sanusi. [S *deep desert*]

Bandits' Cave: Limestone formation in Withwestwa Wood, formerly a base for robbers, now the abode of the Hermit.

Belladonna: A young woman of the Vale of Neume, daughter of the Guardian of the Arrow; her name comes from the tradition of naming guardians after species of plants found in the Vale.

Bewray (Bee-**ray**): Arkhos of Saiwiz, entrusted with the Jugom Ark by the Council of Leaders. Founded Nemohaim and hid the Jugom Ark [FM *to reveal involuntarily*]; also capital city of Nemohaim.

Bhrud achannin Aldh (**Brood** ak-kah-**neen Eld**): A Bhrudwan order pledged to serve the Destroyer, composed of those rejected for the Maghdi Dasht. [OB *brown-bibbed elders*]

Bhrudwo (**Brood**-woe): Continent covering the northeastern hemisphere, a federation of provinces ruled by the Destroyer. [OB *brown land*]

B'ir Birkat (Buh-**air** Bear-cat): Vast province of Bhrudwo, located in the northwestern interior, a land of desert and plateau. [S *golden lake*]

Birinjh (Bear-**arnge**): Vast province of Bhrudwo, located in the northwestern interior, a land of desert and plateau. [OB tableland]

Blessed, the: Informal name for the leaders of the Ecclesia, those chosen for special roles.

Branca (**Bran**-kuh): Large northern river draining Asgowan, Haurn and the far north borders; a tributary of the Aleinus. [OF *river*]

Breidhan Moor (**Bray**-than): Westernmost highlands of

inland Firanes, considered part of the Myrvidda. [OF *white lands*]

Bright-eyes: One of the two Escaignians who travel with the Arkhimm; so called by Leith in lieu of his real name.

Brookside: Small hamlet at the southern end of Loulea Vale.

Brown Army: Colloquial term for the Bhrudwan army which overran Faltha at the end of the Golden Age.

Brunhaven (Brohn hay-vin): Coastal city and capital of Deruys, one of the Sixteen Kindgoms; home of the Raving King. [FM *last home*]

Cache, the: the elaborate network of food supply and storage for Escaigne.

Captain of the Guard: Leader of the Instruian Guard, answerable to the Council of Faltha; currently under orders of the Arkhos of Nemohaim.

Ceau (Say-ow) aka Bright-Eyes: Escaignian who helps rescue Company, accompanies the Arkhimm southwards. [ST *abrupt*]

Central Plains: Vast lowlands of central Faltha, a hundred and fifty leagues from north to south and three hundred from east to west.

Chance Three: the traditional Watcher signal for flight.

Children of the Mist: The *losian* who dwell in the land of the Mist, forced there by the First Men.

Clasped Hands, Book of the: One of the Five Lost Books; a book of ancient tales, including the *Domaz Skreud*.

Cloud, Book of the: One of the Ten Books of Dhauria, preserved in the School of the Prophets.

Clyma II (Cli-mah): Former king of Firanes (971–982), king when the black fly plague covered Firanes. [FI *strength*]

Clymanaea I (Cli-man-**ay**-ah): Only king of that name in Firanes, ascended to the throne in 982; succeeded by his son Prosala I. (FI *arm strength*]

Collocation: Name given by Esacignians to any formal gathering of Escaigne with elders in attendance.

Company, the: the group of northernes who came south attempting to warn Faltha of the coming Bhrudwan incursion.

Council of Faltha: Ruling council of ambassadors from the Sixteen Kingdoms of Faltha, based in Instruere.

Culmea, the (**Kull**-me-ah): Hill country to the south-east of Bewray in Nemohaim, heavily populated. [FM *pasture*]

Dakru (**Dack**-roo): Of the House of Wenta, most famous of the Scriveners of Dhauria, copyists who ensured the safekeeping of the sacred texts. [FM *delicate*]

Dassie aka rock hyrax: small rodent-like animal living in the Valley of a Thousand Fires.

Deorc (Dee-**york**): Lieutenant to the Destroyer, Keeper of Andratan. [JS *spearhead*]

Deruys (Dee-**roys**): One of the Sixteen Kingdoms of Faltha, a coastal land south of Straux. [FM *no regard*]

Dessica (**Dess**-ih-cuh) aka Khersos, the Great Desert: Desert land extending over southern Faltha. [FM *to dry out*]

Destroyer, the aka Undying Man, Lord of Bhrudwo, Lord of Andratan, Kannwar: Rebel against the Most High, cursed with immortality and now makes his home in Bhrudwo. Rules from his fortress of Andratan.

Deuverre (Doo-**vair**): One of the Sixteen Kingdoms of Faltha, located north of Straux in central Faltha; rich, densely populated farmland. [FM *twin rivers*]

Dhaur Bitan (**Dour** Bit-**arn**) aka The Poisoning: Story of the fall of Kannwar and exile from the Vale, contained in the *Domaz Skreud*. [FM *death bite*]

Dhauria (**Dau**-ree-yah) aka the Drowned Land: Names for the Vale of Youth after it was drowned by the sea. [FM *death estuary*]

Dissotis (diss-oh-tiss): Small, cactus-like plant adapted for harsh environments such as the Valley of a Thousand Fires. [FM *little water*]

Docks, the: Warehouse and shipping district of Instruere, outside the main wall of the city.

Domaz Skreud (**Doh**-marz **Scroyd**): The Scroll which recounts the rise of the Destroyer and the fall of the Vale of Youth. [FM *doom scroll*]

Dominie (**domm**-in-ee): Dhaurian name for a scholar who trains students. [FM *schoolmaster*]

Dona Mihst (**Doh**-na **Mist**): City built on the site of the Rock of the Fountain in the Vale of Youth. [FM *misty down*, later corrupted to dunamis, FM *power*]

Druin (**Drew**-in): Youth of Loulea, large boy who bullies others and is keen on Stella. [FI *brown*]

Dunay (**Dunn**-ay): Instruian guardsman; accompanies Arkhos of Nemohaim in search of the Jugom Ark. [ST *red-hair*]

Ecclesia (**E-kle**-zyuh): Name given to the group who began meeting at Foilzie's basement. [ST *called out*]

Ehrenmal (**Air**-en-mall): Town in western Favony on the north bank of the Aleinus River. [FM *bad blood*]

Elders: Rulers of Escaigne, once high-ranking members of the Watchers.

Escaigne (**Ess**-kane): Hidden kingdom in rebellion against Instruere [FM *entangled*]; Escaignians are also known as Cachedwellers.

Escarpment, the aka Timmis-zao: A tall cliff running north-east to south-west across south-western Faltha.

Faltha (Fal-thuh): Continent of north-western hemisphere, an alliance of sixteen independent kingdoms. [CT contraction of *Falthwaite*, itself a corruption of *Withwestwa*]

Falthan Patriots: Name given by Arkhos of Nemohaim to those who joined him in treason against Faltha.

Farr Storrsen (Far Store-sin): Older son of Storr of Vinkullen, a thin, angular man. [FI *far*]

Favony (Fah-vone-ee): One of the Sixteen Kingdoms of Faltha, located on the central Falthan plains north of Straux. [FM *hot wind*]

Fealty, Knights of: Knights said to have driven the Destroyer out of Faltha a thousand years ago, led by Conal Greatheart.

Fealty, Treaty of: Treaty signed by the kings of the Sixteen Kingdoms at the home of Conal Greatheart, establishing the Council of Faltha.

Feerik (Fee-rick): Man of Sivithar in northern Straux, now the Presiding Elder of Escaigne. [ST *foeman*]

Fenni, the (Fen-ny): Race of *losian* dwelling on the moors of inland Firanes. [FN *ancient people*]

Ferdie (Ferr-dee): Husband of Foilzie, property owner of Instruere, recently deceased. [FM *shrewd*]

Firanes (Firr-uh-ness): Westernmost of the Sixteen Kingdoms of Faltha. Named for the sunrise on the heights of the Jawbone Mountains. [FM *Fire Cape*]

Fire, Book of the: One of the Ten Books of Dhauria, preserved in the School of the Prophets.

Firefall, the: the moment in the Vale when the Most High came to the First Men with fire; also applied to subsequent visitations to individuals and groups.

First Men, the: Those called north from Jangela by the Most High to live in the Vale of Youth; name also applies to those exiled from the Vale who settled in Faltha, and to their descendants.

Fisher Coast: Broken, rugged coastal region in southern Bhrudwo, an amalgam of many small provinces.

Fodhram (**Fodd**-rum): A short-statured *losian* race dwelling in the forests of Withwestwa. [FD *woodsman*]

Foilzie (**Foyl**-zee): Widow from Instruere, tenement-owner, shoemaker and stall-holder. [FM *help mate*]

Fountain, Book of the: One of the Ten Books of Dhauria, preserved in the School of the Prophets.

Fountain, Rock of the: Place in the Vale of Youth where the Most High set the fountain of eternal life.

Fuir af Himmin (**Foo**-ir Ahf **Him**-min): Affirmation of the Watchers, used as a greeting. [FM *Fire of Heaven*]

Fuirfad (Foo-ir-**fadd**) aka Realm of Fire, Way of Fire: The lore and religion of the First Men, teachings which enabled them to follow the Most High. [FM *fire path*]

Furist (**Few**-rist): Arkhos (leader) of the House of Landam in exile, founder of Sarista. [FM *to be admired*]

Furoman (**Foo**-row-man): personal secretary to the Appellant Division of the Council of Faltha, headed by Saraskar of Sarista. [ST *tight grasp*]

Gap, the: Narrow pass between Aldhras Mountains and The Armatura, linking Faltha and Bhrudwo.

Geinor (**Gay**-nor): Adviser to the king of Nemohaim, one of his oldest counselors; father of Graig. [NM *charity*]

Ghadir Massab: City of the Sanusi, fabled city of gold, a trading center and slave market on the shores of B'ir Birkat in the Deep Desert. [S *oasis at the river mouth*]

Ghellol: Capital city of Tabul and site of the largest gold mine in Faltha. [FM *gold hole*]

Golden Arrow, Book of the: One of the Five Lost Books; a book of law.

Graig (Grayg): Soldier in the Nemohaimian army, son of Geinor the counselor. [NM *spear*]

Great Harlot: Perjorative Escaignian name for Instruere.

Great South Road: The Straux section of the road between Instruere and Bewray, the major road to the southwestern kingdoms.

Great Southern Mountains: Wide mountain chain separating southern Bhrudwo from unknown lands.

Grossbergen (**Grohss**-berr-gin): Range of the Jawbone Mountains, from which Styggesbreeen flows. [FM *large mountains*]

Haj Kahal (**Harzh** Kar-**harl**): The summer gathering of the Sanusi at Ghadir Massab; part trading, part fair, part sport. [S *summer journey*]

Hal Mahnumsen (Hell): Youth of Loulea, adopted older son of Mahnum and Indrett. A cripple whose name is seemingly ironic. [FI *whole, hale*]

Hamadabat (Har-**mard**-ah-bat): Northern province of the Sanusi, between B'ir Birkat and the Veridian Borders. [S *desert mountain*]

Hands, Book of the aka *Book of the Clasped Hands*: One of the Ten Books of Dhauria, lost soon after the Flood.

Haputa (Ha-poo-tah): Mythical warrior of the Mist, involved in many creation legends, including the story of the water-carrier. [M *the maker*]

Haufuth (**How**-footh): Title of village headmen in northern Firanes. [FI *head*]

Haurn (Hown): One of the Sixteen Kingdoms of Faltha, located north of Asgowan. Annexed by Sna Vaztha in 1006. [FM *horn*]

Hauthius (**How**-thee-yoos): Scholar of Dhauria, author of the *Sayings of Hauthius*. [FM *head scholar*]

Hawkshead: Mountain of southern Nemohaim, part of the Almucantaran Mountains; supposedly Kantara is to be found on its slopes.

Hayne (Haynn): Young man from Loulea Vale, training under Kurr to be a Watcher. [CT *grain farmer*]

Helig Holth (**Hay**-ligg Holth): Huge sinkhole on the edge of Clovenhill, on which the fortress of Adunlok is built. Venerated by the Widuz as the mouth of Mother Earth. [WZ *holy mouth*]

Hermesa (Her-**may**-sah): Girl of Loulea, friend of Stella. [FI *interpreter*]

Hermit, the: Man of Bandits' Cave, drawn south with the Company.

Herza (**Her**-zuh): Mother of Stella, wife of Pell, woman of Loulea Vale. [FI *choice*]

Hinerangi (Hi-nay-rang-ee): Daughter of the paramount chief of the Children of the Mist, brother of Te Tua-hangata. [M *skysong*]

Illyon (**Ill**-yon) aka Freckle: Escaignian woman who helps rescue the Company, and accompanies the Arkhimm southwards. [ST *harbinger*]

Imzad (imm-zhad): single-stringed violin favored by Sanusi tribesmen; originally a Bhrudwan instrument. [S *one string*]

Inch Chanter (Inch **Charn**-tuh): Treikan walled town, hunting and farming community in Old Deer. [OT *small song*]

Indrett (**Inn**-dritt): Woman of Loulea, formerly of Rammr, married to Mahnum. [FI *right hand*]

Inmennost (**In**-men-ost): Capital city of Sna Vaztha and seat of the descendants of Raupa, Arkhos of Leuktom.

Greatest of the northern cities of Faltha. [of uncertain origin]

Inna (**In**-nuh): Northern of two villages founded on an island in the Aleinus River, coalescing into Instruere; also one of the three main gates to the Great City. [FM *within*]

Inner Chamber aka Chamber of Debate: Small meeting hall, an annex of the Hall of Meeting, where the Council of Faltha meet.

Instruere (In-strew-**ear**) aka Great City: Largest city in Faltha and seat of the Council of Faltha. [combination of Inna and Struere, together forming the OF word meaning *to instruct*]

Instruian Guard: Soldiers under the control of the Council of Faltha, charged with keeping the peace in Instruere.

Insusa (In-**soo**-suh): Girl of Loulea, friend of Stella. [FI *warmth*]

Inverell (**Inn**-vuh-**rell**): Town on the Westway in the Bannire, the unclaimed lands between Treika and Deuverre. [WZ *distance between*]

Iron Door: Door guarding the entrance to the Outer Chamber of the Hall of Meeting in Instruere, where the Council of Faltha meet.

Jasweyah (Jarss-**way**-uh): Mountainous kingdom in southern Bhrudwo. [OB *look over*]

Jawbone Mountains aka Tanthussa: Main mountain chain of Firanes (rare form Tanthussa derived from FM *teeth*).

Jethart (**Jeh**-thirt): Heroic figure of western Treika, hated foe of the Widuz, now an old man. [OT *bright hunter*]

Joram Basin (**Jaw**-im): Deep cirque-like basin set between the Sentinella at the head of the Vale of Neume. [FM *jewel*]

Jugom Ark (Yu-gum **Ark)** aka Arrow of Yoke: Flaming arrow loosed by Most High at Kannwar, severing his right hand and sealing his doom. Symbol of unity for Faltha. Name derives from "yoking together" like oxen. [FM *yoke arrow*]

Kanabar (Can-a-barr): Wide inland steppes in southern Birinjh, a province of Bhrudwo. [OB *sulphur brown*]

Kannwar (Cann-wah) aka the Destroyer: Original name of Destroyer, means Guardian of Knowledge. [FM *kenward*]

Kantara (Can-**tah**-ruh): Legendary castle in the sky which comes down to earth once in a thousand years. [FM *thousand*]

Kaskyne (Kass-kine): Capital and largest city of Redana'a. One of the Sixteen Kingdoms; situated on a hill above the southern banks of the Aleinus River at the head of Vulture's Craw. [FM *short rapids*]

Kinnekin (Kin-ee-kin): Largest town of southern Westrau, five days' walk south of Instruere. [ST *connection*]

Kroptur (Crop-tuh): Seer and Watcher of the seventh rank, lives on Watch Hill near Vapnatak. [FM *spell-caster*]

Kurr (Cur) aka Kurnath: Man of Loulea, formerly from the south. Reflects ironic naming practices of Straux. [OF *ill-bred dog*, perh. from FM *grumbler*]

Landam, House of (Lan-dam): One of the four great houses of the First Men. [FM *house of earth*]

Lanka (Lan-kuh): Tall, thin youth from Brookside. Nickname. [CT *lanky*]

Leith Mahnumsen (Leeth): Younger son of Mahnum of Loulea and Indrett of Rammr. Name carries sense of putting aside the past. [CT *forgetful, lethargic*]

Lennan: (**Len**-nin): A young thief of Instruere, imprisoned in The Pinion. [ST *cheeky*]

Lifeblood River: River of southern Faltha whose head-waters are the Thousand Springs. Flows through the Deep Desert and into Sarista.

Longbridge: The mile-long bridge connecting Instruere with Deuverre. Its southern counterpart is Southbridge.

Long-hair: Nickname for Wiusago, Prince of Deruys.

Lonie (**Low**-nee): Youth of Loulea, girl who is friend of Hermesa. [FI *a gift*]

Lore, Hall of: Center of learning in Dona Mihst; latterly a major building in Instruere.

Lornath (**Lorr**-narth): Man of Sivithar in northern Straux, father of Kurr. [ST *loremaster*]

Losian (**low**-si-yin): Properly those who left the Vale of Youth before the fall, forsaking the Most High; popularly, all those races of Faltha who are not First Men. [FM *the lost*]

Losian, Song of (**Low**-si-yin): Ancient document recording all those who left the Vale of Youth before the fall of the First Men. [FM *the lost*]

Loulea, village, Vale (**Low**-lee) aka Louleij: Small coastal village in North March of Firanes, set in vale of same name. [CT *low lea*]

Ma Clothier: A thief and vagabond, she stole from the markets of Instruere and ran a gang of young thiefs who stole to order.

Maghdi Dasht (**Marg**-dee **Darshht**) aka Lords of Fear: One hundred and sixty-nine feared Bhrudwan warrior-wizards. [OB *Heart of the Desert*]

Mahnum (**Marr**-num): Trader of Loulea, son of Modahl, married to Indrett. [FI *man, human*]

Maendraga (man-drag-**uh**): A middle-aged man of the Vale of Neume, the Guardian of the Arrow; his name follows the tradition of naming guardians after species of plants found in the Vale. [FM *holy man*]

Marabout (**mar**-ah-boo): Sanusi holy man, whose words must be obeyed in Ghadir Massab and other cities. [S *holy man*]

Maremma (Muh-**rem**-muh): A vast low-lying area in the Center Plains of Faltha, in the countries of Straux, Deuverre and Asgowan. [FM *death swamps*]

Mariswan (**marr**-ih-swan): Huge birds now extinct. The Jugom Ark is fletched with *mariswan* feathers. [FM *majestic fowl*]

Mariswan, Book of the: One of the Five Lost Books; listing those rejecting the Most High; also known as the *Book of Losian*.

Meeting, Hall of: Largest building in Faltha, the place of public gatherings in Instruere; latterly the home of the Council of Faltha.

Mercium (**Merr**-see-um): Capital city of Straux, the second-largest city in Faltha, on the inland edge of the Aleinus Delta. [AS *merchant*]

Midwinters' Day: Midwinter celebations, held in northern Faltha, asserting the coming of spring.

Mist, The, aka Hinepukohurangi: Forested lands between Deruys and the Valley of a Thousand Fires, often cloaked in mist; home to the Children of the Mist, considered *losian* by the First Men.

Mjolkbridge (**Myoulk**-bridge): Town in inland Firanes, on the southern bank of Mjolk River. Site of the last bridge across the river. [OF *milk*]

Modahl (Mow-**darl**): Legendary Trader of Firanes, father of Mahnum and grandfather of Leith and Hal.

Mossbank Cadence: Complex set of rapids on the

Mossbank River, part of the Southern Run; considered to be impassable by canoe.

Mossbank River aka Fenbeck River: Tributary of the Sagon River, drains most of eastern Withwestwa Wood.

Most High: Supreme god of the First Men.

Mulct (Mullkt): Town of southern Nemohaim, on the banks of the Neume River; home for a time of Bewray. [FM *broken ground*]

Myrvidda (**Mire**-vid-duh): Vast interior moors of northern Firanes. [FN *swampy moor*]

Nagorj (Nah-**gorge**): Southern upland province of Sna Vaztha immediately west of The Gap. [OSV *north gorge*]

Namakhzar (Nar-mark-**zar**): Town and province of the Sanusi, on the Lifeblood River near the border with Sarista. [S *spice array*]

Nemohaim (**Nee**-moh-haym): One of the Sixteen Kingdoms of Faltha, set on the southern Bay of Bewray. Once home to Bewray, guardian of the Jugom Ark. [FM *new home*]

Nena (**Nen**-ya): Wife of Maendraga the Guardian, originally an Aslaman but was exiled. [P *blossom*]

Nentachki (Nenn-**tach**-key): Unit of currency used by the Sanusi; roughly equivalent to a month's wages. [S *cold month*]

Neume, Vale of (Noome): Valley in the Almucantaran Mountains, in southern Nemohaim; supposed location of Kantara. [FM *numinous*]

New Age: Calendar of Faltha, the first year of which was the Destroyer's supposed defeat by Conal Greatheart.

Nimanek (Nim-uh-**neck**): Vartal's lieutanant and one of the four Bhrudwan warriors. [OB *auspicious*]

Nordviken (Nord-**vie**-kin): Southern port of Firanes, at mouth of Kljufa River. [FI *northern raider*]

North March: Area of Firanes bounded by Iskelsee to the north, Wodhaitic Sea to the west, the Fells to the east and the Innerlie Plains to the south.

Otane-atua (oh-tar-nay-ar-too-ah) aka Giantwood: Forest near the border between the Mist and Deruys, scene of a battle between them; also a village. [M *god forest*]

Outer Chamber: Main meeting hall in the Hall of Meeting, site of public gatherings in Instruere.

Parlevaag (**Parl**-ih-vagg): Fenni woman captured by Bhrudwans, slain by Widuz warriors. [FN *storyteller*]

Pei-ra, the (**Pay**-rah): A *losian* race from the mountains of southwestern Faltha, driven out of their home of Astraea by the First Men. [P *the people*]

Perdu (**Purr**-do): Mjolkbridge hunter rescued from death by the Fenni, now serving them as interpreter. [FI *in hiding*]

Phemanderac (Fee-**man**-duh-**rack**): Scholar of Dhauria who leaves his homeland to learn the whereabouts of the Right Hand. [FM *the mandate*]

Philosophers, the: The senior members of the School of the Prophets in Dhauria.

Pinion, The: Longhouse in Instruere, houses the Instruian Guard. Notorious for its dungeon, known ironically as the Pinion Inn.

Piskasia (Pisk-**ay**-zha): One of the Sixteen Kingdoms of Faltha, located south of Sna Vaztha along the banks of the Aleinus. [FM *fish land*]

Plafond (Pluh-**fonnd**): Capital city of Deuverre, at the western end of the basin formed by the Central Plains of Faltha. [FM *plate lip*]

Plonya (**Plonn**-yuh): One of the Sixteen Kingdoms of Faltha, located between Firanes and the wild Widuz country. [FM *floodplain*]

Pohaturoa (Poh-hart-oo-row-ah): Sacred mound on which the reconciliation between Deruvian and the Mist-Children was foretold. [M *sacred hill*]

Porveiir, Mount (**Pour**-vay-**er**): Huge volcanic dome, intermittently active, on the western margins of the Wodranian Mountains in Favony. [FA *pourer*]

Presiding Elder: The head Elder and ruler of Escaigne; formerly a high-ranking Watcher. The current Presiding Elder is named Feerik.

Prosala I (Proh-**sar**-lah) Firanese king, gained the throne on the death of his father in 1020, died in 1030. [FI *procession*]

Pyrinius (Pie-**rinn**-ee-yoos): Dominie (teacher) of Phemanderac, expert harpist and scholar of Dhauria. [FM *fire servant*]

Qali (**Karl**-ee): A type of snow, dry and light, and by association the name of the northern god of winter. [FN *dry snow*]

Rammr (**Ram**-ir): Capital city of Firanes and seat of the King. [FI *straight*]

Raupa (**Rau**-puh): Arkhos of the House of Leuktom in exile, founder of Sna Vaztha. [FM *royal one*]

Raving King of Deruys: Nickname by which the King of Deruys is widely known, attributed to his cryptic speech.

Redana'a (Re-**dar**-na-ah): One of the Sixteen Kingdoms of Faltha, an inland country on the southern bank of the Aleinus River, hemmed in by the Taproot Hills. [FM *red roots*]

Refiner, the: Nickname of the Arkhos of Favony and his father before him, ironically given for their ability to turn gold into dross.

Rehtal clan (**Ray**-tal): Small clan of the House of Saiwiz, remained in the Vale after all others were exiled. [FM *mouse-like*]

Remparer Mountains (Remm-pa-**rair**) aka Ramparts of Faltha, Manu Irion, Man-Eaters: Continental mountain range dividing western from central Faltha. [FM *the ramparts*]

Reveler's Rest, The: A small inn in Kinnekin, set some distance off the main road.

Rhinn na Torridon (**Rinn** nar **toh**-rih-don) aka Tarradale Broads: Coastlands south of Remparer Mountains. [WZ *rack of gentle valleys*]

Rhynn (**Rinn**): Arkhos of Asgowan, one of the Council of Faltha. [FM *rack*]

Right Hand: Mysterious weapon, person or organization mentioned in prophecy as overcoming the Destroyer.

Rivals River aka Afon-yr-Eifl: River of central Nemohaim, with a small port at its mouth.

Rock, Book of the: One of the Ten Books of Dhauria, preserved in the School of the Prophets.

Roofed Road: Section of the Westway carved into the side of the Lower Clough of the Kljufa River.

Rubin (**Roo**-bin): Man of Escaigne, an elder, noted for his baldness. [ST *bold*]

Saiwiz, House of (**Sigh**-wizz): One of the four great houses of the First Men. [FM *house of the sea*]

Sanusi (Sar-**noo**-see): A desert people who dwell in Dessica, the Deep Desert. Scholars are unsure as to whether they are *losian* or have come west from Bhrudwo. [S *sand men*]

Saraskar (Sah-ra-**scar**): The Arkhos of Sarista, and head of the Appellant Division of the Council of Faltha. [FM *sun child*]

Sarista (**Sah**-ris-**tah**): Southernmost of the Sixteen Kingdoms of Faltha and the last to be settled. Saristrians are dark-skinned. [FM *sunlands*]

Saumon (**Sau**-monn): Fishing village in Piskasia, on the eastern bank of the Aleinus River. [FM *rainbow fish*]

School of the Prophets: The University of Dhauria, in which young men are trained in magic and scholarly arts.

Scriveners, the: Group of copyists employed by the School of the Prophets to guarantee the integrity of the sacred texts; led by Dakru.

Sentinella: Twin peaks of the Almucantaran Mountains in southern Nemohaim, guardians of the Jugom Ark.

Sivera Alenskja (Siv-**er**-ah Al-**enn**-skyah): Steep-sided gorge of the upper Aleinus River, south of Sna Vaztha, west of The Gap. [OSV *deep sky rapids*]

Sivithar (**Sih**-vih-thar): City on the southern bank of the Aleinus River, in northern Straux, a river port. [AS *silver thread*]

Sna Vaztha (Snarr **Vazz**-thuh): One of the Sixteen Kingdoms of Faltha, located to the north-east of Faltha. [FM *frozen snow*]

Song of Dawn: Morning birdsong in the land of the Mist, treated as a ritual of worship by the Children of the Mist.

Southbridge aka Straux Bridge: The bridge connecting Instruere with Straux. Its northern counterpart is Longbridge.

Southern Run: Southern fur trapping route across Withwestwa, the earliest that can be used after the spring thaw.

Steffl (**Stef**-fill) aka Meall Gorm: Active volcano in Withwestwa Wood, a well-known landmark by the Westway. Place where the Company rescued Leith and Hal's parents. [FM *the hood*]

Stella Pellwen (**Stell**-ah **Pell**-win): Youth of Loulea, daughter of Pell and Herza of Loulea. [CT *from the stars*]

Sthane (Sthayn): Leader of the smallest clan and member of the Council of Leaders in the Vale of Youth, opposes Kannwar. [FM *spine*]

Straux (Strouw): Most populous of the Sixteen Kingdoms of Faltha, located south of Aleinus River on the central plains. [FM *wheat field*]

Struere (Strew-**ear**): Southern and larger of two villages founded on an island in the Aleinus River, coalescing into Instruere; also the name of the southern gate of Instruere. [FM *instruct*]

Sun, Book of the: One of the Five Lost Books; listing those translated into the presence of the Most High.

Tabul (Tah-**bull**): One of the Sixteen Kingdoms of Faltha, a southern inland kingdom with great mineral resources. [FM *table land*]

Tanghin (**Tang**-in): Man from Bhrudwo who joins the Ecclesia; rapidly promoted to one of the Blessed. [JS *torment*]

Taproot Hills: Mountain range of Redana'a; southern continuation of the Wodranian Mountains. Forms the southern part of Vulture's Craw.

Tapu (tar-poo): An object or activity designated as sacred and therefore forbidden. [M *sacred*]

Te Tuahangata (**Tay Too**-ah-**hung**-ar-tah): Man of The Mist, son of the paramount chief, accompanies the Arkhimm on their journey southward. [M *man who journeys*]

Ten Books of Dhauria: Ten volumes of philosophy, scholarship and moral argument concerning the Most High and his dealings with the First Men. Five books are known to be held in Dhauria; the location of the other five is not known.

Teogothian (Tee-oh-go-thee-yin): A levy placed on

Dhaurians by the School of the Prophets, designed to support the school. [FM *harvest tithe*]

Thousand Springs: A cliff-face below the Escarpment in south-western Faltha, from which groundwater flows in many springs.

Thunderfalls: waterfall on Aleinus River, near The Gap. Drains the river into the Sivera Alenskja gorge.

Timmis-zao (Tih-**mees**-zah-oh): Sanusi name for the escarpment running through south-western Faltha. [S *wall of death*]

Tinei (Tin-**ay**): Wife to Kurr of Loulea. [OF *twist*]

Torrelstrommen River, valley (**Torr**-ill-**strom**-in): Deep river valley in northern Firanes, draining much of Breidhan Moor. [FI *torrent stream*]

Treika (**Tree**-kuh): One of the Sixteen Kingdoms of Faltha, located between Widuz lands and the Remparer Mountains. [FM *forest land*]

Tructa (**Truk**-tuh): Town in southern Piskasia, on the west bank of the Aleinus River. [FM *gray fish*]

Truthspell: aspect of spoken magic allowing the speaker to trap anyone who responds to the truth woven into the words.

Tupuna (too-poo-nuh): Exalted and honored ancestor of the Mist. [M *ancestor*]

Tussoci (**tuss**-sock-ee): Narrow-leaf grass which forms waist-high clumps; suited to semi-arid climates. [FM *sharp grass*]

Vale, Book of the: One of the Ten Books of Dhauria, preserved in the School of the Prophets.

Vale of Youth aka Vale of the Chosen: Vale in the south of Faltha to which the First Men were drawn by the Most High.

Valley of a Thousand Fires: long, narrow land between

the mountains of south-western Faltha and the Deep Desert; hot, arid and filled with volcanic activity.

Vaniyo (Var-nee-yoh): Bhrudwan Trader. [MB *subtle hands*]

Vapnatak (Vapp-nuh-tack): Largest town in the North March of Firanes. Named after the annual weapontake that took place here in the years of the Halvoyan incursions. [OF *weapontake*]

Varec Beach: Fishing village on the coast of North March, Firanes. [FI *sea squid*]

Vartal (Varr-tahl): Aldannin (head trainer) of the *Maghdi Dasht* and leader of the four Bhrudwan warriors. [OB *sunlight*]

Vassilian (Vass-ill-ee-yin): Town on the Plains of Amare where a battle was fought between Nemohaim and Pei-ra; neither side claimed victory. [NM *valiant struggle*]

Veridian Borders: Mountain range on the southern border of Straux, separating the fertile Central Plains from the arid lands to the south.

Vertensia (Nee-moh-haym): One of the southern Sixteen Kingdoms of Faltha, a land of coastal gardens and severe highlands. [FM *garden land*]

Vindstrop House (Vinnd-strop): Main town of the Fodhram, a trading post on the Mossbank River. [MT *wind drop*]

Vinkullen Hills (Vinn-cull-in): Hills to the north of Mjolkbridge, Firanes. [FI *shield hills*]

Vitulian Way (Vih-too-lee-in): Main street in Instruere, connects the Inna (northern) Gate and Struere (southern) Gate. [ST *straightway*]

Voicemaster: Bhrudwan adept at Wordweave, someone who teaches others.

Voiceskill aka Wordweave: The magical ability to weave

different meanings into the words one speaks, thereby affecting the behavior of others.

Vulture's Craw: Central gorge of the Aleinus River through the Wodranian Mountains, dividing Piskasia and Redana'a.

Wainui (Why-noo-ee): Waterfall in the land of the Mist. [M *bigwater*]

Wambakalven (**Wumm**-buh-cal-vin) aka Womb Cavern: Large cave directly below Adunlok, part of Adunlok cave system. [WZ *womb cavern*]

Watchers, the: Secret organization dedicated to protecting Faltha from invasion.

Water-carrier, the: One of the Landstories of the Children of the Mist, concerning Haputa and the formation of the Valley of a Thousand Fires.

Water Chamber: Large reservoir in the Docks area of Instruere, designed to hold Instruian waste until it can be flushed out by the high tide of the Aleinus River.

Wave, Book of the: One of the Five Lost Books; recording the destruction of the Vale.

Wenta, House of (**Wen**-tuh): One of the four great houses of the First Men. [FM *house of wind*]

Westrau (**Wesst**-rouw): One of the two large provinces of Straux, the westernmost and most populous. [AS *west wheat field*]

Westway, the: Former main highway east from Firanes to Instruere, now superseded.

Whanau (far-now): Family group amongst the Children of the Mist, can include grandparents and other relations. [M *family*]

White Palace: Palace of the king of Nemohaim, set on a hill in Bewray.

Widuz (Vi-**dooz**): Small mountain fastness in northwestern Faltha, remnant of a far larger civilization. [WZ *the people*]

Wira Storrsen (**Wee**-rah **Store**-sin): Younger son of Storr of Vinkullen, a solid, blond-haired man. [FI *wiry*]

Wisent (Wih-**sent**): Name of the Fenni clan chief's own aurochs. [FN *bison*]

Wisula (**Wih**-shill-uh): Senior courtier at the Firanese Court. [FI *careful answer*]

Witenagemot (**Vit**-a-**narj**-mot): Dynastic name of the Raving King of Deruys and his house. [OD *soul of the dark sea*]

Withwestwa Wood (With-**west**-wuh): Extensive boreal forest of northern Plonya; part of the forest that extends across northern Faltha. The name was originally given to the whole continent. [FM *westwood*, backform of Falthwaite and Faltha]

Wiusago, Prince (Ar-lay-ee-niss) aka Long-hair: Prince of Deruys, younger but only remaining son of the Raving King of Deruys, companion to the Arkhimm. [OD *wiseacre*]

Wodhaitic Sea (Woe-day-**it**-ick): Western sea bordering Faltha, specifically that ocean partly enclosed by northwestern and southwestern Faltha. [FM *hot water*]

Wodranian Mountains (Woe-**drain**-ee-an): Large mountainous area in east central Faltha, home of the Wodrani. [FM *water men*]

Wordweave aka Voiceskill: One of the word-based powers wielded by an adept in the *Fuirfad*. The Wordweave allows the user to weave another meaning into her or his words.

Workless Day, the: A day of religious observance held once a month in Dhauria, in which the Most High is honored by people resting from their labors.

Worship, House of: Tall tower of Instruere, a monument based on the Tower of Worship in Dona Mihst.

Yawl (yoll): Small dinghy-like boat used by the fishermen of Firanes. [FI *jolly-boat*]

extras

orbit

meet the author

RUSSELL KIRKPATRICK'S love of literature and a chance encounter with fantasy novels as a teenager opened up a vast number of possibilities to him. The idea that he could marry storytelling and mapmaking (his other passion) into one project grabbed him and wouldn't let go. He lives in New Zealand with his wife and two children. Find out more about Russell Kirkpatrick at www.russellkirkpatrick.com.

introducing

If you enjoyed **IN THE EARTH ABIDES THE FLAME,**
look out for

THE RIGHT HAND OF GOD

Book Three of the Fire of Heaven Trilogy
by Russell Kirkpatrick

Achtal came down the path to join the others, wiping
his sword clean as he walked, showing no sign of arrogance or pride that Kurr could see. Apart from the
sweat beaded on Achtal's broad face and the dust clinging to his robe, nothing indicated he had killed some
twelve bandits unaided. Te Tuahangata, who still
breathed heavily from his own exertions, shook his head
in simple disbelief, and Prince Wiusago, his friend, his
enemy, returned the gesture.

"I was raised as a swordsman," the blond man said, still
struggling to control his voice. "I've sparred with the best
in Deruys. Were I to tell them what I've just witnessed, they
would counsel me to stop frequenting taverns."

"I was born a warrior," Te Tuahangata countered

angrily, "and we do not fight as others do. Neither strength nor skill alone makes a warrior. We Mist-warriors are taught to live like fighting men. Larger than life, intimidating in everything we do. That is part of being a true warrior." He sounded as though he was trying to convince himself.

The Deruvian laughed at his companion's words, not unkindly. "Yes, my friend, you are right. I have seen you fight. Gestures, war cries, swinging your club in huge, extravagant arcs, the howling noise it makes, those things are enough to break the spirits of all but the bravest of foes. Yet the Bhrudwan teaches us a different way. He does nothing for show. Everything has an economy about it, which speaks of care and devotion, of calm and heart's peace, of having nothing to prove, unlike you and I. He makes no hasty moves and so comes to no hasty conclusions. He never overcommits himself and so can flow from one move to the next without effort. You, dear Tua, are hot-blooded in all you do. He is cold. While I prefer your way to his, there is much we must learn from him before we can truly call ourselves warriors."

His companion merely grunted, clearly unwilling to accept either the compliment or the judgment implied in the words. But from what Kurr saw, the Child of the Mist had plenty to think about.

A much different and darker set of thoughts occupied the old farmer's mind. He, too, had run some way up the path to give whatever help he could to the Bhrudwan, in itself surprising given that a few short months ago this man had tried to kill him and his friends. And this, really, was the nub of his problem. He had just seen this implacable warrior do something otherwordly, something which must have required the dedication of a lifetime to perform. Yet he and his little band of village peasants had faced four of these monsters, of whom this man was the least, and defeated them. Watching the Bhrudwan kill a dozen bandits brought home to him how unlikely their own victory had been, and he mentioned his concern to the Haufuth as they readied the camel train to move on.

The village headman stood silent a moment, stroking his chin, before answering. "Well, you benefited from some luck, I can see that. From what you've said, had all the Bhrudwans walked across that swingbridge with their captives, you would never have executed your ambush, no matter how clever it was."

Phemanderac spoke up from behind them: he had just finished applying a damp cloth to the swelling on Belladonna's temple. The injury, incurred in the Deep Desert, seemed for some time to have given her a deathly hurt, but had recently healed somewhat. The swelling was still evident, however, and the magician's daughter still had trouble keeping down solid food.

"According to Mablas of Dhauria, who made a study of these things, the Lords of Fear are not only great warriors, but are also masters of the Realm of Fire, and can use illusion, the Wordweave and dark magic to achieve their ends. When Leith first told me of your Company, and how you had overcome four Lords of Fear, I assumed he was being modest about his own abilities, and you were the greatest of your people, life-trained and hand-picked to oppose the Destroyer's servants. But then I saw it was not so, and it became evident you had not overcome the Lords of Fear by strength or by magic. How, then, could you doubt the favor of the Most High rests on you? How else could you have defeated them?"

The Haufuth scowled, and Kurr muttered under his

breath. The lean philosopher had been talking like this for days, ever since their deliverance from the slave markets, in spite of the anger it engendered among his fellow travelers. There had been a time, Kurr admitted, that he had almost been persuaded. Almost he had believed they were the chosen of the Most High, his instruments of salvation destined to bring deliverance to Faltha. To his credit, the Haufuth had never gone along with the words of this outlandish man, words echoed by the equally suspect Hermit, and even by Hal, their own fey prophet. Yes, there were things he couldn't explain, rightly or wrongly, he acknowledged that. He'd seen the castle of Kantara with his own eyes, had witnessed the power of the Jugom Ark. His friend the Haufuth bore the physical scars on his hand in testament to that power. But knowing these things and not being able to explain them fell a long way short of the unquestioning belief others professed.

"Answer me this, then, O Prophet of the Most High," Kurr grated. "If his favor rests on us, where is the Jugom Ark? Where is Leith? Strange way to show favor is that, burying Arrow and Wielder alike under a pile of rubble." He knew his words hurt Phemanderac, he meant them to hurt, because the philosopher seemed not to care for their feelings, so often did he bring up the subject. Phemanderac turned away without a word and busied himself with one of the packs. Perhaps he did care, but not enough. Leith was not from *his* village.

The old farmer returned to the problem. How had the four Bhrudwan warriors been defeated? How had the Company bested even one, this Acolyte, as Mahnum named him?

The question would not leave him, and every time Achtal the Bhrudwan aided them and then deferred to Hal the cripple, unease grew in his mind like a blight taking hold in his apple orchard back on Stibbourne Farm. He remembered giving up hope of anything but a slave's life in that terrible city by the Lake of Gold, until miraculously their purchaser turned out to be the Bhrudwan, complete with camel train. They had been totally in his power then, yet he acted as their servant. What sort of hold did Hal have on the man, and how secure was it? It was as though the Company held the sun in a jar and made it do their bidding. At any time it might break out of its prison and incinerate them all with its power.

Perhaps that was the plan all along.

The travelers took a moment to tend their animals, then set off again to climb the few remaining steps to the top of the pass. Already the huge desert flies buzzed lazily around the pools of drying blood. Achtal did not spare the bodies even a glance: it was as though the people who until a few moments ago inhabited them no longer existed for him. Kurr and the former Captain of the Instruian Guard, who shared with Achtal the vanguard of the camel train, exchanged uneasy glances.

Further down the train the Arkhos of Nemohaim wiped sweaty palms on his red robe. The last few weeks had proven extremely taxing for him, but he was alive, a victory of sorts. Even his dark inner voice was quiet now, sated for the moment by the bandit stepping back on to his sword.

The Arkhos received as deep a shock as anyone to be redeemed from the slave market of Ghadir Massab by the Bhrudwan. He'd fully expected to be killed. Indeed, his captain had made to defend him, but the traitorous Bhrudwan did nothing but lead them to a camel train he had persuaded one of his countrymen to give him. The Arkhos was not clear over that—the Bhrudwan must indeed be high in their complicated hierarchy to have commandeered such wealth—but it proved the perfect disguise. The Bhrudwan even produced their cloaks, packs and swords, having gained them from the slavers as part of the purchase price he paid.

The hatred the Arkhos of Nemohaim bore towards these northerners had not lessened, he knew that, everyone knew that, there was no point pretending otherwise; but while that cursed Bhrudwan served them he could do little but agree to a temporary alliance. Strangely, the crippled boy had suggested it, arguing it would be sensible to recognize the informal partnership originally forced on them because of the attack by the Sanusi of the Deep Desert. In the uncertainty of their rescue it had been agreed to by the northerners, no doubt for the same reason as he gave his swift assent. Sharing the road with his enemies was better than the alternative, which was to lose contact with them—or worse still, to be hunted by them.

The arrangement, therefore, met with the Arkhos's approval. Without their support it was less certain that he would be able to return to Instruere. And he desperately wished to return. He had plans for that city, and for its new leader. The loss of the Jugom Ark did not change that.

The camel train crested the pass; and suddenly the green basin of Maremma lay spread below them like an irregularly patched cloth. A spur of the Veridian Hills stretched a brown finger into the smoky distance, and along this spur, high above the plains, wound their path. Through the town of Fealty it would go, the birthplace of Conal Greatheart and still the seat of his knightly order, then down to Sivithar on the great river, and thence to Instruere; two weeks or more at walking pace. There the travelers would go, having failed in their quest. They were bereft of the Jugom Ark, had lost one of the Arkhimm, and faced an uncertain future.

The Arkhos smiled. He was certain about one thing. The future would involve blood and fire.

The abiding impression created by the Wodhaitic Sea was one of peace. Each morning Leith invariably found his favorite position, lying on his stomach in the prow of the outrigger, letting the silent, turquoise depths slide by mere inches from his face, taking in deep breaths of the astringent salt air. He would spend the day talking with Maendraga, or perhaps with Geinor and his son Graig, while they fished for their evening meal. Then in the evenings, after the warm rains, the glorious red-green sunsets and the swift darkness, Leith talked with the navigator, the only Aslaman willing to make conversation with him.

In spite of all that had happened to Leith, he did not truly appreciate how exotic his life had become until these nights on the ocean. On his travels he had seen so many places unlike the green, rolling hills and chalk cliffs of Loulea, his home: barren, snow-covered moors, cold rearing peaks, deep green woods, wide white deserts. An amazing variety of people had crossed his path, from the ragged villains of Windrise to the laughing Fodhram, the simple but proud Fenni, the sophisticated yet confusing urbane Instruians. Yet the most unsettling land Leith had yet traveled was no land at all, but the sea, the wide, pathless Wodhaitic Sea.

Two weeks on the ocean had given Leith his first

respite, his first chance to really think, since that Midwinter's night many months ago. He found himself relaxing, unclenching like a hand held as a fist for too long—or, perhaps, like the hand learning to hold the Jugom Ark more and more gently. So, for the first time on his journey, he was in a position to appreciate the unfamiliarity surrounding him.

Relentless heat served as a constant reminder that he journeyed far beyond the lands he knew. Coming from a Firanese winter to the warmth of late spring in Instruere felt odd enough, but with so much to occupy them all in the great city of Faltha he hardly noticed the warmth, or perhaps became accustomed to it. The Valley of a Thousand Fires assaulted them with unbearable ferocity, but their journey through the valley lasted only a few days, and they gained some respite at night. But here on the Wodhaitic he found no escape, day or night. The night heat was the worst, leaving him gasping for breath, sweating like a horse after a day's hard riding.

Along with the heat and the vastness of the pitching, heaving ocean came the astonishing skill of their navigator. The archipelago to which they had traveled had been made up of a few dozen tiny islands, none more than half a day's walk around, scattered like crumbs on a tabletop; yet the Aslamen guided their craft straight to them, traveling a hundred leagues or more northwards across the west wind in just over a week. Leith felt sure, in spite of the confidence the Aslamen displayed, they would miss their target and go sailing on forever, until the ice swallowed them or they came to the end of the world; but had since learned in conversations with the navigator that a combination of secrets, wielded by one with experience and skill, made the islands difficult to miss.

The islands themselves were tiny outposts hidden like secrets in the midst of the sea. Leith had expected small mountains rising out of the water, miniatures of the lands he knew; but the island upon which they made their landing was raised no more than a man's height above the waves. As they had sailed through a narrow gap in the coral reef and into a wide lagoon so startlingly blue it seemed to have been mistakenly colored by a child, Maendraga leaned over to Leith and whispered in his ear: "No talking now. This is Motu-tapu, the sacred island of the Aslamen. No word may be spoken until we leave, save the passing on of the Name." Leith nodded his head in earnest reply, though he had been told this before, and had little idea of what the magician meant. All he knew was that Maendraga desperately wanted to bury his dead wife's name, and he had usurped the quest to do so. The Guardian of the Arrow had claimed that traveling on the dugout canoe would be the speediest and safest way back to Instruere, but Leith suspected that Maendraga would have insisted on this particular journey even if it proved the slowest path of all.

Once on the island, little more than a strip of land that cleverly escaped the notice of the sea, the four outsiders were instructed to wait under the palm trees until it was time. There they waited in silence through the long morning and longer afternoon, watching the white clouds gather and lifting their faces to the warm rains; until the evening when, the air washed clean and fires burning along the beach, they were summoned to the Burying.